JUDITH

Books by Stella Wilchek

JUDITH
TALE OF A HERO
ARARAT

JUDITH

by

Stella Wilchek

1817

HARPER & ROW, PUBLISHERS

New York, Evanston, and London

The lines appearing on page 104 concerning the call to arms are reprinted from *The Torah;* all other Biblical quotations are reprinted from *The Holy Scriptures;* with permission of the copyright owner, The Jewish Publication Society of America.

The verse lines appearing on pages 143, 236, and 427, and four prose lines on page 383 are reprinted from *The Ancient Near East: An Anthology of Texts and Pictures,* edited by James B. Pritchard (Princeton University Press, 1958), with permission; for the British Commonwealth, with permission of Oxford University Press, London.

The verse lines on pages 210, 211, and 215, and the excerpts on pages 390 and 391 are reprinted from *Ancient Near Eastern Texts Relating to the Old Testament,* edited by James B. Pritchard (Princeton University Press, 2nd rev. ed., 1955), with permission.

The direct quotation in the law case cited on page 350 is reprinted from *History Begins at Sumer,* by Samuel Noah Kramer, with permission of the author.

The excerpts concerning the exorcism rites on pages 367 and 368 are reprinted from *The Greatness That Was Babylon,* by H. W. F. Saggs, by permission of Sidgwick and Jackson, Ltd., London.

The excerpt on page 392 is reprinted from *Light from the East,* by C. J. Ball, with permission of Eyre & Spottiswoode (Publishers) Ltd., London.

LIBRARY OF CONGRESS CATALOG CARD NUMBER: 69-17287

ACKNOWLEDGMENTS

IN A LONG work of historical fiction, one cannot possibly acknowledge all one's sources. However, I do wish to thank two gentlemen in Jerusalem who were of help to me: Professor Yigael Yadin and Dr. Abraham Malamat of Hebrew University for giving of their valuable time to answer exasperating questions. I also want to thank Major General Moshe Dayan for prudently refusing to answer all questions about territory that was then still in Jordan and Syria. Reputedly it was General Dayan who said that in war there is never a once and for all. With this in mind I wish to dedicate my book to all those whom it may concern.

S. W.

Is there a thing whereof it is said: 'See, this is new'?—it hath been already, in the ages that were before us.

ECCLESIASTES 1:10

PROLOGUE

YOU may well ask why I would have you record a tale that is known to every babe in Bethul—nay, to every one in Judah who was not carried off to Babylon fifty years ago," the old man Isaac said to the young scribe whom he had summoned to the hut after Judith had left. "You may also ask why it must be done tonight. But it is always at this time of the year, when plowing begins after the first hard rain of winter, that Judith spends the night outside the cave where her men are buried.

"Indeed you may ask why I do not attend to the task myself—I, who in my youth was a scribe to captains, governors and kings. But fifty years have passed since Judith took me from the Babylonians. My fingers, which once were nimble at guiding a stylus or a reed pen, have become coarse from pushing a plow, and gnarled and swollen from old age. As for my writing skill—if not for making out Judith's receipts all these years, I should long have forgotten how to trace letters. Therefore you, my boy, shall record the tale for the returning exiles before I die.

"And now, since you are of an inquisitive mind, you may ask what truth is there to tell. Is it not known to all how fifty years ago Judith went down alone into the Babylonian camp and struck off Holofernes' head with his own sword for the glory of her God and the honor of her people? Have not fathers told their sons, and the sons their own sons, how after Judith's brave deed the men of Bethul, though greatly outnumbered, fell upon the Babylonians like eagles and slaughtered them like sheep? And if it was a miracle—what can be truer than a miracle?

"But none of those who handed down the tale from father to son was in the enemy camp when Judith performed her deed—none but I, who was then scribe and interpreter to the Captain Holofernes. The only other who knows what truly happened before and after the deed is the old woman over there. She is Tamar, Judith's handmaiden, who grew up with her and never left her side in eighty years, save for the three nights Judith spent in the Babylonian camp.

"Now Tamar and I shall reveal to you the truth, however each shall tell only his own part. They say that God, in His infinite wisdom, sees past and future as one and knows how the lives of those born at opposite ends of the world will some day mesh. But man has no such foreknowledge and all his wisdom is afterthought. Therefore I shall tell you my story as if I did not know how it would end, and let Tamar tell you Judith's story, until the two become one."

ONE

Now Nineveh was an exceedingly great
city, of three days' journey.

—JONAH III: 3

I WAS born at Nineveh two years after the death of the great King Ashurbanipal (the old man Isaac said to the young scribe), the same Ashurbanipal who took the Hebrew king Manasseh captive to Nineveh and released him only after Manasseh vowed to remain loyal to Assyria. This was but one of Ashurbanipal's great deeds. During his reign Assyria reached her highest peak of glory. He subjugated Phoenicia and Elam. He also carried his armies deep into Egypt and conquered Thebes.

But as a boy I learned more about Ashurbanipal the scholar and builder than about Ashurbanipal the warrior. Until the times of his grandfather Sennacherib, Nineveh had been but a minor city, the capital being Ashur. Sennacherib brought water into Nineveh, adorned the city with parks and broad avenues, had his slaves create a marsh to the north where he could hunt water fowl, and built a splendid palace. But King Ashurbanipal built for himself a palace to surpass that of his grandfather. Both palaces stood in the western part of town, on an island formed by the rivers Tebilut and Husur, which flowed from east to west through Nineveh before emptying below the city gates into the Tigris. The city walls were forty cubits thick and one hundred and eighty tipki high, rendered more formidable yet by a deep moat that surrounded all Nineveh except in the west, where the Tigris ran along the wall. Any fool could see that no army could ever conquer Nineveh and that it would stand for a thousand years. But the safest place was the palace grounds, which were protected by rivers to the north, south and west.

It was in this part that I was born. Until I was twelve years old I

7

never left Nineveh to pass through any of the fifteen splendid gates in the wall, for my parents were slaves at the royal court.

My grandmother had been brought as a hostage to Nineveh in the times of King Sennacherib, after he had invaded Judah and burned all its fenced cities. He burned Lachish then, and so proud was he of his victory that he put up a relief of that battle in his palace at Nineveh, where it could still be seen in my time.

As for me, I would rather contemplate a relief depicting captive musicians from Judah playing the harp, the flute and the kettle drum, for among them was my own grandfather. Of my grandmother I never saw a likeness. She was one of King Hezekiah's own daughters, who had been surrendered as hostages when Sennacherib raised the siege of Jerusalem. Though she was only the offspring of a minor concubine there was the blood of the Hebrew kings in her veins, and through her the same royal blood flows in mine. Had my grandfather not been the finest harp player ever to grace the court at Nineveh, Sennacherib would never have given him for his wife a Hebrew princess meant to be his own concubine. What greater honor could the king bestow upon a slave?

But I never knew either of my grandparents. When I was born my oldest sister was already married, and the youngest of the three ten years old. My mother had thought herself past the childbearing age, and when she was delivered of a son she proclaimed it a miracle. Therefore she named me Isaac as Sarah had named the son of her old age—and also because she hoped that I would bring joy to her latter days, for Isaac means laughter.

Unlike my grandmother, my mother was not a princess but a great singer. As for my father, he followed in his own father's footsteps, playing the harp and teaching the other musicians at court. My three older sisters all had lovely voices, and I too was meant to become a musician. But when my father heard me sing for the first time he placed his hand upon his head in despair, wailing that I had been cursed with a voice that made the listener wish he was born deaf. Even his hope that I might be taught to play the harp was soon shattered, for the only instrument I ever wished to play was the silver trumpet. But about that later.

While I was still a tender babe, I lived with my parents in the court quarters that housed the musicians and foreign artisans. Though we were not freemen, our homes were much better than those of the common kitchen slaves, the bakers, perfumers and sweepers. Indeed the queen held my mother in such high esteem that she gave her a slave of her own, an Ethiopian girl whose parents had been captured in Egypt by King Ashurbanipal.

Though Taia and her elder brother Tarqu were born in Nineveh, they were still thought strangers by the Assyrians, even as we were held to be strangers. Because of this we clung together almost like kin, and Taia became as one of the family. She even learned to cook without boiling meat in milk, for my mother observed the purity laws as she had been taught by her own mother. I would sometimes eat forbidden food at the homes of my friends, but I never touched pork, for my stomach turned at the mere sight of it.

My friends were the sons of the musicians and artisans who had been brought to Nineveh from Phoenicia, Babylon, Egypt, Tyre, Elam, Judah and even from as far away as Greece. The Egyptians were the finest scribes, the Babylonians the shrewdest merchants, the men from Tyre the most skillful carpenters, and none could surpass the Phoenicians at keeping accounts. One of the latter tried to teach me how to fashion two sets of records—one for one's own use and one for the king's tax collectors—for he saw little sense in the paying of high taxes. But I disliked working with figures, my gift being of a different nature, as my parents soon discovered to their great amazement.

Whenever I returned from one of my foreign friends I would speak a few words of his tongue, until in the end I spoke it no worse than he. This was thought proof of my superior mind, though my youngest sister claimed that I learned words as certain birds learn words and that I had no more sense than these birds. But one day my special gift became known to the queen, an event that would change my life forever.

The queen had doted on me from birth, having always held my mother in high esteem as a singer. Indeed when she learned that her favorite was safely delivered of a son, she honored her with a visit to our humble home. However, she was preceded by one of her ladies, who came to see that things might be fittingly prepared for such an exalted visitor.

This lady was a kinswoman of my father, their mothers having been half sisters who were brought together from Judah. But while my grandmother had married a Hebrew slave, her sister became the bride of an Assyrian prince. Now her daughter, an Assyrian princess with Hebrew blood in her veins, was greatly pained to learn that my mother had given me a Hebrew name. Therefore when the queen admired me in my swaddling clothes and asked my name, this lady replied before my mother could utter a word:

"In their delight over being blessed with a son in their latter years, these old people called him Ashur-gives-joy."

Thus I came to be named for a heathen god. But my mother always called me Isaac, nor did she forgive my father's kinswoman for her deceit. Soon that lady and her husband left Nineveh for Harran, where she gave her oldest daughter to become a priestess of the moon-god Sin. Then my mother spoke of her with even greater bitterness. But my father said:

"If King Hezekiah's own son Manasseh erected an altar to Ashtoreth in the forecourt of Yahweh's temple, what should prevent his granddaughter from giving her daughter as a priestess to another heathen god?"

But where it concerned his own children, my father had sterner rules.

We were all brought up as Hebrews, and my married sisters observed the ritual food laws in their homes. My oldest sister, Yael, had wed one of the king's physicians, also a descendant of Judean slaves. Though my parents had thought it a good match, my sister was not content in her marriage. She often came to my mother, weeping that her husband did not fulfill his marital duties toward her. In ten years of marriage he had given her only one child, and that a daughter. But when my father chided her husband, he replied:

"Does a worried man have the strength to please his wife in bed? If a musician sings a false note, none will rip out his tongue. But should I fail at an operation, they would cut off my hand. And what good is a surgeon without his hand? Moreover, the queen suffers from many ills and daily demands new potions of me. Though these potions may not cure her, I must make certain that they do not harm her either. All these demands so perturb me that my stomach churns and prevents me from sleeping at night. As for my manly powers, they have wholly forsaken me, nor can my own remedies restore them."

My second sister, Rachel, was more fortunate in her husband, even though he was of Israelite stock. There was little love between the Hebrews of Judah and the Hebrews of Israel because of the many wars the two kingdoms had waged against each other. My sister's husband was one of the king's charioteers. But in spite of being an Israelite and a soldier by calling, Amnon was a good man. He loved his wife and had her with child every year. And he doted on his children, carried them around on his shoulders and allowed them to ride on the king's horses. Even if my father often called Amnon a simple oaf unfit to be the husband of a fine musician, he had to concede that he made my sister happy.

As for my youngest sister, Abigail, she was the comeliest of the three and a great concern to my parents. Fearful of choosing the wrong husband for her, they turned down suitor after suitor in the hope that someday the right one would present himself. But when Abigail made known her own choice, it was the last man my parents had hoped for.

This came about when I was eleven years old. I had already been studying for six years to become an interpreter, for my schooling began early. The queen, having learned of my great intelligence and my gift for words, had procured for me a place at the library, where the future court scribes were being tutored.

This library, built by King Ashurbanipal, belonged to the temple of Nebo, the god who wrote the fates of men and whose sacred sign was the stylus. While most kings could neither read nor write, Ashurbanipal had studied all the sciences, but more than those he loved the old Akkadian and Sumerian poetry. His scribes traveled all over Babylonia to collect and record these poems, and to prepare new translations, which together with the ancient texts were stored in the library. Each clay tablet was numbered according to its content so that it might be easily found if wanted by one of the scholars. Truly no king before Ashurbanipal had accomplished such a great deed.

For a long time I was the youngest boy studying at the library, and my older comrades tormented me without mercy. I often ran home crying that I would never go back, but I was always forced to return. In the end I was avenged on the older students by surpassing them in knowledge, for their intelligence could not attain to mine.

Even when I entered school as a child of five I knew several tongues besides Assyrian. At home we spoke Hebrew, nor was it the common Hebrew of the Israelite slaves but the pure Hebrew once spoken at King Hezekiah's court. For we were never allowed to forget that we were of the blood royal. I also knew Syrian, having learned it from my Phoenician friends, and even some Egyptian, though I did not master the writing of the latter, the study of Assyrian writing being difficult enough. This meant memorizing many hundreds of signs, which had to be impressed with a stylus on wet clay. Our teachers often crossed out our lessons in wrath and beat us over the ears with our own tablets. No sooner had we become skillful at writing than we were taught Sumerian.

You must understand that Sumerian had long ceased to be spoken, Sumer having fallen before the great king Hammurabi more than a thousand years earlier. But all the great old poems and religious chants were written in Sumerian. It was thought the mark of the learned man to know Sumerian, and the best manner to teach it to young boys by dealing them as many blows as possible. Indeed this proved to be the right way, for in the end most of us mastered Sumerian, even if with many tears.

During these early years of study I found little time to play. I could rarely slip off to the stables, where my uncle Amnon let me ride upon a horse. Nor could I stroll in the garden among the strange tropical plants which Ashurbanipal had brought back from all the conquered lands, tease the apes and peacocks, or stroke the tame old lioness that dozed in the shade beneath a palm tree. And when one day I learned that a new teacher had arrived at court to instruct the brightest among us in Greek, I thought myself truly cursed with this memory for words.

I still recall the day our headmaster presented to us our new teacher. The headmaster was an old man with the evil temper of a dragon. All the boys trembled before him, a feeling that does honor to a teacher. When that revered man entered the room before our new Greek teacher we all bowed low, as we were wont to do, none daring so much as to raise his eyes.

"These are the wretches who will embitter my lord's future days," our headmaster said. "Pray let him not spare the rod with them, for if he does none of these imbeciles will learn a single word of Greek."

And walking about he struck several of the boys with his own rod, as though to set our new teacher a fitting example. We all remained bowed low before this man until he said:

"Stand up before me like men!"

At first I thought we had not understood him, for he spoke our language with a strange intonation, though well. But when he repeated his words we finally unbent our backs, and facing him we gasped with astonishment. Though there were many foreigners at the court in Nineveh, we had never before seen such a man, less still such a teacher.

All our teachers were venerable old men who wore their hair and beards long and carefully curled, whose stiff garments were bedecked with ornaments the king had given them as rewards over the years, and who never appeared in class without wearing their peaked caps and carrying a rod with which to impress upon us the advantages of learning.

But the Lord Hippolytus—for that was his name—looked too young for a teacher. He was clean shaven in the Egyptian manner and his head was bare. His short hair, falling in ringlets over his forehead, was light brown with a golden glint, as if the sun-god Shamash had kissed his brow, and his bright eyes were surrounded by fine lines such as are caused by many smiles.

Nor had we ever beheld a man wearing attire such as his. Instead of the long straight garment with the wide belt around the waist worn by our other teachers, the Greek wore a short tunic and over it a gracefully draped cloak falling from one shoulder and wound over his arm. On his feet were leather sandals with straps tied crosswise up to beneath his knees.

"And now, my young friends," he said—and none of our other teachers had ever addressed us thus—"let us see what we might learn from each other. I shall teach you Greek, if this be the will of the gods, and you shall teach me your tongue."

Need it be said that we worshiped him from that day on and that we should have learned Greek even if it had been difficult—which it was not—for what language is after one has mastered Sumerian?

It was from the Lord Hippolytus that I first learned of the world outside the walls of Nineveh. He had traveled in many lands and often spoke to us of matters other than the Greek language. He had lived in Egypt, and had visited Tyre, Sidon and even Judah. He had seen Babylon, and in the end he had come to Nineveh, having heard of our great library and wishing to translate some of the old

Sumerian poetry into Greek. But more than about poetry the Lord Hippolytus cared about what he called politics—some manner of Greek pastime, if I understood him right. Indeed he often spoke of writing a history of all the peoples he had visited that the rest of the world might learn of *their* politics.

Though we could not comprehend what he said, we boys would raptly listen to him. And even after classes we would follow him about like sheep that we might catch another of his words or see him smile. Truly the Lord Hippolytus was a teacher such as any boy might desire! And if it was said of him that he liked boys better than girls—as Greeks are wont to do—they could never prove that accusation against him. As for me, I can bear witness to the opposite.

Unlike the other students, I was not permitted to eat the king's food, which was prepared in an unclean manner. When I had to spend long hours in school, my sister Abigail would bring me food from home in a basket. On one such occasion the Lord Hippolytus walked into the classroom. Regarding my sister, he halted beside me and said:

"You must indeed be a favorite of the gods to have such a lovely maiden bring your food, Ashur!"

Abigail glanced at him, blushed becomingly and fled away, but not without looking back over her shoulder until she stumbled and nearly fell on her face. Ashamed of her foolish behavior, I said:

"Let my lord pay no heed to my sister, who being a woman is a silly goose like all the rest."

At that the Lord Hippolytus laughed, patted my head and walked away. But the next day, while looking over my Greek lesson, he asked in a passing manner:

"And how is your comely sister?"

What could I reply but that she was in good health, Ashur be praised?

That afternoon, as I sat at home bent over my Greek lesson for the next day, my sister Abigail strolled into the room. She was humming and swishing her skirt and doing all she could to distract me. In the end she approached me to glance over my shoulder.

"Are you practicing your Greek letters?" she asked, though she had never before concerned herself with my practicing letters, Greek or others.

"This is what I am doing, nor do I wish to be disturbed," I replied. But she would not go away.

"And your Greek teacher—what might be his name—"

"The Lord Hippolytus," I said gruffly.

"The Lord Hippolytus, have you seen him today?"

"I have seen him yesterday, I have seen him today and I shall see him tomorrow. Now if you will not leave me alone, I shall call our father and tell him that you prevent me from studying!"

But even that threat would not dismay her.

"The Lord Hippolytus—did he perchance speak of me?" she asked.

"He did indeed."

"And what was it he said?"

I was tempted to reply that he had voiced his distaste of that silly goose, my sister. However, my good nature won out.

"He asked 'And how is your comely sister?' " I said.

Abigail stood entranced for a moment. Then she flushed deeply and ran from the room. I had barely resumed my study when she returned.

"Isaac," she whispered, "what were the words he used?"

"I told you his words," I replied, without raising my eyes from my writing.

"But his very words, my cherished brother!"

At that I threw down my stylus in anger and shouted:

"Small wonder they do not teach girls to read and write if they cannot remember a few simple words from one moment to the next! All the Lord Hippolytus said was 'And how is your comely sister.' "

This answer so delighted Abigail that for the rest of the day she walked about the house singing an old Hebrew tune about love being strong as death—the same song that people now ascribe to King Solomon.

Next day I began to doubt that God had given men better sense than women. The Lord Hippolytus again inquired after my sister, using the very same words as on the previous occasion. Moreover, after classes he fell into step with me and saw me all the way home.

"This then is where you live," he said, gazing at our modest house as if it were a princely mansion.

"Indeed this is my home. My lord did me great honor to bring me to my door. I wish my lord peace."

And bowing I turned to enter the house.

"Will you not ask me in?" the Lord Hippolytus said. "What of your hospitality?"

What choice had I but ask him inside? It was a great honor to have one's teacher visit one's home. My parents bowed down low when I revealed to them who was the guest I had brought with me. Their voices raised in greeting brought my sister Abigail to the door. Upon seeing our visitor she let out a shriek and ran from the room, only to return shortly. How she, who was so slow at every task, had pinned up her hair with a fine new comb in so brief a time I could not fathom.

Knowing what was seemly, my mother bowed again before our guest and invited him to eat with us, though our food might not compare to the king's food.

"Whatever you may serve shall taste to me as ambrosia to the gods," the Lord Hippolytus replied.

My mother glanced at my father in deep consternation. He was no less puzzled than she, but being a man he could not betray his ignorance. Instead he asked our guest to share with him a cup of wine while they waited for their meal.

"I shall gladly have a cup of wine with you, if only you will cease from addressing me as 'my lord.' I am not of noble birth and would rather have grown men call me by my name, Hippolytus. And what, my friend, is your name?"

"Asaph the son of Eliahu," my father replied, bowing low.

"Neither is it seemly that you prostrate yourself before me, Asaph. Men ought not to bow down low before each other—though this may be the only exercise ever performed by Assyrians."

I could see that my father would have preferred being addressed as "my lord," as befits a man of standing. But so amazed was he by our visitor's speech that he forgot himself and asked:

"And what is this thing called exercise?"

"It is what a man does to maintain his strength. Moreover, it is well known that a healthy mind dwells in a healthy body. Ever since I left Greece I have sorely missed the gymnasium. In my despair I have taken to visiting the track of the king's horses early in the morning. There I can strip naked and run around the track before anyone else is awake. Alas, I am not as swift as I was in former times, nor am I as young as I was when I won the foot race at the Olympic Games. Ah, if only you could have seen the finest young men of Greece compete at running, jumping and hurling the discus!"

"And what might have been the purpose of such folly?" my father asked, askance.

"Asaph, my friend," Hippolytus said, "it is in the nature of man that he must prove himself superior to the next. Is it not better that he do this by outrunning than by killing him?"

Even my father had to concede the wisdom of this, while my mother regarded our guest with amazement, and my sister Abigail with such foolish rapture as if a cherub had descended from heaven before her eyes.

If my father had hoped that our visitor would cease from his strange revelations when we sat down to our meal, he was disappointed. Indeed he soon sent Abigail from the room, not wishing to have her ears polluted by these ungodly tales. After several cups of wine the Lord Hippolytus began telling stories such as we had never heard before, nor did we then believe half of them. He spoke of wagers he had placed at chariot races, and of large amounts of silver he had won with the aid of the grooms who knew which horses had been fed forbidden potions that would make them run faster. He told of poets in his country who wrote what he called plays, which were performed in public places. Moreover—if one was to believe his words—these poets did not fear to mock people in high places. And when my father would know whether these men did not even respect the king, he learned that there were no longer kings in Greece.

"Our kings spent so much time murdering their fathers, sons, wives and daughters, or being murdered by them, that the people in the end abolished kingship," the Lord Hippolytus said.

"But how could the people do this great thing?" my father asked.

"And who but the people should decide how they wish to be governed?" Hippolytus answered.

At that my father's face turned ashen. He hastened to the door to make certain that none of the king's spies overheard what was being said in his house. Then he turned back to our guest, asking who ruled the land if there were no kings.

"At first this was done by a council of nobles. But now we have tyrants. These differ from kings only in that they do not inherit their posts but attain them with the help of the people. This pleases the people, for they would sooner be oppressed by choice than by chance."

When my father frowned at such levity, Hippolytus smiled and said:

"Peace, Asaph. I have heard that you Hebrew people have strange, solemn thoughts about righteousness and sin. I know that you have but one god—and that god never laughs. Also you believe that one should not get drunk and that one should go to bed early. I have been a bad guest, Asaph, but I shall take my leave now. Please bid farewell for me to your lovely daughter, whom I hope not to have offended with my coarse talk."

Though he was very drunk, the Lord Hippolytus walked gracefully out the door and into the darkness, where we could hear him singing what sounded like a ribald Greek song. But my father bolted the door behind him, smote his thigh and placed his hand upon his head in despair as he exclaimed:

"Running naked around the track of the king's horses! Placing wagers on chariot races! Preaching rebellion against kings! Getting drunk! And to such men we entrust the teaching of our sons!"

The Lord Hippolytus did not visit our house again for some time. However, this did not prevent him from asking about my sister, or her from asking about him. I found myself caught between them, repeating like a parrot to one what the other had said. This should have driven me to distraction had I not been plagued by troubles of my own.

My father, who had never truly relinquished the hope that I might still become a musician, had bought me a costly silver trumpet for which I had once expressed a wish in a moment of folly. Since he had gone to great expense, I had no choice but to attempt learning to play that trumpet. Teaching me was a task that caused my father no end of grief. He would sing out loudly and mark the beat with his hand, but to no avail. My ear was as bad as ever. But he would not give up hope and continued day after day until—no, not until I was transformed into a musician—but until a second voice from the kitchen joined him in song. It was a rich male voice such as neither of us had ever heard before. Nor did the singer know the Hebrew words but used in their place words of his own, which were neither Hebrew nor Assyrian.

My father silenced me with a motion of his hand and approached the door. I followed after him, and peering over his shoulder I recognized the singer. He was Taia's brother, a tall, beautiful Ethiopian slave, who had risen from overseer of the kitchen slaves to become keeper of the king's harem. This honor had cost him dearly, for they had taken from him his manhood, the Asssyrians differing little from other men who believed that a tall, handsome foreigner would surely defile their women. But Tarqu had already reached manhood when this thing was done to him, and his voice had remained rich and soft like the finest purple linen.

When the young man saw my father in the door, he rose and bowed down low. His skin was almost black, and above his short kilt we could see the powerful muscles in his broad back. Casting an angry glance at her brother, Taia said to my father:

"I told Tarqu not to invent his own words to these songs, which I know are sacred."

But my father replied:

"If God bestowed upon a man such a voice, He would surely delight in hearing him sing His songs. I wish my own son could sing like that. But he croaks like a frog, nor can he learn to play the trumpet. No doubt you know how to play an instrument, Tarqu!"

"Indeed I play the drum, as did my ancestors before me," Tarqu replied.

"Ah, that you were one of my musicians!" my father exclaimed. "But there was never yet an Ethiopian among the musicians at court, nor would the king desire such an innovation. However, if you wish to join me in song, you shall always be welcome to my house."

From then on Tarqu became a frequent guest. Sometimes he came wearing his native garb, but at others he was dressed in the long, richly embroidered robes and the high hat of the harem keeper. Then his manner was stiff and dignified, and I felt shy in his presence. But soon we became great friends, for he loved children. When none was watching he would even allow me a quick look into the king's harem. What I liked better yet was when he took me along to the quarters of the kitchen slaves, who loved to sing and dance after work. Then Tarqu would fetch his drum and beat it for them, while they performed the most astounding leaps and turns. Their throbbing music caught even my poor ear. One day I brought along my silver trumpet, and though I had never mastered our own sacred songs I soon learned to play the music of the kitchen slaves.

I do not know how my father discovered my doings, for I slipped away from home only on such nights when I knew him to entertain at court. Perhaps the people who lived near the slave quarters had complained of the music—music loud enough, they said, to bring their walls tumbling down, as had been known to happen.

One evening, just as Tarqu was beating the drum and I was blowing the trumpet, my father appeared in the court where the slaves met for their revels. His eyes widened in horror when he heard the tune that came forth from our sacred instrument. Snatching the trumpet out of my hand, he struck me across the cheek, caught me by the ear and pulled me all the way home. There he thrust me into the room, bolted the door behind me and locked the trumpet in a chest. His wrath should soon have abated, however, if not for what happened the following morning.

At dawn I was awakened by loud, angry voices. I was amazed to hear Abigail's wailing, for she could barely be roused long after the sun had risen, let alone at such an early hour. I stole to the door and peered through a crack. And there stood my sister, decked out in her best garments, with chains around her neck, bangles on her wrists and ankles, and kohl around her eyes, while my father held her by one arm, shaking her fiercely.

"So you were going out for a stroll, you—you harlot—you who never wants to get out of bed!" he shouted. "A stroll at the break of day, with paint on your face and dressed as if for a wedding! Back to your room, you burden of my old age, and you too!" he added, seeing that I had opened the door. "My daughter slips out at dawn to observe a Greek run naked around the track of the king's horses! My son plays pagan music with an Ethiopian! What is the world coming to?"

Had this been all that was wrong with the world, we should have been happy people. Alas, there was worse turmoil in the world than that caused by a half-grown boy and a girl in love. But my father would not face this until the Lord Hippolytus paid us another visit.

This time my teacher was sober, and his mien more solemn than I had ever seen it.

"Asaph, my friend," he said to my father, who was still startled by that familiar address, "I have come to discuss with you a weighty matter."

Fearing that the Lord Hippolytus had come to ask for my sister Abigail in marriage, my father turned ashen. It would be difficult to refuse the Greek. Not only was it a great honor if a freeman wished to wed the daughter of a slave, it also meant that Abigail's children would be born free. But such were my father's beliefs that he would sooner have Hebrew grandchildren who were slaves than free grandchildren who were Greeks.

"You have a fine son and a beautiful daughter, Asaph," our visitor said. "Surely you will want to do for them what is best!"

My father looked more and more perturbed. Even a heathen stranger should have better sense than ask a father for his daughter *and* his son! But as it turned out, marriage was not what the Lord Hippolytus had in mind.

"I see that you do not understand, Asaph," he said, regarding my father's doubtful face. "Indeed you differ little from the other inhabitants of Nineveh, who will not look beyond the walls of their city. Have you not heard that the Babylonian and Median armies are approaching? They have already vanquished much of Assyria and have taken Ashur. It will not be long before they assault and conquer Nineveh!"

"Conquer Nineveh!" my father exclaimed. "There is no army in the world so powerful that it could conquer Nineveh!"

"The same was said of Troy," the Lord Hippolytus said. "You look puzzled, Asaph, for you have never heard of Troy. And yet it was still a mighty fortress when your own ancestors left Egypt. But today we know of Troy only through the tales of our great poet Homer, who told of the mighty heroes who did battle there, of the blood that was spilled, of the destruction that was wrought, and of how the walls of Troy were razed, the city burned to the ground, and the women and children carried off as slaves. Such might yet be the fate of Nineveh!"

"No man in his senses would believe such a thing," my father replied. "The Assyrian army has always remained victorious in the end."

"My poor friend, the Assyrian army has not won a victory in years. Assyria's glory was eclipsed in the times of King Ashurbanipal. From then on the country has declined. It was truly a miracle that her power lasted so long, for there are rarely more than two strong kings in succession, and Assyria had three: Sennacherib, Esarhaddon and Ashurbanipal. But the royal blood runs thin now, and all the recent kings have been weaklings. It requires a strong ruler to fill his troops with courage. Without such a leader, they will never resist the onslaught of the Babylonians and Medes."

My father tugged at his beard and paced the room greatly troubled, for he could not wholly doubt the Greek's good sense. But then he said with some hope:

"Perhaps the Babylonians will return to their own land now that Ashur has fallen. Perhaps they will be satisfied with casting off the Assyrian yoke."

But the Lord Hippolytus only shook his head, saying:

"Having come so far, the Babylonians will surely not retreat. When I was in Babylon I heard much about their new king, Nabopolassar. He is a descendant of Merodach-Baladan, whom Sennacherib drove out of Babylon and forced to retreat to southern Chaldea. I have heard it said that Nabopolassar vowed to destroy the reliefs which Sennacherib put up in his palace to commemorate this victory. And is not Sennacherib's palace within the walls of Nineveh, not far from where you and I now stand debating?"

"But what has all this to do with my children?" my father asked in despair.

"This too I shall tell you, Asaph. Many nobles have already fled to Harran. This city lies farther to the west than Nineveh and might hold out longer against the Babylonian armies. It is also within shorter reach of Egypt, who has now turned from Assyria's foe into her ally. You too must take your family to Harran, Asaph! Indeed I shall escort you there myself!"

My father stood silent for a long time. Then he spoke sadly:

"Unless the king removed his court to Harran, I must remain with him in Nineveh. But even if I were free to leave, I should not go to Harran."

"Can you think of a safer place then?" Hippolytus asked.

"Of its safety I know little," my father replied. "But it is a place I have longed for all these years without ever having laid eyes on it—the city where my parents were born, Jerusalem. The merchants who travel back and forth by caravan tell great tales of the new king there. Not since the time of King Hezekiah—indeed not since David's time—has one like him sat on the throne. They say he has cleansed the country of evil, strengthened the army and recovered part of the land which the Assyrians took from the former kingdom of Israel."

"I too have heard of this King Josiah," the Lord Hippolytus said. "I was in Syria when he went about smashing the altars of all the gods but his own. But he was still young then and must be forgiven his ignorance. To forbid people the worship of their own gods is a great evil—though there are some in my own country who would do the same."

"For us there is only Yahweh, who gave my people our land forever," my father said proudly.

"Nothing is forever but what men will hold and defend," Hippolytus said. "And even then it is only until the day they die. As for you, Asaph, if the king should grant you leave, it would be wiser if you took your family to Harran. There are rumors that King Josiah might make a league with the Babylonians in this war. If he does, the Egyptian armies will utterly destroy Judah on their march north."

"If it be God's will, King Josiah shall hold back even all the host of Egypt!" my father exclaimed. "It is said of him that he is like the heroes of yore!"

"I have known more than one hero in my life," the Lord Hippolytus replied with a sigh. "None lived to be an old man."

TWO

Prepare thy work without,
And make it fit for thyself in the field;
And afterwards build thy house.

—PROVERBS 24:27

IT may seem strange to you, my boy, that we lived in King Josiah's times (the old man Isaac said to the young scribe). Josiah was crowned king at the age of eight a hundred years ago, after his father Amnon was murdered. In the thirty-one years Josiah sat on the throne of Judah he did only right and walked in the ways of God.

(The old woman, Tamar, who stood stirring a stew on the hearth, glared at Isaac and then spoke.)

Why should it seem strange to the youth that we lived in Josiah's times? There are many alive today who lived then, even here in Bethul. However, one born long after the pride and strength of Judah were broken can hardly picture those times. Nor can he imagine the faith in the future people had then. At times even I doubt my own memories. I was only a child when Josiah died, and there was no king like him afterward. Most of what I remember I learned from my mother, who often spoke of those times when we huddled around the fire on a winter night. But in repeating her tales to you I shall not say 'This is what I remember and this is what my mother told me,' for if one hears a story often enough it becomes part of one's own memory. And one might as well tell it as such.

If you would know Judith you must first learn about her father Merari. He was of the tribe of Simeon, like most in Bethul whose ancestors had moved north after the kingdom of Judah shrank. Having lost their cities in the south, they were content to settle in Bethul. Though the town was small it was protected by a wall, and there was a good spring at the foot of the hill upon which Bethul was built. Also there was enough flat farm land surrounding the hill to feed their families, nor was it too long a journey to Lachish in the west, or even to Jerusalem in the north. As for the Wilderness of Judah to the east of Bethul, the men of Simeon thought it an added protection, for it was known that no foe ever came or went through the wilderness.

But though the tribe of Simeon had lost its inheritance in the south, the people had not lost their pride and fierce temper. Nor was their fame of being mighty men of war without cause. Those who say Merari stood head and shoulders above them, like king Saul, speak the truth. As a child I still lived in the house he had built for himself that he might walk about upright. But that house was not built until after he took a wife.

Before that he dwelled alone in a humble hut. His sister Sarai often chided him for not taking a wife and raising up the seed of their father.

"It is unseemly that a man past thirty years of age should not be married," she would say to him. "Already the people of Bethul speak ill behind your back. They say you visit the harlots by the wall, while your cousin Athara, whom you should wed by custom, is still a maiden."

To this Merari, who in other matters was soft-spoken, would reply by cursing the people of Bethul and his cousin Athara.

"After our father died I worked hard to provide you with a dowry that you might find a husband," he said to his sister. "This left me too poor to pay for a bride of my own."

"Athara's father should ask but little for her, since you are the son of his own brother," Sarai answered.

"I would not give a lame sheep for Athara," Merari would reply to put an end to the dispute.

He had good cause for his refusal. His cousin Athara was not only ugly but also contentious and given to complaints about all sorts of ills. Yet she was strong as an ox, while her two elder brothers were of frail health. Neither of them lived past the age of twenty-two, both dying childless, in the summer when the fever seized them and carried them off. Thus Athara became heiress to all the fields and cattle of her father. But though she was rich Merari would not have her.

Athara's father Shallum had been the older of two brothers. His father had left him the best fields, while Merari's father had received the poorer and rockier portion. Yet Merari often said:

"My grandfather may have given Shallum the richer land, but God gave my father strong sons with powerful backs. We shall make these fields as fruitful as Shallum's if we have to dig out every single rock with our hands!"

But his brother Aaron did not love the land as Merari did.

"If I want to break my back," he said one day, "I can go to Jerusalem and work as a stonemason for the king. At least I shall be paid for my trouble."

This was the year King Josiah had ordered the breaches in the walls of the temple repaired and the laborers paid their wages, for he would not use slave labor. Thus Aaron packed his few belongings and went off to Jerusalem, while Merari stayed behind to tend the land.

He would work from daybreak till dusk then, with only one manservant to help him—the man who was to become my own father. Later he would tell me how Merari stood in the fields, his feet planted apart, to scoop up a handful of soil after the first rains in the fall. He would raise the soil to his nose, and he looked as though he were kissing it. The land repaid him his love with fruitfulness. Soon his harvests were richer than those of his uncle Shallum, who had been heir to the better fields but whose sons had died young, and whose only daughter was an ugly girl.

At times Shallum himself would call on Merari and say:

"Your father's seed and mine shall perish from the earth if you will not marry Athara and have a son!"

To this Merari would reply:

"It pains me that your line of the clan should come to this end. As for my father, he has another son in Jerusalem who has taken a wife and sired sons. But I cannot yet afford a wife."

However, this was but a feeble lie, for shortly afterward Merari bought a horse.

Even in those days, when Judah was not yet as poor as it is today, the common man did not own a horse. The king owned horses. A few of his nobles and horsemen owned horses. But a peasant, if he rode at all, rode upon an ass. However, Merari, though otherwise a

modest man, had always wanted a horse. One summer day, when he
had taken grain to sell in another town—for his fields yielded more
than he needed for himself—he brought back a horse.

He had loaded his grain in sacks upon his donkeys and had gone
with my father to Lachish. There the caravans that came up from
Egypt to Jerusalem passed along the road, bearing such goods as
would come from Egypt: papyrus and fine striped cloth, costly
Egyptian chariots for men of means, camels, slave girls and horses.
Of all the goods Merari coveted only one—a horse. And since there
was silver in his pouch, and since the Egyptian merchant had a glib
tongue, Merari returned to Bethul with a black Arab stallion, a
yearling that pawed the ground, breathed fire and looked as though
it would never allow a man to ride upon its back.

All the people rushed from their houses when Merari led the
horse into town and tied it to his doorpost. And his sister Sarai came
weeping, with her hand upon her head, ready to upbraid him. But
she did not dare go near his hut, for the horse pranced and reared up
like a black demon. Thus she stood at some distance, calling until
Merari came outside.

"Why do you trouble me," he said to his sister, "seeing I am
returned tired from a long journey?"

"You have made us the laughingstock of the whole town," Sarai
replied, "bringing home a beast that will never be of any use to you.
Moreover, you have offended our kinsman Shallum, for it is well
known that for the price of a horse you could have bought three
brides—let alone one such as your cousin Athara!"

"Have I worked hard all my days to deny myself my heart's
desire?" Merari asked. "My silver was well spent, for this horse shall
yet bring me more pleasure than Athara ever could."

"Athara could bear you a son, which this monster never will,"
Sarai said. "Nor will you be able to ride him. If you do, you shall
fall off and break your neck, leaving me and my children to starve
to death."

"You have a husband to look after you," Merari replied, though
it was he who supported his sister's family. "Besides, I shall not
break my neck. I shall yet tame this horse!"

And indeed he did. But the people of Bethul were envious and
mocked Merari behind his back.

"Any day now he will ride up to Jerusalem and proclaim himself
king!"

To speak thus was folly, for there was none in Bethul who honored King Josiah more than did Merari. When Josiah cleansed the land of all heathen gods, Merari went up into the grove where the women worshiped the queen of heaven and cut down her sacred pillar with his own hands. Indeed, if the king had not made the country safe for travel, Merari would have remained unmarried. For he would not wed his cousin Athara, and to marry another would have offended custom. But then, as may happen to the most sober of men, he was smitten by love.

The year after Merari bought the stallion—whom he named Hadad after the storm-god of the Canaanites—the harvest was even richer than the previous year. Merari had built a new storehouse, with a pit dug deep into the ground and calked with lime to keep the mice out. There he stored his grain, for he would not sell early in the season but waited until he learned where there had been a poor harvest. Then he would load his donkeys with sacks and take his grain where it would fetch the highest price.

In those days a man from Judah might venture as far north as the former kingdom of Israel. King Josiah had built up his army and fortified the towns not only in our land but also across the border. Assyria's grip on the conquered nations had weakened, and the prophets predicted the downfall of Nineveh. Indeed some people would have Judah join the Babylonians in war against Assyria, while others would cast their lot with Egypt. Jerusalem was rent by discord—but was there ever a time when Jerusalem was not rent by discord?

None of this could detain Merari from taking his grain north. It was at the time of the grape harvest that he set out on his journey. He had learned that the crop of wheat had failed around Shiloh and Bethel, where once Jeroboam had put up the two golden calves for the Israelites to worship. But much had happened since then. Shiloh had been destroyed. Samaria, the capital of the kingdom of Israel, had fallen, and the people of the land had been carried captive to Assyria by King Sargon. The new inhabitants of the land were people Sargon had brought there from Babylonia, Media and Elam, who had mixed with the Canaanites and the few Hebrews that were left. When they first came to Samaria these strangers were much plagued by lions, for they did not know the god of the land. In the end they begged King Sargon to send them a Hebrew priest that he

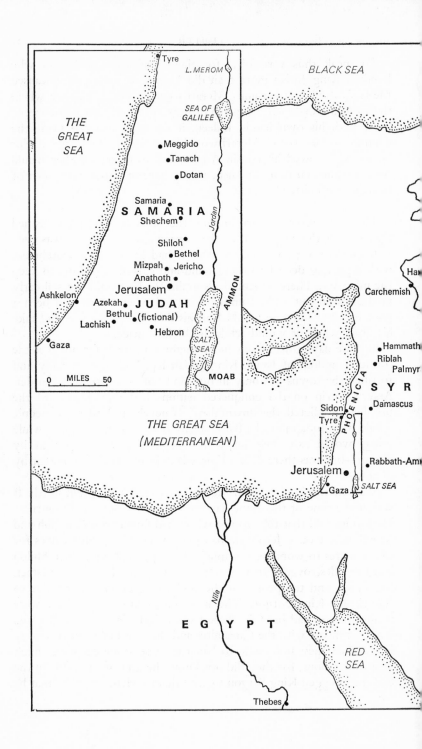

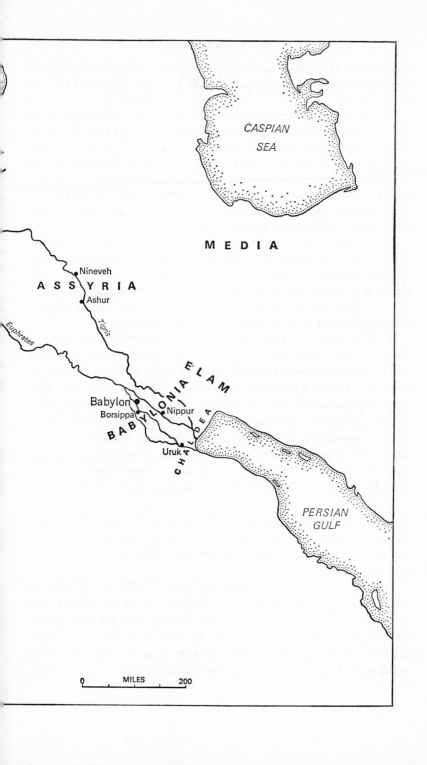

might teach them how to worship Yahweh. But they never ceased from worshiping their own gods beside Yahweh, and thus they still do in Samaria.

To this country Merari traveled with his grain. The trip was long and wearying, through the hills, past Jerusalem and on to the north. Merari rode upon his horse. Behind him came his donkeys laden with grain, and last my father, riding upon a mule. Both he and Merari were armed, for there were outlaws hiding in the woods, and one never knew what one might encounter north of the border. But they traveled safely until, on the eve of the third day, they arrived at a village not far from where once stood Shiloh.

At the time of the grape harvest people would pitch tents in their vineyards for the night. After the day's work there was feasting and dancing around the fire. The older fok sat back and rested, while the young made merry. It was not unlike the harvest feasts in Judah, but here they had one custom Merari did not know. I must tell you about it that you might understand what happened later.

A long time ago there was a bloody war between the tribe of Benjamin and all the other tribes of Israel. Some men of Benjamin had done an abominable thing—they had raped to death the concubine of a Levite who spent the night in Gibeah. When the tribe refused to surrender the guilty men, all the other tribes descended on them and slew a great multitude, even women and children, until only six hundred men were left. Those fled into the hills and saved themselves. But the other tribes vowed not to give them any of their daughters for wives. How this vow was overcome in the end and to what bloodshed it led you can read in our holy books. Though some of the six hundred men obtained wives, there was still a dearth of women. Then the single men went to Shiloh at the time of the grape harvest, knowing that the maidens would come out to dance before the gates. There each seized one for himself and carried her off as his bride.

Every year the people who lived around Shiloh acted out this rape after the grape harvest. Donning their finest raiment and jewels, the maidens would come out singing, dancing and beating their timbrels. The young men would rush upon them and carry them off—but only such young men as were betrothed to these maidens. It is said that nothing unseemly ever happened afterward.

All the young people were married soon, and it is well known that many a babe is born before his time.

When Merari rode into the vineyards of Shiloh one night, the dancing had already begun. The maidens were clad in white, with garlands of vine leaves upon their heads. They swayed and beat their timbrels in time with the singing and the music. Among them was one fairer than the rest, but at first she could barely be seen, for she was small and fragile like a figure carved from ivory. In the glow of the fire her hair shone red and her eyes threw back the sparkle of the flames, but her skin was a milky white. She danced with such skill that the others made room for her, and thus she was revealed before Merari.

The moment he saw her he was smitten, nor could she take her eyes off him. Though he had dismounted he stood head and shoulders above the other men, looking strong and handsome even if no longer in his first youth.

As the dancing continued one young man after another rushed into the circle of maidens to carry one off, until only a few were left. Merari watched bewildered, for he did not know the custom of the land, nor could he fathom why none of the youths had carried off the fairest. Of a sudden Merari lurched forward, swept up the maiden in his strong arms and ran with her toward the woods, as he had seen the others do.

At that the men around the fire ceased from their revels, cried out in fury and began to pursue after him. Even before Merari reached the edge of the woods they caught him. Had he not been big and strong and able to fight many, they would surely have killed him. Thus they barely overcame him and threw him bleeding to the ground, while they shouted:

"Behold this vile stranger from Judah just come to our country and already trying to defile one of our maidens!"

Then they carried off the young woman, who screamed and kicked, a thing she had not done when Merari swept her up in his arms. After the men had left, my father ran to Merari's side, wiped off his blood and gave him some wine to drink. He would have him swiftly depart from the place, but Merari was deaf to his pleas.

"It seems I did a grievous thing," Merari said. "I must discover wherein I erred and make amends, for I may have sullied the good name of a fine and lovely maiden."

And he dispatched my father to find out her name. My father did not gladly go on this errand, for he feared the wrath of the men. In the end he approached one becalmed by wine, who told him that the maiden's name was Shoshanna. Her father was Bela the son of Ahiram, who owned the best vineyards in the country, and also much sheep and cattle. When Merari learned the news, he said:

"Let me seek out this man and offer to pay what penalty he may lay upon me for offending his daughter!"

He would set out on this errand in the middle of the night, bloody and battered as he was. But my father said to him:

"Better let my lord wait until the morning, when he has cleansed himself, for if the maiden's father saw him now, he might indeed take him for an outlaw."

Merari saw the sense of this advice, and thus he and my father slept in the fields with their donkeys.

Next morning Merari washed, shook out his hair and beard, and clad himself in clean garments. Then he swung himself up on Hadad, and together with my father he went looking for the house of Bela the son of Ahiram. Nor was the house hard to find. It was the finest in the village, with a lower and an upper story, and a battlement around the roof so that those who walked there on a cool evening might not fall off and break their necks.

Merari stood a long time gazing at the house. He had never seen such a fine house before, and when he would knock on the door his hand refused to do his bidding. However, in the end he overcame his awe.

The knock was answered by the young handmaiden who had gone with her mistress to the feast the night before. When she recognized Merari she let out a loud scream and shut the door in his face. But he knocked again, until the master himself came to the door. Merari bowed down low before this stately man and said:

"I am Merari the son of Amram, from the town of Bethul in Judah—the same man who offended my lord's daughter last night, though meaning no harm. I am come to beg forgiveness of the maiden's father and to pay what penalty he might see fit to demand."

Then Bela the son of Ahiram stroked his beard and replied:

"Truly my lord must be an honorable man, for he did not steal away like a thief in the night but has come to make amends. But let us step inside, for it is not seemly that we stand debating such a grave matter in the street!"

In his zeal Merari forgot to bend down when he entered so that the beam over the door struck his forehead. Then he stood bowed, for even in this sumptuous home the rooms were too low for him.

"I can see why the men feared for my daughter," Bela the son of Ahiram said. "In the dark my lord must have appeared to them as one of the giants of old!"

"And the maiden?" Merari asked.

"Since she was brought home she has not left her room, nor has she touched a morsel of food. My wife is greatly distraught, Shoshanna being our only child, whom we love dearly."

At that Merari hung his head, looked down at his big, strong hands and said in a low voice:

"If the men told my lord that I tried to defile the maiden, they did not speak truly. Yet my lord's daughter is very comely, and God only knows what was in my heart last night. Therefore let me deal with her according to the law as though I had wronged her and let me take her for my wife—if this would please my lord."

Hearing this my father gave a loud gasp behind Merari, for he knew that Athara had waited all these years for Merari to marry her. If he returned from the north with a strange wife, there would be an outcry in Bethul such as had never been heard before. However, Merari seemed utterly bewitched.

"My lord is but a stranger arrived last night, and I know nothing about him," Bela the son of Ahiram replied. "Yet he must be an honorable man to make this offer. But can he afford to pay the bridal price for a maiden like Shoshanna, who has not only great beauty but also a fine dowry?"

"Neither am I a poor man," Merari said proudly. "Let my lord look outside, and he will see my donkeys laden with sacks of grain, and also my horse, a fine Arabian stallion now two years old and fit for the king himself. The donkeys, the grain and whatever else my lord might require of me I should willingly pay for his daughter. But the horse I would keep. Now if my lord would only consent to let me wed the maiden!"

"And would you not first know the size of her dowry?" Bela the son of Ahiram asked.

"If she would have me for her husband, I should take her even if she owned but the garment on her body!" Merari exclaimed.

At that Bela shook his head in wonder and said:

"Then let us ask her. Dinah!" he called, and in came the young woman who had first opened the door. "Go call Shoshanna, but do not tell her who is our visitor."

Soon Shoshanna herself appeared in the door, but seeing Merari she screamed and fled away. Then Merari said in sorrow:

"I can see that she utterly hates me."

"My young friend knows nothing of women," Bela replied. "If Shoshanna hated him, she would come into the room and speak cold and haughty words. But if a maiden flees away, it only means she wishes the man to pursue after her."

"Has not my lord told me that she wept in her room all night?" Merari asked.

"She did in truth. However, I never revealed why she wept. When the men brought her home last night, she cried: 'O father, the most marvelous man came out of the dark and swept me up in his arms! Now these abominable fiends have beaten him and driven him away. But I shall not put another morsel of food in my mouth until you have found him for me!' "

At that Merari remained speechless with joy.

"My wife and I were much bewildered by this," Bela continued, "for we reared Shoshanna well, nor has she ever acted in such an unseemly manner. Perhaps we erred in not marrying her sooner, but since she is so frail we put it off until now."

"Truly it must have been God's will that she remain unwed until I found her!" Merari exclaimed.

"Then God's will must be strange indeed," Bela said, "for we never thought of marrying our daughter to a giant. The thought troubles me and shall surely distress my wife."

"But is not a big, strong man to be desired over a weakling?" Merari asked, amazed.

"Since my lord wishes to marry Shoshanna, I must reveal to him the truth, for he looks like a man who would want many sons," Bela said. "My wife is of the mixed people and still worships her own gods. However, this is not what I would discuss, for Shoshanna shall surely obey my lord in this matter. Rather I would tell my lord that all the women of my wife's house are very beautiful and built in such a manner as would give a man much pleasure when he lies with them. But they do not bear children well. They rarely have sons, and those who do are wont to die in childbirth. My wife's father told me this before I married her, and I feel bound to tell my lord the same about Shoshanna."

"And did this revelation keep my lord from marrying Shoshanna's mother?" Merari asked. "And should I show less faith and be deterred by what might be?"

"I see my lord's heart is set upon my daughter," Bela said. "Then let us put the question to the maiden and her mother."

No sooner had he spoken than Shoshanna entered, dressed in the fine white linen robe she wore the night before, with chains about her neck, bracelets on her wrists and kohl about her eyes. With her was her mother, a woman no longer young but still of great beauty, with the same fair skin and large eyes, and hair that might once have been red but was graying now. Both women bowed down low before their visitor, and then Shoshanna said to her father:

"My lord has sent for me."

"Indeed I have, Shoshanna. You had already glanced at this young man—as I can tell by the color of your face—is he the one who carried you off last night?"

"He is the one."

"And do you know why he has come here?"

"How should I know such a thing, my lord?" Shoshanna said.

Her father passed his hand over his beard and smiled at Merari. Then he said:

"Merari the son of Amram, who owns good fields and much cattle in Bethul, would have you for his wife."

Shoshanna quickly put her hands over her face to hide her joy.

"And would you have him for your husband?" her father asked.

"If my lord wishes me to marry this man, who am I to disobey him?" Shoshanna said.

Her father laughed and said to Merari:

"Now that my lord has seen of what guile my daughter is capable, would he still have her?"

"I would have her," Merari replied.

"And you, my wife, how does this young man please you?" Bela asked Shoshanna's mother.

"He is so very tall and strong," the lady said, distressed. "Are we to lose our daughter with her first-born?"

"Oh, but I shall not die in childbirth!" Shoshanna cried out before she remembered her modesty.

"We must not keep Shoshanna a maiden forever," Bela the son of Ahiram said to his wife. "And if Merari would still have her, knowing all I told him, he shall have her. Indeed he offered to take Shoshanna without a dowry. But I would never shame my daughter and disgrace myself by accepting such an offer. And now you women had better go and prepare a feast for us, while this young man and I draw up the marriage contract."

A servant ran to fetch a scribe, and Merari and Bela sat down to discuss the terms of the marriage. There was much talk about property, as is only fitting on such an occasion. The bridal price for Shoshanna was to be what Merari had offered—his donkeys and the grain they carried. Moreover, he was to put some of his land in her name. As for Bela, he would give his daughter two precious garments, some jewelry and household goods, and the income from one of his vineyards. Let none in Bethul say that Merari had brought back a poor stranger from Israel! And after Bela died, all his lands would go to Shoshanna, she being his only child. When this was written down, Bela turned to his chosen son and said:

"There is one more thing I would put into this contract. If you will not agree to it, I must refuse you my daughter."

"Whatever my lord might ask of me I shall gladly do," Merari replied.

"No, but wait until you hear what it is," Bela said. "I shall ask of you the same thing my wife's father asked of me when I married her. Shoshanna is frail and might never bear you a son. Yet you, being strong and hale, might become vexed with a wife that can give you no heir."

"I shall always love Shoshanna more than I could love seven sons!" Merari exclaimed.

"You may think so now, but your mind might change in time. Then you will want to take another wife to bear you sons. Though this is your right, I would never have my daughter thus humbled. Rather I would have it written in the contract that if Shoshanna would not share your house with another wife, she should be free to return home and take her dowry with her. Nor should the bridal price be restored, for I would have none think of her as a needy, divorced woman."

"My lord may put in the contract what he pleases," Merari replied. "As for me, I swear before Yahweh that I will not take another wife as long as I live!"

"This last we shall not put in writing," Bela said, "for to make such a vow is utter blasphemy."

The scribe wrote out the contract twice on two pieces of parchment. Then each scroll was rolled up, tied with a fine, twisted rope and sealed. One was to be kept by Merari and the other by Bela that both might have proof of their agreement. My father and the scribe bore witness to the act. Thus the law was served and Merari was the husband of Shoshanna.

The maiden and her mother were summoned, and all sat down to a splendid repast. Shoshanna took her place beside Merari as his wife. While they ate they glanced at each other, and one could see how much Merari desired her. But he had not yet touched her. When the meal was finished Merari rose, bowed down low before Shoshanna's parents and said:

"And now, with your blessings, my bride and I shall leave and head for home."

At that Shoshanna's mother began to weep and would not be comforted.

"Let them stay at least until tomorrow!" she pleaded.

"If this would please my bride I will stay," Merari said. "However, we should be on our way, for it is a long journey and the rains might soon commence. I should be plowing early now that I must provide for a wife."

But Shoshanna too was eager to leave.

"If my lord thinks it wise that we depart this very day, I must do as he wishes," she said modestly.

When she saw that she could not detain her daughter, Shoshanna's mother left off weeping and said:

"My husband has given Shoshanna a fine dowry, neither shall she go empty-handed from her mother. Of my own inheritance I shall give her my handmaiden Dinah. Dinah shall wait on her, sweep her house and grind her flour."

Then Dinah was called into the room and told to fetch her few belongings for the journey to Judah. She was but a slave who could not choose her destiny, nor was she displeased, for she had looked at my father and liked what she saw.

Shoshanna embraced her father and mother, and then her chattels were loaded on the mule, while the donkeys with the grain jars stayed behind as the bridal price. Bela also gave the young couple a tent in which to pass the night, for his daughter was frail and not accustomed to sleeping in the cold night air. There was still room for my father on the mule, while Dinah walked behind him, as befits a woman and a slave. But Merari lifted Shoshanna up and put her on the horse before him, and thus he held her all day against him as they rode homeward.

At nightfall they dismounted, pitched their tent and ate around the fire. Then Merari took Shoshanna's hand and led her into the tent, for he had held her against his body all day and he desired her greatly. And it was on that night, in the tent pitched in the hills of Samaria, that Judith was conceived.

I too was conceived that night. My father had looked at Merari holding his bride in his arms all day as he rode before him, and a man cannot observe another doing this thing without wanting to do it too.

My parents were not married then, nor did they have a tent for shelter. Thus they lay beneath the stars in the cool of the night. My father did not think this a sin, for my mother was only a slave, nor was she a Hebrew woman. She was of the mixed people and shared their beliefs, knowing the names of many heathen gods and tales of their great deeds. These she would later tell to Judith and me, but never before Merari, who worshiped only Yahweh. Nor did he believe that gods were like mortals, enjoying the same sports. Rather he thought that man was created in the image of God and that he must act accordingly.

Next morning they all rose at dawn and continued their journey to Bethul. Merari carried Shoshanna out of the tent in his arms and again held her on the horse before him, where she rode with her head leaning against his chest, like a sleepy child. But my mother walked behind my father, as decreed by custom and decency.

When they reached Bethul all the people came running out of

their houses, more amazed still than on the day Merari had returned with a horse. The woman he carried with him could only be his wife, for he was not the man to take a concubine, nor would he have allowed her to ride with him.

Soon Athara too approached to discover whether the rumor was true. Seeing it was so, she placed her hand upon her head and wailed as though death had carried off her closest kin. Then Merari's sister Sarai drew near and said:

"I always knew you were a fool, my brother Merari, but not such a fool as to insult our father's brother and to forfeit the riches Athara would have brought you. And all because you were bewitched by a Samarian girl!"

Turning ashen with anger, Merari replied:

"Shoshanna is my wife, and you had better learn to honor her as one honors the wife of an elder brother. Moreover, she has not only beauty but also a fine dowry, and shall someday inherit better fields and vineyards than Athara!"

"And what will those fields in Samaria profit you?" Sarai said, for she would speak the last word in this matter.

Then she departed to her own house and all the rest of the people to their houses. But when Merari made a wedding feast, as befits a bridegroom, they all came and ate and drank and feasted for seven days.

Merari, clothed in his finest linen, with garlands about his head, danced with the other men, while Shoshanna sat on the ground and worshiped him with her eyes. And Merari looked upon her in like manner. All said this was quite unseemly, for a man ought to see in his wife only the mother of his sons. So should a woman see in her husband only the father of her children. Still all those who found fault continued coming to the feast every day. In the end even Sarai and her family came, and only Athara and her father stayed away.

Athara had fallen into a fit and said she would surely die of shame if her father did not find her a husband soon. Her father did indeed find her a husband, a strong, handsome man some years younger than she, who had no means to buy a wife and would gladly take Athara, with all her cattle and fields. However, people said there was no handmaiden in Bethul safe from his lewdness. He was married to Athara before the feasting was over in Merari's house, and the bride's father made an even greater feast than Merari. Athara too conceived, and nine months later her son Manasseh, Judith and I were all born within the same fortnight.

When Merari saw that my mother was with child, he asked my father if he had lain with her. And learning the truth he gave my father Dinah for his wife, for he would not have a bastard born in his house. But my father did not have the silver to redeem my mother and thus she remained Shoshanna's handmaiden even though she was wed to a free Hebrew. But Merari and Shoshanna were kind to my parents. Upon their marriage Merari gave them a small plot of land for their own, and to each a new garment. Shoshanna gave my mother one of her own silver chains, for she had been with her since childhood and was to her more friend than servant.

Indeed Shoshanna was in sore need of a friend, for the women of Bethul hated her. Not only was she a stranger and very beautiful, but Merari treated her as no other man in Bethul treated his wife. Fearing for her health since she was with child, he would not let her work. At times his sister Sarai would come and chide him:

"If Shoshanna had not brought her handmaiden, you would grind your own flour to spare her from work!"

But this was a small matter compared to the outcry when Merari built his new house. He built it in the fashion of Bela's house in Samaria so that his wife might not pine for her father's house. Only the rooms were higher to allow Merari to walk about upright. There was a lower story and an upper story, and above them a roof where one could walk about on a summer night. It took many months to build the house, but it was completed in time, for Merari had vowed that his first child should be born in his new home.

Of the three women who were with child then—my mother, Shoshanna and Athara—Shoshanna was the first to give birth. She had grown big with child, and women whispered with glee that her labor would be long and painful if the child took in size after Merari. The last two months Shoshanna's frail body hurt, and she spent all day reclining on her bed. But my mother, who was strong and hale, swept and cooked and washed and ground flour and waited on Shoshanna hand and foot. And Merari set more tongues yet to wag by waiting on her too. He would place food before Shoshanna and beg her to eat, and one could see that he was sick with worry.

It was in the month of Tammuz, in the heat of summer, that Shoshanna went into travail. The women of Bethul had predicted truly. Shoshanna's labor lasted for three days and three nights. Yet she did not cry out once but bit on a sheet, for she would not delight the women with her shrieks. The midwife, who had seen most of the children born in Bethul, had never witnessed such a thing. She said Shoshanna would surely die in defying her pangs. But Shoshanna remained mute until the child's head emerged between her thighs. Then she let out one piercing shriek and fainted. However, she did not die, as the midwife had predicted.

While his wife writhed in travail Merari sat on the floor in another room, praying and tearing his hair, and refusing all food. Just as the sun rose above the horizon on the third day, Shoshanna shrieked, and soon the midwife came to tell Merari that a daughter was born to him. With tears streaming down his face, Merari raised himself on his knees and said:

"Praised be the Lord. Then my wife will live."

Indeed Shoshanna lived. But she was ill a long time, nor did she have much milk to nurse her child.

A few days later my mother gave birth to me. She brought forth easily, her body being strong and supple from work. Moreover, she wore about her neck a likeness of Ashtoreth, the goddess who granted women a fertile womb and easy labor. Shoshanna too had owned such an amulet, but Merari had taken it from her the first night he lay with her. He had crushed it in his fingers and thrown it away in the hills of Samaria. And he had made Shoshanna vow that henceforth she would worship only Yahweh.

Shoshanna's child was hale and gorgeous, perfectly shaped, with pink nails and dark-red hair even at birth, and my mother nursed her at one breast while she nursed me at the other.

And they named her Judith.

A week later Athara gave birth to a boy. This filled her with great glee, and she spread the rumor that God had punished Merari for not marrying her by blessing her with a son while giving him only a daughter. But Merari should not have cared had Athara given birth to seven sons. Moreover, Manasseh proved to be a sickly boy, while Judith was strong and beautiful. She stood at six months, walked at nine and talked at a year. And she was taller than all other children her age in Bethul, for though she had Shoshanna's face she had Merari's build. Her dark-red hair grew thicker every day. Her skin was fair, and in a certain light her amber eyes looked green. Even as a young child she had a long neck and held her head high when Shoshanna carried her about. The other women in Bethul were envious, for none had a daughter to compare with Judith. But since Judith was still too young to speak evil of her, they spoke evil of Shoshanna.

The women never forgot that Shoshanna was a stranger from the north who had stolen the man who was to be the husband of a girl from Bethul. Thus they observed her every move to see if they could trap her in strange practices. But Shoshanna had forsworn the heathen gods, and the only strange thing about her was that she did not fear animals. She loved dogs and cats, allowing them in the house, nor did she tremble before Hadad, Merari's horse, though most men would give him a wide berth. Hadad was still the same old demon, but he was gentle with Shoshanna. Even the bulls in the field would let Shoshanna come near without hurting her. She often walked through the fields, among the cattle, with Judith in her arms, and none of the beasts would harm her. Thus Judith too came to love animals.

But the women spoke of witchcraft and evil practices. No doubt Athara was the source of all these rumors, but she was careful not to let herself be caught. The bulls above all gave the women food for gossip. Shoshanna came from a land where bulls had been wor-shiped—had not Jeroboam put up two golden calves in Bethel—and they said as they did there so Shoshanna did in Bethul.

Again Merari's sister Sarai came to him with tales.

"If your wife lacks good sense," she said to Merari, "you might keep her from the bulls. Were not you the one who smashed the altar of Ashtoreth outside Bethul?"

At first Merari did not understand her words. But when she told him of the gossip in town, he angrily bade her leave his house. But he was troubled by the rumors and spoke about them to Shoshanna.

"If my lord would not have me walk among the cattle, I shall surely obey his will," Shoshanna said. "But Judith loves to play with the young calves, and it grieves me to deny her this pleasure. Who knows if she will ever have brothers and sisters for playmates?"

At that Merari sighed and said:

"If walking among the cattle pleases you and the child, I shall not keep you from it. But remember they are only beasts which God put in this world."

There were few wishes Merari would have refused Shoshanna, for he loved her dearly. Still Shoshanna's sadness increased from week to week. When she discovered that my mother was with child again, she wept bitter tears and spoke:

"You, Dinah, are blessed with a fruitful womb. But I shall never have another child, for my lord lies with me in such a manner as to keep me from conceiving. And if I never bear him a son he will soon cease from loving me."

"Let my lady not trouble herself," my mother said, "for the master loves her more than seven sons. Indeed he loves her better than his god, for the thing he does is a great sin in the eyes of Yahweh."

"But I would not have him sin for me!" Shoshanna exlaimed.

"Such things are between a man and his god, and a woman had better not meddle in them," my mother said. "Moreover, there is nothing my lady can do to make him change his ways."

"Oh, but you could give me one of your potions, Dinah, to mix into his wine! Then he would become greatly inflamed and forget himself," Shoshanna said.

"May the gods do thus and thus to me if I even listen to you!" my mother exclaimed in horror. "If you conceived and any harm came to you, the master would surely kill me if he learned the truth! Have you forgotten your last confinement, your long and painful travail and your sickness afterward? And would you yet have another child? I shall assuredly not help you toward it!"

"No, but I would bear my lord a son," Shoshanna said.

And she pleaded with my mother and even threatened to reveal her secret practices until in the end she gave her the desired potion.

Since his marriage Merari had acquired yet more land and many vineyards, for the Lord blessed all his works and made him prosper. Every year at the time of the grape harvest Merari made a big feast to keep his wife from being homesick. Shoshanna would dance before him, and then they would drink wine and he would carry her into the tent, as he had done on the first night he lay with her.

It was at the grape harvest, when Judith was three years old, that Shoshanna conceived again. She had danced before Merari and had poured Dinah's potion into his wine, inflaming him greatly. Merari was so drunk that night he did not recall his own actions next morning. Nor did he know that Shoshanna had conceived until he could see that she was with child. Then he knew it had happened while he was full of wine. He placed his hand upon his head, wept and said:

"Men are no better than beasts. If any harm should come to you, delight of my eyes, I do not know that I shall go on living!"

But Shoshanna, who kept her secret and knew that Merari was not to blame, replied:

"Let my lord not utter such blasphemy! Surely it was God's will that I conceive again and bear my lord a son."

But in her heart she knew that it was not God's will but the doing of her handmaiden Dinah, and she was afraid.

In the spring, when Shoshanna was big with child, Merari made a vow to God.

"If the Lord will let you live, I shall take the choicest bull calf born in my herd this spring and carry it up to Jerusalem next year to offer it as a sacrifice at Passover. And if the bull does not suffice, let me pay for my sin, if only God would grant you life!"

When Shoshanna's time drew near, my mother called Judith and me—for we clung together, being sisters in my mother's milk—and took us to Sarai's house. But later the story was told me so often it is as though I had witnessed it.

After Shoshanna's pangs commenced and the midwife was called, my mother stepped before Merari and said:

"Surely my lord remembers how the mistress suffered when Judith was born. My lord took away my lady's amulet, but I still have mine. Also I bore my daughter and my younger son with ease. If my lord loves his wife, let him give me permission to put the charm around my lady's neck that it might ease her labor!"

"No," Merari answered. "There is only one God."

But when there was no end to the pangs and he saw that Shoshanna did not have the strength to bring forth the child, Merari came to my mother and said:

"Give her your charm then, Dinah, and let the sin be upon my head. For I can bear it no longer."

But when my mother would place the chain about Shoshanna's neck, she pushed her away, weak and in pain though she was.

"Do not put this abomination on me," she said, "for even if I live my lord would hate me forever after."

And she struggled mightily to give birth but could not. On the fourth day the child died in her body, and she with it. Thus they knew it had been a boy.

Then Merari became as a man possessed. He howled and rent his clothes and cut his flesh—though the last was forbidden to Hebrews —and he threw himself on Shoshanna's body. It took three men to pull him off. But he would not give her up for burial, nor would he eat, but sat on the ground, drinking wine and cursing God and himself.

"Let them come and stone me like a murderer," he cried, "for I killed her with my lust!"

In the end my mother poured another of her potions in his wine to make him sleep. Then the wailing women came, and they took away Shoshanna's body and buried it in a cave in the hills. When Merari woke he went up to the cave and tried to roll away the stone from the entrance to retrieve his dead wife. But it had taken three men to roll the stone before the cave, and even with his great strength Merari could not remove it.

Thus he returned home to drink himself drunk. He did not cease from drinking for a fortnight, while Judith and I remained in his sister's house. Then Sarai came to him and said:

"It is proper to mourn one's wife, but to be drunk continually is unseemly. Can you not see now that it was a sin to love her as you did, for a man must not love his wife as if she were a harlot. Now Shoshanna is dead and your daughter is alive. Would you leave Judith an orphan with neither mother nor father?"

Then Merari bethought himself of his duty. He cut his hair, bathed, changed his garments and had Judith brought home. When he saw her he wept anew, for she had Shoshanna's face. Then he said:

"Now you are doubly precious to me, my daughter, for you are all that is left of her. But I shall never have another child."

From that day on Judith, who had been tended by Shoshanna and my mother, was tended by Merari. My mother saw only to such needs as require the hand of a woman, but Merari saw to the rest. He would take Judith down into the fields with him, and she would trot beside him when he plowed and seeded after the first rains in the fall.

Though Merari had many menservants by then, he still did his own plowing. He was bigger and stronger than any of his men, and when he held the plow it dug deeper into the ground. He would harness his two strongest oxen and walk steadily behind them, his hands on the handles of the plow, the muscles of his bare arms rippling, his black beard blowing in the wind. Those women of Bethul who had no husbands—and many who did—would sigh as they observed him and mutter because he spent his strength on the harlots by the wall. For Merari's needs were like those of any man, but he would not take another wife. In the end the women bade Sarai reason with him.

"My brother," she said to Merari, "the period of your mourning is long over. It is time you should be comforted and take another wife. Also you must think of your daughter. Nor is it seemly that you seek your pleasure with the harlots by the wall."

"And when will you cease troubling yourself with my seemliness?" Merari replied. "Moreover, when I drew up my marriage contract I vowed that I would never have another wife but Shoshanna."

"Fool," Sarai said. "You vowed for as long as she lived!"

"No, my sister," Merari replied. "I vowed for as long as *I* lived. And thus it shall be."

"But what of your daughter if you remain unmarried? You must not take her with you wherever you go—into the fields and to the stables—for these are tasks for men. Rather Judith ought to learn how to sew and cook and sweep that she might know how to look after her house!"

"There are maidservants about the house to sew and cook and sweep," Merari said. "As for Judith, she shall someday inherit all my land. Therefore let her learn to love and tend it!"

Judith did indeed learn to love the land. She would observe her father scoop up a handful of earth and hold it to his nose, and she would do the same, standing with her small feet planted apart, like Merari. Or she would walk beside him holding onto the handle of

the plow, hindering more than helping. But Merari was pleased to
see her act thus. He would teach her the names of all the plants and
trees and show her the first green sprouts coming up in the fields.
And he would speak to her as to one fully grown, revealing to her
the length of time it took for the wheat and barley to ripen, and
how the grain must be cut at the proper time, in the morning, after
the dew had fallen and before the hot winds rose from the southern
desert to wither the harvest. He also took her to the stables and let
her walk among the cattle, as she had done while her mother lived.

The spring Shoshanna died the herd had been increased by many
calves. The most perfect was a young bull, black with a white mark
on his forehead and altogether without a blemish, whom we named
Apis. Though Merari told Judith that the bull had been promised to
God, Judith said he belonged to her.

Merari had not forgotten his vow, though after Shoshanna's
death he had quarreled with God. But in time he relented.

"If she died, she died for my sin," he said. "And should I now
draw God's wrath down on my daughter by refusing what I
promised Him? Rather I shall take Apis in the spring, at the time of
the Passover, and carry him up to Jerusalem for a sin offering that I
might be cleansed and the curse removed from my house."

But to Judith he did not say that her bull must die, only that he
was to be given to Yahweh. For Judith loved Apis and often threw
her arms about him in delight. In the end Merari's sister Sarai came
again to offer more of her sage counsel:

"Like mother like daughter," she said to Merari. "Remember
there is pagan blood in Judith, nor ought you permit such practices
with beasts!"

"No, but I shall not spoil her pleasure yet," Merari replied. "It is
only until the Passover."

In the eighteenth year of King Josiah—that was the year Josiah
ordered the breaches of the temple repaired—the priest Hilkiah
discovered the holy Book of Laws concealed in the walls. And
finding that in their ignorance they had broken many laws, Josiah
rent his clothes and repented of the sins his people had committed.
Then he celebrated a Passover such as had not been celebrated since
the children of Israel left Egypt. And every year thereafter a Passover was celebrated in Jerusalem.

The king and his nobles would give of their wealth to the priests that they might sacrifice for them and share the meat among the Levites and those too poor to bring their own offerings. But many from all over Judah carried their choicest gifts to Jerusalem—the first fruit of their land, a pair of pigeons, a sheep, a ram, a calf, an ox or, if they were wealthy like Merari, even a bull. They would set out days before the feast, for the trek through the hill country was wearisome and not many owned donkeys, less still a horse like Hadad to ride upon.

Two days before the Passover Merari saddled his horse at dawn and put a tether on Apis, the bull, to take him to Jerusalem. He had told Judith of his errand the night before, but being only a child she did not comprehend until she saw Merari mount his horse. Then she stamped her feet and shouted:

"No, but if you take Apis along I too want to go!"

And she continued wailing until my mother hastened from the house and I behind her to learn the cause of Judith's grief. We found Hadad prancing about madly, stirred up by the noise, and Merari barely able to rein him. But Judith lay on the ground, red in the face and kicking her heels as she screamed.

"What shall we do with her, Dinah?" Merari asked my mother in distress.

"This is for my lord to say," my mother replied, though she had often proclaimed that with children a sound slap worked greater wonders than witchcraft.

But Merari had never raised his hand against Judith. Rather he had given way to her in all matters until she had become stubborn beyond correction.

"No, but I want to go with you and Apis!" she shouted.

"Do you not think that I might take her, Dinah?" Merari said in the end.

"Since my lord asks my counsel, let me say that I do not think such a journey meant for a child," my mother replied. "Neither would it be wise to take Judith," she added, glancing at the bull and then at Merari.

"No, but I want to go!" Judith shrieked, bringing some of the neighbors running from their houses.

"I cannot bear to see how my leaving grieves her," Merari said. "There is room for both of us on Hadad's back."

"Let my lord consider the things to be done for a girl child! She must be bathed and combed, and her garments washed and changed. And has my lord ever seen to these tasks?" my mother said.

"I have a married brother in Jerusalem," Merari replied. "Surely his wife would tend Judith for a few days."

"And who would tend her on the journey?" my mother asked.

"No, but I want to go!" Judith screamed.

Seeing Judith's distress, I too began to scream.

"I also want to go! And I shall look after Judith!"

Merari glanced at me and said:

"You, Tamar, are no older than Judith! And could you tend to her needs?"

"Truly I could, my lord." I replied.

Nor was this a lie, for being only a slave I had been taught early to look after my own needs, which were the same as Judith's.

At that Judith clapped her hands with glee and shouted:

"Yes, let us take Tamar, and we shall all go to Jerusalem and offer Apis to the Lord!"

My mother would still dissuade Merari, but he turned a deaf ear.

"I shall indeed take Tamar along to stay with Judith when my errands take me from her," he said. "But you, Dinah, make ready whatever the children might need for the journey, and fill a basket with food, for we must leave before the sun rises and the air turns hot."

Seeing that her counsel would be for naught, my mother went to fetch what was needed. Bread and salted meat and dried grapes, a skin filled with water and one with wine for Merari, and a change of garments for Judith that she might be kept clean. Then my own father, who had also come outside to see us off, lifted Judith up on the horse before Merari, and me behind him. And we set out for Jerusalem, with my parents shouting blessings after us.

The sun was not yet risen when we rode out through the gate of Bethul. It was as fair a day as we might get in the month of Nisan. A gentle breeze came from the hills, and the air was clear and cool. The sky was pale, like the face of a sleeper in the morning, before the sun would restore its color. Descending from Bethul, Hadad haltingly picked his way among the loose pebbles on the steep path.

I clung to Merari's back, while he held Judith with one hand and the reins with the other.

Below us in the fields the golden wheat stood high, but the barley had ripened early and was already cut, ready to be gathered onto the threshing floor. Partridges scurried back and forth among the stacks of barley, picking grain off the stalks. The birds would be fat and succulent when the men began to hunt them after their breeding time. Merari was skillful with the bow and often brought home wild fowl, which my mother roasted for us over the fire.

Once in the valley we turned north and set our faces toward Jerusalem. The meadows about us were still green, for the rains had ceased only a short while ago and the heat of the summer was not yet upon the land. From the lush green grass burst forth a wealth of wildflowers, covering the earth like a many-colored coat. The flowers grew so high and dense they nearly concealed Hadad's legs as he walked. And Apis, the bull, often halted and pulled on his tether as he lowered his head to snatch a mouthful of grass.

It was the time of the year when storks journey north. The clatter of Hadad's hoofs would stir them out of the thickets and into white-winged flight. Judith would shriek with delight as she watched their broad wings flapping toward the brightening sky. As the sun rose the birds in the trees burst into lusty song. Slowly the sky turned from white to blue, but it was not yet hot.

Before we came to the path that served the other pilgrims, Merari reined his horse, looked about him and said in a low voice:

"How lovely the land that God has given us."

But Judith and I were too young then to know how he felt in his heart. We only knew that it was a fine day to journey to Jerusalem.

On the path that cut through the hills we met many pilgrims traveling north. Some carried their first fruit, while others led sheep and goats, which strained at their tethers as they tried to graze by the wayside. But none of the pilgrims brought a bull for sacrifice, nor did any ride a horse. When we passed them along the way—for our progress was swifter than theirs—they nudged each other, pointed at us and whispered.

At noon we halted atop a hill and sat in the shade of a terebinth tree. After we had poured water over our hands we ate the repast my mother had wrapped for us, and Merari drank of his wine. Then he rose, took Judith by the hand and led her to where the hill broke off into a precipice.

"Behold the land, my daughter," he said. "To the east of us, shrouded in the mists of the valley, the Salt Sea, and beyond it the mountains of Moab, where dwell our enemies, the Moabites. To the south and west of us Lachish and Gaza—though we cannot see it from here—and beyond Gaza Egypt, where dwell our enemies, the Egyptians. To the north of us Jerusalem, and north of Jerusalem, beyond Samaria, the land of Hamath, where dwell our enemies, the Syrians. And yet farther to the north and east Assyria, where dwell our enemies, the Assyrians. Judah is but a small country, yet all the other nations covet it continually. But it was given to us by God forever. I would have you remember that always, Judith."

Looking up at her tall father, Judith replied:

"I shall, my lord."

"Ours may be a poor country where we must wrest the harvest from the soil and pray for rain," Merari continued. "But it is a lovely land, where the hills sing the praise of God in the spring, and it is ours. For this we owe thanks. And now let us mount Hadad and ride on to Jerusalem!"

It was on the eve of the second day, after we had spent the first night sleeping in the fields, that we reached the hill south of Jerusalem. When we gained the crest we could see down into the valley of Hinnom, where people had sacrificed their children to Moloch until King Josiah put an end to this evil. From the valley rose Mount Moriah, and upon it the holy city of David. The sun was sinking behind the western hills and the sky was turning a dark blue, from which the houses of Jerusalem stood out white. Above them the walls of the palace and the temple gleamed in the last rays of the setting sun.

The crest of the hill was aswarm with pilgrims, all gazing toward the city. Even strong men like Merari wept, one calling to the other, as if any among them might not recognize the sight:

"Behold, Jerusalem!"

Then we descended the hill and passed the field where the people of Jerusalem buried their dead—for they would not bury them within their walls—and from there we climbed a winding path to the east gate of the city. Now people were streaming toward the gate from all sides, up the slope of Mount Moriah, with their sheep and goats and cattle. The dust they raised was carried off by the evening breeze to hang over the southern hills like a golden haze.

The air was so dry it parched our nostrils, and our tongues clove to
the roofs of our mouths. We all longed for a resting place and a cool
drink. Even Hadad tossed his head, neighed and pawed the ground
when our progress was halted just outside the gate.

A great multitude had gathered there, some listening, others
shouting curses at a young man who had climbed upon a rock and
stood there exhorting the crowd. He was an angry-looking young
man, with an unkempt beard and a coarse robe girdled with a length
of plain cord. His eyes were fierce and frightened at the same time,
as though he did not know whether to stand and preach or turn and
run. For some of the people stood shaking their fists at him.

As we drew near we heard his voice, which was deep and strong
for so frail-looking a young man:

"They say if a man put away his wife, and she go from him and
become another man's, shall he return unto her? Shall not the land
be greatly polluted? But you have played the harlot with many
lovers; yet return again unto me, says the Lord. Lift up your eyes
unto the high places and see where you have not been lain with. In
the ways have you sat for them, like the Arabian in the wilderness;
and you have polluted the land with your whoredom and your
wickedness."

There was an angry growling in the crowd, and some one threw
a stone. The young man flinched, but the stone fell short and he
continued speaking:

"Run to and fro through the streets of Jerusalem, and see now,
and know, and seek in the broad places thereof, if you can find a
man, if there be *any* that execute judgment, that seek the truth; and
I will pardon her. And though they say the Lord lives, surely they
swear falsely."

Merari bent down from his horse and asked the man beside him:

"Who is this young man preaching by the gate?"

"Is there still a man left in Judah who does not know the vile
troublemaker Jeremiah?" the man replied. "He was cursed with a
black vision and continually foresees disaster, even in the midst of
plenty! Has not the king read the law to us? Do we not keep the
Passover? Are not the people come from all the land, even from
Samaria, to offer sacrifice at the temple? What more would he have
us do?"

While he spoke the murmur of the crowd rose even higher, so

that the next words of the young man could not be heard. But the man who stood beside Hadad again plucked at Merari's robe and said:

"My lord must be newly come to Jerusalem, for he sits listening to this mischief maker with his mouth open and amazement in his eyes. Yet has this Jeremiah preached worse things! He has asked that all labor cease on the Sabbath and that no burden be carried in and out through the gates of Jerusalem. Moreover, he has proclaimed at every corner that we must let our slaves go in the seventh year. But how should we prosper if we traded only six days a week and if we freed our slaves? And why should we be troubled by this prophet born north of the border, in the land of Benjamin, who has come south to change our ways? Is there no breaking of the Sabbath in the north? Are there no slaves in the north that he must preach to us in Judah?"

A small crowd had gathered around the man as he spoke, all shouting their approval. But the young prophet raised his voice above those of the others and cried:

"Circumcise yourselves to the Lord, and take away the foreskins of your hearts, you men of Judah and inhabitants of Jerusalem: lest my fury come forth like fire, and burn that none can quench it, because of the evil of your doings. The children have forsaken me and have sworn by them that are no gods: when I fed them to the full, they then committed adultery, and assembled themselves in troops in the harlots' houses. They were as fed horses in the morning: every one neighed after his neighbor's wife. Shall I not visit for these things?"

Now a woman bent down, picked up a stone and threw it at the prophet so that it grazed his cheek and drew blood. Merari turned to her in wrath and said:

"You dare throw stones at a prophet, woman?"

But the woman answered him:

"Would my lord call this man a prophet, who speaks vile words in the ears of our children? Surely the king ought to arrest one who utters such speech in broad places! As for my lord, he had better take his two young daughters where they cannot hear this foulmouth, who casts dirt on all the women of Judah! Had he but a wife of his own, she would teach him to honor women. But what woman would have such a one for her husband?"

At this the other women laughed and smote their thighs. And the men too laughed, though they did not like to hear women speak up before a crowd. Hurt more deeply by their derision than by the stones thrown at him, the prophet stepped down from the rock and was soon engulfed by the crowd that carried him and us through the gate into Jerusalem.

Judith, who had sat silent on the horse before her father, now turned around and asked Merari:

"This wild man—the prophet—what was it he preached?"

Merari sighed and answered:

"He preached against sin, my child."

"And what is that, my lord?" Judith asked.

Merari thought for a while and then he said:

"Sin is when men do what is wrong in the eyes of God."

"But how do men know what is wrong in the eyes of God?" Judith asked.

Merari bent down and pressed his face against Judith's hair.

"Judith, Judith," he said. "The human heart is wiser than the human mind. There is not sin in the eyes of God that the human heart does not recognize. This is why we must make sacrifice: to be purified from our sins."

"Surely *we* have committed no sins!" Judith exclaimed.

But Merari stared straight ahead and made no answer.

Jerusalem was a maze of streets, bewildering after Bethul, where one knew every house and alley, and most inhabitants by name. It took much asking about until we found the quarters where dwelled the king's carpenters and stonemasons, and further inquiry to find the house of Merari's brother, Aaron. His house was small but well put together and handsomely finished, for he was skillful with his hands and had built it himself.

At first Aaron did not recognize his own brother. He had not seen Merari in many years and had not expected him to come riding to his door upon a horse, like a prince. But when Merari dismounted and greeted him by name, the two brothers embraced and shed tears of joy, seeing that each was well and prosperous. Then Aaron called his wife and his three sons—one older than Judith, one the same age, and one younger—and all bowed down low before Merari, while we bowed down low before Merari's brother. The neighbors came forth from their houses to watch this greeting, calling to each other that Aaron the son of Amram had a wealthy visitor, who had come riding upon a horse and had brought a young bull for a Passover sacrifice. Aaron was well pleased with their astonishment.

Then we were led into the house and given water to wash and rugs to sit on. The oldest boy went to look after Hadad, but came back saying the horse would not let him come near. Thus Merari himself had to feed him. Apis too was fed and tethered in the yard, where he bedded down for the night, while Hadad slept standing up. But we had a fine repast inside the house, for it was not every day that a wealthy brother came for a visit. There was much talk about old times, as there will be on such an occasion. Aaron said it grieved him not to have known Merari's wife, but looking at Judith he could see that she must have been very beautiful. When he saw Merari's face turn dark with sorrow, he quickly spoke of other things. In the end he asked:

"And how is our kinfolk in Bethul?"

"Our father's brother is well, thank God, and Athara the mother of a son," Merari replied.

"And is Athara still as ugly as in former times?" Aaron asked.

"Uglier yet," Merari said.

"Then the age of miracles is not past, for such a thing would have seemed impossible," Aaron said, and they both laughed.

After the meal Aaron's wife and sons retired to another room, while Judith and I bedded down where we had eaten. For we would all rise at dawn to go to the temple. Thinking us asleep, Merari and Aaron sat up a long time talking.

"It has gone well with me in Jerusalem," Aaron said. "King Josiah pays his workingmen fair wages. Moreover, I have learned to draw up plans for houses so that I am no longer a common laborer. God willing, my sons too shall someday prosper as builders. And how is it with you, my brother? I can see that you too have prospered, or else you would not come to Jerusalem riding on a horse. Surely you are not a horse thief, nor would you long escape the king's officers!"

And again they laughed, as men will at such jests.

"Indeed God has greatly blessed the work of my hands," Merari said. "My cows calve, my fields bear rich harvests, the grapes in my vineyards hang heavy, and I have a beautiful daughter. However, the Lord not only gives but also requires, and he has taken my wife, who was the delight of my eyes. Still, I must think of my child and would leave her well provided for when my time comes."

Merari paused and then continued haltingly:

"There is a matter I wish to discuss with you, brother. When you went off to Jerusalem long ago, you left me the rocky fields we inherited from our father. I dug up every stone with my own hands until the fields were made as fertile as any around Bethul. They were made so by the labor of my hands and I think of them as mine. But we never drew up a contract where you signed your portion over to me. Know that I would not wish to take your fields as a gift but would pay you the price your share was worth when you left."

Aaron stroked his beard, gazed at his brother and said:

"Need two brothers draw up contracts? I shall here and now give you my hand in token that I shall never lay claim to the land!"

And he stretched forth his hand, but Merari would not take it.

"Cease worrying, Merari," his brother said then. "Your daughter's inheritance shall not be taken from her. Moreover, I have three handsome sons. Who knows but that someday you and I shall cherish the same grandchildren? If it pleases you, you may choose one of my sons for your daughter's husband even now!"

"No, but your word is good enough for me," Merari replied quickly. "Judith is still too young for betrothal. We shall speak of marriage when the time comes."

Then he shook his brother's hand, and they blew out the flame of the oil lamp and went to sleep.

Though the feast of Passover would not begin until sundown, we left Aaron's house at dawn next day. We wanted to find a place in the inner courtyard of the temple, before the arrival of the large crowd. Aaron and his kin also rose early to go with us that they might receive their share of our bull. But when Aaron began to speak of what a sumptuous meal Apis would make, Merari drew him aside and whispered that there would be no meal. He had brought the bull not for a Passover sacrifice but for a sin offering. All the meat would go to the priests alone.

Hearing this, Aaron looked askance at his brother.

"Not only do you come riding upon a horse, like a prince," he said to Merari, "but you would sacrifice a bull for your sin, like the king. Could you not have brought a he-goat, as is done by the humble folk? Was your sin so great that nothing but your finest bull calf will suffice?"

"In my eyes it was great," Merari said. "It grieves me that you should be deprived of your feast, but the bull was promised to God long ago. However, if you would rather not go with me—"

But since they were risen and dressed they all went along. Aaron's wife brought flour kneaded with honey, and Merari took his wineskin, which he would need for the sacrifice. Also we took enough food to sustain us through the day, for the sun was only rising and it was a long time until sundown.

The streets of Jerusalem were teeming with people, as if all had thought to obtain for themselves a place in the inner court. Nor could we find room there when we arrived at the temple. The inner court was so thronged with men and beasts that there was barely room for the priests to pass between them. We counted ourselves fortunate to find a place in the outer court, from where we could get a glimpse of the altar. There we settled down for the day. Merari had never been inside the temple court, and his brother showed him all the great sights.

"Beyond the north wall is the court of the king's palace," Aaron said. "The house of God and the house of the king were built to adjoin each other so that the king might dwell in the shadow of God continually."

"But more than one king forgot that he was dwelling in the shadow of God," Merari said.

"Kings are men, and so are priests," Aaron said. "Therefore it is a pity that they should have all of your bull. However, it is too late now to change your mind, my brother, nor would you, always having been a stubborn man. But come, let us take the children and see if we can approach nearer the altar."

We fought our way through the crowd, Aaron walking ahead of us, and Judith and I clinging to Merari's hands, until we found a spot from where we could gaze into the inner court. Now we could see the steps leading up to the great altar, which King Ahaz had built more than a hundred years before, after the altar he had seen in Damascus. And to the north of the great altar was the old brazen altar made by King Solomon. Over to the south and east stood the

huge sea of brass that had been cast by Hiram of Tyre. It measured
five cubits in height and ten cubits from rim to rim, and it held two
thousand baths. From it water was poured into the movable brass
lavers to purify the victims before the sacrifice.

Aaron told us that the sea had once rested on twelve brazen oxen,
three looking north, three south, three east and three west, all with
their hindermost part toward the inside. But in the days of Tiglath-
Pileser of Assyria, King Ahaz had taken the sea off the oxen and
placed it on the pavement, for he had delivered the oxen as tribute
to the Assyrian king.

Behind the altar was the entrance to the temple, with ten steps
leading up to it. And to either side of the entrance stood a bronze
pillar eighteen cubits high, which had been fashioned by the same
Hiram of Tyre. And the doors of the temple were folding doors,
two panels on the right and two panels on the left, carved with
cherubim and palm trees and open flowers, which had once been
overlaid with gold. But now only the olive wood was left, for the
gold had been cut off the doors by King Hezekiah, when he had
given it as tribute to King Sennacherib. Thus the kings of Assyria
had carried away treasures from the house of Yahweh, yet there was
still much bronze left outside the temple, and much gold within.

We could not enter the sanctuary, for there was room only for
the priests and princes and nobles and such people as knew how to
bribe the proper officials. But Merari was not one to obtain a favor
by bribery. Thus we returned to our own station.

At even the priests came forth from the temple, arrayed in their
costly robes, whose golden embroidery glittered in the rays of the
setting sun. And then King Josiah entered through the gate in the
north wall, followed by his sons, to show himself to the people. A
loud cry went up from the crowd, for the king was greatly beloved
by the common man.

"Long live the king! Long live the great King Josiah, who
brought justice and righteousness back to Judah!"

We stood too far back to see the faces of the king and his sons,
but it was known that they were handsome as all princes of Judah.
For the kings of Judah always took beautiful women for their
wives. King Josiah was but thirty-three years old at that time, and
his three sons still tender youths. Josiah had taken only two wives,
heeding the commandment that the king ought not to take many

wives nor multiply his horses. He owned but two chariots, his garments were simpler than those of the priests, and he walked humbly though he wore the crown of Judah.

After the people had paid the king homage he turned to the altar and prayed long and fervently. Then he turned his face back to the crowd, raised his hands, blessed his people and commanded that the sacrificing commence.

First the victims of the king were purified and slaughtered, and then the common people brought forth their offerings—sheep, goats and pigeons, as befits humble men. The blood of the sacrifices was sprinkled on the altar and the ground about the altar, and the fat burned as an offering to God. But the appointed portions were taken by the priests and the rest returned to those who had brought the offerings, for the meat was to be eaten the same night and the pilgrims were to return to their homes on the morrow.

When Judith saw the fate of the victims she cried out in horror: "They must not kill Apis!"

"He was promised to God," Merari said gently.

"No, he is mine!" Judith cried.

"Judith, did I not warn you that we would give Apis to God?" Merari asked.

"I did not know that he would be slaughtered. But I will not let them kill Apis! He is mine!"

"He is God's, Judith. He is promised. We must give him to God."

"Why can we not give a goat or a sheep, as the other people do? Why must we give Apis, who is strong and beautiful and without a blemish?" Judith wailed.

"This is why we must offer him," Merari said. "Because he is strong and beautiful and without a blemish. If we did not treasure what we gave, how could it be called a sacrifice? Come now, Judith, let go of Apis that I may lead him into the inner court!"

And he tried to loosen Judith's hand from the bull's tether. But she would not let go and Merari had to pry her fingers off. When he had taken the tether from her, Judith threw herself face down on the ground, drumming with her fists on the earth.

"I do not want to give him to God!" she screeched. "He is mine! He is mine! He is mine!"

Merari and his kin formed a tight circle around Judith to keep those next to us from witnessing her unseemly behavior. Merari did not dare look Aaron and his wife in the eye, for he knew they meant him to deal severely with Judith. But this he would never do. Still Judith would not rise from the ground but kept hitting it with her fists, though her wailing grew weaker. In the end Merari filled a cup with water, mixed some of his wine into it, bent down to Judith and gently bade her drink. She turned her face away and would not look at her father, but she was racked by hiccups after her crying, and finally she drank. It was her first taste of wine and she was quickly soothed. When her eyes began to droop, Merari bade his brother carry her to the gate of the court, while he went to do what he had come to do.

Judith had shut her eyes and made no protest when Aaron carried her away. But Aaron's wife shook her head and muttered:

"Woe to the man who someday will have for his wife a girl who is always given her will!"

And she gazed at her own sons with concern, her husband no doubt having discussed with her what was said between him and his brother the previous night.

While Judith lay sleeping outside the gate, I saw Merari gather up his meal offering and drink offering, place one hand upon Apis's head, as the law prescribes, and lead him into the inner court. When he was still some distance from the altar, Merari took a knife and cut the bull's throat with one swift stroke so that his legs buckled under him and he fell to the ground. And I knew he had died quickly. Then Merari and the Levites carried the bull up to the altar. There the priests collected the blood and rubbed it on the horns of the altar, for it was a sin offering, and they spilled the rest of the blood on the ground around the altar. But the fat was cut out of the bull after he was skinned and burned upon the altar that the sweet savor might please the Lord. And the meat was eaten by the priests, but nothing was given to Merari, for it was a sin offering. Then Merari washed his hands, bowed to the priests and returned to us.

But Judith was fast asleep and saw none of this. She did not even wake when her father lifted her up and carried her back to Aaron's house.

"Your heart ought to be eased now, brother," Aaron said to Merari. "For you have shed blood, and blood makes expiation before the Lord."

But Merari looked somber and shook his head.

"Then God is sooner reconciled than I," he replied. "As for me, I shall have to live with my guilt all my days."

When Judith woke next morning she was sullen and would not speak to her father. She ate little and turned her head away when spoken to, and there were tears in her eyes. But she did not inquire after Apis.

Observing her, Aaron's wife turned to Merari and said:

"Surely the child needs a mother. And my lord, still being a young man, also needs a wife. There are among my kin many fine maidens—all virgins—some with dowries that might please even a man like my husband's brother. Will he not let me speak with their parents?"

But Merari only shook his head.

"I thank you for your concern, wife of my brother, but I am bound by vow to remain unwed."

The lady would have pursued the matter further had not her husband said:

"No woman can bear to see a man unwed, less still a wealthy man. However, my brother can well look after his own needs."

Then Merari bade Aaron and his wife farewell. They embraced and blessed each other, saying they must not let so many years pass before they met again.

"Also remember what I proposed last night," Aaron said.

"I shall when the time comes," Merari replied, quickly picking up Judith, who still would not look at him, and carrying her outside.

There Merari placed her on Hadad's back and then swung himself on the horse, while Aaron lifted me up and put me behind Merari. And Aaron's sons came out of the house to see us depart and walk behind us until we reached the east gate. There they halted, shouting blessings after us as we passed through the gate.

The crowd was even larger than the day before, all seeming to depart at the same time. There was much jostling and shouting, and donkeys pushing hard against each other and against people. Now and then we heard the cry of one claiming that he had been robbed in the crush. But we were safe upon Hadad's back, from where we could see the Prophet Jeremiah back at his station by the gate.

There had been great feasting the night before, and much eating and drinking. Many of the people were still drunk and some acted in a lewd manner even as they walked out of the gate of Jerusalem. Pointing at them, the prophet shouted:

"Behold, I will cause to cease out of this place, before your eyes and in your days, the voice of mirth and the voice of gladness, the voice of the bridegroom and the voice of the bride!"

At that the people became greatly incensed and surged forward to pull the prophet down from his rock. But Merari, upon Hadad, forced his way through the crowd until he arrived beside Jeremiah to beat back the attackers with his legs and fists.

"My lord had better cease from provoking these people," Merari said, "for many of them are not yet sober."

However, the prophet would not be silenced but called to the crowd, which pressed around him:

"Thus said the Lord to me: I will make you unto this people a brazen, fortified wall; and they shall fight against you, but they shall not prevail against you. For I am with you to save you and deliver you."

Then a man in the crowd laughed and shouted:

"Perhaps God promised to deliver you, but it is the man upon the horse who is doing His work!"

For Merari had placed himself and Hadad between the prophet and the crowd. Then Jeremiah left off speaking and the people moved on. But Merari bent down and said to the prophet:

"My lord has great courage, but he is only one and they are many. Should the time ever come that my lord needs help, let him remember that my name is Merari the son of Amram, from Bethul in the southern hills of Judah. My house will always be open to my lord as shelter."

Then the prophet raised his hands and said:

"May God bless you and your children. And may you not live to see the evil that shall befall this people."

Merari bowed his head and we went our way. But Judith did not speak to her father, nor did she ask questions, as on the previous day. In the end Merari broke the heavy silence.

"And will you never speak to me again, Judith?" he asked.

Judith only shook her head, but she shook it very lightly. Merari bent down and kissed her on the hair, and tickled her as one will tickle a sullen child to make it laugh. But Judith said:

"No, my lord."

"Listen to me, my daughter," Merari said. "You were asleep when I offered Apis to the Lord. Know then that God was well pleased with the gift, for the smoke from the sacrifice rose straight up to heaven. As for you, I shall give you another bull calf."

"I do not want another bull," Judith said.

"Would you rather have a lamb or a kid then?" Merari asked.

"Neither," Judith replied, for she could be stubborn.

"Pigeons?" Merari asked.

"No," Judith said.

"What would you have then, Judith?"

Judith thought for a while, and then she said:

"I would have a cat in the house, as did my mother."

Merari looked astonished, for he had not known that Judith still remembered her mother's ways.

"Indeed you shall have a cat," he said.

"In the house?"

"In the house," Merari promised, though he knew that his sister Sarai would chide him for permitting such a thing. Was it not an Egyptian custom to keep cats in the house and worship them as gods—and what would the people of Bethul say?

But people found greater faults than that in the manner in which Merari raised his daughter. He never ceased from taking her wherever he went—to watch him plow and reap and harvest the grapes, and also on his journeys to other towns, where he was wont to take the surplus of his harvest. But as Judith grew older and learned to look after herself, I had to stay behind. When she returned she would tell me how people bargained with Merari over the price of his grain, and how he always obtained his price in the end.

"There is no man as wise as my father," Judith would say.

If she still remembered that Merari had taken Apis from her, she did not speak of it. For now she had a cat.

But Judith grew, and when she was seven she stood head and shoulders above the other girls her age. Her beauty increased from day to day. Her red hair was lustrous, her white neck slender and long, her hands and feet beautifully formed, and there was no blemish upon her skin. No other wished to be seen beside Judith, and she had no friends among the girl children of Bethul. Even Sarai's daughters avoided her, for though they were comely they could not attain to Judith. Her only playmate was her kin Manasseh, Athara's son.

But he never ceased to fear Judith. She dashed about the fields wild as a boy, darting in and out among the legs of the cattle, while Manasseh fled shrieking whenever a bull or even a gentle cow came near him. He was shorter than Judith, frail and fine-boned, with a pretty girl's face that should have better served his ugly mother. Whenever he played with Judith, Athara would come running from her house to take him by the hand and pull him into the shade, crying:

"But you must not stay so long in the sun, Manasseh, for if you do your head will hurt!"

Before long Manasseh would claim that his head hurt whenever he wished to cease playing with Judith, though he had never complained of this before. But Judith would mock him and call him a spoiled weakling.

Nor was she wrong. Manasseh was Athara's only child, and she watched over him as if he were made of gold and precious stones. There was gossip in town over why Athara had never conceived again, for the maidservants would reveal the secrets of their mistresses when they met by the spring to draw water. It was at the spring that my mother learned the story.

The husband Athara's father had found for her was a lusty man, handsome and many years younger than his wife. His need for women was known in Bethul, but Athara had hoped he would cease from wenching when he wed her, for she was wealthy and he but a poor youth. However, men do not change their ways. My mother often said that the man a woman wed was the same who would be her husband all her life.

One day, when Manasseh was three years old, Athara went walking with him in the fields at harvest time. There she came upon her husband, lying with one of the maidservants behind a stack of barley. When Athara saw him she began to shriek the way she had shrieked when Merari returned from the north with a bride. She picked up Manasseh, who, frightened by her wailing, shrieked even louder than she, and ran back with him to the house. There she locked herself in her room and vowed she would never again lie with her husband, for she was fool enough to think this a fitting punishment for him. In her madness she even began to dress Manasseh in girls' clothes, vowing she would not allow him to turn

into a lecher. When her father discovered her doings he put an
end to this abomination. But she kept Manasseh so close to her that
in the end he took on the manners of women, for she would not let
him near her husband. The latter would pursue after maidservants as
before, and whenever he got one with child, Athara would drive her
from the house.

But when Judith asked Merari why their kinswoman Athara was
always wroth, Merari replied:

"Her mother ate sour grapes when she carried her, and now
Athara's teeth are set on edge."

But there was no less gossip about the way Merari raised Judith.
When she was seven Merari called the scribe of Bethul and offered
to pay him well if he would teach Judith to read and write. Not
many boys in Bethul were taught to read and write, and to teach a
girl was an unheard of thing. The women clucked their tongues,
and Sarai came to speak with her brother.

"Would you have Judith become recorder to the king that you
teach her to write?" she asked Merari.

"Someday Judith will inherit many fields and much cattle,"
Merari replied. "I would have her know how to keep records, and
also to draw up contracts when she buys or sells. Had I been able to
write I would have drawn up a contract when our brother Aaron
left for Jerusalem. Though he has vowed not to claim Judith's inheritance, my heart is not at ease. Therefore let Judith be well
skilled in all knowledge."

"Out of stubbornness you would not take another wife and have
a son," Sarai said. "But now you would turn your daughter into a
son, teaching her the skills of men. Had you not some shame left,
you would teach her how to wield a sword!"

Upon hearing this, Merari placed his hand on Judith's head and
said:

"May Yahweh grant me that I never see the day when a woman
shall have to take up a sword! Yet should this day come, Judith shall
surely acquit herself well."

Gazing up at her father, Judith said seriously:

"Truly I should, my lord."

Then Merari dropped down on his knees beside her and clasped
her in his arms.

"No, no, my daughter," he said. "But this day will never come.

King Josiah has strengthened the army and fortified our cities. If war should once more come to Judah, we will be well prepared. However, it is not us whom God has chastised with war now, but our former oppressors. We must give thanks that this time the battle is far away from our homes!"

For now it was known even in Bethul that the armies of the Medes and the Babylonians were standing at the gates of Nineveh.

THREE

And Jonah began to enter into the city a day's journey, and he proclaimed and said: 'Yet forty days, and Nineveh shall be overthrown.'

—JONAH 3:4

INDEED all the world knew that Nineveh was besieged and would soon be overthrown (the old man Isaac said to the young scribe). The only people who did not know were the inhabitants of Nineveh. For such is the nature of men that they will blind themselves to disaster until it is upon them.

The streets of Nineveh were thronged in those days. Many who dwelled in the open country had fled within the walls, bringing with them much cattle. The king had laid up huge stores of oil, grain and wine, and there was enough water in town to weather a long siege. For weeks slaves were treading mortar and molding bricks to strengthen the walls. All the brave warriors had been called up to man their posts at the walls, the turrets, the towers and rooms at the gates. Day and night the clang of weapons was heard in the streets. Let the enemy come, the people said boastfully. They shall dash their heads bloody on the walls of Nineveh, for none can ever conquer our city!

Indeed there was much feasting in Nineveh, as if life were to continue forever. Never had there been so many banquets at court, so many people drinking themselves drunk and so much harlotry. With the arrival of the enemy at the gates a wild fever of gayety seized the city, and many a young maiden forgot her modesty. My father was greatly troubled over my sister Abigail, whose love for the Lord Hippolytus was still increased. And he, claiming concern for our safety, now called at our house every day.

In the end my father said to him:

"My lord is but a stranger newly come to Assyria. If he wanted

73

to leave, the enemy, seeing that he is a Greek, would surely grant him safe-conduct that he might return to die in his own land!"

"It matters little where a man dies, if only he dies honorably," Hippolytus replied. "Many Greeks have fought for pay in foreign armies. And though I am not come here as a soldier, I too am in the pay of the king and my loyalty is unto him. But even should I forget this debt, how could I leave knowing that you and your kin must remain behind? Moreover, the fortunes of war might still change. It is said that soon the Egyptian armies will come to aid us in breaking the siege of Nineveh."

"I too have heard this rumor," my father said. "However, there is an old saying among my people, who more than once vainly waited for help: do not trust in Egypt, that broken reed that pierces the hand of the one who would lean upon it."

"If this be so, then we shall die together," the Lord Hippolytus said, as if dying were a small matter in the life of a man.

But none in Nineveh truly thought that he might suffer the fate the people of Ashur had suffered two years earlier, when Ashur had been captured and the inhabitants slaughtered by the Median armies, even before their Babylonian allies reached the city. And though now both armies had pitched camp before the walls of Nineveh, it was known that the Babylonians dealt leniently with their captured foe.

Indeed the enemy had made but small progress since the beginning of the siege. A number of skirmishes had been fought between the attackers and the Assyrian troops stationed outside the walls. Many people—I among them—had mounted the walls to observe the battles, as though they were spectacles put on for their diversion. For they were still certain that none could breach their defenses.

The Medes and Babylonians had pitched camp to the east of Nineveh, where they would have to ford only the moat to assault the walls, for in the west the city was protected by the broad bed of the Tigris. As far as the eye could see the flat land was covered with tents and war machines: heavy chariots drawn by swift steeds, huge armored battering rams, movable siege towers from whose heights the archers could loosen their arrows upon the defenders on the wall, and a wealth of scaling ladders for the final assault by the foot soldiers. The mounts of the feared Babylonian horsemen were tethered to the tent posts, neighing, tossing their manes and churning up clouds of dust as they pawed the ground. For it was the month of Ab, and the hot midsummer air was aswarm with flies. Among the dull brown tents and the dull brown earth, the armors and shields of the Babylonians glared red, as though they had daubed them with blood. But it was not yet blood, only the color of their good fortune. And yet, for all the threatening sight, it seemed as though the enemy would do no more than ride to and fro before the walls to impress us with their might until, overcome by terror, we surrendered.

But none seemed to consider surrender. Indeed my parents sang at more banquets in the king's palace than ever before. During the past two years the king had led his army against the invaders as they advanced north along the Euphrates, winning a battle here, losing a battle there. As for the terrible loss of Ashur, those who knew about such matters blamed it on treachery, cowardice of the defenders, ill fortune or inclement weather. Surely it could not happen in Nineveh! Was not the king returned to his own palace to embark upon an unceasing round of celebrations? And was not the palace an impenetrable fortress, protected by rivers to the north, south and west of it? As for the fighting men defending the walls of Nineveh, were they not known to be the best and bravest in the world? Why, then, should we tremble before a foe, even if their numbers were as the sand of the sea?

As the days went by and the massed troops before the gates of Nineveh failed to attack, the vigilance of the defenders slackened. Many officers slipped away to banquets, while their men returned to their homes to spend a night with their wives. The need for carousing was blamed on the high heat of summer, and wine in the beleaguered city was getting dear.

One night when my parents had gone to sing at the palace my sister Abigail and I were alone in the house. Our servant Taia had bedded down in the yard to savor the cool of the evening. But none of us slept, for the sound of revelry and the clang of weapons in the street did not abate until dawn. I did not fall asleep until after my parents returned home shortly before the morning watch.

When I was wakened by loud shouts in the street I thought I had slumbered but briefly. But when I opened the door to glance outside I found the sky lined by the first gray of dawn. And still I thought myself asleep and the shouts in the street but an evil dream.

"Every man to the walls! All soldiers to their battle stations! The river gates are open! The palace is in danger!"

How could the river gates be open unless there had been treachery? But were not the most loyal troops stationed at the gates that protected the very palace grounds? And how had the enemy crossed the Tigris in the west when all these weeks they had threatened Nineveh from the east?

I staggered out of the room, still dazed by sleep. My parents were up and awake, my father looking distraught, my mother weeping. Abigail had slipped on a garment and stood with her hair falling tangled into her face, but her hands trembled so she could not comb it. Taia had run into the house, struck by such terror her eyes seemed all white in her black face.

Through the open door we could see foot soldiers running past our house, followed by mounted horsemen and war chariots manned by archers and their shield-bearers. Though it was not yet light we recognized them as ours. Those on foot staggered as if the alarm had roused them from deep slumber. And all the time the shouts in the street grew louder:

"The river gates are open! The river gates are open!"

"But how can such a thing have come to pass?" my father moaned, holding his head. "There is no way to open the river gates but from within, and how could the enemy get there without first scaling the walls?"

By then all the neighbors had come running from their doors. There was much shouting of men, wailing of women, and howling of children. But none knew yet what had happened in truth until a man staggered in from the street, out of breath and looking half mad. He fell to his knees in our forecourt and gasped:

"The gods have performed a miracle for our enemies! The Tigris ceased flowing during the night, and now the Babylonian soldiers are come in under the river gate and have opened it from within! They are followed by their horsemen and their chariots, for even now the water in the river bed is no higher than their thighs, and they shall slay us all!"

At that my mother broke into loud lamentations, clutching my sister and me to her bosom, but my father said:

"Surely the man is bereft of his senses! How could the Tigris cease to flow when it is nearly his time to flood?"

But I, being only twelve years old and proud of my great intelligence, said:

"Did not God part the Red Sea for the Hebrews to cross over? What if the Babylonian gods wrought a similar miracle?"

Even in his distress my father found the strength to fetch me a terrible blow for speaking such blasphemy. I held my ear and tears came to my eyes while I harbored bitter thoughts against my father—may God forgive me.

But more and more people were crowding into our court, each bearing out the tale that the Tigris had ceased flowing. Soon we heard the clash of weapons as they met in battle, and saw a red haze rising in the distance as the first houses went up in flames. Before long Assyrian soldiers came charging down the street, turned back in flight, while their own officers pursued after them, shouting: "Stand, stand!" Yet they kept fleeing away.

Then the people around us also turned to flight, each running off in a different direction to seek a safe place. My mother wanted to follow them, but my father said:

"There is no place to hide, and soon the streets will be running with blood. Better let us stay in the house. Since ours is but a humble dwelling, perhaps the soldiers will pass it by."

But no sooner had we locked ourselves into the house than there was a loud pounding on the door. Abigail covered her mouth to keep from screaming, and we crept back into a corner of the room, not daring to breathe. The door gave way to the powerful thrust of a shoulder, and framed in it stood the Lord Hippolytus as we had never seen him before. He had put off his teacher's robes and strapped on his battle dress, which—we could see—he had carried with him from Greece. From beneath a gleaming, crested helmet his short curls fell onto his forehead. His bronze armor ended just below his waist, above his brief kilts. He carried a small, round shield and a short, broad sword, and he wore leather boots instead of sandals. As he stood there he looked like the Greek gods he had so often described to us in school. And even her distress, my sister Abigail gazed upon him with admiration.

"You did well not to flee into the street, Asaph," Hippolytus said to my father. "The city is full of prancing horses and bounding chariots. The horsemen are charging with swords and spears, and so many are slain that those who tried to escape are stumbling over heaps of carcasses. Indeed they too shall soon be corpses, for those who are not run through by swords shall be run over by chariots and trampled underfoot by horses."

"But what shall become of us, where shall we go?" my mother wailed.

"You had best remain where you are," the Lord Hippolytus said. "The slaves in their humble quarters are safer today then the king in his palace. Being old, you and your husband might be spared by the Babylonians, and your son is but a child. However, your beautiful daughter had better be hidden. I have found some valiant warriors who would make a stand with me at the temple of Nebo. The library there is sturdily built of stone and we might be able to hold it even against greater numbers. Let me therefore take Abigail with me, for she will be safer with me than with you. At any rate, I would not allow her to be captured alive."

Hearing this, Abigail wanted to rush toward Hippolytus, but my father restrained her.

"Let my lord not think me ungrateful," he said. "But if we are to be taken captives, let us be taken together. We are musicians, and the Babylonians love music no less than the Assyrians. We shall carry our instruments to make known our trade, and Abigail shall raise her sweet voice in song when they come for us."

Hippolytus glanced back over his shoulder at the fleeing soldiers and the sky turned a flaming red by the rising sun and the raging fires.

"You have never seen battle-crazed soldiers, Asaph, but I have," he said. "Let me tell you then that the first to enter this house will not look at your daughter and say 'Behold, a fine singer,' but 'Behold, a comely woman.' And he will deal with her as one deals with a comely woman. Therefore it is better that she come with me!"

He stretched out his hand to my sister and she strained toward him, but my father would not release her.

"No, but we shall stay together," he said stubbornly.

"If this is your wish, Asaph, so be it then," the Lord Hippolytus said. "I can no longer tarry, for the brave warriors in the library count on my sword. Farewell—and if the Egyptians do not arrive to aid us in time, may they all languish forever in the nether world, while we meet in the Elysian Fields!"

And he raised his sword in a last salute and plunged into the street.

But Abigail let out a loud scream and threw herself on the floor, clinging to the skirts of my mother as she wept with despair. While she still lay prostrate, wailing and tearing her hair, another bearer of ill news arrived. Through the door, which had remained ajar, we could see a young boy running toward our house, his clothes blackened by smoke and his face bloody. Not until he entered the room did we recognize him as my sister Rachel's oldest son. He could barely speak and told his tale with many sobs.

When the alarm was sounded, his father had hastened off to join his chariot crew, leaving my sister and the children alone in the house. As always my sister Rachel was big with child. In her terror her pangs had seized her, though she had completed only eight months. Her oldest had run for the midwife, but all the midwives had fled, and so had the neighbors who lived about them. He had then tried to reach the palace and fetch my older sister's husband, who was physician to the queen. But the palace was surrounded by enemy troops, engaged in bloody battle with the defenders. Then the boy had bethought himself of his grandmother and had made his way through the back alleys to our house.

Weeping and clinging to my mother's skirt, he cried.

"I beg you to come with me, for my mother is in great pain and there is none to help her!"

Without a moment's thought my mother replied:

"Indeed I must go."

And she took the hand of her grandson and turned to the door.

My father ran after her and caught her by the arm.

"Are you mad, woman?" he asked. "You will never be able to get through the streets, and both you and the boy will be killed! As for Rachel, she has born five children and, God willing, shall bear her sixth, even without help!"

"What do men know?" my mother replied. It was the only time I heard her speak sharply to my father. "My daughter is in travail with none to comfort her! And should I remain here without coming to her aid?"

And she took a firmer grip on her grandson's hand and ran out into the street with him.

"Come back, come back, come back!" my father shouted after her.

But she did not even look around, and the last I saw of her was her back.

When my father returned from the door his face had become as stone. He neither wept nor lamented, but gazed down on my sister Abigail, who still lay on the ground, and spoke sternly:

"Cease your weeping, daughter, for it is of no avail. Those of us who are left must prepare for whatever may come. Get up from the ground, Abigail, and fetch your mother's and your own jewels. Bind them into your skirt that we might not leave home empty-handed when they come for us. And you, Isaac and Taia, fill as many baskets as we might be able to carry with food, to keep us from starving on the way. But I shall prepare our instruments for us. Let us pray that all our captors are deaf that they might mistake even Isaac for a musician."

While I followed Taia to the kitchen to fill my father's orders, I wondered how he knew what people who fear being carried off must do, though he himself had never gone into exile. Abigail too rose from the ground and went to do what my father had commanded her. Thus my father was alone in the room when the Babylonian soldier burst through the door. Taia and I were concealed behind the kitchen door, neither of us daring to breathe. As we peered out through a crack in the door, I could feel her heart pounding against my back.

The soldier who entered our house was an archer who seemingly had gone off on his own to plunder. He had slung his bow over his shoulder and carried his unsheathed sword in his hand. His shield and armor were red, not from dye but with blood, and so was his beard. From a deep gash in his forehead blood trickled over his face, nearly congealing the socket of his left eye. But his right eye was clear enough to let him notice my silver trumpet on the table. He gleefully snatched it up and shook it in the air, no doubt pleased with its value rather than its fine workmanship.

Observing him, my father had backed against the wall in terror. The soldier looked around the room, and finding nothing more of value there, he walked up to my father, seized him by the beard and shouted:

"Where did you hide your jewels and the women of your household?"

I could understand his speech well, though he spoke in the singsong manner in which our tongue was spoken in the south.

"Answer me!" he yelled, pulling hard on my father's beard.

"Mercy, my lord!" my father pleaded. "I am but a poor man, a musician and slave at court, who has no jewels. As for my women, they all fled, leaving me behind. There is none but myself in the house." He spoke loudly that we in the kitchen and Abigail in the next room might hear him and remain concealed.

"Scum of a liar!" the soldier shouted, menacing my father with his sword. "Would you have me believe that an Assyrian who dwells in his own house on the palace grounds has no wealth?"

"Let my lord know that I am not a rich Assyrian but only a humble Hebrew slave!"

"Hah," the soldier sneered, "today many a prince would proclaim himself a Hebrew slave to save his life!"

"But I can prove it to my lord," my father said, raising his hands in supplication. "Behold, I am circumcised!"

And then my father did a thing I had never thought he might do—he raised up his skirt and discovered his parts before the Babylonian soldier. But that one only laughed a terrible laugh and exclaimed:

"Indeed you are circumcised, scum, but so are the wretched Egyptians circumcised, who have threatened to fall on our backs! Who knows but that you are one of their spies? At any rate I had better slay you and take your member as proof of my great deed!"

At that threat my father dropped his skirt and screamed, trying to jump past the soldier to gain the door. But even before he could take one step the soldier seized him by the throat and ran him through with his sword so that he fell to the ground. Then, laughing his terrible laugh, he raised up my father's skirt and struck off his member.

Seeing my father lie on the ground in his blood, I let out a piercing shriek. I should have screamed again had not Taia put her hand over my mouth from behind. But while I was thus silenced, my sister Abigail, who had observed the bloody deed from the other room, went on screaming and screaming. The soldier, who had first turned toward the kitchen, now turned the other way, for he recognized the voice of a woman. As he entered the room where Abigail was concealed, her shrieking rose to a high pitch before it was choked into moaning. This was the last I heard, for Taia, her strength increased many times by her fear, picked me up as though I had no weight and carried me out through the door which led from our kitchen into a back alley. Holding me against her with one arm, her other hand still placed over my mouth, she began to run, and ran on wildly before she finally put me down without ever stopping to run. Then she seized my hand and dragged me along.

I stumbled after her, no longer screaming, for my voice had died inside of me. Nor did I know where we were running until we entered a large shed. Gazing about me I saw that we were in the quarters of the kitchen slaves, where in happier times I had gone to make music.

Now all the slaves were cowering in corners, shaking with terror. From outside came the clang of weapons, the screams of wounded men and the wild neighing of horses charging into battle. But the wailing inside the shed was even louder. The only one who did not appear wholly consumed by fear was Tarqu. He had taken off the gorgeous robes of the harem keeper and put on his native garb, the short kilts that left his upper body and his legs bare. When Taia saw him she released my hand and threw herself at her brother's feet, weeping loudly and telling him in their own tongue what had befallen us.

Tarqu came to where I lay on the ground, raised me up and spoke kind words to me. But I could not answer, for my voice was gone from me.

Then Tarqu turned to his sister and said:

"This is a bitter day for the boy. But he lives, and he will be safe here. There will be great slaughter among the princes today, but I do not think that we shall be harmed. A conqueror has little use for nobles, but he cannot do without skilled slaves."

Tarqu was right. While the battle still raged on the palace grounds some soldiers broke into our shed. When their officer saw that all who huddled there were slaves, he seized us as booty to be shared out later among the warriors. He left two sentries at the door to keep us from fleeing, while he and his troop returned to the battle.

Even without the sentries at the door none could have escaped, for there was no place to go. Indeed some of the slaves who had fled the burning palace came to join us. The sentries willingly let them in, for they increased their booty. From these we learned the fate of the king and his court.

When the king saw that the palace could no longer be held by his troops he fell upon his sword rather than be taken alive by the foe. But the queen, who lay ill in her quarters, was discovered and carried off by the Babylonians, together with her ladies in waiting. The men who had remained in the palace were all slain. Thus I knew that my sister's husband—the queen's physician, who never left her side when she was ill—had also perished. As for my sister Yael, she had either been killed or carried off with the other ladies.

But, lying on the ground in one corner, I could no longer mourn. Nor could I mourn when Tarqu returned from the door to tell us that the temple of Nebo was in flames and the roof about to cave in. Beneath it would be buried King Ashurbanipal's library, the tablets on which were recorded the world's science and the loftiest poetry, and also my beloved teacher, who had carried laughter within him like precious wine in a golden vessel.

Toward evening the officer who had posted the sentries returned with his troop. They were grimy and covered with blood, and many were wounded. All carried with them treasures they had looted from the palace, objects of gold and silver and ivory, and also weapons. Moreover, they brought food which they shared out among the slaves, for they understood that horses and slaves must be fed to be of service.

Taia crouched down beside me and tried to make me eat, but with the first bite I remembered my father lying dead in his blood. My stomach turned and I vomited on the floor.

Then Tarqu said:

"Let him be, Taia, for he cannot hold food. If he does not die of grief, his will to live will prevail in the end and he will eat."

But I still believed I should die. Indeed I longed for death. What right had I to go on living, with my father slain and dishonored and the women of my house either dead or carried away to be slaves and harlots?

After the soldiers had fed us they cast lots for the slaves, this one taking a girl, the other a boy. But the commanding officer, who had first choice, took Tarqu, the biggest and strongest of all. Then Tarqu threw himself at the feet of his new master and begged not to be parted from Taia.

"Indeed I shall also take your wife, for together your worth to me is threefold," the officer said, not knowing that they were brother and sister nor that Tarqu could never father children.

Still lying prostrate before the officer, Tarqu said:

"The gods will greatly reward my lord if he will also let us keep the boy." And he pointed to where I lay on the ground, immobile with grief.

"Is he not dead then?" the officer asked, kicking me with his boot.

I opened my eyes and looked at him, but I remained motionless, nor did I open my mouth to speak. The officer bent down and shone his torch in my face. Then he said to Tarqu:

"This boy is fair-skinned and not your son. What is he to you? Moreover, he seems both feeble-minded and dumb, for he neither speaks nor is there light in his eyes. Rather than waste good food on him I ought to kill him here and now!"

Tarqu raised himself up on his knees and caught the officer by his kilt.

"I pray my lord not to slay the boy! Though he seems dumb now, yet he is very bright. It is only terror that took away his voice, for he has witnessed grave things today. Moreover, he is of great value, being of royal blood!"

It was a good thing I could not speak then, for in my bitterness I should have called Tarqu a liar, though I was indeed of royal blood. However, he had made it sound as though I belonged to the royal house of Assyria. Indeed this is how the officer understood his words, for he drew his sword, exclaiming:

"Then he shall surely die!"

But holding onto his kilt Tarqu whispered so as not to be heard by the other soldiers:

"The boy's father was one of the royal princes who fled to Harran, leaving his wife and child behind. Who knows but that he might someday become king over the remnant of Assyria. Let my lord consider the ransom a king would pay for his son were he to find him alive!"

Gazing about him, the officer sheathed his sword and said softly:

"Because of your clever pleading I shall spare his life. But I will not be burdened with looking after a weakling such as he. Therefore, you had better see that he arrives alive in Babylon, or else it shall go badly with you."

"Let my lord trust in me," Tarqu replied. "If he lives through this night he will not die."

We spent the night in the shed, but early next morning our captors drove us outside. A heavy cloud of smoke lay over the city. Many houses had burned to the ground, while others still stood smoldering, their beams thrust into the air like naked bones. The palace and the temple lay in shambles, while soldiers climbed over the rubble to seize yet more loot. Wherever one looked carcasses littered the street, bodies whose scorched flesh stank in the heat of day, and others with heads and limbs hacked off. Among them the living wandered in a daze, stumbling over the corpses. Some carried what meager belongings they had saved, others their children or old upon their backs.

The fighting in the city was not yet over, but some of the streets that led to the gates had been captured and cleared by the enemy. Those were the ones through which our captors led us away. Now and then we had to make our way around a wrecked Assyrian chariot, some with their horses and crew lying dead beside them. It seemed that the invaders had carried their own dead out of sight so that it looked as if only Assyrians had perished in the battle. Whenever we passed a woman lying dead upon the ground, with her skirt thrown back over her head, I averted my face and wept.

We were not the only ones being led from the city. There were many others like us. Where the enemy had captured men of standing he had stripped them naked and chained them to each other by their necks and their wrists. However, we noticed that this was done only by the Medes. The Babylonians treated their captives with greater mercy and even allowed the women and children to ride in carts drawn by oxen. Thus a long, wailing column of downcast people moved through the smoldering town.

It was on this day that I walked out through the Ninlil Gate for the first and last time in my life. As we were marched to the Babylonian camp, I looked back once more at the city of my birth, where I had lost all those I loved. The turrets and towers were still in flames. Against the black columns of smoke and the red sky I could see the enemy soldiers breaking down the walls that had been meant to stand for a thousand years. Then I turned my head away and did not look back again.

In the camp the scribes took down a record of the booty. Each soldier was to be rewarded according to the length of his service. Many had been in the field since King Nabopolassar first went up against Ashur. These would soon return home, while fresh troops would come up for garrison duty in the conquered lands. But the king would remain at Nineveh, to pursue from there after the Assyrian army, which had escaped to Harran.

The officer who was now our master had served his term. He led us to the meeting ground for those bound for Babylon. There the men milled about in disorder, each clutching his booty or driving it before him, according to its nature. But their number was so great, and so was the confusion after the battle, that one could see it would still be days before they began their homeward trek.

During their wait the soldiers settled down where they found space, some guarding the captives while others went to forage for food. The prisoners too received their fill, with special care given the women and children. Nor did the soldiers torture their captives, as had been the custom of the Assyrians. Nowhere did I see men being flogged, flayed, or impaled on poles around the vanquished city.

Soon I discovered whence came this restraint. For though I still had not regained my speech I had not lost my hearing, and I could listen to the talk around the campfires at night. Thus I learned that it was the crown prince of Babylon, who—after leading his troops in assault against Nineveh—had forbidden all needless cruelty. Indeed some Babylonian soldiers muttered among themselves because they were denied the same liberties as the Medes. But others praised the prince for his great valor.

It was on that night, when I lay speechless on the ground, with my soul sick unto death, that I first heard the name of Nebuchadrezzar.

The following day I took food for the first time. Until then, whenever a morsel passed over my lips, I would again see the back of my mother as she ran from the house, my father lying defiled in his blood, and I would hear the shrieks of my sister Abigail. Then my throat would tighten and I could not swallow. But in the end hunger vanquished my grim memories. I took some milk and a piece of bread Taia had soaked in it, and for the first time I slept that night without screaming in my sleep.

I was wakened by the shouts of another. My master had sat up late drinking with the other officers, and when his comrades retired to their tents he still lingered by the fire to empty another cup. Thus he was roaring drunk when the soldier leading the woman passed by the fire. It was his voice that tore me from my slumber.

"No, but you must let me have her! She is much too good for such a one as you!"

Rubbing the sleep from my eyes, I saw that the man addressed by my master was one of those simple peasant oafs who were pressed into the king's service. However, he was not as simple as his appearance, for when the officer wanted to seize his woman from him, he said:

"Let my lord remember the king's law, whereby a soldier is entitled to booty even as an officer! I have proof drawn up by the camp scribe that this woman is my lawful property."

And he held up a clay tablet, which he had tied with a string around his neck. But while he spoke the woman cast languid glances at the officer, for she would sooner have for her master a highborn man than a simple peasant. She was dressed in fine garb such as was worn by the ladies at court, and she had put kohl around her eyes and painted her lips, no doubt hoping to take the fancy of some noble lord. Also she was young and comely, though not as comely as she might have appeared to our drunk master.

"Ah, but I would not seize her from you!" that one exclaimed, moved not by honesty but by his fear of the king. "See, I am willing to trade you my woman for yours!"

And he caught Taia by the arm and pulled her near the fire.

"But mine is much comelier than yours," the soldier replied. "I am not such a fool as to make a bad bargain. My captive is an Assyrian princess, who should fetch a good price in Babylon should I decide to sell her."

Crouching on the ground beside me, Tarqu muttered:

"The fall of Nineveh created much new nobility. I knew this wench when she was still the handmaiden of a royal concubine. No doubt she stole her mistress's robes to pass herself off for what she is not."

Thus he spoke, forgetting that he saved me through a similar device. However, our master had not forgotten it, for now he said:

"Indeed I can offer you an equal bargain. Not only will I give you this Ethiopian girl, who is strong and healthy enough to help you work your land and bear you many children—thus increasing your wealth—while the one you have will never survive the march to Babylon. I shall add to the deal this boy, who is himself an Assyrian prince. His father escaped to Harran and will someday redeem him for a high ransom, making you rich beyond your fondest dreams!"

I shuddered with dread at the thought of being parted from Tarqu, while Taia burst into tears as she turned around to gaze at her brother. But he only shook his head as if to tell her not to worry, the bargain would never come about. And indeed the soldier was as shrewd as he looked simple. Seeing that the officer was mad about possessing his captive, he said:

"Even if this runt be in truth an Assyrian prince, he will not live, as anyone with eyes can see. Pressed by my lord's higher rank, however, I shall surrender to him this comely princess if he will also add the tall Ethiopian slave to the bargain. Though it pains me to give up a treasure such as mine at a loss!"

And he pushed the woman nearer the fire, where the flames gave off more light. She pulled down her breastcloth a bit to display her splendid bosom, and with the other hand raised up her skirt to show off her small, well-formed feet. Her sight so inflamed our drunken master that he shouted:

"Take these three then, you thief, and give me the maiden, for I shall go mad if I do not possess her this very night!"

The soldier would not release the woman until the bargain was put into writing. Then Tarqu, concerned that we remain together now that the deal was made, pushed me forward and said:

"It would never do to rouse a scribe at this time of the night! The boy knows how to write. Let him draw up the contract, and let my lords affix their seals to it."

Thus it came about that I drew up the contract for my own sale. The clay tablets were not yet dry when our former master pulled his purchase into the tent with him. But our new master herded us before him, muttering:

"Let us hasten away from here before this fool changes his mind!"

And he drove us on with such speed that Tarqu had to carry me on his back, for I was still too weak to walk. Our new master did not let us rest until we reached the opposite side of the camp, where he allowed us to bed down for the night. My eyes closed with weariness, but I still heard Tarqu and Taia softly arguing between themselves. When Taia learned that the woman for whom we had been traded was not a princess, she chided her brother for not having revealed the truth. For Taia, being a woman, should also have preferred a highborn master. But Tarqu replied:

"It is not my task to prevent one Babylonian from deceiving another. Moreover, we are in better hands now. Our former master should have drunk and gambled us away one by one. But a peasant knows a good bargain."

On our long trek to Babylon I learned to honor Tarqu for his wisdom and love him for his kindness.

I soon lost count of the days we tramped southward along the bank of the Tigris, through the endless plains that in the distance seemed to merge with the sky. After some days we saw on the right bank of the river the ruins of Ashur, left there by the conqueror as another monument to destruction. The city that in olden times had been the foremost in all Assyria was now become a dwelling place for jackals, and wild beasts lay down in the midst of it.

Much of our progress was made at night, for at the end of Ab the days were so hot that even the hardened Babylonian warriors grew faint beneath the sun. Many slaves died along the way. The nearer our captors came to their homes the more they desired to see their wives and children. Thus they became careless of their prisoners, driving them on harder and harder.

At times Taia and I were allowed to ride in one of the carts drawn by oxen. But there were not enough of them, and mostly we were forced to walk. If not for Tarqu I should have been among those who perished along the way. I often wished he would leave me behind, but he had resolved to carry me with him to Babylon. Whenever I fell by the wayside he would hoist me upon his back and carry me. I was not heavy, having lost much weight, and Tarqu had the strength of three. And though the spirit of many captives broke, his remained unbent. He even sang as he walked along. His voice brought cheer to all but me, for often he would unwittingly sing the songs he had learned by listening to my father. But when he saw me weep bitterly, he changed to singing the gay songs of the slave quarters. Then I wept even harder, remembering our happy times there. In the end Tarqu ceased singing and said to me:

"If you would live, you must forget the past and think of the future. You are young and well skilled in many tongues and in writing. Someday you might still attain to a high position. Did not I attain a high position? Did not your father attain a high position? There is many a master who would rather put a wise slave over his household than a foolish son."

But when I considered the future I thought of a different matter. All I could think was that someday I would find the man who had slain my father and ravished my sister that I might have my revenge upon him. An eye for an eye, a tooth for a tooth. I burned his ugly face upon my memory that I might recognize it, even if finding him took me a lifetime. An eye for an eye. A tooth for a tooth. I shall kill him. I shall kill him.

Indeed these were the first words I uttered when my voice returned to me.

"The gods be praised, he can speak," Tarqu said.

"I shall kill him. I shall find him and I shall kill him."

"And who is it you will find and kill?" Tarqu asked.

"The man who slew my father."

Tarqu sighed and shook his head.

"Even if you were free to go about the land—which you are not—how would you find that man among the many thousand times thousands of Babylon? How would you recognize him?"

"He had a deep gash in his forehead, which will leave an ugly scar when it heals," I replied.

"There are countless soldiers with scars upon their foreheads. And all men look alike when they are grimy and bloody from battle," Tarqu said.

"No, but I shall find this man. Even should I forget his face, I shall always remember his dreadful laughter. Truly I shall find him and kill him!"

"If this thought gives you comfort, then keep on thinking it," Tarqu said. "It will restore your desire to live."

After passing Ashur we crossed from the east bank of the Tigris to the west bank, continuing south to the former borders of Babylonia. There the distance between the Tigris and the Euphrates narrowed, and we proceeded west until we reached the river on whose banks lay the city of Babylon. On the way we passed Sippar and Cutha, where the inhabitants came out to greet the returning soldiers with timbrels and dances, the women throwing flowers and languid glances at them. The soldiers to whom these cities were home remained behind with their captives, while we continued south.

Our new master, whose name was Iddina, had told us that his own land lay outside Borsippa, a city some distance downstream from Babylon. Nor would he pass through Babylon but went around it, professing a deep dislike for the city.

"Babylon is crowded and ugly," he said, "a place where people hurry about day and night, jostling each other out of the way as they go about their business. Only a madman would wish to live there!"

And he gave Babylon a wide berth so that we saw only the outside of the wall and the moat around it. Neither wall nor moat was of dimensions to fill us with awe, for during the past years of strife nearly all building work had ground to a halt. Thus to us, who came from Nineveh, Babylon from afar appeared old and shabby, even if it overawed our master Iddina.

The farther south we went the worse became the heat. But when I asked Tarqu why the Babylonian soldiers had hastened back rather than lingered in our own pleasant clime, he replied:

"As you grow older you will understand that men would sooner suffer the hardships of their homeland than live in the most pleasant of strange places."

Once more Tarqu was right. When our master Iddina reached his own meager plot he wept and fell upon the ground, kissing it even before he embraced his mother and brothers and sisters. Then he showed them the rich booty he had brought home from the war. They all laughed and smote their thighs when he told them how he had traded one frail maiden for three sturdy slaves.

Pointing at me, Iddina's mother said:

"Only two sturdy slaves. For surely this one shall serve for nought!"

Then Iddina revealed to her that I was an Assyrian prince who would someday fetch a rich ransom.

"Moreover, the boy can read and write, and we might hire him out as a scribe. At any rate he can herd the cattle and feed the fowl."

Since Iddina's mother had never owned slaves but knew well

their price, she treated us as one would treat a treasured possession. For she knew that if any of us fell ill and died, her loss would never be restored. Also because I was said to be a prince who could read and write I was handled gently, for Iddina's kin were simple folk who stood in awe of royalty and learning. Most of the time I was given no harder task than feeding the fowl. Few of the peasants had ever need of a scribe, but after the day's work they liked to gather around and hear me recite our ancient tales, though they laughed at my strange northern speech.

As for me, who was born and bred in a city, I learned to live with the seasons and understand such work as is done on a farm: the plowing and seeding, the tending of the canals whose network spread from the Euphrates through all the land, the opening and closing of the sluices to water the fields at their appointed time, the feeding of cattle, shearing of sheep and harvesting of grain. Though Iddina's plot was small it was fertile, and in a good year it bore two crops.

Our master never went to Borsippa, for he hated that city almost as much as Babylon. He claimed Borsippa was full of wily merchants ready to cheat a simple man, and of priests who induced the women to give to the temple presents they could ill afford. There was an ancient temple of Nebo in Borsippa, but like most temples in Babylonia it too was in bad repair.

"If only the gods granted us peace that we might rebuild our land and that our sons need not go to war, as did we and our fathers before us," Iddina often said.

Nor did he speak of sons without good reason. On the way south from Nineveh he had lain with Taia and she had conceived. When she bore him a fine son, Iddina—who was a good man and also too frugal to buy a bride—took her for his wife. Thus Tarqu became his kin, though he remained his slave, and I too was treated as though I were one of the clan. Iddina's father had died long ago, leaving his oldest son the head of the house. His mother ran the household and reared his younger brothers and sisters, dealing me no more cuffs than she did them. Indeed these simple folk, so different from my own lost kin, were kind to me in their way and taught me to love them. And in my heart I knew that in spite of my bitter fate I had been more fortunate than most captives. Indeed I should have learned in time to forget the past—for it was peaceful on Iddina's farm—had not fate overtaken us again.

The following year the Euphrates flooded Iddina's fields. All his seed was washed away and he was left to face famine, with no silver to buy grain for food, nor seed for the coming season. At such times the merchants from Borsippa would journey about the land to offer loans at high interest to those who could give them surety for their silver. But if the peasants could not repay the loan, as happened often, the merchants would seize their land.

It was such a merchant who called on Iddina that fateful spring, bringing about a new turn in our destinies.

This happened two years after the fall of Nineveh. There was not yet peace in the land. King Nabopolassar had led his army north to join the Medes in an attack upon Harran, where Prince Ashur-u-ballit of Assyria had proclaimed himself king. When Harran was attacked, Ashur-u-ballit fled still farther west to Carchemish, to wait there for help from Egypt, which—as always—was slow in coming.

But to those of us in Babylonia the war was far away, our own troubles being nearer our hearts than those of the troops in the field. It was a bitter day when Iddina told Tarqu and me that he must sell us that he might buy food for his family, and also seed for the coming season.

"It grieves me to do this thing," Iddina said, "but being the head of the household I must provide food for the others. My neighbors are selling their own children to keep from starving to death. And though Tarqu is become my kin, yet he is not of my blood, and neither are you, Ashur."

At the thought of being sold to yet another master I began to weep, but Tarqu said:

"Iddina must do what he must do, nor would I have my sister and her child die of hunger. Only one thing I would beg of you: if you sell us, sell us together, for though Ashur is already fourteen years old, he still needs someone to look after him. Nor would I wish him to die of hard work after I carried him all the way from Nineveh on my back."

Thus even in this calamity Tarqu thought to provide for me.

"I shall do my best that you might stay together," Iddina replied. "There is a merchant from Borsippa coming to see me today. His wealth is great, and he might wish to buy both of you."

It was I who helped the merchant from Borsippa dismount his camel when he arrived outside Iddina's door. The moment I laid eyes on him I was seized by a strong dislike of this man. He was old and fat, and his effort to dismount led to much wheezing. Though he was said to be wealthy, he wore old and dirty clothes. Crumbs of food stuck to his beard, and the small eyes in his oily face were shrewd and hard.

Iddina and his brothers bowed low before the merchant when he entered their home. After his visitor was seated, Iddina said:

"I ought to offer my lord refreshments, but there is no food left in the house. Indeed this is why I must sell my two faithful slaves." And he bade us step forward that the prospective buyer might examine us.

The merchant squinted, stroked his beard and said:

"You speak of two slaves, but I see only one. Surely you do not expect to find a buyer for this runt?" And he pointed his fat finger at me.

Iddina turned pale, for he needed the sum which both would bring him to see him through the year.

"The boy may look like a poor purchase," he said in the end, "but let my lord know that he can read and write, not only Babylonian, but also Sumerian, Syrian, Hebrew and Greek. Moreover, he is the son of an Assyrian prince who fled to Harran and who shall someday buy him back at a high ransom."

"These days there is a surfeit of Assyrian nobility in Babylonia," the merchant replied. "As for the princes who fled to Harran, they are now fled to Carchemish, and only the gods know where they will flee from there. Also, I am but a poor man who can ill afford owning a prince. Rather I need a strong slave to carry the merchandise in my warehouse—bales of linen, coils of rope, sacks of grain and heavy jars of wine. What I do not need is a scribe—for of what value is a scribe in Borsippa, the city of the god of writing, where there are more scribes than an honest man has use for?"

Only when Iddina revealed that I also knew how to keep accounts did the merchant seem tempted, asking whether I knew how to keep two sets of books. Though I had never been good at the science of numbers I said I could, for if I was to be sold I would be sold together with Tarqu, even if I disliked our buyer.

But that one was not yet resolved to take me, offering to pay the full price for Tarqu, but only a fourth for me. After much bargaining, weeping and swearing by the names of all the gods, Iddina sold me in the end for a third of Tarqu's price.

Once more I was called upon to draw up the contract for my own sale. Then Tarqu and I bade Iddina and his family farewell. Many tears were shed. Taia clung to her brother as he embraced her for the last time. Iddina too wept, not only because he loved us but because with our leaving he would again become a poor peasant. His mother, who had dealt me many cuffs, folded me in her arms and said between sobs:

"Though you were of small help to me and often did mischief, I love you no less than my own children. As I looked at you I often thought that but for the grace of the gods *we* might have lost the war, and the enemy might have carried off *my* sons. I wish I could give you and Tarqu some food to take on your journey, but there is none left." And turning to the merchant she said: "I pray my lord not to let the boy starve. When my son brought him home he was skinny as a mongrel in the street. I have fattened him, though he eats no more than a sparrow."

"And would I let my investment starve to death?" the merchant replied with indignation. "But if you are done embracing these slaves as though they were flesh of your flesh, we shall be on our way, for we want to reach Borsippa before nightfall. With the famine in the land there are many desperate men lying in wait along the roads, and I have a young wife at home whom I do not wish to leave a widow before her time!"

Then he poked Tarqu and me with the rod he carried to spur on his camel, and with Taia following behind us part of the way, her hand placed upon her head in mourning, we set out for Borsippa.

The sun was sinking behind Ezida, the temple of Nebo in Borsippa, when we entered the city through the north gate. As I saw the ziggurat of the temple in white outline against the red sky, tears welled up in my eyes, for I remembered my school days in another temple of Nebo. Then I had thought that I should grow up to be a scribe, while now I was being carried to Borsippa to be a sweeper of floors. But when Tarqu turned to me and said:

"Do not weep but be of good cheer, for we are still together," I replied:

"I am not weeping. It is only the setting sun stinging my eyes."

And even in my sorrow I rejoiced at once more setting foot in a large city that teemed with life. All the ships traveling upstream on the Euphrates from the Southern Sea docked in Borsippa before they continued north to Babylon. Every spring there was a great, solemn procession when the god Nebo was brought forth from his temple, loaded upon a barge and borne toward Babylon, there to take the hand of his father Marduk for the celebration of the new year. Though we had lived near Borsippa we had never gone into town to see the festival. Now I comforted myself with the thought that there would be some diversion to balance the hardship ahead.

Nor did I doubt that I was headed for hard times. Though our new owner had promised not to let me starve, he had given me but the crumbs from his meal, while Tarqu, who was of greater value to him, was well fed. Had Tarqu not secretly given me of his share, I should have fainted with hunger along the way. Even so I stumbled along slowly. To make me hasten, the merchant struck me with his rod, leaving a smarting welt on my back. Though I was born a slave I had never been struck in this manner before. However, being no longer a child I bit my lips and did not cry out, only adding one more hatred to the one that smoldered in my heart. If it pleased God I would someday pay back the merchant in kind.

But now, with the sounds, sights and smells of Borsippa about me, I forgot about the welt on my back. It was a long time since I had seen gorgeously garbed women in the street, their necklaces, bracelets and anklets jingling as they walked along. The men, with long curled beards and hair, were also handsomely dressed in robes with wide belts and pleats in the back, and pointed, tasseled caps upon their heads. The bazaars that lined the streets were still open, and though there was famine all around Borsippa, yet within the gates of the city there was great wealth and goods such as were brought by ship from every part of the world.

Our master halted outside a bazaar where a young woman sat upon a rug, minding the store. When she saw him she came forward, bowed down low and said:

"Praised be the gods that brought my lord safely home to me."

But when she rose I could see there was no joy in her eyes, rather chagrin at seeing her husband back so soon.

"And did my lord have a pleasant journey?" she asked, while she observed Tarqu and me out of the corner of her eye.

"The journey was hot and dusty, and these two wretched slaves delayed me on the way so that I was nearly caught by darkness.

Who knows what mishap might have befallen me had not the thought of you, my turtledove, spurred me on to hasten home."

He patted her cheek with his fat fingers, and though she did not flinch I could see that she loathed him.

Indeed she was much too young for that old man, I thought, and quite comely, with large, black eyes, a soft, pink mouth and big round breasts that pressed enticingly through her garments. As I stood staring at her, Tarqu seized my arm and whispered:

"Such thoughts are unseemly for a mere boy and a slave." For he knew what was in my mind.

I quickly lowered my eyes, but only until the talk between the merchant and his wife turned to me.

"And did my lord bring me the present he promised me?" the woman asked in a wheedling voice as she slipped away from her husband's caresses.

"I did indeed, my love! Behold, I brought you your very own slave!" the merchant replied, pointing at me.

"But my lord promised me a maidservant!" his wife wailed. "One who would cook my meals, wash my clothes and comb my hair in the morning, and to whom I could talk while my lord went off on his journeys! Instead he brought me this boy who, I am certain, does not even know how to kindle a fire! As for this black giant, I am afraid of him even in my lord's presence and shall surely not suffer him in the house with me when I am alone!"

"No harm shall come to you from the Ethiopian, my doe," the merchant replied, "for he was made a eunuch long ago. But the boy Ashur shall serve you well. Even if he cannot cook, he can fetch and carry for you and also keep you from boredom, for he can read and write and knows many amusing tales. Moreover, he is an Assyrian prince, whose father shall someday buy him back at a high ransom. And though I paid a handsome price for this boy, I shall give him to you as a present so that the ransom money will be yours."

"And will my lord put this in writing for me?" the lady asked.

"Need a husband and wife draw up contracts?" the merchant asked. "Let those two be witnesses that the boy is yours!"

Tarqu and I nodded as he looked at us, though we knew that if this gift was ever disputed before a judge, the law would not favor the lady. But if Tarqu had said that it was not his task to prevent one Babylonian from deceiving another, surely it was not our task

to prevent a husband from cheating his wife or—for that matter—
her from cheating him.

That the latter was in the lady's mind became clear to me after I
had been her slave for less than a week. While Tarqu helped our
master in the bazaar, I spent my time working for our mistress,
whose name was Harshinana. She made me sweep the yard and the
house, cut kindling for the hearth, and draw water to fill the trough
in which she took her daily bath. Indeed even while she was
washing herself she would call out to me to bring her yet more
water for her ablutions.

So as not to look at her I would clumsily back into the room,
holding the heavy water pitcher in my arms. The temptation to
peep at my mistress as she sat in her bath was great. But this I would
not do for fear of having her husband catch me at it. Thus I remained with my back to her while she sprinkled herself with perfume and slipped into her robes. Yet her scent and the rustling
noises as she dressed caused me no end of divine agony.

When she was dressed Harshinana made me assist her in the
kitchen with such tasks as I was able to perform. Every now and
then she would ask me:

"Is it true that you are a prince?"

Since this lie had once before assured my being treated well, I
nodded in assent. Then Harshinana would glance at me in a manner
in which a mistress ought not to look at a slave, and say:

"Indeed you are handsome enough to be a prince!"

I would blush and cast down my eyes, but never lower than her
splendid bosom.

One night Tarqu, who having been keeper of a harem knew
much about women, spoke to me sternly as we lay in our wretched
quarters.

"Harshinana is a young woman who has an old husband. Such
women are always bent on mischief. Though you are but a boy,
Ashur, this will not prevent her from using you for her pleasure. I
pray you to resist temptation when it is offered you, for you can
come to great harm from a woman older than yourself. I have seen
it happen more than once."

I promised to let virtue be my guide. But every night at bedtime
I would picture what might happen if our master left on another

journey. Then my dreams would be troubled and I would spill my seed in my sleep.

However, our master remained at home to guard his wife. Nor was there much need for him to travel, for people in need of silver would offer to sell him all manner of goods at low prices. Among them were former soldiers fallen on hard times, who were forced to sell the booty they had carried with them from Nineveh. On occasions when I was summoned to help in the bazaar, I would see there vessels of gold and of silver, perfume jars of blue and green glass, and artfully wrought bracelets and earrings which showed the hand of Assyrian craftsmen.

"Before long we shall also have a surfeit of goods from Egypt," our master said, rubbing his hands with glee. "The Egyptian armies are on their way to Carchemish, where they are certain to be beaten in battle, as has been their fate for years now. But the spoil will fall to our victorious soldiers, who shall soon offer to sell me scarabs carved of precious stone and fine Egyptian gold chains. May Nebo bless the weapons of our troops and grant them a great victory at Carchemish, for I know many customers willing to pay high prices for Egyptian jewelry!"

FOUR

After all this, when Josiah had prepared the temple, Neco king of Egypt went up to fight against Carchemish by the Euphrates; and Josiah went out against him. But he sent ambassadors to him, saying: 'What have I to do with thee, thou king of Judah? I come not against thee this day, but against the house wherewith I have war; and God hath given command to speed me; forbear thee from meddling with God, who is with me, that He destroy thee not.'

—SECOND CHRONICLES 35:20,21

I F the report that Pharaoh Necho was going up against Carchemish filled the merchant of Borsippa with glee, it brought gloom to us in Judah (the old woman Tamar said to the young scribe).

Three years before, when Nineveh had fallen and the power had passed from Assyria, there had been great rejoicing in our land. All had clapped their hands at the fate of the Assyrians, for upon whom had not their wickedness fallen continually? We thought that a new golden age was to begin for Judah now that our oppressors lay in the dust. For the first time in many years we were free of foreign garrisons, and the land was indeed ours.

But those who understood the fate of nations knew that this would not continue long if the Egyptians went up to Carchemish, for there was no way for them to go north except through our country. Indeed there were many in Judah who said the Egyptian armies must not be allowed to pass through. Merari was one of them.

"Should we assist the allies of these accursed Assyrians and aid them in regaining their power that they might again place their yoke on our necks? No, but the land is ours now, and so it shall remain!"

Thus, when King Josiah called up all those fit to bear arms, Merari was among the first to go. He was well skilled in the handling of weapons, nor had he ever shirked his duty of giving one month out of the year to serve in the king's army. Only then had he left the running of his household to his servants, proclaiming that the good of the nation came first. He had risen to the rank of captain of hundreds over the men of Bethul, and it was his task to provide the prescribed number of soldiers for the king.

When King Josiah issued the call to arms, Merari swung himself 'upon Hadad and rode to Lachish to furnish himslf with the needed weapons, for there was no armor maker in Bethul. He returned with a shining new coat of mail, a peaked helmet upon his head, a bow slung over his shoulder, a spear in his hand, and a sword strapped to his waist.

Gazing at him with admiration, Judith exclaimed:

"There is no man as handsome and brave as my father!"

But his kinsman Shallum did not think highly of Merari's act, nor did he conceal his thoughts.

"Does it not suffice that you would serve the king, Merari?" Shallum asked. "Must you buy your own armor? Has not the king arms and shields enough for his men?"

"And am I a pauper to take from the king what he can ill afford to offer?" Merari replied. "There are not enough swords and shields among the men of Judah, neither are there enough soldiers, for our great Moses made provisions that we should have no army in times of distress!"

Observing Merari with amazement, Shallum asked:

"How has Moses, who has been dead these six hundred years, a hand in this?"

"You, Shallum, who never served in war, do not know that in calling the men to arms I must speak thus: 'Is there anyone who has built a new house but has not dedicated it? Let him go back to his home, lest he die in battle and another dedicate it. Is there anyone who has planted a vineyard but has never harvested it? Let him go back to his home, lest he die in battle and another initiate it. Is there anyone who has spoken for a woman in marriage but has not yet married her? Let him go back to his home, lest he die in battle and another marry her. Is there anyone afraid and disheartened? Let him go back to his home, lest the courage of his comrades flag like his.' And after I have thus spoken to the men, I may turn around and march off into battle—alone!"

"Truly the law of our great teacher Moses is not a matter for mocking!" Shallum said with indignation.

"I am not mocking," Merari replied. "Rather I am filled with despair. Since the call for troops reached us, there has been such buying and selling of vineyards around Bethul as never before. Nor is there a maiden so ugly or poor that she would not find one who would gladly wed her now, even if he had three other wives whom he could ill afford to keep, less still please. How are we to halt the Egyptian armies, whose numbers are as those of grasshoppers, if we have no soldiers?"

"Then you are truly of a mind to join in this madness and be killed?" Shallum asked.

"I am not of a mind to be killed," Merari said. "But if this be the will of God, so be it. My duty to my king and my country comes before my life."

"And what of your daughter?" Shallum asked.

"What of my daughter?"

"If you fall in battle, what will become of her, and she but a child of ten?"

"I shall leave her well provided for," Merari said gravely. "I had it put in writing—sealed and duly witnessed—that all I own shall be hers. As for my faithful servants, whom I always treated well and paid promptly, they will continue serving Judith as they served me."

Shallum shook his head and gazed at Merari as though he doubted his good sense.

"Son of my brother," he said, "you are an honest man blinded by his own honesty. If you should fall, remember that you have a living brother who has sons. Is it not the law that the land shall go to the male heirs?"

At that Merari turned pale and said:

"My brother Aaron swore to me never to seize Judith's fields!"

"And how many men have broken a vow for great riches?" Shallum asked. "Though Aaron may not know your wealth, there might be those who tell him of it. If he came to claim the land as his own, who would speak for Judith?"

While Merari began to pace to and fro in distress, Shallum observed him with cunning. Then he spoke:

"I can see that you are troubled, son of my brother, as well you should be. However, there are ways to protect your daughter should you fail to return. Am I not one of the elders of Bethul who sit in the gate and judge the cause of the people? Let Judith be betrothed to my grandson Manasseh, and I shall defend her cause even against your own brother!"

"But Judith is still too young for betrothal!" Merari exclaimed in distress.

"Many a maiden is promised at ten," Shallum replied. "She need not marry until she is grown—unless you fall in battle, may God grant you many years!"

"But I thought to betroth her to one of my brother's sons, who are closer kin to me than Manasseh," Merari said.

"And would you tarry in Jerusalem on your way to war to draw up a contract with your brother?" Shallum asked. "Moreover, her husband might still take Judith's land from her and find himself another wife. But such a thing shall never happen if she weds Manasseh! Rather your fields and mine shall again be joined together as they were in the time of my own father."

And when Merari still would not consent, Shallum continued:

"I know what is in your heart. But Manasseh does not take after his father, who has caused my daughter no end of grief. Truly my grandson is a docile youth who does not pursue after girls. He has always been ruled by his mother and would be ruled by his wife. Therefore let us draw up a contract of betrothal for the children before you go off to war, Merari!"

After some brooding, Merari said:

"But first I would ask Judith if she would have Manasseh."

Shallum placed his hand upon his head in despair.

"Ask a woman—and yet one ten years old—if she would have for a husband the man her father chooses for her?"

"I raised Judith to think her own thoughts and do what is right," Merari said, "nor did I ever force her in any matter. Surely then I would not force a husband on her!"

Merari called Judith the same day and bade her sit beside him on the rug by the hearth.

"You are but a child, my daughter," he said, "yet there is a grave matter I must discuss with you. Soon I shall go off to war, where I might be slain in battle."

"May God prevent such a dreadful thing!" Judith exclaimed.

"Amen," Merari said. "It might come to pass, however, and you are young to be left an orphan with no male kin to speak up for your rights. Therefore it might be wise to betroth you before I leave."

"Betroth me, my lord?" Judith asked with amazement, for her father had never before spoken to her of betrothal. "But I am not yet of childbearing age!"

"You need not marry for a long time to come, Judith," Merari replied. "You need marry only if I were to die—which God forbid—that you might have a husband to protect you. Since it is the custom to marry a kinsman, lest the land be dispersed among strangers, I thought to betroth you to Manasseh. But I would not do so without your consent. And would you have Manasseh for your husband when you grow up?"

Judith had sat looking modestly down into her lap, as was seemly for a maiden when such a thing was discussed. But now she gazed straight at her father and replied:

"When I grow up I would have for my husband a man such as my lord. But since there is no other like him in the world, let me marry Manasseh, though he is frail and afraid of cattle and the sun."

This answer pleased Merari well. He folded Judith in his arms, kissed her and said:

"Unless I die in battle—which God forbid—it is yet many years before you will be married."

The following day a scribe was called to draw up the contract between Merari and Manasseh's father. But Shallum, the boy's grandfather, also affixed his name to the parchment, for the land that would someday go to Manasseh was his. Indeed there was so much talk about the land that none thought to protest when Merari had it written into the contract that Manasseh must never take another wife besides Judith, even as Merari had promised to take but one wife. As for the land, if Judith died childless before Manasseh, her fields would become his. But if Manasseh died before Judith, his land would be hers. If there was a son when Manasseh died, half would go to the son, half to Judith until her death that she might never rely on the charity of her children. If there were two sons, there must be three shares. And if there were daughters, they too should be provided with dowries.

Then the face of Manasseh's father grew dark, for he could see that if his son died before him he would be left to depend on

Judith's charity. But having been a bad husband to Athara, he could not hope for an inheritance from his wife's father.

When all the terms were drawn up, Merari said:

"If I die in battle, let Judith be married. But if I live, my daughter shall not be wed until the proper time."

"And when will that be?" Shallum asked.

"When I think her old enough for marriage," Merari replied.

And though Shallum pressed him, he would not fix a date for Judith's wedding in the marriage contract.

Not many days after the contract was sealed, a royal herald came to Bethul to summon the soldiers. Merari nailed the order to the gate, and all men who were not too old, too young or too fearful, or had built houses, bought vineyards or taken wives, answered the call. My own father was among them, for wherever Merari went he too would go.

The men who left Bethul next morning were a ragged troop. Few owned weapons other than axes, and none rode upon a horse, like Merari. With his fine coat of mail, his gleaming helmet, plaited shield and newly burnished sword he looked like a hero of yore among the men. Gazing at him, Judith exclaimed time and again:

"There is none to equal my father!"

But Shallum, who had come with us to bid our men farewell, only shook his head as he watched them file down the narrow path, past the spring, and head for the road to Jerusalem.

"God, in His infinite wisdom, created brave men fools, lest they have the good sense to be cowards," he said. "But the greatest fool of all is our King Josiah. Why would he prevent the Egyptians from going up in battle against the Babylonians and Medes? Let them all slay each other, and may their carcasses find no burial and be devoured by vultures! What have we to do with their wars?"

The men had left before the barley harvest, for it was in spring, when the rains ceased and the roads were no longer muddy, that the Egyptians went forth to war. Of Merari's menservants none but the old and feeble or young and tender stayed behind. Thus it fell to the women to gather the harvest that year. When the barley turned golden we moved down into our summer house in the fields. Every morning we rose at dawn to commence work before the hot sun licked the dew off the blades. Some of the young boys helped us cut the stalks and tie them in sheaves, and so they did in Shallum's fields, which bordered ours. But Manasseh, Judith's betrothed, was not among them, for his mother would not allow him to work in the sun.

As for Judith, though she was but ten years old she stood over the servants to keep them from faltering at their tasks, as she had seen her father do. Even then she was nearly as tall as the grown women, and only her voice betrayed her as a child. But her demeanor was that of a mistress, and when her aunt Sarai came to claim the share Merari dealt her every year, Judith watched narrowly that she receive no more and no less than her due. Then Sarai placed her hand upon her head and wailed:

"Not enough that my brother Merari is a madman gone to fight the war of strangers, he has sired a daughter with a heart and a fist of stone! God forbid that we ever need rely on her charity!"

But Judith said:

"Those who would not work should not eat."

For Sarai and her daughters had not come to help with the harvest.

When the barley was gathered onto the threshing floors, the grain winnowed and stored in the pits, and still there was no word from the men, the anguish of the women increased. Many crept up to the high places which King Josiah had desecrated, to sacrifice and pray there for the safety of their husbands and sons. The Baalim were always as near as the next hill, but Yahweh dwelled far away, in the temple of Jerusalem.

My mother was among those who sought out the sacred groves, but she never revealed to me what she did there. She would not have Judith find her out, and she knew there was nothing I could conceal from Judith.

However, at night, when we huddled around the oil lamp in the summer house, my mother would tell us tales of the old gods now that Merari was not here to prevent her. She would speak of Baal, who made the grain grow and the cattle multiply, and his sister and spouse Anath, who fought as well as any male god. She told us of Mot, the god of death, how he slew radiant Baal, causing the fields to wither and the cattle to languish. And she recounted how Anath descended to avenge the death of her brother and spouse, how she hacked Mot to pieces and scattered his remains over the fields. Then the rains began to fall again, the fields to grow and the cattle to bear young. And glorious Baal rose, for, however often he was slain, he would always return to life.

"There is none who can slay Baal," my mother whispered, while the flickering oil lamp cast strange shadows on the wall, and Judith and I shuddered with pleasure and dread.

But in the end Judith would remember that she was Merari's daughter and say to my mother:

"Do not speak to me of strange gods while my father is away at war, Dinah, lest you draw the wrath of God on him by your impious talk. Let the sin be on your head!"

Then my mother said:

"Though it was but yesterday that I suckled her at my breast, she already speaks to me as if she were my mistress."

"But I am no longer a child!" Judith replied, pouting. "Indeed I am betrothed to be married!"

At that my mother frowned and muttered:

"May God grant that your father return alive, for no good can come of betrothing you to a boy like Manasseh, who still sits on his mother's lap when he should be reaching under the skirts of the maidservants."

She should never have dared speak in this manner before Merari. Though he visited the harlots by the wall when the need was upon him, he would not suffer coarse talk in his house.

But in spite of all the forbidden dealings we prayed with great fervor to Yahweh in those days. We prayed for the hale return of our men and for victory for King Josiah and the troops. But it was not to be.

One evening a herald on horseback came from Jerusalem. As he rode from village to village he shouted to call out the mourning women and make a great lamentation. For our army was beaten in the Valley of Jezreel and our great King Josiah fallen in battle at Megiddo. As for our soldiers—some were killed, some wounded and some fled homeward, but who had lived and who had died would not be known for many days.

Every day we went to stand by the road that led to Jerusalem, hoping that we should see our men return. But when they came in

straggling groups Merari was not among them, neither was my
father. None of the men knew what had befallen them. There was
great confusion after King Josiah was slain, and each had fled by a
different way to save himself from the Egyptians. But we would not
yet surrender hope.

The time of the wheat harvest passed, and the second months of
vine tending, without my father or Merari returning home. Then
Shallum came to the house—for we had moved back into town—
and spoke to Judith of the contract her father had made for her.

"I inquired again of all the men who returned from war," Judith
replied. "And though none is certain that my father lives, yet there
is none certain that he is dead. Therefore let me wait yet a little
while before I marry Manasseh. If my father is not returned by the
time of plowing, I shall do as you wish."

Even then Judith knew how to address men in a manner that
would make them bow to her will. Thus Shallum returned to his
own house, while Judith and I resumed our daily vigil by the gate.

It was after the harvest of summer fruit, on a Sabbath eve when
the first light rain of the season had fallen, that we saw Hadad climb
the path to Bethul, with Merari sitting hunched upon his back. But
my father was not with him. Merari did not raise his head until
Judith ran toward him, shrieking with joy. The master's hair and
beard, which had been all black when he left, were streaked with
gray. His helmet was battered, and though he still had his sword and
spear, he seemed to have lost his shield. When he dismounted we
saw that he was grievously wounded in one leg, for he dragged it
behind him as he approached us, leaning on his spear.

Bending down, he folded Judith in his arms and wept. Then he
turned to my mother, who had followed after Judith and me, and
said:

"Rend your garments, Dinah, put ashes on your head and sit in
the dust, for your husband is fallen in battle. But he died bravely
and a hero."

Then my mother and I rent our clothes, beat our breasts and set
up a great lamentation, weeping all the way as we returned to our
house. Merari limped behind us, leaning on his spear and on Judith's
shoulder. When my younger brother learned that his father was
dead, he too wailed and rent his clothes. Then all our neighbors

came to mourn with us and to praise my father, as one praises the dead. And they gave thanks that at least Merari had been spared. Though he was returned alive, Merari's grief was great. And sitting with us on the ground in mourning, he revealed to all what had happened at Megiddo.

"When we arrived at Jerusalem the troops were already assembled. However, the number of men who had answered the call to arms was small. Not only had many found means to escape serving, but some declared they did not wish to go up in war against the Egyptians, our neighbors who often sided with us in war. Among those who spoke against the king was his own oldest son, Eliakim. He was known to lend a willing ear to the Egyptian envoys and the Hebrew princes who sided with them. But there were also many others who warned Josiah not to make war on Pharaoh Necho. While our troops were thus delayed by those who would weaken our hands, the Egyptians advanced boldly along the Sea Road and toward the pass at Aruna, which offered them the shortest route north.

"But when our own troops at last departed Jerusalem, they could not progress swiftly. There were among them but ten chariots, counting the two of the king, and no more than a hundred horsemen. The captains, greatly perturbed, asked Josiah how they could dare engage the Egyptian army, whose chariots, horsemen and troops were as the sand of the sea. Then King Josiah replied: 'Indeed we must not engage them in battle. Rather we must make haste to reach the pass at Aruna before our foe. There the road becomes so narrow that chariot will have to go after chariot, and horse after horse, and they will emerge from the pass one at a time. But we, who know our hills better than these Egyptians, shall take our posts along both ridges of the pass, from where our archers and slingers shall rain down arrows and stones on them. Those Egyptian soldiers who come through the pass alive shall be slain one by one as they emerge. What if our forces are small? Did not Gideon vanquish the great army of Midian with but three hundred men?'

"When the king mounted his chariot and moved to the head of his troops, the captain would not have him take the lead, for if he were seen and slain by the enemy, the soldiers would turn to flight. But Josiah replied: 'Am I as vain a fool as was King Ahab to go into battle dressed in my royal garments, thus making of myself an easy target? Nor shall I fly the royal standard or break formation when we engage the Egyptians in battle. How, then, would they know me among my charioteers?'

"Though the captains ceased from warning Josiah, they muttered among themselves that it should be a small matter for the Egyptians to pick out the king by his bearing. But the rest of the troops were much heartened by Josiah's great courage. Thus we continued north through the hills of Samaria, past Bethel, Shiloh and Shechem, going round the mountains to cut off the Egyptians where the pass led into the Valley of Jezreel, not far from Megiddo. And King Josiah sent five horsemen ahead to spy out from the ridge of the mountains how far the Egyptians had come. The horsemen brought back the report that the foe was already halfway through the pass, their spearhead approaching the exit while their rearguard was still in Aruna.

"Then King Josiah urged his soldiers to even greater haste, hoping to seal off the western mouth of the pass. When at noon we reached the Valley of Jezreel, the troops were so faint they would have fallen down in the fields to rest had not the sight before them turned them to stone. For the Egyptian army was come forth into the valley, their chariots massing as though about to attack us. But King Josiah kept our soldiers from flight, shouting: 'It is only their vanguard come through the pass! The rest of their troops are in Aruna and will not reach Megiddo before sunset! We can still vanquish them and seal off the rest in the pass!'

"But though our men closed in fighting ranks, with the chariots in front, the horsemen behind them, and the archers and slingers following last, they were become as pillars of salt and would not advance. Then King Josiah did what he had vowed to forego. He broke formation and rode in his chariot before his troops, crossing the field from left to right as he shouted: 'Follow me, follow me, we can yet wrest victory from them!' And whipping his horses he would turn his chariot to face the foe.

"But then the Egyptians knew who was the brave leader of our troops. One of their archers, standing upon a chariot, drew near and shot his arrow. And he smote the king between the joints of his armor, above his left shoulder blade, so that the arrow pierced through his back into his chest. And Josiah toppled over and fell out of his chariot. But while the horses broke and ran away, the king still tried to raise himself from the ground, shouting even though his life ebbed away with his blood: 'Stand, stand!'

"When the Egyptians saw that they had smitten our king, their chariots bore down on our troops. These broke and began to run this way and that to escape. Yet many were overtaken and slain. Now our own chariots, of which there were only nine left, drew near King Josiah, and so did some of the horsemen and troops who had not fled. For they would not let the Egyptians seize the king and defile his body as the Philistines had defiled the body of King Saul.

"I was among those who placed King Josiah in his second chariot. It was then I lost my shield and was wounded in the leg, while Dinah's husband, who was among the brave men to make a stand, was killed. But the battle was lost. The Egyptians came pouring forth from the pass and filled the valley like grasshoppers. Then our chariots turned back together with the remnant of horsemen to carry our wounded king to Jerusalem. But his mind was clouded and he kept on shouting whenever he woke from his faint: 'Fight, fight!' Not until he saw the walls of Jerusalem did he know where he was. Then he murmured: 'All is lost.' And Josiah died and they buried him with his fathers.

"As for me, my wound festered and a fever seized me. For many days I did not know where I was, nor what had befallen me. Neither could I tell the woman who had taken me into her house and nursed me to seek out my brother Aaron. When my senses returned to me, Prince Jehoahaz had been anointed and made king in his father's stead, while his older brother Eliakim, who had been a friend of the Egyptians, was passed over. However, the people did not cease from mourning, for Jehoahaz was too young to sit on the throne in these troubled times. Nor was he a good and righteous man, as had been his father. And all those who sided with the Egyptians said it would not go well with him.

"Then I made haste to leave Jerusalem, for I saw there was bloodshed ahead. There were rumors that Pharaoh Necho would soon send troops to Jerusalem to place his own favorite on the throne, and no man who had fought against the Egyptians would be safe. As for me, if I am to die by the sword I would die in battle against a foe, but I would not be slaughtered like a sheep by my own countrymen. Rather I shall bide my time in Bethul until another righteous king who needs my sword arises in Judah!"

It happened as Merari predicted. No sooner had Pharaoh Necho established his seat in Riblah—which is in Syria—than he dispatched troops to capture Jehoahaz. Their numbers were small, but there was treachery in Jerusalem. After having been king for only three months, Jehoahaz was carried off in chains to Riblah, and thence to Egypt to die there. In his stead Pharaoh Necho made Eliakim king of Judah, and he changed his name to Jehoiakim. Moreover, he put a fine of a hundred talents of silver and one talent of gold on the country. This tribute Jehoiakim exacted from the people of the land. The poor suffered grievously from the taxation, but the rich complained even more loudly.

Indeed some in Bethul refused to pay their taxes, saying there was enough gold in the king's treasure house to pay the tribute. The tax collectors who came to Bethul were often beaten so that in the end they were loath to come. Nor did they think it worth the trouble to visit Bethul escorted by soldiers.

Moreover, all the soldiers were needed in Jerusalem. There was no end to the spilling of innocent blood while Jehoiakim slew all those who had opposed him. Under his reign the people of Judah soon forgot King Josiah's godly rule and returned to the worship of heathen gods. And when Jeremiah stood in the gate of the temple, predicting Jerusalem's downfall because of her sins, the people tried to kill him. But the prophet escaped with his life.

We in Bethul had a few years of peace, to plow, to seed, to harvest and to pay taxes—those who would pay taxes—to marry, to beget children, to bring forth and to die.

Merari's leg never recovered from the wound he had received at Megiddo, and all his days he walked with a limp. When the winter rains came the wound would often pain him so that he had to lean upon a cane. But he continued to work as before, holding on to the handles of the plow as he walked the furrows of his fields. And still the women would sigh as they watched him.

For a while my mother hoped Merari would take her for his wife now that her own husband was dead and she was almost mother to Judith. But when her period of mourning was accomplished, Merari called her to him and said:

"I know what is in your heart, Dinah, but it cannot be. For I would not break my vow. Indeed I told the same to the woman who nursed me when I lay wounded in Jerusalem, lest I forget myself and make her such promises as men make in times of war. However, there is another matter I wish to discuss with you. Though you are not a Hebrew woman, your husband was a Hebrew who died a hero in battle. Therefore I shall deal with you as I would with a Hebrew woman who was my slave. You have served me more than seven years since my wife died, and I shall give you back your freedom. Fetch me a scribe and let me put it in writing that for the sake of their father, you and your children shall go free."

But my mother replied:

"Where would I, a poor woman, go if I were free, and how should I live? Even if out of his goodness my lord gave me fields, I should soon lose them, never having learned to look after property. Moreover, my lord has always treated me kindly. My children were born in his house, and I suckled his own daughter at my breast and love her no less than mine. How could I part with her after rearing her like a mother? Therefore I pray my lord not to send me away but to let me remain with him forever!"

"Is this truly your wish?" Merari asked.

"It is truly my wish," my mother replied.

Then Merari made her stand in the door and pierced her ear with an awl as a sign that of her own will she would remain his slave forever. And all her life she wore an earring to remind him of it.

But as for weddings, there were none—neither for Merari nor for Judith. Now that her father was returned from war Judith was free from marrying Manesseh till the time Merari would give his consent. Until then they were only playmates.

At times they were joined in their games by a youth named Joab, Manasseh's kin by his father's sister. Joab was as strong and ruddy as Manasseh was frail, but Manasseh doted on him and often brought him gifts he himself had fashioned, small likenesses of animals molded in clay or carved in wood. There was none in Bethul who did such work or had shown Manasseh how to do it. But he was clever with his hands, bragging that if he had silver or gold he would make a gorgeous bracelet for Joab. But Manasseh never brought Judith gifts, though she often allowed him to play with her rich, red hair, a thing that pleased him no end. He would plait it or put it up for her in ringlets, making of it a better task than any maidservant. But though none had ever told us, we knew that there was something strange about Manasseh and that our elders must not learn of his deeds.

Joab, who was strong as an ox if no brighter, would truly have been a better match for Judith than frail Manasseh. However, Manasseh was Judith's kin and she was promised to him. But she gave little thought to marriage, still preferring to play rough games with her betrothed. Whenever she chased a cow toward Manasseh to make him run away screaming, he stamped his foot and shouted:

"If you will not cease from teasing me, Judith, I shall not marry you!"

Then Joab, who worshiped Judith, would say boldly:

"If Manasseh will not have you for his wife, I will."

But Judith only laughed and replied:

"Rather than marry either of you I would remain with my father, whom I love better than I could ever love a husband!"

Indeed it seemed that Judith would remain with her father a long time yet. Merari's health was good, and unless war came to the very gates of Bethul, his lame leg would keep him from ever again going out into battle. But for four years there was peace in the land.

King Jehoiakim paid tribute to Egypt until Pharaoh Necho was beaten by the Babylonians at Carchemish. Then the pharaoh returned to his own country and came forth no more, for the king of Babylon had taken from him all the land from the Brook of Egypt unto the River Euphrates.

But Judah had a new overlord.

FIVE

For, lo, I raise up the Chaldeans,
That bitter and impetuous nation,
That march through the breadth of the
    earth,
To possess dwelling-places that are not
    theirs.

—HABAKKUK 1:6

THOUGH I, in Borsippa, was far removed from the war (the old man Isaac said to the young scribe), the four years that were years of peace in Bethul were bitter years for me. For it is in the nature of man that if trouble does not pursue him, he will seek it out.

It took me no longer to find trouble than it took my master to go off on his next journey. He had heard of a ship that had run aground and sunk a day's journey from Borsippa, and of some brave men who had dived into the Euphrates and brought up such goods as they could lay their hands on. Now these men were selling the goods they had so courageously salvaged to those who would handle doubtful merchandise, my master being one of them. Thus he entrusted his store and house to Tarqu and me, lacing his pleas to deal honestly in his absence with such threats as would strengthen our virtue, and departed on his errand.

The lady Harshinana had long been waiting for this event, and, I confess, so had I. My mistress had never ceased from showing me more favors than one would show a mere kitchen slave. She fed me larger portions than the master assigned me, and also used me as her confidant.

"Why should I not speak to you of my troubles?" she said when in the name of decency I begged her to desist. "My lord promised me a maidservant to whom I could talk while he was away, and instead he brought me you. Moreover, you are but a child, and what harm can there be in unburdening my heart to you?"

What harm could come of it the lady knew better than I, for

such things are not discussed between a man and a woman, even if the man is only a boy.

"Ah, but you do not know what sorrow it is for a young woman to be the wife of an old man," Harshinana would sigh when I sat with her in the kitchen. "I thought that my lord, being a rich man, would give me beautiful garments and much jewelry. But he gives me barely a length of cloth to cover my back, and as for jewelry, I may keep it only until a buyer comes along who offers him a good price. Since he never puts anything for me in writing, I cannot prevent him from taking away the gifts he has given me. It is true that he himself goes about in tattered clothes, but he is an old man who cannot live much longer, while I am still a young woman!"

I would sit in silence and merely nod my head, for it would be unwise of me to answer my mistress one way or the other. Moreover, she was right in all she said. Our master was an old miser who doled out food sparingly and made his wife account for every half shekel she spent.

"Still, I should be content if he were a good husband to me," my mistress continued, "one who knew how to please me as a husband ought to please his wife. But he has wasted his strength in his younger years so that now he cannot even give me a son. Someday I shall be left a widow with no offspring to gladden my later years! But he would still have his pleasure and forces me to do abominable things which I had better not describe to you, for you are but a boy who has never yet lain with a woman. Or have you, Ashur?"

I blushed and looked down on my hands and shook my head, but I was greatly troubled by all that talk.

"Ah, but you will someday, you will," Harshinana said in a low voice that sent shivers down my back. "Then you will know what pleasures I am made to miss!"

When our master went off on his journey, Harshinana considered the time come to show me what pleasures she was made to miss. No sooner had she embraced her husband and commended him to the protection of the gods on his perilous journey than she turned to me and said:

"Whenever my lord leaves home I am sorely afraid that some stranger might break into the house and force his wiles on me. Therefore you shall not sleep with Tarqu tonight, Ashur, but spread your blanket before the door of my chamber. Thus I shall feel safe and not be troubled in my sleep."

And who was I, a mere slave, to refuse such an order?

I shall not describe to you what the lady Harshinana and I did that night, for those who know about such things know—as for the others, let them find out for themselves. Moreover, all old men who profess to remember every sigh and sweet embrace are liars. I shall only tell you that I spread my blanket before Harshinana's chamber door every night while our master was away on his journey. Would I had been on it.

Tarqu, who did not believe that I was but a sentinel at our mistress's door, was angry with me and full of dire warnings.

"You had better come to your senses before it is too late," he said to me. "There are many tales I could tell you where striplings like you came to everlasting harm through an older woman."

But I closed my ears to Tarqu's wise counsel. The fruits of my sin tasted sweeter to me every night. Not only did the embraces of my mistress increase in fervor, but she also made me believe that she might raise me from my lowly position if she were left a widow.

"My husband is an old man who cannot live forever," Harshinana said. "If only I could entice him to name me his heir, I should look forward to a pleasant future. But the old miser will not put anything in writing."

One night, when I lay in her bosom, she whispered to me:

"Consider how happy we could be together, Ashur, if you—who can write—would make out a will in my husband's name. I would only have to borrow his seal while he lies sleeping and impress it on the tablet to render it lawful. Then, if some unfortunate accident befell him on one of his journeys we should both be free and rich."

Though I was foolish then, I was not so foolish as to become party to such a plot. Indeed the mere thought of it made the hair rise on the back of my neck. Still, I would not lose the favor of my mistress, and I replied:

"To make a document legal a number of witnesses are required. Where would my lady find men willing to swear that they saw her husband seal a will he never made?"

"Such men might be found more easily than you imagine,"

Harshinana replied. "The promise of silver does marvelous things to a man's memory."

Perhaps I should have succumbed to her pleas in the end had not the master returned one night to find me occupying his rightful place. Harshinana had not expected her husband at this late hour, for none in his right senses traveled after dark, less still if he carried things of value with him. Later we were to learn the cause of this fateful folly: the men who sold the stolen goods at low prices would often pursue after their buyers and rob them of the merchandise they had so cheaply sold them. Thus the master had made haste, driving his camels day and night to reach the haven of home.

Tarqu slept soundly after a day's hard work, and when he was roused by the master's arrival in the court it was too late to warn me. Oil lamp in hand, the old man broke in upon Harshinana and me. Though the fright put an instant end to what we were doing, there was no denying what it had been.

"Hah, filthy harlot!" the merchant shouted, striking Harshinana with his rod upon her head and shoulders, while she tried to protect her face from his blows. "Is this how you reward me for having raised you from wretched poverty to being my rightful wife? But I shall deal with you as one deals with an adulteress! I shall have you bound and thrown in the river, you fornicating whore!"

And he went on striking her, while she screamed "Mercy, my lord, mercy!" and I tried to hide my nakedness under the bed covers.

Then Harshinana threw herself at her husband's feet, and shedding many tears, she said:

"No, but let my lord listen to me! Would I deceive a good and kind man like my husband? It was this wretched slave who forced me! I only commanded him to sleep outside my door, fearing someone might break in upon me while my lord was away. But this slave stole into the room while I lay in deep slumber and slipped into my bed. When I woke he had already mounted me! Who knows what he might have done had not the gods brought back my lord in time to save my virtue!"

These lies from a woman who only a short while ago had spoken to me of love left me speechless. Nor should I have been saved had I found words with which to describe her wretched deeds and plans to my master. As he turned to me with a murderous gleam in his eyes, I remembered how Tarqu had once told me that a man would sooner believe a lie from a comely woman than the truth from the mouth of his best friend. Surely the master would rather think I had forced his wife than that she had made a fool of him.

"Hah!" he screamed, hitting me now. "I should have known that there is no foreigner who would not defile our women if given a chance! Yet it never entered my mind that a mere boy might commit such a lewd deed. But you shall be punished according to our law!"

At the thought of being drowned in the river I began to weep and to plead for my life, hopeless though I knew such pleading to be. Therefore I was astonished when the master said:

"Out of the kindness of my heart I shall spare you. Also I paid much silver for you and would not cause myself a loss on top of the harm you already did me. But you shall not go unpunished, nor shall you ever again defile a Babylonian woman. Go rouse Tarqu, Harshinana, and bid him run for a surgeon that he might render this wretched knave harmless forever!"

When I understood what was in his mind I let out a terrible scream and tried to bolt for the door. But the master caught me by the hair and held me fast, while he urged his wife to hasten.

"Do not reveal to Tarqu what happened but tell him that I returned ill from my journey and must be attended this very instant!"

Without casting another glance at me, Harshinana left the room. I twisted and squirmed in my master's grip, but though he was old he was strong, and I could not escape him. Thus I stood weeping and covering my parts with my hands until Tarqu entered, bringing the surgeon with him. When Tarqu saw me standing naked in the room he knew what was to be my fate, though the wretched woman had not told him. But the surgeon, surly because he had been roused from sleep, looked about him and said:

"I see no sick person here, only one possessed by demons." For I was still writhing and screaming. "I am a surgeon, not one who practices exorcism. Go fetch such a one and pay him the high fee these scoundrels demand, while an honest surgeon must work for a pittance, always in danger of having his hand cut off should he fail!" Indeed he sounded much like my sister's husband, who had been royal surgeon at Nineveh.

But, shaking me as he held me by the hair, my master replied:

"The wretch is possessed by nothing but lewdness. While I was gone on a journey, this Assyrian scum sneaked into my wife's bedchamber, thinking to force her. With the help of the gods I caught him before he accomplished this vile deed. And now I would have you see to it that he may never again threaten the virtue of a Babylonian lady!"

Hearing these words, Tarqu approached the door, for he would not witness my punishment. The master detained him that he might aid in holding me down during the surgery. But Tarqu shook his head and said:

"This my lord cannot make me do."

"Would you defy me, wretched slave, and have me punish you too?" the merchant screamed.

"What is to be done to Ashur was done to me long ago. And though my lord might cut off my ear, pluck out my eye, tear out my tongue, cut off my hand or beat me unto death, he would only be squandering his silver," Tarqu said, knowing well that our master's greed would prevent him from harming his property.

"I shall deal with you later, scum!" the merchant roared so as not to lose face before the surgeon. "Now go and attend to your mistress, who no doubt sits weeping over having been humbled by this Assyrian filth!"

Tarqu left the room, his head bowed in grief. But the surgeon, pulling away my hands with which I still covered myself, looked astonished and said to my master:

"Surely this boy is not an Assyrian. Rather he must be an Egyptian or a Hebrew!"

My master, who had never seen me naked before, looked down at me and let out a howl of fury.

"Not enough that he tried to ravish my wife, he also deceived me and his former master by proclaiming himself an Assyrian prince! Cursed be the day I ever laid eyes on him! He not only injured my honor but made me pay for him above his value! Make haste then, surgeon, and do your work, lest I strangle the wretch in my fury and lose all!"

But the surgeon could not yet proceed, for while he held both my hands with his, he had none free to wield his knife. Even when my master would assist him, they could not subdue me until the merchant picked up a heavy pitcher and brought it crashing down on my head. Then all about me went dark.

When I woke I was in my own quarters, with Tarqu's mourning black face bent over me. But I had lost forever the power to know the pleasure men value above all else and which I had tasted all too briefly.

I fell back into the state in which I was after seeing my father killed and defiled at Nineveh. Not only was I feverish and in pain for days, but I would not eat. The evil woman who had caused my misery never inquired whether I was still alive, but Tarqu brought me food. I turned my face to the wall when he coaxed me to eat.

"To please me you must eat, Ashur," Tarqu would say. "I did not carry you on my back from Nineveh that you might die in Borsippa."

"Would you had let me die on the road," I replied. "I would sooner be dead than live as a eunuch!"

Thus, in my bitterness, I struck out at the one who tended me. But Tarqu did not reprove me. He only sighed and said:

"I understand your grief, Ashur, for I too have felt it. However, one goes on living, and after a while one finds that there are still many good things left in life: a savory meal, a brimming cup of wine, a pleasant spring day, a joyful song. As for you, Ashur, there are yet other rewards that come to those who can read and write. Is it not said that writing is the father of wise men and the mother of orators? Therefore consider your good fortune!"

"I desire but one pleasure," I replied. "And that is gone from me forever."

"Out of every evil some good will come," Tarqu said. "Now that you have discovered what snakes women are, at least you never need fear being tempted again. Your body will heal in time, and so will your mind, if you let it."

Again Tarqu proved right. For if a man had all his limbs cut off and only his heart kept on beating, yet would he want to live. But even after I knew that I wanted to live I would not admit it for a long time. If I did not bewail the loss of my manhood I would brood over the slave mark my master made the surgeon burn upon my wrist while I lay senseless. Though I was born a slave I had never been marked and might have passed for a freeman. But now my lowly station was plain for everyone to see. Thus, even long after my pain and fever had ceased, I was loath to show myself in the street.

While I lay ill Tarqu not only did my work but tried to cheer me up in every way. One day he burst into our wretched room to tell me that there was a man in the kitchen who would greatly divert me if only I would rise and go there.

"This man came to our door while the mistress was out and offered to foretell my future if I let him have a few crumbs of food," Tarqu said. "Indeed he is a famous soothsayer from Uruk, fallen on hard times."

"He cannot be so famous if he must beg for food," I replied sullenly. "I was taught to believe that the future is known only to God. And though I ceased to believe in God after what befell me, I believe still less in what a man might foretell."

"Do not speak thus before you see this soothsayer," Tarqu said. "He has beheld the goddess Ishtar with his own two eyes, and so dazzled was he by her glory that he was blinded in one of them!"

How Tarqu, who in many ways was so much wiser than I, could believe such lies I could not fathom. But he continued:

"Get up from your blanket and follow me to the kitchen, Ashur! The soothsayer poured oil on the water for me and predicted that I should go on a long journey, that I should rise to a high position, indeed that I should again serve a king! He might yet prophesy such marvels for you!"

"No doubt he will," I said. "All soothsayers promise that one shall go on a journey, that one shall rise to a high position and that one shall serve a king."

But in the end I was persuaded to follow Tarqu to the kitchen. There the soothsayer sat on the floor by the hearth, picking his teeth after the meal Tarqu had served him. He was short and gaunt, and much too young for a soothsayer of renown, but his robe, though rent in places, was of fine material, as if its owner had indeed seen better days. His left eye was closed and swollen in an ugly manner.

"I brought you my young friend," Tarqu said. "And though he scoffs at prophecies, yet I hope you will predict a pleasant future for him."

"For a cup of wine I shall predict for him the most pleasant of futures—if this be the will of Ishtar, who in her goodness granted me a glimpse of her, though the vision cost me the sight of one eye!" the soothsayer replied.

"To look at your eye, the goddess must have shown herself to you but yesterday," I said.

"Indeed it was not long ago that she appeared before me," the soothsayer said. "But the priests of Uruk are a jealous lot and would not believe that Ishtar favored me over them. Their hatred of me was such that I had to flee Uruk. This is the cause of my wretched state, which, I trust, shall last but briefly. And now, if you will give me a fresh pan of water and some oil, I shall see what the future holds in store for this handsome youth."

Tarqu fetched fresh water and stole some oil out of Harshinana's pitcher. Pouring a few drops onto the water, the soothsayer creased his brow, waved his hands in the air, muttered incantations and acted altogether as though he could indeed gaze beyond even the next moment.

"I see a splendid future for this young man," he said in the end. "He shall go on a journey. He shall rise to a high position. Indeed he shall serve princes and kings!"

I turned to Tarqu and said with scorn:

"Did I not tell you that he knew but one oracle?"

"And would I lie if the goddess decreed the same future for you and your friend?" the soothsayer said. "But wait, there is still another thing in store for you!" And his one eye became glassy as though he did truly behold some marvelous vision. "Not only will everything I predicted happen to you, but the goddess Ishtar herself will descend from on high to take you by the hand and change your fate forever!"

I was very angry then and said to Tarqu:

"Have you made me rise from my blanket only to listen to such folly? I had better leave the kitchen before the mistress returns, and so had your guest, for I do not know how she might deal with us if she found that we stole of her food and oil."

This seemed wise counsel to Tarqu. He bade our visitor farewell and hurried him out into the back alley just as Harshinana entered from the street. Seeing me, she gave me a hateful glance and said:

"If you are well enough to visit my kitchen while I am out, run and fetch me some wood! Then go help the master in the store, for after your vile deed I would not have you in the same room with me!"

And she gave me a cuff to hurry me on my way.

As I passed Tarqu, I muttered:
"Behold me rising to a high position."

From that day on I spent more time in the bazaar than in the kitchen. Since I could no longer serve Harshinana's pleasure, nor would I write her a forged will, she had little use for me. Moreover, she would convince her husband that she hated the sight of me. Thus, whenever the master was around, she would kick or strike me, and more than once she begged him to sell me so that she might never again be reminded of how I had humbled her.

Her husband would have granted her wish had he been able to find a buyer for me. But I was not strong enough for heavy work, and none of his customers would buy a scribe, who were plentiful in Borsippa. Thus he used me for sweeping his floors and dusting his merchandise. Though I detested these tasks, I learned to distinguish between jewelry wrought in Phoenicia and that made in Babylon, between pottery vessels from Uruk and alabaster vases from Egypt, between mantles of Babylonian wool and many-colored garments from Judah, between wine made of our own dates and imported wine pressed of grapes.

For a while my master made me keep his accounts, but I made many mistakes, some willfully. Then he would curse and threaten to sell me. But I did not care, though I was saddened by the thought of parting from Tarqu. Still I would have preferred this to being in the same house with the vile woman who had caused my ruin.

But a year passed and nothing came of my master's threats. While I continued as his slave, I saw his bazaar expand and his reputation spread abroad. Indeed some buyers made the boat ride down from Babylon to visit his store.

It was such a man who entered the bazaar one afternoon while I stood sweeping the floor. I could tell that he was of noble birth, for his garments were of the finest linen and he wore sandals upon his feet. His hair and beard were dressed in the latest fashion, framing a slender face with large, somber eyes. Looking about him, he picked up a perfume jar here, a bracelet there, but clearly not finding what he had come for. My master followed him about like a hungry dog, pointing out such objects as he thought this fine gentleman might fancy. But in the end the man said:

"None of this is what I came for from Babylon. Rather I was told by a friend that I might find here loot sold by soldiers who fought at the battle of Nineveh."

At that my master grew pale and exclaimed:

"As Nebo is my witness, I buy from them in good faith and do not inquire where they obtained the goods! Nor would I know if they came by them in an unlawful manner."

The man smiled his sad smile and said:

"Fear not, my friend, I am not one of the king's officers come to discover thieves who stole what was rightfully the king's spoil, though there must be many of them. Rather I have come to discover whether any of the soldiers sold you some clay tablets he carried away from the library at Nineveh."

Hearing these words I left off sweeping and drew closer, for the man spoke of the place where I had spent many good years—though then I had thought differently. But my master asked, astonished:

"And what sort of clay tablets might these be to merit a journey down from Babylon?"

"Clay tablets on which there is written ancient Sumerian poetry," the man replied.

"Let my lord know that I deal in goods which are useful to men," my master said with indignation. "What use is there in poems written on clay, and in Sumerian, which none can understand? I would rather show my lord a fine piece of Egyptian linen or some gorgeously tinted perfume flasks for the fortunate lady who is my lord's wife!"

But the man only shook his head and turned to the door.

"Sumerian poetry!" my master exclaimed, putting both his hands to his head in despair at losing a customer over such a trifle. Then his gaze fell on me and he called after the man: "No, but wait, my lord! Though I have no Sumerian poetry in my bazaar, I have a slave who claims he can read and write Sumerian!" And he caught me by the arm and pulled me into the light, where our caller might see me better.

The gentleman gazed at me full of doubt, for as I stood there, broom in hand, I hardly looked like a learned person. But he spoke kindly to me, asking:

"Is it true that you know Sumerian, my boy?"

"It is true, my lord," I mumbled.

"And where would one as young as you have learned this ancient tongue?"

"I was taught it at the same library my lord spoke of before," I replied. "These clay tablets my lord would buy—I read and copied these very tablets at Nineveh."

The gentleman regarded me with ever-greater astonishment.

"What, then, are you doing here, sweeping floors?" he asked.

Lowering my eyes, I said:

"I am but a slave and must do such work as my master bids me do."

But the merchant would not see me lower my value in the eyes of a buyer and said quickly:

"I let this boy keep my accounts, but whenever he added two and two the result was five, which will never do in business. As for his knowledge of Sumerian, what use have I, a humble man, for that? But my lord, who is a learned man as I can well see, could put this lad to good use! For not only does he know Sumerian, he also knows Syrian, Hebrew and Greek. Moreover, he is not a mere slave but an Assyrian prince, whose father fled to Carchemish and will someday buy him back at a high ransom. I paid for him three times the price of a common slave. But seeing how much my lord values one who knows Sumerian, I am willing to suffer a loss and sell him the boy for only twice the price of a common slave!"

I opened and closed my mouth, remembering that it was not my task to prevent one Babylonian from deceiving another. And I was curious to discover whether the gentleman would think me worth such a high price. But he only sighed, stroked his beard and said he already owned three slaves, which he could ill afford. When he again turned to the door to leave, my master called after him that he was willing to sacrifice me at one and a half times the market price of a slave, even if all the world laughed at him for being such a simpleton.

"Let my lord consider how he would rise in the eyes of his friends if had an Assyrian prince to wait on him!"

"Though I am well aware of my own small worth, I would rather have my friends value me for what I am than for what I own," the gentleman replied. "Moreover, my wife, a lady who knows the value of silver better than I, would be greatly dismayed if I spent so much on indulging myself. For truly we have no need of yet another slave."

Then the merchant exclaimed in despair:

"Who am I to stand in my way of learning? Let my lord take the boy at the fair market price then, and if his wife is not pleased with the purchase, my lord can always sell him in Babylon. Surely there is a greater demand for scribes there than in Borsippa, where they abound!"

And so eager was the merchant to sell me that he declared himself willing to accept half the sum now and a written promise for the rest, to be paid later. But I knew as well as my master that even at half the price he had already made a profit on what he had in truth paid for me.

Thus the deal was concluded, and for the third time since I was carried away from Nineveh I had to prove my writing skill by drawing up a contract for my own sale. Thus I learned that my new master's name was Nabukasir, and that he owned a house in Babylon and much land outside the city walls. All this would ensure that he would redeem his note in due time. Then the contract was witnessed and sealed, and once again I had a new master.

After putting down my broom I was ready for the journey to Babylon, for I had no possessions to carry with me. However, I asked leave to say farewell to Tarqu, who stood splitting wood in the yard for the cause of my downfall. When it came to me that I might never see him again, I burst into tears and threw myself at his chest, bemoaning our cruel fate. Though he too shed tears he spoke cheering words to me.

"Was it not you who scoffed at the words of the soothsayer? And now you are to go on a journey even before me! Surely the rest of the prediction will still come true!"

As we embraced one last time, I promised to speak a good word for Tarqu to my new master if I found favor in his eyes. Perhaps he had a wealthy friend in Babylon who might wish to buy Tarqu. Then I returned to the store, where I bowed to my former master with as little respect as I dared show. And, giving the kitchen a wide berth, I followed my new lord with a heart in which mingled sadness, joy and hope for a better future.

My lord Nabukasir had come by boat from Babylon, but since the journey upstream was slow and perilous, he hired a man with two mules to take us back. It was I who haggled with the mule driver over the price, for seeing that my lord was a stranger in town, he would charge him too much. My new master thanked me, saying he had never learned to bargain and was always being deceived, much to the distress of his wife. Hearing this, I was not a little worried over how she would feel should she ever learn the truth about me.

The price of transport settled, we commenced our journey to Babylon. I had meant to walk behind my lord's mule, as befitted a slave, but he said to me:

"Come, mount behind me, my boy, for you are not heavy and neither am I. Surely the beast will be able to carry us both."

Thus I found myself riding to Babylon like a prince, beneath the shade of the palm trees and willows along the bank of the Euphrates. On our right I could watch the heavy barges loaded with grain, timber, pitch and many other goods going up to Babylon, and the small, round boats made of animal skins and steered by oars drifting downstream. Every now and then we crossed on a shaky bridge over one of the many canals that spread from the river across the country, a network of water bringing fruitfulness and abundance to the land.

There was much traffic on the road, with mules, donkeys, camels, oxcarts and chariots going back and forth between Babylon and Borsippa. Once again King Nabopolassar had called up his army. Troops of horsemen passed us on the way, all splendid young men, their red coats of mail and pointed helmets gleaming in the sun. But my master only observed them with sorrow and murmured:

"Will there never be peace in the land?"

Sitting behind each other, we spoke little until we halted at an inn along the road. The owner stepped before his door to usher my master inside with many bows. But when I would follow the mule driver for a meal of scraps behind the kitchen, my master bade me join him.

"Come sit with me, my boy," he said. "There are many questions I wish to ask you."

The innkeeper gazed at my lord as though he doubted his good sense. But Nabukasir seemed little perturbed by what the man might think of him and invited me to share with him the rug meant for the use of patrons. After we were seated, he inquired about the food.

"My lord is indeed fortunate," the innkeeper said. "This morning a chariot ran over one of our pigs. It is already roasting on the spit, its meat succulent and fat enough to please the gods!"

When I heard these words my stomach turned, and I wondered how I would refuse such a treat should my master offer it to me. For though I was gone from home for many years now I had never yet tasted pork. But much to my amazement my lord said:

"If this is the only kind of meat you can offer us, I shall rather have some bread and pulse, and a jug of grape wine, if you have the latter. However, my servant might wish to taste of your pig—"

"It would be unseemly for me to eat meat while my lord goes without it," I said quickly, grateful for having been offered this simple excuse. "Moreover, my stomach does not take well to pork, as I see neither does my lord's."

But while the innkeeper walked away, muttering under his breath, Nabukasir said:

"It is not my stomach that prevents me from eating pork, but the laws of my God. For I am a Hebrew."

My mouth dropped open and I stammered:

"Let my lord forgive me for gaping at him, but I would never have taken him for a Hebrew!"

Nabukasir laughed and said:

"How, then, would you expect a Hebrew to look?"

To this I knew no answer, for was not I myself a Hebrew, passing as an Assyrian prince? Had I not feared that Nabukasir might take me back to Borsippa if he learned the truth, I should have revealed to him my deception even then. But I vowed in my heart to make my confession as soon as we reached Babylon. I would throw myself at my master's feet and implore him not to send me back. Moreover, I would advise him not to honor his pledge, for the merchant had sold me under false pretenses. Let the scoundrel go to court and claim his silver if he dared!

Having thus appeased my uneasy mind, I was able to answer calmly the questions my master put to me.

"How is it that you were chosen to be taught all the tongues you claim to know?" he asked. "One does not find many learned men among princes!"

I swallowed hard before I made my reply.

"Ever since King Ashurbanipal made it a kingly task to study writing, it was also thought fit for princes. Moreover, I was born with a special gift that made the learning of languages easy for me."

"And is it true that you also know Hebrew?"

I nodded, hoping my lord would proceed to different matters, but he continued:

"I was never taught the tongue of my forefathers. And though I bought you because you know Sumerian, you shall teach me Hebrew, and also my son—if God grants me one—for my wife is with child. Of course, my wife, being a Babylonian lady, may think this folly, as she thinks many of my deeds. And do you know the language well? And who taught it you?"

I was not a little confused by all these sudden revelations, and also by my fear of betraying myself too soon. Therefore I said I had been taught Hebrew by a Judean slave at the court of Nineveh—may God forgive me.

"As for Greek, I learned it from a Greek scholar who had come to study at our library," I added, hoping to make my master desist from further questions. But to no avail.

"Indeed most Hebrews at Nineveh were slaves, were they not?" Nabukasir continued. "But the few Hebrews who dwell in Babylonia are freemen. My father's father came here as ambassador to bring gifts from King Hezekiah to Merodach-Baladan. He never returned to Judah but became a loyal servant of the king of Babylon and even followed him to Chaldea when Sennacherib drove him back. My own father was born in Chaldea and so was I, though I no longer remember living in the south. For we all returned to Nippur when King Nabopolassar seized the throne, and later to Babylon, where we have lived since. But though my father had taken a Babylonian wife, he raised me a Hebrew, and so shall I raise my son a Hebrew. If the child be a daughter, my wife shall bring her up according to her own beliefs. But in the male line the faith of my forefathers shall live on."

I sat with my head bowed, not knowing what to say. For my lord spoke with pride of his ancestors, though his blood was twice thinned, while I, a Hebrew of the blood royal, passed myself off as an Assyrian. Then I renewed my vow to reveal the truth as soon as we reached Babylon.

You must not think that Babylon was then what it would become later. Nimid-Enlil, the outer wall, was not yet built, and Imgur-Enlil, the inner wall, though seven yards thick, was made of crude, un-baked brick and still in need of repair. And so were the many temples of Babylon. Only of late had King Nabopolassar begun to rebuild Esagila, the temple of Marduk, and Etemenanki, the great Tower of Babylon. But the royal palace looked decayed, for the king was often gone on campaigns and had not yet found time to oversee the repairs.

Even as far as I could think back Babylon had been at war. In the tenth year of his reign King Nabopolassar had gone up against the Assyrians in the town of Quablinu, and had taken the town. And when the Assyrians pursued after him as he returned, he had battled them at Madanu and thrown them into the river Zab.

In the eleventh year the king had gone up against Ashur, but had been unable to take the city. He had retreated as far as the town of Takritain, on the banks of the Tigris. And though surrounded by Assyrians he inflicted a great defeat on them, and the king of Assyria and his army returned north.

In the twelfth year the Medes came down from the mountains and attacked Ashur, but when King Nabopolassar came to their aid they had already taken the town. However, Nabopolassar and Cyaxares, the king of the Medes, met before the town and made a pact of friendship. And Cyaxares gave his daughter, the princess Amytis, as wife to the crown prince Nebuchadrezzar.

In the thirteenth year the inhabitants of the country of Suhu rebelled against Nabopolassar, and he called up his army and marched against Suhu. But the Assyrian army came downstream and the king of Babylon returned to his own country.

In the fourteenth year the Babylonians and Medes went up against Nineveh and took it.

In the fifteenth year Nabopolassar went up against Rugguluti.

In the sixteenth year he went up against Harran.

In the seventeenth year the king went to the aid of his troops who were being besieged by the Assyrians and Egyptians at Harran. The enemy failed to take the city and he returned.

In the eighteenth year, in the month of Elul, the king again mustered his army. That was the year my lord Nabukasir bought me from the merchant in Borsippa and carried me with him to Babylon. There had not been a year of peace since King Nabopolassar sat down on the throne.

Small wonder that Babylon was in ill repair. The walls of the houses looked as though smitten by the plague, for the people had patched them with old, faded bricks. The teeming streets were unpaved and narrow, and stank because they were poorly drained. Thinking back, I recalled that Nineveh had been a marvel compared to Babylon. And yet there was also an air of great wealth about the city, for all the important trade routes ran through Babylon. Indeed she was second only to Tyre in luring merchants from every part of the world. Borsippa had been a truly Chaldean city, but Babylon— the gate of god—was a city of many peoples. There was no foreign tongue that was not heard in the streets, a thing that filled me with delight because of my special gift.

My master and I dismounted on the western bank of the Euphrates, dismissed the mule driver, crossed the bridge King Nabopolassar had built over the river, and entered Babylon through the old Ishtar Gate. From there we proceeded on foot past the king's palace and along the Processional Way toward the part of town where my master lived. This was a fine old quarter surrounding the temple of the Ishtar of Akkad. Many noble families had their homes there, as did some court officials and also the wealthiest merchants—the true nobility of Babylon. The houses, some three stories high, were spacious, built around courtyards with gardens and fountains, and in better repair than the houses near the city wall, which suffered in every siege. Moreover, this part of town was set upon a hill and offered a splendid view of the king's palace to the north and the Tower of Babylon to the south.

As I followed my master through the well-tended streets, my heart ached and rejoiced at the same time, for it was almost as if I had returned to the palace grounds at Nineveh, where I had spent my childhood.

After some more walking we reached my master's house, which was enclosed by a high wall bordering on three streets. This wall was shaped like the teeth of a saw so that light and shadow played upon it in the most pleasing manner. I could see that it had been designed by a builder of fine taste, and that the garden behind it was equally well appointed. There were palm trees and arbors for shade, and a fountain into which water trickled from a jug held by a female figure sculptured in clay. The walk of baked brick that led up to the house was swept clean, showing the firm hand of a good housewife.

In the door stood a young slave girl, who, seeing the master approach, bowed low in greeting.

"Peace be with my lord," she said, while she glanced at me out of the corner of her eye. Alas I could no longer return her anticipation.

"And how is the mistress?" my lord asked after greeting the girl.

"She has been resting all morning, for the child is heavy within her. I shall run and tell her of my lord's arrival!"

While the girl ran ahead, I entered the house behind my master. The large room from which corridors led to the other parts of the house was richly furnished with ivory tables, carved chairs and couches covered with fine rugs. Looking about me, I wondered why my master had told the merchant in Borsippa that he could ill afford another slave. Perhaps he was better fit to bargain than I had thought him.

Observing my admiring glances, Nabukasir smiled his sad smile and said:

"This is indeed one of the finest houses in town. But then my wife's father has great wealth and could give his daughter this handsome dowry. As for me, my own income barely suffices to let me keep such a sumptuous home."

While he still spoke to me, the lady who was his wife entered the room. She was a young woman, not as comely as my former mistress, but with the handsome looks of good breeding. She was clad in fine, embroidered garments and slippers, and her hair was done in the latest fashion, piled in small curls on her head and behind her ears. The latter were well shaped and large, a sign of a bright mind.

"Let my lord forgive me for not bowing down before him," the lady said, "but I am faint from the weight of the child."

My master embraced and kissed her with great affection, while she observed me over his shoulder. Being a good wife she would not yet press him with questions, but in the end she asked:

"And did my lord discover what he went to seek in Borsippa?"

"If you mean the tablets of Sumerian poetry, Margidda, my dear, I did not," my master replied. "However, I found this young slave who was taught to be a scribe and knows Sumerian. I bought him at quite a fair price!"

"Oh, my lord!" the lady Margidda exclaimed in distress.

"I know well what you think of my squandering silver, my good wife," Nabukasir said.

But the lady quickly broke into his speech, vowing that it was far from her mind to fault his actions. I could see that she would rather not discuss such matters before a slave and a stranger. However, my lord continued:

"It is true that we already have three slaves and shall have to hire a wet nurse when the child is born. But this youth has knowledge the others lack. He can read and write, and shall assist me in my work. Moreover, if our child be a son, he will serve as his tutor!"

The lady Margidda only shook her head and sighed.

"It will be many years before the child learns to read and write— if Marduk grants us a son. As for my lord's work, has he not told me that he is sick unto death of it and would sooner give it up? And how shall I defend before my father the purchase of yet another slave after he paid for our kitchen maid?"

"Even your father will be pleased to learn how cheaply I bought an Assyrian prince!" my master replied.

"An Assyrian prince!" the lady exclaimed, gazing at me with new awe, for like all women she doted on royalty. "But why did my lord not tell me the youth was a prince?"

"And think, Margidda, I paid for him no more than for a common kitchen slave, and he being of royal blood and able to read and write!"

My heart sank then, for now that my lord had defended his buying me by telling his wife that I was a prince, I could not reveal the truth to him. The thought of living as a Hebrew in a Hebrew's house had seemed to me sheer bliss. But rather than making my master an utter fool in his wife's eyes, I resigned myself to remaining an Assyrian prince.

As the months went by I often thought of Tarqu and his wisdom. Though I was bereft of the one great pleasure, there were many others left me. Indeed I never thought that I might still know such contentment.

I was given a clean room, good food, and was treated well. But though the lady Margidda always spoke kindly to me, I never forgot in her presence that I was a slave. I often thought that if only my former mistress had treated me thus I should never have lost my manhood. I, in turn, displayed before the lady Margidda my finest manners. In the end she told her husband that none could doubt I had been raised at court. Which was indeed the truth.

However, I had little dealing with the mistress, for she had her own maidservant to wait on her. As the time of her confinement drew near, she spent most of the day reclining on her couch in the bedchamber. Early in the month of Kislev she gave birth to a daughter. Though my master had hoped for a son, he was filled with joy at seeing his wife safely delivered of her first child. But the mistress was greatly distressed over not having born her husband an heir. Soon she summoned a dream diviner to soothe her troubled mind and to learn from her dreams the cause of her misfortune. For she would make certain by the omens that her next child would be a son.

Being a Hebrew, my master scoffed at such beliefs. But he let his wife have her way, saying one must indulge a woman after childbirth. Nor would he prevent her from raising their daughter according to her own practices.

By then there were few matters my master would not discuss with me. Indeed he treated me not like a slave but like a trusted friend. This came about because I aided him in his work, whose nature I soon discovered. Nabukasir was born the son of a wealthy merchant, who thought that a knowledge of writing might later profit his son in conducting his business. However, my lord used his learning for a different end. Of late he had engaged in rendering the old Sumerian poems into new Akkadian that their beauty might not be lost to the world. In this I was allowed to assist him. There was no greater joy for us than to debate the meaning of some unknown word until we found for it the only right translation. I spent long happy hours in my master's room on the upper floor, where he kept the clay tablets he had gathered over the years. Some were new copies of the old poetry, but others were quite ancient. And yet I often thought that I had seen these tablets before, for they had such marks as clay tablets acquire from much handling. But whenever I would ask my lord where he had found them, I remembered that it was not my task to question him.

Indeed Nabukasir concealed some of his work from me. His face would be grave when he bent over his writing board, pressing his stylus into the soft wax. As soon as the board was covered with script he would lock it away in a chest, never once offering to let me read what he had written. But I loved him too much to pry into what he would not reveal to me of his own will.

I had as good a cause to love my new master as I had had to hate my old one. Though I had not confessed to Nabukasir that I was a Hebrew, I knew that I could not long conceal that I was a eunuch. But I would never admit that this had been my punishment for sharing the couch of my former mistress. Therefore I invented another tale, saying my manhood was taken from me when I was first captured at Nineveh, at the time when they put a slave mark on me. Then Nabukasir said:

"The first is done forever. But I shall have a surgeon remove the slave mark from your wrist, for I am certain that you will not betray my trust by running away. Also you may let your hair grow long again. Why should one who has such learning be looked upon as a common slave?"

After the wound healed, there was only a thin scar left on my wrist, which I hoped to conceal someday beneath a silver bracelet. My master paid me the legal wage that I might buy myself a handful of dates or a cup of wine when I walked in the streets, but I saved my silver.

Now that I was allowed to roam about freely I took up the search for my father's slayer. There were many soldiers abroad with scars on their foreheads, but the face of one looked like the face of the other, and I had only the memory of the killer's terrible laughter to steer me to him. Thus I would follow now one, now another until I heard him laugh. But I never discovered the right one.

Not all my pastimes were so grim. Often I would wander down to the wharves, where the big ships unloaded their goods, where the merchants had their bazaars, where anything under the sun was traded, and where the price of grain, dates, silver and gold was established according to the demand. Then I would sit on the pier and watch the sailors swarm off the ships and head for the nearest alehouse or brothel, envying them because I could not partake of the same pleasures.

But there were other joys left me. My master would allow me to attend the gathering of his friends, all men of high rank, some of whom could even read and write. Soon I came to know all the noble lords who came to Nabukasir's house, and there was not one among them who had coarse manners. But one day, in the month of Tebet, as my master and I sat warming ourselves by a charcoal brazier, I heard the clang of weapons on the stairs, and then the slave girl screech and laugh as a girl will when touched in an indecent manner. The next instant a tall young soldier burst through the door of my master's room, spread his arms wide and shouted:

"Nabukasir, you old son of a camel, are you still sitting with your nose bent over your writing boards while your former comrades conquer the world?"

My master jumped up, his face beaming with joy, and clasped the young soldier in his arms.

"Then the king and his army are returned to Babylon," he said. Taking a step back, he gazed at the crest on his visitor's helmet. "And my friend Holofernes has been made a captain over thousands!"

When I first met the Captain Holofernes I knew what people meant when they proclaimed a man handsome as Gilgamesh.

Let me tell you who never heard of mighty Gilgamesh that he was one of the great heroes of yore, a king of Uruk who was two parts god and one part human. There was none who could match his strength but Enkidu, the savage man whom a harlot had lured from the steppe where he dwelled in peace with his beasts. After meeting in battle, he and Gilgamesh became great friends and performed many brave deeds together, slaying the Bull of Heaven and the monster Humbawa. But when Enkidu died, Gilgamesh was overcome by fear of death and set out to learn the secret of eternal life from the wise boatman Utnapishtim, who had survived the great flood and had become immortal. Though Gilgamesh never learned the secret of immortality, he received from the boatman the plant of eternal youth. But the sea serpent stole the plant from him, and thus snakes shed their skins and remain young forever, while man must grow old in his own skin. As for Gilgamesh, he returned to Uruk a sadder and wiser man, knowing that eternal life is only for the gods.

The words with which the harlot first described Gilgamesh to Enkidu fitted the Captain Holofernes well.

"Look thou at him, regard his face;
He is radiant with manhood, vigor has he.
With ripeness gorgeous is the whole of his body . . ."

Indeed the Captain Holofernes was radiant with manhood and full of vigor the day he burst into my master's room. He took off his helmet, ungirded his sword and threw both down on the table, making me fear for our writing tools. Then he stood stretching his arms and shaking out his thick hair, which hung down to his shoulders. His face was clean-shaven, in the fashion of young men whose cheeks and chin are still firm, nor did he wear the long robes to which his rank entitled him. Rather he was clad in the short kilts of the common foot soldier, which allowed him to display his splendid legs. In spite of the winter cold his arms too were bare, save for thick silver bracelets circling his wrists.

Striding about the room as though unable to remain idle for even one moment, the captain picked up a clay tablet here and there, glanced at it and asked with a frown:

"Is this the work in which you engage, Nabukasir? What, then, of the tale about the battle at Nineveh, which you promised the prince?"

I observed the captain with amazement, for I would never have thought him able to read. He looked like a warrior born and bred, and where it concerned writing even the commander of the host relied on his scribes.

"The prince bade me convey his greetings to you and remind you of your promise, Nabukasir," the captain said. "And also of your debt."

"My debt to the prince can never be repaid," Nabukasir replied with a sigh.

"If you truly wished to repay the prince you might join him in battle, as he would have you do," the Captain Holofernes said.

"I served in the army of my own free will," my master said. "It would have been a small matter for me to buy an exemption. But I fought at Nineveh. I fought at Harran. Indeed I put off my wedding until I returned from war. But now I have a wife and child, and I would spend my life with them and with my work."

"Has not the prince a wife and child, and yet he remained a soldier?" the captain asked.

"The prince shall someday be king of Babylon," Nabukasir said. "But I am only a poor landowner who would not increase his lands by conquest, and an even poorer soldier, who despises war."

"If you were as poor a soldier as you say, Nabukasir, you would not have been among the troops that entered Nineveh below the Water Gate," the captain said. "Nor would you have covered me with your shield when my own shield-bearer was killed. But for you I should be dead these six years!"

I must have stood with my mouth open, for the captain suddenly laughed out loud, and pointing his finger at me, he asked:

"Who is this imbecile staring at me?"

"This is my servant Ashur, whom I bought at Borsippa from a merchant unable to value his skills. Behold a young man who studied at the library in Nineveh!"

The captain laughed even louder, smote his thigh and said:

"Then you salvaged more from that wretched library than these battered clay tablets!"

Hearing these words, I knew where I had first seen my master's ancient tablets. No doubt my face betrayed amazement, for the captain turned to me again and asked:

"You did not know that your master tried to save the library at Nineveh?"

"I did not know to this day that my lord fought at Nineveh!" I replied.

"He never told you that he was one of the brave warriors who entered the town below the Water Gate?"

While I shook my head, my master said:

"I take little pride in having been a warrior."

"In what, then, do you take pride? In these old writings?" And the captain picked up a tablet at random and dropped it back on the table. "Rather than play with broken tablets you ought to write of how bravely we fought then! Or if you will not write the tale, tell it to this slave who, you say, can write. Better yet, let me tell him of our great deeds! For I can see that if I fail to do so he shall perish of curiosity, thus causing you a grievous loss of silver!"

"To tell you how strong a fortress Nineveh was would be folly," the captain said, "for you lived there at the time of the siege. From the month of Sivan until the month of Ab our armies lay before Nineveh. Though we fought three battles during that time, all we achieved was to have the Assyrians mock us from the walls. Slowly the spirit of our soldiers sank, as happens when a siege drags on and there is no hope of an imminent victory. Then Prince Nebuchadrezzar stepped before his father, King Nabopolassar, and said: 'If my lord will let me have his best and bravest troops, I shall deliver Nineveh into his hands within a fortnight.'

"And he proceeded to reveal his plan to the king. Since we had pitched camp to the east of Nineveh, the Assyrians had braced themselves against an attack from the east. They had stationed their strongest troops on the walls there, and we had been unable to breach their defenses. What we must do, Prince Nebuchadrezzar said, was to surprise them and attack from the west.

"He would take a large troop of soldiers some distance north of the city and have them dig a canal connecting with the marshes which Sennacherib had made there. The soil that was scooped out of the ground he would have them put into sacks. Then he would ferry the bravest warriors to the west bank of the Tigris, from where they would march downstream under cover of darkness until they reached Nineveh. In the meantime those who remained behind would pile the sandbags into the river, forcing it through the canal into the marshes. Thus the water level would be reduced so that it would be lowest just before the change of the morning watch. When the river sank to about thigh level the soldiers who lay in ambush west of Nineveh would wade across and enter the city below the Water Gate. They would have little time until the river rose again, but once the guards were slain and the gates opened, the other men could swim across with the help of inflated goatskins. Then they would storm the royal palace, creating great confusion among the defenders, who would think that the entire Babylonian army had attacked from the west.

"Surely the Assyrians would hastily summon troops from the eastern wall. But Nineveh being an exceedingly large city, it would take some time before these arrived at the other side of town. While these troops were removed from battle, the Babylonian and Median armies were to make a great attack on the eastern wall, with scaling ladders, sappers and battering rams, and break into Nineveh from the east. Then the invaders from both the east and the west were to advance toward each other, choking the Assyrian defenders between them.

"When the older captains heard this plan they smote their thighs, tugged at their beards and said such a thing could never be accomplished. However, the prince prevailed and the king allowed him to select his troops. He chose a company of skilled archers to pluck the defenders off the wall and a company of crack spearmen for the battle after we entered Nineveh. I was among the archers. And your master Nabukasir was among the spearmen.

"In the end the prince's plans were accomplished. But while the battle raged we had many moments when we thought we would fail. The waters of the river returned faster than we had expected, and many of our soldiers who could not swim were drowned. And the Assyrian troops who guarded the Water Gate made a brave stand in the chambers beside the gate. There was a fierce battle before we could rout them, and in the darkness it was hard to tell friend from foe.

"During this part of the battle I lost my shield-bearer. Just as an Assyrian soldier rushed me with his sword, your master stepped between us and held his large shield over me. Together we fought our way out of the crush.

"About the slaughter, the carcasses piled in the streets, and the flames consuming the houses I need not tell you, for you were there that night. Our brave band who had entered Nineveh beneath the Water Gate surrounded the palace of Ashurbanipal, making a stand there until we were relieved by our troops from the east. By then they too had scaled the walls and broken down the gates as they poured into Nineveh. But we advanced south toward the old palace built by King Sennacherib. It was on the way there that we passed the temple of Nebo.

"Our troop had split into small groups of two and three, who clung together for safety. Many of our soldiers had fallen, while others had strayed off to plunder and rape, though the prince had forbidden that this be done before the battle was won. I remained with your master, who had saved my life and whom I hoped to repay yet before the day was over.

"When we reached the temple of Nebo we found it surrounded by soldiers breaking down the walls and setting fire to the wood-work. Nabukasir caught one of them by the arm and shouted:

" 'Cease from your bloody work, you savages!'

"But the soldier replied with scorn:

" 'We are burning the temples of the accursed enemy! Here, take a torch and help us in this glorious task!'

"Nabukasir flung away the torch the soldier handed him and threw himself in the path of the others.

" 'Do you not know that this temple houses the world's finest library?' he shouted. 'All the great old poetry, our own heritage—'

" 'We must obey our orders,' the soldier said. 'And our orders are to make Nineveh a desolation and a heap of ruins.'

"Then the soldiers pushed Nabukasir out of the way as they continued their work. But he followed after them, screaming:

" 'Beasts! Does it not suffice that you slaughter the old, rape the women and dash children to pieces? Must you also burn the books?'

"The soldiers became angry and would have turned on him had I not jumped before Nabukasir, shouting:

" 'Pay no heed to this man's words! He fought bravely today and has become crazed by battle!'

"And I pinned his arms behind his back and held him fast until the soldiers were done setting fire to the temple. But when they moved on and I released your master, he struck me a terrible blow that sent me staggering back. Then he ran toward the burning temple, shouting that he was going to save the books!

"I knew then that he was indeed bereft of his senses. Sitting down on the ground I held my head in despair, for I had failed to save the man to whom I owed my life. Suddenly a shadow fell over me. Looking up, I beheld a young captain, whose face I could not recognize, for it was smeared with soot and blood. He angrily ordered me to rise and join the battle, which was yet far from won.

" 'Let my lord know that I am not resting but mourning,' I said. 'The man who saved my life today ran into the burning temple and shall surely perish there!'

" 'If his greed for gold and silver is such that he will risk death in the flames, let him perish,' the captain said.

" 'It is not for loot he periled his life, but to save the books,' I replied.

"The eyes of the captain glowed strangely in the light of the flames as he exclaimed:

" 'Is there indeed a man who would do this thing? No, but he surely must not die!'

"And he too dashed into the burning temple.

"Then I knew that I had met with another battle-crazed madman. But not much later I saw a figure staggering out through the smoke. When I ran toward it I recognized the captain, carrying Nabukasir on his back. This was no small task, the captain being short and squat and Nabukasir a full head taller than he.

"'Help me with this fool,' the captain said to me. 'Though he is nearer death than life, he will not release the tablets he clutched to his chest.'

"Together we placed Nabukasir on the ground. But as soon as he recovered his senses in the fresh air, he jumped up and headed back for the temple. When the captain would detain him, Nabukasir turned around and struck him a hard blow. The captain stood stunned for an instant. Then he gazed about him and said:

"'The gods must indeed love a madman to prevent others from witnessing this deed. As for the young soldier here, if he wishes to live he will forget what he saw. I did not risk my life to save a man from the flames only to have him slain for striking the crown prince of Babylon!'

"Then I bowed low to the ground, and even your master dropped his accursed tablets and bowed low, saying:

"'Let my lord forgive me, but I did not recognize him.'

"The prince wiped his bloody face with his arm and said:

"'As we look now, our own mothers would not recognize us. But let us join the remnant of our troop, for there are still some of the foe holding out in the temple. They might come forth from the flames and engage us in battle. If they are as brave and fierce as the Greek mercenary I helped you slay before you were overcome by smoke, they might yet vanquish us. Indeed it pained me to slay the Greek, for he was a man of great beauty and would have made a splendid slave at my court. But when I bade him surrender he cursed me in our own tongue, using such words as I did not think a foreigner would know, nor are they seemly for me to repeat.'"

At this point the Captain Holofernes broke off his account to exclaim:

"May Ishtar strike me dead if the boy is not weeping! Surely there was nothing in my tale to make you weep!"

"Let my lord know that I am weeping for the Greek," I said. "He was not a mercenary but my own revered teacher, who only came to Nineveh because he loved books. Had he and my master met in times of peace they would have become great friends."

"It is a bitter world where two men who love poetry must slay each other in battle," Nabukasir said sadly.

"It is also a world where those who would rather hold a stylus than a sword lose wars," the captain said. "As for the Greek, he should have remained in his own land."

"The Lord Hippolytus traveled the world over to see the many nations, learn of their customs and write of their politics," I said. "Now that he is dead none will accomplish this task—unless another Greek puts his mind to it."

"Why anyone should wish to write about a nation other than his own I do not know," the Captain Holofernes said. "But then the Greeks are a perverse people. And now I had better take my leave. There are a number of ladies in town who already offered sacrifice in thanks for the safe return of the army, and I must not disappoint them."

After the captain left, my master and I did not resume our work. Nabukasir sat sorting the clay tablets which the captain had thrown into disarray, while I stood licking my lips, eager and yet too shy to ask further questions. But as always my curiosity vanquished my good sense.

"Far be it from me to doubt the words of the captain," I said, "but is this great tale he told really true?"

"The Captain Holofernes may sometimes lie concerning the number of foes he has slain—as all soldiers will—but in this matter he spoke the truth. We did enter Nineveh beneath the Water Gate, and the crown prince did indeed rescue me from the flames."

Nabukasir sighed, shuffled the clay tablets on his desk, and looked up at me.

"It is a grave thing to owe a man one's life and yet not be able to repay him," he said.

I did not know what to make of my lord's words, but he continued of his own will:

"The prince would have me write an account of our glorious battles and conquests. But I saw much wanton destruction and savage slaughter in the war, and these things I cannot praise. And though I write about them every day, what I record would not please the prince."

These then were the writings my master concealed from me, I thought.

"If this be so, why write at all, my lord?" I asked.

"Because I must not turn my eyes from evil, like all the others who say 'It is nothing, it is nothing.' We fought at Nineveh and Harran to throw off the Assyrian yoke and to bring back freedom and justice to our land. Yet look around you! Do not the strong oppress the weak, as before? Do not the rich exploit the poor, as before? Do not judges find for those who bring them the better gifts? Is this what we fought for?"

When I heard these words the blood drained from my face and my knees shook.

"Let my lord consider his wife and his infant daughter!" I exclaimed. "Would he leave the lady Margidda a widow, his child an orphan, and me to be sold to another master? I beseech my lord to throw his writing boards in the fire before the king throws my lord in the fire! Is it not better to please the prince, to whom my lord owes his life, than to be dead?"

My master smiled at my zeal and shook his head.

"You have the heart of a slave, Ashur," he said. "But a man who has risked his life in battle may also risk it for his beliefs. Moreover, only you and I know of my writings, and you would not betray me."

I nodded in assent, though I was not certain how I would act when seized by fear.

"Truly I should prefer to please the prince," Nabukasir continued. "He earnestly desires to do justice and to be remembered only for his good deeds. But until these are accomplished I cannot write of them, even though the prince spoke to me of his great plans for Babylon.

"When the battle of Nineveh had been won and we returned to the camp the prince put me in a tent near his own that he might summon me whenever he longed for my company. This often occurred late at night, when he was roused by evil dreams. It was on such a night that he spoke to me of how he would rebuild Babylon. He would lay out straight streets, with gates opening in the wall at the end of every broad avenue so that commerce might flow freely in and out of town. He would erect a higher, stronger wall of baked brick outside the one his father had built. He would restore the temples that had fallen into disrepair and offer sacrifices to all the gods that they might bestow on him their blessing, a long life, a just rule, and peace and prosperity in his kingdom.

" 'Truly I have greater need of the gods than any other man,' the prince said to me, 'for I was not born to be king. But my elder brother, who was bold and handsome and the delight of my mother's eyes, died when he was thirteen years old. And I, who was destined to be a priest, became crown prince of Babylon. But my mother never ceased mourning her favorite son, and my father observed me with sorrow, for I did not have the bearings of a royal prince. Then I prayed to the gods for the strength to become a prince such as had never lived before.

" 'I put away the stylus I had been taught to wield and the books I loved so well. And though I was fat and my hands lacked skill, I learned to string a bow, wield a sword, and ride a horse better than any other youth my age. To toughen my body I did not sleep in a tent, as befitted my station, but in the open fields like the least foot soldier. At night I studied our laws that I might learn justice and statecraft, and our battle records that I might learn strategy.

" 'My father was well pleased with me and soon called me his true heir. But my mother never forgot her favorite son, and her heart turned toward my younger brother, who resembled the one who had died. Though she accorded me the respect a mother must show the crown prince, I could read in her eyes that she thought me a usurper. And in my heart I knew that she was right. But I shall yet become a worthy successor to my father, though to follow after the king who freed Babylonia from the Assyrian yoke is no small task!'

"Thus the prince honored me with his confidence," Nabukasir said. "As for me, I could not comprehend why he felt unworthy, for surely he was a brave warrior, nor could I fathom why he felt guilt for his brother's death. To dispel his morbid thoughts I would speak to him of the books he loved so well. He knew all the old poems by heart, nor did he remember with pride that we had burned the library at Nineveh. 'In war one must often destroy what one reveres,' the prince said. 'But I shall make restitution to Nebo—whose name I bear—and build him a larger and costlier library in Babylon when I become king. And you, my friend, shall collect for me again all our old writings!'

"Indeed the prince's love for all things Babylonian is so great that he changed my name. For my father had named me Abraham, after

one of our ancestors who was born in Chaldea. But when I told the
prince that I was a Hebrew, he said to me: 'You are no more a
Hebrew than I. You and your father were born in this land of
Babylonian mothers, and you know our language and poetry better
than most of my subjects. Therefore I shall charge you with writing
the chronicles of our great and just wars!'

"Though I bowed low and thanked the prince for the honor my
heart was heavy, for I did not glory in the terrible deeds I had seen
done in Nineveh. But a crown prince of Babylon cannot be refused.
Thus I began keeping a record and continue doing so to this day.
But how I shall ever dare show it to the prince I do not know."

All through the winter the army remained in Babylon, and the
Captain Holofernes was a frequent guest in my master's house. But
he never came when Nabukasir dined his learned friends, claiming
that their talk would put him to sleep and that he might disgrace
his host by snoring.

"Not since they chained me in the tablet house did I listen to
such grave debates," the captain said.

He and my master would laugh, but I could make nothing of his
words.

There were other puzzling things about the Captain Holofernes.
When he spoke to the lady Margidda his manners were those of a
nobleman. But when he went after one of the slave girls he used
such words as would make a swineherd blush. Or again he would
recite long parts of the epic of Gilgamesh from memory, but the
next instant he would disown his learning by using the crude speech
of a southern peasant. I often wondered where he had learned the
one and the other, for he looked a warrior born and bred who had
the air of neither a scholar nor a farmer.

Though my own master also was born in the south, he had long
ceased to speak in the singsong manner, while the Captain Holofernes only had to open his mouth to reveal himself as one born in
Uruk. When I made mention of this to my master, he laughed and
said:

"The captain has lived in Babylon long enough to forget the
speech of the south. But his way with words delights the women
even more than his splendid looks, and thus he takes great pains to
preserve it."

"Then it is true what they say in town about the captain and the ladies?" I asked, once again falling prey to my curiosity.

"Indeed he is beloved by many," my master replied. "But the gods love him even better, for he causes them to receive double sacrifice: once when the ladies bring offers of thanks for seeing him safe back from the war, and once when the ladies' husbands offer sacrifice, beseeching the gods to send him off again."

Whether the gods were swayed by the sacrifices of the aggrieved husbands I cannot say, but in the month of Sivan, only six months after the previous campaign, King Nabopolassar called up his army again, and so did the crown prince Nebuchadrezzar. When the Captain Holofernes came to my master's house resplendent in full armor, Nabukasir thought that his friend had come to bid him farewell. But the captain said:

"This time we shall not be parted by war, Nabukasir, for Prince Nebuchadrezzar has summoned all the brave warriors who fought by his side before."

My master's face turned dark and he said:

"I served my full term, nor do I owe a feudal debt on my estates. I fought at Nineveh, I fought at Harran—"

"The prince knows well your past bravery," the captain said, "nor would he press you into service. But remember that he carried you out of the flames, and then consider if you would refuse to join him the first time he leads his own army."

"One soldier more or less will neither win nor lose the prince a battle," Nabukasir said.

"One soldier more or less may matter little to Prince Nebuchadrezzar. But one friend more or less matters greatly, the prince having but few friends. And though he has taken me into his guard, he has not taken me into his heart as he has you. Moreover, he wishes you to witness his first campaign so that you might write a record of it."

Then my master threw up his hands in despair and exclaimed:

"Cursed be the day I learned to write, for where others are called for their skill with the sword I am called for my skill with the stylus!"

But he brought forth his armor and weapons, bade me help him clean and polish them, embraced his wife and child, and went off to war as even unwilling men have done since times of yore.

The following month King Nabopolassar returned from the mountain country, where he had gone to make war. But Prince Nebuchadrezzar and his army remained in the field all through the hot summer, for three months, until the month of Elul.

While the lady Margidda wept and prayed, I stood in the gate of the royal palace, with the sun beating down on my head and the fierce west wind parching my lips, to wait for the mounted messengers who brought news from the front. From them I learned that the prince and his army had seized the fortified cities in the mountains, had set them on fire and taken much spoil from the conquered peoples. My heart was heavy as I thought of my master made witness to the carnage, when his sole wish was to spend his days musing over the old poems.

Once there was a letter from my lord among the royal mail. But even a learned man like Nabukasir wrote only what all soldiers write from the front: that he was tired, dirty and crawling with vermin; that he longed for a bath and a good meal cooked in his own kitchen; and that he missed his wife and child. Though the letter was loving, the lady Margidda worried, fearing her husband might bring back a slave girl wise in the ways of foreign women, who would displace the lawful wife in his favors. Such a thing had happened to more than one of her friends.

In the month of Elul the prince and his army returned to Babylon, and also my master Nabukasir, thin and weary from battle, but without a concubine. When I told him of his wife's concern as I poured his bath water and laid out his clean garments, he smiled sadly and said:

"A man whom Prince Nebuchadrezzar honors with his friendship has little time for such diversions. While others spent the nights in the arms of some comely captive, I spent mine listening to the prince rave about his plans for the future. Even when I was so weary from battle that I could have slept wherever I fell down, the prince remained awake, pacing his tent as though driven by evil demons. Had I not seen him with my own eyes, I would never have believed a man to possess such endurance.

"When he did not speak to me of his grand dreams he spoke to me of his wife, the beautiful princess Amytis, who was pining away in Babylon for the mountains of her homeland Media. And though we in the field lived in wretched discomfort, choked by the heat and dust, and bitten by flies, the prince was troubled over how his wife bore the fierce Babylonian summer, and whether the heat would harm the child she carried. In the seven years of their marriage Amytis had borne him only one child—a daughter—as clever a girl as he had ever seen but cursed by the gods with his features. If only his wife would give him a son this time, Nebuchadrezzar would build for her such gardens as had never before been seen in the world, to make her forget the mountains of her homeland.

"But I would sooner listen to the prince rave than have him plague me with questions about the chronicles I was to write. Nor could I tell him that where he saw glory, justice and righteous wars I saw only wanton slaughter and destruction. Indeed what could I reply when the prince said to me: 'Do we not free the oppressed nations from the yoke? Do we not take the land from the rich and share it among the poor, teaching them to till their fields and to conduct their business in the Babylonian manner, which is the best and wisest in all the world?' "

My master sighed, passed his wet hands over his eyes and shook his head, as if to shake off the memory of all he had seen and heard. When he looked up again there was a faint smile about his lips.

"And now hand me a piece of soap, Ashur, that I might scrub the last trace of battle grime from my body," he said. "Then I shall anoint my skin, sprinkle my hair and beard with perfume, and render to my dear wife such services as she had to forgo these past months. But tomorrow I shall return to my work, and for a while at least be spared accounts of how this old, battered city might be turned into the foremost in the world."

My master had his wish. The following year he was allowed to spend with his family and his work. Immediately upon the return of the crown prince, King Nabopolassar had led his army in another campaign. But though Prince Nebuchadrezzar remained in Babylon, matters of state left him little time to trouble my master. Moreover, the princess Amytis had borne him an heir, who was given the name Amel-Marduk. No doubt the prince spent many hours with his architects, planning the gardens he had promised his wife.

For my master and me these were tranquil months of fruitful work, broken only by visits of the Captain Holofernes, who grew

more restive with every passing day. He longed to be in the field
with the troops, but being a member of Nebuchadrezzar's guard he
had to remain near the crown prince, while other soldiers were free
to join King Nabopolassar in his campaign.

"Will you never have your fill of battle?" my master asked the
captain when he complained of his unwanted idleness.

"Will you never have your fill of old clay tablets?" the captain
asked in return. "I am as much a soldier as you are a scholar, nor
were men put in this world to be idle. If I remain in town much
longer, my weapons will rust, my flesh grow flabby, and I shall
become afraid of death."

"As I look at you, my friend," Nabukasir said, "your sword
gleams as though it were furbished every day. Your body should be
the pride of any man, and as for death, I have heard that since you
cannot seek it on the battlefield, you now court it in the bedchamber. It is said in town that no lawfully wedded wife is safe
from you. One day an irate husband will catch you and have you
thrown in the river, as you so well deserve."

"You, whose nose is always buried in old tablets, know little of
the thrill of risking one's life in conquest—be it of a foe or a
woman," the captain replied. "If these foolish husbands but knew
how to please their wives, the ladies would not stray after other
men!"

"Truly I do not know whether I act wisely in letting you into
my house, Holofernes," my master said. "I too have a comely wife."

At that the captain turned grave and said:

"May Ishtar strike me dead if such a thought ever entered my
mind! Did you not hold your shield over me, giving me back my
life? I should as soon lie with the wife of the one who first gave me
life!"

"Like all men who scoff at the gods, you swear freely by their
names," my lord said. "I trust my wife, even if I do not trust
you."

"These are vile words to speak to a faithful friend," the captain
said. "Therefore I shall now leave you to molder with your old clay
tablets and never visit you again!"

In spite of his grave words the captain had spoken in jest. He
soon came back to my master's house, more fretful than before. The

king's army had returned with much spoil from their campaign against the city of Kimuhu on the banks of the Euphrates, while he had been made to miss the looting. But my master, who had brought back nothing from the previous campaign, would not pity him.

"Not everyone is as foolish as you, my friend Nabukasir," the captain said. "You are so loath to touch a dead body that you will not strip a fallen enemy, nor would you hack off a hand to retrieve a precious bracelet. And though I do not care to cut off the limbs of living men, as was done by those wretched Assyrians, what good are his hands to a dead man? As for his ornaments, they are the due of the victor. How would people know that I fought bravely if I did not wear the bracelets of those I vanquished?"

And the captain stretched forth his splendid, strong arms to display the bracelets circling his wrists. They were made of silver overlaid with gold, with artfully hammered rosettes in the center—the work of one of the most skillful silversmiths at the royal court of Nineveh. Bending over to look at them more closely, I said:

"I knew the man well who did this work."

"Indeed I prize them highly among my trophies," the captain said, slipping one off that I might see it the better.

But rather than look at the bracelet I stared at a scar on the captain's wrist—a scar like my own, such as would be left by cutting off a slave mark. I did not know what to think, nor could I tear my eyes away from the scar. But when the captain caught me staring at him, I stammered:

"Was my lord injured in battle?"

The captain glanced at his scar and laughed aloud.

"This scratch I caused myself when I was a boy. As for being injured in battle, no enemy has yet touched me with his weapons. Do you not know what my soldiers say of me, Ashur? They say the Captain Holofernes is lucky as one who has been pissed on by a red dog!"

"My friend Holofernes thinks himself invulnerable," my master said. "But only the gods are immortal."

"This may be true," the captain replied. "But before I left Uruk a soothsayer predicted that my fate would not be accomplished until the goddess Ishtar descended from on high to take me by the hand. Since I do not believe that this will ever come to pass, I must indeed be immortal!"

I gaped at the captain with even greater amazement than before and said:

"Let my lord know that I was made the same prediction by a soothsayer who claimed the goddess Ishtar had appeared before him, dazzling him so that he was blinded in one eye."

The captain slapped his thigh and roared with laughter.

"Indeed he must be the same scoundrel, who knows but one divination. When I met him he still had both his eyes. But a priestess caught him peeping at her as she stood disrobing, and in her wrath she scratched out one of his eyes. Afterward the priests of Uruk, whose power is such that even the king fears them, drove him out of town. I hear he has been wandering all over Babylonia since, lying about how he lost his eye and raking in much silver by telling his poor victims what they wish to hear. As for me, I would throw all soothsayers into the fire, for they know as little of the future as the gods themselves!"

"You had better keep such words from the ears of the prince, Holofernes," my master said. "Nebuchadrezzar has great faith in the meaning of dreams and omens. Nor are you free of these beliefs, my friend, or else you would not wear an amulet of Ishtar about your neck."

The captain flushed and placed his hand upon his chest, as if to conceal what he wore beneath his garments.

"I wear this amulet because it was given me by my mother when she saw that I was old enough to seek out women," the captain said. " 'Someday, my son, when you take a wife, hang this chain about her neck, and she shall bear you seven sons,' my mother said to me. But for a soldier to take a wife is folly. Indeed I would rather have other husbands worry about their wives when I return from war than worry about mine when I leave. As for begetting seven sons, I must have a greater number in Babylon, though they may call another man father."

"Someday even you, my friend, will grow a beard and take a wife," my master said.

But the captain only slapped his thigh with mirth and exclaimed: "Indeed I will, when the goddess Ishtar descends from on high!"

King Nabopolassar returned from the war in the month of Shebat, leaving only a garrison in the city of Kimuhu. But the following year the Egyptian army seized that city and slew the entire Babylonian garrison. To show his strength, Nabopolassar led his troops north on another campaign in the month of Tishri.

While the king was away the crown prince remained as regent in Babylon. During this time he sent for my master. Upon his return from the palace Nabukasir locked himself in his chamber and would speak with no one. When at last he let me enter, I saw that he had taken his wax-covered writing boards from the chest and spread them on his desk. Rubbing his red eyes, he said to me:

"The prince would have me write an account that surpasses even those of the Assyrian kings, all in praise of his just and righteous deeds. But in reading over my records I do not see how I can alter even one single word. No, rather than bend the truth I shall renounce all honors the prince would bestow upon me! Should another royal messenger come to summon me, I would have you tell him that I am wasting away with a mortal disease. Indeed I shall not rise from my bed until the prince ceases to vex me!"

This excuse seemed to me both foolish and dangerous, but my master would not listen to reason. However, fate has a way of smiling upon madmen.

Many months passed before the prince sent again for my master. In the month of Shebat King Nabopolassar returned to Babylon, and soon the rumor spread in town that the king was grievously ill. The last time he came forth from his palace was in the month of Nisan, to take the hand of Marduk at the Akitu Festival. For without this ceremony all Babylonia would have to forgo the celebration of the new year.

Those who saw the king said he had become frail as the shadows who wander about the nether world. An evil demon was ripping his bowels so that he could hold neither food nor drink. Yet there were many who would not believe in the king's sickness. He had ruled in strength for twenty years, and every year he had gone forth to war. But in the twenty-first year of his reign the king of Babylon remained in his own land. Then the people knew that the evil rumors were true, and they began to fear and tremble. The Egyptian army had recaptured Qumarati on the Euphrates and might yet come downriver to threaten Babylon.

At that time, when there was unrest and fear in Babylon, and much hoarding of food and silver—for people were beginning to lay up stores against a siege—the prince sent again for my master. But Nabukasir bade me tell the royal messenger that he was sick in bed. By nightfall he was truly ill with a fever, as happens sometimes when a man believes in his own sickness.

While my master lay abed the Captain Holofernes came to see him.

"Then you are really ill and not feigning sickness, Nabukasir!" the captain exclaimed.

"And why should I be feigning sickness?" my master asked with the wrath of the liar.

"Because even you must have heard that the prince is mustering every soldier in Babylonia to go up against Carchemish and drive those accursed Egyptians from our land forever!"

"Is this, then, why the prince sent for me?" my master said, almost relieved. "No, but I fought at Nineveh, Harran and in the mountain cities! I shall not go to war again now that my wife expects another child. Moreover, I myself am sick, as you can well see, and I would have you bear witness of it before the prince."

"I shall indeed inform the prince that you were seized by the worst sickness that can befall a man—that of turning into a woman," the captain said. "The prince will be well rid of you, for this war will not be won by women!"

Though the insult did not rouse my master from his bed, the thought that the Captain Holofernes would confirm his sickness to the prince aided his swift recovery. A day after the captain's visit my master rose from his bed to resume his work. Yet neither of us could keep his mind on the task. There was a continuous clanging of weapons and stamping of feet in the street as soldiers marched to their camping grounds, and a clattering of wheels and horses' hoofs as chariots rolled past our house.

But after a while our ears became accustomed to these martial sounds and we paid no heed when one of the chariots came to a halt before our garden gate. Thus we were taken by surprise when the slave who split wood and fetched water burst into my lord's chamber on the upper floor, wildly flailing his arms but unable to utter a word. As I approached him to shake him back to his senses, he suddenly seized me around the waist and threw me face down on the floor so that in falling I bruised my knees and hands. I had just uttered the first loud curse when he put his arms around my neck as though to strangle me, and hissed in my ear:

"Silence, the Prince Nebuchadrezzar!"

I knew then that he had taken leave of his senses. But when I raised myself to my knees I saw a man entering the room who made me fall flat on my belly again. For it was indeed the Prince Nebuchadrezzar.

The last princes I had beheld had been those of the royal house of Assyria—all handsome men with splendid bodies, strong arms, fine hands with long, tapered fingers, boldly curved noses like those of eagles, and large ears, as befits men of intelligence and breeding. Nebuchadrezzar was wholly unlike these princes. He was short of stature—shorter even than I—and though he was still young, his stomach bulged above the belt to which his heavy sword was strapped. His arms were not the firm arms of a warrior of renown, and the fingers of his hand, which rested on the jeweled knob of his sword, were short and broad. Had I not known of his grand design to capture Nineveh I should have taken him for an imbecile, for his ears were very small and set close to his head. But the strangest part of his face was his straight nose, turned up at the tip, no doubt a cause of endless embarrassment to the prince. When he took off his helmet—for he was wearing armor—I saw that he was beginning to go bald.

All this I observed from beneath lowered lids as I lay prostrate, for I would not have dared raise my gaze to the crown prince. But the prince paid heed neither to me nor to the slave who had announced him. He turned to my master, who had jumped up from his stool to bow low before his royal visitor, and said:

"I was told you were at the threshold of death when I summoned you to the palace. And since your life is precious to me—having snatched it from the flames—I would not leave for war without bidding you farewell before the gods called you to your fate. However, I find you swiftly recovered, having deceived both me and the gods!"

"As Yahweh is my witness, I was ill only last night," Nabukasir replied. "Let my lord ask the Captain Holofernes, who called on me as I lay stricken! Also my slave Ashur, an honest youth and skilled scribe who assists me in my work, can attest to the truth of my words."

And my master pointed to where I lay prostrate on the ground. I quickly lowered my eyes as the prince's gaze fell on me.

"I would neither have you swear to the truth by strange gods, Nabukasir," the prince said, "nor would I have you call your slaves by foreign names. From this day on, let this boy's name be Marduk-sharusur."

"It shall be as my lord commands," my master said, bowing low.

Thus my name was changed a second time, and I was called after another heathen god. But the prince paid no further heed to me and turned back to my master, saying:

"And now, since the gods restored your health, Nabukasir, you shall accompany me to war!"

"When I fought beside my lord in the mountains, he promised me that I should henceforth be free from serving in war so that I might engage in my work. And would my lord break his word?" my master said.

Stealing a glance at the prince, I saw him frown and draw himself up to his full height. But he was still a head shorter than my master.

"The crown prince of Babylon does not break his word," Nebuchadrezzar replied. "Nor did I summon you to arms as your commander. Rather I beg you to join me as my friend, as one of my bravest captains, and as a warrior who fought beside me at Nineveh! To you and Holofernes shall go the honor of riding with me in my chariot. Not only will you protect my life, Nabukasir, but also my ears, for you will restrain your friend from using in my presence language unseemly coming from one trained for the priesthood."

I gaped in surprise, and even my master looked astonished.

"Then my lord knows about the Captain Holofernes," he said.

"There is little I am not told, Nabukasir," the prince said, "whether I wish to hear it or not. For if I raise a man to a high place, there will instantly arise ten to advise me that this man is not deserving. And when I made Holofernes a captain in spite of his youth, some whispered in my ear that he was a shirku, a temple slave who had cut off his mark and run away from the temple Eanna in Uruk. I had the temple records searched and found no proof that Holofernes or any of his house had ever been temple slaves. Though simple peasants, his parents were freemen. And if a boy who was meant to be a priest runs away to become a soldier it may be a disgrace, but it is not against the law. However, I did not come to discuss your friend, Nabukasir, but to pay you a sick call, which has now become a call to arms. For surely you will not forget your duty and honor!"

"My wife is with child and well gone into her time. I should like to see a son born to me before he is made an orphan," my master said, in one last attempt to weaken the prince's heart.

"If the gods grant you a son, Nabukasir, how will you defend before him that you sat in your room bent over old clay tablets while we fought for the freedom of our land?" the prince asked.

My master bowed his head and remained silent. But the prince began to pace the room in great agitation, speaking with such fervor that he forgot his careful northern speech and betrayed himself as a true Chaldean:

"I know your thoughts, Nabukasir! You think we go to war spurred by the same lust of conquest as these wretched Assyrians! You fear that we not only wish to drive the Egyptians from our land but that we shall pursue after them and conquer Egypt! Yet what need have we of Egypt, where people rely for the fruitfulness of their fields on the rising of the Nile and starve when the river fails them? As for us, have we not made our land fruitful by the labor of our own hands, building canals and dikes to water our soil? Do our fields not bear a hundredfold? Could we not feed the whole world and still have grain to spare? Need we take spoil from others if we can trade them wheat and barley for goods we lack in Babylonia? Indeed, are those goods not brought to our very doorsteps, for all the caravan routes lead through Babylon? And what of the silver we obtain by taxing these caravans for protecting the safety of the roads on which they travel? Need we covet alien lands? Surely only a fool would go to war if he can keep the peace, for in peacetimes sons bury fathers, but in times of war fathers bury sons. Give me peace and I, who next to the gods loves beauty best, shall make of Babylon a marvel that will astonish the nations! Let later generations remember me not for the lands I conquered but for the temples I built! But if we win this one last battle, we shall have peace forever!"

So amazed was I by this speech that I raised myself up on my knees to gape at the prince. His face had turned crimson, his forehead glistened moist, and there was foam in the corners of his mouth. His eyes shone as the eyes of one who is seized by ecstasy, and his body trembled so that I feared he would indeed fall to the ground. But he recovered and stood gazing at my master in silence, waiting for an answer.

"My lord has great visions," Nabukasir said softly. "May the gods grant him to see them accomplished."

"If I have need of the gods, I also have need of men's swords," the prince said. "I have need of brave warriors by my side. I also have need of my friend. The king is gravely ill, and the diviners find no hope in the omens nor can the physicians offer him balm. Since I have known the king's end to be near I have been pursued by the evil dream of a great mountain crashing down and burying me beneath it. In my dream I can feel its weight on my chest nor can I recover my breath upon awaking. What if the king should die while I am at war? What if there should be sedition in Babylon, and a usurper attempt to seize the throne? No, but I must drive out the Egyptians while the king still lives! Let him go to his fate knowing that our land is free at last. And would you, Nabukasir, whom I carried out of the flames and gave a new name, refuse me your sword in these grave times?"

Then my master replied with tears in his eyes:

"This I would not do, my lord. Let us then go up together against the Egyptians and fight this last battle that our sons may enjoy their freedom in peace!"

For the second time since I became his slave my master bade me fetch his weapons and help him polish them. While we were engaged in this task, the Captain Holofernes came to visit.

"I see that none but the highest can make you fulfill your duty," the captain said. And when my master pretended not to understand, he added: "It is well known at court that the prince called on you in your house. There are many at court who curry his favors now that the king is near his end. But the prince would never honor any of them as he honors you, Nabukasir, who cause him no end of vexation. Surely you must have strange powers over him, and thus it would be wise of me to gain your good will. Let me therefore help you polish your weapons, for I see that you handle them with distaste and will injure yourself even before the enemy has his chance at you."

The captain took off his belt and bracelets to work on my

master's armor. But I, remembering the rumor about him, paused in my task to stare again at the scar on his wrist. When the captain noticed my curious glances, he said to my master:

"Someday I shall gouge out the eyes of your wretched slave! And what are you gaping at now, imbecile?" he asked, turning to me.

I was afraid to repeat the rumor to the captain, but my master came to my aid and told him the words of the prince. At that the Captain Holofernes laughed and said:

"The slave mark I am said to have cut off was but a birthmark. Indeed I can still furnish the midwife who saw it on my wrist when I was born. When she discovered it she set up a great cry, shouting: 'Behold, the babe is born with the sign of Ishtar on him!' For the mark was in the form of the eight-pointed star of Ishtar. Then all the women ran together to marvel at the miracle, while the midwife hastened to summon a priest from Eanna.

"Now, these priests, who must fan the foolish beliefs of women— for that is whence comes their wealth—sent one to examine me. When he found that the birthmark was in truth shaped like the star of Ishtar he would carry me with him to the temple. But my parents were freemen and could not be compelled to surrender me. Then the priest offered to tutor me in the rites of the goddess when I reached the proper age, nor would he charge a fee for it.

"Until then I was allowed to remain with my family. I grew up with the sons of our neighbors—only taller and stronger—and there was none I could not beat in a fight. Indeed what I liked best was to play at war. And when the Assyrians besieged Uruk when I was six I hoped in my heart that they would take the city and burn down the temple Eanna and all the priests in it so that I might never have to go to school. It was the only time I ever thought treason in my heart.

"But the siege was broken, and the priests came to take me away. Though I screamed and kicked, they dragged me up the many stairs to the great white temple so that I arrived bloody even before they began to beat me. Nor did they cease from beating me until they made me hate every written word. Since I ran away more than once, they chained me in the tablet house to make me study. In the end they taught me to read, though they could not compel me to write. And the only poem I would recite of my own will was the tale of Gilgamesh, for I dreamed of growing up to be a mighty hero. Nor did I ever doubt that I should someday be a soldier.

"Though how I would accomplish this I did not know. My voice broke, my beard began to sprout, I lay with my first woman, and still these priests beat me and would not let me go. Then, when I was fifteen, that wretched soothsayer prophesied that Ishtar would descend from on high to lead me to my fate. This only confirmed the priests in their belief that I was meant to serve the goddess.

"But I had other plans, and fate came to my aid. My older brother had reached the age to serve in the king's army. But my father had died the year before, leaving him the head of the household. At the time of the harvest, when the king mustered his army, my brother was sorely needed at home. Then my mother thought to do what was done by many. She spoke to one of the priests who was known to act as go-between, and he set a day when the recruiting sergeant would come to our house to receive a gift for substituting another name for that of my brother.

"It was thought best that my brother be out harvesting with the women that day. Thus I was fetched from the temple and given the task of delivering the silver to the sergeant. But after the others had left the house I hid the silver in my mother's bed, thinking that a poor widow might put it to better use than for bribing a sergeant. Then I went to the barnyard, seized our old, black he-goat, cut off his beard, and with some pitch pasted it to my chin. Though I was only sixteen then, I was tall and strong enough to pass for twenty, except that my beard was not yet grown. Admiring myself in my sister's mirror, I found myself most handsome with my new beard— even if it would not curl and reeked in the most dreadful manner.

"When the sergeant arrived, saying he had come to fetch what was agreed upon, I replied: 'Here I am, ready to follow my lord wherever he wishes to take me.' Looking bewildered, the sergeant asked my name, and when I gave him my brother's, he said there must be some mistake, for he had received the message from the priest. But I said I knew of no messages. In the end he took me away with him, cursing the priest and those dumb peasants who put him to much trouble for nought.

"There was a motley crowd outside the city gate of Uruk, where all the recruits gathered. Some were simple oafs from the farms, others sons of merchants and artisans, and a few from priestly or noble families. The last wore finer garments than the rest, and some had brought their own weapons—bows of the best wood and swords with jeweled knobs. These youths had chosen to become soldiers of their own will, for their fathers could have bought them exemptions. However, they had taken care to bribe the sergeants that they might receive choicer food and gentler treatment.

"As for me, I was thrown together with the other peasants. Since they all smelled of the barnyard, the odor of my beard went unnoticed. I only hoped we would be marched off before my mother returned from the harvest and found me gone. If Ishtar ever favored me, she favored me that day. Soon we were herded onto the road that led to Babylon.

"As the sun rose in the sky and the heat increased, the pitch on my face began to soften. Having been cheated of his bribe, the sergeant took a keen dislike to me. When he thought I was lagging behind, he caught me roughly by the beard to pull me along. But my beard remained in his hand, and he would have fallen on his back had I not seized him. As we stood nose to nose, none of the other recruits saw what had happened, nor could they hear what was said.

" 'Hah, so you thought you could cheat me out of my silver, you cur!' the sergeant hissed. 'But I shall yet have you tried before the officers for what you did!'

"But like many of his rank he was not very bright. Though I was younger than he, I had been taught by the priests and knew how to bewilder simple people. Therefore I whispered in his ear: 'The officers will never believe that a wise man like my lord could have been fooled by one as young as I. Moreover, I shall say that my lord received silver to substitute my name for that of another recruit. And my lord knows well that the penalty for such a deed is death!'

"At that the sergeant turned ashen, for he would rather not have his records examined. He pressed his hand in which he held my beard against my chin, and muttered: 'You lout will yet curse the day you joined the king's army in such a devious manner!' Then he kicked me to make me fall in step, but he did so subtly, for he was not meant to mistreat soldiers.

"When we reached the camp where the recruits were trained, the sergeant thought of many ways to torment me. He made me run until I fainted from weariness, and kept me practicing with the bow long after my comrades had retired to their blankets. But the end of it was that I became a better soldier than the rest, and a crack archer. By the time I was twenty years of age I was chosen to be among the troops that assaulted Nineveh.

"As for the mark of Ishtar on my wrist, I had not been a soldier for a week when I cut it off with a knife. The wound bled badly and later festered, but I suffered in silence until it healed. Still, it might have been a mark of good fortune. After all the battles in which I fought, the scar on my wrist is my only one.

"But now let us complete our task, for if we wish to defeat the Egyptians we shall have to go up against them armed with keen weapons and not with tall tales!"

Before my master went off to war he charged me with the care of his clay tablets, the running of his household, and the welfare of his wife. For though I was still young he thought highly of my good sense.

"I shall not be returned from war when the time comes for my wife to give birth," my master said. "Therefore it shall fall to you, Marduksharusur (for that was how I was called now) to fetch the surgeon and have the child circumcised if it be a boy."

My master took me to the surgeon of his choice to tell him of his wish. But the surgeon refused to perform such an operation unless my master left him a written order, sealed before two witnesses, lest he be accused of having mutilated a Babylonian male.

Nabukasir asked his wife's father and the Captain Holofernes to act as his witnesses. The captain only shook his head at such folly. But the lady Margidda's father, a Babylonian nobleman of great wealth who was known to lend silver even to the king, spoke sternly to his daughter's husband.

"It is not a good thing to put such a mark on a Babylonian child, my son."

"But he will be a Hebrew, if God grants me an heir," my master replied.

"He will be the child of a Babylonian mother and of a father who is himself three parts Babylonian. Do you not think it is time you left off being a Hebrew, Nabukasir, and allowed your son to be a true child of his native land?"

"If I had brothers I might be persuaded by my lord," Nabukasir replied. "But my father is gone to his fate, leaving me the last male of my house. If I fall in battle, I will die happier knowing that my son will grow up a Hebrew. Moreover, it is written in my marriage contract that if Margidda bears me a son, he shall be raised in the faith of my forefathers."

"So be it then," the lady's father said. But I could see that he was not pleased with the matter.

Not many days after this debate my master donned his armor, blessed his wife, his daughter and his servants, and went off to war. And again I stood in the gate of the palace to wait for news from the battlefield.

There were many reports of glorious victories to brighten the last days of the dying king. Prince Nebuchadrezzar had marched with his troops to Carchemish, had crossed the river, engaged the Egyptian army in battle and beaten them into nonexistence. As for those Egyptian troops who had escaped before they could be engaged in battle, the Babylonian army overtook them in the district of Hamath, defeating them so that not one single man escaped to his own country.

The day I brought home this glorious news I found the lady Margidda in travail. The slave girl had already fetched the midwife, who was tending the mistress in her chamber. While I waited for the birth I paced up and down in the garden, covering my ears to shut out the screams of the mistress and muttering such prayers as I could remember and hoped might be fitting for the occasion. After many hours the slave girl came running to tell me that the lady Margidda had been delivered of a son. At the thought of how glad my master would be, I wept for joy.

When the infant was seven days old I called the surgeon, holding the babe in my arms, while he performed the circumcision. Again I wept, for I would never thus hold a son of my own and this boy was the only son I would ever know.

To please her husband the lady Margidda gave her son the name my master would have him bear—David. But we all knew that if Prince Nebuchadrezzar ever laid eyes on the boy he would change his name. However, that event seemed a long time off.

The prince and the Babylonian army had marched to Syria to drive out the last Egyptian garrisons so that Babylonia might never again be menaced at her borders. While the crown prince was still in Syria, King Nabopolassar died. He died on the eighth day of Ab, in the twenty-first year of his reign. There was great mourning in Babylon. People slashed their faces and went about with their hair disheveled, for Nabopolassar had been a strong king who had freed Babylonia from the Assyrian yoke.

But the month of mourning was cut short. The crown prince, accompanied by only a small group of his close friends, rode back across the Syrian desert and arrived in town only three weeks after the king had died.

And on the first day of the month of Elul, Nebuchadrezzar sat on the royal throne of Babylon.

SIX

And it shall come to pass, that the nation
and the kingdom which will not serve the
same Nebuchadnezzar, king of Babylon, and
that will not put their neck under the yoke
of the king of Babylon, that nation will I
visit, saith the Lord, with the sword, and
with the famine, and with the pestilence,
until I have consumed them by his hand.

—JEREMIAH 27:8

WHEN Nebuchadrezzar sat on the royal throne of Babylon (the old woman Tamar said to the young scribe), a new era began in Judah. Jehoiakim, who had served Pharaoh Necho for four years, now became Nebuchadrezzar's servant. But the king of Judah did not gladly bow his neck under the yoke of the Babylonian king, for it was the pharaoh who had placed him on the throne of his father. However, the prophet Jeremiah celebrated Nebuchadrezzar's victory at Carchemish in a great song, proclaiming before the nations that God had chosen the king of Babylon to rule all the lands, even Judah. And Jeremiah was much hated by those in Jerusalem who had sided with the Egyptians.

We knew of these things, for men would visit Merari's house to discuss with him the doings of the princes and prophets in Jerusalem. And Shallum, Merari's uncle, said:

"This Jeremiah is a madman, truly he is a man of contention to the whole world! Has he forgotten the fate of the prophet Uriah when he spoke against Jehoiakim and his mighty men in Jerusalem? Even though Uriah fled to Egypt, did not the king have him brought back and slain with the sword? And whither would Jeremiah flee, who speaks even stronger words against the king? Who would dare hide him?"

"I would dare hide him," Merari replied.

"Then you are a greater madman yet than the prophet, for you do not share his beliefs," Shallum said. "You, Merari, would not have the Babylonians rule the land!"

"Neither would I have the Egyptians rule the land, for it is ours,"

Merari replied. "But a prophet speaks with the tongue of God and must not be restrained by force."

"I had better leave your house, Merari," Shallum said. "If your words became known to the king, his wrath would fall on all of us."

"Let your heart not be troubled," Merari replied. "King Jehoiakim would not send troops here to fight the last remnant of the tribe of Simeon. Indeed he fears us more than he fears the Babylonians! Moreover, the king has trouble enough in Jerusalem."

Then all the men who had come to Merari's house departed to their homes, for they dreaded being overheard by the king's spies. But Merari continued speaking his mind as before, and from him Judith learned to act in like manner.

Judith and I were fourteen years old when the Egyptians were defeated at Carchemish. But though the Babylonian army marched along the Sea Road as they pursued after the Egyptians, and though they left garrisons behind when they departed, we in Bethul never saw a Chaldean. Still the women whispered among themselves that all the Chaldeans were gorgeous young men, horsemen riding upon horses, each a governor and captain to look upon. And many envied those living in towns where there was a garrison of Babylonian soldiers.

Though Judith judged these women no better than harlots, yet at that time she began to put up her hair and to wear the jewels she had inherited from her mother. Sometimes I would find her sitting before the mirror, her cheeks cradled in the palms of her hands as she gravely stared at herself. Then she would turn to me and ask:

"Tell me the truth, Tamar—am I as comely as some would have me believe?"

And I would reply:

"You are very beautiful, Judith. Can you not see it in the mirror?"

"And does Manasseh ever say he finds me beautiful?"

Then I would sigh, avert my eyes and answer:

"Joab says you are the comeliest maiden in all of Judah."

"How would Joab know, never having left Bethul?" Judith said. "Moreover, he is betrothed to my cousin Rebeccah and had better not look upon me with lewdness!"

But Judith was still half child then, and if one day she was troubled over whether Manasseh found her beautiful, the next day she would tease him as if he were only her playmate. Nor was it difficult for her to forget that some day she was to marry Manasseh. He did not hasten that day, as some other youth might have, and Merari never spoke of Judith's marriage.

Merari still took Judith with him wherever his work called him—into the fields, into the vineyards and on his journeys. And now that Judith was become skilled in writing, he let her keep his accounts. Soon she knew better even than her father how much grain there was in the storage pits and what was the value of their fields, their vineyards and houses. For they owned two houses, the large winter house in Bethul and the small summer house in the fields below, where we lived at harvest time.

But in spite of his great wealth Merari retained his simple ways. He treated his servants justly, paying each his due at nightfall, and never forgot that his riches came from God. And when in the fifth year of King Jehoiakim—which was the first year of Nebuchadrez-zar—a great fast was proclaimed before the Lord and people from all over Judah went to Jerusalem, Merari was among the first to journey there.

This was after the plowing and seeding had been completed and before the first green shoots pierced the soil. There had been much rain that year, and even a few snow flurries during the night. We were glad to be in the winter house in Bethul, which was built solidly against the icy wind and where braziers in all the rooms kept us warm.

My mother looked with misgiving upon the master's journey to Jerusalem. His lame leg had troubled him because of the rain and the cold, and often he was in great pain, though he would not speak of it. But when my mother cautioned him against the strain of travel, Merari replied that he would not go on foot but ride upon Hadad.

"Hadad too is getting on in years," my mother said. "Who knows but that he will slip on the icy path, causing my lord to break his neck!"

"I am not yet ancient that I should sit by the fire while those many years older than I go up to Jerusalem," Merari replied. "Should I not join in the fast—I, who have so much to be grateful for, and also much to repent?"

"It is ten years since the mistress died," my mother said. "And will my lord never cease from blaming himself?"

"Is a sin lesser because ten years have passed over it?" Merari asked.

Then my mother placed her hand upon her head and said:

"Let my lord deal with me as he pleases, but let him listen to me, for I can no longer bear to see him suffer. It was not my lord's doing but mine that Shoshanna conceived on the night of the grape harvest!"

"Do not speak folly, Dinah," Merari said. "You may believe in your own witchcraft, but it takes a man to get a woman with child."

"However, it took one of my potions to make my lord forget himself that night," my mother said. "Shoshanna poured it into my lord's wine, for she would bear him a son. Now let my lord do to me as he pleases, but let him cease from tormenting himself!"

Merari turned pale and approached my mother with his hands stretched forth, as though to strangle her. But when she did not flinch he bethought himself, covered his face with his hands and ran out of the house. Though it was a bitter cold day and he had not taken his cloak, he did not return until nightfall. Then my mother knew that he had gone up to the cave in the hills where Shoshanna was buried.

My mother sat fanning the fire in the brazier when Merari came home, leaning upon his cane and dragging the leg that had been wounded at Megiddo. For a long time he stood looking down on her. Then he said:

"It took great courage to tell me what you did, Dinah. But you were only God's tool to punish me. I would deceive Him to save Shoshanna's life for my pleasure. Had I trusted in His mercy, my wife might have borne me a son and lived. But I broke God's law, and he took Shoshanna from me."

Then Merari retired to his own chamber and locked the door behind him. But my mother mumbled:

"As Yahweh is my witness, I told him the truth. But he would not let go of his guilt!"

The next morning Merari departed for Jerusalem. He was gone from one Sabbath eve to the next. When he returned he had many strange tales to tell us.

The previous year the prophet Jeremiah had dictated to his scribe Baruch all the oracles he had proclaimed against Judah from the time he first received the call from God. And he had bidden Baruch read all these words to the people of Judah on a fast day, when they came to make supplication before Yahweh. For Jeremiah was detained and could not go into the house of the Lord.

The day Merari went up to the temple he found Baruch standing in the new gate to the Lord's house, reading aloud to the people from the book Jeremiah had dictated to him. He read of all the sins King Jehoiakim and the people had committed—how they had returned to worshiping Baal and Ashtoreth, and how they burned their children in the Valley of Tophet, as a sacrifice to Moloch. He also accused King Jehoiakim of plotting rebellion against Nebuchadrezzar, whom God had appointed ruler over all the nations. Surely this act would draw the wrath of the Babylonian king on Jerusalem and he would come against their city with all his men of war to destroy it utterly.

The people feared for Baruch when they heard him read these words aloud. But, though the scrolls in his hands shook, he went on reading until Jehudi the son of Nethaniah came into the upper court to fetch him into the chamber of the princes.

"From then on we heard but rumors," Merari said. "Some claimed Baruch was slain, and so was Jeremiah. But others said that the princes had fallen to quarreling among themselves, some taking the prophet's side. The latter had helped Jeremiah and Baruch escape. As for the book, some whispered that it was hidden in the chamber of Elishama the scribe. But others said it had been taken to the king, to deal with it as he pleased. And if it be true that the king read the book, the lives of Jeremiah and Baruch are worth less than the chaff left after the threshing!"

In the following days Merari's manner altered strangely. At nightfall, when we were wont to gather around the brazier, he would stand near the door as though listening into the darkness. But when Judith asked him whether he was expecting a visitor, Merari quickly walked away from the door and replied:

"And who would wish to go visiting on such a cold night?"

Yet in a little while he would return to his listening post at the door.

On the fifth day after the master had returned from Jerusalem snow fell, muffling all sound so that the stillness of the winter night was even deeper than before. Thus we heard no footsteps before we heard someone coughing outside. Without waiting for a knock, Merari leapt toward the door and flung it open. He reached outside with both hands, pulled two men into the room and quickly shut the door behind them.

"Then my lord received the message," Merari said in a low voice. "May Yahweh grant my lord peace this very day."

"Amen. And may He bless the house of Merari the son of Amram, and keep it from such danger as our visit might bring it," the older of the two men replied.

Judith and I rose and bowed low before our visitors, for we knew who they were, though it was ten years since we had seen the prophet. Merari bade them sit near the brazier to warm their stiff limbs and ordered us to fetch food and wine for our guests. But Judith and I stood transfixed, gaping at the two men.

Both were clad in simple, coarsely woven robes, tied around their waists with cords. In spite of the bitter cold they wore no woolen overgarments, no doubt because neither owned one. In the light of the fire we could see that what had looked like snow in the prophet's hair and beard was in truth white hair. He looked much older than his forty years. His face with the piercing eyes beneath the bushy eyebrows was blue from the cold, and his long nose and thin lips were almost purple. He was shivering so violently that Merari had to help him sit down on the rug by the brazier.

The young man Baruch seemed no less frozen, but there were red blotches showing through the blue where his skin was broken out. He was shorter than the prophet, with a thin, stringy beard. In spite of his youth he was already growing bald, and his teary eyes squinted as though he did not see well. He had hidden his hands in the sleeves of his garment for warmth, and tucked the two parchment scrolls he carried under his arms.

"Make haste, children!" Merari urged us on. "Can you not see that our guests are utterly famished and frozen?"

But when we turned to the kitchen, the prophet raised his hand to detain us, saying to Merari:

"Let the maidens not tell the others in the house of our presence, which places my lord and his household in great danger. Indeed had I known that there were children in the house, I would never have accepted the invitation the young lad brought to Baruch. As for that lad, he too was but a child who might yet reveal my lord's name to an officer of the king!"

Thus we learned that Merari had sent word to the prophet, and we knew why he had stood waiting by the door. But Merari replied:

"The lad is my own brother's son. He can be trusted."

The prophet sighed and shook his head.

"These are bitter times in which a man may not trust his own brother. There are many in Jerusalem today who would betray each other!"

"No, but my brother is an honorable man," Merari said. "As for my own household, there is only the mother of this young hand-maiden in the house. She has served me for sixteen years, suckling my own daughter and raising her after my wife died. She too can be trusted."

And again Merari urged us to go on our errand. When we roused my mother and told her who our late guests were, she clutched the amulet she wore about her neck and whispered in terror:

"May the queen of heaven protect us! The master must be mad to ask these men into his house! It might be better to turn them out and denounce them before they bring down the king's wrath on all of us!"

But Judith seized my mother by the arm and hissed that if she dared betray her father's sacred hospitality she would strangle her with her own hands. And she looked as though she meant her words.

"Truly you are your father's daughter, Judith, and just as mad as he," my mother said. "However, if he wishes to destroy the house he built, who am I to prevent him?"

And she stirred the fire on the hearth and warmed up some stewed fowl she had prepared the day before. Then she carried the kettle into the room, while Judith and I followed behind her with bread and wine for our guests.

Baruch had sat down by the brazier beside Jeremiah and had placed the two scrolls in his lap. He held his head in his hands, moaning:

"Woe is me! The Lord has added sorrow to my pain! I am weary with my groaning, and I find no rest."

"If you are weary with your groaning, then cease from it," the prophet said harshly. "You suffered no harm even though you read my book to the people. What more would you want?"

"That we might complete our work in peace, and that it might find favor in the eyes of those who read it," Baruch replied.

"Do you seek great things for yourself?" Jeremiah asked. "Seek them not! For evil shall befall even those who accomplish great things in our time, and their work shall be utterly destroyed. But you, Baruch, shall yet live to write of their vain doings!"

"Amen," Merari said. "May we all live to look back on these times in disbelief. But now let my lords put aside their troubles and refresh themselves! As for the book, I shall hide it in a safe place."

Merari stretched forth his hands to receive the scrolls from Baruch's lap. But instead of handing them to his host, Baruch broke into renewed lamentations. And unrolling the scrolls he showed them to be clean, with not a single word written on them.

"But what of the book?" Merari asked, bewildered.

"The king sent Jehudi to fetch the book out of the chamber of Elishama the scribe," Jeremiah replied. "And Jehudi read it to the king and to all the princes who stood beside him. Now the king was sitting in his winter house, before his brazier. And Jehudi had not read more than three or four columns when the king seized the book from him, and cut it with his penknife, and cast it into the fire of his brazier, until all the roll was consumed. And though Elnathan and Delaiah and Gemariah entreated the king not to burn the roll, he would not listen to them. Then the king commanded that Baruch and I be arrested. However, the Lord was with us and we escaped."

"Has it come to such a pass in Jerusalem that they burn books?" Merari asked with bitterness.

"And would people who burn their own children in the fire not burn books?" Jeremiah asked. "Who can restore the lives of these children once they are dead? But the word of God does not perish in the fire, and a book can be written again. Indeed I shall dictate to Baruch all the words that were written in the book the king burned, and add many more to it. As for King Jehoiakim, who sought to keep away Nebuchadrezzar by burning my prophecies about the king of Babylon, his dead body shall be cast out unburied, and he shall have none to sit on the throne after him!"

We saw that the prophet had fallen into an ecstasy, for his eyes had become glassy and there were red patches on the cheeks of his haggard face. Even after he fell silent, the left corner of his mouth and his left eye went on twitching, and though he placed his hand over that part of his face he could not stop the quivering.

We women had remained standing in the back of the room, too awed to break in upon the discourse of the men. When Merari beckoned to us to serve the food, Judith was the first to approach the prophet, offering him bread and salt.

"And who is this lovely maiden?" Jeremiah asked, wakened from his ecstasy.

"My own daughter Judith," Merari replied.

"What right have we to endanger this child?" Jeremiah asked in despair.

"But I am not afraid," Judith replied, speaking so boldly that even Merari looked amazed at her words. "Will not God protect the righteous?"

"The maiden is very young. May the Lord reward her faith," Jeremiah said. "As for us, we shall leave at dawn and seek shelter elsewhere."

"Let my lord eat and recover first," Merari said quickly. "As for his leaving, we shall speak of this on the morrow."

After the prophet and Baruch had refreshed themselves, they bedded down for the night in the master's chamber. But Merrari stayed up with us to discuss what must be done and where we might hide the prophet and Baruch. Then my mother said:

"Why would my lord hide these men? Does not Jeremiah say that the king ought to bow his neck under the yoke of the king of Babylon? And does not my lord say that Judah ought to remain free and not serve strange kings?"

"If I refuse the prophet shelter, the king's officers might find him and put him to death," Merari replied. "And though I do not share Jeremiah's beliefs, I do believe that a man ought not to be put to death for the words he speaks. Moreover, I offered the prophet my hospitality, and such an offer is as sacred as an oath before Yahweh and must not be broken."

"Then let my lord hide the two men in the house where we store the grain," my mother said. "It is shut up for the winter, and none but my lord has the key to it."

"And would you have them freeze to death, Dinah?" Judith asked in anger. "They could not light a fire there, for it might spread and consume them, together with the grain. No, let us rather hide them in the chamber on the roof! It is used in the summer only, and even then none of the maidservants ever goes there. We can put two beds, a table and some chairs there, and board up the windows to keep out the cold. After dark the prophet and Baruch could walk about on the roof in the fresh air. But late at night, when everyone is asleep, they might descend into the house below and warm themselves by the fire. And the prophet shall dictate to Baruch all he wishes him to write in the book, and none shall hinder them!"

Merari looked at Judith with great pride and said:

"You speak wisely, my daughter, though you are but a child."

"I am no longer a child," Judith replied.

But seeing her father gaze strangely at her, she flushed and quickly lowered her eyes. Merari passed his hand over his eyes, as if to wipe away a memory, and said:

"If Yahweh did not grant me a son, he gave me a daughter with the courage of a man and the beauty of a cherub. How could one so blessed refuse to hide His prophet? Therefore let us do as you propose, Judith!"

It was done accordingly. Though Jeremiah would search for shelter elsewhere, he was weary unto death and his health was frail. His cough had worsened overnight, and in the morning his face was aflame and he had a fever. The master made him stay in his room and remained there with him, for he would have the servants believe that it was he who was ill. Only my mother was allowed into the chamber. She mixed such potions as she knew to be helpful and fed them to the prophet. But he never learned of the charms she mumbled over them to increase their power. And Jeremiah recovered and moved upstairs into the room with Baruch.

We helped Merari carry the beds and chairs up on the roof, for we dared not ask the help of the menservants. But it was Judith who took the two men their food. Sometimes she would glance over Baruch's shoulder as he wrote—for she could read—and see how in writing he altered the prophet's words until they sounded as dull as Baruch. And Judith said it would be better if Jeremiah wrote his own book. But the prophet's hands were heavy like those of a man who was wont to work the fields, while Baruch had the nimble fingers of a scribe. Once, when Judith spoke of her observation to Merari, he said:

"It were better if you spent less time upstairs, Judith, for you must not torment Baruch."

"But I never even speak to Baruch!" Judith exclaimed. "How can my lord accuse me of tormenting him?"

"It is not with words you torment him, Judith," Merari said. "But Baruch is still a young man, and you are very beautiful."

When Judith understood his words, she flushed deeply and said: "Are they not sworn to live without women?"

"It is only the prophet who vowed not to take a wife," Merari replied. "But even a man sworn to live alone may feel tempted. Nor is it seemly that my daughter be the cause of it."

Merari sighed as though Judith's beauty was a cause of grief to him. Then she ceased from tarrying longer than need be in the chamber on the roof. But she spent again much time before the mirror, asking me often whether she was in truth beautiful.

The prophet and Baruch remained with us for many months. None of the servants knew about them. My mother and I cleaned the upper chambers, allowing the maidservants to tend only to the lower floor. We spread it about that the master kept his silver in his room and would have none but his most trusted servants near it. Though such a rumor might attract thieves, it was better than have it known the Merari was hiding one sought by the king.

During the winter none wondered why the room on the roof was shuttered, and in the spring we moved down into the summer house earlier than in previous years. Merari would reap his harvest early, for there were again rumors that the king of Babylon was to march against Egypt, and who knew but that the war might spread to Judah. But Jeremiah and Baruch remained alone in the winter house, and none troubled them there.

As for Judith and me, we always looked forward to moving down into the fields. Summer meant warm evenings when one lingered by the spring and met with the village maidens who came there to draw water, to gossip, to discover who was betrothed and who was with child, and to see how the others had changed during the winter. We were then sixteen years of age, and those who were to be comely had become comely and those who were to be ugly had remained ugly. But Judith was comelier than any other maiden in Bethul.

She was almost fully grown, with the face of Shoshanna, but nearly as tall as Merari. There was no other maiden in town who came up to her shoulder, and even among the youths none attained to her height. Next to her Manasseh looked like a frail child, and many snickered at the thought that someday he would be Judith's husband. But the most aggrieved was Joab. He was mad for Judith and followed her about with the eyes of a sick calf, though he was betrothed to her own cousin Rebeccah.

Whereas Judith had formerly sneered at the way men looked at her, she now began to relish such glances. She would tie back her red hair to display her lovely ears and the fine earrings Shoshanna had left her. And she would put kohl around her green eyes to enlarge them, but she never painted her cheeks or her lips, for her beauty did not require such devices. When she walked away from the spring with a jugful of water on her head, there was not a man who would not turn and stare after her, though she wore no jingling bangles around her ankles to attract their eyes.

That year at the grape harvest Judith came out for the first time to dance with the maidens at the feast. She put on a white linen robe, placed a garland of vine leaves upon her head, and beat upon a timbrel as she swayed in the circle around the fire. But where Shoshanna had been so small that the others had to make room that she might be seen, Judith towered above the maidens as a cedar towers above junipers, and she moved as stately as a queen. And even those men who were betrothed or had wives looked upon her with lust.

Merari's mien turned dark when he saw the looks on the faces of the men. He scowled and drank much wine, and he kept wiping the sweat off his forehead with his arm. In the end he summoned Judith out of the circle of dancers and bade her sit beside him.

"Is my lord not pleased with my dancing?" Judith asked, hurt.

"Indeed you dance too well, my daughter," Merari replied. "Nor would I have you stir lewd thoughts in the hearts of men."

By his speech we knew that the master was very drunk. Later we had to lead him to the house, but he shut the door of his chamber against Judith and would not let her help him disrobe. Then Judith retired to her room and we to ours, for I slept with my mother. But she said to me:

"Take your mat, Tamar, and sleep in Judith's room tonight. The men are drunk and have looked upon her with lewdness. Who knows but one might take it into his head to steal into the house and force her. Therefore sleep lightly, my daughter, and if you hear a noise, call out to me in a loud voice and I shall come running."

I did as my mother bade me. Judith was lying in bed when I entered her room in the dark, but she sat up and asked:

"Who is it?"

However, she did not seem frightened, even before I made myself known to her. "Then it is only you, Tamar," she said and rolled over on her side.

I stretched out on my mat beside Judith's bed. But though my mother had warned me to sleep lightly, I was so tired after the feast that I fell asleep before I knew it. Whether I was wakened by a noise or by the feeling of a presence in the room I cannot say. But suddenly my eyes flew open and my heart beat against my ribs as I perceived the dark shape of a man in the pale square of the open door. At first I did not find my voice, but when it returned to me even I was startled by its shrillness.

My mother must have lain awake to respond so swiftly to my screams. She came running with a lighted oil lamp in her hand, nearly colliding in the door with the man, who had turned to leave. When she shone the lamp in his face, I was amazed to see Merari. For he had not made himself known when I began to scream but had turned to steal away like a thief.

"Let my lord forgive me, but I did not recognize him in the dark," I stammered.

Merari made no answer but stood gazing at my mother, and she at him. He was still fully dressed, and he swayed as though in a stupor. But when he spoke his voice was steady, and I could hear that he was no longer drunk.

"Who told you to sleep with Judith?" he asked me.

Before I could answer, my mother replied:

"I bade Tamar sleep with Judith. The men drank much tonight, and I feared one might steal into Judith's room and force her before she wakened. Indeed she did not cry out now—though it was only my lord who came into the room."

I looked at Judith then. She had sat up in bed, but she did not look as if she had just been startled from sleep. Her eyes were wide open, and she sat scowling at me and my mother.

"And would you protect me from my own father, who only came to see if I was asleep after the feast?" she asked sharply.

"No, but you did well, Dinah," Merari said quickly. "Truly another man might have broken in and taken Judith in her sleep. As for you, Tamar, henceforth you are to sleep with Judith every night. I may come from time to time to test your watchfulness. And even if you recognize me, you are to cry out. If you watch faithfully, I shall reward you with a silver bracelet."

From then on I slept with Judith. I even learned to sleep lightly that I might earn my silver bracelet. But the master never came again.

When we returned to our winter house in town, Jeremiah told us how his heart had ached when we moved into the fields below.

"But for the call from God I would never have gone to Jerusalem," the prophet said. "I would have remained in Anathoth to help Hanamel, my uncle's son, work his fields. Though many years have passed since my youth, I still feel the clean smell of freshly cut barley in my nostrils. And after the first heavy rain of fall, my hands itch for the handles of a plow. But instead of tilling the pure soil I must wallow in the human filth that is Jerusalem. However, Hanamel promised to sell me one of his fields. God willing, I shall return to live on the land someday."

Then we understood what had caused the prophet's broad hands and knew why he let Baruch do his writing. As for the new book, it was nearly completed, leaving Jeremiah more time to spend with us. And there were many things he would discuss with Merari.

In the month of Kislev—after plowing had followed the first rains of winter—Nebuchadrezzar captured Ashkelon. We heard that he took the king of Ashkelon prisoner, turned the city into a heap of ruins, and marched back to his own land in the month of Shebat.

The same month the weather in Bethul turned cold. At night, after the servants had retired to their quarters, Jeremiah and Baruch would come down from the roof to warm themselves by the brazier. For they did not dare light a fire in their room lest the smoke rising through the door betray them. They had been with us then a full year, and we had become so accustomed to their presence we nearly forgot our fear, for none had come to search for them.

While Judith and I served them food and wine, the men would sit around the fire discussing the future of Judah. Often these debates became bitter, for Merari would speak one way and Jeremiah another, while Baruch contented himself with cursing the day he was born. But we would tremble at hearing two men who held each other in high esteem shout at each other in wrath. Then Jeremiah would say he had no right to remain in the house of a man who did not share his beliefs, endangering all his household. But in the end Merari would prevail upon the prophet to remain with us.

It was after the fall of Ashkelon that the two had another quarrel.

"Did my lord not say that Nebuchadrezzar was a prince of peace?" Merari asked the prophet. "Why, then, has the king of Babylon come to our land to make war?"

"And has Nebuchadrezzar made war on Judah?" Jeremiah replied. "Did not his army march peacefully through the land, without destroying towns and taking captives?"

"What, then, of the tribute our king must pay Nebuchadrezzar? Does that not make us vassals of Babylon? Did I fight at Megiddo to keep away the Assyrians, only to have Judah seized by the ᴌabylonians?"

"Would my lord rather see Judah under the yoke of Egypt?" Jeremiah asked.

"I would see all our foes consumed by the plague," Merari replied.

"Amen," the prophet said. "However, this is not God's will. Rather it is His will that Nebuchadrezzar rule over all the nations. Therefore let us bend our necks under his yoke and live in peace as part of his kingdom."

"And whence comes my lord's certainty that this is God's will?" Merari asked. "Did not the same God give us our land forever?"

Then Jeremiah replied in wrath:

"Are you then as blind as all the others who cannot see that if we wish to keep our land forever—as God promised us—we must serve the king of Babylon? For if we fail to do so, Nebuchadrezzar will surely come against Judah with all his mighty men of war and utterly destroy our land! But it will be our own folly that will bring about our downfall!"

Another winter passed and there was no war. In the spring when the earth turned green, the storks journeyed north, and the turtle was heard in the land, Merari's sister Sarai came to the house to inquire about a certain matter.

"My brother," she said, "this is the second spring that the room on your roof—which you built at great expense for your pleasure—has stood boarded up. There are those in Bethul who wonder what might be the cause of this?"

"If those who wonder are none but my own sister," Merari replied, "let her cease troubling her mind over my affairs. As for the room, the roof sprang a leak two winters ago, and I have not yet seen to its repair. However, I shall refurbish the room this spring and give it to Judith for her own that she and Tamar may sleep there."

"And why can Judith not sleep in the chamber where she has slept these seventeen years?" Sarai asked.

"Because the young men have taken to standing beneath her window, calling up to her such offers as are not seemly for me to repeat, concerning my own daughter. But the room on the roof is well set back from the parapet, and none will trouble her there."

"If you are so concerned for Judith, then let her be married to Manasseh, to whom she has been betrothed these six years," Sarai said.

"No, but she is still too young!" Merari exclaimed.

"My own daughter Rebeccah, who is no older than Judith, is to be married to Joab after the harvest," Sarai said. "Why can your daughter not be married?"

At that Merari became angry and said:

"Your daughter Rebeccah had better be married soon, or else she may be a mother before she is a wife. As for Joab, I shall be glad to see him wed, for he is one of those who stand beneath Judith's window!"

Then Sarai stamped her foot and returned to her own house. But she did not fail to stir up trouble, for a few days later Merari's uncle Shallum came to call on him.

"Nephew," he said to Merari, "is it true that you will not let Judith be married to my grandson Manasseh? Did we not sign a marriage contract before witnesses?"

"And who told you such lies?" Merari replied. "I never said Judith will not be married to Manasseh!"

"Then let them be married," Shallum said. "I am getting on in years, and I would yet see a son born to my grandson before I die."

"No, but Judith is still too young," Merari said.

"Your own wife Shoshanna was no older when you brought her home a bride," Shallum said.

"Times were different then. Moreover, I was a man well past thirty, while Manasseh is but a child."

"Now you speak as my own daughter Athara," Shallum said. "Indeed whenever I say 'Let Manasseh be married,' she falls into a faint, or else she wails: 'Not enough that my wretched husband embittered my life, will you now tear from my bosom my only son, who is but a child?' I pray you, Merari, is there madness in our family that both you and Athara should speak thus? Do you not wish to see a grandson born to you, who has but one daughter?"

"But there is yet time," Merari said. "Moreover, remember, Shallum, that both your sons died before they were twenty-two. Let Manasseh pass this fateful age before he is married to Judith, for I would not have her a widow before she was a wife."

Then Shallum smote his thigh in anger and left Merari's house.

But from that day on the people of Bethul, who had formerly not concerned themselves with Merari's doings, paid much heed to the room on the roof that had stood boarded up for the past two years. No doubt Sarai had told her daughter Rebeccah, who had told all her friends, that Judith was to have the room on the roof that she might not be vexed by the young men. This only attracted more young men to the house. It became so bad that Jeremiah and Baruch feared to step out onto the roof until the morning watch, just before darkness gave way to dawn, when the people of Bethul slept the soundest.

Still someone saw them. Even as we were about to move down into the summer house for the harvest, Merari's sister Sarai and his uncle Shallum came to him. Their faces were white with fear, and they tightly shut the door behind them before they spoke to Merari. Then Sarai placed her hand upon her head and wailed:

"I always knew that you were mad, Merari, but I never thought you were mad enough to call down disaster on us all!"

"If there is a mad person in this house it is you, Sarai," Merari replied. "For I do not know whereof you speak, and neither do you."

"Your sister speaks of the two men who were seen walking on your roof last night," Shallum said.

"What two men, and who is the fool or knave who claims having seen such men?" Merari asked.

"I may not reveal his name to you," Shallum said. "But he swears he saw two men on your roof just before the morning watch, one of them taller than the other. And the tall one raised his hands to heaven and threw back his head, as though he were conversing with the Almighty."

"Whoever saw such visions must himself have been walking in his sleep," Merari said. "What else would he have been doing in the street at that hour? Or perhaps there were two angels on my roof!"

"No angels have visited mortal men since the times of the patriarchs," Shallum said. "As for your two angels, Merari, I do not wish to know who they are, nor do I wish to behold their miraculous presence with my own eyes. I only entreat you to send them away under cover of darkness—as they must have come to you—before it becomes known to the king that you are hiding his enemies. For not only will you and Judith be killed and all your lands seized, but also we, your nearest kin, will suffer from the king's wrath!"

"I should surely follow your counsel, Shallum, if I but knew whereof you speak," Merari replied.

"Among a stubborn people you are the most stubborn, Merari," Shallum said, nearly weeping with rage. "Let the crime be upon your head then! When they come to arrest you and your—angels— I shall disclaim all knowledge of your deed. And so will your sister Sarai!"

"Amen," Merari said mockingly. "And now, for your own safety, you had better leave my house."

But after Shallum and Sarai had departed, Merari's face turned dark with worry. The Passover was nearly upon us and the time come to move into the fields for the harvest. But though Merari was afraid to let the prophet and Baruch stay alone in the winter house, he would not ask them to leave.

"They are my guests," Merari said. "Their lives are more sacred to me even than the life of my own daughter."

And when he asked Judith's counsel, she too insisted that they must continue hiding Jeremiah and Baruch.

Merari put off moving from one day to the next, until in the end he decided to spend the summer in town. He and Judith went down into the fields every day to harvest, as did the poor people who owned but one house within the walls of Bethul. As for the summer house, he let his sister Sarai use it that year.

When people asked questions—as people will—Merari replied that the summer house was easy to enter by stealth, and that he would not have Judith tempt any of the youths to do so. As for the daughters of his sister, they were all so ugly they would be safe even if they slept in the open field.

Nobody in town really believed Merari's words. But people held him in high esteem and pretended not to know what went on in his house. Yet there were some who begrudged him his wealth—though it was earned honestly and by hard work—and others to whom the sound of their speech was more precious than their neighbor's life. Thus the rumor got abroad that Merari was hiding fugitives from the king.

One evening, after the master and Judith had returned from work and had sat down to their evening meal, Sarai's daughter Miriam, who was two years younger than Judith, came running into the house. She was out of breath and red in the face, for she was fat even then, and she had run all the way up the steep path from the fields.

"My mother bade me tell my lord that there are three officers of the king walking among the people in the fields, asking whether they have not seen two strange men," Miriam panted. "Surely the officers will come into town to go from house to house. Let my lord be prepared to receive them as befits officers of the king!"

And Miriam was off before Merari could ask her another question. No doubt her mother had warned her to make haste, lest she be in the house when the officers arrived.

Judith and Merari looked at each other, and though they would appear calm, I saw they were greatly troubled. But my mother placed her hand upon her head and began to wail aloud, until Merari sharply bade her be quiet. Then he said:

"If it were already dark, the prophet and Baruch could hide in one of the alleys until the officers searched our house. But it will not be dark for a while yet, and thus they must remain inside. However, the officers will first visit the houses near the gate. By the time they arrive here, night will have fallen. Then it will be safe for Jeremiah and Baruch to leave."

"But how are they to escape once the officers enter our house?" Judith asked.

"You and Tamar are both strong," Merari said. "You will let Jeremiah and Baruch down from the roof into the back yard. But Dinah and I will detain the officers in the lower chambers with food and drink, which—if I know the king's officers—should not be a difficult matter. Nor will they suspect us of such a daring deed while they are in the house. And now run and fetch strong ropes from Hadad's stable and some old rags to put under Jeremiah's arms when you let him down, lest his flesh be bruised. Then carry your own bedding and trinkets to the roof chamber, to make it appear as though it were used by women. But make haste, for the officers may soon be upon us!"

I ran to the stable for ropes while Judith carried our blankets and garments up to the chamber on the roof. She even took her mirror and the clay jar with the kohl for her eyes. When I arrived on the roof with the ropes, she bade me descend again and put our room in order, lest the disarray she left behind arouse the suspicion of the officers.

While I was thus engaged I heard a pounding on the door below, and the voices of strange men. My hands began to tremble so that I could barely finish my task, but in the end it was accomplished, and I returned to the roof.

Judith had led the prophet and Baruch out on the roof, near the parapet. Both men were ashen, but while Jeremiah contained his fear well, Baruch's teeth chattered and his knees knocked together. But when it came to decide who would climb down first, Baruch refused to go until the prophet had saved himself. But neither would Jeremiah go, saying if one of them was to be caught, it ought to be he. Thus they stood arguing even in this calamity, until Judith harshly bade them cease from it. They stared at her with amazement, not being accustomed to orders from a woman, less still from one so young. But Judith said:

"If my lords will make haste, they will have much time to argue. But if they argue now, they will not live to resolve their differences. The officers are already in the house below, and my father may not be able to detain them much longer. Therefore, let Baruch climb down first, for he is the younger and more agile. Then let him stand in the yard below and assist my lord in his descent, lest he fall and break his neck!"

Baruch handed the two scrolls to the prophet. Then Judith and I fastened the ropes under his arms and let him down into the yard back of the house. We could see the glow of fires in the fields below, for there darkness fell before it reached the top of the hill. Soon night would creep uphill to envelop our fugitives in safety.

After Baruch had dropped to the ground, we hoisted up the ropes to let the prophet down. But Jeremiah had walked away and stood listening near the trap door which led from the roof to the floor below. When Judith beckoned to him to make haste, he shook his head, signaling with his hands that the officers were already ascended to the upper floor. It was too late for him to escape.

My bowels turned to water and I began to weep, for I could see us all slain with the sword. But Judith tossed the ropes down to Baruch in the yard below, motioning to him to take them and hide behind Hadad's stable. Then she ran toward Jeremiah, who stood with the scrolls in his hands as though he were turned to stone and was resolved to be thus taken. Judith seized his arm and pulled him with her into the chamber, while I ran after them.

"No, but you must not be found with me, my daughter," Jeremiah said, trying to shake off her grip.

"If my lord will do as I say, he will not be found," Judith replied.

"Would you perform a miracle, child? Listen, the men who have come to seize me are already on the stairs! And where would you hide me?"

"I shall hide my lord under the bed, while I lie upon it, pretending to be ill!"

"No, this I will not do!" Jeremiah exclaimed with indignation.

"I cannot compel my lord," Judith said. "But if he is taken, what will become of his book?"

Jeremiah gazed at the scrolls in his hands, in which Baruch had written all the words he had dictated to him. We could see that he would do for his work what he would not do for himself. Handing the scrolls to Judith, he crouched down on the floor, slid under the bed and then stretched his hands forth to take the scrolls and hide them with him.

But Judith threw a blanket over the bed so that it was covered to the ground. Then she lay upon it, loosened her dress and her hair, and bade me sit on the ground before the bed and fan her. No sooner had I taken my place than the door to the chamber flew open and in strode an officer in full armor, followed by another two and by Merari.

"Then it is truly the maiden's room!" the officer exclaimed.

"Did I not tell my lord so?" Merari said.

Though he must have been astonished by the sight before him, he hid his amazement well. But Judith bowed her head as she lay on the bed and spoke in a weak voice:

"Let my lord forgive me for not rising before him, but the weakness of women is upon me and I am faint."

Then I fanned her harder than before, for it was a warm night.

Gazing at Judith in the manner in which men would look at her, the officer said to Merrari:

"I cannot blame my lord for hiding a maiden of such beauty. Surely there is none to rival her even in Jerusalem! Let me commend her to the king that he might find a place for her in his harem."

Hearing this, Merari turned ashen and said:

"My daughter is already betrothed, and the marriage contract signed and sealed before witnesses. The king would not wish to bring a sin upon his head by taking a maiden lawfully promised to another!"

"I only thought to do the maiden honor," the officer replied. "However, I see that my lord has great regard for the law."

We did not know whether he spoke in mockery, for the other two officers walked about the room, picking up our clothes, trinkets and paint pots as though they expected to find a man concealed beneath them. Then one of them discovered the inkpot and reed pen, which in our haste we had forgotten to hide. My breath stopped and I ceased moving the fan. But Judith cast me a warning glance, and I returned to fanning her.

"And what might be the purpose of this in the maiden's room?" the officer asked, holding up the inkpot and the pen.

But Merari replied calmly:

"God granted me a daughter whose learning is equal to her beauty. Indeed she can read and write and has kept my accounts these last years. If my lord wishes to see them, I shall gladly show him my books."

"Only an honest man would make such an offer," the first officer replied. "As for the maiden, it is the more a pity that she should waste her life in a small village. If she were not betrothed, I should myself take her for my wife!"

He approached the bed and stood gazing down on Judith, but he did not touch her. Perhaps he was ashamed to deal dishonorably before the other officers. Perhaps he feared they would fall to quarreling among themselves over such a lovely prey. Or perhaps he had been taught to respect women in their time of the moon. Whatever kept him from touching Judith also saved his life, for Merari would surely have slain him.

Merari's face, which had been ashen before, had turned so dark a red it looked nearly purple. The veins on his forehead and neck stood out like thick cords, and one could see the blood pulsing in them. The master stood with his arms hanging down and his fists clenched as he observed the officer's every move. And he had the strength to kill a man with his bare hands.

However, the need did not arise. The officer turned to his comrades and said:

"There is none concealed here. This man has shown us his house freely, and we searched his stable even before we knocked on his door. Let us depart and hasten on to the next village, for we might yet accomplish the journey before it is too dark. If we surprise the people in their houses after night has fallen, we might catch this accursed Jeremiah and his scribe!"

"Is it the prophet my lord is searching for?" Merari asked.

"It is he," the officer replied. "Though he is sly, he will not be able to evade us forever. But when we catch him, it will go badly with him!"

"Amen," Merari said. "May all the enemies of the king suffer his fate!"

Then he stood aside from the door to let the officers step out before him. One still lingered to glance back at Judith, but she had wisely turned her face to the wall.

"I shall escort my lords to the gate and down the hill, for the path is treacherous and their horses might stumble in the dusk," Merari said. And turning to Judith, he added: "When I return, I shall look in on you and see how you feel, my daughter."

We knew then that Merari meant us to remain in the room until he returned to tell us that the danger was past. When we heard the sound of hoofbeats as the officers rode away, Judith bent down, raised up the blanket and spoke under the bed:

"Let my lord be patient a little longer and remain where he is until my father returns. These officers cannot be trusted, and their departure might be a ruse. But once they have descended the hill, they will not mount it again in the dark."

After a long wait we heard Hadad neighing in the yard below. But Judith would not let Jeremiah come forth even now, for we did not know whether Merari had returned alone. When we heard the steps of two men on the stairs, Judith and I looked at each other in fear. However, it was only Baruch entering the room with the master. He had come out of his hiding place behind the stable, and there was straw clinging to his robe and his beard. His face, always broken out, appeared covered with even more boils since we had let him down. He entered the room with his hand placed upon his head, lamenting loudly.

"Have the officers gone for good?" Judith asked her father.

"I put them on a rarely traveled path that will take them to the next village the long way," Merari replied. "With the help of God, all three will break their necks before they get there. But you, my daughter, did well to pretend being ill, for who knows what that accursed henchman of the king might have done to you! As for Jeremiah, Baruch says you did not let the prophet down into the yard and already mourns him for dead. But he was not found in the house. Where then is he?"

"In this very room," Judith replied.

And rising from the bed, she threw back the blanket, bent down and assisted Jeremiah in coming forth. Then Baruch's mouth flew open in amazement, while Merari turned ashen at the thought of the danger through which we had passed. But soon his expression changed, for a grown man coming forth from beneath a bed would make one laugh, even if that man is a prophet.

Merari passed his hand over his mouth to hide his smile, while Judith and I fell to giggling after the great fear that had weighed upon us for the past hours. Even Baruch ceased his lamentations, though he did not quite smile. But as Jeremiah glanced from one to the other, his eyes filled with tears, and raising his gaze toward heaven he exclaimed:

"O Lord, you have enticed me and I was enticed. You have overcome me and have prevailed. I am become a laughingstock all the day. Every one mocks me."

Then Merari ceased from smiling, while Judith threw herself at the prophet's feet to beg his forgiveness. But Jeremiah put his hand on her head and said:

"One as young and brave as you, my daughter, should not have to cease from laughter because of me. However, the danger is not yet past, for I have enemies even among my familiar friends. It is not just that I, who have neither wife nor child, should endanger the life of another man's child. Therefore Baruch and I shall depart at dawn and find another hiding place."

Nothing Merari said could alter the prophet's resolve. But when Judith asked where they would go, Merari said quickly:

"We had better not know, for what we do not know we cannot be made to tell."

"These are wise words," Jeremiah said, "nor shall I reveal to you my plans. However, the time may come again when I may need my lord's help—not to save my life, but to save the Word of God. If King Jehoiakim persists on his treacherous course, Nebuchadrezzar will come against Jerusalem, seize the city and carry away the king, his household and all the treasures of the temple. For this is how he has dealt with other rebellious nations. As for the vessels of gold and silver, let the king of Babylon carry them away. They are but dross in the eyes of God. But the Tablets of the Law, which God gave to Moses, must not be taken as spoil to the temple of Marduk in Babylon. They shall be hidden even from Nebuchadrezzar. If it comes to pass that Nebuchadrezzar marches on Jerusalem, I shall send to my lord a messenger with the words: 'The time is come.' Then—if it pleases my lord—he is to follow that messenger whither he takes him, for I shall need the help of one who is strong in body and righteous in spirit."

"It shall be done," Merari replied.

Then Jeremiah and Baruch bedded down for a few hours. But at dawn they rose, embraced and blessed us, took the two scrolls of the book and departed—whither we did not know.

When Merari returned from the gate—for he had escorted the prophet and Baruch to assure their safe departure—he complained of a great weariness. He said his blood was pounding in his ears like a drum, and he asked for a cup of wine to refresh himself. But before my mother could fetch it for him, he began to sway as a drunken man and fell down in a faint. Then terror overcame us, and Judith threw herself on the floor beside her father, thinking he was dead. But soon Merari opened his eyes, gazed about him and asked in a whisper what had happened.

When we told him that he had fainted, he said such a thing ought not to happen to one as strong as he. And he arose from the floor and would not rest but went straight down into the fields, for the harvest was not yet fully gathered. However for many days his left hand would not do his bidding and he spoke with a slight stammer that never left him. But my mother said it was a sign from Yahweh to remind Merari forever that he had sheltered one of His chosen.

The house seemed empty now that the prophet and Baruch were gone. From habit we would still listen for hoofbeats or look out for spies of the king. But none troubled us, and in the end we came to think that the officers who had searched our house had indeed broken their necks in the dark woods or else had been torn by wild beasts.

At times Judith and I would climb on the roof and sit in the chamber that had housed the two fugitives. We would speak of their stay with us, and Judith would toy with the inkpot and the reed pen, which they had left behind. But as time passed it came to seem as though they had never been with us.

Our daily life continued as before. Not long after the harvest Joab was married to Sarai's daughter Rebeccah. There was a great feast in the house of the bridegroom, with music and dancing and much food and drink. All the kin of the bride and groom came to the house, even Merari's uncle Shallum, his daughter Athara, her husband Ephraim and their son Manasseh. Then folks fell to jesting with Merari, inquiring when *his* daughter would be married. But he replied:

"Behold Manasseh, and does he look like a bridegroom to you?"

And indeed he looked like a child, for his mother still led him around by his hand, though he was already eighteen years old.

But Joab, at twenty-one, looked and acted like a grown man. He ate mightily, got drunk with wine and danced in a circle with the other men. However, his eyes were not on his bride but on Judith. Then my mother muttered:

"It is a good thing that Rebeccah cannot read thoughts, or she would know with whom her husband will lie when he climbs into her bed tonight."

After the feast all the guests returned to their own homes. And before the month was over Rebeccah was with child.

But our life continued as before, with plowing and seeding and harvesting, with tending the flocks and threshing the grain and pressing the grapes, and moving from the winter house to the summer house, and back again.

And Rebeccah was delivered of a child—a daughter—but still there was no talk of Judith being married to Manasseh. Time and again Merari's uncle Shallum, and Ephraim, Manasseh's father, would come and reason with the master. But Merari knew only one answer:

"First let Manasseh be twenty-two, and then they shall be married."

The year Rebeccah had her first child, in the month of Kislev, at the time of plowing, the news reached Bethul that Nebuchadrezzar had marched with his army to Egypt. The king of Egypt met him in open battle, but neither won a victory, and Nebuchadrezzar returned to Babylonia.

The following year Nebuchadrezzar remained in his own land. There was great rejoicing among those in Judah who would not serve the king of Babylon. They said he was not equal to his father Nabopolassar, who had gone forth to war every year, until the year he lay upon his deathbed. Then Pharaoh Necho sent ambassadors to all the kings who had become servants of Nebuchadrezzar, and made great promises to those who would side with him. And Jehoiakim, king of Judah, rebelled against Nebuchadrezzar and refused to pay him tribute.

At that time Jeremiah came forth from his hiding place to warn the people of Judah against their king's folly. But the prophet did not send word to Merari.

The following year we learned that the king of Babylon had mustered his army in greater force than ever before. Many feared that Nebuchadrezzar would come against Judah. But he marched no farther than to Syria before returning to his own land.

Then there was great jubilation in Jerusalem. The king and his princes proclaimed that Nebuchadrezzar feared the power of

Pharaoh Necho, for he had gone up against the Arabs but not against the kings who had allied themselves with Egypt. And Jehoiakim ordered those who had sided with Nebuchadrezzar slain with the sword.

Even in Bethul there was bad feeling among familiar friends. Some sided with Jehoiakim, some with Jeremiah, and some like Merari would have none meddle in their affairs.

Merari was become one of the elders who sat in the gate. He was known to deal honestly, taking no gifts and passing just verdicts, even if those who came before him did not share his beliefs. At that time Merari began to warn that we must make provision for having water in town, in case of a siege. For there was enough grain in the storehouses to last for many months. He would have the men dig a deep shaft in the midst of Bethul, and build a secret tunnel to the spring at the bottom of the hill. But some said such a thing could not be done; others said they were in the midst of harvesting and could not spare the time for digging shafts. And still others proclaimed that the Babylonians would never come against Bethul, for no enemy had ever troubled himself with conquering our village. Moreover, the rains would soon commence and fill the cisterns in town.

After the first heavy rain in the month of Kislev, when the air turned cold and the plowing began, a stranger knocked on the door of the winter house. He looked weary and his sandals were caked with mud as if after a long journey. But he would neither rest nor give his name, but asked to see the master. When Merari and he had bowed down before each other, the stranger simply said:

"The time is come."

"Then we shall leave for Jerusalem at dawn," Merrari replied.

"No, we must leave this very day," the man said. "Nebuchadrezzar's army is already departed from Babylon, and it is known that they will come up against Jerusalem. Therefore let us make haste, lest we fail to accomplish our task!"

So Merari and the stranger departed. But we spent many troubled days waiting for the master's return. He had not taken Hadad but had gone on foot, fearing to be noticed if he rode into Jerusalem on a horse. When he returned he was so weary he could barely stand upright, but leaned heavily upon his staff, dragging his lame leg behind him.

After Merari had washed and refreshed himself, Judith sat down at his feet to ask him many questions. She would know how matters stood in Jerusalem and whether it had been difficult to find the prophet.

"Jerusalem is preparing for a siege," Merari replied. "Also the city is full of spies, watching all coming and going, for it is rumored that there is a plot afoot to murder King Jehoiakim. Now that the Babylonian army is marching on Jerusalem, there are many who would rather surrender than see the city sacked. But Jehoiakim has vowed not to bow his neck under the yoke of Nebuchadrezzar."

"If the city is so heavily guarded, how was the great task accomplished, and where were the tablets taken?" Judith asked.

"This I must not tell you, my daughter, for I would not burden you with the danger of such knowledge. Nor would I reveal to you the names of the priests and officers who lent their assistance. As for the Tablets of the Law, they were brought down from a mountain and are returned to a mountain. And there they shall repose until another righteous king sits on the throne of Judah!"

But it seemed that such a time would never come again.

Only a few days after the master's return we learned that King Jehoiakim had died—in what manner none knew—and that his son Jehoiachin was become king. Jehoiachin was eighteen years old when he sat on the throne of Judah. Few believed that the young king could make his army hold out against the Babylonians. Indeed some whispered that his father had been murdered and Jehoiachin placed on the throne because it would be less shameful for so young a king to surrender.

Now that Nebuchadrezzar's mighty army had laid siege to Jerusalem, none dared walk in and out of the gate even in Bethul. Day and night a watchman stood guard on the one tower of our wall, to sound the alarm if he should see soldiers approaching from the north. But Merari rounded up all the young men who were fit and brave enough to fight, putting over them Joab as their captain. And he gave Joab his sword, for he, Merari, was become too lame to go out into battle. But he could still shoot an arrow and hit a target at a great distance.

Every day Merari would climb the tower in the wall and Judith would go with him to look down into the valley below. There had been much rain that winter, and already the shoots were rising green from the black soil. Merari feared greatly that the Babylonians might come and devastate the fields around Bethul. And, though his storehouses were filled with grain, he loathed the thought of losing his crops and seeing his fields trampled and burned.

Nor would Merari relinquish his plan of providing water for Bethul. Though the cisterns in town were full to the brim, he set the men to digging the shaft of which he had spoken so often. Now that they were confined within the walls, none had an excuse for shirking the work. But the digging was soon abandoned, for in the month of Adar—three months after the Babylonian army had come against Jerusalem—the young king surrendered to Nebuchadrezzar.

And Jehoiachin went out before the city to Nebuchadrezzar, he and his mother and his wives and his servants, and his princes and his officers, and the king of Babylon took them in the seventh year of his reign. And he also took another ten thousand captives, all the craftsmen and smiths and those who knew building—even Merari's own brother Aaron and his wife and sons—Nebuchadrezzar carried away to Babylon. But he made Mattaniah, an uncle of Jehoiachin, king of Judah and changed his name to Zedekiah.

Zedekiah was twenty and one years old when he began to reign. His grandfather's father Hezekiah had reigned five and thirty years in Jerusalem. His son Manasseh reigned five and fifty years. His son Amon was slain by his own servants, having reigned but two years. However, his son Josiah reigned thirty and one years in Jerusalem. Four kings reigned one hundred and thirteen years.

But Zedekiah was the fourth king to sit on the throne of Judah in the twelve years since King Josiah was slain in battle at Megiddo.

SEVEN

Nebuchadnezzar the king, unto all the peoples, nations, and languages, that dwell in all the earth; peace be multiplied unto you.

—DANIEL 3:31

BECAUSE Babylonia was in the midst of war (the old man Isaac said to the young scribe), the crowning of Nebuchadrezzar was not a cause for great celebration. No sooner had he secured his throne than Nebuchadrezzar returned to Syria to establish his rule there. His army marched about unopposed until the month of Shebat, when the king returned to Babylon.

Though the Captain Holofernes had been among the small troop of horsemen that accompanied Nebuchadrezzar back to Babylon, my master Nabukasir remained in Syria. He did not come home until his son was eight months old. The boy already knew how to sit upright and crawl about on the floor, and when the strange man who smelled of sweat and war picked him up and clasped him to his bosom, he screamed as though he had been seized by a demon. Then the master's face became more somber than before, and handing the child back to his nurse, he muttered:

"This wretched war detained me so long, I am a stranger to my own son!"

But the lady Margidda threw her arms about her husband, exclaiming among tears:

"The boy is only a babe who knows no better! But I and all the household are thanking the gods for my lord's safe return!"

And she gazed at the master with great pride, for he wore upon his helmet the crest of a captain of thousands, and about his neck such ornaments as Nebuchadrezzar had bestowed upon him for bravery.

But more than love and admiration the master craved a bath upon his return. I bade one of the kitchen slaves fetch hot water and pour it over the stones in the bathroom that my lord might ease his weary body in the steam, and a new bar of soap, with which to scrub the grime off his body. While he disrobed I stood admiring the golden chains the king had given him, but Nabukasir said with a sigh:

"With each of these chains the king ties me to himself as with fetters. But who would dare refuse gifts from the king of Babylon?"

When Nabukasir took off his undergarments I cried out in horror, for there was an ugly, red scar running from his chest across his ribs toward his back. I could see then that the Captain Holofernes had lied to us when he said the master was well and had remained with the troops in Syria only to tend to the king's business. Rather he must have been grievously wounded and unable to travel.

"Now the war has also left its mark on me, Marduksharusur," my master said. "Yet should I praise God if this were the only mark. For senseless killing and burning leave worse marks on a man, even if these cannot be seen with the eye. Neither do I believe that the battle at Carchemish, which was to have been our last, will remain our last. Nebuchadrezzar has been king only six months, but already he is changing. As he marched about unopposed in Syria, with all the kings prostrating themselves before him, I could see how his pride increased and how he gloried in his power. And though he speaks of peace, he will soon invent another cause for war."

Then I knew the master had not changed. I went to see that none was listening at the bathroom door, for even a friend of the king may not speak against him.

To all but me the master was a proud hero returned from war. Though the lady Margidda screamed and fainted when first she saw his scar, she soon spoke boastfully of it to her friends. And when Nabukasir was chosen to escort Nebuchadrezzar at the Akitu Festival—when the king took the hand of Marduk to celebrate the New Year—the mistress's pride knew no bounds, for indeed only few men were so honored by the king.

And now spring was again come to Babylon—the glorious brief time in the month of Nisan when one need not seek shelter inside the house from the winter cold, nor yet hide from the scorching summer sun and the fiery south wind that dried one's nostrils and made even the skin of the young shrivel, as though they were ancient. Into the bright blue sky above Babylon rose the doves of Ishtar from their cotes in the forecourt of the goddess's temple, to circle above the city like white clouds. It was said that if their droppings fell upon a man walking beneath, he would lie that very day with the woman of his choice. However, this belief was but another Babylonian folly, for more than once such droppings alighted on me.

It was the first time Nebuchadrezzar would take the hand of Marduk to celebrate the New Year—the day from which the true beginning of his reign was to be counted. King Nabopolassar had died after the previous Akitu Festival, and we were still in the last year of his reign. The soothsayers proclaimed a multitude of favorable omens. The Euphrates had risen but little, and there was no danger that the river would flood this spring, devastating the fields and bringing pestilence to the land. After these floodings, when the air turned hot of a sudden, many children were seized by a dreadful fever that racked their bodies and left them unable to move their limbs. Those who did not die remained crippled forever, bereft of the use of their arms or legs.

But this was to be a perfect spring. Already before the middle of Adar pilgrims began to pour into Babylon. There had been little building during the reign of Nabopolassar, and lodgings were hard to find. Soon all the choicer hostels clustering around Esagila, the temple of Marduk, were filled with visitors to the city. These strangers were easily recognized in the street by the way they walked with their heads thrown back and their faces turned upward to stare at Etemenanki, the Tower of Babylon. Many came from small villages and had never been to a big city. They would get in the way of the king's horsemen, be nearly run over by chariots, or lose their wives and children in the maze of Babylon. Then their cries of anguish would add to the noise and confusion that was an unceasing part of the city's life.

The merchants did splendid business during these holidays, disposing of goods they had not been able to sell all year. And so did the street vendors of food—of date cakes and thin sesame wafers, of salted fish and pickled pork and honey and beer and wine—which they offered to the visitors at outrageous prices.

The odor of food and the sweet smell of perfume that people had poured over their bodies lent the very air of Babylon a festive scent. And every day there was another procession to one of the countless shrines of the city, with the priests carrying the image of their god through the streets to the playing of music and the chanting of singers. Then all traffic came to a halt, and it was impossible to move either forward or backward.

On such a day the Captain Holofernes would come to my master's house, cursing the priests, the gods and the visitors in the same breath.

"You, my friend, shall someday be burned for cursing the gods," my master said to the captain. "As for the people celebrating the New Year, would you deprive them of their pleasure—you who are out reveling day and night?"

"Far be it from me to speak against revelry," the captain replied. "However, if I wished to spend my days prostrate, I would sooner spend them prostrate with a woman in bed than prostrate before some god!"

Then I went to look for listeners at the door, fearing that between my master and the captain I should someday be tried with the one for treason or burned with the other for blasphemy. But none was there to eavesdrop, for during these weeks of rejoicing even the kitchen slaves spent their days in the street, gawking at the processions and the visitors.

On the second day of Nisan, when the festival began, all work ceased in Babylon. The high priest of the temple Esagila rose at dawn, washed with river water, entered into the presence of the god Marduk and recited a long prayer that ended with the words:

> "Lord of the countries, who dwells in the temple
> Eudul, who grasps the hand of the fallen,
> Grant mercy to your city, Babylon!
> Turn your face to the temple Esagil, your house!
> Establish the liberty of the people of Babylon, your
>   subordinates."

After adding some secret recitations, he opened the gates of the temple and summoned the lesser priests and the singers that they might perform the prescribed rituals.

The same ceremonies were repeated on the second day. On the

third day three skilled artisans fashioned two images of cedar wood and tamarisk, clothed them in red garments, and adorned them with gold and precious stones. These images were given food offerings until the sixth day, when the god Nebo reached Babylon on his journey by barge up the river from Borsippa. Then their heads were struck off, and in the presence of Nebo they were burned in a fire.

The great celebration began on the fourth day of the festival. This was the day when the high priest stepped before the god Marduk at even to recite the Enuma Elis, the poem of the creation of the world.

"When on high heaven had not been named
Firm ground below had not been called by name . . .
No reed hut had been matted, no marsh land had appeared,
When no gods whatever had been brought into being . . ."

The poem went on to tell of the creation of the gods, and of the battle between Tiamat, the goddess of chaos, and Marduk, the wise one. How Marduk prevailed over Tiamat, how he split her body to create heaven and earth, how he made the moon and the stars, how he divided time into months and days, and how in the end he conceived of creating man.

"Blood will I mass and cause bones to be.
I will establish a savage, 'man' shall be his name.
Verily, savage-man will I create.
He shall be charged with the service of the gods
    That they might be at ease!"

Then the gods delivered to Marduk the one who had incited Tiamat to rebel and had caused great bloodshed and havoc among the other gods. From his tainted blood man was fashioned, nor has he ceased causing havoc on earth to this day.

But the high point of the festival came on the fifth day, when the king visited the temple. On that day my master Nabukasir rose as early as the high priest to prepare himself for escorting the king. He had summoned his barber to the house, and after taking his bath he suffered the long ordeal of having his hair and beard curled and perfumed. He even allowed the barber to lengthen his beard by adding a false hair piece to it, as was the fashion.

Then Nabukasir dressed in an undergarment of fine Egyptian linen—the sort of garment that could no longer be obtained, since we were at war with Egypt. Over it he slipped the red woolen tunic which the lady Margidda had lovingly embroidered with gold thread. On his head he put a tasseled cap and across his chest a sash that held up his broad bronze girdle. His wrists were circled by silver bracelets adorned with hammered rosettes and stones of lapis lazuli and about his neck he hung all the chains and ornaments the king had bestowed upon him.

When my master was fully dressed, all the members of the household gathered around to admire him and to envy me, for I was to go with him to the palace, opening for him a path through the throng that had gathered since dawn along the Processional Way.

Many had spent the night sleeping in the street that they might obtain a place near the road where the king would pass and receive of the free food that was distributed on that day to celebrate the New Year. I had feared that I would have to fight my way through the crowd, but all stood back in awe when they beheld my master. He looked a man of distinction and so, for that matter, did I, having put on weight, as will happen to one in my condition. And I too was dressed in fine clothes, though not as sumptuously as my lord.

At the east gate of the palace the guards let us pass unchallenged into the first of the five courts. The buildings around this court housed the garrisons that guarded the royal residence. This was where the Captain Holofernes spent his days, except when he was off duty. Then he retired to his own house in the New Town, on the western bank of the Euphrates—far from the palace, so that the ladies visiting him there might not be recognized in the street.

We found the captain idly leaning against a wall while he observed the coming and going of the many chamberlains and courtiers. When he came to greet us, my master asked him why he was not dressed for the festive occasion.

"I am not to walk in the procession," the captain replied, "for the temple grounds must not be defiled by soldiers bearing arms, and the king must go there without his guard. I should soon change this evil practice, for more than one king was slain at prayer. However, Nebuchadrezzar does not believe that anyone might wish to harm him, though there are some who whisper that the king's own younger brother would seize the throne from him if he could find men to aid him. Prince Nabu-suma-lisir is his mother's favorite.

Indeed she made him hope that she would persuade his father to name him his successor, but King Nabopolassar would not pass over the rightful heir. As for Nebuchadrezzar—he dotes on his family and would not believe them capable of evil—neither the queen mother, who plots with his worthless brother, nor the queen Amytis, who even today, when all Babylon rejoices at the return of spring, sits in her chambers weeping for the mountains of her homeland instead of being thankful that the king put many men to laying out the gardens he promised her, while his own palace stands in great need of repair."

The captain spoke the truth. During his discourse we had passed through the double gateway into the second court, around which lived the officers who administered the kingdom. We were about to enter through a massive gateway into the third court—the largest of them all—to the south of which lay the throne room. None had challenged us, for the Captain Holofernes was well known to the soldiers who guarded the gates. As we passed from the third into the fourth court, around which were grouped the king's own quarters, I could see that the buildings were still in bad repair, while to the north of the palace grounds rose the new, staggered terraces of the gardens which Nebuchadrezzar was building for the queen.

It was only after we had entered the fourth court that the Captain Holofernes suddenly took notice of my presence, for only the most exalted courtiers were allowed there.

"I see that your slave Marduksharusur has stolen in with us," the captain said to my master. "Truly he is as curious as a cat and shall no doubt end as badly as many of these despicable beasts. But we shall leave you here, for I am not invited to the king's reception room. Rather I shall escort this shameless slave back to the gate before he is thrown in prison, thus causing you a loss of silver."

And bidding my master farewell, the captain seized my arm and marched me back to the gate of the first court. But he was not as vexed as he would have me believe, for he proposed that I come with him to the gate of the temple Esagila, where we could watch the king enter into the temple grounds.

We made our way through the crowd back to where I had come from with my master, and turning west walked along the wall that surrounded the courtyard of the Tower of Babylon. Prayers and sacrifices had commenced at dawn, and when we reached the gate of Esagila, the rituals inside were still being performed. We could

smell the sweet scent of incense and the pungent odor of roasted
meat and hear the chanting of the priests. But we could not see
them, for they were within the temple. Thus we amused ourselves
by observing the crowd while we waited for the royal procession.
There was a multitude of food vendors, storytellers, singers, dream
diviners and soothsayers about—New Year's Day being the day
when Marduk fixed the fates, a propitious time to discover what the
future held in store.

Finally a rising murmur warned us of the king's approach. The
crowd about us began to strain forward, one jostling the other,
those at the back converging upon those in front, with children
screaming and women fainting, until I thought we would be
crushed to death even before the arrival of the procession.

"Come, let us stand with our backs against the wall, lest these
savages utterly mangle us," the Captain Holofernes said. "Though
little harm may come to you, I still have parts left I would not wish
to lose in the crush."

Those standing nearest the captain guffawed, for people will
forever love coarse talk. My pride was hurt, though I knew it was
the captain's manner to speak thus and he meant nought by it. But I
found little time to sulk, for the king appeared on the Processional
Way.

Nebuchadrezzar had resolved to restore the ancient custom where
the king ascended on foot the tall temple tower to prove his youthful vigor. And though he would not climb all the way to the top of
Etemenanki, he went on foot. In spite of the heavy crown and gold-
encrusted garments, the king walked with great vigor and majesty.
His sumptuous coronation robes were richly embroidered with
designs of pine cones, the tree of life and winged genii to ensure
good fortune and fertility. His golden crown was set with precious
stones, and in his right hand he carried the scepter of white and
brown onyx, while his left rested on the gilded knob of his ceremonial sword.

Though the king's eyes shone with joy at the shouts of acclama-
tion, the Captain Holofernes scanned the crowd with narrowed
eyes, muttering:

"A crowd is but a savage beast best governed by fear and force.
Only a fool would trust it. But an even greater folly is to trust the
priests, into whose hands the king is about to deliver himself."

By then the artisans of the temple had arrived in the open gate, bearing golden vessels with river water to pour over the king's hands. When Nebuchadrezzar entered the Exalted Courtyard, the artisans formed into ranks behind him to escort him up to the temple, while the courtiers and chamberlains slowly filed through the gate. Though I craned my neck, the short figure of the king, surrounded by the priests, soon vanished from my sight.

"Ah, how I would like to witness the ceremony!" I exclaimed.

"This wish I do not share," the Captain Holofernes said. "But to appease your wretched curiosity I shall describe it to you. When the king reaches the presence of the god Marduk, the high priest will take away his scepter, crown and sword and place them before the god. Then the priest will strike the king's cheek, drag him by the ears and make him bow down to the ground, while the king speaks these words: 'I did not sin, lord of the countries. I was not neglectful of your godship. I did not destroy Babylon. I did not command its overthrow. I did not neglect the temple Esagil, I did not forget its rites. I did not rain blows on the shoulders of the subordinates. I did not humiliate them. I watched out for Babylon; I did not smash its walls.' After the king has spoken these words the high priest will bless him and restore his scepter, crown and sword. Then the priest will again strike the king's cheek. If, when he strikes the king's cheek, the tears flow, it means that Marduk is friendly. If no tears appear, the god is angry: the enemy will rise up and bring about the king's downfall."

When the captain ceased speaking I saw that he had turned ashen, and I knew that his hatred of the priests had not abated since his youth. But before he could curse them in his customary manner the king returned to show himself to the crowd. As he became visible to those nearest the gate a loud roar of joy went up, for on his cheek were the red marks of the priest's five fingers. Then all knew that the high priest had slapped the king with vigor, thus ensuring a favorable fate for Babylon.

A strange sound beside me made me glance at the Captain Holofernes. He had turned paler yet, and he stood gnashing his teeth so that his cheekbones worked in his face. Suddenly he swung around, and with a retching sound he vomited against the wall of Esagila.

A priest who had come to the gate turned toward the captain, wagged his head and said:

"To celebrate the New Year is the task of the pious. But to be drunk so early in the day and to vomit in the presence of the king is utterly unbecoming to a captain of the guard!"

The captain was still retching while the priest walked away. But when he recovered his breath he began to swear so horribly that I covered both my ears with my hands, lest I be called as a witness against him if he were brought to trial for blaspheming the gods.

Though the ceremonies were far from over, the Captain Holofernes declared that he would not waste his day standing in the gate of the temple. He could see more than a dozen courtiers whose comely wives were pining away in solitude, and he felt honorbound to console them. Thus he departed, leaving me alone by the gate.

There I remained until sunset to see the high priest and the king offer the evening sacrifice. But the true revelry began when darkness fell over Babylon. The men got drunk with date wine and barley beer, and the harlots who plied their trade in the name of the god and for the profit of the temple had their busiest night of the year. While the king and his retinue returned to the palace for the banquet that closed the festivities, I wandered about the streets of Babylon, which on that night were lit by so many torches that darkness was turned to daylight. And I too drank wine and ate roasted meat, and joined in the singing and the revelry, until I utterly forgot that this was a heathen feast and I a Hebrew. But since I could not enjoy the company of the temple harlots, I returned to the palace gate to wait there for my master, lest he find none to assist him if he came forth drunk.

It was near the morning watch when my lord staggered out of the palace gate. Though I sat half dozing on the ground, with my back against the wall, I jumped up and ran toward him. But he was not drunk, only weary unto death, and he leaned on my shoulder all the way home.

"Truly the king is driven by demons," my lord said to me. "Though he has tended to ceremonies since dawn, he still had the strength to pace back and forth after the banquet, while he spoke of his plans for Babylon. The old courtiers muttered among themselves about the unseemliness of his behavior. They would have preferred to nod after the meal rather than listen to Nebuchadrezzar's long discourse. Nor could they understand half his words, for as he became inflamed with his visions he lapsed into Chaldean speech, which only those born in the south can comprehend.

"However, the king, oblivious of his guests' bewildered faces, raved on about his great building plans. But when one of the courtiers asked him if he would install stone reliefs depicting his great deeds on the walls of his palace—as was done by the Assyrian kings—Nebuchadrezzar replied: 'Why should we, who have much clay and brick, use stone to embellish our palaces? Let our monuments be built of what our own land renders us! As for the battle scenes the Assyrian kings put on the walls of their palaces—of cities being sacked and burned, of men being impaled, flayed and hacked to pieces, of women and children being driven into capitivity—we shall not depict such abominations, for the Babylonians are a peace-loving people!' "

Two months after he had spoken these words the king mustered his army, went off to war, and turned Ashkelon into a heap of ruins.

My master, not being fully recovered from his wound, was allowed to remain in Babylon. But his heart ached when he learned that yet another city had been destroyed, and he spoke bitter words, though there were many who proclaimed that Ashkelon had sealed its own fate by remaining the last Egyptian stronghold in what was now the Babylonian empire.

The king and his army did not return from the campaign for nine months. And for nine months my master was left in peace to enjoy his home, the embrace of his wife and the company of his children. His little daughter, born in the eighteenth year of Nabopolassar, was now four years old, and as lovely a child as one could imagine. She was raised in the faith of her mother to believe in all the deities of heaven—in Marduk, Nebo, Ishtar and all the minor gods and goddesses—and she was taught to observe the omens that she might not bring down misfortune on her head. But the boy David, who was a year and a half, and already walked and spoke a few words, was taught none of this.

As for the lady Margidda, she continued inquiring of her dream diviner about omens concerning her son. But the master knew nothing of this. Nor did I inform him, for to sow discord between a man and his wife is evil, neither could my lord be troubled by what he did not know. Was it not enough that he troubled himself over the deeds of the king?

Nebuchadrezzar and his army returned to Babylon in the month of Shebat, carrying the king of Ashkelon with him as his prisoner. But unlike the Assyrian kings, who had humiliated their captives and sometimes even displayed them in cages at the city gate to the mirth and mockery of the people, Nebuchadrezzar assigned the king of Ashkelon and his wives quarters on the very palace grounds. There they lived, being treated like royal prisoners. Many of the older courtiers found fault with such leniency. But others said to give Nebuchadrezzar time—he had been king less than two years and, though he was wise at making war, he still had much to learn about ruling.

Again my master was summoned to celebrate the New Year with the king, and again Nebuchadrezzar vowed never again to look upon the destruction of another city, only to lead his army in war against Syria the following month. And so he did in the third year of his reign. But even before he reached Syria, Nebuchadrezzar had to call a halt to the march and return with a troop of faithful men to Babylon. For his younger brother, Nabu-suma-lisir, had sat down on the throne and proclaimed himself king.

This happened on a hot day in the month of Tammuz, when the south wind brought the dust from the desert to toss it over Babylon like a yellow blanket. My master and I sat in the upper chamber where he kept his clay tablets, engaged upon our task of translating the old poetry. Though it was daytime we had lit the oil lamp, having been forced to shut the door against the wind and the dust. The lady Margidda had taken the two children and their nurse for a visit to her father's house. Thus the silence in our secluded room was complete, and we did not learn until evening what had happened at the palace.

Aided by the queen mother, who had gained him the support of some disgruntled courtiers, Prince Nabu-suma-lisir had sat down on the throne of Babylon. The courtiers had long been dismayed by the king's great building plans, which could only lead to a rise in taxes that would weigh more heavily on the rich landowners than on the poor people. Nor were they pleased with the manner in which the king conducted his wars. Whereas Nabopolassar's cam-

paigns had been brief, Nebuchadrezzar had taken the army into the
field for many months so that the men were absent at harvest time.
The few hirelings left had demanded higher wages and diminished
the gains of the landowners, who for fear of the king did not dare
raise the price of grain. Thinking to seize power while Nebuchadrezzar was absent from Babylon, these disgruntled men had rallied
behind his younger brother to make him king.

Having learned of this calamity, my master summoned a few of
those loyal to the king to his house. Together they found a way to
bribe the guards which the rebels had put at the city gates and send
a messenger to Nebuchadrezzar. Though my master often spoke
harsh words against the king, he had not forgotten that Nebuchadrezzar carried him out of the flames, nor had he ceased loving the
king in his heart.

But it was nearly three months before Nebuchadrezzar returned
to Babylon. He entered the town without a struggle, for when the
guards on the wall beheld their rightful king, they threw open the
gates to him. As for the officers who had cast their lot with the
rebels, some fled Babylon, while others fell upon their own swords
rather than be taken alive. Thus only Prince Nabu-suma-lisir and his
evil counselors were left. The latter Nebuchadrezzar put to death,
but he did not raise his hand against his brother, nor against the
queen mother.

Of this the Captain Holofernes, who had returned with the king,
spoke bitterly to my master.

"After we seized the palace without a battle, all those who had
spoken treason threw themselves at the king's feet," he said. "But
the queen mother had fled to the women's quarters, and the prince
had barricaded himself in his chambers. I begged the king to let me
deal with his wretched brother as he deserved, for it would have
been easy to break into his apartments with a few soldiers and split
his accursed head. But Nebuchadrezzar replied: 'My brother was
used by those older and wiser than himself for their own ends.
These wretches shall surely pay for their crimes! But I will not have
it said after me that Nebuchadrezzar had to slay his brother that he
might sit on the throne of Babylon. I shall pardon the prince and
give him leave to repent his error for the rest of his days. As for the
queen mother—should I defile myself with the blood of her who
bore me? Though she loves my younger brother better than me, she

does so only because through me she lost her favorite first-born.'
Thus the worst evildoers remained free to invent more mischief!"

The following day my master went to the palace, where Nebuchadrezzar uttered many bitter words about the rebels, saying he
did not know why they should have betrayed him after he had
granted them many privileges. Then my master spoke freely to the
king about the grievances of these men and told him how his long
campaigns weighed heavily on the land, the men who served in the
army being needed in Babylonia at harvest time.

"You speak true words, my friend," the king replied. "Nor must
you doubt that it grieves me to tear away these men from the
bosoms of their wives and from the fields where they are needed.
But am I to abandon a war in the midst before it is won? Let me but
secure our borders against Egypt and ensure the loyalty of the
Syrian kings, and we shall cease forever from making war! However, I can see that it is not wise if I absent myself from Babylonia
for too long. Therefore I shall bring back the troops from Syria as
soon as our yearly tribute is collected. I shall be gone but a month
or two. When I return, you Nabukasir shall gladden my heart by
showing me all your writings—a task for which I excused you from
serving in my army!"

This request filled my master with dread, for he knew that the
king must never read what he had written. In his despair Nabukasir
uttered a lie, pretending that he was at work on an epic about
Nebuchadrezzar's great deeds, which would yet take many months
to complete.

At that the king's eyes lit up and he exclaimed:

"Surely our conquest of Nineveh will make a tale to rival the
deeds of Gilgamesh!"

And he dispatched my master home to his work, while he returned to join his troops in Syria.

But now my master sat in the upper chamber moaning as he held
his head in his hands.

"I do not know what evil demon twisted my tongue to make me
lie to the king," he said. "As for writing an epic about his deeds,
such epics ought to be written long after the hero is dead. For only
then can it be known whether he was in truth deserving. As for
Nebuchadrezzar, he has sat on the throne of Babylon three years!"

Still, my master brought forth his wax-covered writing boards from the chest where he kept them under lock, and together we thought to put the battle of Nineveh into verse. But my heart was not in the work, for I would rather not remember the grimmest part of my past, nor would I glorify it. As for my lord, if the truth must be told, he was but a poor poet. To write an epic of one's own is not the same as to translate the work of another. After we had labored for many days, Nabukasir pushed away the tablets in disgust, exclaiming that he would sooner prove his loyalty to the king with the sword than with the stylus.

"If one is skillful with the sword one can wield it at will," my master said. "But a stylus cannot be forced to do one's bidding."

When Nebuchadrezzar returned from Syria and my master had nothing to show him—for in his wrath he had smashed all the tablets—he offered to follow the king when next he went to Syria.

This was to be an unbloody campaign. All the land was now under the yoke of Babylon, and the troops marched about unopposed. Nebuchadrezzar called up the army in the month of Elul, after the harvest, for he had not yet forgotten the uprising of the previous year. Nor did he muster a great force but took only as many men as were needed for a show of strength. The rest of the army was left behind at the charge of some loyal officers, to guard Babylon against another attempt at secession. Among these men was the Captain Holofernes, who cursed his fate for having been left behind while my own master went off with the king.

Neither of us expected my lord to be absent for long. Indeed the Captain Holofernes continued to be a frequent visitor in our house. At times I wondered whether he had taken it into his mind to seduce the mistress, for men will often covet the wives of their best friends. Thus I always busied myself around the captain when he came to call that he and the lady Margidda might not be alone together.

But the captain did not come to court his friend's wife. Rather he came to play with his friend's son. He would pick up the boy David, carry him about on his shoulders or toss him in the air, until the child shrieked with delight. But when the lady Margidda inquired whether he would never take a wife that he too might have sons, the captain replied:

"A man can have sons without taking a wife. As for getting

married, I vowed not to do so until the Lady Ishtar descends from on high to take me by the hand. For if I am to believe the oracle, it is she who desires me for her husband."

"I beg my lord not to mock the gods in my house!" the lady Margidda exlaimed. "It might bring misfortune down on our heads."

"Let all the misfortunes befall me," the captain said. "Neither let my lady be concerned about the gods. Most of the time they are too drunk to listen to the speech of mortals."

Then the lady Margidda covered her ears with her hands and fled from the room in terror. And when not too many days later it became known that the king had sent for more troops to join him in Syria—for he was to lead them in war against Egypt—the mistress was certain that this evil turn of events had been caused by the captain's impious words.

When the king left with the army, none had thought that he would go to war against Egypt. Rather it was believed that he went to Syria only to collect the yearly tribute. Now some said his taking but a few troops had been a ruse to deceive the Egyptians. But others declared that the army was ill prepared for a major war. Surely the sudden calling up of unskilled soldiers meant that the Egyptians had moved first.

The only one who rejoiced at the news was the Captain Holofernes, for it meant an end to his idleness. He came to bid the lady Margidda farewell, promising to bring her a fine linen garment from Thebes, and some wooden toys for the children.

"As for you, Marduksharusur," he said, "since a comely slave girl could be of little use to you, I shall bring you a roll of papyrus covered with Egyptian letters, for you would read even the lies written by our wretched enemy."

When I wondered aloud whether this sudden war would lead to an easy victory, the captain only laughed and exclaimed:

"I saw the Egyptians run at Carchemish! Surely if we could drive them back from there into their own country, it should be a small matter to push them across the border from Gaza!"

Again the tramping of soldiers was heard day and night as troops were rounded up and marched off to Syria. And again women wept and carried sacrifices to the temples so that the gods might bless the arms of their men and bring them back alive and victorious.

For many weeks no news came from the front. And when the couriers began to arrive they would speak to none but the king's officers at the palace. But bad news, however tightly guarded, will out. Soon it was known that Nebuchadrezzar and his army had suffered a bitter defeat. Though the Egyptians too had sustained great losses, they had succeeded in turning back our troops.

For days hordes of women waited by the Ishtar Gate to see whether their husbands and sons would return among the living. Few were as fortunate as the lady Margidda, whose husband knew how to write and whose letters were carried to Babylon with the royal mail. Thus we learned that the master had survived, though he did not write whether he was well or wounded.

I too went to stand in the gate, for it was not seemly that the lady Margidda mingle with the common people. Nor would the master wish her to see him return to Babylon in defeat. Yet many days passed until at the end of the month of Tebet, on a cold winter evening, the first ragged soldiers approached the Ishtar Gate. Only then did we begin to know how bad the defeat had been, for not half of those who had left came back. And most of those who returned were wounded, with rags bound around their heads, arms or legs. They staggered along leaning upon their spears or upon each other, while the badly wounded lay moaning on oxcarts, one thrown above the other, so that one could not tell the living from the dead. Between them ran the women, looking for their sons and husbands, crying when they found them, weeping even louder when they did not, asking here and there if their men had not been seen, if perchance they were still alive, straggling in the back, or if they had been taken captive.

But the king did not enter Babylon until after night had fallen. Only then did Nebuchadrezzar ride into town, surrounded by his guard, and enter the palace, whose gates were swiftly shut behind him. There was no victory celebration, no music and dancing in the street, and no women coming forth with timbrels and wreaths of flowers. But many went about with their faces slashed and their hair disheveled, in mourning for their fallen men.

Though I had seen my lord Nabukasir return from other wars, I had never seen him as he was now. For days he would not speak to anyone. The mistress's handmaiden told me that the lady Margidda sat weeping in her chamber, for her husband had not yet lain with

her though he had been absent for many months. None of his
wounds was as bad as the one he had sustained in the previous war,
nor could the suffering I saw in his eyes be caused by bodily pain.
But I did not dare ask the cause of his torment, until one day he
spoke to me of his own accord.

"I fought in many wars, Marduksharusur. But never have I seen
such slaughter as I saw in this last one. Or perhaps the slaughter
seems worse when one suffers defeat. Nor can I blot from my mind
the memory of fields running with blood and littered with the bodies
of the dead and the dying, of soldiers with limbs hacked off and
bowels spilling from their split bellies, of men and horses screaming
in agony.

"Since we beat the Egyptians in battle at Carchemish, they had
built up the strength of their chariot corps and their mounted
troops. When we met their army not far from Gaza, they exceeded
us in men and equipment. Indeed they were swarming all around us,
throwing our ranks into confusion. Had the king not fought at the
head of his troops, who knows but that they might have turned us
to flight. There was not a man among us who was not wounded—
even the king—except the Captain Holofernes.

"Of him it was told that he led a troop of a hundred brave
warriors to harass the Egyptian flank. Soon he was surrounded
by a force that outnumbered his soldiers ten to one. But when the
Egyptian captain sent a messenger to demand his surrender, they say
that Holofernes raised himself up in his saddle—for he was on horseback—broke wind loudly and shouted: 'Take this answer to your
captain!' Then he and his men fought their way out of the ambush.
When they reached the rest of the Babylonian forces, of the hundred only seven were alive. And among them only one whose skin
was not even grazed: the Captain Holofernes. This has strengthened
the soldiers in their belief that he is invulnerable. And even I, who
do not believe in such follies, have come to believe it. For no man
may challenge death that often and still emerge unscathed.

"Nor did the captain's spirit flag on the long, bitter trek home.
Most of the time we marched by night, avoiding the big cities, that
our wounds and weakness might not be witnessed by the vassals of
Babylon. But when I asked the king why we had gone up against
Egypt when we were so ill prepared, he said:

" 'You, who know little but would find much fault, may now
learn why we could not delay this campaign. While we were col-

lecting tribute in Syria, I received word from our spies in Egypt that Pharaoh Necho was building a canal from the mouth of the Nile to the Red Sea that he might carry his fleet across land to the Great Gulf south of Chaldea. This thing I could never permit, for the southern coast of Babylonia is not fortified against enemy attacks. What choice had I but to threaten the border of Egypt from the north that they might not threaten the border of Babylonia from the south? Or would you rather have the Egyptians conquer our ᵈd, devastate our cities, carry away our gods and defile our wou.　-and worse yet, teach them the indecencies of their own: to walk abo.　ⁱn sheer garments revealing their breasts and their legs; and to starve　ᵐselves for the sake of slender bodies, until in the end they would ru.　ˢe to bear us more than a son or two, lest they lose their shapely hip　ⁱ'

"Yet I know that　ıe war was not waged to keep the Egyptians from defiling our v)men," my master continued, "but rather to keep them from sei　ıg our trade routes."

"My lord did ɪ ȼ speak of this to the king?" I asked in horror.

"Indeed how　ɔuld I? No, I only bemoaned our heavy losses, for these even Neɔuchadrezzar could not deny. But the king said: 'Though we lost many brave warriors, the losses of the Egyptians were three times as great. But it was a grave error to go to war with unskilled troops and poor equipment. Nor shall I ever repeat this blunder. Rather than muster the army every year, I shall train men and horses, and amass many chariots that we might at all times have an army ready for battle. Thus we shall never again suffer defeat from lack of preparedness!'

"I knew then that we will never have peace in Babylonia," my master said. "It may be a great evil to call up the army every year. But to have a standing army is an even greater evil. For how could these troops be paid except with plunder won in war, and how could men trained to fight be kept in Babylonia without stirring up rebellion? But when I spoke of this to the king he called me a foolish dreamer who had better study his clay tablets than mix in affairs of state. Thus the king and I parted in bitterness. The only good to come of our discord is that he will not torment me for some time with the epic I promised to write for him."

Many months passed and the king did not send for my master. The building up of his army left Nebuchadrezzar little leisure for small diversions. All through the fifth year of his reign the king stayed in his own land, gathering together chariots and horses in great numbers. Those who brought horses to Babylon and bred them became rich. Those who brought in iron for weapons became rich. Those who were skilled in the building of chariots became rich. And the makers of armor and saddles and bridles and wheels and axles and helmets and boots were busy day and night, hiring many men to work for them and paying them well. These men spent their wages for goods they had never been able to buy before, thus bringing wealth to others.

But my master said bitterly that the country was growing rich from preparing for war, and that the people rejoiced in their wealth as if someday they would not have to pay for it with the blood of their sons.

In the sixth year of his reign, in the month of Kislev, when the new charioteers and horsemen had been trained, Nebuchadrezzar marched with his troops to Syria to show his strength that none of the vassal kings might be tempted to fall away. For it was known that after the battle at Gaza Pharaoh Necho had sent ambassadors to the Syrian kings to win them away from Nebuchadrezzar. But when those kings beheld Nebuchadrezzar's new armed might they bowed their necks again under his yoke. Only Jehoiakim, king of Judah, refused to pay his yearly tribute to Babylon.

Neither my master nor I believed this report. How would the king of so small a country dare defy the king of Babylon? And when Nebuchadrezzar did not go up against Judah but only made war on the desert Arabs, taking much plunder from them and returning to Babylon in the month of Adar, we knew that there had been no truth to the rumor.

Then my master rejoiced, for there was still love left in his heart for the land of his ancestors, and he would rather not choose sides in a war between Babylonia and Judah. As for me, though I had never revealed myself as Hebrew, I too rejoiced. I knew the might of the Babylonian army. And I knew that if they ever went up against Judah they would utterly destroy Jerusalem, where my own grand-father's father, Hezekiah, had sat on the throne. Thus I was not too grieved when I learned that Nebuchadrezzar had made war only on the Arabs, even though that campaign caused me a great loss of silver.

You may well ask how I, a mere slave in Babylon, could lose silver in one of the king's wars. Indeed you might ask whence came this silver. But I told you earlier that my master always paid me the wages prescribed by law for a slave. And since he was well pleased with me and loved me almost like a son, he doubled them in time. By investing his silver wisely, many a slave had amassed enough to buy back his liberty.

But it was not my own liberty I considered as I added shekel to shekel. For of what value was liberty to me, who had no kin left, nor could he take a wife and beget sons that his seed might be continued on earth? It was not *my* freedom I thought to buy but that of my friend, who had remained in bondage to the merchant at Borsippa, while I had met with a much kinder fate.

I had written to Tarqu once but had never received an answer. Perhaps the tablet I sent by messenger had been lost. Or perhaps Tarqu's master had withheld it from him out of spite. And when I had begged my own master to buy my friend, he sadly shook his head, replying that he could ill afford even the slaves he owned.

I saw then that if I wished to free Tarqu from his cruel master I would have to provide the silver myself. Though how I might increase my savings to thirty-five shekels—which was then the price of a slave—I did not know. The swiftest way to multiply one's silver was by lending it against interest, but such dealings were forbidden to a slave by law.

Once again my learning proved my good fortune. As I strolled along the wharves one day, as I was wont to do in my idle hours, I heard a merchant shouting for a scribe who knew Syrian. This merchant, having received a shipment of goods from Tyre accompanied by a letter written in the Syrian tongue, stood cursing beside the vessel that had brought his merchandise.

"Is Babylonia not the greatest nation on earth?" he shouted at the man who had delivered his goods. "Does not even the pharaoh of Egypt write to the other kings in our tongue? Why, then, must these Syrians write to me in their wretched language and script?"

And he called for a scribe to translate the letter for him. I took this as an omen to make the acquaintance of one who knew how to multiply gains, for there was none in the world to surpass a Babylonian merchant for shrewdness. Thus I offered myself to translate his letter, refusing payment in the hope that he would show himself beholden in some other manner. And indeed he invited me into his warehouse for a cup of wine.

"My lord must be a man of means to refuse my silver," the merchant said as we seated ourselves on a rug before a low table.

By the way he had addressed me, I knew that he took me for a freeman. There was nothing about my appearance that revealed the slave, nor would I tell him the truth yet but said:

"I am not a public scribe. Why, then, should my lord pay me for a small favor? But as for my being a man of means, though I have some small savings I am not wealthy, not being as clever at business as my lord."

Observing me with his shrewd, black eyes, the merchant stroked his beard and said:

"A man who must keep his warehouse stocked with much merchandise if he would make but a modest living is often in need of a loan. And though there are many who would press their silver on me, I would rather borrow from friends who served me well. Therefore if my lord should wish to invest his silver with me, I would be glad to pay him the customary increase."

Though in my heart I rejoiced at the offer I feared to do an unlawful thing, for I would not lose what little I had saved. Therefore I replied:

"My lord does me great honor, but I should not dare risk such a thing."

At that the merchant frowned, telling me to forget my concern—he always paid the interest agreed upon, nor had he ever embezzled silver entrusted to him.

"I did not mean to offend my lord," I said. "Rather I spoke for myself, for the law forbids that I lend silver against increase."

The merchant quickly glanced at my wrist and my head, to see whether I bore a slave mark or a tonsure. But finding me free of any sign that would betray me as a slave, he sat knitting his brows for some time before he spoke:

"I need not have known what you revealed to me. Indeed your master must think highly of you to let you walk about unmarked. Nor do you seem a common slave but a learned man fallen on hard times, who had to sell himself into bondage. I am not one to hold misfortune against a man. Neither would it be unlawful to accept your silver, for if you died tomorrow your master would be your legal heir. And how can it be unlawful to increase the inheritance of a freeman?"

I saw that the merchant was a sensible man with a clear mind. Thus we drew up a contract, naming my master as the lender of my silver. Even if Nabukasir knew nothing of my dealings, he would not be the poorer for them. Moreover, I thought to take back my loan after a while. But as time went by and my silver increased so did my greed, proving true the old proverb: the giving of a loan is like making love; the receiving of increase like having a son born.

In the end I was no longer content to take increase but would let the merchant use my silver to finance caravans, which brought a higher profit. This was how I came to acquire a share in a camel. If the beast was sold at a good price, the gain would bring me that much nearer to buying Tarqu's freedom. But no sooner had the caravan bearing my camel arrived in Babylon than Nebuchadrezzar returned from his campaign, bringing with him all the camels he had plundered from the Arabs. Since these camels had cost the king nothing he sold them cheaply in the market place, causing the price of camels to drop overnight. While those who purchased the beasts at a low price praised the king, those who had brought in camels at great cost cursed him.

"Surely the king will utterly ruin the country," the merchant said to me when next I visited him. "How are we to pay our taxes if he undersells us, depriving us of our meager profits?"

But when I wept with despair at my loss, he counseled me not to be disheartened, for one who would gain in business must also be willing to lose.

Then I confessed that I did not weep for my silver but for my friend, whose freedom I had thought to buy. And when the merchant would know more about Tarqu—for he found it strange that I should wish to buy another's freedom rather than my own—I said:

"But for my friend I should not be alive today. Twice he snatched me from the jaws of death, when I had utterly lost the will to live. But I have failed to repay his kindness and find him a good master, one who would count himself fortunate to own a slave like

Tarqu. For not only is my friend a man of great beauty, but he also has the strength of three, being able to lift a heavy sack of barley as if it were filled with the lightest lamb's fleece."

"Indeed I could use such a slave myself," the merchant said, as I had hoped he would. "Those who unload my merchandise from the ships are weaklings who stagger under the loads and often drop them. Only last week I lost two precious Egyptian vases made of the finest alabaster. Now that the king has forbidden the bringing in of Egyptian goods, I must buy these vases at twice their former price in Tyre and bring them to Babylonia concealed in sacks of barley. Therefore, if you will travel to Borsippa and buy your friend for me, I shall give you a letter to a merchant there, who will finance the purchase against my future payment."

I took no offense because the merchant would not trust me with the needed silver, for thirty-five shekels was a great sum. Indeed I welcomed it when he signed his letter before witnesses, for trust between friends is a good thing, but a sealed contract is better.

Taking this letter home with me, I begged my master to let me visit Borsippa. I had served him faithfully for nine years and knew he would not deny me a short leave from Babylon. Indeed he put his permission in writing, for though I did not look a slave and would not be stopped at the gate, my former owner in Borsippa might stir up trouble if he recognized me.

Then, armed with two letters, I set out on my journey to Borsippa. I still had enough silver left to buy passage on a ship that had unloaded wood from the Sea Lands in Babylon, and was now taking a cargo of sesame seeds back to Uruk. It was a lovely day in the month of Iyar, some two weeks after the end of the New Year Festival, when the heat was not yet upon the land and the breeze that swelled the sails of the ship did not parch one's mouth and nostrils. As we slowly drifted down the Euphrates I could see the grain standing high and yellow on either side of the river, with blades as broad as a man's hand. The barley had ripened early, and after the harvest the fields would be plowed and seeded again, to yield a second crop.

Among the sailors aboard ship were some from Tyre, the best in all the world. They were pleased to discover that I knew their language and conversed with me at great length, boasting of their city which—they said—could never be conquered. Though Tyre

stood in the midst of the sea, she had her own source of sweet
water, nor would she ever lack for provisions, which could be
brought from Egypt, Cyprus or Greece.

"Though Nebuchadrezzar conquer all the world, he shall never
conquer Tyre!" the sailors said. "He may have a powerful army,
but they do not know how to sail ships, nor do they control the
Great Sea."

But it was too fine a day to discuss the king's wars, past or future.
I would sooner savor the sight of the rich fields and orchards along
the river's edge, of tall date palms swaying in the breeze and willows
trailing their branches in the water, of the rhythmic swinging back
and forth of the shaduf—the pail fastened to the long pole with
which water was scooped out of the canals to irrigate the fields—
and the movement of men and donkeys along the path by the river.

I thought of how I had been but a poor slave dressed in tatters
when I rode up that path nine years ago, sitting on a donkey behind
my master, and how I now returned dressed in fine garments, and
with a letter for the purchase of my dearest friend. And I pictured
in my mind how my former master and his wretched wife would
bow down low when I entered their bazaar—for surely they would
not recognize me—how they would haggle with me over Tarqu's
price but would sell him in the end, lured by the profit. Only then
would I make myself known to them so as to savor my triumph
doubly. Then Tarqu and I would fall into each other's arms, shed
many tears, and depart together for Babylon to live happily ever
after.

The sight of the great temple of Nebo beyond the walls of
Borsippa tore me from my daydreams. Remembering my wretched
state when I had first beheld this temple, I had to blink back my
tears. But when one of the sailors stared at me curiously, I repeated
what I had said to Tarqu many years ago:

"It is but the sun getting in my eyes."

After we had docked in Borsippa I bade my sailor friends farewell
and set out to find the merchant to whom I bore the letter. He
greeted me with great courtesy, read the letter, stroked his beard
and said:

"I shall gladly do as my friend in Babylon bids me. But first you
had better find out whether this slave has not been sold already.
Nine years are a long time, and much has changed in Borsippa."

Though this thought should have troubled me earlier, I had never allowed it to enter my mind. Now I hurried toward the bazaar of my former master as if my haste could make up for the delay of nine years. My heart beat easier when I saw that the store was still where it had been. I approached the woman who sat in the entrance and spoke to her in a haughty voice, but whn she looked up I saw that she was not Harshinana. Though my former mistress might have aged in nine years, she could not have become as old and ugly as the one before me. But since one could never be certain with a woman, I asked to see the master.

The woman rose and disappeared into the store which I had swept so often, while I wondered whether the merchant had divorced Harshinana and taken another wife—though why he should take one old and ugly I could not fathom. But when the woman returned with her husband I saw that this was not the man who had caused me to lose my manhood. My former master had been fat and confident, but the one before me was haggard and worried-looking. He seized me by the arm and pulled me inside his bazaar to praise his wares to me.

"I did not come to make a purchase but to see the former owner of this store," I said. "Can my lord tell me where I might find him?"

The man and the woman exchanged a glance of concern. Then the man replied:

"If my lord were impious enough to disturb the dead, he might find him lying in the ground. Indeed he has been buried these five years."

"Dead!" I exclaimed, my heart filled with the woe that comes with having one's triumph snatched away. "But surely his wife must be alive, for she was still a young woman! And how did her husband die? And did she inherit his fortune after all?"

Again the man and his wife glanced at each other as if frightened by my many questions.

"We bought this store in a lawful manner from the widow Harshinana, and have a sealed and witnessed contract to prove it. But whither she went we do not know, nor do we know how her husband died," the man said to me. "And now, if my lord does not wish to buy anything, I must look after my own business."

Seizing him by his garment as he turned, I exclaimed:

"There is one purchase I wish to make! I would buy the slave Tarqu who belonged to the former owner!"

"I know of no such slave," the man said.

"But surely my lord must have seen him—a tall Ethiopian of great strength and beauty!"

"If ever there was such an Ethiopian, he was sold before we bought this store. As for us, we can ill afford a slave. Business has not been good, what with the king bringing in much plunder and selling it cheaply in the market."

Neither he nor his wife would say more to me, but pushed me out of the store and shut the door in my face. And when I went from neighbor to neighbor, inquiring about my former master, his wife and Tarqu, all looked strangely at me, but none would answer my questions. In the end one of them said:

"Surely my lord has been gone from Borsippa a long time not to have heard the story. But I shall not repeat it, for I will not spend my days in court bearing testimony to things of which I know nothing. As for the slave Tarqu, I remember him well. Soon after her husband's death the widow Harshinana sold him to a slave dealer, who carried him off with his caravan, whither I do not know."

Great as was my despair then, I still had one hope left of finding Tarqu. Perchance he had let his sister and her husband know of his fate. I hired a donkey to ride out to the farm which had belonged to my first master Iddina, for I remembered that it was a long trek on foot. But the distance was not as great as it had seemed to me when I was a young boy with sore, bare feet and a welt on my back inflicted by the merchant's rod.

It was a long time since I had breathed the barnyard smell of dung, chicken droppings, and the damp pelts of cattle, and heard the creaking of the shaduf as it swung across the fields. Iddina's land had been good land that bore richly except in the years when the river brought up the flood. I could see that this was a good year, for the grain stood almost as high as my head.

Again I gave myself over to daydreams. Surely Taia would be astonished to see me again. She had known me since I was a babe, and like her brother she had once saved my life. Again I marveled at my own ingratitude, for I had never even sought to discover whether she was still alive. Her own first-born would now be nearly as old as I was when I was carried away from Nineveh.

The house where the family had lived in former times still looked the same. I knocked at the door, expecting Iddina's mother to bid me come in. But the voice that answered was that of a man, and when I entered I found that all the people within the house were strangers to me.

My inquiries were answered with another tale of woe. Two years after Iddina had sold Tarqu and me to raise silver for seed, there had been a plague of locusts that had destroyed his fields. Then Iddina had obtained a loan by pledging his farm. But he had been unable to redeem his pledge and had lost his land, his house and all his possessions. His mother had died of grief. His younger brothers and sisters had sold themselves into slavery, while Iddina and Taia had earned their keep by hiring themselves out to work on other farms. But such was their plight that they had to sell their first-born into slavery and put up their younger children for adoption that they might not starve to death. However, they continued near their former home until about a year ago, when they received a letter from Babylon. Since neither Iddina nor his wife knew how to read, they went to Borsippa to find a scribe. That was the last anyone saw of them. They never returned from Borsippa, nor did any of the neighbors know where they had gone.

Then I relinquished all hope of finding Tarqu again. It would be as fruitless to search for him as it had been to search for my father's slayer among the many thousand times thousand inhabitants of Babylonia. As I rode back to Borsippa I let my tears flow freely, nor did I pretend to myself that it was but the sun getting in my eyes. For I had let the years slip by, thinking that while I lived in Babylon time stood still in other places so that I would find everything unchanged if ever I wished to go back. But time is of one piece, and men who think it will halt for them are but simple-minded fools.

After my return to Babylon I still grieved for many weeks. But even though I had given up hope of finding Tarqu, I continued to save my silver and to take increase on it, for once acquired the habit can never again be broken.

And there were other things to take my mind off my loss. The boy David was now seven years old, of an age to be taught reading and writing. Thus the lie my master had told his wife when first he brought me home turned to truth, for I had indeed become his son's tutor. I also taught the boy Hebrew, and he grasped the language with the ease of a young child.

As for my lord Nabukasir, he never mastered Hebrew. Though he could read and write the words, when he spoke them aloud the sound grated on one's ears. He made me think of some bright boys with whom I had gone to school. Though they could converse brilliantly in their own tongue, they were never able to learn another.

But not all my time with David was given to studying. The boy loved to hear stories, and holding him on my knee I would tell him the tale of Gilgamesh and Enkidu, and of Utnapishtim, the wise boatman who built a ship for his family and his beasts and who survived the great flood to become himself immortal. But the tale David loved best was the one about the happy land of Dilmun, where the lion did not kill, the wolf did not tear the sheep, and there was neither sickness nor old age nor death.

It was on a mild day in the month of Heshvan, before the raw winter months came to Babylon, that I sat in the courtyard with David upon my knee. The lady Margidda had taken her daughter and the nurse to visit one of her women friends, as was her custom. It was quiet and peaceful in the garden as I sat rocking the boy in my arms. My singsong voice, the trickling of the fountain and the rustling of the palm trees had made him drowsy so that he put his face against my chest and fell asleep. These were for me golden moments. With the soft body of the child leaning against me, I pretended that he was my son, and the courtyard in which we sat my courtyard, and the fountain my fountain, and the palm tree my palm tree. Then I only need close my eyes to imagine that what had happened to me had never happened, that I was still in Nineveh, and that I would soon hear the voice of my mother calling me.

The voice that tore me from my dream was not that of my mother but that of my master, rising to such a furious pitch that I stiffened with terror. I had never heard him utter such curses, which woke the boy in my arms so that he started with a frightened whimper.

"Let him put me in prison then!" my master shouted within the house. "Let him throw me in the fire! Let him have me torn limb from limb! But he shall not force me to go up with him in war against Judah!"

Though I could not see to whom my lord was speaking I could well imagine who was his visitor. I quickly put David down and hastened to shut the door which led into the garden, lest any of the neighbors overhear my master's rash words. But even before I could seize him, the boy ran past me through the door into the room where his father stood shouting at the Captain Holofernes:

"Should I, a Hebrew, bear arms against my own people?"

"Pray keep your voice down, Nabukasir," the captain replied. "The king's plans are not yet known save to a few of his captains. Nor need you go shouting all over town that you are a Hebrew at a time when these wretched Hebrews provoked the king to make war on them. Indeed you are not a Hebrew but a Chaldean, like the king, and your loyalty should be unto him. Did he not carry you out of the flames on his own back?"

Then my master wept with rage and exclaimed:

"Shall I never be rid of this debt?

　" 'Do we build a house forever?
　　Do we seal contracts forever?
　　Do brothers divide shares forever?
　　Does hatred persist forever in the land?
　　Does the river forever rise up and bring on floods?
　　The dragonfly leaves its shell
　　That its face might but glance at the face of the sun!' "

"For one who calls himself a Hebrew, you know our old poetry well," the Captain Holofernes said. "But you would leave out the most important part." And looking hard at my master, he added:

　" 'Since the days of yore there has been no permanence.
　　The resting and the dead, how alike they are!' "

David stood leaning against me, and I could feel the trembling of his slender body. He had never heard his father and the Captain Holofernes raise their voices at each other. And, though he could not understand their words, he was frightened. Then the captain's glance fell on the boy. He approached David, picked him up, and holding him so that they were face to face, he asked:

"Now you tell me, my boy—are you a Hebrew or a Babylonian?"

Glancing from the captain to his father and back again, David whispered with trembling lips:

"A Babylonian, my lord."

"Even a small child can see the truth!" the captain said to my master. But that one replied:

"Does it not suffice that the king torments me? Must you torment my son? Put the boy down and cease from asking him questions to which he cannot know the answers!"

Turning to me, my master bade me take David from the room. I led the boy to the kitchen and bade the cook give him some date cakes and honey that his thoughts might be turned from what he had heard. Then I crept back to the room where my master and the captain stood arguing, for my heart was heavy, and I would learn the cause why Nebuchadrezzar planned to march against Judah. I remained standing in the open door—not hidden so that they might not suspect me of eavesdropping—yet in such a manner that I could swiftly depart if I were so commanded.

"And would Nebuchadrezzar go up against Jerusalem if this wretched Hebrew king had not refused to pay him tribute?" the captain shouted just as I arrived at the door.

"What is the tribute of a poor country like Judah to one as great and rich as Babylonia?" my master asked.

"Surely even you must know that the king would not wage this war for plunder," the captain replied. "But if the king of Judah goes unpunished for refusing his tribute to Babylon, there will soon be rebellion among all the vassal kingdoms! While one is powerless, many banded together are strong enough to drive our garrisons out of Syria. And without our garrisons, we would soon have those wretched Egyptians at the very walls of Babylon. Truly the king has no choice but to make war on Judah if he would have us keep our liberty, which was bought with the blood of many brave soldiers!"

"Let him do then what he must do," Nabukasir said. "But of what use would *I* be to him on this campaign?"

"Indeed you would be of great use to Nebuchadrezzar, for it is known that you learned the Hebrew tongue from your insolent slave Marduksharusur, who stands listening in the door to what is not meant for his ears. If you could persuade these Hebrews to cease their defiance, you might save Jerusalem—which is so dear to your heart, though you never even beheld it—and also spare the king the loathsome task of having to destroy yet another city, which he has vowed never to do again."

"Jerusalem refused to surrender even to the great king Sen-nacherib," my master said. "But if the city defied Nebuchadrezzar, I would have to attack the walls with the rest of the troops, seize the palace, and set fire to the temple of my own God! This thing even the king of Babylon can never make me do!"

And my master strode angrily from the room. The Captain Holofernes remained behind, pacing to and fro just as angrily, his boots clattering on the baked-brick floor and his long sword whip-ping against his thigh. Suddenly he swung around, pointed his finger at me and shouted:

"How would you, who thinks himself so wise, tell the king that your master refused to bear arms for him? And should I be the one to be charged by the king with slaying the man who saved my life at Nineveh?"

Seeing that the captain had spoken in greater earnest than he would have it appear, I gave the matter some thought, and then I replied:

"If the captain truly seeks my advice, I should speak thus to the king: 'My lord knows well that Nabukasir fought bravely for him in many campaigns, to which the scars on his body bear witness. But it might not be wise to make him go to war against those whom he still considers his own people. Strange things might happen in his heart were he to set foot on the soil of his forefathers, and to tempt a faithful servant to become a traitor is tempting the gods. As for a man who can speak to the Hebrews in their own tongue, there are others in Babylon who could serve the king better than Nabukasir. His slave tells me that my friend speaks the language poorly, and that he should wreak havoc rather than good were he to be made ambassador.' "

When I finished this speech, the captain gazed at me with admiration and said:

"Truly, Marduksharusur, what was taken from you in your members was restored to you in the nimbleness of your tongue! Unless I utterly confuse your words in repeating them to the king, they might yet get your master exempted from this campaign!"

A few days later the Captain Holofernes returned with the good news that my counsel had saved my master.

"Not only did I repeat to the king all your words," the captain said, "but I added some of mine. 'As for employing Nabukasir to deal with the Hebrews,' I said, 'why take the pupil if one can have the teacher? Does not the slave Marduksharusur speak the Hebrew tongue better than his master? And if he were to shout the orders for surrender to those defending the walls of Jerusalem, and one should take it into his head to shoot him with an arrow, would not the loss be smaller than if Nabukasir were killed?' Thus, by my words, was the king persuaded to bestow upon you the honor of traveling with the army as the royal interpreter!"

The blood fled from my face, for when I thought of the ruse to save my master I had not planned to go to war in his stead.

"My lord has given the king evil counsel," I said to the captain. "I have never been on a campaign and will surely perish of fatigue long before we reach Jerusalem. If the king would have an interpreter who is also a warrior, let him use one of the Israelite charioteers who were captured at Nineveh and pressed into service in the Babylonian army."

Frowning, the captain gazed at me with suspicion.

"How does a common slave know so much about our army?" he asked. "If you had not served my friend Nabukasir these nine years, I should take you for a spy. But then spies are bold men, while you have the heart of a woman. As for those Israelite charioteers, I would not lead them to war against Judah, for strange things might happen in the hearts of these men were they to set foot on the soil of their forefathers," the captain said, turning my own words back upon me. "I should sooner trust an Assyrian like you, Marduk-sharusur, even though you love your Hebrew master. But I, who also love your master, know well that one might cherish one Hebrew and yet despise the rest of them. Moreover, your service to the king shall count in your master's favor, for Nebuchadrezzar knows how my friend dotes on you, nor shall the king fail to value his sacrifice."

"My lord might well call me a sacrifice," I said. "Indeed I shall be no better than a lamb being led to slaughter!"

But slapping my back, the captain only laughed and said:

"Have you forgotten that my fate and yours will not be sealed until the goddess Ishtar descends from on high? Unless she has moved her seat from Uruk to Jerusalem our lives will be safe! And now you had better settle such business as needs looking after, for the army is to march for Judah early in the month of Kislev!"

I had no choice but resign myself to my fate. If I was destined to follow the Babylonian army to Jerusalem, it must be the will of God. How else would I ever see the city where my grandfather's father had ruled as king? Deep in my mind there was also another thought: I would be traveling with many thousands of soldiers. Perchance I might yet discover among them my father's slayer—though how I would deal with him if I found him I did not know.

As for settling my affairs before my departure, the only one needing attention was my investments. If I failed to return alive from this campaign, my master would be my lawful heir. And though I trusted the man who handled my silver, I thought it wise to leave my master the contracts I had made with the merchant that all might be in writing if matters ever came before a judge.

My master was deeply distraught when I delivered my clay tablets to him. Like many a rich man's son who never had to tend to business, he despised dealing with silver. But I said I would sooner add my fortune to the inheritance of David, whom I loved like a son, than leave it in the hands of the merchant, who was but a friend in sharing my profits.

Then my master embraced me and said:

"If you were to go to war against any other nation, I would lend you my own sword. But I shall not have my sword carried against Judah."

"My lord's sword should serve me for nought but to inflict injury upon myself," I replied. "Moreover, I am to render services of peace to the king—should I live to carry them out."

Of this I was not at all certain. Therefore I shed many tears as I bade the lady Margidda and the little maiden Hegala farewell. But when I embraced the boy David I thought my heart would break. He too wept—not because I was leaving but because he wanted to come with me. And even as I walked away from the house I heard him calling after me:

"When I grow up I too shall go to war against Judah! I too shall go to war against Judah!"

And now I was a soldier in the army of the king of Babylon, however, a soldier armed with a stylus rather than with a sword.

The Captain Holofernes had provided me with a donkey. But I had never ridden much before, and after two days my seat was so sore that I preferred to walk. Yet not having walked long stretches since I was carried away from Nineveh, I soon found my soles covered with blisters and my legs buckling under me. Then I abandoned all shame and went to ride in the oxcarts with the harlots—for wherever the army went the harlots and dream diviners followed, that the soldiers might not be utterly without the comforts of home.

As for the army, it was indeed one to strike terror into the hearts of an enemy. First went the chariot corps, with four men to each chariot—one driver, one archer and two shield-bearers to cover them. The chariots were solidly built, with eight spoked wheels, sturdy axles, and two horses to draw each one.

Behind them came the troops of horsemen riding upon their horses, each a governor and captain to look upon. The manes of their horses were braided, and there were tassels on their harnesses and saddles. According to their designation, the horsemen carried spears or bows, and swords girded about their waists. All were shod in boots, Babylonia being a rich nation. The muscles on the bare arms of the riders bulged as they held the reins, and their short kilts revealed their sinewy legs. All were handsome young men, but the most handsome among them was the Captain Holofernes.

Last came the foot soldiers—thousands upon thousands marching in columns ten abreast and twenty one behind the other. Their gleaming metal helmets were padded with sheep's wool and lined with oxhide to protect the heads of the wearers. Their coats of mail were made of scales of sturdy leather, one scale overlapping the other, like the scales of a fish. The leather was dyed red to ensure good fortune, and so was the leather covering their shields of plaited wicker. And even the foot soldiers wore boots, Babylonia's wealth exceeding that of all other nations. The wooden spears of the spearmen had metal tips. The archers' quivers were filled with metal-tipped arrows. The slingers carried their slings and stones, and all wore girded about their waists the long, straight swords needed for close combat.

The Captain Holofernes, who was over the horsemen, would ride back and forth along the columns of soldiers, more splendid to look upon than all the rest. His eyes shone, and when he opened his mouth in laughter his teeth sparkled white through his black beard.

He had grown the beard when he turned thirty years of age, for it was no longer seemly that he walk about with his chin naked, like a youth or a eunuch. The captain would jest with the soldiers as he passed them, and then he would gallop back to where I rode in the oxcart with the harlots and roar with laughter, shouting that the space I took up among them was a waste to me and to them. But the harlots would call out to him such proposals as are not seemly for me to repeat, offering to do all these things for him without pay, if only they might boast of having been honored by his embrace.

However, not only the harlots and I followed after the army. There was also a multitude of camels and pack asses loaded with provisions, with grain, oil and wine, with dried meat and dates, with harnesses for the horses, and spare wheels and axles for the chariots. For many chariots broke down on the march and had to be mended, while their drivers stood by, cursing bitterly and proclaiming that they remembered how chariots had been better in olden times. There were carts for carrying the battering rams, which were dismantled for the transport, and for the high towers from which the archers covered the battering rams when they moved to attack the walls of a city. There were physicians to treat wounds suffered in battle or toothaches sent by evil demons. There were scribes to keep account of the pay to the army, and others to write out orders for provisions, which were sent ahead to the vassal towns along the route of the march. For it was impossible to carry along enough food for such a numerous army. And there were quartermasters who handled the food and who all lived in terror of the king, for now and then he would come unannounced to make certain that none of them stole more than was seemly to sell to the soldiers for his own profit.

Though I saw the king from afar every year at the New Year Festival, I had not seen him from close by since his visit to my master while he was still the crown prince. I was amazed by how much he had aged in the seven years of his reign. Indeed he appeared old enough to be the father of the Captain Holofernes, though there were but a few years between them. But his vigor was undiminished even by his stouter girth, and he consented to ride in a chariot only because it was not fitting for the king to ride among his horsemen.

When the army struck camp at night, a separate place was fenced

in for the king that he might not be troubled by the multitude. But
he would often come forth to walk about the camp, to converse
with his captains and soldiers, to harass the quartermasters, and to
wake the scribes. For whenever an evil dream woke the king, he
would not return to sleep but would pass the night reading dispatches from the governors of his vast kingdom, or dictating dispatches to them. Where before one scribe had sufficed, two were
needed now, for there were few who could go without sleep like
the king. Moreover, his temper had become short so that he often
raised his voice in anger at those who could neither think nor act as
swiftly as he. At that time they began to say about Nebuchadrezzar
that he was as ugly as the dragon Humbawa, that he roared like
Humbawa, and that he needed no sleep like Humbawa. Some even
whispered that the king had no need of a woman, like Humbawa,
for he never summoned a harlot to his tent. But the queen had borne
him a daughter and a son, thus giving the lie to these slanderers.

Creeping along the northern edge of the Great Desert like a long,
deadly snake that churned up clouds of yellow dust as it moved
along, the Babylonian army came nearer Judah every day. On the
twenty-first day we reached Tadmor, and a few days later Damascus came in sight like the dream of a thirsty man, with its green,
luxuriant gardens, swaying palm trees and the clear, rushing water
of its rivers.

After the long trek across the desert many soldiers plunged into
the rivers with their garments on, but the Captain Holofernes was not
ashamed to strip naked to bathe himself, and wash his hair and his
beard. The only thing he kept on his body was the chain with the
image of the goddess Ishtar, which his mother had given him to
hang about the neck of the woman whom he would have bear him
seven sons. As I observed the captain swimming in the river—for he
was a good and fearless swimmer—and beheld his body, firm as if it
were cast in copper, I wondered whether our fates were truly
linked together. Save for the scars on our wrists, we had not a thing
in common. As for the captain, he gave little thought to our fate,
drying himself after his bath and singing such songs as "Oh,
Gardener of the Garden of Desires" and "I Saw Two Harlots in the
Market Place." He had a fine voice that should have pleased my
father, though he might have frowned at the tunes.

At Damascus the army pitched camp to allow the soldiers a respite and to replenish its water and provisions. I spent my days mingling with the troops and searching out soldiers who had scars on their foreheads. But as in my early days in Babylon I never discovered the one whose dreadful laughter I still remembered.

While we were encamped, all the Syrian kings came to prostrate themselves before Nebuchadrezzar and to kiss his feet—all but the king of Tyre, who felt secure in his city that stood in the sea. It was at Damascus that Nebuchadrezzar learned from his spies, who had returned from Judah, that King Jehoiakim had died, and that his young son Jehoiachin had been made king over Judah. There were some who believed that the former king had been murdered to make surrender less dishonorable and that Jerusalem would not resist. But others warned that this might only be a ruse used by the Hebrews to confuse the Babylonians.

Before breaking camp at Damascus, the king met with his captains in secret talks, whose contents were soon known, as is common with secret talks. There had been a great debate over which route to take to Jerusalem. The captains preferred to go by way of Megiddo and down through the pass along the Sea Road, which was the least difficult approach. The spies had revealed that there had been much rain in the north of the land, and the flooded marshes along the other routes might slow progress and make it dangerous. But the king would take the army from Megiddo to Tanach and thence to Dotan that he might approach Jerusalem from the north, by way of Samaria. When the captains showed themselves wary of crossing the hill country, where the enemy might lie in ambush, Nebuchadrezzar commanded the priests to search the omens. The priests gazed at the stars, examined the livers of sacrifices, cast the sticks, and delivered the omens which suited the king's plans.

Thus, after the army broke camp at Damascus, we proceeded south across the Syrian mountains, past Lake Merom, through Hazor and on down through the hills until, passing Mount Tabor on our left, we entered the Valley of Jezreel. And there before us opened the rich plains where so many battles had been fought— where Pharaoh Tutmoses had battled the King of Kadesh and all his allies; where the armies of Barak and Deborah had vanquished Sisera by the Brook of Kishon; where the Philistines had beaten King Saul in battle and had taken his body to nail to the walls of Beth Shean;

and where King Josiah had fallen a hero in trying to hold back all the host of Egypt with a handful of men.

The land was barren now, for it was winter and the fields were flooded by the rains. But the road on which the army moved was raised above the fields so that the chariots rarely became mired in the mud. The worst suffering was caused us by the small marsh flies which suck one's blood and make the skin swell. Many soldiers were seized by the evil marsh demons who rack travelers with fevers against which even the exorcisers are powerless. Some of the sick died on the way and were buried outside Megiddo, in the ground where the fallen soldiers of many nations lay buried. It is said that they all shall rise when the last great battle on earth will be fought on this very site.

From Megiddo the army headed west as though to return whence it had come, following the slow rise of the land toward Tanach. Though the sky was cloudy the air was clear, and looking south one could see the Mountains of Samaria rising in range after range. But in the distance they looked neither high nor worthy of the concern the captains had professed.

Not until we entered the Dotan Pass did the hills close in on us. Though they were not steep, their dense forests were capable of concealing an enemy lurking beside the narrow road. But the pass soon opened into the Valley of Dotan, which spread between the ranges from east to west. There, where they could not be taken by surprise, the troops pitched camp for the night.

Next morning the soldiers proceeded without dismay until they arrived at the southern edge of the Dotan Valley, where the road suddenly began to curve and rise steeply into the high hills. Then a change came over the troops. While they had been loud and boisterous before, shouting and singing as they marched along, they now fell silent, glancing forward, sideways and back over their shoulders at the hills rising on either side of the road. For they were men born in the vast plains of Babylonia, where one could observe the movements of troops in the very distance, and they dreaded the thickly wooded hills from which an enemy might swoop down on them when least they thought of it.

Moreover, the road was become so bad now that the chariots broke down more often than before, hampering the movement of the troops. The horses stumbled and slipped in the mud caused by the daily rains. At night the soldiers in their soaked garments huddled around the fires, starting at every strange sound, and cursing the war and the Hebrews who had forced them to come to this savage country. However, we had not yet reached the border of Judah, which was still some distance to the south of us.

On and on, upward and upward, the army trekked through the hills without encountering resistance. Though the soldiers were drenched much of the time and in great discomfort, none had yet been wounded in battle. Nor was I summoned to render my services until we reached the place where once the city of Samaria had stood, before it was destroyed by King Sargon. From the mound there was a splendid view of the valley and of the high hills in the west. Though bare now, the fields in the valley looked rich and fertile, and there were groves of olive and fruit trees on the hillside. It was easy to see why King Omri had chosen this site to build himself a fortress.

It was in Samaria that I was first called upon to prove my skill as interpreter. But when I spoke to the people of the land in Hebrew they looked at me askance, or laughed and poked each other in the ribs. For these were the sons of the people whom King Sargon had brought to Samaria after carrying away the Israelites. These strangers had mingled with the Hebrews who were left, and as they had mingled so had their tongues, until in the end they spoke neither the one nor the other, but a mixture of all.

When the Captain Holofernes saw that they did not understand me, he said:

"It seems that you speak Hebrew even worse than Nabukasir, and that you deceived me into obtaining this post for you that you might steal your master's glory!"

"Did I not beg my lord to find another interpreter for the king and to let me remain in Babylon?" I replied.

I was not only angry with the captain, but also hurt in my pride. For these Samarian peasants did not understand the fine Hebrew that was spoken at court in the times of King Hezekiah, when the Prophet Isaiah had preached in the land. But by good fortune Nebuchadrezzar had not yet commanded my services. He led the army straight up the road toward Jerusalem, without inquiring of every peasant along the way how far it was from one village to the next, as did all his captains. For it was they who had to soothe and calm their soldiers, who were wary of this unknown land.

And still the road rose steeply, past ancient Shechem and Mount Gerizim, between the encroaching hills that did not recede again until we reached the Valley of Shiloh, where in times of yore the sons of Benjamin had carried off the maidens who came to dance before the walls at the time of the grape harvest. The valley opened toward the east, circling the foot of the hill where once Shiloh had stood. The soil of the fallow fields was black from the rain that ran off the hills to water the valley below. When we arrived there early in the morning, white patches of mist floated above the fields like the souls of dead men who had found no burial. But the mists succumbed to the rising sun, and the army pitched camp in the valley before continuing to Jerusalem.

The soldiers had heard that the daughters of the land were of great beauty. But when they went looking for them they found that the peasants had fled with their women into the woods. But they discovered much of the famous wine of the region and carried it back to the camp with them, to drink themselves drunk at night.

Next morning we continued to Jerusalem. And still the road climbed up the hills until it leveled off not far from Ramah. It was from there that one could first see Jerusalem. The news spread back from column to column until it reached the rearguard, where I rode in one of the oxcarts. Then I dismounted and walked the last stretch on foot, for I would not have my first glimpse of the sacred city in the company of harlots.

My heart beat wildly when I saw houses in the distance, but soon they disappeared again between the hills that broke like low waves across the almost level plain. To the south and west of us there were still more mountain ranges, but they were far off, nor would the army have to cross them. For now we were on land higher than Jerusalem.

Not long after we had passed the road that led off east toward Anathoth, Jerusalem came fully in sight, lying below us to the south. And when I beheld at the summit of Mount Moriah the Temple of the Lord and Solomon's Palace, I wept with joy and sorrow. Joy for seeing at last the city where my grandfather's father had sat on the throne, and sorrow for having come to the land of my forefathers with the host of a conqueror.

But when those about me asked why I wept, I said it was from fatigue after the long march. Nor could I pretend that it was the sun getting in my eyes, for the sky was gray and the wintry hills a dull yellowish brown beneath the slight drizzle. I had heard that from where I stood one could behold the Salt Sea in the east, but it was hidden by the mist.

While I stood gazing at the land of which I had only heard tales as a boy, the entire Babylonian army had poured forth from among the low hills to engulf Jerusalem like a rising flood. The people of the land had fled within the walls, barred the gates and put soldiers on the towers. But I wondered whether the hearts of these men who would defend Jerusalem did not freeze at the sight before them.

For the army of the king of Babylon had drawn near the walls with its thousands upon thousands of soldiers, with their countless chariots manned by four men each, and their horsemen upon horses riding in pairs. Soon the soldiers would mount the battering rams and the movable towers from which the archers could aim at those on the walls. But the men of Jerusalem did not open their gates, neither did they send ambassadors to offer their surrender. And Nebuchadrezzar's army pitched camp and made ready for the siege.

A month passed and a second month, and still the defenders of Jerusalem would not open the gates. None had come forth from the walls but some deserters who fled in the dark of night. These were trapped by the earthworks the Babylonians had thrown up all around Jerusalem, and taken before the king to be questioned. Since I acted as their interpreter, I know all they revealed.

They said the city could hold out a long time yet, for there was enough water in Jerusalem since King Hezekiah had built a conduit from the Gihon spring to the pool of Siloam. Also the people had driven their livestock within the city and had laid up much provisions, pulse and grain, wine and oil, for the harvest had been good. There were many who believed that the Egyptians would soon come to their aid and who wished to fight the king of Babylon. But one prophet, Jeremiah by name, weakened the hands of the soldiers by proclaiming that God would give all the nations into the hand of Nebuchadrezzar and that Jerusalem too should fall to him.

And when the king would learn more about this Jeremiah, the deserters told him that the prophet had fled Jerusalem and had lived hidden many years—where none knew—for King Jehoiakim had sought his life. But now Jeremiah was returned to Jerusalem, urging the new king and his princes to surrender.

"Truly we must reward this man," Nebuchadrezzar said. "If we take Jerusalem by force, let every soldier look out for him that he might not be slain."

But when he had heard all the deserters had to tell, Nebuchadrezzar resolved to wait yet a little while before storming the walls. Perchance the Hebrew god would deliver Jerusalem into his hand without a battle. Moreover, the king knew that the losses of the attacker always exceeded those of the defender, and he was loath to see his soldiers killed.

As for the Captain Holofernes and all the other captains, they hated this sitting war. They continually had to employ their soldiers digging trenches and throwing up earthworks—even if those should never be used—lest the men fall to quarreling among themselves out of boredom.

The troops suffered sorely from the daily rains. They were always wet and cold, their boots covered with mud and their swords rusty so that they found no respite from polishing their weapons. To make matters worse, the people who dwelled around Jerusalem had taken their cattle and women within the city. The soldiers could find neither without wandering far afield, and this they did but rarely for fear of an ambush. When they found women these were plain peasant women, who pleased only the country lads among them. But those who came from the big cities—from Babylon, Borsippa, Nippur, Uruk and Lagash—grumbled and longed for women who knew how to dress, put up their hair, paint their eyes and perfume their bodies, and whose speech they could understand.

When the men did not speak of women they spoke of food. They cursed the army cooks and dreamed of the day when they would sit down to a meal prepared by their wives or mothers—above all a meal of roast pork, for there was hardly a pig to be found in all of Judah. Listening to the men, one would have thought that the greatest hardship caused them by the war was that they could not obtain their familiar food.

Yet there were greater hardships. The dampness and cold caused many soldiers to be seized by fevers that brought on coughs and pains in the chest. Some began to spit up blood, their breath would come rattling through their lips, and they would die. While they had blamed the fevers of the plains on the marsh demons, they blamed this new plague on the demons of the hills.

Swearing bitterly, the Captain Holofernes said:

"If not for the tales of this Hebrew god which the deserters planted in the king's ear, we should long have seized Jerusalem! At any rate it were better to attack this wretched city, for we are losing more men to sickness than we would lose in battle. Moreover, the king promised that the troops would be back in Babylon for the New Year Festival. But it is already the month of Shebat, and we are still besieging this accursed Jerusalem!"

It was not until the third month after the army had encamped before Jerusalem—and still the city had not surrendered—that the omens for an attack were propitious. Whether the omens were sent by the gods, or whether the priests too had tired of the siege and wished to be back in Babylon for the New Year, I do not know. But on the first day of Adar the priests informed Nebuchadrezzar that the time was ripe for Jerusalem to fall into his hands. How this was to come about—whether by attack, ruse or negotiation—the omens would not reveal. And when the Captain Holofernes learned that Nebuchadrezzar would offer the city yet one more chance to surrender, he uttered such curses as were new even to me, a scholar and student of the Babylonian tongue.

But this was to be my great moment. The king summoned me to his tent and dictated to me the conditions of surrender that I might translate them into Hebrew. And Nebuchadrezzar swore by all his gods that if King Jehoiachin and his wives and his mother and his princes would come forth and surrender to him, he would not attack Jerusalem, neither would he sack and burn the city. But he would take prisoner only those who had caused the rebellion and carry them away captives with the king to Babylon. Neither would he allow his soldiers to loot Jerusalem but would take for his booty only such treasures from the palace and the temple as were the custom for the conqueror to take. Moreover, he would spare the lives of the people and would share among them the land taken from the rich, that those who had not sown this year because of the siege might harvest doubly the following year. But if King Jehoiachin would not heed his words and surrender, Nebuchadrezzar would attack Jerusalem with all his armed might, break down the walls, burn the palace and the temple, and turn the city into a heap of ruins as he had done to Nineveh and Ashkelon.

And the king added still more threats lest his offer of mercy fail
to persuade Jehoiachin and the princes.

After I had recorded all these words on a clay tablet, I was given
a scroll of parchment that I might translate them into Hebrew. And
the king named me his ambassador, ordering me to shout his message
up to the defenders on the walls of Jerusalem. When I learned of
this honor my knees began to knock together, for my voice was
weak, and I would have to approach near the wall lest my words be
carried away by the wind. But I did not dare reveal my fears to the
king. Rather I sought out the Captain Holofernes to bewail my new
exalted position. But he only mocked me, saying:

"Do you not know, Marduksharusur, that it is the hallowed
custom not to harm a herald when he approaches the wall waving a
palm branch over his head?"

"A custom is hallowed until one takes it into his mind to break
it," I replied. "As for me, I would rather have a shield-bearer than a
palm branch to protect my head, for one of the archers on the wall
might yet use me to test his aim!"

Then the captain laughed even louder and said:

"It pleases me to see that you are more steadfast in your cowardice than most men are in their courage. Therefore I shall entreat the
king to furnish you not with a shield-bearer but with a battering
ram that you might ride up to the wall and proclaim his word
concealed behind the turret. Even if your death would be no great
loss, your mad master would assuredly mourn you like a son.
Moreover, your worth as a slave shall soon rise to forty shekels,
which is too great a sum to lose to the whim of a Hebrew archer!"

I was to deliver the order for surrender on the following morning, allowing King Jehoiachin until sundown to come forth and
prostrate himself before Nebuchadrezzar.

I slept poorly and woke long before the changing of the morning
watch. Creeping out of the tent that I shared with some other
scribes, I carried the scroll with the order for surrender near one of
the campfires. There I read once more all the words Nebuchadrezzar had dictated to me, fixing their sequence in my mind that my
tongue might not stumble on such a solemn occasion. Then I returned the scroll to the tent and went to find a basin with water for
my morning ablutions. But even after I had washed my body,

combed my hair and dressed myself in clean garments, it was not yet light nor time for my errand.

It was then I thought of climbing one of the hills from where I could gaze upon Jerusalem. If King Jehoiachin refused Nebuchadrezzar's offer, this might be the last time I could see the holy city before it went up in flames. Also, I might be killed on my mission— but of this I preferred not to think.

Thus I borrowed one of the pack asses, and as the sky above turned white I headed for the high hill to the north and east of Jerusalem. The soldiers were beginning to come forth from their tents, scratching their heads, their beards, their backs and such parts as men scratch, or walking about in search of a place to relieve themselves. But none challenged me until I came to the edge of the camp, and even there the guards let me pass. I might have been a spy or a deserter, but at this early hour the guards cared little, or else they recognized me from having seen me ride in the oxcarts with the harlots.

My donkey was a docile beast that picked its way through the underbrush without much stumbling to carry me up the slope as the sun rose behind the mountains. Rain had fallen the night before, but now the sky was clear and the light so bright that in looking upon it one felt blinded. To rest my eyes I halted in a grove from where one had a view toward the east. There I saw for the first time the Salt Sea, its northern tip shimmering blue-green in the Valley of the Jordan, between the Mountains of Moab and the Wilderness of Judah. But I could not tarry long and rode on until I reached the crest of the hill. Reining my ass, I gazed across the Kidron Valley, down on Mount Moriah and on the city that had stood unconquered since the times of David. My heart grew heavy within me as I beheld the Babylonian army encompassing Jerusalem all around. For looking back on the three hundred years in which the walls had been breached but once—and that time by a king of Israel—the defenders of Jerusalem might become arrogant and refuse to surrender.

I tried to etch all I saw upon my memory. Now that the sun was risen in the sky, the houses to the south stood out white against the hillside of Millo, the land that David had filled in when first he took the city from the Jebusites. Across from where I stood on the hill was the temple court. Stairs led up to the entrance of the temple, which faced east toward the rising sun, even as the doors of the great temples in Babylon. At either side of the entrance a tall pillar of bronze gleamed golden in the sun. Bordering on the southern wall of the temple court was the court of the palace. This court surrounded the palace of Solomon, where save for the time Athaliah had seized the rule a prince of Judah had sat on the throne since the beginning of the kingdom. The land north of the city looked strangely flat now, though it had seemed all hills when we passed through it. I turned around to gaze once more east toward the Mountains of Moab, from which Moses had seen the Promised Land into which he was never to set foot.

And here was I—a Hebrew slave born in Nineveh and made a eunuch in Babylon—gazing upon the same promised land, perhaps to witness the end of the promise this very day. In the distance, where people had not been kept by fear of our army from plowing and seeding, the fields were turning green. For it was already the month of Adar, only one month before the gathering of the first fruit. I let my eyes roam over the terraced vineyards, over the backs of the hills covered with dark-green forests, the olive trees standing old and gnarled on the slopes, and the walls of Jerusalem with their barred gates, meant to protect the houses of the people, the palace of Solomon, and the temple of Yahweh.

Then I prayed for the strength to lend persuasion to Nebuchadrezzar's words so that what I beheld might not be destroyed. Having prayed, I shook the reins of my ass and returned to the camp.

No sooner had I entered my tent than I was summoned before Nebuchadrezzar. Once more the king spoke to me of my grave mission. Then he mounted his chariot to show himself before the walls of Jerusalem. The captains grumbled among themselves, for Nebuchadrezzar was flying the royal standard that would make him an easy target. But he said:

"Should the king of Babylon display fear while asking the king of Judah to surrender?"

I followed on foot behind the king's chariot. When we passed beyond the earthworks which the soldiers had thrown up all around Jerusalem, I saw that the Captain Holofernes had been true to his word, for there was a battering ram awaiting me. The long poles that jutted out through the opening in the turret had been removed lest the defenders believe we had come to attack the walls—though even they would not think the Babylonians mad enough to attack Jerusalem with one battering ram. In place of the poles a palm branch had been mounted on the turret, and the four men who wheeled the battering ram forward carried no weapons. Neither did they carry shields, for they were concealed by the sturdy leather sides of the battering ram, and by the high metal turret in front. But I stepped between the soldiers, and riding inside the turret I approached the walls of Jerusalem.

I peered out through the hole from which the poles had been removed. The nearer we came to the wall the higher and more formidable it appeared to me. Behind the battlements I could perceive the glinting of helmets, and when I heard the clang of weapons I prayed that the defenders would honor the palm branch mounted on the turret. We were near enough now for them to hurl firebrands down on us, nor had we brought along a water carrier to put out the flames if we were hit.

But the men on the wall did not move to attack us. Then I unrolled my scroll and began to read in a very loud voice all the words that Nebuchadrezzar had commanded me to speak. As I read I was overcome by the great occasion, for surely I would never again read the order for surrender to a city such as Jerusalem. And since the soldiers with me did not understand Hebrew, and since those on the wall did not know the words the king had dictated to me, I began to make such changes as I thought would do the most good. Rather than threatening that Nebuchadrezzar would make Jerusalem a dwelling place for dragons—as the king had commanded me—I spoke of such things as concern men: the lives of their children and the honor of their women. Surely the defenders of Jerusalem would not wish their women defiled by strangers and their sons made eunuchs. Nor did I mock them or use indecent words as had Rabshakeh when he shouted Sennacherib's order for surrender at the time of King Hezekiah. And having said all the king had commanded me and added such words as I thought would strengthen the cause for surrender, I bade the soldiers who were with me wheel the battering ram back to our lines.

Then began the long wait. None had answered me from the wall, nor did we know whether King Jehoiachin would surrender, or whether the Babylonian army would storm Jerusalem on the following day. All morning long the soldiers milled about behind the heaped-up earthworks to observe the gate through which the Hebrew king might come forth. Some got drunk while they waited and fell to quarreling among themselves. In the three months of the siege there were not as many hurt in fights as were on this day of waiting.

Nebuchadrezzar had returned to his tent to sacrifice with the priests and to pray that his gods might grant him a bloodless conquest. But I remained near the earthworks to see if King Jehoiachin would come forth, for then my services would be needed.

All day there was no rain. The sky above Jerusalem remained a bright blue as if to remind the people what joys of life they stood to lose in resisting. Yet noon passed and none came forth from the gates. Then the Captain Holofernes and the Captain Nabuzaradan, who was one of his close friends and among those who would use force, rejoiced and said:

"Tomorrow these wretched Hebrews will regret having defied the king of Babylon!"

But as the sun sank and the sky turned dark blue above Jerusalem, the east gate in the wall swung open. And King Jehoiachin came forth with his wives and his mother, with the princes and chamberlains and priests, to bow down before Nebuchadrezzar.

But I, who all day had prayed for their surrender, did not rejoice but felt downcast and ashamed. Then I discovered that I had hoped they would resist and fight. I was filled with amazement, for had I not spoken strong words to bring about their surrender? However, this was not the time to search my heart, for the officers who had gone to meet Jehoiachin and put him in fetters were calling for an interpreter.

When I drew near and beheld the Hebrew king my heart became heavier yet. He was but a boy, no older than I had been when I came to Babylon, riding on the ass behind my master. But though his lips trembled and tears began to roll down his cheeks when they put him in fetters, Jehoiachin tried to bear himself regally. He did not wear the garments of kingship but was dressed in a clean, white linen robe, and he was handsome as all princes of Judah, of slender build though not tall. His hair was cut short in the Hebrew fashion, and his beard not yet grown. But he was a man in other ways, for both his wives were with child, and behind them walked a nurse carrying an infant in his swaddling clothes. The wives had rent their garments, scattered dirt on their heads, and approached lamenting and weeping loudly, as did the king's mother. Behind them came the princes, the nobles, the priests and the captains—all the men Nebuchadrezzar had ordered to surrender—each in the raiments of his calling. And yet some distance behind them followed a man alone, clothed in a simple, coarsely woven robe gathered in the waist by a crude cord. His beard and hair were gray, and his deep-set eyes burned as though he had a fever. It was plain to see that he did not belong to the king's retinue, for those who walked in the rear would turn around and shout insults at him, calling him a vulture, a dog and a traitor.

Made wary, the Babylonian captains bade their soldiers seize and detain the man. But he struggled, shouting in Hebrew that he wished to look upon the face of the king into whose hands Yahweh had given all the nations. Then the soldiers, not understanding his words, began to beat him with their fists. I approached in haste to restrain them and ask the man's name, for I thought I knew who he was. When I addressed him in my fine Hebrew he gazed at me with amazement and said:

"Truly the king of Babylon must be one of Yahweh's chosen to have an interpreter who speaks our tongue as it was spoken in the times of the prophet Isaiah! As for me, my name is Jeremiah the son of Hilkiah. God sent me to the Hebrews that I might lead them back into His ways. But they love me little for it, as my lord can well see."

Then I told the soldiers to show that man all honor, for he was the same Jeremiah whose life the king had wished spared if Jerusalem fell by force. And I myself led him to the tent of the scribes and bade him wait there while I hastened after King Jehoiachin, for it would be my sad task to translate his words when he humbled himself before Nebuchadrezzar.

Since that memory still smarts like an old wound, I shall say little of it. I shall not describe the sumptuous garments in which Nebuchadrezzar had dressed himself, nor the throne on which he sat, nor how Jehoiachin was made to crawl up to that throne on his knees to kiss the feet of the king of Babylon. All this is but custom that has not changed since times of yore, for the victor must keep his place, and so must the vanquished. Neither would the humbled king have shown himself more merciful had victory been his. When all the prescribed rituals had been accomplished, the Hebrew king, his wives, his mother and all his retinue were taken to the tents that had been set aside for them. There they would be kept prisoners until the army broke camp and returned to Babylon.

I remained standing in the entrance of Nebuchadrezzar's tent, for I had not yet told him that Jeremiah had come to pay him homage. But the king sat thoughtfully upon his throne, and I did not dare break the silence, neither did his captains, until he spoke:

"I should rather have captured the father than this boy who knows nothing yet of kingship, though he already knows how to beget children. In this he is truly a man."

And Nebuchadrezzar sighed, for though he was twice the age of Jehoiachin, the queen had borne him only one son and one daughter. There was also a rumor that no children were born in the house of women since Nebuchadrezzar sat on the throne. But the king continued:

"Surely many Hebrew princes shall be born in Babylon. If they are handsome as their father they shall please me well, for next to the gods I love beauty best."

Then one of the captains—a veteran who had served under King Nabopolassar—spoke up and said:

"If my lord would listen to my counsel, he would slay this Hebrew together with his seed and seize his lands, rather than raise enemies in the bosom of Babylonia. No royal prince ever ceases to dream of kingship, and these princes of Judah pride themselves on having held the throne for more than three hundred years!"

The other captains shouted their assent, but Nebuchadrezzar bade them be silent.

"Have I not sworn before my gods to spare the life of the king and his family? I shall surely not break my word and display fear before a mere boy and unborn children. Neither shall I make the young king pay for the treachery of his father, for it was Jehoiakim who was my sworn vassal and not his son! Nor shall I seize his lands, but put them in the hands of a steward that he may keep them in trust for Jehoiachin's sons. For these lads shall be born and raised in Babylon, and shall be married to Babylonian princesses when they are grown. Who knows but that someday a king of Babylonian and Hebrew royal blood shall sit on the throne of Judah!"

Nebuchadrezzar's eyes glistened, and there was foam in the corners of his mouth, as happened when he was overcome by his visions.

"However, while these princes grow up in Babylon," the king continued, "we must find a loyal Hebrew to keep the land for us. I know well that some of you would sooner see me place a Babylonian governor in Jerusalem. But how can I banish a faithful servant to this savage country, where he will become ill from the cold and the unaccustomed food, and be made to miss the glorious festivals of the gods? Moreover, consider how unhappy his wife would be here! No, I shall rather appoint a worthy Hebrew to rule over Judah."

It was then I bethought myself of Jeremiah waiting in the tent of the scribes. When the king granted me leave to address him, and I revealed who had come to seek his ear, he exclaimed:

"Truly the god of these hills favors me to have sent me the one who proclaimed me victor over Judah even before I set foot in the land!"

And Nebuchadrezzar commanded that Jeremiah be brought before him.

I ran to Jeremiah and brought him into the tent where Nebuchadrezzar sat on the throne. Drawing near, Jeremiah bowed down low, but he straightened up again and looked at the king as one accustomed to royalty. Indeed it was known that the Hebrew kings had sought his counsel, even if they quarreled with him on many occasions.

Tired of sitting so long, Nebuchadrezzar descended from his throne and walked around Jeremiah to gaze at him with wonder. Custom required that one appear before the king arrayed in fine garments, but Jeremiah wore a robe of coarse sackcloth tied with a cord, neither did he wear shoes. There was about him the smell of poverty and of those who sleep together with others in crowded quarters.

"Has he been newly released from prison?" the king asked at last.

When I translated the question for Jeremiah, he answered that he

had walked freely about Jerusalem since the death of King Jehoiakim.

"Then why is he not dressed as is seemly in my presence?"
Nebuchadrezzar asked.

And Jeremiah replied that the clothes on his body were all he
owned.

"Aha!" Nebuchadrezzar exclaimed. "He has hastened to me that I
might reward him for defending my cause! Let my servants fetch
one of my own garments to put on him, as befits a man honored by
the king, and some golden ornaments to hang about his neck!"

But when the servants returned with the king's garments to put
them on Jeremiah, the prophet stepped back and raised his hands in
horror.

"What need have I of royal robes who was called to preach to the
people of modesty and virtue? Should I not look to them a picture
of corruption in such garments?"

I thought it best not to translate these words to the king, but said
simply that Jeremiah was sworn to walk about in sackcloth all his
days, mourning the sinfulness of his people.

Then the king's astonishment knew no bounds, and he said:

"Though I have heard of men who would refuse earthly riches, I
never yet beheld one with my own eyes!"

And again he circled around Jeremiah, while the prophet stood
motionless, looking down on him, for he was a full head taller than
Nebuchadrezzar. When the king had gazed his fill, he asked:

"If he has not come to gather his reward, why has he come?"

And Jeremiah replied through my mouth:

"I came to beg but one favor: when the king seizes the golden
vessels from the temple, let him allow the priests to carry these
vessels out, lest the Babylonian soldiers enter and defile the sanctuary of Yahweh. As for me, I desire nothing of the king."

Having heard this request, Nebuchadrezzar said:

"I shall indeed do as this Jeremiah says. Has not his god delivered
Jerusalem into my hands without requiring the life of one single
Babylonian soldier? Nor shall I take all the vessels but leave some
behind that the Hebrews may continue serving Yahweh. As for
Jeremiah, would not a man who asks nothing for himself and who
proved his loyalty toward me make a perfect ruler? He could
neither be bribed with gold by the wealthy nor be threatened with

death by those who aspire to rebellion, for he has already braved death many times. Therefore let Jeremiah govern Judah!"

At these words Jeremiah recoiled in even greater horror than when offered the king's garments, and replied:

"Who am I to rule over Judah? Am I of royal blood that I should sit on the throne of David? Indeed I was not even born here but north of the border, in Anathoth, in the country of Benjamin. How could I rule over those who despise me for a stranger and hate me for what I preach to them? Long ago it was ordained by God that none but a prince of Judah should rule in Jerusalem. Let the king of Babylon appoint such a one in my stead!"

"Truly this man is marvelous to refuse not only riches but also power, which is of greater value than all the riches in the world," Nebuchadrezzar said. "But as for appointing a prince of Judah ruler—the sons of Jehoiachin are yet unborn or still too young to sit on the throne, and I must carry the father as hostage to Babylon, for these were the terms of surrender."

Then Jeremiah revealed that there was still one royal prince left in Judah, the youngest son of King Josiah, Mattaniah by name. Matttaniah was twenty-one years old and had never hoped to sit on his father's throne, for the kingship had already passed on to his brother's son. If the king of Babylon would make Mattaniah king, the young man would forever remain his loyal vassal.

"Truly there is no end to Jeremiah's wisdom," Nebuchadrezzar said. "I know well what it means to be the younger son who might never hope to be king. Therefore I myself shall crown Prince Mattaniah as king over Judah tomorrow!"

The very same evening the Captain Holofernes and the Captain Nabuzaradan entered Jerusalem with a troop of soldiers to search all the houses along the road which Nebuchadrezzar would take to the palace the following day. There might still be archers lying in ambush upon one of the roofs, from where they could easily kill the king of Babylon. But early next morning the captains sent word that they had placed guards all along the way and put soldiers in every house to protect the king's life.

Then Prince Mattaniah and such nobles as had been found free of ties to Egypt were summoned to Nebuchadrezzar's tent, all having surrendered with King Jehoiachin the previous day. And Nebu-

chadrezzar commanded them to walk behind his royal chariot into
Jerusalem to make the people understand that Mattaniah was to be
king by the grace of Nebuchadrezzar.

Again I was called upon to act as interpreter. Standing near
Prince Mattaniah, I saw that he too was handsome, as were all
princes of Judah. But though he was only three years older than
Jehoiachin he looked like one who had indulged himself much for
lack of better occupation. When his father fell at Megiddo, Mattaniah was but a boy, nor had he ever hoped to be king. Now his
eyes shone even as he humbled himself before Nebuchadrezzar, and
no doubt he rejoiced in his heart over the fate of his elder brother's
son.

Nebuchadrezzar, arrayed in his royal robes, the golden circlet on
his forehead, the ceremonial sword girded about his waist, sat on the
throne below which Prince Mattaniah humbled himself. Not until
the king descended from his throne to mount his chariot could it be
seen that he was even shorter than the Hebrew prince. Then
Mattaniah smiled a secret smile of contempt, for he was still too
young to know that the content of a vessel was not determined by
its outward shape. I should have whispered into the prince's ear: Be
not misled by Nebuchadrezzar's appearance into thinking him
weak. But I was there to act as interpreter, not to counsel princes.

The king had mounted his chariot and set out for Jerusalem,
surrounded by his captains and followed by Mattaniah and the
Hebrew nobles. When we passed through the east gate into the city
there was a big throng in the street, waiting to see the king of
Babylon enter. The captains drew closer about the royal chariot,
looking left and right, before, behind and above them, for in spite of
all the precautions they still feared for the king's life. But Nebuchadrezzar showed no fear as he rode through the crowd. Moreover, the people were cheering him loudly, a sight that filled me
with great astonishment, for had not the king come as conqueror to
Judah?

But then I remembered how the people had been divided against
themselves. Many had been oppressed by the king and the princes
whom Nebuchadrezzar would carry away captive to Babylon. To
those and to the poor, who were to share among themselves the land
of the rich, Nebuchadrezzar must have come as liberator. Thus
there was much cheering along the road. If there was also mourning

and lamentation, the captains had seen to it that the sight might not offend the king's eyes. For he truly believed that he had come to Jerusalem on a righteous mission and that Yahweh had delivered the city into his hands.

As on the previous day the sky was an unblemished blue and the air so clear that one could see all the land around Jerusalem. The hills were turning green and the orchards stood in bloom, for Nebuchadrezzar had forbidden his soldiers to cut down the groves of fruit trees. Seen from close by, the houses within the walls were not as white as they had looked from the distance, nor were they large and sumptuous as those of Babylon. Many were in bad repair, but the gardens around them lent a cheerful air and the flowers gave off a sweet odor. Though I had never been to Jerusalem, I felt as if I had been here before.

We ascended the steep streets until we arrived outside the palace grounds. There the captains jumped from their horses to form a guard around the king as he entered through the Hall of Pillars into the inner court. Though as a child I had heard much of this hall I gaped in astonishment, for I had never beheld the like of it before. In Babylon all great buildings were made of brick, for there were few forests in the land and lumber was dear. But here even the porch that led to the hall was adorned with pillars of precious cedarwood. As for the hall, its width was that of ten chariots standing abreast—or so it appeared to me—and its length even greater. The roof was supported by rows of pillars of cedarwood, each ten times the height of a man my size. These same pillars had stood there for almost four hundred years, ever since King Solomon had brought cedars from Lebanon to Jerusalem. And no enemy had ever burned them down.

While Nebuchadrezzar passed swiftly through the Hall of Pillars without glancing left or right, I walked with my mouth open and my face turned upward so that I stumbled over my own feet and nearly fell down flat. But when we entered the courtyard of the palace the king halted to marvel at the foundation stones of the buildings, for they were of a size even Nebuchadrezzar had never seen. Above the foundations were three rows of smaller hewn stones, all of costly rock in shades of pink and white, and above them beams of cedarwood. But when the king would know the size of all the stones, and the height of the pillars in the great hall, and the length and width of the buildings around the courtyard, none could answer him. Then Nebuchadrezzar raised his voice as he was wont to do when displeased by the dullness of those about him, and shouted:

"Is there not one among these men who knows anything about the house they inhabit? Surely the ignorance of these Hebrew princes surpasses even that of our own!"

Trembling before the wrath of the king, the Hebrew nobles whispered among themselves. And one hastened to fetch a young man of a priestly family who, they said, knew much about measurements.

The youth that was brought before the king was even younger than Mattaniah, and so thin that his bare arms appeared all bone. His hair was a bright red such as I had never seen, and in his pale face his veins showed blue through the tender skin of his temples. When I repeated to him Nebuchadrezzar's questions he began to tremble and gasp, but no sound came out of his mouth. Then one of the nobles whispered in my ear:

"He is wont to lose his speech when overcome by terror."

"Let my lord not be afraid of the king," I said, "for his heart is inclined toward those who have knowledge."

The youth recovered and answered, speaking so softly and swiftly that it was difficult for me to translate his words:

"If the king will forbear with my ignorance, I shall reveal to him all he wishes to know: the great hall through which the king passed is the Porch of Pillars. The length of it is fifty cubits and the breadth of it thirty cubits. All the pillars there are of cedarwood, as are the beams above them. The building to the north of the courtyard is the house of the forest of Lebanon. The length of it is a hundred cubits and the breadth fifty cubits. Its height is thirty cubits, and its roof is supported by four rows of cedar pillars, with cedar beams upon them. This is the house of the guard and also the treasury, but there is not much gold left in it, for it was plundered many times: by Pharaoh Shishak at the time of Rehoboam; by King Jehoash of Israel at the time of Amaziah; and by all the kings of Judah who had to pay tribute to foreign overlords. To the west of the court is the throne room, and beyond it the house where the king dwells. As for the foundation stones, they are stones of ten cubits and stones of eight cubits, which were quarried in the quarries outside Jerusalem. To do the work King Solomon raised a levy of thirty thousand men, ten thousand in turn being sent to Lebanon for one month and spending two months at home. And he had three score and ten thousand who bore burdens, and four score thousand that were hewers in the mountains, and three thousand three hundred who were overseers over the workmen, aside from the chief officers. It took them thirteen years to build the house."

When the youth had finished speaking he was out of breath, and so was I. But Nebuchadrezzar said:

"Truly the knowledge of this young man is astounding. Ask him his name!"

The youth replied that his name was Ezekiel, the son of Buzi.

"I shall take this Ezekiel with me to Babylon that he might assist me in the building of my palaces," Nebuchadrezzar said before he turned to continue on his way.

When Ezekiel heard these words his eyes opened wide and so did his mouth, but no sound came out of it. Then his face turned ashen and he fell into a faint. While some crowded around to tend to him I hurried after the king, who had already passed through the entrance into the throne room. But when Nebuchadrezzar asked for Ezekiel, I pretended that the young man had fainted with joy upon hearing of the honor that the king had bestowed upon him.

Ezekiel soon recovered his senses. When I glanced behind me I saw him entering the throne room, where the new king of Judah was to be crowned. Ezekiel tried to draw near, but Nebucha-drezzar's captains, his retinue, and the Hebrew nobles who had come with Mattaniah had all crowded into the room so that there was not a breadth of empty floor between wall and wall. Looking down one saw nought but feet, but looking up one saw the walls of cedar-wood, covered with carvings of knops and open flowers, of pome-granates and lilywork. The wood smelled sweet, stronger even than the many bodies in the room, and the carvings delighted the eye. But even the beauty of the walls could not attain to the magnifi-cence of the throne.

King Solomon had made the throne of ivory, overlaid with the finest gold. Six steps led up to the throne. On either side of each step stood a lion, and two lions beside the arms of the throne, fourteen lions in all. I had never seen the likes of it, neither in Nineveh nor in

Babylon. My knees buckled under me at the thought that my own grandfather's father had sat on this very throne. But now Prince Mattaniah would sit on it.

Nebuchadrezzar took the hand of the prince and bade me draw near that I might translate the oath he would have Mattaniah swear. Thus the solemn words passed through my mouth even before they were uttered by the prince. And Mattaniah swore by Yahweh that he would faithfully keep his covenant with the king of Babylon; that he would not stir up rebellion, neither would he solicit arms and horses from Egypt; that he would pay his annual tribute to Babylon; that he would honor the garrisons left behind by the king, and that he would rule Judah in justice, neither shedding the blood of the innocent nor oppressing the poor.

Then Nebuchadrezzar placed Mattaniah on the throne, and he changed his name to Zedekiah lest he forget who had made him king of Judah.

After bowing low before their new king, the Hebrew nobles went to the king's house to feast at a banquet given in honor of the great occasion. Though Nebuchadrezzar too was to be present, my services were no longer needed, for there would be no more weighty talks. Thus, begging leave of the king, I hastened out of the throne room and through the courtyard toward the north gate that led to the temple grounds. For I would not leave Jerusalem without having seen the temple where my grandfather had made music before he was carried off to Nineveh.

When I entered the temple court and passed the great brazen sea that stood on the right side of the house, to the south and east of it—the same brazen sea that King Ahaz had taken from the twelve brazen oxen and set on the pavement—my eyes beheld a strange spectacle. At the top of the stairs that led to the temple stood the Captain Holofernes and the Captain Nabuzaradan, their arms spread around one of the tall brass pillars so that they looked as if they were about to lift it up and carry it away.

The two captains were not at the banquet, being in charge of the soldiers who stood guard in the courts of the palace and the temple. Now all these soldiers grinned under their beards as they observed their captains. But at the foot of the stairs stood a group of ancient Hebrew priests—for all the younger ones had been taken captive—

who did not grin but murmured among themselves, fearful of what these two heathens might attempt.

Seeing me approach, the Captain Holofernes shouted down to me:

"You, Marduksharusur, ask these priests what is the weight and worth of these brass pillars!"

The priests only shook their heads at my question, and one answered:

"The weight of these pillars, and of the brazen sea, the ten lavers, and all the pots, shovels and basins of brass was never known, for King Solomon left them unweighed. All this brass was accounted as nothing in his time!"

Then I knew that Solomon's wealth was truly without measure, for each pillar was five times the height of the Captain Holofernes, and the capital upon it, which was adorned with a network of pomegranates, was again one time the height of him. As for its girth, it was such that the two captains could not encompass it with their outstretched arms.

But the Captain Holofernes was not pleased with the priest's answer, and said to me:

"You, who pretend to great knowledge, can you not ascertain the weight of this column by its height and width? Surely its value in brass must be beyond accounting!"

"I was never good at the science of numbers," I replied. "But even I can see that the pillar should be too heavy for my lords to carry away between them."

For they still stood with their arms thrown around it.

Dropping his arms, the Captain Holofernes glared at me and said:

"Being royal interpreter has made you forget that you are but a common slave, Marduksharusur. But the day will yet come when I shall rip your shameless tongue from your mouth!"

Then he and the Captain Nabuzaradan turned toward the temple doors, which were made of cedarwood, two folding leaves on the left and two on the right, carved with figures of cherubim, palm trees and flowers. But the moment the captain touched the door one of the priests set up a loud cry, pleading with me to remind the captain that Nebuchadrezzar had promised to keep the sanctuary undefiled by soldiers. When I called these words after the captains, they turned around and came down the stairs.

"Truly this Jeremiah must have cast a spell over the king to make him give such a promise," the Captain Holofernes said. "No doubt the temple is filled with more gold and silver than these priests would admit!"

"I did not know that my lord believed in spells," I said.

"Neither do I believe in them," the captain replied. "But I would never trust a man who refused royal garments to walk about clothed in nothing but righteousness. However, since we must honor the king's promise, let us go and search the treasury rather than the temple, for none can claim that we might defile it with our unclean weapons!"

And the two captains departed toward the house of the forest of Lebanon. But I walked around the temple to gaze up at the walls, each three stories high, with windows cut in them all around. One of the priests told me that all the stones for the building had been made ready in the quarry, and there was neither hammer nor ax nor any tool of iron heard in the house while it was being built. But when I asked to be shown the inside of the temple, the priest glanced at my naked chin, and turning away his eyes, he muttered:

"The king of Babylon promised that Yahweh's house should not be defiled. And none who is not whole in his parts may enter the temple."

The blood rushed to my cheeks, for I had never thought that I might be denied entry to the temple where my grandfather had sung the praise of God. And I wondered whether this was the punishment for having concealed all these years that I was in truth a Hebrew.

But I had little time to brood about my misfortune, for the king was approaching the temple. Nebuchadrezzar had entered the courtyard through the gate that led from the palace onto the temple grounds, nor did his visit appear of a ceremonial nature. He was accompanied neither by Zedekiah nor by any Hebrew nobles but only by a few of his own captains.

The priests bowed low and stood in respectful silence while Nebuchadrezzar walked about, gazing up at the temple, and curiously touching the stones and all the things that were made of brass. Then he bade me ask the priests where pillars of this great size could be cast, and who was the man that had cast them. The priests replied that the pillars and the sea of brass had been cast in the plain of the

Jordan, in the clay ground between Succoth and Zaretan. The name of the man who had wrought this work was Hiram, the son of a woman of the tribe of Naphtali and a man of Tyre, himself a worker in brass.

"I wish I had a craftsman like Hiram to embellish my palace," the king said with a sigh. "But a man of such skill is born only once every thousand years."

Nebuchadrezzar tenderly touched the pillars, which shone a golden red in the afternoon sun, before he turned to approach the doors of the temple. When the priests saw that he would enter the temple, they set up a loud cry, while Nebuchadrezzar's captains mounted the stairs and drew their swords to drive them back. But when the king would know the cause of their anguish and I reminded him of the promise he had made Jeremiah, Nebuchadrezzar said:

"Indeed I shall not break my word, neither shall the temple of Yahweh be defiled by weapons. None of my captains shall pass through the door. As for me, I shall enter. But I shall ungird my sword before I step inside."

The king ungirded his sword, and since I was the one who stood nearest him—his captains having pursued the priests down the stairs—he handed it to me. A loud gasp went up from the priests and captains alike, but Nebuchadrezzar said:

"Let none come after me, for the word of the king of Babylon is sacred before the gods!"

And approaching the folding doors he pushed them open with his two hands and entered the temple. The doors, being heavy in their hinges, closed again behind him, while those outside remained staring at the closed leaves. Thus we all stood like pillars of salt when the Captain Holofernes returned from the treasury in search of me, for he needed my services as interpreter. Seeing the sword in my hand, the captain turned ashen and shouted:

"How does the king's sword come to be in your wretched fist?"

I stammered that Nebuchadrezzar himself had handed it to me before he entered the temple. But when the captain saw the others standing with their drawn swords at the foot of the stairs, he roared:

"Fools! Have you let the king enter alone into this place where one of those wretched Hebrew priests might slay him? Let us hasten after him before it is too late!"

But none of the captains would follow him, not daring to disobey the king's command. Then the Captain Holofernes seized me by the arm and said:

"You at least shall come with me! If the priests have locked the king into one of their secret chambers—and all temples abound in secret chambers—you shall make them reveal to me the hiding place before I hack them to pieces with my sword!"

I struggled as the captain pulled me along, begging him not to make me enter, for one who was not whole in his parts was not allowed inside the temple.

The captain's eyes turned red with fury as he shouted at me:

"Have you gone mad, or are you become a Hebrew like your master that you should fear this Hebrew god?"

He snatched the king's sword out of my hand and held it in his right, while he seized me by the scruff of my neck with his left. Then he pushed one leaf of the folding door open with his foot and dragged me inside. I covered my eyes with my hands, waiting for the thunderbolt that would destroy us both. But instead of thunder I heard the Captain Holofernes catch his breath and say softly:

"May I meet the goddess of death this very day if there is not more gold in this temple than in Marduk's temple in Babylon!"

I prayed in my heart to God, saying:

"Lord, as You are my witness, I did not defile Your temple of my own will. As for this heathen swearing by the goddess of death in Your house, let the sin be upon his head."

And having thus absolved myself before the Almighty, I lifted up my eyes and looked around. Then I too gasped in wonder, for there was indeed more gold inside the temple than I had ever seen.

The walls were covered with cedarwood so that not a stone was to be seen. But all the carvings of knops and open flowers were overlaid with pure gold. And so was the floor of the house overlaid with pure gold. At the far end of the temple, before the double doors of the Sanctuary, there was an altar of cedarwood overlaid with pure gold. And at either side of the altar a candelabra of pure gold. The walls of the Sanctuary from without, and the richly carved doors of olive wood were overlaid with pure gold. As for the inside of the Sanctuary, it could not be seen, for none but the high priest was allowed to pass through the locked doors. But I knew from the tales that had come down to me through my father that the Sanctuary within also was overlaid with pure gold. And so were the figures of the two cherubim, which were carved of olive wood and whose wings spread ten cubits, the outer tips touching the walls of the Sanctuary and the inner tips touching each other. Beneath the two cherubim was the ark of the covenant, and within it the two tablets upon which Yahweh had written the Law with His own finger.

"Did not Ezekiel claim that all the gold of the temple was carried away by conquerors?" the Captain Holofernes asked. "But being of a priestly family he can be trusted as little as all the other priests, who were shrewd enough to leave the outer doors of the temple of crude wood that none might suspect the treasures within."

I could have told the captain that the outer doors also had been overlaid with gold, until my own grandfather's father, King Hezekiah, had cut it off and sent it as tribute to Sennacherib. Indeed how could I ever forget this when my own grandparents had been part of that tribute? But this was not the time to instruct the captain, for he had raised his voice, shouting loudly through the house of Yahweh:

"My lord! My lord the king! If these wretched priests have not slain my lord let him answer me!"

The Captain Holofernes gazed around and above him, thinking the king might be in one of the upper chambers. When he received no answer he poured forth all the oaths he knew—which were without number—so that I covered my ears against his blasphemies. But the captain, still holding me by the scruff, shook me as one shakes a puppy dog, and pointing his unsheathed sword at the doors of the Sanctuary, he said:

"Let us go see if the king does not lie murdered in his blood beyond that door, for it is known that this Hebrew god requires human sacrifice."

"No!" I screamed then, not only to deny that awful lie but also to protest against entering the Sanctuary. "Let my lord not open that door! None but the high priest may enter into the holiest place without being struck dead. For beyond these doors is the ark and the Tablets of the Law, which Yahweh engraved with His own finger."

The captain glared down at me with deep distrust and asked:

"How come you have knowledge of all these things, Marduk-sharusur? Were you not brought up to revere Ashur?"

I stammered that I had learned all I knew from the Hebrew priests, and that I should not step beyond the doors even if the captain killed me. Then I threw myself flat on the floor, thinking that if the death blow had to be struck let it be the captain who dealt it, for he might yet miss, while the Almighty never missed. But the captain only uttered another curse and walked away from me. Presently I heard the sighing of the doors in their hinges as he pushed them open to enter the Sanctuary. But I lay with my face pressed to the ground and my hands covering my head, waiting for the end.

Some time passed and there was no lightning, neither was there a thunderclap. Then I heard again the opening of the doors and the tread of the Captain Holofernes, sounding heavier than before. I did not look up until he was beside me, kicking me with his boot and commanding me to rise and help him. When I raised myself on my knees and saw that the captain carried the limp figure of the king in his arms, I let out a scream and fell down again. I thought Nebuchadrezzar struck dead by God, for there was neither blood nor injury on him. But the captain kicked me again and said:

"Get up, you fool! If this Hebrew god did not strike me dead, he shall surely not trouble himself with such a one as you. The king is only fallen into a faint. And small wonder, for all temples reek of myrrh and frankincense, which benumb and suffocate a man. Moreover, the doors of the Sanctuary fell shut behind the king so that he was enclosed in complete darkness. Run now and open the temple door that the king may recover in the fresh air! I will not carry him outside in my arms lest these Hebrews think him dead and rise in rebellion even before we depart from Jerusalem!"

I did as the captain bade me, while he carried the king near the door and laid him down flat on the floor. Nebuchadrezzar's face was ashen, but by and by his color returned and he began to breathe. However, when he opened his eyes they were glazed as if he were seeing visions, and he did not seem to recognize us. Rising heavily to his feet, he stared straight ahead and said in a low voice:

"I beheld the face of Yahweh."

Then the king walked out the door and down the stairs without touching the sword, which the captain held out to him. The latter shook his head in wonder, exclaiming:

"May Ishtar strike me dead if the madness of the one God is not catching like the plague! Let us leave this temple before we too are overcome!"

When we emerged from the door—the Captain Holofernes with his own sword girded about his waist and the king's sword in his hand—the priests at the foot of the stairs shook their fists at him. But they did not dare go near him, for he looked as though he could wield two swords at the same time. Nor was he afraid to cut a path straight through their midst, even though the other captains and the king were already departed and he was alone among the priests.

"Let these scoundrels curse me! They are no better than our Babylonian priests," the captain said. "They proclaim that they keep the two tablets on which their god wrote with his own finger concealed in the ark, threatening death to any who would enter the Sanctuary. In this the priests deal wisely, for if any entered he would discover what I discovered: there is neither an ark nor stone tablets. The Sanctuary is empty."

Aware that in entering the temple I had broken not only God's but also the king's command, I spent all night in terror of the punishment that would befall me. And when I was summoned to Nebuchadrezzar's tent next morning my bowels turned to water, for I was certain that it was to hear my death sentence. Nor was I relieved to find that the Captain Holofernes had already been summoned into the king's presence before me. I threw myself at Nebuchadrezzar's feet, imploring him to pardon my trespass, for I was but a slave who had to follow the orders of those above him. Looking perturbed, the king said:

"I was told that the Captain Holofernes and you entered the temple against my command. But I cannot recall seeing you there, and though I trust the words of those who informed me, I shall take it as a sign from Yahweh that he concealed you from me. Therefore I shall show you no less mercy than the Hebrew god, who let you escape with your lives rather than strike you dead. However, you shall not go wholly unpunished. Rather than having a day of rest, the Captain Holofernes and his soldiers shall assist the priests in carrying the precious vessels from the temple. But none of the soldiers shall enter the temple. They shall stand in the door and take the vessels from the hands of the priests, who being old men might weary themselves with much climbing up and down the stairs. As for you, Marduksharusur, you shall work with the scribes on the record of the booty."

And the king dismissed us from his presence. Once outside the tent, the Captain Holofernes broke into laughter, smote his thigh and exclaimed:

"Surely the king knows why he put me in charge of receiving the vessels! I am the only one among the captains who has seen the treasures of the temple and cannot be deceived by the priests!"

But before we went to the temple, the Captain Holofernes sought out the Captain Nabuzaradan and charged him with bringing out the treasures from the house of the forest of Lebanon. For it was already the third day of Adar, and there was need for haste if the troops were to be back in Babylon for the New Year Festival. Then the captain rounded up all the priests that were left in Jerusalem and made them bring the holy vessels to the temple door, from where his soldiers handed them down the stairs to pile them on the pavement of the courtyard.

While this was being done, I stood among the scribes with my clay tablets to make a record of the loot. And when all was counted, there were thirty basins of gold, a thousand basins of silver, nine and twenty knives, thirty bowls of gold, silver bowls of a second sort four hundred and ten, and other vessels a thousand. All the vessels of gold and silver were five thousand and four hundred. Piled on the ground in the courtyard, they gleamed and glistened in the sun like Humbawa's treasure.

But since this was a Babylonian accounting, a second record was made after the first had been completed. Then the two records were compared, and when it was found that the second contained all that was in the first, there were copies made, while all the captains and soldiers swore that none had laid hands on what was the king's. Then the vessels and knives were counted once again, until it appeared that the counting of vessels and making of records and swearing of witnesses would take longer than the entire campaign.

But when at long last the records were presented to Nebuchadrezzar, he would take only half of the golden vessels, leaving behind the other half, and all the vessels of silver and the nine and twenty knives. Then a great uproar arose among those who had spent all day collecting and counting the booty, each proclaiming that the king had been bewitched or had gone mad. Indeed some of the

captains murmured that the power ought to be taken out of
Nebuchadrezzar's hand so that they might break down the walls of
Jerusalem, burn the temple and the palace, and carry away all the
people captive while the Babylonian army was still in Jerusalem.
Those most in favor of destroying Jerusalem were the Captain
Nabuzaradan and another young captain, Neriglissar by name, who
on many other occasions had sided with the king.

As for the Captain Holofernes, he cursed in his accustomed
manner, saying that the war would cost Babylonia more than it
would render in spoils. Not only had the king forbidden to plunder
the people, he had also forbidden to force the women. Thus the
soldiers had to buy their favors with gifts of food and trinkets,
leaving behind more in Jerusalem than they would carry away.

"May Ishtar grant that each of these Hebrew harlots be left with
a Babylonian bastard to avenge such injustice!" the captain said.

But all was not as the captain would have one believe. There were
among the soldiers good men who honored the king's orders and
bad men who forced the women and took whatever they could lay
their hands on, for none of the Hebrews dared resist. There were
also those—the worst of the lot—who were neither good nor bad
but did according to their company.

Of these things the king did not hear. But he learned of the
murmurings of his captains and summoned them to his tent to chide
them.

"I was told that some of you would break down the walls of
Jerusalem, burn the temple and the palace, and carry away the
population," he said. "But I vowed that none of these things would
be done, nor would such deeds be wise. A loyal Jerusalem is a strong
southern fortress against Egypt. But a city cannot stand without
walls, nor without the temple of the god of the land. As for taking
captives—I shall carry with me only the princes and nobles who
caused the rebellion, and the skilled smiths, carpenters and craftsmen who shall assist in the building up of Babylon. These men
shall prosper in our country, being a burden neither to us
nor to themselves, but enriching both. As for the poor and unskilled, they should serve for nought but to take the bread out of
the mouths of our own poor and unskilled. Even if I let them go
free they would not improve their lot but add only to the number
of our needy, for the poor carry their poverty with them and

spread it about like a disease. And as for the precious vessels and knives which we shall leave behind—the Hebrews are aware that we know their number and that they cannot be concealed from us. But to bring all the gold and silver into Babylonia at one time would only cheapen its worth, thus causing grievous losses to many of our faithful servants. And now that I have quelled those doubts which you had no right to have, I command you to prepare for breaking camp tomorrow. I promised my soldiers that they would be home for the New Year, and the king of Babylon does not break his promises."

And now the Babylonian army was marching home, with their chariots and battering rams and siege towers and thousands upon thousands of foot soldiers, with their pack asses and camels and oxcarts, whose number was now swelled by the pack asses and oxcarts of the captives. The latter had been allowed to take their possessions with them, for Nebuchadrezzar would not bring the poor and needy to his land. There were of the prisoners three thousand three and twenty: King Jehoiachin and his wives and his mother, the princes and nobles and men of might, the craftsmen and smiths and carpenters, the wives and children of these men, and a few Hebrew harlots. For they, like the Babylonian harlots, would follow their business halfway across the earth.

Seeing the weariness of these men, some of whom led their children by the hand, while others carried them on their backs, and the dejection of the women, who took turns riding in the oxcarts, I was reminded of the time I was carried away from Nineveh. Just so had the prisoners walked then, weeping and wary of the future. I would mingle with the captives and try to comfort them, promising that they would find the Babylonians more lenient masters than the Assyrians had been. But they observed me with contempt and then turned their heads away, mumbling that I knew nothing of what it meant to be carried away from one's home.

Though at times I thought to confess that I differed but little from them—being myself a captive Hebrew—I never revealed myself. For in my heart I was glad that I need not share their fate but was the royal interpreter, dressed in fine garments and permitted to stand before the king. Later I would be ashamed of being glad, and at night I often wept with despair over not knowing my

true place. Then I would punish myself the following day by
walking with the captives, but soon my weakness would win out
again and I would return to riding in the oxcarts with the harlots,
while I cursed myself, and the day I was unmanned, and the day I
was born.

As for the captives, they were not inclined toward me but always
fell silent in my presence, knowing that I understood their speech
and thinking me a spy for the king. Though Nebuchadrezzar had
forbidden such dealings, there was much trading between the
captives and the soldiers, the prisoners bartering some of their
possessions for extra shares of food. In the end there was hardly a
soldier who had not taken something off the captives, even if it was
but a small token to bring home as a remembrance of this war that
had been won without a battle. But the Captain Holofernes remained disgruntled, saying to me:

"This war has been for nought, nor have we brought back anything of value. As for the golden vessels, Nebuchadrezzar will place
them in the temple of Marduk, where they will bring pleasure only
to the priests. We might at least have broken down the brazen
pillars and carried them with us to Babylon, to beat them into
helmets and shields! But when I spoke of this to the king, he replied:
'Hearing your words, Holofernes, I wonder whether savage Enkidu
ever became human. Do you not know that pillars of such beauty
are worth many times their weight in brass? If only I could carry
them with me to Babylon that I might feast my eyes on them
forever! But they are too heavy for transport, and thus I shall have
to content myself with the work of my own craftsmen until
another man is born who can fashion such work. One thing I shall
do, however: I shall obtain from Lebanon just such timber as we
saw in Jerusalem, even if I have to drive out the enemy who seized
that country!' "

Though I knew well the meaning of these words, I would not
think of the next war now that we were barely returned from the
last. I already longed to be home, where I could bathe in my
master's house instead of sharing a pan of dirty water with the other
scribes in my tent. I was eager to return to my daily chores, to
embrace the boy David, to inquire about the increase of my silver,
and to be spared the sight of these weeping captives who made my
heart ache.

And when one day at noon the walls of Babylon came in sight, and beyond them the terraced gardens of the queen with their swaying palm trees, and I saw the top of Etemenanki gleaming in the sun—for the king had sheathed its summit in glazed blue tile—and I beheld the white doves of Ishtar rising into the spring sky; and when we passed beneath the Ishtar Gate, on which many men were at work to repair and enlarge it, I wept with joy and shame—joy for being back in Babylon, and shame for calling this city where I was a slave, in this country where I was made a eunuch, home.

EIGHT

What is my strength, that I should wait?
And what is mine end, that I should be
    patient?
Is my strength the strength of stones?
Or is my flesh of brass?

—JOB 6:11,12

NOW that Nebuchadrezzar's army was departed from Jerusalem, life in Bethul returned to its former course (the old woman Tamar said to the young scribe). Those who had predicted that the Babylonians would never come against Bethul cursed Merari for making them dig the shaft in the middle of town, saying that it would yet be the cause of many broken necks. Some demanded that Merari's own servants fill in the hole, and were scornful when he begged them to complete the task. But Merari was as stiff-necked as his neighbors. Since neither would do the work, the shaft remained there to remind all of how the Babylonians had not besieged Bethul. And they called it Merari's folly.

But soon people turned their minds to different matters. None truly knew the number of the captives Nebuchadrezzar had carried away. Though Jeremiah made it known that the king of Babylon had led only three thousand into exile, some claimed that Nebuchadrezzar had carried away ten thousand prisoners. Nor would they believe that the king of Babylon had left behind most of the precious vessels. But each believed according to the side he had taken before the war.

Thus nothing was changed, nor was Zedekiah a better king than the one before him. Soon the poles of Ashtoreth went up again all over the land. On every rooftop people poured out libations to the deities of heaven, and they burned their children in the Valley of Tophet as in former times. Judges accepted gifts, merchants falsified weights, masters would not free their Hebrew slaves in the seventh year, men committed adultery and women harlotry, and there were sodomites plying their trade in the very shadow of the temple.

All this we knew only from such tales as a stray traveler would bring to Bethul. From these travelers we also learned that new prophets had arisen who proclaimed that the captives would shortly return from Babylon, together with the vessels that were carried away. For there was a rumor that the captains of his own army had revolted against Nebuchadrezzar and that there was turmoil in Babylon.

But Jeremiah warned the people not to trust these prophets, who prophesied to them such lies as they wished to hear. Indeed he wrote a letter to the captives in Babylon, counseling them to prepare for a long captivity and to live in peace in the land where they had been taken. Later we heard that there was among the captives one Shemaiah, who complained to the priest Zephaniah in Jerusalem about the letter Jeremiah had written and asked that the prophet be put in prison. But Jeremiah remained free. As for his accuser, it was whispered that he was burned in the fire by the king of Babylon.

These were the rumors we heard in the beginning of King Zedekiah's reign. But not even Merari, who was wont to worry over such matters, paid much heed to these tales. For it was the year Manasseh was twenty-two years old, and his grandfather Shallum came to Merari, demanding that he and Judith be married now.

"Not until after the harvest," Merari replied, stammering as he would when he was upset. "Was it not at the time of the barley harvest that your own two sons were seized by the fever and died, each in his twenty-third year?"

"Nephew, I am an old man," Shallum said. "I do not know how many years God will grant me yet. Therefore I would see my grandson the father of a son that I might die knowing my seed continued on earth. But I had better send the boy's father to deal with you, Merari, lest I perish of vexation even before the wedding."

The following day Manasseh's father came to call on Merari. Now it was known that Ephraim was no better than a servant in the house of his wife's father because of the grief he had brought to Athara. For he had never ceased from pursuing after every maidservant in town. If Manasseh should die before him, his wife's father would turn out Ephraim like a dog unless there was a grandchild of his blood born in the house. Thus Ephraim was even more eager than the old man to see Manasseh married to Judith.

Merari despised Ephraim and had not asked him into his house
since they signed the marriage contract for their children, the year
King Josiah was slain at Megiddo. But, being a good host, he now
bade his visitor sit with him on the rug by the hearth and called for
a jug of wine that they might not discuss with parched throats such
a weighty matter.

My mother sent me to wait on the men, but she would not let
Judith enter the room where her marriage was being discussed.

"You might as well let me enter," Judith said, tossing her head.
"My father will never consent to my marriage. Nor do I much care
to marry Manasseh, who would still rather play with my hair than
kiss me!

"It is a good thing your father did not hear you utter such speech
of harlotry," my mother said.

But in truth she cared even less for this marriage than did Judith.
And sending me off with the jug of wine, she bade me keep my
distance from our guest after I had served him.

Soon I understood her words of caution. For when I bent over to
refill Ephraim's cup, his hand slipped under my skirt and up my leg
toward my buttocks. The blood rushed to my cheeks and I stepped
back quickly, but I could not keep from glancing at Ephraim from
beneath lowered lids. Though he was no longer young he was still
handsome in a coarse way, with dark shadows under his eyes that
betrayed a knowledge of many women. And though one knows
such a man to be utterly worthless, there is something about him
that will tempt women.

But Merari, not being a woman, could barely conceal his disgust.
He watched in silence as his guest downed his third cup of wine, in
this manner postponing the unwelcome debate. Ephraim's face was
flushed from the wine. There were drops clinging to his beard, and
his thick lips glistened red and moist. He wiped them with his hand
before speaking:

"You know why I have come, Merari. My son and your daughter
ought to be married this year. In truth they should have been
married already, for they are both in their twenty-third year.
Therefore let us set a date."

"Not before the barley harvest," Merari replied.

"You need not fear that Manasseh will die at the barley harvest,"
Ephraim said. "His mother would never permit him to work in the
sun with the other men."

"This is hardly a matter for boasting," Merari replied surlily, stammering as he spoke. "It was folly betrothing my daughter to a weakling like your son. But they were both children then, and I was leaving for war and did not know whether I would return alive. However, now I am willing to buy back the marriage contract from you by giving you some of my choice fields."

"Why should I take part of your land, Merari, if in the end all will come down to your daughter and my son?"

"Not if Judith remains childless and Manasseh dies before her. Then all the land will be hers, while you, Ephraim, will go empty-handed."

Ephraim only shook his head, wiping his lips that were moist from his fourth cup of wine. Then he spoke with the thick voice of one who has drunk too much:

"If my son dies, am I not his nearest kin, he having no brothers? And would I shirk my duty to raise up his seed on earth? Neither would Judith have to disguise herself as a harlot like Tamar when she would have her dead husband's father lie with her!"

When I heard Ephraim utter such speech before the master, my bowels turned to water. Glancing at Merari, I saw that his face was become dark red and that the veins throbbed in his neck. He rose from the rug with his fists clenched, stepped close to Ephraim and stammered:

"Be gone from my house!"

Unclenching his fists, he bent over as if to seize his guest by the throat. Ephraim jumped to his feet, staggered backward and shouted drunkenly:

"You would appear righteous before me, Merari, but I know well the reason why you will not let your daughter be married!"

"Be gone before I strangle you!" Merari cried hoarsely, pursuing him.

No sooner had Ephraim escaped through the door than Merari reared up like a horse struck by a whip and crashed full length to the floor. I dropped the jug of wine and ran to him. When I knelt down beside the master, he dug the fingers of his right hand so hard into my arm that tears came to my eyes. But when he tried to raise his left he could not do it. Then he pulled me down to him and whispered, stammering so that I barely understood his words:

"Swear . . . swear . . ."

"But what, my lord?"

"Never . . . leave . . . her. Judith . . . never . . . day and night . . . take no husband . . . swear . . ."

My dread was such that I would have sworn to anything.

"If you break your vow," Merari said, his voice ebbing, "I shall return from . . . I shall return . . ."

He tried to say more, but his head rolled back and his voice went out with his life.

My shriek of terror brought my mother and Judith running from the kitchen. When Judith saw her father on the floor she dropped to her knees beside him. Taking his head in her arms she spoke to him, nor would she let go even after she saw that he would answer her no more. My mother tried to loosen her arms from around Merari, but Judith spat at her like a furious cat. She held Merari's head against her bosom so that her red hair spilled over him, mingling with the black hair of his beard. For Merari was not yet sixty years old when he died, and though his temples had turned gray, his beard and his bushy eyebrows had not changed color. But his face, which had been dark red when he crashed to the floor, was ashen now. It was a dreadful sight to behold this tall man lying still on the floor, with his head cradled in the arms of his daughter.

Judith neither wept nor screamed but just sat glaring at us, as though she defied any to take Merari from her. Then my mother pulled me aside and whispered:

"There is nought we can do until her eyes close from weariness. She is like her father in that she cannot let go of what she loves. Neither shall we call the wailing women yet lest they spread evil tales about her, for they would think it unseemly that she sit thus without shedding a tear. But now tell me what was said in this room, for I saw our visitor fleeing from the house in terror."

When I repeated to my mother Ephraim's lewd words, she cursed him, saying:

"May he come to an evil and untimely end for speaking thus to the master! He might as well have taken a knife and driven it into Merari's heart! But we cannot prevent him from fetching Judith to become his son's bride, for it is written in the marriage contract that upon her father's death she is to marry Manasseh. Though this contract was written fifteen years ago, when Merari went off to war, it was witnessed and sealed, and such a contract cannot be broken."

Not until Judith's eyes closed with weariness did we let it be known that Merari was dead. Then my mother and I did what had to be done. We rent our garments, scattered dirt on our heads and ran out in the street with our hands placed upon our heads in mourning. And we called for the wailing women to come and lament over the death of Merari, who had walked the earth like a prince and had stood head and shoulders above all other men, even after he was become old and lame.

Judith remained sitting on the floor of the room where Merari had died and where we had placed him on a bier. There she sat staring at her dead father, but she did not weep or lament, neither did she dishevel her long red hair, which fell down almost to her waist. Nor did she shed tears when her aunt Sarai and all her daughters came to the house with their hands upon their heads, even Joab's wife, Rebeccah, who was again big with child. But Sarai embraced Judith, weeping loudly, and said:

"You are my nearest kin now that my brother Merari is dead, and my brother Aaron carried away captive to Babylon. And remember we always honored your father and he looked after us, for we are needy!"

Then my mother said under her breath:

"Her grief is in her mouth, nor is she ashamed to ask for charity even before her brother is buried."

But we had little time to heed Sarai. Soon all the people of Bethul came to the house to mourn Merari, even those who had been at odds with him over digging the shaft in the middle of town. However, Judith would speak to none, nor did she answer when Shallum would comfort her by saying that she should not long live alone but should soon come to share his house as his grandson's wife. Only Athara, who stood among the wailing women trying to outwail them all, did not approach Judith, neither would she allow Manasseh to go near her.

"Judith is unclean from touching the dead," Athara said to her son. "Keep yourself from her till she be purified of her uncleanness."

And Manasseh did as his mother bade him.

When the men lifted the bier to carry Merari up into the hills where he was to be buried in a cave beside the burial cave of Shoshanna, his wife, everybody observed Judith to see if she would try to prevent them. But my mother had mixed a soothing potion into the cup of consolation she had offered Judith. Thus Judith was in a stupor and consented without a struggle to everything that was done. She followed silently after Merari's body, towering above the mourning women as her father had towered above the men. Her face was pale and her large green eyes remained lifeless as she watched a heavy rock being rolled before the mouth of the cave into which Merari's body had been carried.

Then my mother and I led Judith home, put her to bed and watched over her all night, lest she come to and do herself some harm. But even the following morning, after the potion my mother had mixed in her wine had lost its power, Judith did not weep or lament. She rose from her bed, washed her face, went to the door, and looked up at the bright sky, saying:

"We shall have a rich and early harvest. My father will be pleased."

I glanced at my mother, who observed Judith with concern. But when Shallum came to the house to inquire after Judith and found her up and about, he said:

"The truly pious accept the will of God. And since Judith has been comforted, let the wedding take place before the month is over, for a feast of joy cancels all grief and mourning."

While Shallum's household was busy preparing for the wedding feast, Judith continued in her own house as if nothing had changed. She rose early, put the maidservants to work, bade the men clean the storehouses for the new harvest, and went down into the fields to see when the barley would be ready for reaping. She walked through the stables, counted the cows that were to calve and the ewes that were to bring forth lambs, and ministered to such beasts as were sick. And every day she fed Hadad and walked him about the yard, for though he was old he still had a fiery temper that terrified the menservants. Thus Judith performed all the tasks which had been Merari's. She worked from sunup till sundown, eating little and growing very thin in the month between her father's death and her wedding day. Nor did she speak much, but sank wearily into bed after her day's work, concealing her grief from the world. But

I, who slept on a mat beside her bed—for I had made the vow to Merari—sometimes woke in the middle of the night to hear her moan as one in terrible pain.

When I spoke of this to my mother, she went to Judith and said:

"I suckled you at my breast, Judith, and after your mother's death I raised you like my own daughter. Now if there be such a thing as you would confide only in a mother, tell me."

But Judith remained silent. Then my mother continued:

"If you would not be married yet, let me go and speak to Shallum. Should he refuse to listen I shall speak to Athara, who will surely do all she can to keep her son from marrying, even if not to help *you*."

But Judith shook her head and replied:

"It matters little whether I marry now or next year, for I shall feel the same then. Nor does it matter whether it be to Manasseh or to another. As for the wedding feast, let it be soon lest it hold up the harvest."

"Never have I heard such speech from a maiden," my mother said. "You speak like one who does not know what a husband is for."

"I know well what a husband is for," Judith said. "But I have never known a man I would truly want to marry. Let me be Manasseh's wife then, for we have been betrothed since childhood, and he is gentle and will do me no harm."

"Now you speak like an utter fool," my mother said. "If you would grieve for your father as is seemly and not shut the pain in your heart to treasure it, you would soon come to your senses and know that someday you will want a man instead of a memory!"

Then Judith turned pale, and pointing at the golden ring in my mother's ear, she exclaimed:

"You forget that you are but a slave in my house, Dinah! You have no right to speak to me thus! As for me, I shall do what I think right."

"Who am I to gainsay my mistress?" my mother said, bowing down low. But there was bitter mockery in her voice. "Let me therefore prepare your robes and your jewels that you may go to your wedding as befits a joyful bride!"

The wedding feast was the most lavish Bethul had ever witnessed. It was not every day that the richest maiden in town was married to the grandson of the richest man in town. For days the maidservants in Shallum's house cooked and baked and roasted meat and stewed fowl, and the men brought up many jugs of wine from the cool storage pits so that all who came to the wedding might make merry. In those days, when there were still people of wealth in Judah, a wedding feast continued for seven days. There was no end to the victuals and wine needed for the guests. All this was provided by the bridegroom, while the bride brought only her dowry and such jewels as her father had given her as presents.

But Judith was wealthy in her own right. She was an heiress who owned much land, and cattle and menservants and maidservants, property that would remain hers if she ever was divorced through no fault of her own. In this at least Merari had dealt wisely, my mother said, for she did not believe that Judith would long remain married to Manasseh.

"Marrying a strong and hale maiden to such a one as Manasseh is a jest in the eyes of men and a sin in the eyes of God," my mother said.

But to Judith she said none of this as she prepared her for the wedding. She bathed Judith, washed her hair, anointed her body with precious oil and poured perfume over her. She dressed her in the finest white linen garment, whose borders were embroidered with gold thread, and on her feet she put embroidered slippers. She enlarged Judith's green eyes with kohl, and after braiding her long red hair she draped the veil around her head. The veil, gossamer sheer with a border embroidered with gold thread, fell down at the back almost to the floor. Upon Judith's forehead my mother placed the diadem Shoshanna had worn at her wedding to Merari. And she put in her ears Shoshanna's golden earrings set with precious stones, and about her neck gold and silver chains, and a stomacher set with beryl and lapis lazuli, and bracelets on her wrists and rings on her fingers and silver bangles with little bells upon her ankles so that Judith made a tinkling noise as she walked.

When she was thus attired Judith went to her bridegroom's house. The people stood in the street to gape at her, men, women and children, all saying that they had never seen a bride of such beauty. For Judith was tall as a palm tree and moved stately as a queen, her jewels glittering in the sun and the silver bells on her ankles tinkling as she walked. But her face was ashen beneath her dark-red hair, making her green eyes with the kohl around them seem huge. She did not smile as she walked through the streets, neither did she glance left or right. And when all the guests gasped at her beauty as she entered Shallum's house, she still did not smile.

Athara broke into loud weeping when she saw Judith. She had never forgotten that Judith's mother had taken away the man she had hoped to marry, and now Judith was come to take away her son.

But Manasseh came forward to greet his bride. Though his beard was grown he looked like a pretty child beside her, for he barely came up to her shoulder, and his hands and feet were like those of a young girl. He too was dressed in white linen, with a garland upon his head, earrings in his ears and bracelets upon his wrists. He blushed when Judith bowed down low before him, for she had often teased him and chased cows after him, but now she was come to be his wife. And he too bowed down before her and led her to the seat of honor, where she was to sit beside him while his grandfather read the marriage contract to the guests.

First, however, Shallum had to bid his daughter cease from her weeping that he might make himself heard. Even while he read the contract aloud there was whispering among the guests, who were astounded by the terms. For Merari had made it plain that his property was to remain Judith's forever.

While the contract was being read I looked about me and caught Ephraim gazing at Judith in a manner that made my skin crawl. But when I glanced at the faces of the other men I saw that all observed her in like manner, save Joab, who looked like a sick calf and seemed about to weep. The only man whose eyes were not on Judith was her own bridegroom. He sat staring down into his lap, but now and then he glanced up at his mother or his cousin Joab. And when he saw Joab gaping at Judith he blushed and let his gaze drop again.

My mother whispered in my ear:

"There will be many children begotten upon Judith tonight, yet she will bear none. But we must look to her good name, and there is a thing I would have you do."

Then, as the feasting began, with the guests falling to the food and drink, the musicians strumming the harps and beating the timbrels, and people singing the old love songs that were sung at weddings, my mother pulled me into a corner and handed me a small, sealed vial.

"Conceal this vial in your bosom," she said to me. "When you assist Judith in undressing later at night, break it and sprinkle the contents on the sheet of the bridal bed. But do not let Judith catch you at it."

"Is it a potion to ensure that she conceive?" I asked.

"Ask no questions but do as I bid you," my mother replied. "Nor fail in your task if you love Judith."

Then I remembered the vow I had made Merari, and I asked my mother where I was to sleep that night.

"Surely you cannot sleep with Judith in the bridal chamber," my mother said. "Bed down on the floor outside the door and call me when you hear her stir in the morning, for I shall be keeping a vigil in the yard outside. Make sure then that you remember my instructions and follow them faithfully!"

But it took a long time yet before the singing and dancing, eating and drinking were over, and the guests went home to return next morning for the second day of feasting. Many were drunk, but none more so than the bridegroom's father, who proclaimed aloud that there would be a grandson born to him before the year was over. The louder Ephraim boasted the louder his wife wept, until all thought she would surely perish of joy.

As for Judith, she barely took a morsel, though she had a cup of wine. When the time came to go to her bridal chamber her face turned even paler, and leaning heavily on my arm she said:

"The wine has made me drunk and I shall be sick."

But she contained herself, not wishing to be disgraced before the other women, who called after her such lewd remarks as are made at the wedding of a virgin.

While I helped Judith take off her jewels and garments, the men brought Manasseh to the door of the bridal chamber. When Judith heard the voices and laughter of the men, she shuddered and put her hands over her face. Then I quickly took the vial out of my bosom, slipped my hand under the blanket of the bridal bed and emptied the contents of the vial. But when Judith dropped her hands from her eyes and looked at me I pretended that I was only smoothing the sheets. And I carried the vial outside concealed beneath her trinkets and clothes.

I found Manasseh before the door, looking not like a bridegroom but like one about to enter a lion's den, while all the men laughed and joked and tried to push him forward. Just then there was heard a piercing shriek as of a woman in travail, and a maidservant came running to tell Manasseh that his mother had fallen upon the ground in convulsions and that she wanted to see him before she died. Manasseh ran off after the maid, leaving the men to frown, grin and offer to take his place while he comforted his mother. Ephraim, who was very drunk, tried to outdo them in lewdness until he remembered that Manasseh was his son and the woman who went on shrieking his own wife, and he too went to her. Then the last guests went home, muttering that they hoped Athara would recover lest the wedding feast be cut short by mourning.

In the end only I remained, not knowing whether to enter the bridal chamber and comfort Judith or wait outside for Manasseh's return. I listened at the door, but I heard nothing stir within, and thinking that the wine had put Judith to sleep, I bedded down outside the door.

I dozed off but was awakened from time to time by another shriek from Athara. As for Manasseh, he did not return until it was almost dawn. I pretended to be asleep, but I saw his father lead him by the arm, push him into the bridal chamber and shut the door behind him. Then Ephraim bent over me so that I feared he would force me, but he only touched my shoulder and whispered:

"Should Manasseh come forth from the room, show him that you are awake and he will return."

But neither Manasseh nor Judith came forth until the sun rose in the sky and the first guests returned to the house. When I heard a stirring in the bridal chamber I ran to fetch my mother, who had slept all night in the yard. She came into the room just as Athara entered through another door, both approaching the bridal chamber. Then my mother said to Athara:

"Praised be the Lord that one who only last night was on the threshold of death should be so swiftly recovered."

"Praised be He," Athara replied. "And what is your business here so early in the morning, when you should be at home looking after the house of your mistress?"

"I have come to look after a weightier matter—the good name of my mistress," my mother said. "Since I suckled her at my breast and she has neither father nor mother, I came to fetch the sheet from her bridal bed."

Athara smiled and said:

"Let us both go then to fetch this sheet and show it to all the people, for I too am concerned about the chastity of my son's wife."

My mother scratched on the door, and Judith's voice bade her enter.

Judith and Manasseh sat on the rug before the bed, both fully clothed, their faces pale and weary. The bed did not look as if two had spent their wedding night in it, but then Judith might have smoothed it after rising in the morning. Athara smiled when she saw the bed, and approaching it she threw back the coverlet. Then she gasped and turned pale, for there was on the sheet a large, brown stain as of dried blood. Manasseh blushed deeply when his mother turned to glower at him, while Judith quickly glanced at me. But my mother ran to the bed, pulled off the sheet and held it up in triumph, exclaiming:

"Come then, Athara, and let us display the sheet before the wedding guests, as you proposed! Let all know that your son married a virgin!"

And my mother walked out swiftly. But Ephraim, who had followed the women into the room, embraced Manasseh, blessed him and said:

"God willing, a son shall spring from your loins!"

And Shallum too blessed Manasseh, saying to Athara:

"You may well weep with joy, my daughter, for this is a great day for all of us!"

But later, while the feasting continued, with all the guests celebrating even more heartily now that they knew the marriage had been sealed, Judith pulled me aside and said:

"Who bade you do this thing?"

And I replied that my mother had commanded me to do it.

Then Judith called my mother to her and said:

"You had no right to shame me thus before Manasseh and Athara, for they know the truth. Nor did I have to prove myself a virgin, for I was never seen with a man other than my own father."

"Fool," my mother replied. "Righteousness has never yet shielded one against a hatred such as Athara bears you. Even as I came to get the sheet from your bridal bed, she too was on her way to do the same. Had I not made provision, she would have called you a harlot before everyone. And Manasseh would never have dared tell the truth—as he will not tell the truth now—for he fears his father's wrath as much as that of his mother. Nor would it have helped your cause that you were seen only with your father, for the imagination of men is evil. Your father was a strange man who would not take a wife after your mother died, neither would he let you be married at the appointed time. These same people who dance and make merry at your wedding feast would have stoned you to death, as is done to women who commit the sin of which they would have accused you. But the land that your father cleared with his own hands and made fruitful would have gone to Shallum and his heirs!"

Then Judith turned ashen and said:

"You did well, Dinah. but none must ever learn of this."

"And would I reveal such a thing?" my mother said. "Neither will Athara, for she would not admit having kept her son from you on your wedding night. As for this boy you took for your husband, you had better come and live with him in your own house, for you need not take bread from the hand of his kin, being wealthier than they. Nor will you ever spend one joyful day in the same house with your husband's mother."

But Judith only shook her head, set her jaw and replied:

"This I shall not do. No other man shall ever live in the house which my father built that he might walk about in it upright!"

That night when the guests returned to their own homes Athara again fell into a fit. And so she did every single night of the wedding feast, keeping Manasseh by her side until dawn. But toward morning he always went to the room he shared with Judith and slept there until it was time to rise.

Though I never discovered another stain on the sheets I would search Judith's face to see whether she was not become a wife. She had worked hard in the fields and had often swung herself upon Hadad—much to the horror of the other women—and they say that such maidens do not bleed in their bridal bed. But her face was as closed as her lips, and though she met my glance evenly her eyes revealed nothing to me.

While the wedding feast was still in progress, my mother came to tell Judith that she had better fetch Hadad to her new home. The men feared to enter his stable, and he would surely starve to death if she did not look after him. Then Judith begged her uncle Shallum to make room for Hadad in one of his stables. But Ephraim, who heard her make that request, laughed and said:

"Let us put Hadad in the stable with our she-ass! Though he is old and half blind, there is a thing for which neither man nor horse needs keen sight. Hadad might yet beget a foal upon our ass. Then she and Judith shall be delivered of a young the same year!"

Judith made no reply but fetched Hadad and put him in the stable with the she-ass. Whenever she went to feed the horse I went with her. According to my vow to Merari I always stayed at her side, save when she slept in the room she shared with her husband. Sometimes Ephraim would come to the stable to watch Judith walk Hadad, gazing upon her as no man ought to gaze upon his daughter-in-law. And he made many coarse remarks about what Hadad was doing with the she-ass, but Judith never answered him, and in the end she even ceased to blush.

Manasseh kept away from the stables, never having overcome his fear of animals. And when it was time to harvest and Judith asked him to go down with her into the fields, Athara replied in his stead:

"My son is of delicate health as am I, nor is he accustomed to work in the sun. I do not know what can be in your mind to make this request, unless you would be left a widow before your time!"

Judith sighed and said:

"Manasseh has a grandfather and a father to look after his inheritance. Thus he may stay home and play with his toys. But I must look after my own land."

And Judith tucked up her skirts and followed her servants down into the fields, to tend to the tasks which Merari had performed before he died. But Manasseh stayed at home playing with his toys. He had many figurines of wood, and some even of silver, which he had carved himself. None had shown him how to do this work, for there was no silversmith in Bethul, all jewelry having been brought from Jerusalem before Nebuchadrezzar carried off the workers in silver. However, Manasseh knew how to fashion things of beauty with his fine hands. He would gather flowers in the garden and arrange them in vases more deftly than any woman. And he would play endlessly with his garments, bracelets and earrings, while Judith worked with the men in the fields below.

That year the harvest was richer than ever. The early rains had been plentiful, and the late rains had come in their proper season. The barley stood high and ripe, and the wheat was turning yellow. Judith helped cut the long stalks with the sickle, tie them in sheaves and load them on oxcarts after they had dried in the sun to take them to the threshing floor. There she stood among the other women swinging the winnowing fork, with her red hair blowing in the evening breeze that carried off the chaff like a golden cloud, while the heavy grain fell back to the ground. At such times she seemed happy, as if she had forgotten that her father was dead and that she was married to a husband who was not a man.

When she returned from the fields, Manasseh would gaze at her in dismay, exclaiming:

"Oh, Judith, your hair!"

And he would fetch a comb, run it through her red tangles and braid her hair better than any maidservant could. Judith would let him amuse himself in this manner, being fond of him as one might be fond of a child. But Athara would look in in disgust, saying:

"Judith's hair is filthy and will cause warts on your hands, Manasseh! Come let me wash your fingers and pour oil over them lest you suffer grievous harm."

But for once Manasseh would not listen to his mother.

"Judith's hair is like the finest purple silk," he replied. "And it smells of the sun and the fresh grain!"

And he would continue combing her hair. Judith would hide a smile, for though she would not dispute with her mother-in-law, she knew how to vex her without using words. Nor did she consent to quarrel until Athara began to taunt her for being barren. For though the she-ass had conceived, it soon became plain that Judith had not.

"Your mother at least bore a daughter," Athara said to Judith. "But you cannot do even that. It is already the time of the grape harvest, and you have not yet conceived. When I was married that long I was four months with child!"

At first Judith kept her peace. But one day she replied, overcome by vexation:

"If you truly long for a grandchild, I shall give my handmaiden Tamar as a concubine to Manasseh that she might bear a child upon my knees to be counted as mine."

"Alas, this thing cannot be," Athara said dolefully. "Your father had it written in the marriage contract that Manasseh must not take another wife besides you, neither may he take a concubine."

Then Judith said with a smile:

"It is written in the contract that Manasseh may not *take* a concubine. It is not written that I may not *give* him one."

I remembered then how Judith had gone to observe her father judge the cause of the people in the gate, and I saw that she had learned there a thing or two. Athara paled at the thought of having to keep her son from two women, and she taunted Judith no more.

As for Ephraim, he would not be put off so easily. Whenever he came to the stable and saw the belly of the she-ass swelling, while Judith remained slender as a reed, he would say:

"Are you not yet with child, Judith? Is my son such a poor gardener that he cannot make you render fruit? Though Manasseh may not know how to plow a field, yet should he know how to do much sweeter plowing! But then perhaps the fault is mine for instructing him in neither."

And Ephraim would gaze at Judith in his manner until she turned crimson with vexation and led Hadad back into the stable.

This continued until the following spring, when the she-ass was delivered of a foal. It was the time when shoots rise green from the fields and the first blossoms appear in the terebinth trees, when cows give birth to calves and ewes drop their lambs. Every day Judith ran to the stables to count the young born on her land and on Shallum's land. She would pick up the newborn lambs and press them to her bosom, her lovely face flushed by longing.

One evening at sunset a manservant came to the house bringing the news that the she-ass with whom Hadad had mated had dropped her foal. Judith let out a shout of joy and hastened to the stable, while I ran after her, for I too would see the newborn mule. In the door we met Ephraim coming in. He inquired where we were running, and when I called the answer back over my shoulder, I saw that he did not enter the house but remained standing in the door, his hand shading his eyes against the setting sun. But I hastened on after Judith, for she was swifter than I and had already entered the stable.

I found her there, kneeling in the straw beside the newborn wet gray mule. The mother moved skittishly around, but without harming Judith, for she had a way with beasts. Judith fondled the mule and cooed to it, and then she spoke words of praise to Hadad, who stood behind a gate in a separate stall in the stable, neighing and pawing the ground and demanding Judith's attention.

When Ephraim entered the stable neither Judith nor I paid much heed to him, for we thought he too had come to see the foal. But he seemed out of breath, as though he had been running, and said to me:

"Just after you left, Tamar, a maidservant came from Merari's house, shouting that your mother was taken ill of a sudden and that she would have you come to her. Therefore make haste, for her illness may be grave!"

I jumped up, glancing from Ephraim to Judith to see if she would come with me, for my mother was almost mother to her. But Judith remained kneeling in the straw with her arms around the foal. When she saw me linger, she said:

"Do not tarry, Tamar, but be on your way! If your mother be indeed gravely ill, send word and I too shall come!"

Then I picked up my skirts and ran out of the stable and through the dusky streets to Merari's house. There I found my mother standing over the hearth in the kitchen, stirring food in a pot. She looked up and asked in amazement:

"What brings you here all disheveled and out of breath?"

"Then you are well!" I exclaimed, throwing myself at her bosom.

"And why should I not be well?"

When I repeated to her Ephraim's message, she ceased stirring the stew on the hearth and asked:

"Where is Judith?"

"She was in the stable when I left her."

"And Ephraim?"

"He too was in the stable."

My mother dropped the spoon and cried:

"Let us hasten back to the stable, but run ahead, Tamar, for I am no longer young and we might be too late!"

When I understood why Ephraim had thought of a ruse to send me away, I ran back, with my breath hurting in my chest and my hair flying. In the street I came upon Hadad, racing past me as though possessed by a demon, neighing, rearing up and stumbling, for his sight was almost gone. What few people were about scattered left and right out of his path, but I had no time to tarry and hastened on to the stable.

When I entered and beheld the sight before me I began to scream, nor could I cease from it until my mother came upon me from behind, shook me and slapped my face.

The gate to Hadad's stall stood open. And there upon the straw lay Ephraim with his head bashed in, his brains spilling out and blood all over his face and his garments. But Judith stood with her back pressed against the wall of the stall, her arms spread wide and her fingers clawing the brick. Her face was white, her eyes dark with terror and her mouth agape, but no sound came out of it. And there was blood on the hem of her skirt.

"Be silent," my mother hissed at me, quickly glancing back over her shoulder to see whether my screams had brought anyone running. Then, stepping over Ephraim as if he were but a piece of carrion, she entered Hadad's stall and approached Judith.

"Did he touch you? Did the wretch harm you?" she asked.

Judith did not reply, nor did she nod or shake her head but remained standing with her outstretched arms supporting her against the wall. My mother bent down swiftly, examined the blood on Judith's garment, lifted up her skirt, glanced at her thighs and murmured:

"Praised be the queen of heaven, there is no mark on her!"

And pulling the amulet she wore around her neck out of her bosom, she kissed it and whispered:

"Thank you, lady, for avenging Merari's death and bringing the dog to his deserved end." Then she raised her glance and spoke to the air: "As for you, master, leave Hadad's body and return to your grave, for the carrion shall trouble your daughter no more."

When I heard my mother commune with the dead the hair rose on the back of my neck. Though I knew her to have understanding of charms and sorcery, I had never seen her practice it. Then it was I who glanced fearfully at the door lest one of the men enter and overhear her words, for they would surely burn her for a witch.

But Judith stood as before, neither speaking nor moving. And when my mother could not pry her fingers from the wall, she struck Judith hard across the cheek. Then Judith let go of the wall, covered her face with her hands and began to weep loudly. But my mother pulled her to her bosom and asked in a low voice:

"Did you scream when he would force you, maddening Hadad so that he kicked the swine to death?"

I do not know whether Judith whispered an answer or only nodded, for she stood with her face hidden in my mother's shoulder. But my mother bade me run to the house and fetch Ephraim's widow and his son. And she ordered me to bring a sheet that we might cover the body, and to lock up the dogs lest they be crazed by the smell of blood.

"If any ask you how it happened, say only that Hadad went mad, broke the gate of his stall and killed Ephraim."

I did as my mother bade me. Running to the house I rent my garments and disheveled my hair to let them know that I bore bad tidings. When I shouted the news through the door, Athara set up a wailing as if she had not hated her husband all her married days but had loved him with utter devotion. She ran to the stable even before the men, while I and Manasseh followed after her.

Though Manasseh's face was ashen he did not weep. But when we entered the stable he gasped, covered his eyes with his hands and turned away retching. Athara cast one glance at her dead husband, shrieked and advanced on Judith, who still stood with her face buried in my mother's shoulder. She grasped Judith's long hair with both her hands, and pulling it viciously she cried:

"If a man owns an ox that is known to gore and that ox kills another man, the owner of the ox is put to death for not taking better care of his beast! Just so should they do to you for bringing this murderous horse to our stables!"

She yanked Judith's head back and would have scratched her face—for Judith made no resistance—had not my mother spoken up.

"Beware of slandering Judith, Athara, lest you force me to reveal the truth and make you the derision of Bethul, and your husband even more despised in death than he was in his lifetime! For he followed Judith and Tamar to the stable, telling my daughter that I had fallen ill and had sent a maidservant for her. Even if you search high and low for the maidservant who bore this message you will not find her. But you need not search your imagination to discover what your husband wanted with Judith alone. Also give praise that he did not succeed but was killed by Hadad, for had he defiled his own daughter-in-law he would have been stoned to death by the people!"

"And who would believe such lies about my cruelly murdered husband?" Athara cried.

"There is many a handmaiden in Bethul who could bear witness to how your husband raised her skirts," my mother said. "As for Tamar and me, we would submit to the ordeal to prove the truth of our words. If you will not let go of Judith's hair now and act as is seemly for a bereaved widow, Athara, I shall tell the men that your husband tried to ravish the wife of his own son, and they will throw his body to the dogs!"

Pushing Athara away, my mother put her arm around Judith to lead her from the stable. But Athara said bitterly:

"I am powerless against you, Dinah. You have spun a clever web of lies to conceal that there is a curse on this girl who sucked your witch's milk, for she has brought death to two men in one year. But she shall never harm my son!"

Athara turned to Manasseh, who still stood trembling and retching near the door. But when his mother would put her arms around him, he screamed and fled into the night. He did not return until after his father's body had been carried into the house, washed and placed on a bier. Then the wailing women came to lament over Ephraim, whom all had despised, just as they had wailed over Merari, who had walked the earth like a prince. And Judith too sat in mourning, with her garments rent and dirt scattered on her head. But she did not regain her speech until after Ephraim was buried.

It was when Ephraim's body was taken to his burial cave in the hills that Hadad was discovered. None knew how the old horse had found Merari's grave. But he had climbed the hill during the night and had tried to crash into the cave, for the marks of his hoofs were on the rock before the entrance. And there he had fallen down and died. The men wanted to cut up his carcass and feed it to the dogs. But Judith, who had not spoken since she was discovered in the stable with the dead man, regained her voice and said:

"You shall not deal thus with the horse that carried my father in the battle of Megiddo!"

And she had Hadad buried in the ground outside Merari's burial cave.

Immediately after her husband's burial Athara made Manasseh move out of the chamber he shared with Judith. Now that his father was dead Manasseh need no longer pretend that he was sleeping with Judith. As for his grandfather Shallum, he was become feeble in the past year and spent most of the time upon his bed, his straying mind confounding the past with the future so that he did not know what went on in his own house.

Though she slept alone now, Judith would not allow me to move my mat back beside her bed. I continued sleeping outside her door, my ears becoming witness to what went on in the house after dark. I often heard Athara call for Manasseh at night. Since her husband's death she was plagued by evil dreams, and she also pretended to be in pain. Of the latter none believed her, for she had complained about her delicate health since her youth, and yet she had always been strong as a mule. But Manasseh would rise at her first wail and run to her room to spend many hours sitting beside her bed.

As for Judith, she was kept busy by her work. Now that Ephraim was dead and Shallum too feeble to look after his land, Judith had to tend his fields as well as her own. Thus when harvest time came she moved down into her summer house, while Manasseh remained with his mother in town. But Judith stood over the servants to see that they worked diligently and that they left the gleanings and the tenth part of the crop for the needy, the orphans and widows, just as Merari had done. Of that which was harvested Judith kept a strict account, recording every bushel of grain on potsherds, which she stored in sealed jars. And so she did after the grapes were picked and pressed, and the wine was put into clay jugs to be stored in cool pits. She impressed a seal on the handle of every jug, marking the year of the harvest that they might know the old wine from the new. And when she saw that there was much grain—more than was needed to feed her household, seed the fields the following season and store against a bad harvest—she filled sacks with the grain and had them carried on donkeys to neighboring towns to sell it there at a good profit. Then all proclaimed that they had never seen a woman deal as wisely, less still one so young, for Judith was but twenty-four years old.

When Judith returned to her husband's house in autumn—for she would not have it said that she did not live with Manasseh—she found her mother-in-law lying abed. Athara wailed that she was in great pain and would surely die, while Manasseh sat beside her, weeping and holding his head. And he beseeched Judith to think of a remedy, for he had come to rely upon her for everything.

Now Athara had never done Judith a good turn, nor did Judith bear her great love. But knowing her duty, she said:

"Let us send to Lachish for a physician, for there is none in Bethul who has much understanding."

But Athara shrieked that she could stand the pain no longer and must have a potion to ease it. And she bade me ask my mother mix her one. Then I knew she was indeed in great pain, for she feared my mother and knew how much she hated her.

But when I spoke to my mother she replied that she could not prepare a remedy without seeing the patient. She came to the house, and when she emerged from Athara's room there was a strange smile on her face. Pulling Judith aside, she said:

"Athara has shammed illness for so long that in the end her lying words were turned to truth. But you need not send for a physician. If one who is past the childbearing age bleeds from her womb and her belly swells, she will not live. Athara was struck in her bowels for begrudging you a child and keeping her son from you. But that which grows in her own womb will kill her with a pain as of a woman in travail. The gods are just."

Then Judith raised her hand, exclaiming:

"Let it be known before Yahweh that I never bade you put a curse on her, for I would not deal with the spirits of the nether world!"

"Do not speak rashly, for you may yet call on them," my mother replied.

"Remember, Dinah, that I am Merari's daughter," Judith said haughtily. "Also consider the fate of witches!"

But my mother only smiled, drew her garments about her and returned to Judith's own house.

And it happened according to her prediction. Athara did not rise again from her bed but grew worse, with her belly swelling and her pain increasing until she shrieked like a woman in travail. In the end Manasseh could no longer bear being in her room, and it was Judith and I who tended her. The maidservants refused to go near Athara's bed, murmuring that there was a curse on her. Some even whispered that she was with child by her own son, who had spent all summer in the house with her, while his wife lived in the fields below.

As for Manasseh, he would stand in the door of Athara's room but refuse to enter even when her pain was soothed by my mother's potions and she did not scream. For the room reeked of blood and excrement and of a woman dying, and from childhood on Manasseh would vomit at loathsome odors. Thus Athara spent her last days being nursed by Judith, whom she had always hated, while her own beloved son cowered before the door, unwilling to look upon her death.

Now Judith had to bear the double burden of two households and two dying people. For Shallum too was near death, with his eyesight and much of his mind gone. Now and then when he heard Athara scream he would ask whether Judith was in travail, and when the screams ceased he wished to know whether she had borne a son. In the end, to please him, one of the maidservants brought him a male infant—for Shallum could no longer see—and placed his hands upon his head that he might bless the babe. I feared Judith would be angry when she discovered the deception, but she only sighed and said:

"God gave Shallum a long life that he might see his children die before him. At least let him go to his grave thinking that his seed will continue on earth."

These were hard days and nights for Judith. Manasseh was of no help, though it was his own mother and grandfather who were dying. When the smell of death became too strong in the house he would shut himself in his room to play with his figurines and carve new ones. And they were all wondrously beautiful.

But if Manasseh would not aid Judith, his cousin Joab often came to the house to offer his help. Though his own wife Rebeccah had already borne him four daughters, he was still in love with Judith. He would follow her about as in former times, until she said to him:

"If you will not cease from your folly, Joab, you will give me a bad name in town. Already the maidservants snicker behind your back. God only knows what gossip they spread when they go to draw water from the spring in the valley!"

But Joab replied:

"Is it a sin to visit the house of my kin to comfort them in their grief? Moreover, I do not come to see you but Manasseh, who is almost brother to me, for we grew up together!"

"Then go sit with Manasseh instead of following me about as a calf follows its mother," Judith said, her voice harsh, for she had many burdens to bear and her patience had become short.

From then on Joab took care to spend some time with Manasseh, who was glad of it, for he loved his cousin. One morning as I made up the bed in Manasseh's room, I found under his blanket a new figure he had carved. When I picked it up to gaze at it my hand began to shake, for it was a perfect likeness of Joab. And Manasseh had hidden it under his blanket to sleep with it. I called Judith and asked her what to do with the thing Manasseh had fashioned, for this was idolatry and worse. But instead of smashing the figure Judith bade me put it back where I had found it. Then, sighing so deeply it sounded like a sob, she said:

"Ever since my father died my life has been broken in two, so that what followed after his death bears no likeness to what went before. Moreover, death pursues me like my own shadow. As for Manasseh, he is just one more burden on my shoulders. Perhaps God devised a test for me, though for what purpose I do not know."

But when I repeated Judith's words to my mother, she said:

"Judith cherishes her burden as did her father before her and would test her strength against it. If only Athara and Shallum died and took Manasseh with them! Then Judith might find a husband fit for a woman of her strength and beauty."

Hearing these words I placed my hand over my mouth in horror. For my mother had mentioned Manasseh in one breath with the dying, and I was certain that she was inventing charms against him so that he too might die.

Shortly before the barley harvest Athara and Shallum died within the same week. And they were buried in the hills beside their kinfolk. This was two years after Merari had fallen dead and one year after Hadad had killed Ephraim. Now both Judith and Manasseh were wealthy heirs, she owning all of Merari's land and he all the land of his grandfather. If Manasseh died everything would belong to Judith, making her the richest woman in Bethul—perhaps in all of Judah.

But Manasseh was in good health, and Judith, fearing the curse on her, looked after him even better than his own mother had. She treated him as the child she did not have, running after him with a cloak when he went out on a cold day or warning him to stay out of the sun when it was hot. By then it was no secret to anyone that he was no husband to her. And when Joab continued coming to the house people whispered among themselves that he was her lover, for they could not believe that a hale woman of such beauty should live as she lived.

Then Judith asked Manasseh to bid Joab stay away, for he would not listen to her. But Manasseh replied:

"How can I ask this thing of Joab if he is the only kin left me and I love him with all my soul?"

And he entreated Judith to show Joab all due hospitality and to sit down with them to their meal when he came to the house. In the end Judith relented to keep Manasseh from whining in her ears. But the maidservants who waited on them would run to the kitchen laughing behind their hands, for the three were indeed a strange sight to behold, with Manasseh mooning over Joab, Joab mooning over Judith, and Judith gazing down into her lap.

But Joab never touched Judith, for she would not consent to such a thing. As for Manasseh, all he ever did was adore Joab with his eyes—though what he did on his journeys to Jerusalem was a different matter. None of us was meant to know his secret. But he always took a manservant along, for he would not travel alone, and servants will talk.

Manasseh first journeyed to Jerusalem a year after his mother had died, when he had become comforted and would cheer himself by buying new furniture. He had always delighted in placing tables and chairs this way and that in a novel manner, and in the end it was he who proposed that they move into Merari's house.

"Why should the house that your father built at great expense be kept by your slave Dinah when it might serve our own pleasure?" Manasseh asked Judith. "We could furnish it with new tables and chairs, put rugs on all the floors, place beautiful vessels of silver in the cupboards, and even buy a knife or two that we might live as befits people of our wealth."

But Judith replied:

"The house was good enough for my father, and thus it shall remain. Nor shall we move into it. If you wish to make changes, make them in your own house, though what you propose is but a waste."

"Then what shall we do with all our silver?" Manasseh asked, for though they never spoke about it they knew there would be no children to inherit their wealth.

"We shall use it to buy more fields," Judith said.

"And for what will these fields serve us when we already have much land?"

"To raise more wheat and barley and store it against the years of famine, which never fail to come," Judith said. But her storehouses were full to the brim and she sold much of her grain, earning even more silver with which to acquire fields.

Manasseh stamped his foot like a child and exclaimed:

"If you want to add field unto field until you own all of Judah, please yourself! As for me, the yield of my land is mine and I shall do with it as I please!"

Then Manasseh ordered asses saddled for himself and his servant, and also two pack asses, and he rode off to purchase such things as he fancied in Jerusalem. But Judith said bitterly:

"When it comes to taking our grain to Lachish, Manasseh is too frail for the journey. But to indulge his childish whims he has the strength to ride to Jerusalem!"

My mother only shook her head when she learned of Judith's doings and said to me:

"Merari is dead, and Judith has neither husband nor child to cherish. Thus she pours all her love into the soil. But only a man can be satisfied with owning land. To a woman it is as nothing!"

Yet Judith continued buying fields, while Manasseh brought precious things from Jerusalem: carved chairs with high backs and armrests and low tables inlaid with ivory; rugs and wall hangings woven in intricate patterns and brilliant colors, and fine embroidered garments for Judith. These she wore once or twice to please him and then put them away, for they were not the kind she would wear for standing over the servants in the field. Neither did she wear the silver combs and gold bangles Manasseh bought for her. But then he obtained all these things more to please himself than to please her, for it gave him joy to look at them.

For himself Manasseh bought many new garments, and rings and bracelets and perfume and kohl for the eyes. What he did with the latter I do not know, but I could well imagine it, for whenever he returned from Jerusalem there were dark circles of weariness beneath his eyes. His servant told tales of how Manasseh would slip out of the inn at night not to return until morning. Nor was there a need for him to tell more. Everyone knew that in Jerusalem there were many harlots plying their trade, both male and female. But Judith closed her ears to these tales and pretended that Manasseh returned worn out from the journey. And instead of speaking to him in anger, she spoke angrily of the useless things he brought home.

Another two years passed and Judith's wealth increased, for everything she set her hand to was blessed by God. But she was twenty-seven years old and had no child, though she had much land, many menservants and maidservants, and great herds of cattle and sheep.

Every spring when the young of the flock were born Judith would play with them as she had in her childhood. She would pick up the lambs and press them against her bosom, standing in the meadow with the wildflowers coming up to her waist, her long red hair gleaming in the sun and her eyes sick with longing, so that in looking upon her one's heart could break. But she remained silent in her pride, and her loneliness was greater than before.

At harvest time we moved down into the summer house. Judith would often fetch water from the spring at the bottom of the hill upon which Bethul was built, though she had many handmaidens to do this task. But if she searched for the gay chatter of her youth at the spring she could no longer find it there. All the women her age were married and had children. The maidens who now came to the spring were more than ten years younger than Judith. They would fall silent at her approach, not only because she was older but also because they were awed by her great wealth. And they would not resume their chatter until after Judith had filled her jug, placed it on her head and walked away from the spring. Then they would whisper and giggle and make faces behind her back, now one and now the other trying to imitate the way Judith walked, proudly, with her head held high and her back straight. Yet in spite of all their mirth they knew that Judith was still more beautiful than any of them. But even the ugly ones among them were soon married and with child, and when they came to the spring with their bellies swelling it was like a reproach to Judith. However, she suffered in silence until the following year, when she turned twenty-eight at the time of the barley harvest.

The hot weather commenced early that spring. There were days when the air was so dry that each breath burned in one's nostrils, and the hot wind from the desert flung a yellow veil before the sky, turning its deep blue to a pale green. Judith would stand looking at the sky with her hands upon her hips, sniffing the wind and biting her lips, for the barley was not yet ripe for the cutting and the desert wind might wither it before the harvest. And she would walk through the fields, parting the stalks with her arms so that she looked as if she were swimming through the barley, while the sweat ran down her cheeks and her neck into her garments. But such was the heat that her clothes were barely damp before they were dry again.

When Judith returned from the fields her eyes were red. She paced the house, finding fault with everything and chiding the maidservants until I thought her time of the month was near. She had been testy at such times even when she was younger, but now she was almost as bad as her female kinfolk, who were known for their vile temper. Thus I kept out of Judith's way when her trouble was upon her, knowing she would be herself again once it passed.

But this time she would not leave me in peace, tormenting me until I ran to my mother in tears. Then my mother returned with me to the summer house—for she always remained behind to watch over the house in town—and said to Judith:

"It is six years since your father died, not yet long enough for you to forget that he taught you to treat your slaves with kindness and justice—for were we not all slaves in Egypt? Then why do you walk about stiking them like one consumed by her own venom? And why are your eyes red as though from weeping?"

Judith frowned and bit her lips, but she did not forget that my mother had suckled her at her breast, and she answered with restraint:

"It is I who must see that my household will not starve to death, for my husband will not concern himself with this task. Should I not weep when I see that we shall lose the harvest?"

"The harvest is not yet lost," my mother said. "Nor would your household starve if it were, for you have laid up provisions. Neither are you weeping over the harvest, for there were other years when the harvest was poor and yet you did not weep."

"It is the dust in the air," Judith said.

"There has been dust in the air before without turning your eyes red," my mother said. "Nor is it wise of you to lie to me, Judith, for I can see into your heart."

"Then tell me what you see there," Judith said, gazing at my mother with her red eyes.

"No, you tell me, Judith. You tell me why you pace back and forth like one possessed, why you stand sniffing the wind like a she-ass in her season, why you strike your maidservants and why your eyes are red? Is it that the hot wind has stirred up your blood and reminded you that you are a woman?"

Turning her head away that we might not see her tears, Judith answered softly:

"My youth is going from me and I have no child. Am I not like these fields that will wither before the harvest? I would have a son."

"Then take a husband," my mother replied harshly.

"I have a husband," Judith said.

"If you would call Manasseh your husband and still have a child, you must find a lover," my mother said. "Would not Joab, your husband's nearest kin, gladly fulfill Manasseh's duty toward you?"

"Beware of how you speak to me, Dinah," Judith said, her voice trembling with wrath.

"If you will not accuse Manasseh of his sin nor take a lover, how would you have a child?" my mother asked.

"I would have a child by my husband," Judith replied.

Then my mother smote her thigh, saying:

"Do fish fly? Does snow fall in the summer? Are you Moses that you would strike water from a stone?"

But Judith looked hard at my mother and said:

"You know ways, Dinah. You have means. Give me a potion that will change Manasseh so that I may have a child by him!"

"Just so your mother spoke to me, and a year later she lay dead in the ground!" my mother exclaimed in horror. "May Yahweh do thus and thus to me if I should also bring your blood on my head!"

"You have often told me that I am my father's daughter," Judith said. "I have nought of my mother but her face, nor shall I die in childbirth. If you gave her a potion, knowing she was frail, you will assuredly give *me* such a potion!"

"Judith, your father was a lusty man who loved his wife more than his life and had to guard against getting her with child lest he lose her to death. It was a small matter to slip him a potion that would weaken his will. But there are no potions to turn such a one as Manasseh into what he is not! A sick body can be healed, but a warped soul only the gods can restore. And Manasseh's sickness is not in his blood but in his soul, which his mother snatched from him out of the hatred she bore men—your father because he took another woman for his wife and her husband because he humbled her all his days."

"Then make her release his soul," Judith said.

My mother took a step back and raised her hands before her as though to ward off Judith's request.

"Athara is gone to the nether world—may she be tormented forever by evil demons—and none can follow her there."

"You have ways, Dinah," Judith said softly.

"I know not whereof you speak," my mother said, averting her eyes.

"Remember the day Ephraim was killed by Hadad? Though my speech had fled from me, my hearing remained keen and I heard you converse with the dead in my very presence. If you could do so when I did not bid you do it, you can do so now when I have need of your charms."

My mother was silent a long time before she answered:

"Did you not vow that you would never deal with the spirits of the nether world? Are you then like King Saul who put away those who divined by ghosts, only to inquire afterward of the witch of Endor?"

"I would have a child even if I have to pursue Athara to the nether world to wrest Manasseh's soul from her," Judith replied. "I would have a child, you hear, I would have a child!"

"So be it then," my mother said. "But let Tamar be my witness that you came to me. I never offered of my own will to do what you require."

"Let her be a witness," Judith said. "And now tell me what I must do."

"Have Tamar fetch your bridal garments, your jewels and your

veil from the house in town. You are to dress and adorn yourself as
for your wedding. When you have done so, go to the spring at the
bottom of the hill between the middle and the morning watch,
when the night is darkest. Take Tamar with you and let her carry a
torch, but do not light the torch before you reach the spring lest
any of the servants who sleep in the fields see you. From the spring
a narrow path leads up the hill to the east of Bethul. Make sure you
take the right path, for the entrance to it is overgrown by brambles.
This path will lead you behind the caves where the dead are buried
and up to the top of the hill. Few use it, for people fear to walk
above the dead. Do not be afraid, neither be startled by what you
may encounter, but obey all orders that may be given you along the
way."

"Who will be there to give me orders?" Judith asked with pale
lips.

"If you would seek out the dead you must not ask questions but
obey commands. These are the rules of the nether world," my
mother said. "And now make sure that you follow my instructions,
nor let any know of your plans lest we all be slain before dawn."

I went to fetch Judith's bridal garments from Merari's house,
where she had returned them after her wedding. There they lay in a
chest as though still waiting for the maiden Judith to be married.
My mother folded them for me into a basket to make it appear that
I was carrying sheets to the summer house.

Only Judith and I lived in the house, while the servants slept in
huts and tents in the fields. As for Manasseh, he always remained in
Bethul, for he could not bear the sun. Moreover, his eyes and nose
ran whenever the grain stood high. Thus none observed me when I
spread Judith's wedding dress on her bed and laid out her jewels and
ointments on the table.

Judith returned from the fields at sunset, her face streaked where
the sweat had run down her dusty skin. Upon entering she said:

"If the hot wind does not abate overnight we shall begin reaping
tomorrow. It is better to save what is ripe of the crop than to lose it
all."

But I replied:

"I brought what you sent me for, Judith."

She gazed at me blankly, her thoughts still on the harvest. Then she frowned and quickly walked into her bedchamber, where I had spread out her garments. Bending over the bed she touched them, but not like a woman recalling her happiest day. Then she said:

"It is many hours yet until the middle watch. Let us eat and rest, for we have a long climb before us."

After darkness had fallen we waited until the fires in the fields died down and the singing of the servants faded away. Then Judith bade me bolt the door of the house, bring an oil lamp to her room and help her dress. And I did what my mother had done for her on her wedding day six years ago: I anointed and perfumed her body, braided her hair and helped her slip into her inner and outer garments. I put the chains about her neck, the jeweled corselet about her waist, the bracelets on her wrists, the veil on her head and the diadem upon her veil. But she would not wear her anklets with the silver bells for fear one might hear her walk. When I had dressed her I fetched a basket in which to hide the oil lamp, for we would need a flame to light the torch when we reached the spring.

Then Judith and I slipped outside, pausing to let our eyes become accustomed to the black of night. It was the time of the new moon, when sky and earth melt into one in darkness. But a few stars glittered above, while below the stalks of barley rustled in the steady hot wind.

Judith wordlessly beckoned to me to follow her. We cut a path across the fields, I clinging closely to Judith, for I had never been out in the fields so late at night and I feared the demons that dwelt there. Whenever I heard a rustling in the stalks or the cry of a wild beast I would clutch Judith from behind. But she shook me off and swiftly strode on, her veil billowing in the wind and her bracelets jingling softly.

When we reached the spring at the foot of the hill we halted. We had come into the trees and far enough from the fields to light the torch. Afterward I blew out the oil lamp and set the basket down in the cave of the spring, for we would have no need of it until we returned. Judith raised up the torch to search for the entrance to the path of which my mother had spoken. As she held the torch above her head her jewels caught its glow and the precious stones in her diadem glittered in the dark. The flame lent fire to her red hair and threw dark shadows around her eyes, which she had enlarged with kohl, and she looked like some goddess descended from above. But she addressed me impatiently:

"Why do you gape at me? Hurry and find the path, or we shall never reach the hilltop before dawn!"

I began to pull at the brambles until my hands bled, fearing we would still be discovered. But in the end I found the entrance to the path and we began our ascent.

Again Judith preceded me, climbing swiftly up the steep incline. Now that we were in the woods the rustling was louder, and the fluttering and slithering sounds around us made my hair stand on end. I knew that halfway up the hill the burial caves would be on our left. Then I clutched Judith's garments so tightly she could not shake me off. The higher we climbed the deeper became my terror, for I had never seen my mother practice sorcery. All my life I had gone only where Judith went, and she had never yet gone to consort with witches and raise the dead.

As we approached the summit we could see a faint glow as of a distant fire among the trees, and hear the murmuring of voices. Suddenly a figure clad in white swung out from among the trees and barred our way. I screamed in terror, certain that it was the soul of one of the dead, for I had neither seen nor heard it approach. Even Judith stood stock-still, and I could feel her trembling through her garments. Then the apparition spoke, and though its face was concealed by its tightly drawn veil, the voice sounded familiar. But it was not my mother's voice.

"I shall take your crown," the white figure whispered, raised her arms, snatched the diadem from Judith's head and disappeared among the trees.

We had proceeded but a few steps on the path when a second figure emerged from among the trees and demanded Judith's chains. As we neared the red glow that filtered between the tree trunks, figure after figure swung out from the darkness, seizing Judith's corselet, her bracelets, her veil and her embroidered slippers, until there was nothing but her garments left on her body.

When finally we reached the top of the hill we beheld a startling sight. For there assembled in the firelight was a multitude of women, all virtuous housewives from Bethul who looked neither left nor right in their daily lives. But now they were come to the grove atop the hill to drink wine, pour out libations and celebrate such rites as they pretended to abhor at other times. Nor could their purpose be mistaken. In the midst of the clearing stood a stone altar with four horns, and behind it a high pole of smooth, polished wood—the altar and pole of Ashtoreth, the queen of heaven. Though Merari had smashed these abominations when King Josiah destroyed the heathen idols in Judah, the women of Bethul had raised them again in the grove atop the hill and had installed a priestess to celebrate the rites.

The priestess was my own mother. She was dressed in white robes, with a crown on her head and chains such as I had never seen her wear about her neck. She stood near the altar surrounded by women, who sang and swayed as though already overcome by wine. When she saw Judith she raised her hand to keep her from coming closer and called out to the women:

"Seize her clothes and bring her before me naked!"

Judith paled and turned to flight. But she was already ringed about by women who caught hold of her hair and her arms, undid the pins that held her garments together and pulled them off her, leaving her naked in the firelight. When they released her arms Judith folded them over her bare breasts and tossed her long hair forward to hide her shame. The women around the altar ceased from their revels to gape at Judith, for her body was perfect without a blemish and of such beauty as is praised in our love songs. But my mother, standing before the fire on the altar, beckoned to the women to bring Judith forward.

Again she was seized—for she would not go of her own accord—and dragged to the raised platform of the altar. There the women released her and stepped back to form a half circle around her. My mother, looking like a terrible stranger in her priestly robes, approached the top of the stairs that led down from the platform. Facing Judith, she said:

"What is it you seek here?"

But Judith stood dumb, her head lowered and her arms folded over her bare breasts.

"Have you not come to seek the soul of your husband?" my mother asked. And when Judith only nodded without raising her eyes, she added: "If you would retrieve his soul you must speak the words."

Then Judith looked up at my mother and mumbled:

"I have come to seek the soul of my husband."

Stretching forth her hand to Judith, my mother said:

"Ascend, stand by the pole of the goddess and let us beseech her to wrest your husband's soul from the dead and make him into a whole man that he might beget a son upon you!"

Judith dropped her arms from her breasts, took my mother's hand and climbed the steps to the platform. Now the glow from the altar was fully upon her, the rosy light of the flames dancing over her breasts, her white belly and her thighs. Her hair had come undone and fell down halfway over her round, shapely hips. The flesh of her long legs was firm, for in spite of her wealth she did not spend her days reclining idly upon a couch, and her breasts the high breasts of a maiden who had never borne a child. As she stood there naked before the eyes of all the women, her nipples rose to a dark point, as if every glance were a touch. She shuddered and raised her arms to cover herself again. But then she only cupped her hands over her modesty, and in the end she let them fall to her sides.

My mother led Judith to the pole of the goddess and laid her hands on the smooth pillar that was broader at the base and tapered toward the rounded top. Then, muttering charms and incantations, she set a caldron filled with a dark-red liquid upon the fire of the altar, while woman after woman came forward to bring an offering: the eyes of a cat, the tail of a pig, the foot of a toad, the heart of a snake and other things loathsome and unclean.

Among the women was Judith's own cousin Miriam, the younger sister of Rebeccah, Joab's wife. Miriam was twenty-six, and though she had been married two years she had not yet conceived. I also recognized the harlots who lived by the wall. One brought in a small flask the seed of a youth who had lain with his first woman. A midwife offered the foreskin of a newborn male, and a wailing woman the nail of a dead man who had begotten seven sons. All these things my mother tossed into the caldron as she muttered incantations.

But Judith stood with her eyes closed, her hands caressing the smooth hard pillar of Ashtoreth. She seemed fallen in a trance when my mother touched her shoulder and handed her a cup of wine.

"Drink it all, Judith," she commanded. "Then turn and face the altar that we may summon the dead."

Taking the cup in both her hands Judith emptied it, while my
mother raised her hands, threw back her head and called into the
air:

"Athara, hear me, Athara! Come forth from the evil place where
you dwell and look upon this maiden from whom you would withhold your son! Her beauty shall yet prevail over your wickedness
and she shall conceive seven times!"

My mother handed Judith a fresh cup, and calling upon Ashtoreth, she bade her pour wine upon the ground as a libation. The
other women also drank and poured out libations until the earth
looked as if it were running with blood. But Judith was made to
drink a third and fourth and fifth cup, until she had emptied seven
cups and poured out seven libations. By then she swayed drunkenly,
nor did she any longer attempt to conceal her nakedness but stood
boldly in the firelight.

Now the women drew near to whirl around Judith in wild
dances. Indeed some looked upon her as lewdly as men and tried to
touch her in an indecent manner. But my mother drove them away
with curses. Then, glancing up at the sky, she said:

"The stars are growing pale, marking your time to leave. But first
I shall give you two things."

She fetched a small flask, filled it with the brew from the caldron
and handed it to Judith, saying:

"When you become purified after your next moon, pour this into
your husband's wine and he will lie with you. Until then, pray daily
to the goddess that she may bless you and make you fruitful."

Then my mother took off a chain on which hung the likeness of
Ashtoreth cast in silver and placed it about Judith's neck. Judith's
hand went up to where the amulet lay between her breasts. She
shuddered, but perhaps it was only the cold metal on her hot skin
that startled her.

Afterward my mother bade me lead Judith through the crowd of
swaying women and shield her from their glances and touches. At
the edge of the clearing Judith's garments were restored to her. And
as we descended through the woods all the rest of her belongings
were returned—her slippers, her bracelets, her chains, her corselet,
her veil and her diadem—until she was again fully clothed. Yet she
was not the same Judith who had climbed the hill. Then she had
walked boldly ahead of me, carrying the torch. But now I carried

the torch while Judith leaned upon my shoulder, swaying and
giggling and making dance steps on the perilous path, for she was
very drunk. And so afraid was I that we should both break our
necks that I even forgot to be afraid of the evil spirits.

My heart was eased when we arrived at the spring and I found the
basket where I had left it concealed in the cave. After relighting the
oil lamp I drowned the torch in the water and turned toward the
open fields. But Judith headed east and began to climb the path that
led to Bethul. I thought she had become confused in her drunkenness, but when I would stop her she told me that she would spend
the night with her husband in town. Seeing that she would not obey
my mother's instructions, I exlaimed:

"You must wait until after your next moon, Judith! Nor must
you go to Manasseh before you have made him drink the charmed
potion!"

But Judith only laughed, tossed away the flask my mother had
given her, and spoke drunkenly:

"I was purified from my uncleanness three days ago. As for this
potion I am to give Manasseh—did you not see how the women
glanced at me? Should I then use charms on my husband, who is a
man and has never yet seen me naked? I shall use on him only the
charms of my own body, which I never used on him before!"

And she continued staggering drunkenly up the path to Bethul,
stumbling over loose stones, but neither slowing down nor halting.

"This is madness, Judith!" I called out as I stumbled after her.
"How will you enter Bethul at this hour, when the gate is locked?"

"Is the richest woman of Bethul to be kept from entering the
town when she pleases? I shall pound on the gate and bid the
watchman open up!"

Then I knew that she was indeed mad, and since I could not
detain her I must follow her. Climbing the steep path after Judith, I
became drenched with sweat. Not only was my blood inflamed by
the wine I had drunk, but the hot wind was still blowing steadily.
Judith arrived at the gate before me and began hammering on it
with both her fists while she shouted:

"Open up, open up! Let Judith the daughter of Merari enter
Bethul!"

She was swaying from her effort when I reached her, and I

caught her just as the watchman unlocked the gate and shone his torch upon us. But Judith's head had fallen on my shoulder, and I pretended that she was sick and I was taking her to my mother. Only after we entered Bethul did I remember that my mother was not in town. I wondered how she had slipped out unobserved, for the watchman had not suspected my lie.

But soon my thoughts returned to Judith, who, having recovered, let go of my arm and skipped ahead of me like a newborn kid in spring. It was a good thing that none saw us proceed in this unseemly fashion toward Manasseh's house.

The door of the house was not locked, for there was always a dog in the yard to guard against thieves, and a servant sleeping outside Manasseh's chamber to wait on him when he woke. But knowing Judith the dog did not bark, and when we entered the house the startled servant sat up on his mat, his eyes wide with terror and his mouth open in a soundless scream. My oil lamp shed enough light to reveal Judith decked out in her bridal garments, her jewels, her veil and her diadem. The servant must have thought himself caught in some dreadful dream. I ran to his side and softly bade him leave. In his stupor he obeyed me, snatching up his mat and staggering out into the yard as I hastened to bolt the door behind him.

I had spoken softly so as not to awaken Manasseh. But Judith was as boisterous as before, singing and dancing as she began to strip off her bracelets, her diadem, her veil, her chains, her stomacher, her slippers and the pins that held her garments together. As I watched in horror she let her clothes drop all around her on the floor until she stood as naked as she had stood in the firelight before the pillar of Ashtoreth. Only the chain with the image of the goddess was left on her body.

Seeing the look on my face, Judith laughed again. Then she placed the diadem upon her tangled red hair, snatched the oil lamp from my hand, and thus stark-naked save for the silver chain around her neck and the crown on her head she entered Manasseh's chamber.

Without thinking I began to gather Judith's garments from the floor, trembling in the dark as I listened toward Manasseh's chamber. Suddenly there was a hoarse cry as of one caught in an evil dream. The door flew open, and in the faint glow of the oil lamp I saw Manasseh running from the room, his sheet wrapped around him, his face white as the sheet. He ran past me out into the yard, leaving the door open as he fled into the night.

I stood with my knees knocking together, fearful of what I should encounter if I entered the chamber. But when I heard a retching sound within I dropped the garments I had gathered from the floor and ran into the room.

Judith lay on her belly across her husband's bed, her diadem fallen from her head. Her face was bent over the edge of the bed and her naked body writhed as she vomited on the floor.

"Judith," I whispered. "Judith."

But she could not cease from vomiting until all the wine she had drunk was purged from her. Then she rolled over on her back, her face ashen and the kohl around her eyes smeared across her forehead and her cheeks. As she raised her hand to wipe her mouth, her fingers touched the amulet of the goddess between her breasts. She caught it in her hand and tried to slip the chain off her neck, but it became entangled in her long hair. When I would help her she flung me away with such force that I fell to my knees. Then she began to pull viciously on the chain until it broke, cutting a deep gash in the skin on her neck. Her blood spilled onto the bed, but not in the manner in which she had thought to spill it. She crushed the amulet of the goddess in her strong hands, cursing and sobbing all the while, and then she flung it away into the farthest corner of the room. Still sobbing she rolled over again on her belly. Her shoulders continued to shake until the wine she had drunk suddenly soothed her and she fell asleep from one instant to the next, like a child.

I fetched a rag and wiped up the vomit from the floor. Then I sat down by the bed to wait for dawn, and there I fell asleep.

What woke me was Judith stirring and moaning on the bed. When I opened my eyes I saw her sit up and look about her blankly until her gaze dropped down on her nakedness. The sight of her bare body brought back the memory of the past night. She snatched up the sheet and covered herself up to her neck. There was a dark-brown crust where the chain had cut her, and the skin around it was red and swollen. Her hand went up to touch the cut and she winced with pain, but when our eyes met she quickly averted her gaze.

"Is the east wind still blowing?" Judith asked.

"It is blowing," I replied.

"Then we shall reap today." She paused and put her hands to her head, moaning. "The heat has made my head ache. Fetch me a pan of cold water that I may wash my face. And bring my working clothes, for I must hurry down to the fields and set the servants upon their tasks before the sun rises in the sky."

Thus Judith spoke as if she knew nothing of the previous night, and I ran to do her bidding.

Manasseh had stolen back while I was drowsing beside Judith's bed and had hidden himself in the room that had once been his mother's. His servant was not about to help him dress, nor had he eaten yet. He came to the door in his undergarments as I returned with the pitcher of water. When he saw Judith's garments scattered all over the floor—for I had not had time to pick them up—he blushed deeply, lowered his gaze and muttered:

"Is Judith angry this morning?"

"Why should she be angry?" I asked. "Her sole concern is for the harvest and she bade me hasten, for she would go down in the fields."

And I walked past Judith's robes and jewels as if they were invisible to my eyes.

When I entered the chamber I found Judith pacing back and forth, the sheet wrapped about her body. Her pale face was smeared with kohl and streaked where the tears had run through it, and her brow furrowed as though her head ached badly.

"What made you tarry?" she asked, snatching the pitcher from my hand. I saw that she was already in a temper. "If all will idle today as you idled, we shall not save one single blade of barley!"

She began to wash her face, scrubbing viciously. Whenever she touched the cut on her neck she winced and bit her lips, but she would not cease from her haste. Then she threw on her garments, twisted her long hair into a coil, tied it at the back of her neck, and strode from the chamber.

In the outer room Manasseh had silently picked up Judith's garments and jewels and piled them into a basket. Now he stood with his head lowered, like a child that had done mischief and hoped his punishment would not be too severe.

Seeing Manasseh, Judith blushed but made no mention of the previous night. Rather she asked:

"Why are you not dressed yet, seeing that we must hurry down to the fields to save what we can of the harvest?"

Manasseh raised his head and gaped at her.

"Surely you would not have *me* help with the harvest, Judith!"

"Surely I do," Judith replied, her face hard. "I cannot be in your fields and mine at the same time, and the hands of the servants will slacken in the heat if none drives them on."

"But I never worked in the fields, nor can I bear the hot sun!" Manasseh exclaimed.

Then Judith furrowed her brow, touched her fingers to the cut on her neck, winced and said softly:

"If you are not man enough for anything else, at least be man enough to stand over the servants in the field."

Manasseh pulled back from her and answered with trembling lips:

"But I cannot leave the house today! Joab went hunting partridges and promised to bring me one, which we shall roast and eat together."

"If Joab has no more sense than to hunt partridges in their season, you ought to know better than to accept such an ill-gotten gift," Judith said.

"How can I refuse Joab's gift when he is the only kinsman left me and I love him with all my soul?" Manasseh replied.

"For such love Sodom was destroyed," Judith said, her face white with fury. "And now dress yourself and come with me, for you have already made me lose much time!"

Then Manasseh ceased to resist her, for he knew that she had not forgiven him. And he also knew that if she were to accuse him of his sin he would be dealt with according to the law, which was death.

While Manasseh dressed inside his chamber, Judith pushed open the outer door and stood staring up at the sky, which was nearly colorless behind the yellow haze of dust. The fiery east wind sent in a blast as from a heated furnace.

"Manasseh!" Judith called, her voice shrill as that of her aunt Sarai. "What in the name of God is keeping the fool?"

Manasseh emerged pinning his robes together, for he was not used to dressing without help. He went on fussing with his clothes as he stumbled after Judith through the streets of Bethul.

Some housewives were already about, shaking out the garments in which they had slept. A few had been at the hilltop the night before and had seen Judith standing naked before the pillar of Ashtoreth. These stared at her askance, seeing that she had defied the rules of the goddess. But Judith held her head high, looking straight ahead, as if she did not know that her husband was stumbling after her.

Now that I saw these women it suddenly dawned on me in what manner they had left Bethul unobserved. Surely they had climbed out through the windows of the harlots' quarters, which were built into the wall. And yet there was not one among them who would not thumb her nose at the harlots at other times. As for their husbands—whether they knew of their wives' doings I could not tell.

Just as these women pretended never to have trafficked with the harlots, so Judith pretended now never to have had any commerce with them. She strode out through the open gate of Bethul and down the path which she had stumbled up drunkenly the night before. In the east the sky was turning brighter behind the haze, but only a few birds raised their voices in song. The air was hot and dry, and the whining of the wind louder even than the rustling of the brittle stalks in the fields.

Walking behind Manasseh, I saw the sweat run down his neck and stain the garment on his back. From time to time he halted to catch his breath with a terrible gasp, for he had trouble breathing in hot weather. But when Judith glared back at him over her shoulder, her eyes fiery as the wind, he staggered on.

Judith ran ahead of us, shouting into the huts and tents of the servants to rouse those who were not yet up and cursing them for their idleness. They came forth, yawning and stretching, their mouths falling open when they saw Manasseh following Judith. But Judith gave them no rest to gossip and set them to work, the men to cut the barley, the women to glean and to tie the stalks in sheaves. She left Manasseh behind in his fields to stand over his servants, while she hastened on to her own.

That day I too labored among the maidservants, following the rows of men who stood with their backs bent as they swung the sickles. To cut the barley was madness, for it was not yet ripe. The harvest would be lost whether it was reaped now or not reaped at all. But Judith would not rest, neither would she let her servants rest.

Though the sun remained a pale disk behind the haze as it rose into the sky, I thought we would all perish from the heat. The wind blew dust in our eyes and our nostrils, and sweat caked our hair and garments. As the day wore on many a handmaiden fainted, while strong men sat down and wept, for the work was not only hard but wasted.

Judith alone did not grow weary, nor would she cease in her work to eat or drink. She screamed at the servants when their hands slackened, and when one came running to tell her that Manasseh had fainted in the heat, she cursed terribly. But she would not go to him and only commanded that he be carried to the summer house and that one of the old women who were too feeble to work look after him.

Not until dusk, when all the barley was cut and tied, and the men and women sank down on the ground too tired to drag themselves to their huts, did Judith and I return to the summer house. My sole wish was to douse myself with cold water and fall on my mat to sleep forever. But when we entered the house the old woman who tended Manasseh rose from his bedside and said:

"It is a good thing you are come, Judith, for your husband is dying."

"Do not speak folly," Judith replied. "All that ails Manasseh is that he hates to work in the fields. However, none of those who labored all day long is dead of the work."

"No, but he is in truth dying," the old woman said. "I should have fetched you sooner, but I dared not leave him alone, nor do I have the strength to run across the fields in this heat."

Judith approached the bed on which Manasseh lay and spoke to him. But he neither opened his eyes nor answered her. Bending down, she put her hand on his forehead and said:

"He is burning with fever, Tamar." Though she would appear calm, her eyes were frightened. "But his sickness cannot be caused by the heat, for did we not all work in the fields? Surely he fell into this fit out of spite! Still, we must keep him from getting worse. Therefore run and fetch your mother from town that she may cure him!"

But I replied:

"I barely have the strength to walk across this room, Judith, less still to climb the hill to Bethul. I shall fall by the wayside and perish of the heat just as Manasseh is perishing of it!"

Then Judith struck me, shouting:

"Neither you nor Manasseh will perish! If I am cursed with useless servants I shall go to Bethul myself. But sit you by Manasseh's bed and wipe his face with a rag dipped in cool water until I return."

And Judith strode angrily out of the house, leaving me to marvel at her strength.

I bade the old woman fetch me a pan of water, for I was too faint to get it myself, and sat down beside Manasseh's bed. There was sweat on his forehead and red patches on his cheeks. His lips moved feverishly, but I could not make out his mumblings. Though he was covered up to his chin with a blanket, his whole body shivered in spite of the stifling heat. When I wrung out the rag and pressed it to his forehead, his eyes flew open, he sat up and screamed:

"Mother!"

I dropped the rag in fright while the old woman fled through the door. Had I not feared Judith I too would have fled. Instead I cowered beside the bed, the rag pressed against my mouth as I watched Manasseh fall back to resume his mumbling and tossing. Nor did I dare touch him again for fear he would call for his mother, whose ghost might still be abroad after having been summoned from the nether world the previous night.

Thus Judith found me when she returned with my mother from Bethul. Judith looked weary now, her lids drooping, her skin parched, her hair lackluster. But my mother, not having worked in the fields, looked fresh, nor did her appearance betray the manner in which she had spent the night. She wore her plain servant's clothes, her only jewelry the golden earring she had worn from the day she refused her freedom. Approaching Manasseh's bed she gazed down on him, felt his cheek and forehead, and asked me:

"Has he spoken?"

"He called for his mother," I whispered.

"Ah."

There was a strange look in my mother's eyes, but Judith said in a temper:

"What profits all this talk? You had better tend to him!"

My mother opened her mouth as though to reply, but then she shrugged and bade me fetch a cup of wine from the kitchen. Though I was weary I obeyed her command swiftly, fearful that Judith would strike me again if I tarried. Out of a small flask my mother poured a few drops into the wine, swirling them in the cup.

Then she placed her hand under Manasseh's head and raised it so that his lips met the rim of the cup. But no sooner had he touched it than he pushed it away, his body arching and his head dropping back on the bed as he shrieked:

"Mother, mother, mother!"

My hands flew to my mouth and I jumped away from the bed. Even Judith shuddered, though she remained rooted where she stood. But my mother poured the wine out on the ground, saying:

"I can do nothing for him. He will die as Athara's two brothers, at the time of the barley harvest."

"He must not die," Judith said. "He shall not die!"

"Would you decide over life and death, Judith—you, a mortal woman who only last night prayed to the goddess for her heart's desire?" my mother asked.

"I know not whereof you speak," Judith replied, looking hard at my mother.

"Last night you beseeched Ashtoreth that you might be blessed with a child. And though you broke my commands, the merciful goddess would still grant you your wish: behold, she let Athara remain abroad that she might carry Manasseh with her to the nether world. But you shall be free to take a husband who can give you a child!"

Then Judith's face turned ashen and she whispered:

"I never prayed for Manasseh's death. And now leave my house, Dinah, and do not defile it again with your sorceries!"

Judith took the rag from me and sat down on the floor beside Manasseh's bed to tend him herself. But my mother beckoned to me to follow her outside. There she made me tell her what had happened after Judith and I returned to Bethul last night. When she heard that Judith had ripped off the amulet to crush it in her fingers and toss it away, my mother only shook her head, muttering:

"Just so did her father. Yet it was to no avail, for the goddess owned this land long before the Hebrews brought their fierce god of wrath with them to drive out all other gods. As for Manasseh, he is beyond being saved by any god. The sign of the nether world is upon him."

But Judith still believed differently. When I returned to the room I found her kneeling beside Manasseh's bed, wiping his face and neck, imploring him not to die, promising that he should never again work in the fields, and holding his hands in hers as she had not held them since they were children. And Manasseh, who had always taken care not to touch Judith even when he combed her hair, was too weak to withdraw his fingers. Nor did he know her but kept on screaming for his mother.

Toward morning, when daylight began to seep through the dusty haze outside, Manasseh's trembling ceased. His head rolled back, his limbs stiffened and he died.

When the wailing women came Judith was still dressed in the sweat-caked garb she had worn the day before while working in the fields. Nor had she slept since her drunken slumber after the rite on the hilltop. Her eyes were dull as she sat on the ground with her strong hands lying idle in her lap, the damp rag dropped from her fingers and staining her skirt. I feared to approach her and wished my mother were here to do what must be done. But Judith had forbidden her to return. Thus when the wailing women came Judith had not rent her garments and scattered dirt on her head, nor was she weeping. Because of this some said afterward that she was glad Manasseh had died. But I had seen Judith mourn before, and I had never seen her weep.

The wailing women made up for Judith's silence by weeping all the more loudly, for Manasseh had died in the flower of his youth, in his twenty-ninth year. They fetched widow's garments for Judith and brought dirt to scatter on her head. But when the other women came from Bethul to join in the weeping, those who had taken part in the rites kept away from Judith. And even those who knew nothing of the secret rites whispered that there was a curse on her—for had not all her kin died within a short time? Now all the fields that had belonged to Merari's father and his brother Shallum were again united in one hand. But it was the hand of a widow, and there was no male heir.

Still all the people came to witness Manasseh's burial, for none would slight the richest woman in Bethul. Manasseh had died at dawn and was to be buried before nightfall. The long climb up to the burial caves was wearisome, with the afternoon sun burning through the haze and the east wind blowing as fiercely as on the two previous days. The leaves had withered on the trees, and from the hill I saw that the young vines had shriveled in the vineyards on the southern slopes. The grape harvest was gone the way of the barley harvest. It would be a bitter year.

What Judith thought as she stared with empty eyes out over her parched lands I do not know—whether she grieved over the lost crops, or over her husband's death, or whether she was too tired to grieve at all. It was the fourth time she had climbed the hill in the past two days, and the heat had become even worse than before.

But when Manasseh had been placed in his burial cave and the stone rolled before it, the wind suddenly shifted from east to west, stirring up the dry leaves that had dropped from the trees and hurling them through the air like a rustling shower. Within a brief span the air cooled off, as it will when the wind shifts, and by the time we returned to the valley below the sun had set and a chill lay over the land.

At the foot of the hill Judith stopped at the spring and scooped up a drink of water with her hands. She had taken no food all day, and whence came her strength to walk about I could not fathom.

But the people returned to their homes in Bethul. There would be no harvest this year, and no need to move into the tents in the fields. Judith alone walked back to her summer house, and I behind her. I was deadly tired, having slept little, but the cool breeze refreshed me, and to cheer Judith I said:

"The heat is broken. We shall have a stretch of fair weather."

But Judith replied:

"The heat broke too late. The land is parched. The vines are withered. The crop is lost. Tomorrow we shall lock up the summer house and return to Bethul. There is nothing more I can do in the fields."

Next morning we returned to Bethul. When we came to Manasseh's house Judith would not enter but bade me call the servants, have them sweep all the rooms, bar the windows and doors and bring her the keys. Then she went to the stables and fetched the mule Hadad had begotten, for she had resolved to return to Merari's house, and the mule was all she would take with her. As for the precious things Manasseh had brought from Jerusalem—the tables inlaid with ivory, the chairs with armrests, the many-colored rugs and wall hangings, the silver cups and knives, Judith left them behind. And so she did with all the figures Manasseh had carved. Nor would she take her jewels and bridal garments but bade me lock them up with the rest of the things.

Thus Judith returned in widow's garb to the house she had left six years before as a bride. When my mother met her at the door, bowing low before her, Judith said:

"Be gone from my house, witch!"

But my mother stood in the door, by the post where Merari had pierced her ear with the awl, and replied:

"Would you drive me from the home where I have lived these thirty years? Tamar is my witness that I never offered to do what you bade me do!"

And I nodded, for my mother spoke the truth.

"Stay then," Judith said. "But do not practice your abominations in this house."

My mother had readied her old room for Judith, but she would not use the chamber where she had slept as a maiden. She bade me carry her bedding up to the room where the prophet had lived for two years, and there she dwelt henceforth. All she had was a hard bed, a table and a chair. Nor would she put off her widow's garb after the time of mourning. And on the shelf where other women kept their perfumes, their ointments and their trinket boxes, Judith kept the potsherds on which she tallied her accounts.

Though there was no harvest that year, Judith did not suffer like the rest. Her storehouses were filled with grain and her cellars with wine and oil. Those who had need of flour came to buy from her, and if they lacked silver for payment they would turn over to her the deeds for their land. Thus Judith acquired still more fields and her wealth increased. But in spite of it she lived frugally, eating little and watching over the food prepared in her kitchen that there might be no waste. Toward her aunt Sarai she remained charitable, nor did she forget the orphans and the needy, for this had been Merari's way.

Judith's providence was much respected, and soon even the elders of Bethul came to seek her counsel. As for the young men, the only one she could not bar from her house was Joab, he being her kin. But his visits vexed her exceedingly, and after he left she would often rub the scar on her neck until it was red and swollen.

"I am your dead husband's only male kin," Joab would say to

Judith whenever he called. "You should by rights become my wife that I might raise up his seed."

"You already have a wife," Judith would reply.

"A man may have two wives and more if he can please them equally," Joab said. "Moreover, the law requires that I provide for my widowed kin."

Then Judith raised her eyes heavenward and exclaimed:

"Am I not cursed enough without being cursed by foolish kinsmen? This law is meant to keep poor widows from hunger and harlotry! It was not made for rich widows. As for sharing a home with your wife Rebeccah, I would sooner earn my bread in the shadow of the wall than live under one roof with her!"

Then Joab said:

"If such a thing were seemly for a man I should do the same, for it is better to dwell in a corner on the housetop than under one roof with a contentious woman. But remember, Judith, if you would marry again the right is mine and you may wed no other."

To this Judith replied:

"Have no fear, Joab. I shall never take another husband after Manasseh."

At the time of the next barley harvest we heard rumors that Nebuchadrezzar would again come against Judah. In the nine years since Zedekiah sat on the throne there had been many such rumors. Zedekiah was weak and would one day listen to the princes, who urged rebellion, and the next day to Jeremiah, who counseled submission to Babylon. In the end the Hebrew king would always remain loyal to Nebuchadrezzar.

But things looked different the year after Manasseh's death. There was a new ruler in Egypt, Pharaoh Hophra, who would stir up the small nations under the yoke of Babylon, promising to aid them if they rebelled. Though Judah was a poor nation it was precious to both the pharaoh of Egypt and the king of Babylon. While there were Babylonian garrisons in Judah the pharaoh's caravans could not proceed along the Sea Road. And if Egypt should gain dominion over Judah, the Babylonian caravans would meet the same fate. Thus Egypt and Babylon coveted Judah.

As for Zedekiah, he had sworn by Yahweh to remain loyal to Nebuchadrezzar when the king of Babylon put him on the throne.

But his nephew Jehoiachin, the former king, was still alive in Babylon, and the captives who had been taken there with him continued to reckon time by his reign. Even in Judah many believed that Nebuchadrezzar would someday return the former king or one of his sons to the throne. But Zedekiah wanted to see his own heirs rule Judah. And since his throne was not assured while there was still a royal Hebrew prince alive in Babylon, he cast his lot with Pharaoh Hophra.

But the people of Bethul did not truly believe that war might come to their gates. Our town was set on a hill near a narrow pass that led from the wilderness to the road to Lachish. No enemy had ever come this way or troubled himself with the villages beyond Lachish. Still there was talk in town, one asking the other whether he would rather side with the Babylonians or with the Egyptians. And when they asked Judith whose side she would choose, she replied in Merari's words:

"May both be taken by the plague. However, let us prepare for war. Though we have but few men who draw the sword, we sit safely upon a hilltop, protected by our walls. Our storehouses are filled with grain so that we can withstand even a long siege. All we lack is a safe source of water. Therefore let us complete the shaft my father began digging nine years ago and bring in water from the spring at the bottom of the hill."

Then the people smote their thighs in laughter, saying:

"The Babylonians will never come against Bethul! But if they come they will arrive in winter, when the cisterns in town are filled with rain water. Why, then, should we dig shafts at the time of the barley harvest? And later we must reap the wheat, the olives, the summer fruit, the pulse and the grapes, and lay up stores. Where shall we find time to do useless work? As for Zedekiah, he will still weaken and bow his neck under Nebuchadrezzar's yoke!"

Then Judith sighed and said:

"If these people did not listen to my father, a forceful man who sat in the council of elders, why should they listen to a weak woman?"

NINE

Is not this great Babylon, which I have built for a royal dwelling-place, by the might of my power and for the glory of my majesty?

—DANIEL 4:27

WHEN I returned to Babylon from the brief campaign against Judah (the old man Isaac said to the young scribe), I felt as though I had been absent a lifetime. After the small towns through which the army had marched, Babylon seemed even bigger and noisier than before, and the number of inhabitants doubled since my departure. All were rushing about madly engaged in their business and increasing their gains. As for the war that had come to such a swift and unbloody conclusion, those who had not taken part cared little about it, and less still about the fate of the captives who had been brought to Babylonia.

The only one who could not hear his fill of the campaign was my own master. He made me tell him every last thing about Jerusalem, until I was sorry that he could not meet Ezekiel the son of Buzi, who would have satisfied his curiosity better than I.

But Ezekiel, together with most of the captives, had been shipped to the small town of Tel-Abib on the river Chebar, not far from the city of Nippur south of Babylon. Nebuchadrezzar had wished to keep the young man at court that he might counsel his architects in the building of his palace. But shortly after leaving Jerusalem Ezekiel had fallen into a fit from which he had not recovered. He remained lying on one side and would not turn over on the other, neither would he answer when spoken to. And when one raised up his right arm—for he was lying on his left—it remained stretched heavenward and would not return until it was put down by force. All this I witnessed with my own eyes on the march from Jerusalem to Babylon, when I saw two men carrying Ezekiel upon a litter.

335

Then I pleaded with the king to let the young man continue with the rest of the captives. If leaving Jerusalem had brought him to this state, being torn from his family might be his death. Nebuchadrezzar granted my request, but at the same time he commanded that a few Hebrew princes be chosen to remain at his court in Babylon. And the king appointed me to teach these men the language of the land after we returned.

Though this would leave me little time with my master, I was secretly glad of the king's command. Since my return from Judah my master's manner toward me was strangely altered, for he was not pleased with what I told him of the campaign.

"I can see that your mind was poisoned and that you would make Nebuchadrezzar appear more righteous than he is," my master said to me. "But I, who have been to war, know well how conquered towns are sacked and how captives are dealt with. Nor do I believe your words, for you would not reveal the truth to me knowing that I am a Hebrew."

It was then I learned that people will listen only if a witness tells them such tales as they would believe. Though my master was a learned man, in this he did not differ from others. Afterward he no longer spoke to me freely as before, nor would he dictate his writings to me but worked in secret, locking his wax-covered writing boards into a chest. Then I knew he had forsaken the epic he had promised the king, and I prayed that affairs of state might keep Nebuchadrezzar from remembering it.

When the king finally summoned my master to court it was not to see what he had written but to act as judge upon the writings of others. True to Nebuchadrezzar's promise, we had returned for the New Year Festival. In celebration of the new year and his recent victory, the king gave many banquets in his palace. On these occasions he honored such men as had served him well: the chamberlains, architects, sculptors and painters—and since the queen was fond of music and poetry—the sellers of songs and writers of poems. Every year there was a contest among the latter, the one who was chosen winner receiving a golden chain to put about his neck. The most distinguished men at court acted as judges, but the king rendered the final verdict.

When the tablet naming my master one of the judges was delivered to our house, Nabukasir creased his brow, tugged at his beard and paced the room for some time before saying to me:

"After he carried away half my people captive, Nebuchadrezzar would have me rejoice with him! Should I not be wholly without honor in spitting upon their suffering? Therefore I would have you take my answer to the king, Marduksharusur—since you are in his good graces—and tell him that I shall not set foot in his palace while there is yet one Babylonian garrison on the soil of Judah!"

Hearing these words I turned ashen and my knees buckled under me.

"My lord had better command me to throw myself in the river, thus sparing the king the trouble of having me slain for bringing him such a message!" I exclaimed.

"You speak truly," my master replied. "It would be cruel to make you the bearer of my words. Rather I shall write them on a clay tablet and seal them in an envelope, which you may deliver at the gate of the palace."

Then I placed my hand upon my head in despair, saying:

"To utter such words as my lord would say to the king is folly. But to put them in writing is sheer madness, for what is written down can never be denied. I would sooner deliver the message by mouth, for I might yet think of a manner in which to transmit it without arousing the king's ire."

But I had no intention of doing this. Rather I would gain time to invent an excuse for my master's refusal. In the end I resolved to pretend before the king that my lord had gone mad, for surely his defiance was the act of a madman. But when I sought out the Captain Holofernes to discuss my plan with him, he spoke against it.

"At times I believe that Nabukasir would force the king to snuff out the life he snatched from the flames," the captain said. "But let us return to the house and reason with your master, for he is in other matters not without good sense. Still, I loathe the thought of advising a friend to attend these poetry readings, for I know them to be utterly tedious."

"Has my lord been one of the judges?" I asked in great amazement, thinking this office most unsuitable for the captain.

"Ishtar forbid that I should ever have to judge such nonsense!" the captain exclaimed. "I only had the ill fortune of being on guard duty in the banquet hall during one of these contests. Never have I seen such unseemly conduct by so many courtiers of high rank! Indeed it was their loud disputes that kept me from falling asleep. Over the merit of a poem they would call each other names and pull each other's beards—those who had beards. As for the love songs, these were judged by a council of eunuchs who know nothing of love!"

I became very angry and said:

"One need not know of love to tell whether a love song is written well!"

But the captain only laughed and said:

"Since you esteem your understanding of writing so highly, I might recommend you to the king as one of the judges. Many of them turned into great enemies after these contests, slandering each other in such a manner that more than one ended up being thrown in the fire."

"My lord already procured for me the post of royal interpreter," I replied. "I beg my lord not to procure for me any more honors. Rather let us hasten back and reason with my master lest he be thrown in the fire without ever judging a poetry contest!"

But when the Captain Holofernes and I returned to the house Nabukasir would not listen to us, speaking bitter words not only against the captain but also against me.

"I always treated Marduksharusur as a friend rather than a slave," my lord said. "But since he has become one of the king's favorites he despises serving a Hebrew."

Then the captain said to my master:

"Now I can see that you have in truth gone mad! Not only has Marduksharusur remained loyal to you, but on the march back from Jerusalem he spent so much time comforting the captives that some of our officers suspected him of being in league with these Hebrews. Nor would he enter the temple in Jerusalem but forced me to drag him inside, making even me suspect that he had turned Hebrew because of you!"

Then my master's face softened and he asked:

"Why did you not make mention to me of these matters, Marduksharusur?"

"My lord was not inclined to believe my words," I replied. "But now that the captain has reassured him of my loyalty, let me persuade my lord not to vex the king!"

However, Nabukasir remained stubborn in his defiance. Then I followed the captain outside to see what might be done. To pretend that Nabukasir had gone mad would be folly, the captain said. But I might say that my master had caught a loathsome skin disease, which made it unseemly for him to present himself before the king.

"If need be you shall swear to the truth of your story by Marduk, Nebo and Shamash," the captain said, "for what matters the false oath of a slave?"

Indeed it mattered little what I swore to by the names of these heathen gods in whom I did not believe, though I did not tell this to the captain. But the king required no oath of me when I delivered to him the news of my master's sickness. Rather he said:

"Though I do not believe your words, Marduksharusur, I shall not inquire into their truthfulness. If I found that Nabukasir was deceiving me I should be forced to have him slain. And this I would do as little as slaying the son to whom I gave life. Nor have I forgotten what your master did for me when my brother tried to seize my throne. Therefore return home and tell Nabukasir to tend to his illness and also to the words he utters, lest the one or the other be the cause of his death. As for you, I would soon have you begin instructing the young Hebrew princes in our language. Perchance I shall find among them one who might take your master's place in my heart, making me forget his bitter ingratitude."

Though my errand had been successful, I returned home with a heavy heart, knowing that my master would not rest until he provoked the king into slaying him. Nor was I wrong in my misgivings. No sooner had I entered my lord's chamber than he threw his arms about me and begged my forgiveness for ever having doubted my loyalty.

"To show you that my trust in you is restored," he said to me, "I shall dictate to you my latest writings. I would have you transfer them onto clay tablets, which are more durable and also simpler to store than my wax-covered writing boards."

And Nabukasir unlocked his chest, brought forth his writing boards and spread them on the table before me. I had read no more than one or two when the hair rose on the back of my neck and my bowels turned to water.

"My lord spoke to the Greeks at court while I was away," I whispered in horror.

"Then you too know these Greek thoughts!" Nabukasir exclaimed.

"I learned of them long ago from the man who taught me Greek at Nineveh. Only because he was well beloved by his pupils did rumors of his teachings never get abroad, or the king of Assyria would have slain him for preaching rebellion. Nor would Nebuchadrezzar pardon my lord if he learned of these writings. Therefore let us burn the writing boards rather than transfer the words onto clay tablets, which would have to be smashed with an ax if one came to search the house. Even then one might learn their contents from the bits and pieces! But if my lord must keep these dangerous writings, let us copy them on a roll of papyrus—which is easily burned—and seal that roll into a jar to keep it from the eyes of spies!"

"And where would you find papyrus now that the king has forbidden the bringing in of Egyptian goods?" my master asked.

"Let me but go down to the wharves," I said, "and I shall buy my lord whatever Egyptian merchandise he desires at three times its former price."

"Go then and get this roll of papyrus, but let me not hear of your unlawful dealings," my master said, for though he would defy the king he would not break the king's law.

The merchant who invested my silver for me found my request in no way strange. He dealt in many scarce and forbidden goods, and his warehouse was stocked with merchandise from all the lands. Though he was glad that the king had not brought back much loot from Judah with which to glut the market, he had many complaints about the state of the nation.

At the beginning of his reign Nebuchadrezzar had conceived many great plans for restoring the old temples in town, for building new ones, for enlarging his palace and strengthening the walls around Babylon, and for improving the streets that traffic might flow back and forth more freely. Now that the winter was past, summer not yet come and the air mild and clear, the king's workingmen were out in force widening the streets and planting the broad avenues with palm trees. The queen had complained that she could not bear to gaze upon the ugliness of Babylon, and there was nothing Nebuchadrezzar would not do to please her. But making the city more beautiful only added to its noise and turmoil. The air was filled with the sound of hammers and axes, and with the dust of bricks being dumped from oxcarts onto the ground. Chariots became stuck in the ditches dug across the streets, and walkers fell into them and broke limbs. Indeed there were suits in court brought by those who held the king responsible for their injuries, and it was known that some had received rewards.

My friend the merchant was in a black mood when I called on him to obtain the roll of papyrus. The street before his store was torn up, delaying the transport of merchandise from a docked ship into his warehouse, thus causing him grievous losses.

"Perhaps you, who are a sensible and learned man, can tell me where all this building will lead!" the merchant said to me. "In olden days, when a man fell on hard times he would sell his wife, his children and even himself into slavery, as is only fitting—for why else did the gods give us the poor but that we might have servants to do our menial tasks? But now that the king has resolved to build Babylon all over again, these men who formerly became slaves leave the land and come into town to do the king's work, for which they receive ample food for themselves and their kin. Nor has the king brought slaves from his last war to take their place but only more men to do his building. There are not enough people left to work the land, and since the times of King Nabopolassar the price of a slave has risen from thirty shekels to thirty-five. Soon it will rise to forty, and then what will become of the price of grain, which surely must go up with the price of labor? How will the people eat? How will one make a profit? Yet everyone spends more than ever before, and those who were once content with our good native barley beer and date wine must now have imported wine made from grapes, which costs ten times as much as our own!

"Also the women have gone mad and would all have gardens like the queen. My own wife has made me move to the new town west of the river, claiming that our children will grow up stronger and healthier if they are surrounded by flowers and trees. And I, who grew up strong and healthy in the old part of town, consented in my madness so that now I must hire a litter at great expense to get to my warehouse, whereas before I could walk there at my leisure. Moreover, I lose half a day in crossing Babylon, for all the streets are torn up. Indeed the crush of litters, donkeys, oxcarts and chariots has become such that compared to crossing our city it must be utter bliss to traverse the nether world pursued by all the demons!

"And still there is no end to the building and to people pouring into town, with prices and taxes rising faster than one can amass the silver. But if our mad king—may he live forever—will persist in drawing all these men from the land to wage his wars and do his building, our prosperity will increase in such manner that our sons will starve to death!"

I was glad to pay the exorbitant price for my roll of papyrus and flee from the presence of my friend the merchant. If I was to be burned for listening to forbidden speech I would sooner be burned with my master, whom I loved, than with the merchant, who was but a friend in business. Nor could I fathom how the increasing wealth of our land could lead to its downfall, never having had a great understanding of figures.

But as to what the merchant had said about the new town west of the Euphrates, I knew that he spoke the truth. The houses there had been built hastily, and every day another collapsed, burying its tenants beneath it. Though the builder was put to death before such a house, others continued building in the same manner, for human greed always outweighs concern for one's fellows.

Nor was the new town with its uniform houses a pleasant sight to behold. Indeed it was said that if a husband came home drunk late at night he might wander into his neighbor's house and lie with his neighbor's wife without discovering his mistake until daybreak. For the women too had all come to look and talk and dress alike.

Then I was glad of living in my master's lovely house in the old part of town. And if my life there was equally periled, at least it was not collapsing walls that would cause my death.

When my master began dictating to me what he had written on his wax-covered writing boards, I beseeched him to let me copy his words in the Syrian tongue and script. Most learned men could not yet read it, though it was coming into use just then. Since the Hebrews used the same script, some Babylonians would later claim that a small band of captives had perverted the writing of all Babylonia.

When we had finished for the day, my master would erase his words from the writing boards, while I concealed the roll of papyrus in an earthenware jar that rested on a tripod in a corner of the room. The jar had a tightly fitting cover and was too heavy to be moved by any of the slaves. My master's writings would be safe there unless the one who knew all his secrets would denounce him. And this thing I would never do.

Still, I was glad when I was summoned from my dangerous work to teach our language to the young Hebrew princes who had remained at Nebuchadrezzar's court. I arrayed myself in my finest garments to present myself before my noble charges. But when I met the Captain Holofernes in the first court and revealed to him my errand, he jeered at me and at the king's folly, saying:

"Why it should please the king to converse with all these strangers I do not know, for surely they cannot have knowledge of matters that are not better understood in Babylonia. Moreover, they will in the end defy him just as your own master has, for it is known that these Hebrews are the most stubborn of peoples!"

The princes who were to be my pupils had been quartered in one of the buildings around the second court, which housed the king's high officials. The chamberlain entrusted with their care was a man by the name of Ashpenaz, who spoke a few words of Hebrew and might have come of Israelite stock. He was shorter and thinner than the Babylonians, with a worried face made gaunter by his long, curly beard, which he wore in the Babylonian fashion.

"Marduk be praised that my lord has come!" he exclaimed when I presented myself to him. "Perhaps my lord will be able to persuade these young men to cease from their folly. Since they were entrusted to me they have refused to eat the king's food, saying that it is prepared in an unclean manner. The king's own food! They turned a deaf ear to all my pleading, for their stubbornness is beyond belief. And how will I answer the king if he finds them looking famished? Would he not accuse me of having stolen their appointed rations and have me thrown in the fire? It is only through some miracle that I discovered in the kitchen a woman who knows how to prepare such food as they would eat. Even then they made me take them to the kitchen that they might observe the cooking. Has my lord ever heard of such a thing? Are not these Hebrews the most contrary of people? But at least their food agrees with the princes. My lord will find them plump and ruddy, though they still refuse to eat of the meat that has been boiled in the common pots."

Thus chattering excitedly Ashpenaz led me into the chamber where the young princes were reclining on rugs. They rose and bowed down before me as one bows down before a teacher, and I bowed down before them as one bows down before royal princes. There were of them four, all dressed in simple white linen robes. They were handsome as all princes of Judah, slender and of perfect limbs though not tall, with fine faces, bright eyes and beards worn short in the Hebrew fashion. Three were quite young, but one was older even than I. Thinking it difficult to teach a new language to one no longer young, I turned to Ashpenaz and inquired why he had chosen one older man. And he told me that the one called Belteshazzar had some understanding of dream divining, in which the king put great store. Knowing that this practice was forbidden to Hebrews I was amazed, but I said nothing then. Moreover, Ashpenaz had gone on to introduce the other princes to me by name:

"These three young men are Shadrach, Meshach and Abed-nego. I trust that in time my lord will learn to tell them apart, though they resemble each other."

And indeed they did, being of the same family. No sooner had Ashpenaz commended them to my care and retired than I addressed them in Hebrew:

"I see that my lords' names have already been changed to Babylonian names."

They smiled, and the one who seemed to me the youngest replied:

"Indeed our new names seem to please the king more than our former names, which were Daniel, Hananiah, Mishael and Azariah."

"Then we already have a thing in common," I said, "for my name too was changed by the king. But have my lords been well seen to? I was told that they were not pleased at first with their fare."

Then the one whose name had been Daniel and who was now called Belteshazzar replied:

"Our God has seen to it that we should not starve. There was found in the royal kitchen a woman who knows how to prepare ritually pure food. And if this were not miracle enough, the woman is not a Hebrew but an Ethiopian— Is my lord ill?"

I saw Belteshazzar, whose name had been Daniel, gaze at me in a strange manner, for the blood had fled from my cheeks. But I shook my head, thinking that there must be in this world more than one Ethiopian woman who knew how to prepare food in the Hebrew fashion.

"Nor is this yet the end of the miracle," said Shadrach, whose name had been Hananiah. "For this woman has a brother who is chamberlain over the house of women, he being a eunuch. And when she learned that we were Hebrews she fetched her brother that he might make our acquaintance. This man, a tall Ethiopian of great beauty, knows the tunes of many of our sacred songs, though he does not know the words. And he said that Azariah, our youngest, whose name the king changed to Abed-nego, reminded him of a youth he once knew."

Then the room began to spin around me so that I could barely maintain myself on my feet, for God had also performed a miracle for me, the least deserving of His creatures. I could not keep the tears from running down my cheeks, even though Belteshazzar, whose name was Daniel, observed me with his piercing eyes as though he could see into my heart.

"If my lords would give me leave I should seek out this man," I said, "for it seems to me that I know him, having met him many years ago and still owing him a great debt."

Daniel's eyes were upon me as though he knew all I concealed, but he only said:

"Let my lord go then and see if he knows that man. As for our instructions—we shall yet weather another day without knowing the Babylonian tongue."

Before I hastened away I cast another glance at the young man Abed-nego, who had reminded the tall Ethiopian of the youth he once knew. Abed-nego was slender and handsome as all princes of Judah, while the man I had seen in the mirror this morning had a fat face and a naked chin—nay, two chins hanging beneath his plump cheeks. But perhaps when I left Borsippa ten years ago I had still looked like Abed-nego, I too being of the blood royal of Judah.

While these thoughts tumbled about my mind I hastened through the third and fourth courts to the entrance of the Women's House. None would suspect my calling there, for it was plain to behold that I was a eunuch. I gave the sentry at the gate some silver and bade him fetch the keeper of the king's harem.

My wait was so long that I feared the chamberlain had refused to see one who had not given his name. But when finally he approached the gate I knew him at once. He was arrayed in fine robes such as he had worn as keeper of the harem at Nineveh, before he became a lowly slave in Borsippa. Though his hair had turned gray he was still handsome. His dark skin gleamed with precious oil, and he moved with the dignity befitting one of his station. His face had aged, but his eyes were as kind as before though puzzled when he saw me standing in the gate. I could not speak for the sobs rising in my throat but threw myself weeping at his feet to kiss the hem of his garment.

"The sentry told me that my lord asked for me," he said in his familiar voice that made me weep all the harder. "But I cannot recall having met him before. However I can see that he is in great distress and has no doubt come to ask some favor of me. If it be because of some kinswoman in the king's harem—a younger sister perchance— I shall plead my lord's case if it is not of an indelicate nature."

Then I raised my tear-stained face, and looking up at him I exclaimed:

"Have I changed so much that you no longer recognize me, Tarqu?"

Hearing me pronounce his name he started and said:

"It is a long time since any called me by this name, for I am known here as Ardia. Outside of my nearest kin there is only one who would call me Tarqu, and I long relinquished all hope of ever seeing him again."

Lifting me up from the ground he clasped me in his arms, and we stood shedding our tears of joy together. Then he took me by the hand and led me inside the court of the Women's House, for the sentry stood gaping at us with great curiosity, and what we had to tell each other was not meant for his ears.

This was the first time I had set foot inside the fifth court. There were many women walking about, attended by their slave girls. Some of the ladies were ancient—perhaps the last of the concubines left from the times of King Nabopolassar—while others were young and comely. But though there were many young women abroad, I saw no children in the court. However, my mind was so taken up with my joy that I did not long dwell on this strange discovery.

Tarqu led me to his fine quarters, which were a long way from the hovel we had shared at Borsippa. When we were seated on a rug and a slave girl had served us wine and honey cakes, Tarqu bade me tell him all that had happened to me since I left Borsippa. Having learned of my good fortune and of how I had discovered him in the end, he said:

"Were you not the one who scoffed at the soothsayer's predictions? And are we not met again, I as keeper of the king's harem and you, Ashur, as royal interpreter?"

"Indeed many strange things have come to pass," I replied. "And just as your name is no longer Tarqu mine is no longer Ashur, for the king himself changed it to Marduksharusur long ago. It is the only name by which I am known now." Then, dropping my gaze, I added: "Nor does any know that I am born a Hebrew, not even my own master."

And I told Tarqu how it had come about that I had concealed this from my lord. Then Tarqu shook his head and said:

"This is not a good thing you are doing. If you should be discovered someday, you will be suspected of evil reasons for your deceit."

But I would no longer speak of my own life. Rather I would have Tarqu tell me all that had happened to him since last I embraced him ten years ago, as he stood splitting wood for the lady Harshinana in the yard of the merchant at Borsippa.

"Then you have not yet heard the story," Tarqu said to me. "I should have thought it was known in all Babylonia, for at the time there was much talk about it. However, so many people were haled into court to testify that in the end none would discuss the matter any longer. Bearing testimony in court is a task for idlers with which men of business do not wish to be troubled. There is wisdom in the old proverb: Do not wander to the place of strife. It is in strife that fate may overtake you and you may be made a witness to testify in a lawsuit not your own.

"But let me go on with the story. After our master in Borsippa had sold you, he did not buy another kitchen slave for his wife. Nor would he give her the silver he had received for you, though he had made her a gift of you when first he brought us to his house. But having nothing in writing, Harshinana could not claim what was rightfully hers. Thus she came to hate her husband even more than before, nor did he bear her great love, for he never believed that she had been without guilt in what happened between you. He gave her still less silver than before, and nothing at all when he left on a journey. At times there was barely enough food for the two of us in the house. I would have starved had I not stolen from the mistress, as even the most honest of slaves would have been forced to do.

"Thus we continued, with the master and the mistress hating each other more every day. Often the old vulture would beat her, and since she could not repay him in kind she vented her venom on me. But when her husband went on a journey Harshinana would leave the house for many hours. Though the master charged me with watching her, I could not follow her all over town, being only a slave who had to obey her.

"In the fourth year after you were sold the merchant left on another journey to buy merchandise from a ship that had foundered not far from Uruk. When many days passed and he did not return, the spirits of the lady Harshinana rose, for she hoped that he had met with an ill fate.

"One night, toward the middle watch, there was a knock at the door. Thinking it was the master come home I went to open. But when I shone the lamp outside I saw three strange men in the yard. I should have shut the door in their faces, for they looked as though they would think nothing of running a man through with a knife. But just then Harshinana came running to inquire who had knocked at the door. And when one of the men called inside that he had news of her husband—news that would be most welcome to her ears—she bade me let them enter. I obeyed with great misgivings, for I could see that they were villains. No sooner had I shut the door behind them than they told Harshinana that her husband was dead, having been murdered on his way back from Uruk.

" 'And what reward will you give us for bringing you this news, now that you are fallen heir to your husband's wealth?' one of the blackguards asked.

" 'Am I to reward you for telling me that I am left a widow in my youth!' Harshinana exclaimed, disheveling her hair, rending her garments and acting in every way as though a most beloved husband had been torn from her bosom. 'Nay, but you had better leave my house before I scream for help and denounce you, for no doubt it is you who killed my poor husband and robbed him of his goods!'

" 'You need not act before us in this manner,' another of the men said. 'It was told us by one who knows you well how often you wished your husband dead. Indeed you said it would be worth a

great deal of silver to you if ever he failed to return alive from one
of his journeys.'

"'May the person who slandered me thus come to an untimely
end and find no burial!' Harshinana cried. 'As for me, I always
worshiped my husband and wished him no ill. And now leave my
house before I order my slave to drive you out!'

"The men muttered among themselves, throwing sidelong glances
at me. But then, frightened by my size and also by Harshinana's
threat to set up a loud cry, they fled into the night. I thought that
once they were gone the mistress would begin to dance for joy. But
she was careful to keep up her mourning before me that I might
never testify against her.

"As for our unbidden visitors, she did not denounce them to the
king's officers, nor did she open her mouth before the neighbors.
Moreover, she threatened to sell me into the mines if I revealed to
any what I had heard. Then she took possession of all the merchandise in her husband's bazaar and also of his silver, whose hiding place
she had always known though she had pretended otherwise. But
when any of the neighbors inquired about the master, Harshinana
said he had joined a caravan traveling to Tyre, and that it would be
many months yet before he returned.

"However, the gods willed otherwise. The master's body, which
the murderers had thrown in the river, was washed ashore near
Uruk and recognized by one who had done business with him. That
man also knew what merchandise the master had carried with him.
Not many days later a man trying to sell some of these same goods
was arrested by the king's officers. When questioned in a persuasive
manner he gave away the names of his two accomplices in the
murder. The three were the same men who had called at our house
late at night. They put the blame for their deed on the lady
Harshinana, saying she had bidden them kill her husband that she
might inherit his fortune. And to prove their claim they confessed
that they had visited her after the deed, naming me as a witness.

"Word was sent from Uruk to Borsippa, and an officer came to
the house to arrest Harshinana as an accomplice in her husband's
murder. Then the three men were brought to Borsippa that they
might be tried for their crime in the city where their victim had
lived. And thus it came about that I was made a witness in a lawsuit
not my own.

"For many days there was no other talk in Borsippa than of the trial. All the neighbors were haled into court to testify whether Harshinana's marriage had been good or bad, for she denied having had any part in the murder. But she could not deny that the men had visited her, for I was made to swear by Marduk, Nebo and Shamash, and fearing the gods more than the mistress I spoke the truth.

"As for the other witnesses, some swore that they had heard quarreling between husband and wife, while others said that her husband had not given Harshinana enough for the household, even though he was a wealthy man. And I, being sworn to tell the truth, confirmed this.

"Now, there were three judges listening to the case. After they had heard all the testimony, two said Harshinana ought to be slain together with the murderers. For even if she had not killed her husband she had been guilty of concealing his murder. However, the third judge said:

" 'A woman whose husband did not support her—granted that she knew her husband's enemies, and that after her husband had been killed she heard that her husband had been killed—why should she not remain silent? Is it she who killed her husband? The punishment of those who actually killed her husband should suffice.'

"And the judge went on at great length, arguing that Harshinana had neither hired her husband's killers nor had she rewarded them for their deed or sheltered them in her house, until he persuaded the other two judges of her innocence. And she was allowed to go free, while the three men were put to death. Thus was proved another old proverb: At the gate of the judge's house the mouth of a sinful woman is mightier than her husband's.

"Since there was no other kin left, Harshinana was now the lawful heir to her husband's fortune. No sooner were we returned home from court than she struck me, saying she would sell me to the next slave train passing through Borsippa because I had testified against her. And so she did the very next day, not even giving me time to send word to my sister and her husband.

"If not for the fear that I should never see them again—for they had visited me in Borsippa from time to time—I would have rejoiced at leaving the town where I had known nothing but bitterness and loss. Though Harshinana sold me with the plea that I be sent to the mines in the far north where they dig for iron, the slave dealer knew that I would fetch a better price in Babylon, where the king was buying up strong slaves to do his building.

"Thus I was taken to Babylon and became one of the king's slaves. I did not mind the hard work, for we were fed well so that we might work speedily, the king requiring great haste in everything he orders done. I was glad of working in the open air and often sang while wielding the pickax or carrying bricks. One day I was heard by the queen, who often came to observe the building, and she had me fetched to the Women's House that I might sing for her and her ladies.

"But when the queen learned that I had been keeper of the harem at Nineveh, she begged the king to appoint me a place in the Women's House. And Nebuchadrezzar made me the keeper of his own harem and changed my name to Ardia. As for the man who had held the post before me, he was thrown in the fire for having been party to one of the harem intrigues, of which there are many. Thus out of Harshinana's ill will toward me came my good fortune.

"After attaining my high position I sent to Borsippa for my sister and her husband, who had fallen on bad times. From them I learned that Harshinana had sold the store, had married the judge who had gained her acquittal and had moved with him away from Borsippa to escape the gossip about them. Wherever they are now, may they live out their lives in mutual fear of each other, for two linked in a dishonest deed can never again trust each other.

"But let us give thanks to the gods for having dealt mercifully with us. And if ever we should meet again the soothsayer who predicted our good fortune, let us reward him richly, for he spoke the truth!"

"Indeed we owe thanks to our gods," I replied. "But as for the soothsayer, he told us what he tells everyone, his predictions coming true once and failing a hundred times. Moreover, he prophesied that my fate should not be accomplished until the goddess Ishtar descended from on high—and even you, Tarqu, cannot believe that this thing will ever come to pass!"

Now that I had found my old friend again, my pleasure in going to the palace every day was increased a hundredfold. Though I was still Nabukasir's slave, being royal tutor bestowed upon me a certain freedom, and I spent many nights with Tarqu. Of late I sought excuses for not returning home, for there was bad blood between the master and the mistress, and also between the mistress and me.

While the husbands of many of the lady Margidda's friends had been made courtiers and even governors by Nebuchadrezzar, her own husband had by his contrary actions kept the king from appointing him to office. This filled the lady Margidda with bitterness, which was still increased when I attained my new office. At times I heard the master and the mistress arguing behind the closed door of their chamber.

"Your own slave holds a royal post," the lady Margidda would say, "while you who fought by Nebuchadrezzar's side no longer find favor in his eyes. And I, who spoke proudly of the high station you would attain, am made the laughingstock among my friends. But it is all because out of your Hebrew stubbornness you will not write for the king what he wishes you to write!"

My master made harsh answer, telling his wife that she was a foolish woman who cared nothing for him but thought only of her vanity. And he stalked out in anger to visit a tavern and spend the night with one of the temple harlots. Though this was done by most men of my master's station, he had never done so before, preferring to seek his pleasure in the bosom of his own wife. But he too was become embittered, as will happen to one who labors at a task for which none offers him praise or thanks.

I hoped his evil mood would pass in time. And when one day the mistress's handmaiden came running from the garden, wailing that a snake had dropped from a tree between the master and his wife—a certain omen that they would be divorced—I chided the girl for her folly. Nor do I believe what followed would have happened had not the Captain Holofernes moved in with us.

This came about after the army returned from Carchemish. In the month of Tebet Nebuchadrezzar had marched north to collect his yearly tribute and display his force of arms. The troops returned the following month, and with them the Captain Holofernes. Though many of my master's friends had ceased visiting him when they learned that he was no longer in the king's favor, the captain continued coming to the house as before. Nabukasir had saved his life at Nineveh, and such a debt is forever.

On a cold day in the month of Shebat when I had not gone to the palace but was sitting by the brazier, telling the boy David his favorite stories, I heard a loud crash in the street, followed by a torrent of oaths in a familiar voice. Curious to learn what had incensed the Captain Holofernes I hastened to the door, and glancing outside I beheld a strange sight: for there, piled high on a chariot, was the captain's armor and weapons and garments and bedding, and crouched on top of all this the captain's hunting dog, growling horribly at the crowd that had collected. As for the chariot, its side was dented and the spokes of one wheel bent so that it stood leaning sideways, its load threatening to topple off at any moment.

Running out to assist the captain, I shouted:

"Has my lord's house burned down?"

"Worse than that," the captain replied. "My brother has come from Uruk to visit me, bringing with him all the women of my family. They have caused such confusion in my house that I fled to seek shelter with your master. Should he refuse me I would sooner sleep in the open field than share a house with those females! What is more, when I drove away in great haste I collided with another chariot, driven by one of those worthless sons of rich men who have recently acquired great wealth. Not only do these men buy their sons exemptions from serving in the king's army, they also buy them chariots with which to endanger the lives of their fellow citizens. Indeed times of peace are more perilous now than times of war, for in war a man may guard against his enemies, whereas in peace his own countrymen deprive him of life and limb! When I was the age of those striplings I still bowed down low before the nobles who drove past me in the street, but today all those worthless youths have chariots—and Egyptian chariots to boot! No matter that the king has forbidden the bringing in of Egyptian goods—they go to Tyre for them. But the silver paid for these chariots ends up in the coffers of the Egyptians, who use it to arm against us! And why must these misfits have Egyptian chariots? Because they are smaller and lighter than our own—they say—because they are easier to swing around, because they do not wear out the horses so that one can go for longer stretches without changing them! But when two such scoundrels driving Egyptian chariots meet in the street, they halt, jump off and embrace each other like long-lost brothers, while we, their elders and betters who go to war with Egypt, must fight against weapons bought with our own silver!"

The captain added many more oaths to those he had already

uttered. The crowd that had swelled to a great size listened with rapture, for it was not every day that they heard such marvelous swearing. In the end the shouting woke my master, who had retired to his chamber for his afternoon rest. When he learned of his friend's ill fortune he bade the captain bring his gear into the house and stay with him as long as he pleased.

When the Captain Holofernes was made comfortable and I had fetched a jug of wine for him and my master, he continued his tale of woe:

"Ah, had my brother only come alone, he could be made to understand that I must have the house to myself when the ladies of my acquaintance visit me. But how can I explain such matters to my pious mother, who shudders at the thought of a man consorting with married women?

"Do not misunderstand me—I was glad to see my mother, who is getting on in years and whom I neglected to visit for a long time. But no sooner had she embraced and kissed me than she began to quarrel with my old, deaf servant, accusing her of stealing from me—for how else could one explain my being so thin? Then my slave woman, who not only serves me faithfully but is also unable to recognize my female visitors, having weak eyes in addition to being deaf, threatened to throw herself in the river. What trouble I had to reconcile her with my mother! But my mother, resolved to find a culprit for the lack of fat on my body, now turned on my elder brother and chided him for withholding my due share of silver brought in by the fields which the king bestowed upon me for my services. My brother in turn replied that he sent me more than he uses for himself, his wife and all his children, and that no doubt I wasted my fortune on harlots and wine. To this his wife and my two sisters added their wisdom, nor was there an end to the bedlam until they all went to sleep.

"But no sooner did the women wake refreshed this morning than they went shopping in town. May Ishtar strike me dead if they did not visit every clothes merchant, perfumer and hairdresser, buying from them goods with which to clutter my simple soldier's home! There are garments thrown about, and jars of ointment and paint for the face, while these women sit before mirrors, putting on the false hair pieces they bought and painting their eyes and their cheeks until they look like temple harlots who have seen better days. Even my own mother, a widow well gone into her years who should have better sense, has pinned up her hair and reddened her lips so that I blush with shame whenever I glance at her!

"But now the women have resolved to see the sights of Babylon, and also to visit a number of midwives to inquire after remedies for such ills as beset women in their middle years. May I not see the end of this day if I accompany them on these errands! Let me borrow Marduksharusur to escort my women—for it is not seemly that they wander about alone—let him show them the sights and take them to the midwives! As for you and me, Nabukasir, we shall take my brother to the Tavern of the Prancing Lioness, for he has heard much about it and greatly desires to go there!"

Though I had never set foot inside, I too had heard of this tavern. It had been opened by a wily alewife who had conceived the clever thought of having wine served to her patrons by naked slave girls, dressed only in the heads and tails of lionesses. All these girls were said to be virgins who had never lain with a man, nor were they allowed to consort with the patrons—or so the story went. This the men found greatly exciting, though why a woman dressed in a beast's tail and head should rouse men thus I do not know. But then not being whole in my parts, perhaps I cannot understand such delights.

However, my master had his own doubts.

"I do not think it wise for us to visit this tavern, Holofernes," he said. "I have heard rumors that outlaws congregate there and that it was they who provided the silver to open this tavern, for they would learn from the merchants who carouse there when their caravans leave Babylon. More than one such caravan has been robbed along the way and the merchants murdered. Also it is said that some priestesses of Ishtar break the law and visit the tavern, though they must not set foot in a winehouse. Any day now the king's officers will arrest all they find there, and it would be better if we were not among them!"

The captain only laughed and replied:

"You need not fear to visit the Tavern of the Prancing Lioness! Indeed you could hardly be safer in Nebuchadrezzar's own bed-chamber. Many of the king's chamberlains have lain with these virgins who have never known a man, confiding in them such secrets as men will reveal in their moment of weakness. As for the king's officers, they have accepted free wine and silver from the alewife, nor would they dare arrest any of her patrons!"

Then my master agreed to visit the tavern with the captain and his brother. But to me fell the task of taking the ladies around town. The captain had spoken truly in warning me that these women would faint at the sight of a snake, but when it came to seeing the sights of a strange city they had the strength his foot soldiers might envy them. Though I returned home weary at night, the women were still fresh and eager to see more.

As for my master, he visited the Tavern of the Prancing Lioness every night until the captain's brother departed. And to my great amazement he continued going there alone afterward.

Barely a month passed before the lady Margidda's friends began whispering in her ear that her husband was seeing a priestess of Ishtar, for women delight in bearing such tales to their friends. The mistress spent many hours weeping in her chamber, fearing that because her youth was gone from her her husband would take a concubine. He could never bring her to live in the same house with his wife, for the mistress's father—like many a father who loved his daughter—had written this into the marriage contract. But none could hinder the master in what he did outside the house.

Nor was he different from other men who thought that a new woman would bring back their youthful vigor. And he, who had never troubled himself with his garments, now chose them with great care, perfuming his body before he dressed, and spending many hours in the hands of his barber. He even allowed the latter to use such dyes as would conceal the few gray hairs on his head and in his beard. I saw then that where it concerned women a learned man was no better than a fool.

But for the friends of the lady Margidda all this should have mattered little, for such affairs are known to pass swiftly. However, these vipers spread the tale that the mistress's rival would not rest until the master divorced his wife and married her. The lady Margidda's unhappiness increased from day to day, while the children, seeing their mother weep continually, also became downcast. Thus our happy home turned into a dwelling place of misery.

In my heart I cursed the Captain Holofernes for luring my master to the tavern where first he met the cause of our trouble. Indeed such was my chagrin that I would avoid the captain when I went to teach my princely charges at the palace. In the end he chided me for my sullenness.

"Though I was often vexed by your insolence, Marduksharusur," he said one day, "I would rather listen to your shameless speech than have you pass me like one whose tongue was ripped from his mouth. What makes you act thus toward an old comrade-in-arms with whom you went to war against Judah?"

Though I knew the captain to be mocking me, I blurted out what mischief he had caused in the house of the man who had saved his life at Nineveh. Then the captain smote his thigh in anger, exclaiming:

"May Ishtar strike me dead if that wretched harlot has not sunk her fangs into your master! But does he not know that such a woman is for the pleasure of one night and not to take the place of one's rightful spouse? Neither is she as young as your master thinks her, for a woman of her calling knows how to enhance her face with paint and keep her skin youthful through the use of many ointments. Moreover, she is not a priestess of Ishtar, as she would have your master believe; she only invented this lie to enhance her station when she came to live in Babylon. I knew her well when I was still an acolyte at the temple Eanna in Uruk, for she was one of the temple harlots. There was not a man at the temple with whom she had not lain, from the high priest down to the last water carrier. No doubt she learned from them many tricks with which to beguile a simpleton like your master. But to think of taking such a woman for one's wife is madness!"

"Since my lord knows all these evil things about the lady, would he not warn my master of his folly?" I asked.

But the captain frowned and replied:

"Unless a man wishes to lose a friend, he must never tell him that the woman he loves is a harlot. Therefore let us hope that your master's god will still enlighten him. As for me, I must keep silent."

After instructing my charges in their lesson for the day, I sought out Tarqu in his quarters. There I opened my heart to him, pouring out my sorrows, to which he replied:

"This world would be a happy place if not for the women in it. Was it not a woman who lured savage Enkidu from the steppe, where he dwelt in peaceful bliss with his wild beasts? Was it not a woman who caused you to be made a eunuch? Even the women in the king's own harem provoke no end of trouble—though they are not without cause. In Nineveh, where the king knew how to please the ladies, my task was an easy one. But here it requires the guile of an ambassador to prevent these women from murdering each other in their venom. Nor is there an end to their need of physicians, for—as the proverb tells us—a restless woman in the house adds ache to pain!

"But I can see that you learned restraint, Marduksharusur, for you never inquired why there are no children in the Women's House. Now that we are discussing these matters I shall reveal the secret to you, knowing that you will not open your mouth.

"There are in the king's harem many comely young women, maidens sent him by his allies in the hope that he would beget sons upon them, thus strengthening the ties between their nations. But Nebuchadrezzar's only son was begotten upon the queen. And even she bore him only one other child, the princess Naq'd.

"From time to time the king visits his other wives, if only out of courtesy, for many of these ladies are of royal blood and must not be humbled. Yet after his visits all tell the same tale: how they anointed and perfumed their bodies to receive the king; how they enlarged their eyes, painted their cheeks and put on their finest garments; how they sang and danced before the king, and how when the time came for him to embrace them he would turn pale, his brow would be covered with sweat and he would hasten away, pretending that there were pressing matters of state that needed his attention. The following day the king would send the lady he had visited some precious gift—a fine bracelet or necklace, or a costly garment. Moreover, he has built many bathrooms in the Women's House, and privies with seats of marble. But the ladies would sooner have the king honor them with his embrace than regale them with golden dippers to scoop up the water for rinsing their privies.

"There is among them a princess from Elam, a woman of great beauty, whose bitterness is even deeper than that of the others. She had hoped to take the queen's place in Nebuchadrezzar's favor, the queen being no longer young and having borne him but one son, a weakling. This princess has uttered many dangerous words in her chagrin, saying to me: 'The king has raised up the tower of

Etemenanki. He has raised up the outer wall around Babylon. He has even raised the roof of his throne room to a new height. But when it comes to raising what counts most among men, he cannot do it. And we who adorn ourselves for his visits and do all manner of things to please him are made to look like fools. But if we dared act like the queen—who pretends that her trouble is upon her whenever the king desires her company, barring her door to him—his desire would be greatly fanned!'

"Nor are these words untrue," Tarqu said. "It is known in the Women's House that the queen detests her husband and shudders at his touch. Before her father, Cyaxares, made an alliance with Nabopolassar, giving his daughter as a wife to the crown prince Nebuchadrezzar, Amytis was betrothed to one of her princely kinsmen. And though Nebuchadrezzar worships the queen and would give her an army and even half his kingdom, she differs little from any other woman who would sooner be the concubine of some handsome princeling than the wife of a great and mighty king whom the gods blessed with everything but handsome looks.

"Yet in spite of her loathing—or if one were to believe the Elamite princess, because of it—Nebuchadrezzar desires the queen more than all the other women. As for the princess, she has taken to seducing the young maidens in the harem, forcing me to avert my eyes if I would not be drawn into her intrigues and end up being thrown in the fire like my predecessor. Thus it is not without cause when I say that women are the worst troublemakers in this world!"

Then I understood that Tarqu's task was even more perilous than mine. For I had to conceal the doings of one alone, while he had to conceal the doings of many. Nor was the tale he had told me the only secret he knew.

When he led me back to the gate, we passed in the court a woman strolling with her arm about the shoulder of a youth who was not yet a man, but neither was he a child. To walk about thus with a young man was unseemly in any place and more so in the king's own palace. When I halted to gape at this woman, who was quite comely though no longer young. Tarqu glanced at me and asked:

"Do you recognize the lady?"

"How should I recognize her, never having set eyes on her before?" I replied.

"Indeed it is a long time since last you saw her at Nineveh. Her mother was your own father's kinswoman—the same who moved with her husband to Harran, where she gave her daughter to become a priestess of the moon-god Sin. The woman you see strolling about is that priestess, and the youth her son Nabonidus. The old king brought her to Babylon after he conquered Harran, and though she was married to an Assyrian prince, there are some who whisper that Nabonidus is Nabopolassar's son. But the lady has always wisely denied such rumors, for the queen mother would see her younger son Nabu-suma-lisir king if Nebuchadrezzar died, nor would she suffer another son of her dead husband to live. As for Nebuchadrezzar, he too would not show Nabonidus much love if he thought him a rival for his throne.

"But the youth betrays little desire to be king. He would sooner be a priest and bring back the worship of the moon-god Sin, as his mother would have him do. Even as a young boy Nabonidus was given to strange pleasures. While others played at war he would dig in the ground, happy to unearth old, broken jars or clay tablets written in Sumerian. Thus he seems harmless enough. But as for his mother, no doubt she harbors in her bosom such dreams as every mother has for her favorite son.

"However, the less we discuss these things the better, my friend, for if one of the king's spies heard us we might spend our last moments on earth together in the fire!"

Even while I nodded in agreement, I stared with wonder at Nabonidus. For though there might be in his veins the blood royal of Babylon, he was descended through his mother from my own ancestor Hezekiah, who a hundred years ago had sat on the throne of Judah.

Soon I was reminded of what Tarqu had said about women being the cause of much trouble. I am speaking of the snake who had taken my master's fancy and did not rest until she had induced him to divorce his lawful wife.

Or rather I should say that it was the lady Margidda who sought this divorce. She could no longer bear the mockery of her friends, who would give her no rest but came every day to weep with her in her grief. Each told a different tale and offered different counsel, all speaking at the same time, until they would have thrown the calmest person into confusion. In the end the lady Margidda fled with her children to her father's house, begging him to take such steps as would set her free from her husband.

Then my master's father-in-law came to heap bitter blame on his head for having brought the woman who had borne him children to this state. And he said he would use all his power at court to obtain for his daughter not only her divorce but also the right to keep the children—a man who ran after a harlot not being a fit father for them. Moreover, he would make my master restore to the lady Margidda the dowry she had brought with her—which included our lovely house—and make him pay the full sum which the law required a man to pay his divorced wife who had borne him children. He would also persuade the judge to seize in trust the lands that would someday go to David, lest his father write them over to a son born of his second marriage.

Sick at heart for doing what was wrong yet not being able to do otherwise, my master wept over losing his children but consented to everything to be quit of the quarreling. Neither did he know enough about business to understand that these arrangements would leave him nearly a pauper. All he would have left were the crown lands which King Nabopolassar had bestowed upon his father. These had to remain in the family and could never be sold. However, the income from these lands was poor, the tenant who kept them for my lord being a thief and cheating him of his profits. Since my master loathed lawsuits and would not take the scoundrel to court, he had to be satisfied with his meager share.

To this day I believe that my master's divorce would never have come about had the Captain Holofernes been in Babylon to speak against it. Though the captain had refused to warn my lord earlier, he would now have denounced this harlot who had snared him. But Nebuchadrezzar had marched with the army along the banks of the Tigris to prevent the king of Elam from invading Babylonia, and the Captain Holofernes was with him on the campaign. By the time he returned, my master was divorced from the lady Margidda and married to his second wife, whose name was Baltesha.

It was a bitter day when I moved my master's possessions out of the house where we had lived since he brought me from Borsippa, nearly twelve years ago. Among his few belongings I was the most precious, for he owned little more than his garments, his armor and his stack of old clay tablets. To me fell the task of seeing that the slaves did not drop the heavy jar which concealed my lord's most dangerous writings. If that jar were broken in the street and its contents revealed, we would both end up in the fire rather than in the new part of town—this being a bad enough fate.

I had never thought that some day I might live with my lord on the western bank of the Euphrates, where one house looked like the next, one garden like the next and one woman like the next. Nor was my new mistress, the lady Baltesha, pleased with the simple dwelling my lord had bought. On her way to and from the temple of Ishtar she had often passed our former home, and thinking it my master's property, she had coveted it in her heart. Now her chagrin was all the greater for not finding him the wealthy man she had thought him. Before long she began to taunt her new husband, boasting that she could have made a better match, her tongue that had beguiled him with sweet words now being sharp and bitter like that of many such women. But my master was still smitten by her beauty, which in truth was great. He would suffer her taunts in silence and give her more silver than he could spare that she might buy herself the trinkets and garments she craved. Soon his need for money became so dire that I proposed to visit his tenant farmer and press him for his payments.

But since my lord would not take his just claims to court, I had to obtain a document with which to threaten that thieving scoundrel. I asked Tarqu whether he did not know a chamberlain at court who might aid me in this matter. After speaking to such a man, Tarqu said:

"Since the land is kept by a tenant, you may not set foot on your master's own property without a written order from a judge. This even my friend at court would not dare obtain unlawfully. What he can obtain for you is an imprint of the king's seal on a clay tablet. You may write above this seal whatever pleases you, but make certain that your words are neither unlawful nor blasphemous. Surely your master's tenant cannot read, but even he will be able to recognize the king's seal. This will strike terror in his heart, allowing you to deal with him as you wish."

Tarqu made good his promise, and I wrote above the king's seal the old proverb: Do no crime, then the fear of the gods will not worry you. This could not displease the king even if I were discovered. Then I concealed the tablet in my garments and set out for the crown lands beyond the outer wall of Babylon, which King Nabopolassar had bestowed upon my lord's father. When I beheld the rich, fertile fields near the river and the plenteous crop upon them I was filled with even greater wrath against the scoundrel who was cheating my master of his rightful share.

Nor was the thief frightened when I presented myself before him but would have thrown me off the land had I not shown him my tablet. He frowned at it as though he could read, but all he recognized was the king's own seal. He might have called a scribe to read it for him, but having a troubled conscience he feared to reveal his dishonesty before others. Thus he only gnashed his teeth, saying:

"The fox had a stick with him—whom can I beat? He carried a legal document—what can I challenge?"

But he let me enter his house, where we haggled until nightfall over the sum he owed my master. Whenever I made a request, the scoundrel set up loud lamentations, claiming that there had been a flood, a drought, locusts or weevils devastating the crop. In the end I threatened to examine the yield of his neighbor's fields and accordingly make him restore my master's loss threefold, as the law required. But if he could not make restitution, I would have him dragged through the fields by a team of oxen. Then he gave in, cursing me and the day he had rented my lord's fields and the day he was born.

The silver I brought back soon ended up in the hand of the lady Baltesha. Nor was she grateful but accused me of having taken a bribe from the tenant for accepting a smaller share for my lord, making me regret that I had failed to do so. Surely after twelve years of faithful service I had a better right to my master's silver than Baltesha, who had filled his life with bitterness in the few months she had been his wife.

There was little love between the mistress and me. Indeed she would have forced me to do all manner of menial tasks had I not been in the good graces of the king. Also she hated me for sharing with my lord his love for the old writings, while she did all in her power to entice him away from his work. And if the truth must be told, I hated her for robbing me of the time my master used to spend with me in translating the old poetry. Now he would recite the poems to his new wife, while she reclined upon a couch, gazing into a mirror to inspect her skin and her teeth, for like all such women she lived in terror of losing her looks. Nor did she have the good grace to conceal her boredom but suffered my lord's reading only to keep him from working with me.

Thus I spent more and more time away from home, pretending that the king had charged me with many new tasks. Indeed many new duties had been added to my old ones. Daniel, whose name had been changed to Belteshazzar, had spoken of me to the young king Jehoiachin while visiting him in his quarters. And Jehoiachin had asked that I come and teach him, his wives and his children the Babylonian tongue.

The Hebrew king had been given a house in Nebuchadrezzar's own garden, where he lived with his kin in comfort if not in splendor. They received food rations such as befit royalty and were given slaves to perform their menial tasks. But they were not allowed to leave the palace grounds or to consort with the Hebrews who had been taken to Tel-Abib lest they stir up rebellion among them.

Both Jehoiachin's wives had been with child when taken captive, and the first Hebrew princes were born in Babylon. The two boys already walked and talked. Indeed they had learned the Babylonian tongue from their slaves, nor would they answer in Hebrew when spoken to. This greatly angered Jehoiachin's mother and led her to claim that children were more perverse now than in former times. However, it did not hinder her from also wishing to learn Babylonian, for the queen Amytis had taken to visiting the royal Hebrew ladies in their quarters. She would often bring the crown prince Amel-Marduk with her that he might play with the Hebrew princes, whom she thought better company for him than the sons of the Babylonian nobles.

Amel-Marduk was a strange boy, as pretty as his older sister was ugly. Though his speech was insolent, he was shy at heart and lived in dread of his father, who seized by despair over having sired this weakling often roared at him in fury. This would throw the boy into even greater terror and send him to hide howling in his mother's lap. Indeed what Amel-Marduk liked best was to play with younger boys, who could neither hurt nor tease him. Thus he was happiest when taken along to visit King Jehoiachin's small sons. As for the queen Amytis, she had never ceased feeling an exile in her husband's country and soon came to love the Hebrew ladies like sisters. And when spring came and all Babylon rejoiced at the New Year Festival, they would sit together and weep for the hills of their homelands.

But my main task remained teaching the Babylonian tongue to Daniel and the three young men, whose names had been changed to Shadrach, Meshach and Abed-nego. Being younger, they learned the language more swiftly than Daniel. Even after he had mastered it he needed but open his mouth to reveal himself a Hebrew, and for many months he still required my aid as interpreter. Thus it came about that I was present when first he ministered to the king.

After Nebuchadrezzar returned from his war against Elam, a feeling of unrest swept the land. From Tarqu, who knew the comings and goings of all courtiers, I learned that there were daily secret dispatches from the provinces. Also the number of spies in the land had nearly doubled, for there were rumors of rebellion. But none knew whether the unrest was caused by the king's captains being displeased over the manner in which Nebuchadrezzar waged his wars—for many still held that he should have destroyed Jerusalem—or by the landowners being angry because of the men the king drew from the land, or by the merchants grumbling over their increased taxes.

The king spent many sleepless nights pondering matters of state, and even when he slept he was plagued by evil dreams so that he woke up screaming and bathed in sweat. Then he would summon his dream diviners that they might reveal to him the meaning of his dreams. But their dread of the king was such that they pretended not to understand his dreams, until he threatened to have every one of them thrown in the fire.

Learning of this threat, the Captain Holofernes laughed with glee and exclaimed:

"It would give me great pleasure to carry out this execution, for I do not believe one single lying word of these scoundrels! But if all dream diviners in Babylonia were slain, life in the land would come to a total halt. It has become so that none from the king down to the last slave can go about his daily tasks without the counsel of his dream diviner!"

In this the captain spoke the truth. Not only the rich but also the poor inquired into their dreams. For the latter the dream diviners had devised a new way: they would assemble in a circle those who wished to consult them and have each tell his dream. Since most had had a similar dream at some time they would soon fall to explaining their dreams to each other, while the scoundrel whose task it was to divine the meaning was free to spend his time counting his silver.

But the king's own soothsayers were not the sort who had to content themselves with small offerings from slaves. Most were ordained priests and exorcisers who had studied the secret tablets that could be read only by the initiated. It was such a man, clad in his costly robes and tall hat, that I saw hastening down a corridor in the palace one day as I strolled with Daniel after our lesson. Behind him followed his acolytes carrying the implements for his rites, and after them several of the king's chamberlains, all chattering in great excitement.

Seizing one I knew by his garments to ask him where all were running, I learned that the king had spent a dreadful night. Not only had he been plagued by evil dreams, but he had wakened with a headache so severe that he was barely able to open his eyes and raise his head from the pillow. Nor could he speak, and when he tried to rise from his bed to relieve himself, his face had turned ashen and he had fallen to the ground in a faint. As for nourishment, what little he had taken he had brought up again, until it had become clear to all that he was seized by an evil demon, for there had been no sign of sickness upon him the previous day.

Having told me this, the chamberlain hastened after the others to the king's bedchamber. But when I translated his words to Daniel, he smote his thigh in anger and said:

"The Babylonians are wise in many ways. They know how to observe the course of the stars in the sky. They know how to divide time into months and years. They know how to build great buildings, conduct commerce, govern nations and wage wars, but when it comes to their belief in ghosts their folly is beyond measure! There are neither ghosts nor familiar spirits, nor are there gods besides Yahweh, from whom proceed sickness and health, wisdom and folly. As for the king, he would be better served by a physician than by a dream diviner. Even I could sooner cure him than these sorcerers!"

"Then let us follow the chamberlains to the king's bedchamber and offer my lord's assistance," I proposed.

But Daniel hesitated and replied:

"These Chaldeans would not take it kindly if I robbed them of the king's trust. Since they are powerful men I would rather not vex them, for they might harm not only me but also my people."

"Let us at any rate go and observe the rites," I said. "There will be so many in the king's bedchamber that another two will hardly be noticed."

We found the door to the chamber ajar and none there to guard it, for the sentries too had crowded into the room. The exorciser had lit the incense upon his censer, and the raised ivory bed of the king was shrouded in blue haze. But even the screen of smoke could not conceal Nebuchadrezzar's ashen face, nor the dark circles under his eyes and the deep creases running down from his nostrils into his tangled beard. His long hair was matted with sweat, for he had not allowed his barber to come near him all day and touch his aching head. Though the king's face was turned toward the exorciser, he seemed neither to see him nor to hear his chanting.

". . . whether it be a ghost that was slain by a weapon or a ghost that died of a sin against a god or a crime against a king—a forgotten ghost, a ghost whose name is not uttered or a ghost that has no one to care for it—whether it be an evil spook or a buried ghost or an unburied ghost, or a ghost without a brother or sister, or a ghost with no one to mention its name, or a ghost whose family was nomadic, or a ghost which was left in the desert, appoint it to the keeping of the ghosts of his family!"

By the words I knew that this was the rite for driving out an unknown ghost that might have taken hold of the king. While the acolytes scattered more incense on the censer, the priest raised his arms heavenward to summon the help of the sun-god Shamash. All his helpers chimed into the chant, and even the chamberlains in the room mumbled prayers. Only Daniel stood with his brow furrowed and his lips pressed together as though he tried to keep himself from opening his mouth.

Having finished his prayer, the priest glanced at the king to see whether he was eased. But Nebuchadrezzar lay with his eyes closed and his face twisted in pain as before. Then the priest pulled from a basket such things as he needed for another spell. He lined up on the stand before him an onion, a date, a piece of wick, a wad of wool and some goat's hair. Then he addressed himself again to the ghosts:

". . . whether it be the curse of his father, or the curse of his mother, or the curse of his elder brother—"

At this the king moaned loudly and covered his face with his hands.

". . . or the curse of the murder of a man he does not know—
   By the conjuration of Ea,
   Let the curse be peeled off like this onion,
   Let it be wrenched apart like this date,
   Let it be untwined like this wick."

As the priest proceeded to peel the onion, wrench apart the date, unwind the wick, pluck the wad of wool and scatter the goat's hair, he chanted:

"Like this onion which I peel and throw in the fire, which the fire consumed entirely, whose roots will not take hold in the soil, whose shoots will not sprout, that will not be used for a meal of a god or a king, so may the oath, curse, sickness, weariness, guilt, sin, wickedness, transgression—"

During the last words Nebuchadrezzar sat up on his bed and let out one loud, agonized scream before he fell back on his pillow. While the priest halted in the gesture of tossing the peeled onion into the fire to glance at the king, Daniel suddenly spoke up loudly in Hebrew:

"Why do they not cease from tormenting the king? Can they not see that his soul is in agony?"

There was a sound in the room as if all the chamberlains had gasped at the same time. They turned to stare at the intruder who had dared interrupt the sacred rites. The priest made a motion with his head bidding the guards drive us out, but just then the king opened his eyes and muttered:

"Who is this man and what did he say?"

Being the only one in the room who understood Daniel's words, I prostrated myself before the king's bed and replied:

"This man is the Hebrew prince Daniel whose name my lord changed to Belteshazzar. He meant well in speaking aloud, not wishing to see the king suffer. Indeed this same Belteshazzar told me that he could sooner cure the king than all his exorcisers."

Addressing the king in Babylonian, I forgot that the chamberlains and priests in the room could understand my words. They converged upon Daniel and me and would have harmed us had not the king suddenly said in a clear, strong voice:

"Let Belteshazzar approach and divine my trouble. As for all the others in the chamber, let them depart!"

The courtiers and priests withdrew, muttering among themselves and casting angry glances at Daniel and me. When I saw the king frowning at me for having remained behind, I said:

"Though Belteshazzar understands the Babylonian tongue, he still speaks it poorly. If the king wishes to converse with him he will have to suffer my presence."

Then Nebuchadrezzar commanded us to draw near the sumptuous ivory bed upon which he lay propped up on his pillow. Bowing down low, Daniel gently touched the king's hand and forehead.

"It is not a fever that troubles the king, nor are his eyes clouded," he said to me. "Pray ask him if his limbs ache."

When Nebuchadrezzar shook his head at my question, Daniel said:

"Surely the sickness is not of the body but of the soul. But perhaps the king would reveal to me the cause of his torments?"

To this question Nebuchadrezzar replied:

"It is the ghost of one murdered in childhood."

Then Daniel spoke through my mouth:

"The king has seen his priest trying to exorcise this evil spirit. In this he was doomed to fail, for there are no ghosts!"

Nebuchadrezzar closed his eyes again and said with a deep sigh:

"To lay a ghost the priest must know his name that he might fashion an image of the dead one, inscribe his name upon his thigh, put a dog's tooth in his mouth, break his legs and throw him down on the ground. But though I know the name of the one who torments me I would not reveal it. Is it not enough that I murdered my elder brother? Should I also have his ghost defiled?"

When I heard these words the blood fled from my face and my teeth began to chatter so that I could barely make myself understood in speaking to Daniel:

"Surely the king is sicker than my lord thinks him! Though he has no fever he is raving and speaks of having murdered his elder brother who died in childhood. If the king had performed such a crime, would it not be known in all the land?"

Gazing at Nebuchadrezzar as though he could see into his heart, Daniel said:

"Ask the king how he murdered his brother—whether he stabbed him or strangled him or poisoned him or pushed him down a precipice so that he fell, breaking his neck?"

And when tremblingly I asked this question, Nebuchadrezzar replied:

"I did none of these things, and yet I caused his death." The king leaned back upon his pillow and closed his eyes. I thought he would say no more but he continued: "My elder brother, the first-born of my father and mother, was but a year older than I. He was a child of great beauty, with graceful movements and the heart of a lion—a son to delight his mother's eyes and an heir any king would desire. My mother loved him more than her life. My father loved him with pride, and I too loved him—let the gods be witness that I did! From earliest childhood on I tried to be like him, but being short and fat I could never equal his feats. He knew how to bend a bow and ride a horse long before others his age. He feared nothing, and women looked at him with lustful eyes even before his beard was grown. None doubted that he would be a great king when he sat on the throne after my father.

"At that time, however, my father Nabopolassar was not yet crowned king in Babylon. We still dwelled in Uruk, where he had first been acclaimed ruler. There my brother was taught all the skills needed by one who would someday rule Babylonia and lead the army in war, while I was taught to read and write that I might become a priest. This was as it should be, I being the second son. Nor did I ever fail to honor my elder brother, who was strong and handsome and the delight of my mother's eyes.

"He too loved me, even if he teased me at times, for I was short and fat, and my nose was turned up so that my mother was ashamed of me before the other women. But I always did my brother's bidding, he being the elder and the crown prince. He showed me how to wield a sword, though I was clumsy, and taught me how to swim in the river, where we went at times, slipping away from our tutors.

"It was in the spring of the year when my brother turned thirteen and his beard began to sprout that the waters of the river ran red, an omen sent by the gods to warn us of a pestilence. My mother forbade us to go near the riverbank lest we be struck down by the evil plague demons. But the sky was blue and the air pleasant, and I whispered to my brother: 'Come, let us slip away and go swimming.' But he replied: 'Have you forgotten that our mother forbade us?' Then I said: 'I can see that you, who are so brave in other things, are afraid of the river demons!' And he replied: 'The crown prince of Babylon is afraid of nothing!'

"Thus we stole away and went down to the riverbank. We took off our garments and immersed ourselves in the water that was red and muddy, as though a stream of thick blood were running through the riverbed. Nor were we refreshed by the swim but dressed swiftly again and returned home, not daring to look at each other for having broken a command.

"All though the night my heart was heavy with fear and foreboding, for it was I who had enticed my brother to come with me. When next morning he did not rise from his bed, having been seized by a fever, my despair was complete. But I did not dare reveal our trespass, and neither did he.

"His fever increased as the day wore on. Even after the exorcisers had been summoned to drive away the evil spirits he continued tossing and raving on his bed. The following day his limbs grew stiff—first his feet, then his legs and thighs, then his arms, and he was in such torment that he screamed continually. My remorse became such that I threw myself down beside his bed and confessed having lured him to the river. But he, though feverish and in pain, opened his eyes and said: 'I am the crown prince of Babylon! It was I who said we ought to go down to the river! If I allowed my younger brother to rule me, would he not wish to sit on my throne?'

"Nor would he change his testimony. But the numbness of his body spread until he could no longer breathe, and he died strangled by the evil river demons. And I, who had caused his death, became crown prince of Babylon.

"Though my father grieved bitterly over the death of his first-born, he became comforted when I labored hard to equal my dead brother in manliness. But my mother never consoled herself, nor did she believe the words of my dying brother but knew in her heart that it was I who had caused his death.

"I have tried to atone for my crime with many pious deeds. But the ghost of my dead brother often rises to remind me that I seized the throne from him. Also he stirs up the soul of my younger brother that he might deal with me as I dealt with him, and he sends me evil dreams in which I see a high tree chopped down until only a stump is left in the grass or a tall image toppling over and crashing to pieces. Nor have I been able to father more than one son, a weakling. Thus the kingdom will be cut off from my seed after me, for the gods do not favor one who murdered his brother."

When Nebuchadrezzar ceased speaking his face was wet. Gazing closely at him I saw that what glistened on his cheeks was not sweat but tears. While I gaped in wonder, the king covered his face with his hands and sobbed like a child.

Daniel stood knitting his brows and stroking his beard until the king's weeping subsided. Then he spoke:

"Let the king not add sin to sin by claiming that he killed his brother when he never committed such a deed."

"But I lured him down to the river, and only the gods know what was in my heart that day!" Nebuchadrezzar exclaimed.

"The fate of mortal men is decided by God," Daniel said. "No man—not even a king—may claim that the desires of his heart can alter God's will. If the king had done his brother violence he might indeed say he murdered him. But all he said was: 'Let us go swim in the river.' And was not my lord's brother the elder and wiser? Was he not the stronger? Was he not meant to sit on the throne of Babylon? Had not he too heard the command of my lord's mother, and did he not know the omens? Knowing all this, was it not he who should have said: 'No, let us not break our mother's command'? And did he not claim until his death that it was he who enticed my lord, knowing well what was the duty of an elder brother? Nothing happens on earth that is not willed by God. Even as my lord and his brother went to the river, God saw that the weaker was the stronger, and that he was better fit to be king. Has God not given all the nations into the hand of Nebuchadrezzar? Would He have dealt thus with a murderer?"

"Then you truly think that I am without guilt in my brother's death?" the king asked at last.

"A man cannot kill with his thoughts," Daniel replied. "Only

God can think a man dead. Therefore let my lord's soul be eased and let the memory of his dead brother depart from him!"

Nebuchadrezzar sank back on his pillow, closed his eyes, and as he lay there the deep creases in his face lost their sharpness until he appeared to be smiling. Thinking him fallen asleep, Daniel and I backed toward the door. But before we reached it, Nebuchadrezzar opened his eyes again and said:

"Let my servants prepare my bath and fetch my barber, for my head no longer aches. As for Belteshazzar—henceforth he is to be the foremost of my dream diviners, being free to come and go in my own chambers as he pleases!"

From that day on Daniel held the highest office in the kingdom. There was none other who could gain the king's ear day or night. Many of the priests and chamberlains hated him bitterly for having risen above them, while others tried to buy his good will with gifts. All wished to discover how he had gained the king's favor, but neither he nor I would reveal the secret. The king had spoken to Daniel as one speaks to a physician and such confidences are not to be spread abroad.

However, the priests and exorcisers believed that Daniel had used some powerful magic. Shortly after Nebuchadrezzar was recovered from his illness it became known that the queen, who had not conceived since the birth of the crown prince, was with child again. The king heaped Daniel with rich presents and precious garments, and sacrificed not only to his own gods but also to Yahweh, hoping that the child would be a son better fit for the kingship than his first-born. For it need not be the oldest who succeeded the king if he appointed a younger son his heir.

As Daniel rose at court I rose with him as his interpreter. I barely found time to visit my master in his house west of the river, which seemed to me even more modest now that I was accustomed to dwell in the palace. Indeed the king put it to me that he would buy me from my master, but I threw myself at his feet, saying:

"I pray my lord not to do this thing, for I am the only possession of value left my master. Should he sell me, the silver will soon end up in the hand of his new wife, who will desert him when he has nothing more to give her. But my master will be left to beg in the street since he does not know how to do any useful work."

"Your master deserves no concern, having not only defied his king but also abandoned the mother of his children for a harlot! And why do you, who are yourself but a slave, consider his welfare?"

"Because I love my master even as my lord the king loves him. Surely the king, who is much wiser than I, knows that we do not love others according to their merit. And my master would never willfully hurt anyone!"

"I have known other such men who mean to hurt none yet harm many," Nebuchadrezzar said. "However, you speak truly in saying that we do not love others according to their merit. Therefore I shall not buy you from Nabukasir but rather pay him for your services. Let none say that Nebuchadrezzar stole slaves from his subjects, breaking the law of his own land."

The king did as he had proposed. And thus it came about that I lived in the royal palace during the fateful tenth year of Nebuchadrezzar's reign.

It may be said that one's customs are the customs of those about one. Soon I acted and talked like all the other courtiers, using language understood only by those initiated into affairs of state. However, I must confess that as much time was given to court gossip as to pondering grave matters. The chamberlains spoke to me of many things, but none dared mention Daniel, and it was from Tarqu that I learned how much he was hated by the Chaldeans. These were men born in the south of Babylonia, even as Nebuchadrezzar himself. Previously they had held the highest offices at court, the king differing little from other men in that he placed the greatest trust in those who came from his own part of the country. But lately they had been supplanted by a Hebrew who had been brought captive from Judah.

Now that the king had a Hebrew dream diviner, other people of standing also wished to be counseled by one. Many Chaldeans who had long practiced this art lost their clients. In the end some began using Hebrew garb and mixing Hebrew words in their speech to gain back their following. This filled me with great mirth, though I should have known better than to laugh about a rise of ill feeling toward the Hebrew people.

But then they were not the sole objects of ill feelings. There were at Nebuchadrezzar's court men of many nations—from Assyria,

Media and Elam, from Egypt and Ethiopia, from Sidon, Tyre and Ashkelon. There were Arabs from the Great Desert, Hebrews from Judah, and even some Greeks—the same Greeks from whom my master had first learned the dangerous thoughts I had recorded for him on the papyrus scroll. Being able to speak many tongues I conversed with all these men. And though they dwelled together and could observe each other from close by, yet did I find but few among them who would not willingly believe the worst of the others. Thus the strangers in the land despised each other as much as the Chaldeans despised them.

All this hatred only added to the unrest that had seized the country since Nebuchadrezzar returned from his war against Elam. Moreover, the Captain Holofernes spoke to me of discontent among the king's older captains. Who would assure them that Nebuchadrezzar, having appointed a Hebrew to the highest office at court, would not appoint another stranger commander of the host, passing over men who had fought under his father Nabopolassar to free Babylonia from the Assyrian yoke?

In the seclusion of his room Tarqu revealed to me that even the queen mother used her gold to stir up rebellion against the king. She had always coveted the throne for her younger son Nabu-suma-lisir, hoping he would succeed Nebuchadrezzar, whose own heir was a weakling not fit to rule Babylonia. But now that the queen Amytis was with child again and might bear a strong, healthy son, the hopes of the queen mother might never find fulfillment. Thus she too fanned the embers of discontent.

The king knew well of the unrest in the land, but he had full trust in his army. And when he called up his soldiers for a campaign against Lebanon and his captains asked for a war council, Nebuchadrezzar granted their wish. From behind the grilled window of Tarqu's room, he and I observed the captains arrive at the palace. I had not seen so many soldiers in one place since I accompanied the army to Judah. When I spoke of this to Tarqu, he said:

"Neither have I ever seen so many captains enter the palace. Nor are they wont to attend a war council fully armed with their swords, shields, spears and even their bows and arrows, which must encumber them greatly during the long talks."

Now I understood that it was the clang of weapons rather than the milling crowd that had disturbed me, for the third court was often thronged by people. Indeed many of the captains did not enter the throne room but remained in the court, assembling themselves into ranks while yet more armed men streamed through the gate. I wondered why the sentries did not prevent these soldiers from crowding into the court when I saw that all the sentries had disappeared. Even as I noticed this strange occurrence so did Tarqu. Turning pale, he seized me by the arm and shouted:

"It bodes ill if the guards at the gate of the king's own court are gone! I must hasten to the Women's House and have the eunuchs barricade the entrance! These men have come to the palace with evil intent and may not respect the women's quarters. But if any should enter and force one of the women, I shall have to answer for it to the king!"

We left Tarqu's room and hastened through the corridors to the Women's House. On the way we met many chamberlains and courtiers running this way and that in great agitation. They too had perceived the multitude of armed men at the palace, yet none seemed to know what they had come for, nor would those who knew it reveal their knowledge. But each man was fleeing to his own apartment to barricade himself behind his door.

No sooner had we reached the Women's House and Tarqu had bidden the eunuchs bar the gate than a great clamor of warriors uttering the battle cry went up in the third court. Peeping out through a crack in the wooden gate I saw soldiers advancing in closed ranks toward the entrance to the king's throne room.

At the noise of shouting the queen Amytis, heavy with child, came hastening from her quarters into the harem court, and from another part of the Women's House the queen mother. The two ladies met near the gate, where they halted to glare at each other. It was plain to see that there was hatred between them, and they would have exchanged harsh words had not Tarqu approached them, bowing down low and saying:

"Let my ladies return to their apartments, for these madmen may yet break into the court!"

But the queen mother, a stately woman well gone into her years, replied haughtily:

"You need not be concerned for my safety, Ardia. No harm shall come to *me* from these men!"

And after another hateful glance at her daughter-in-law she

returned to her chambers. But the queen Amytis followed her ladies, who had surged screeching into the court to fetch her back.

"Indeed no harm will come to the queen mother," Tarqu muttered. "Is it not her own gold that helped incite this rebellion and her own favorite son who heads it? Even if these rebels fail in their wicked plot, Nebuchadrezzar will never raise his hand against his mother. But may the gods protect the queen Amytis and her unborn child if the king should be slain!"

Now the noise outside the barred gate had become even louder. The clang of sword striking upon sword mingled with the screams of men being hurt or fanning their courage with the sound of their own voices. All the eunuchs who had gathered near the gate of the Women's House fled at the sound of battle. I too trembled with fear, but being a veteran of the war against Judah I took heart and entered one of the chambers beside the gate, from where one could gaze into the third court.

There I beheld what I had not seen in four months with the army in the field—a bloody battle. All the captains who had remained in the court had conspired against Nebuchadrezzar, but those who had entered the throne room were loyal to the king. These brave men had surged outside as the others tried to force their way in. The king too had seized a sword and shield and was fighting at the head of his men. By his side was the Captain Holofernes, striking left and right with his sword while he shouted at the top of his voice. I could see his wide-open mouth, and though I could not hear his words I knew all the oaths pouring from his lips. There was none who could draw near him but that he struck him down with his sword, being taller and stronger than most. And even from where I stood I could see on his face an expression of rapture such as another man might display only in the arms of a woman.

The king too fought bravely, though he was short and fat and his movements lacked grace. Soon the court was strewn with men writhing in their blood, and the air rent with the screams of the wounded. Slowly the king and his brave soldiers pushed the aggressors out through the gate into the second court. When they barred the gate behind them, there were still a few of the rebels left inside the third court. Those were now trapped between the two barred gates, while the king's warriors converged upon them with a shout of fury to make an end of them. As they battled viciously in the midst of the court one broke away and came running toward the gate of the Women's House. When he came closer I recognized the king's younger brother, Prince Nabu-suma-lisir. He had nearly reached the barred gate when the Captain Holofernes perceived his flight and came pursuing after him. The prince furiously struck the gate with his sword. The half-rotted wood, never having been meant to withstand armed assault, splintered and the prince slipped through the breach into the court of the Women's House.

Standing behind the gate, Tarqu had not observed the battle and did not know that the Captain Holofernes was pursuing the prince. With his arms spread wide he stepped before Nabu-suma-lisir and said:

"I pray my lord not to defile the harem!"

But the prince, no doubt wishing to seek refuge in his mother's chambers, cried:

"Out of my way, you castrated black dog!"

And before Tarqu could swerve or step aside, Nabu-suma-lisir ran him through with his sword. When I saw my friend sway and fall to the ground while a stream of blood gushed from his chest and spilled over his garments, I shrieked and sank to my knees, covering my eyes to blot out what I had already seen. But even before my hands reached my face the Captain Holofernes jumped through the breach in the gate.

"Stand and fight, you cowardly bastard!" he called after the fleeing prince.

When Nabu-suma-lisir did not halt, the captain gave chase and ran his sword through the prince's back, inflicting upon him the shameful death of one taken in flight.

But I fell to the ground and wept bitterly. Though Tarqu had been avenged the very instant he died, this could never bring my dead friend back to me.

The rebels were soon driven from the palace grounds by the troops loyal to the king, but the battle in and about Babylon continued for many days. Even after the rebels laid down their arms the slaughter was not ended. As happens in times of upheaval men denounced each other, and many innocent people were slain together with the guilty. The hatred persisted long after the executions had ceased, for men can forgive strangers for rising against them in war, but they can never forgive their own countrymen.

As for me, I cared little about those who died but wept for only one. I rent my garments, scattered dirt on my head and sat on the ground with Taia and her husband in mourning for Tarqu. During those bitter days long-banished memories returned. I saw again the back of my mother as she ran from our house, heard my sister Abigail scream as she was being ravished, and remembered my father lying dead and mutilated in his blood. Like Tarqu, he too had been a peaceful man who loved his family and had never harmed anyone. Then I knew that a sword in a warrior's hand made no distinction between the good and the evil.

When Nebuchadrezzar learned that Tarqu had died defending the Women's House with his bare hands, the king ordered that he be given a royal funeral and a splendid grave furnished with many costly things that might please the living but could not profit the dead. And in honor of her dead brother the king gave Taia a house where she might dwell with her husband for the rest of their lives.

But the Captain Holofernes received no reward, for the king had commanded that Prince Nabu-suma-lisir be taken alive. Some even proclaimed that the captain's life was spared only because he was one of those who had fought at Nineveh. But others whispered that the king was glad to know his treacherous brother dead, even if his mouth spoke otherwise.

I too believed the latter, for Nebuchadrezzar did not let any of the rebels go unpunished. From Daniel I learned that even some of the Hebrew captives at Tel-Abib had been thrown in the fire. It was discovered that they had given silver to the rebels, hoping that if Nebuchadrezzar was overthrown they would be allowed to return to Judah. What they did not know was that many of the rebellious captains had counseled that Jerusalem be destroyed. Thus I learned of another human folly—that of misguided men aiding the cause of their worst enemies.

Many days passed before the streets of Babylon became safe to traverse and I could visit my master in the western part of town. I was glad to find him well and unharmed, but when I told him of the battle and of how my best friend had been slain I wept again. Nor did I find much to cheer me in my master's house.

Since I had last seen my lord, his marriage had taken a turn for the worse. He had hoped that his new wife would bear him a son to make him forget the one he had surrendered. But the lady Baltesha, having conceived by many lovers and often having taken measures to cast off the fruit of her womb, could no longer conceive. Thus she turned more shrewish every day and demanded more gifts and silver of my master, knowing that if he divorced her as a childless wife she would receive but little.

As for my master, he now pined away for the children he had abandoned. He bade me stand in the gate of his former house that I might catch a glimpse of them and report to him how I found them. I waited in concealment until the lady Margidda left on an errand. Then I knocked on the gate and bribed the nurse with silver to let me visit the children.

David, who was now ten years old, had grown much in the past year so that he was nearly tall enough to throw his arms about my neck. As I held him I wept bitterly, for it seemed to me that I was forever losing those I loved. But when I spoke to him of his father, he would not listen to me but turned his face away, saying that his father was an evil man who had made his mother shed many tears. However, when I left with a heavy heart, the maiden Hegala came running after me and whispered among sobs to tell her father that she loved him as before.

My master too wept when he heard how his children had grown and how handsome they were so that in the end I was glad to return to my duties in the royal palace.

In the tenth year of his reign—the year of the army rebellion— Nebuchadrezzar stayed in his own land. He had slain many of his captains, and it required time to rebuild the strength of his army. Thus the campaign against Lebanon was put off until the following year.

There were many changes in the land. Some governors who had been party to the revolt were thrown in the fire, while men who had proved their loyalty rose to their posts. Among them were my former pupils Shadrach, Meshach and Abed-nego. This caused further ill feelings among the Chaldeans, the princes being not only Hebrews but also young for holding such high offices. But trusting in the words of Daniel, who had vouched for their loyalty, the king had great faith in them.

Before the new governors were installed there was a period of court mourning, for the queen Amytis had given birth in her eighth month to a stillborn boy. Nebuchadrezzar grieved bitterly, confessing to Daniel that he feared the gods had required of him the life of his son for the life of his younger brother. Daniel spent long hours soothing the king and assuring him that God would not avenge one who had sought to slay the rightful ruler.

As for me, I believed what many others whispered at court: that the queen mother, crazed by grief over losing her favorite, had bribed the cook in the Women's House to put a potion into the queen's food that she might miscarry. Thus she was avenged upon the king, whom she hated bitterly though he was the fruit of her own womb.

When the period of mourning ended, all the affairs of state were resumed with great haste. The events of the past months had further increased Nebuchadrezzar's impatience and shortened his temper. His hands, which had always been steady, now shook when he carried a cup of wine to his lips, and though before he had often gone unarmed, he now did not ungird his sword even when he sat down to a meal. I recalled with wonder that it was only four years since the king had handed me his sword to enter alone and unarmed into the temple of Jerusalem.

But I had little time for meditation. Having assumed their new offices, the three Hebrew princes required my aid with some legal documents written in the Akkadian script. Thus I was kept busy day after day, with no time even to visit my master across the river. But knowing him well paid by the king for my services I felt at ease.

During this time my own wealth too was increased by those who found me helpful in gaining them the ears of the new governors. In accepting their tokens of gratitude I only followed a hallowed custom, nor was my friend the merchant displeased by the sums of silver I invested with him. Indeed I gained more wealth in the year after Shadrach, Meshach and Abed-nego were appointed governors than in all the previous years. I would have bought back my freedom then had I not feared that my silver would soon end up in the hand of the lady Baltesha. Thus I continued as Nabukasir's slave, knowing that my wages would profit him more than my silver.

It was not until the time of the New Year Festival, when all Babylon was out celebrating and only the most pressing business of state was conducted that I found time to pay my master a visit. I put on festive garb and joined the crowd that surged back and forth across the bridge that King Nabopolassar had built to connect the east bank of the Euphrates to the west bank. Lately Nebuchadrezzar had further strengthened that bridge and had added many new wharves along the east bank of the river so that the large vessels coming from the south might dock there with ease to unload their wares.

As always early in the month of Nisan the air was balmy, the sky blue and the white doves of Ishtar were circling overhead to drop their lucky omens on those who believed in them. Being seized by the holiday mood, I stopped along the way to buy some honey cakes as a gift for my master. If fate smiled upon me, the lady Baltesha would be visiting her friends at the temple of Ishtar, leaving my master and me free to discuss such things as pleased us.

But when I knocked at the door of my master's house, it was his wife who opened. Glaring angrily at me, she asked what I wanted.

"I have come to wish my lord a prosperous new year," I replied.

"Your master no longer lives here," Baltesha said.

My mouth dropped open and for some time I found no words to utter. In the end a stammered:

"But where else would he live if not in his house?"

"This is no longer his house but mine," Baltesha answered. "Nabukasir and I were divorced last month. It is only seemly that he should treat me no worse than his first wife and leave me the house to live in."

I was about to reply that the house my lord had left the lady Margidda had been her own, but I thought better of it. Rather than quarrel with Baltesha I would learn where my master had gone. But when I asked her for his new abode, she shouted:

"Go find out for yourself!" She shut the door in my face, leaving me standing in the street with the honey cakes in my hand.

But I, who stood before the king, who dealt with governors and chamberlains, who indeed had fearlessly shouted the order for surrender to those defending the walls of Jerusalem, did not dare pound on the door and demand that Baltesha answer my question. For ever since a woman caused me to lose my manhood I feared them worse than lions. Rather I returned to the palace and begged the Captain Holofernes to help me find my master. When he heard my bitter tale he drew on his great knowledge of curses before he said:

"Come let us return together to the New Town. And if that harlot refuses to reveal to me Nabukasir's dwelling place she shall yet regret the day she was born!"

As we neared the house where the lady Baltesha was now sole mistress, I proposed that the captain approach the door alone. Baltesha might speak freely to him, whereas she might not open her mouth before me out of spite. Thus I concealed myself in a cranny of the wall while the captain pounded on the door.

Again it was Baltesha who opened. Though I could not see her, I could tell by the way she greeted the captain that she was pleased by his visit. But he returned her greeting curtly and said:

"I was told that my friend Nabukasir no longer lives here."

"Then you have come to see *me*, knowing that I am a divorced woman now and wealthy," Baltesha said in the voice women use when they would have a man make them an indecent offer.

"No, I have not come to see you," the captain replied coldly. "I have come to discover where Nabukasir lives, since in his shame he did not let me know of his move."

"Ah, but we need not discuss this matter in the street," Baltesha said. "Come and rest in my house, where I shall wait on you myself, for my slave went to the market and will not return for some time. Only this morning I put fresh sheets on my bed and perfumed them with myrrh and aloes as though I knew of your coming!"

"May Ishtar strike me dead if I set foot in the house you stole from my foolish friend!" the captain exclaimed. "Nor do I have a mind to do any of the shameless things you propose. What are you but a palace that crushes the valiant, pitch that soils its bearer, a shoe that pinches the foot of its owner? Which lover did you love forever? What do you want with me? Has my mother not baked, have I not eaten that I should taste the food of stench and foulness?"

Hearing the captain's speech I clapped my hand over my mouth to keep from laughing aloud. Though I had heard my lovesick master recite poetry to the lady Baltesha, I had never expected the captain to do the same in his anger. For his words were the words Gilgamesh spoke to the goddess Ishtar when she bade him be her lover.

"And now you had better tell me where your former husband lives, harlot, or it will go badly with you!" the captain shouted.

"Go look for him yourself, you base drunkard," Baltesha replied in a fury. "Neither threaten me, for I know many powerful men at court who can protect me from scum like you!"

Their wrath having made them lapse into the speech of the south, they sounded like a soldier and a harlot quarreling in the market place at Uruk. But the captain continued:

"I piss on these powerful men of your acquaintance! Also in case you have forgotten, I know who you are and where you come from. Should I reveal that you never were a priestess but only passed yourself off as one in Babylon, the king will have you thrown in the fire. But if you prefer to remain a priestess I shall make it known that you were wont to visit taverns, in which no priestess must set foot, and you will be impaled before the wall! So you had better reveal to me this very instant where I might find Nabukasir!"

"Go then and look for him in the artisan's quarters behind the temple Esagila," Baltesha shouted, "and may you both die an untimely death and find no burial but be eaten by dogs!"

I heard the door slam and the tread of the captain as he approached my hiding place. As we made our way back to the Old Town, the Captain Holofernes walked beside me in grim silence, neither would he look at me. In the end he said:

"You had best forget what you heard. Though you may think I knew Baltesha too well, I never lay with her after she married Nabukasir, nor would I touch her now. She was the wife of the man who gave me back my life at Nineveh, and if I lay with her I would feel as though I defiled the bed of my own father. As for Nabukasir, you had better seek him out alone, for I fear he lives in such squalor that he would be ashamed to have me see his quarters. If you find him in need let me know, for that harlot may well have taken from him everything of value."

The artisans' quarters behind the temple Esagila were made up of decayed buildings, some three or four stories high, in which many people dwelled together in poverty and squalor. One found there more harlots and panders than artisans, and even among the latter but few who had succeeded in their chosen trade. There were sellers of songs whose wares none would buy, writers of poetry who could gain no hearing, artists whose wall paintings found no patrons, sculptors whom none bade cast images, singers, dancers and sundry musicians living from day to day by doing such odd tasks as came along.

In former days I had sometimes visited this part of town to drink wine in a tavern and listen to the tall tales of the artisans. They all lived for the day when they would be summoned to recite their poetry or sing and dance before the king, to adorn the palace with wall paintings or cast precious images for the many new temples Nebuchadrezzar was building. But whenever one was chosen the others would speak ill of him, saying that his work was in truth inferior to theirs and that he had gained his good fortune through the offices of a courtier's wife or a courtier with whom he had lain. The fortunate one, for his part, would soon disown them all, pretending not to know them when they met in the street.

I had never thought that someday I should find my own master living among these people. It took much asking around before I discovered the shabby house where he lived on the second floor. When my knocking brought him to the door I barely recognized him. His beard was unkempt and his garments besmirched, since he had none to look after him, Baltesha having taken from him even his kitchen slave. The blood rushed to his face when he saw me and he would have slammed the door had I not pleaded with him to let me in.

Seeing the room in which he lived I wept without shame. He did not even own a bed but slept on a mat on the floor. His only chair was a stool without backrest and arms, but there was a table with a few writing implements on it, and along the wall a shelf stacked high with clay tablets. On the table stood a jug of cheap date wine next to a bowl half filled with sesame wafers and pulse.

Since I was still holding the honey cakes I had bought as a New Year gift, I held them out to my master, saying:

"I have come to wish my lord a prosperous new year."

Only after these words had escaped my lips was I struck by their folly. But my lord graciously took my present, saying:

"It grieves me that I have nothing to give you in return, Marduk-sharusur. All I can offer you is a cup of wine while you tell me how you discovered my hiding place."

Then I recounted how I had found him with the aid of the Captain Holofernes, adding that the captain wished to assist my lord in any way he could. For I would not shame him by offering my own silver. But my master replied:

"Though my home is modest I am content here, nor do I lack for anything, having enough silver to take care of my needs."

"What silver?" I asked. "Except my lord speak of the silver the king pays for my services, which surely is not enough to support a man of my lord's standing."

"The silver Nebuchadrezzar pays me for your services I wrote over to Baltesha, for she would have me sell you and give her the proceeds. But this I would never do! No, rather than sell *you* I sold my fields!"

"My lord sold the land which King Nabopolassar bestowed upon his father to remain in the family forever!" I exclaimed, the blood fleeing from my face. "Does not my lord know that the crown lands must never be sold? Let him give me this ill-gotten silver that I may redeem the fields, and I shall provide another income for my lord's needs!"

"I no longer have the silver I received for the land," my master replied. "I gave half of it to Baltesha that she might leave me in peace."

"Then all is lost, for one might sooner wrest a treasure from the monster Humbawa than silver from the hand of the lady Baltesha," I said, placing my hand upon my head in despair. "But if I knew the name of the man who bought the fields, I might persuade him to return them until payment can be made."

"He is the same tenant who tended my fields, having come into a rich inheritance," Nabukasir replied.

"The scoundrel's inheritance was the profits he stole over the years, thus becoming an heir to my lord in his lifetime. Nor would he willingly deal with me, hating me from before. Therefore let us pray that none search the land records while my lord lives. After his death these lands will have to be returned by the thief to my lord's son without pay, for they belong to the rightful heir. And now with my lord's permission I would like to ask why he did not send word to me of these calamities before they took a turn for the worse?"

"How could I send word to you with the city in turmoil and men slaying each other in the street? Nor would I reveal how the woman for whom I abandoned my lawful wife and my children tormented me, turning all my days into darkness! Nothing I did found favor in her eyes—neither the words I spoke, nor the gifts I bought her, nor the manner in which I embraced her. Indeed she taunted me with tales of other men who had pleased her better, adding that she had a mind to seek them out again since I was not man enough for a woman of her passion."

"Why, then, did my lord give her the house and all the silver when he could prove adultery? Baltesha should have been bound and thrown in the river, as she so well deserved!"

"And how was I to prove that her taunts were true? Should I lower myself to creep after her and catch her in bed with another man? And having caught her, should I stand up before the world, accusing her and proclaiming myself the fool who was married to this woman? Besides she threatened to denounce me for having spoken words against the king. Nor could I have denied her accusations, for I made rash remarks before her, not thinking to conceal my thoughts from the one who lay in my bosom."

"Then it was indeed best for my lord to part from this evil woman, no matter what the cost. As for an income, let my lord entrust me with the rest of his silver that I may invest it wisely for him."

"This I shall gladly do," my master replied, "for I find little delight in such dealings. But now that I have neither wife nor household, I shall be free to spend all my time with my writings!"

"Indeed I see that my lord salvaged his old clay tablets," I said. "And though I do not see the jar in which we concealed the scroll of papyrus, I trust that it is well hidden in this room."

But lowering his eyes, my master muttered:

"If you would know the truth, the scroll is still in my former house."

The thought that this piece of writing—put down by me in the Syrian script and tongue—was still in the house of the lady Baltesha filled me with such terror that my knees buckled under me and I had to sit down on the stool.

"Why in the name of all the gods did my lord abandon his most dangerous writings in the hands of his worst enemy?" I asked in dismay.

"Baltesha knows nothing of that scroll," my master replied. "But when I removed from the house such things as I needed most, she did not leave my side for fear I would take what she would keep.

Since she was full of hatred toward me I did not dare remove the cover from the jar and pull out the scroll, for Baltesha would have known that it contained some forbidden writing and would have denounced me. Thus I left it there, planning to visit the house some-day when she was out and ask the kitchen slave, whom I always treated with kindness, to let me fetch something I had forgotten. However, the thought of stealing into my house fills me with such loathing that I put it off from one day to the next."

Knowing not only my master's life but also mine in the hands of the lady Baltesha, I said:

"Since my lord is so loath to do what must be done, the task of retrieving the scroll has fallen to me. Now let my lord pray while I go and see how this can be accomplished!"

By the time I left my master darkness had fallen so that I had to put off my errand until the following day. Early next morning I returned to the New Town across the river and concealed myself in the shadow of a wall near Baltesha's house. Since the New Year Festival was not yet over, I hoped she would go to see one of the many processions in the Old Town across the river. Nor was I disappointed, for she soon emerged from the house, dressed in her most gorgeous robes.

When she rounded the corner of the street I quickly approached the house and knocked at the door. The kitchen slave, a young Elamite girl, peeped out through a crack and exclaimed in surprise upon recognizing me, for she had not seen me in many months. But when I told her I had come to fetch something my master had forgotten, she would not let me in.

"You are fortunate that you were kept by the master," she said. "The mistress scolds and beats me, and if she learned that I allowed you to take something from the house, it would go badly with me."

"But the thing is of no value to her," I said, "nor does she know of its existence. I have come for a scroll of papyrus written in the Syrian script, which I brought as a gift for my master from the war against Judah. I stored it in a jar to preserve it from dampness and mice, and when my lord moved out in great haste he forgot to take it with him. If you do not believe me, you may stand beside me as I retrieve it from the jar. I shall show it to you, and also give you some silver for wine and honey cakes. As for the lady Baltesha, she need never find out that I set foot in the house."

The girl was persuaded by my words and let me enter. When I pried the lid off the jar and showed her the scroll, her heart was eased. Though she could not read she recognized the Syrian script and believed that I had told her the truth. I gave her the promised silver and left the house in great haste, pleased by having accomplished my task with such ease.

But I had not yet walked ten paces from the house when the lady Baltesha appeared around the next corner. No doubt she had forgotten something and had returned home, missing my presence in the house by a few moments. The blood fled from my face and I bowed down low to make it return to my cheeks. Baltesha halted, stared at me with deep distrust and said:

"What are you doing so near my house at this time of the morning?"

Having recovered my composure, I replied:

"Though I am a slave, there is no law that prevents me from strolling about where I please within the walls of Babylon."

"I should have made Nabukasir give you to me that I might teach you how to curb your insolent tongue!" Baltesha said, scowling at me. "And what are you hiding under your arm? Have you perchance been inside my house and stolen something for your wretched master?"

She approached me and would have snatched the scroll from under my arm had I not quickly stepped back, saying:

"Since my lady would know what brings me here so early in the morning—I was told that a Hebrew who lives in the New Town has a scroll of the sacred writing which my lord Belteshazzar, the king's own dream diviner, wishes to read. What I carry here is this same scroll, written in Hebrew letters, as my lady can see for herself!"

And I unrolled part of the scroll, knowing that Baltesha could not read.

"Now let my lady not detain me, for my lord Belteshazzar, the king's own dream diviner, greatly desires to study these writings."

I hastened away while Baltesha still stood benumbed by the name of the mighty man I had mentioned. As soon as I turned the corner I picked up my garments and began to run, heedless of the curious glances people cast at the portly eunuch acting in this unseemly fashion. I feared that Baltesha would soon recover her wits and with them her suspicion. If she entered her house and questioned the slave girl, who would surely betray me if threatened with a whipping, she might yet come after me. But if I gained the safety of the royal palace and concealed the scroll there, Baltesha could never prove her accusation. For what was the word of a harlot against the word of one who was interpreter to the king's own dream diviner and secretary to three royal governors?

Since I never heard that Baltesha made inquiries at the palace, I assumed that she had believed my words. But I was still afraid to keep the scroll in my room, for much thievery was going on in the palace and it might be discovered by chance.

Therefore, after some days had passed, I purchased another large jar in which to conceal the scroll and took it to my master. None of the wretched folk living in his house would break into his room, thinking him as poor as themselves. He had never revealed to them that the sumptuously clothed eunuch visiting him was his own slave, who brought him the interest on the silver he invested for him. Indeed Nabukasir refused to learn in what manner these gains were made, fearing it was done unlawfully. For though he spoke against the king, he would not break the king's law.

Soon my master found new occasions to pronounce bitter words against the king. In the twelfth year of his reign, after he had rebuilt his army, Nebuchadrezzar went up against Lebanon. Upon his return from the war he put up an inscription to prove before the world his just and righteous actions. Since I read the words with my own eyes, I shall repeat some of them to you:

". . . this Lebanon over which a foreign enemy was ruling and robbing it of its riches—its people were scattered, had fled to far regions. Trusting in the power of my lords Nebo and Marduk, I mustered my army for an expedition to the Lebanon. I made that country happy by eradicating its enemy everywhere. All its scattered inhabitants I led back to their settlements. What no former king had done I achieved: I cut through steep mountains, I split rocks, opened passages and constructed a straight road for the transport of cedars. I made the Arahtu float down and carry to Marduk, my king, mighty cedars, high and strong, of precious beauty and excellent dark quality, the abundant yield of the Lebanon, as if they were reed stalks carried by the river. Within Babylon I stored mulberry wood. I made the inhabitants of the Lebanon live in safety together and let nobody disturb them. In order that nobody might harm them, I erected a stela, showing me as everlasting king of the region . . ."

There were more lofty words, ending with the king's prayer:

"O Marduk, my lord, do remember my deeds favorably as good deeds, may these my good deeds be always before your mind so that my walking in Esagila and Ezida—which I love—may last to old age. May I remain always your legitimate governor, may I pull your yoke till I am sated with progeny, may my name be remembered in future days in a good sense, may my offspring rule forever over the black-headed."

But after reading these words, my master said bitterly:

"Indeed Nebuchadrezzar always achieves his aims: he drove out the enemy from the Lebanon; he made the scattered inhabitants return to their land; and he also brought back the timber he wanted for building his temples and palaces!"

Though the king continued his yearly treks to the conquered countries that the might of his army might not pass from their memory, the following years were truly great years of building in Babylon. Nebuchadrezzar erected many new temples, restored his palaces and completed the great outer wall around Babylon for which his father Nabopolassar had laid the foundations.

The soil dug from the moat around the wall was used to make bricks, which were baked in ovens as soon as a sufficient number had been made. These brick ovens were kept hot day and night that the work might be accomplished with the speed commanded by the king. For mortar the workmen used hot bitumen, starting with parapets on either side of the moat and then going up to erect the actual wall. Between every thirty courses of brick they laid rush mats, and on top of the wall they constructed along each edge a row of one-roomed buildings facing inward, with enough space between them for a four-horse chariot to turn. When the work was accomplished all were certain that no enemy could ever conquer Babylon and that it would stand for a thousand years.

But the king also remembered his debt to the gods. In Babylon alone he rebuilt twenty temples, the foremost among them Esagila, the temple of Marduk, and Ezida, the temple of Nebo. On the wall he put the inscription:

"Nebuchadrezzar, king of righteousness, humble, lowly, who has knowledge of the fear of the gods, who loves justice and righteousness, who seeks after life, who puts in the mouth of the people the fear of the mighty gods; who maintains Esagila and Ezida, true son of Nabopolassar, king of Babylon, am I . . ."

Nebuchadrezzar also widened and paved the Processional Way with large limestone flags set in bitumen, bordered on either side with slabs of red breccia veined with white. And the edge of each block was inscribed with the king's name.

The Processional Way ran between high brick walls, which the king thought to cover in time with enamelled brick. And so he proposed to do with the two arches of the Ishtar Gate. As for his throne room, whose roof he had raised so that it seemed to touch the sky, men were already at work there to sheath the walls with glazed bricks. These bricks were made to form images of lions, daisies, and high columns of scrollwork in brown, gold and light blue on a dark-blue background. Nor was there anywhere a relief of a battle scene, for Nebuchadrezzar was a ruler who loved peace.

All this splendor of Babylon was enhanced by the terraced gardens the king had built for his wife Amytis. The trees and shrubs there had now reached such a luxurious height that they were visible at a great distance from Babylon, astounding the visitor who approached the city. It was with just pride that Nebuchadrezzar had written:

"I made the city of Babylon the foremost among all the countries and every human habitation; its name I have made elevated to the most worthy of praise among the sacred cities . . ."

In the end even the work on Etemenanki was completed, with all seven stages of the great tower rebuilt. There was one sanctuary at the bottom and another sanctuary at the top. A spiral way ran around the outside of the tower by which the summit could be gained, and about halfway up there were benches to rest on for the devout pilgrims who wished to make the ascent.

Indeed this ascent—which I made more than once—was well worth the effort. Gazing down upon the city one saw the many wide, straight streets running to the gates, the two high walls encircling Babylon, the king's three palaces, and the terraced gardens of the queen rising green and luxuriant in the eastern part of town. One saw the many ships docked at the strong new wharves, the restored bridge across the Euphrates, the large expanse of the New Town on the west bank, and the movement of people, chariots, litters, donkeys and oxcarts in the teeming streets. Beholding all this, the viewer could well understand Nebuchadrezzar's proud words:

"Is not this great Babylon, which I have built for a royal dwelling-place, by the might of my power and for the glory of my majesty?"

Though most of the work I have described to you was not completed while I lived in Babylon, I saw the beginning of it. And I also witnessed how the land prospered in spite of the many wars, or—as my master would have it—because of the many wars. Nor would he cease from speaking against the king, even though Nebuchadrezzar's manner toward those about him hardened from year to year. In the end the king passed a decree that all must worship the same gods and do so where they could be seen, for a man who did not fear the gods might soon despise his ruler.

Even the Captain Holofernes was forced to visit the temples, doing so with much grumbling and many curses. However, he did not dare defy the king. Nebuchadrezzar had not forgotten that the captain had killed Prince Nabu-suma-lisir against his orders, and many younger and less distinguished officers rose in rank above him. In former times this would have troubled the captain little, but lately he was become embittered by his lack of advancement. It was now twenty years since he had fought at Nineveh—twenty years since I was carried away from the city where I was born. Indeed I had now lived the better part of my life in Babylon.

In the thirteenth year of Nebuchadrezzar—the year of the fateful edict concerning the worship of the gods—I had nearly forgotten that I was a slave. Nor was my faith as strong as it had been when the teachings of my father were still fresh in my mind. I felt barely troubled when I bowed down before the heathen images that were carried past me in the street, as did all other loyal subjects of the king.

However, some Hebrews refused to honor idols, among them the three governors to whom I acted as secretary. Nor did their defiance go unnoticed by the Chaldeans, who had never forgiven mere captives for rising to these high positions. Though Shadrach, Meshach and Abed-nego worshiped Yahweh in secret, they could not conceal it, the Chaldeans having more spies in the land than the king himself. They arranged it so that one day all three governors were present when the image of Marduk was carried by on a float. And when Shadrach, Meshach and Abed-nego refused to bow down before the god, their enemies hastened to bring charges against them before the king.

One morning as I sat working in the antechamber of Meshach, a sentinel came to fetch him that he might answer the charges. For Nebuchadrezzar would not condemn a man without giving him leave to repent. But knowing that these Hebrews had refused to eat the king's own food that they might keep faith with Yahweh, I had small hope of their recanting. Nor were my misgivings ill-founded. An hour passed, and then another and another, without bringing the return of Meshach.

My heart heavy, I was about to end my work for the day when suddenly the Captain Holofernes entered the room. He cast a furtive glance about him and asked in a whisper if I was alone. Then he said in a low voice:

"Some Chaldeans have brought certain charges against your master, which I had better not reveal to you. But let us hasten to his house that he may learn the bad news from me rather than from those who wish him ill and would search his room for proof of his guilt."

At these words my bowels turned to water. I had little doubt that the captain spoke of the hidden scroll—though how the Chaldeans had learned of its existence I could not fathom. I would have run ahead and warned my master, but the captain had gripped my arm with such force I thought he would break it in two. Holding me thus he led me from the palace, pretending all the time that we were engaged in the most pleasant conversation. As for me, I kept my mouth closed, fearing to reveal more than the captain knew.

My master exclaimed in surprise when he opened his door to our knocking. But the captain pushed me past him into the room so that I nearly fell on my face, slammed the door behind us, and leaning his back against it as though to block the way of escape, he said harshly to my master:

"Where is that accursed scroll with your treasonous writings?"

My master gasped, turned pale and spoke to me with contempt:

"I never thought that you would betray me, Marduksharusur."

Sinking down on my knees and clasping my master's skirt, I exclaimed:

"Let my lord know that I did not open my mouth!"

"Ah, then there *is* such a scroll," the captain said. "You had better destroy it, Nabukasir, before it falls into the hands of your enemies!"

But seeing that I had revealed nothing, my master said:

"Truly, I know not whereof you speak, Holofernes. There is no such scroll."

The captain's face grew dark as he said:

"This is an ill time for playing games, Nabukasir. Three men who defied the king are about to be burned in the fire. If proof is found of your guilt, you will assuredly join them!" Then, raising me up from the ground where I crouched at my master's feet, the captain seized me by the throat and spoke to me: "Your master is as stubborn as these other Hebrews who would not recant, even though the king himself beseeched them. Therefore *you* had better reveal to me the hiding place of this scroll if you wish to live!"

Since my master had not opened his mouth, my lips too remained sealed. But I could not keep my eyes from straying to the heavy jar that rested on a tripod in the corner of the room. Following my glance, the captain suddenly let go of my throat, swiftly crossed the room, picked up the sealed jar and dropped it on the floor so that it broke into many pieces. With a terrible look at my master and me, the captain retrieved the scroll and unrolled it, only to exclaim:

"It is written in Syrian!"

"Then you see for yourself that it is not what you were led to believe. Rather it is a gift Marduksharusur brought me from the war against Judah," my master said, having learned from me the ruse I had used to rescue the scroll from Baltesha's house.

"Had Marduksharusur brought you such a gift I would assuredly have heard of it," the captain said, "for he would have boasted of his thoughtfulness. As for you, slave," he added, seizing me again by the throat, "you had better tell me what is written on this scroll lest I have it read by someone at court who knows the Syrian tongue. And if it contains treason and it was you who wrote these words, your death will be a slow and painful one!"

Seeing the fear in my eyes, my master sighed and said:

"Translate the words for the captain, Marduksharusur. But let him know that it was I who conceived of them while you only acted as my scribe."

I unrolled the scroll, took a deep breath and began to read through my chattering teeth:

" '. . . the time has passed for any one man among us to have absolute power. Kingship is neither pleasant nor good, when it allows a man to do whatever he likes to do without any responsibility or control. Even the best of men raised to such a position would be bound to change for the worse—he could not possibly see things as he used to do. The foremost vice of a king is pride, because excessive wealth and power lead to the delusion that he is something more than a man. Moreover, a king is the most inconsistent of men: show him reasonable respect, and he is angry because you do not abase yourself before his majesty; abase yourself, and he hates you for a subservient scoundrel. But the worst is that he may break his own laws, force women to serve his pleasure and put men to death without trial. Contrast this with the rule of the people. . . .' "

Glancing from time to time at the captain, I saw his face turn paler and paler until he snatched the scroll out of my hand, shouting:

"Enough of this treasonous talk! Neither think me too ignorant to know the source of this mischief! I too have spoken with the Greeks whom our mad king delights in keeping at his court. I know well that these Greeks, in the perversion of their minds, conceived of a government in which they would have the people elect their own officials. If this thing ever came to pass—may such gods as are sober protect us from it!—can you not see where it would lead? At present only the judges and high officials are corrupt, which is as it has always been. But if these honorable men had to obtain their offices through election, would they not in turn have to bribe the people with silver and promises, thus turning all the land to corruption? Nor is this form of government as new as those wretched Greeks would have it. In times of yore our own land was ruled in this imbecile manner. Did not the great Gilgamesh himself have to ask approval of the assembly of elders before going to war? And when these feeble-minded old men refused him their votes, did he not turn to the council of warriors for this approval? Should we, who long abandoned this cumbersome way of governing our country, return to it because of the foolish counsel of strangers? Did not Babylonia reach her mightiest power under strong kings—in olden times under the great Hammurabi, and now under our own king, Nebuchadrezzar?

"As for these words you dictated to your wretched slave, Nabukasir, give thanks to your god that they fell into my hands. Even now some Chaldeans are on the way to arrest you, having learned of your writings from the harlot you once called your wife!"

With these words the captain ripped the scroll in half and tossed it upon the lighted brazier. My master let out a loud scream and tried to throw himself after it, for such is the love of a man for the words he has written that he would thrust his hands into the fire to save them. But seizing my master from behind the captain held him fast as the papyrus caught fire, the flame shooting up bright and red to consume the writings until only some charred, brown pieces of coarse ashes were left.

While my master wept with rage and despair, the captain said:

"Twenty years have passed since we fought at Nineveh, Nabukasir, and yet here I am again trying to keep you from hurling yourself into the flames after some written words! But even now you are not safe from the fire, for you may yet burn if the Chaldeans discover these fresh ashes. Let Marduksharusur sweep up the broken pieces of the jar—for Baltesha revealed that it was a jar where you first concealed your writings—empty the brazier, and bury the broken jar and the ashes in a secret place. But you and I shall sit down to a cup of wine and a game of dice that the Chaldeans may discover us thus when they come to question you."

While my master and the Captain Holofernes sat down by the table, I placed the last traces of my lord's treason in a covered basket, which I carried down to bury it in an empty lot. Returning from that errand, I saw in the distance three men whom I recognized by their tall hats, broad swords and sumptuous garments as the feared Chaldeans. I swiftly hid myself in the shadow of a wall, for it could only harm my master if the secretary of the three Hebrews who had incurred the king's wrath were found with him. There I remained, trembling and praying, to wait for the Chaldeans to emerge again.

While I stood thus concealed I saw some of the folk who had observed the Chaldeans enter my lord's house gather in the street. More than one raised his voice in anger and shook his fist at the house, for many hated the powerful Chaldeans. Indeed I feared that my lord had spoken to the artisans about the Greek manner of government, which was certain to find favor in the eyes of these shiftless men. As for me, I wished they would disperse rather than call down yet more suspicion on my master.

After a long time the three Chaldeans emerged, accompanied only by the Captain Holofernes. By the look on his face he was speaking to them like one who had witnessed an outrage. No doubt he was berating them for having questioned a man as honorable as my master. The captain waited until the Chaldeans turned the corner before he went back to the house. Then I ran after him to inquire if all had gone well.

"So far so good," the captain replied. "But knowing these Chaldeans, I fear we have not yet seen the end of the matter."

Nor was the captain proved wrong in his judgment. The Chaldeans had long sought to halt the advancement of the Hebrews, who in the short years of their captivity had become bankers, builders, dream diviners and even governors in the land. Now that Shadrach, Meshach and Abed-nego had been condemned to the fire, the Chaldeans thought to prevent others from rising to their positions. And since they knew that my master had once been in the favor of the king, they filled Nebuchadrezzar's ear with tales, saying that though they had found no proof against my lord they still thought him disloyal to the king. In the end, to appease them, Nebuchadrezzar commanded my master to witness the burning of the three governors that he might be warned of the fruits of disloyalty.

I was amazed to learn that the Captain Holofernes had offered himself to take this message to my lord. When I inquired into the truth of the rumor, the captain not only confirmed it but told me that I too had been ordered to witness the execution, having worked closely with the condemned men.

It was with a heavy heart that I went with the captain to fetch my master. But even before we entered my lord's chamber, the captain shouted the king's order loudly enough to be heard by all the neighbors. Then, pushing his way into the room past my ashen-faced master, he shut the door behind him and whispered:

"The words I shouted were only meant to mislead the neighbors, Nabukasir. You are not to witness the execution but rather to assist the king with your sword!" And when my master gazed at him greatly baffled, the captain added: "Nebuchadrezzar desires the death of his three Hebrew governors as little as he desires *your* death. Not only does he hold them in high esteem, but Belteshazzar, his dream diviner on whom he relies for his soothing counsel, has threatened to hurl himself into the flames with them. Therefore Nebuchadrezzar decreed that the three Hebrews should be saved by a miracle performed by their god—"

My master's face darkened with anger as he broke into the captain's speech.

"Mock me, if you must, but do not mock my God in my house!"

The captain replied:

"Fool, can you not see why the king wishes to do this thing? It was he who gave the order that all must worship the same gods. Were he to make exceptions, there would soon be rebellion in the land! The first to rise against him would be the same Chaldeans who even now wish to force his hand. But if the god of these Hebrews were to perform a miracle for them, none could accuse Nebucha-drezzar of having weakened before mere men! However, in this the king needs the aid of those whose lips will remain sealed. Surely you, who calls himself a Hebrew, would not betray the plot. As for your slave, he would not dare reveal it, nor would any believe him if he did. And now listen closely to what the king would have us do: Nebuchadrezzar ordered that one of the brick ovens outside the wall be heated exceedingly, for it is there that these Hebrews are to be burned. Three Chaldeans have been charged with binding the prisoners and escorting them into the oven to carry out the execu-tion. The only other witnesses are to be the king, you Nabukasir and I, who will guard the king that day."

"Did I not understand that Marduksharusur too was to be present?" my master asked.

"Indeed he is to be present, but not as a witness. Rather he shall appear before these three men as an angel," the captain said.

"Even if it pleases my lord to mock me," I broke in, "it is not seemly to make mirth of so grave a matter as the burning of three righteous men!"

"You had better curb your insolent tongue until I have done speaking," the captain said. "The three Chaldean executioners are men whom the king suspects of wishing to deprive him of his power—the same Chaldeans who brought charges against Shadrach, Meshach and Abed-nego. When they lead the prisoners into the brick oven, the king, Nabukasir and I shall follow after them. Once inside, we shall draw our swords, fall upon them from behind, slay them and toss them in the fire, which will consume their bodies until no trace is left of the manner in which they died. As for Shadrach, Meshach and Abed-nego—since they are not to know of the plot, the king would have them led to safety by an angel. Marduksharusur is to be that angel. He knows their tongue, and surely these men will expect an angel sent by their god to address them in Hebrew!"

Unable to contain myself any longer, I spoke up:

"My lord is jesting again. I cannot appear before the three governors as an angel, for they know me well, having seen me every day. It is also unseemly that pious and honorable men should be thus deceived!"

"Your folly exceeds even your insolence, Marduksharusur," the captain said. "Just because these men are honorable they must be deceived, for they have taken it into their minds to die for their faith, and such men will not listen to reason. As for you, you will be disguised in a manner that would deceive even your own mother. You shall wear a high turban, a beard tied around your chin, and a garment with wings attached to it, such as the priests use for their secret rites at the temple. And you are to sing one of the Hebrew songs you learned from Ardia, who knew such songs."

"I shall gladly do all I can to save these worthy men," I replied. "But let my lord not ask me to sing before them. My father, who had a great love for music, often lamented that my voice raised in song made the listener wish he had been born deaf. If I sang before these saintly men, they might yet prefer death in the flames!"

"Now it is you who make mirth," the captain said. "As for me, I know nothing of music. But I have looked death in the face more than once—as these men will tomorrow—and I know that in such a moment men are not concerned about the voice of a singer. And now let your master furbish his sword, which he has not used in many years, and let you sharpen your wits, for tomorrow three lives will depend upon the faithful performance of your tasks."

If you doubt my words you need but read the records to discover their truth. Is it not written that the three mighty men who bound Shadrach, Meshach and Abed-nego to throw them in the fire were themselves consumed by the flames? Is it not written that Nebuchadrezzar gazed into the furnace and proclaimed to all his satraps and captains that though three men were tossed in the fire he now saw four walking in it, the appearance of the fourth being like a son of the gods?

As for this fourth man, whose appearance was like a son of the gods, I hardly need describe to you the fears and tortures he suffered standing so close to the fire while singing a sacred Hebrew song in his wretched voice. He was exceedingly hot in his sumptuous garments and his false beard, which had been tied to his naked chin. Moreover, he dreaded that the wax which held together the feathers of his wings might melt, leaving him exposed as the impostor he was. Only because of the thick smoke in the furnace, and in their confusion at seeing the Chaldean executioners fall into the fire, did Shadrach, Meshach and Abed-nego not discover the deception but believed that a miracle had taken place. In their exaltation they joined me in song so that my wretched voice was drowned out by theirs.

I was relieved when Nebuchadrezzar called them forth from the furnace to display before all his mighty men that not a hair on their heads was singed. And while all still stood astounded, the king decreed that Shadrach, Meshach and Abed-nego might continue worshiping the god who could perform such miracles and that any who spoke against them should be cut in pieces and his house made a dunghill. Then Nebuchadrezzar raised them to even higher positions and commanded all his chamberlains to escort them back into town.

Only after they were departed was I allowed to divest myself of my cumbersome disguise and to come forth from the hot furnace.

The king did not betray with as much as a wink of his eye that he
knew of my deception, neither did my master nor the Captain
Holofernes. For there was still the entourage left that would escort
Nebuchadrezzar on his ride back.

When we arrived at the palace my master bade the king a cool
farewell. All the time there had been few words exchanged between
them, they having been estranged for many years. But the king bade
my lord enter the palace and share with him and the captain a cup
of wine. They were all parched, having spent much time in the
furnace not only in slaying the Chaldeans but also in wiping their
weapons clean and tossing the bloody rags in the fire that no trace
of their deed might be discovered. Since I too had aided in the plot,
the king allowed me to follow my master into the banquet hall that I
might wait on him.

Having completed his ablutions, Nebuchadrezzar sat down with
his guests at the richly carved banquet table. He dismissed all the
other slaves and charged me with serving him and his company.
When I handed the king his first cup of wine he did not drink it but
poured it out on the ground as a libation to the gods. Then the
Captain Holofernes also poured out his cup of wine. But my master
only gazed down into his lap without following their example.

Frowning at my lord, the king said:

"Your heart has not changed since I last spoke to you, Nabukasir.
Indeed I believe now that you are in truth a Hebrew, for you are as
stubborn as the three who would sooner have died in the flames than
deny their god. As for me, my own gods must have decreed that I
should continually save Hebrews from the fire, only to have them
reward me with ingratitude. But let us not unearth old quarrels on
this occasion, for it is twenty years since we did battle at Nineveh.
Do you remember how bravely we fought, how we waded across
the river in the darkness and entered Nineveh below the Water
Gate? Ah, we were young then! What dreams we had!"

"Indeed we had great dreams," my lord said softly. "We dreamed
that there would be peace in the land after we drove the Egyptians
back to their own country. Yet in the past twenty years there were
but two of peace: the year after the Egyptians defeated us at Gaza,
when the king stayed in his own country to rebuild his army; and
the year the captains rose in rebellion and shed more blood within
Babylon than they ever shed on the battlefield."

I trembled when I heard my master speak such words to the king, and the Captain Holofernes also gave him a warning glance. Though Nebuchadrezzar had saved the lives of three Hebrews that day, it was folly to strain his mercy. But having downed two cups of wine in quick succession, the king was in a mellow mood.

"In former times your words would have vexed me, Nabukasir," he said. "But now you are no more than a gadfly tormenting a bull. Though your sting hurts, I can suffer it knowing that my name will be remembered long after yours is forgotten. As for gratitude, I have learned that this is not to be expected of men. In spite of all the great things I did for my country I am not beloved by men, and as for women, they look upon me with revulsion."

"There is not a woman in the land who would not feel honored by the embrace of the king!" the Captain Holofernes exclaimed.

Nebuchadrezzar emptied yet another cup, and when he opened his mouth it was the wine that spoke through his lips:

"Indeed there is not a woman who would not be honored by the embrace of the king. But were the king to put off his royal robes and walk among them as a mere man, he would have to pay for their favors or force them to his pleasure. You, Holofernes, whose looks make the bowels of women yearn for you, do not know what it means to be regarded with loathing. There are those who tell me that were I to enforce the law that demands that adulteresses be thrown in the river, the bodies of those who lay with you would stem the flow of the Euphrates, causing a flood and drowning all Babylonia!"

"My enemies have slandered me in the ears of the king," the captain said. But he looked as pleased as any man would be with such slander.

"As for me, my only concern is the queen," Nebuchadrezzar continued drunkenly. "This may not be a seemly matter for me to discuss, even among friends. But why should my wife love me if my mother hates me and my son loathes me? Only my daughter Naq'd, whom the gods cursed with my features, has tender feelings for me. How I wish that she had been born a male! But she may yet bear a son to sit on the throne after me. I shall marry her to a strong, hale husband of fine features that he might beget upon her a worthy heir. Nor need such a husband be of royal blood if he fulfill these requirements."

The king gazed a long time at the Captain Holofernes. But just as the captain's face began to flush, Nebuchadrezzar lowered his eyes to stare glumly into his cup of wine. He had placed his hands on the table before him, where they trembled and twitched as though they had a life of their own.

"There are many who wish to see me dead," Nebuchadrezzar muttered, "and many others who would care little if I were slain. I have brought greatness and wealth to the land, and still the people have small regard for me. Those whom I love hate me. Those upon whom I bestow honors betray me. Those whom I have made powerful would force my hand. And yet all bring their troubles before me and would have me solve them! The captains would have me increase the army. The priests would have me build more temples. The governors would have me fortify the walls around their cities and place troops along the roads that their caravans might travel in safety. And if all this did not suffice, the youth Nabonidus, with whose care my father charged me, vexes me with pleas for workmen to dig up old temples when I have barely enough to build new ones! But in the end none gives me thanks. As for the three Hebrews I saved from the fire, even they praise their god for my deed, believing it was he who saved them by a miracle!"

Then my master said:

"If Nebuchadrezzar, king of Babylon, king of the world, slew three of his own men and proclaimed a lie before all his nobles to save some Hebrews—if the king's heart was moved by God to such deeds, is this not a greater miracle than if an angel had descended to save these men?"

The king gazed at my master a long time before he spoke:

"I see that I shall receive no credit. I would have been happier as a priest. My sleep would have been untroubled, for all the rites of priesthood are prescribed: what to do and what not to do; what to say and what not to say; when to pray, when to eat, when to fast, when to sacrifice, when to sleep, when to wake, and in what words to address the gods. But none furnishes the answers for a king and he must lie awake nights, troubling himself over the welfare of his land and his people, over the strength of his army and the weakness of his defenses, guarding against rebellion by those who hate him, worrying about who will sit on the throne after him. Why did my elder brother die, leaving me to bear this burden?"

And with tears in his eyes Nebuchadrezzar rose and drunkenly staggered from the table. Looking after him, my master mumbled: "Ah, how he loves to be king!"

The warm feelings that had once bound Nebuchadrezzar to my master were not rekindled, for my lord had spoken many words to the king which had better remained unsaid. Though Nebuchadrezzar's mind had been benumbed by wine he did not easily forget, his memory being one of the marvels of Babylon. But to prove before the Chaldeans that his trust in Nabukasir was restored, the king invited my lord to join him in a lion hunt. My master and the Captain Holofernes were to share one of the royal hunting chariots, whose drivers were skilled at keeping a steady rein on the horses among the roaring beasts.

Save for his delight in tormenting me, I do not know what made the Captain Holofernes propose that I be the fourth man in the chariot to hand him and my master the arrows for their bows. Hearing this, I exclaimed in horror:

"Let my lord save such honors as he would bestow upon me for those who hate me! The only lion hunt I ever witnessed was the one depicted in King Ashurbanipal's library. And the last time I saw a live lion was as a boy at Nineveh. There the king kept a tame lioness who was old and gentle, neither did she have teeth left, who allowed the children to pet her like a cat. As for me, I bear no ill will toward lions and would gladly let them live if they would do the same unto me!"

But the captain only laughed and replied:

"One who fought in the war against Judah and whose fate shall not be accomplished until the goddess Ishtar descends from on high is surely not afraid to hunt lions!"

The memory of that lion hunt still makes my blood run cold—the roaring and stench of the wounded lions, the gleeful shouts of the hunters as they raced hither and yon in their chariots, and the frightened neighing of the horses. Moreover, when our driver swung the chariot around I was thrown from it so that I fell right in the path of a charging lion. As I lay there, too terrified to scream even though death grinned at me from behind the bared fangs of the beast, I heard all the men laughing with glee in the hope of seeing me torn asunder. Nor would I have lived to tell this tale had not the

Captain Holofernes jumped from the chariot, pulled the lion's tail so that the beast turned around in a fury, caught it by the beard as it reared up to attack him and, standing face to face with the lion, run him through with his sword. But later he claimed that he had saved my life only to prevent my master from losing forty shekels, which was now my value.

When I asked my lord whether it was truly worth risking one's life for forty shekels, he replied that this was hardly the cause for the captain's brave deed.

"Never have I known a man with a greater wish to look death in the face than the Captain Holofernes," my master said. "But how save by vanquishing death can a man prove himself immortal?"

After the lion hunt the king no longer troubled himself with my master, his mind being taken up by graver matters. As for me, I was allowed to return to my former post. But since the three Hebrew governors now had many scribes, I found more time to spend with my lord.

The gains from the silver which my friend the merchant had invested for him had greatly improved my lord's position. Though he could have lived in comfort now he refused to move from the artisans' quarters.

"Why should I leave this place, where I have been happier than in my former dwellings?" my master asked. "Indeed my happiness is such that I am thinking of marrying again."

My face turned pale at the thought that one of the harlots who lived in the quarter had ensnared my lord and offered to share with him his newly gained wealth. For, though Nabukasir was a learned man who could read and write, and who would counsel the king how to govern his country, yet where it concerned women and money he had the sense of a newborn babe.

Seeing my troubled face, my master laughed aloud and said:

"You need not worry that I shall make another bad choice, Marduksharusur. This time I resolved to take a Hebrew maiden for my wife. Nor shall I marry one who has already been perverted by living in Babylon. Rather you and I shall travel to Tel-Abib, where the captives live among themselves, and you who speak Hebrew well shall aid me in choosing a bride who will make me a good wife!"

"And how does my lord propose to find such a maiden, neither he nor I knowing a soul in Tel-Abib?" I asked. "I have heard that the Hebrews do not give their daughters lightly to a stranger but would know all about him, whether he is righteous, honest and well able to provide for a wife. Even if my lord took along the needed silver, would he dare approach a strange house, knock on the door and inquire whether there was a Hebrew bride for sale?"

"You speak as one who knows nothing about Hebrew customs," my lord replied, unaware that I knew more about such customs than he. "When the time came for the only son of my forefather Abraham to be married, Abraham sent a servant back to Chaldea that he might fetch a bride for Isaac from among his own kinsmen. It was by a well where she came to draw water that this faithful servant discovered Rebeccah. If he could find a bride for his master's son in this manner, should I not be able to do the same?"

I placed my hand upon my head in despair, exclaiming:

"All this happened in times of yore, if indeed it ever happened! But times and maidens have changed, and one who may look comely drawing water from a well might yet turn out to be a nagging wife!"

But my master would not be dissuaded. He dispatched me to find a boatman who would ferry us down the Euphrates to Nippur and thence along the Chebar Canal to Tel-Abib. Had the cause of our journey been a different one, I should have rejoiced at the thought of traveling down the river. It was spring, when the heart yearns for distant places, and I had not set foot on a boat since I went to Borsippa on my fruitless search for Tarqu.

I took great care in selecting the boatman who would take us in his coracle to Tel-Abib, for there were many who would agree to a fare but afterward quarrel bitterly with their passengers. Worse yet were others who, once their passengers boarded their boats and were helpless in their hands, would talk incessantly. Such men would not only inquire into the lives of their fares but also reveal so much of their own that upon parting one knew more about them than their own wives.

Though the boatman I chose seemed a taciturn fellow, once on the river he proved as loquacious as the rest. No sooner had my lord and I settled back to enjoy the sight of the rich fields watered by the rising and dipping shadufs than the boatman opened his mouth not to close it again until we debarked. After telling us all about his wife and his concubine, about the trouble between them and their children, and about the grim fate of a poor boatman having to support the large family with which the gods had blessed him, he inquired why we were traveling to Tel-Abib. But even before my lord or I could reply—not that we would have revealed the true purpose of our journey—the boatman provided his own answer:

"No doubt you wish to visit Tel-Abib because you love music and have heard that these Hebrews are fine musicians. But you had better give up all hope of hearing them sing, for they have hung up their lyres, refusing to sing their songs in an alien land. Though why they call Tel-Abib an alien land I do not know, for they have turned it into a small Judah. They have built their houses in the Hebrew fashion, they dress in the Hebrew fashion, they wear their hair and their beards in the Hebrew fashion, and they speak Hebrew among themselves, refusing to learn our language. But why they should display such longing for their country I cannot fathom. I, who was a foot soldier in the war against Judah, know well their wretched hills! I remember many a night we huddled shivering around the fire, our garments soaked by rain and our boots caked with mud, while we listened to the howling of the spirits in the woods. Nor have I ever rid myself of the cough with which one of the demons struck me. Truly if these Hebrews had good sense they would be grateful for having been brought to our glorious country!"

These memories having brought on a fit of coughing, the boatman paused long enough for my lord to ask a question:

"You who cannot see why the Hebrews long for their own land, did you not long for *your* country when you were in Judah?"

"Ah, but I was longing for Babylonia!" the boatman exclaimed, regarding my master as if that one were bereft of his senses.

Then my master saw that it was useless to pursue the debate. Nor did I open my mouth in defense of the Hebrews, for I too remembered the cold, wet nights and dreadful climb through the hill country. Gazing at the fields on the riverbanks where the wheat and barley stood higher than a man, I wondered why anyone would wish to live in a country other than Babylonia, until I remembered the wise words Tarqu had spoken many years ago: that men would sooner live among the discomforts of their own country than as strangers in the most delightful alien land.

After a pleasant journey down the willow-lined Chebar Canal, my lord and I debarked in Tel-Abib. Then we saw that the boatman had spoken the truth, even if he had done so in too many words. Save for the missing hills Tel-Abib truly looked as if a part of Judah had been transplanted to Babylonia. The Hebrews had built houses and planted gardens, and had given their sons and daughters in marriage so that many children had been born during the eight years of their captivity. While the older people spoke Hebrew among themselves, most youngsters spoke Babylonian, having learned the language from the merchants and tradesmen who passed through Tel-Abib. Soon we were to hear that a number of youths who had come to Tel-Abib as children had run away to Babylon when they reached manhood, unwilling to live the life of their elders in this new land.

But those who had remained in Tel-Abib continued observing their customs with greater fervor than before, these customs being their only link with their homeland. Seeing this I had great doubts that any would surrender his daughter to be carried off by a stranger to Babylon. However, my lord turned a deaf ear to my doubts and bade me ask the way to the nearest well, still determined to search there for his next wife. I asked directions of a youth, who was astounded by my knowledge of Hebrew, for he could tell by our garb that my master and I were Babylonians. Indeed he trailed us to the well, curious to discover what such noble gentlemen might seek there.

Having arrived in Tel-Abib at sunset, we had come at a good hour to observe the village maidens drawing water. When they saw two strange Babylonians draw near they gaped at us with curiosity, whispering and giggling behind their hands. But when I addressed them in Hebrew to ask whether there was among them one not yet betrothed who would wish to marry my lord, they broke into shrieks of mock horror, each snatching up her water jug, placing it on her head and fleeing. One, who was young and comely, kept glancing back over her shoulder to deny with her beckoning eyes the message of her fleeing feet.

"Let us follow her," my master proposed, "and see if her father might be as easily enticed as the maiden, who, I can see even now, would make me a splendid wife!"

How my lord could see this thing I could not fathom, but then I knew him not to have much sense in these matters.

As for the maiden, she knew well how to lead on men while

seeming reluctant, as is the manner of women. Whenever she gained too much on us she would halt, making certain that we saw the house she entered. Since my master persisted in his folly, I had no choice but to knock on the door and ask to be admitted.

The man who answered my knock resembled my own father so much that I jumped back in surprise. But he was even more startled by the sight before him, turning pale as he stammered:

"If my lords be officers of the king, let them know that their servant obeys all laws, neither does he leave town without permission nor has he failed to pay his taxes!"

When I assured him that we were not officers of the king but had come to purchase a Hebrew bride for my master he regarded us with even greater fear, no doubt taking us for scoundrels or madmen. But seeing that we were Babylonians he did not dare refuse us entry into his house.

The room where he bade us sit on the rug while his wife fetched a jug of wine was poorly furnished, betraying that these people might find good use for the bridal price my lord was willing to pay. But when the maiden's father inquired who had sent us to him and I revealed that we had simply followed his daughter from the well, he shook his head, saying that this was a most unseemly manner to choose a bride. Though these people were captives and poor, they would not have their daughters treated like harlots. Indeed his words reminded me much of what my own father had said concerning my sister Abigail and the Lord Hippolytus. Neither would he be persuaded when I named the price my master was willing to pay for a bride, nor by the promise that his daughter would be treated with kindness and lack for nothing, be spared all hard work and even given her own kitchen slave.

Then I turned to my master, saying:

"This is a poor but proud man who will not be bought by silver but would rather marry off his daughter in the traditional manner. Therefore if my lord's heart is set on this maiden—though he had but a brief glimpse of her—let us return to Babylon, where I might persuade one of the Hebrew governors to vouch for my lord's good name, and to put it in writing for him. Surely such a document would be of greater value to this Hebrew father than all the silver offered him by my lord!"

Not wishing to coerce the man by fear, my master agreed to my

proposal. Now that he had discovered the great new love of his life
he was inclined to be patient and court her in the accustomed
fashion. The maiden's father was glad to see us leave, but my master
was much elated, saying to me:

"Did I not tell you that I would discover a fine bride by the well?
However, since the wedding is not to be today, let us stroll about
Tel-Abib and see what there is to see!"

Darkness had not yet fallen, and there was still a crowd abroad in
the streets, all seemingly headed for the market place in the center
of town, from where could be heard laughter and shouting. When
we arrived there we found men and women jostling each other, and
only because we were recognized as Babylonians did the people
open a path for us. Advancing toward the source of the laughter, we
came upon a clearing in the throng, where a man had fallen down
on the ground in an ecstasy. My hand flew to my mouth in amazement as I exclaimed:

"But this is Ezekiel, the son of Buzi!"

For I recognized him by his bright red hair and beard.

"You know this man?" my master asked in surprise.

"Indeed I do. This is the same Ezekiel who recited before
Nebuchadrezzar all the measurements of the temple and the palace
in Jerusalem, astounding the king with his great knowledge."

Though I had spoken in Babylonian, a young Hebrew who stood
beside us understood my words, for he addressed me, saying:

"And does my lord not think it utter folly that Ezekiel, who even
knows how to draw plans and could become a wealthy builder in
Babylon, should wish to be a prophet? Instead of living in luxury he
lives in the lowliest hut, and though his comely wife—whom you
may observe weeping beside him on the ground—tries to provide
for him with their small means, he will not eat her cooking but has
taken to eating all manner of things too loathsome to describe. Also
he falls into faints and has visions of fearful beasts, and he predicts
that Jerusalem shall be utterly destroyed. Yet in spite of this
prophecy he wishes to return there! Small wonder that men laugh
about him and his visions! But then my people has always been beset
by these madmen who call themselves prophets, a plague unknown
among the Babylonians."

While the young man ranted on, Ezekiel moaned and writhed on
the ground, his white-skinned, bony arms threshing about him. But

his young wife knelt weeping by his side, cradling his head in her arms.

"When it comes to seeing one of their fellows suffer, these Hebrews are no less unfeeling than the Babylonians," my master said to me. "Come, let us draw near and help raise the prophet to his feet, for one who sees visions should not be mocked."

A gasp of astonishment went up when the people beheld the two Babylonian visitors approach the supine man. Seeing by his glazed eyes that Ezekiel could not hear my words, I bent down and spoke to his wife in Hebrew:

"Let me and my lord help you take your husband home, mistress. It is not seemly that he lie in the dust, the laughingstock of the whole village."

Raising her tear-stained face, which was in truth very comely, the woman looked up at me and asked:

"Why would two strangers show me this kindness?"

"I am no stranger to your husband, having known him since Jerusalem was taken," I said. "Indeed his learning greatly pleased the king, who would have kept him at his court had not Ezekiel preferred to remain with his people—a love for which they reward him ill indeed!"

"No prophet is honored by his own people," the woman replied. "However, if my lords would help me with my husband, Yahweh will bless them for their good deed."

My master and I placed our hands under Ezekiel's arms and raised him from the ground, half carrying and half dragging him to the hut which his wife pointed out to us. There we put him down on a worn mat, where he rolled over on his left side and remained rigid, staring at us with unseeing eyes.

"I saw him so once before," I said to his wife. "Has he been in this state for long?"

"Ever since he learned the bad news from Jerusalem," the woman replied.

"What bad news?" I asked, my blood running cold.

"I need not keep it a secret," the woman said. "No doubt the Chaldean spies know more about this matter than we in Tel-Abib. There are rumors that King Zedekiah is plotting rebellion against the king of Babylon!"

I glanced at my master to see whether he understood the words, for the woman spoke to me in Hebrew. By the pale color of his cheeks I could tell that he understood her only too well.

"If this be true," he said, "Ezekiel's prophecy will surely be fulfilled. Nebuchadrezzar will never suffer one whom he made king to rise up against him!"

At that Ezekiel's unseeing eyes began to perceive us. When he spoke I knew that he had heard what was said even though he had appeared deaf and mute.

"It is not the king of Babylon but the Lord of hosts who shall destroy Zedekiah," Ezekiel said. "Did I not witness with my own ears how Zedekiah swore by Yahweh that he would remain loyal to Nebuchadrezzar? What man may hope to go unpunished breaking such an oath? But why should the fate of the Hebrew king trouble the two Babylonian noblemen who showed me such kindness?"

"We are troubled because my master, having had a Hebrew grandfather, proudly calls himself a Hebrew," I replied, without revealing that I, who had a Hebrew father, kept this a secret. "As for me, though my lord may have forgotten my name he may remember that it was I who translated his words to the king of Babylon in Jerusalem."

"Indeed I remember not only that event but also the many wise words of caution my lord called up to those defending the walls of Jerusalem," Ezekiel said. "Perchance my lord has come to Tel-Abib on a similar mission, trying to warn the captives against becoming a party to Zedekiah's plot?"

When I revealed the true cause of our visit and told how my master's suit was turned down by the father of his chosen bride, Ezekiel said:

"I would gladly aid your master in obtaining the maiden of his choice. But I am not regarded highly among my people, and the word of a Hebrew governor will carry more weight. Indeed I myself need the help of a man of influence, for I greatly desire to return to Jerusalem. A man born in the lovely hills of Judah can never be happy in this wretched, flat land where the eye must roam endlessly in search of a resting place like the soul of one unburied. However, it is not to escape the fate of the other exiles that I wish to return. Rather I hope that I might dissuade those would-be rebels from secession. Now that the youthful vigor is gone from Jeremiah, he needs one to help him with this task!"

"Let me speak to Daniel, whom the king calls Belteshazzar, and see whether he might not gain my lord permission to return," I said.

Ezekiel received my offer with many words of gratitude, and bade us spend the night and share with him and his wife what little they had. But seeing that these were poor people, my master would not take bread out of their mouths, nor would he insult them by offering payment. Thus we took our leave and sought shelter for the night in an inn, where we were served the best Hebrew meal I had tasted since I left my mother's house. But the memory of what I had learned from Ezekiel turned the food to ashes in my mouth. If his words were true, it would not be long before the Babylonian army again marched on Judah.

No sooner were we returned to Babylon than I approached Daniel with Ezekiel's suit.

"Not only would my lord help fulfill Ezekiel's deepest wish," I said, "he would also render a service to Nebuchadrezzar if one whose words might quell the brewing rebellion were sent to Jerusalem."

"If news of this insurrection is already known in Tel-Abib," Daniel replied, greatly perturbed, "the rumor will soon spread all over the land. The fear that their sons must again go to war against Judah will harden the hearts of the Babylonians against my people. As for the Chaldeans, it will afford them yet another occasion to call any they hate a Hebrew and do away with him. I have no fear for myself, being in the king's favor. Nor do I fear for the Hebrews in Tel-Abib but for those who have come to live in Babylon, and for the Babylonians who befriended them and those who took Hebrew wives."

Hearing this, I did not mention that my lord wished to engage Daniel's good offices in helping him to obtain a Hebrew bride. Rather I hastened home, hoping that I might yet dissuade my lord from his latest folly. But I found my master in the company of the Captain Holofernes, nor was he inclined to discuss his marriage plans. He had learned from the captain, who had chanced upon the lady Margidda in the street, that the maiden Hegala was betrothed to a youth from a Babylonian family of distinction. But my master showed little regard for the high repute of this family, saying:

"I too have heard of this shiftless young man who is to be the husband of my only daughter! He has never engaged in a single day of honest occupation but only wastes his father's fortune. Moreover, he is known to spend every night in another tavern, from where he will soon bring home a concubine to embitter the days of my poor child!"

Listening to these words, I marveled at how great would seem to a man his own faults when found in the bridegroom of his daughter.

"However, I cannot break up this betrothal," my master continued, "for my children no longer call me father."

Let me explain my master's words to you. When the lady Margidda was first divorced from her husband she grieved for him, as is the manner of women who truly cherish a man. But after some time she became comforted and begged her father to find her another spouse. Her father chose for her a Babylonian nobleman of high rank, who was a desirable match though no longer young. This man, twice widowed yet childless, gladly adopted the lady Margidda's children as his own. At that time the boy David was fourteen years old, tall, handsome and looking so much like his father that tears came to my eyes whenever I saw him. For I would still call at the house to speak with the children and bring news of them to their father. But when I visited them after their mother was married again, and called the boy by the name he had borne all his life, he pouted and said:

"My name is no longer David the son of Nabukasir, but Ziria the son of Shumkenum."

"Would you deny the name of your own father?" I asked, appalled.

"The man of whom you speak is not my father but one who calls himself a Hebrew and who is known to have plotted treason against the king. As for me, my father is the lord Shumkenum, as loyal a Babylonian as myself!"

I never found it in my heart to repeat these bitter words to my master. If he discovered that his own son had cast off his name, he did not learn it from me. But he also knew that his daughter had never ceased loving him, and it pained him all the more to have no voice in the choosing of her bridegroom.

"I should give Hegala a rich dowry that she might leave the scoundrel whenever her heart desires," my master said. "But I am not a wealthy man, nor would her mother allow her to accept

anything from me. However, you, Marduksharusur, shall take some
of my silver to the house of my former wife, pretending that it is a
wedding present from you. None will take such a gift amiss, you
having known the maiden since she was born. Besides it is no secret
that you own more silver than is needed by one who will never have
sons. As for me, I shall stand across the street from the bridegroom's
house on the wedding day to catch a glimpse of my daughter when
she is brought there, and to curse the day I abandoned my lawful
wife and my children! But God willing, I shall yet have children by
my future wife!"

And when, upon the captain's inquiry, my master revealed to him
his own wedding plans, the Captain Holofernes smote his thigh in
anger, exclaiming:

"Are you mad, my friend, to pick a Hebrew bride at this time?
Have you not heard that there is rebellion stirring in Judah? Soon
there will be another campaign against that wretched country,
whose king continually plots with the Egyptians, who will not cease
from inciting our vassals until we have slain every last one of them!
As for this Hebrew maiden you wish to wed, you would do her an
even worse service than yourself. If there is war with Judah, the
Hebrews in Tel-Abib will be little troubled, but woe to those in
Babylon! The Babylonian ladies turn into lionesses whenever their
husbands and sons are torn from their bosoms, claiming that from
every war their men bring back strange wives and new diseases.
They will surely scratch out the eyes of any Hebrew woman they
catch in the street!"

Hearing these words, I told my master that Daniel had voiced to
me similar fears.

"Is a man to choose his bride by the wars of the king?" my lord
asked wrathfully. "At any rate I shall not marry until after my
daughter's wedding, when my need to console myself will be even
greater!"

Though Ezekiel was given leave to return to Jerusalem, his word
did not prevail with the king of Judah. Not long after the wedding
of the maiden Hegala—which we observed standing across the
street from the bridegroom's house, my master weeping bitterly
when his lovely daughter was brought there by her mother and her
adoptive father—Nebuchadrezzar mustered his army for another
war.

King Zedekiah, stirred up by Pharaoh Hophra, had risen in revolt against the king of Babylon and had refused to pay his yearly tribute. No sooner was it known that there would be war against Judah than the Chaldeans began to keep a strict watch on any who had commerce with the Hebrews in Tel-Abib, fearing that through the captives the king of Judah might learn the strength and strategy of the Babylonian army. Even my master had more sense than to pursue his suit for a Hebrew bride while suspicion and hatred ran high in the land. Preceding every war the king's men went about arousing the people that they might more willingly surrender their sons. And though many wealthy men bought exemptions for their sons, others thought it a matter of pride to serve their country in war.

The one war in which my master least wished his son to serve was a war against the land of his forefathers. But knowing David too young to bear arms, my lord lost little sleep worrying. One can barely picture his despair when the Captain Holofernes came to the house while the army was being mustered to tell my lord that his son had enlisted of his own will.

"But David is only seventeen years old!" my master exlaimed.

"I was no more than sixteen when I joined the army," the captain replied. "And only twenty when I fought at Nineveh."

"You always wanted to be a soldier," my lord said. "Moreover, you had great strength of body even when you were still a youth. But David was taught to read and write, not to wield a sword. Nor can I fathom how his mother could permit such a thing!"

The captain's face turned somber as he replied:

"Your son cast off your name, wishing to be a true Babylonian. Neither has he forgotten that you, whom Nebuchadrezzar carried out of the flames on his own back, refused to serve the king. Ziria only wishes to prove his bravery that none might accuse him of weakness because of his Hebrew blood. Neither should his father, who fought bravely in many campaigns, begrudge his son the same honor."

"I never taught David to look to war for honor," my master said. "Nor did I tell him of the battles in which I fought. It was you, Holofernes, who filled his mind with tall tales and gave him his first wooden sword, which I broke over my knee in wrath. I charge you, as a captain in the king's army, to have my son released from service for which he is still too young!"

"This I would not do even if I were commander of the host," the captain replied. "No male, however young, must be denied his test of manhood."

"There are more ways than one to prove oneself a man," my master said. "And as for being commander of the host, Nebuchadrezzar might yet appoint you to that position."

"In this you are mistaken," the captain said grimly. "I learned this morning that Nabuzaradan and Neriglissar, who fought under me as captains of hundreds in the first war against Judah, are to command the troops."

"Then you see that men are not rewarded according to their merit by Nebuchadrezzar," my master said. "Nabuzaradan is the king's kinsman, and as for Neriglissar, he is the husband of the Princess Naq'd."

Biting his lips, the captain blurted out:

"Had I wished to advance in this manner, I too could have married the princess! Do you remember the night after we saved the three Hebrews from the fire, when we sat drinking with the king and he described the husband he sought for his daughter? Know then that later the king spoke to me of that great honor. But I replied: 'Who am I to be the husband of the king's only daughter? I am of peasant stock, and were I to beget a son to take the place of the crown prince, the Chaldeans might wish to prevent one who was not of royal blood from succeeding Nebuchadrezzar. Therefore let the king find for his daughter a husband more deserving of a royal princess!' "

My master shook his head and said:

"To despise the hand of a princess exceeds in folly everything I ever did in my life! Small wonder the king did not appoint you to higher rank. Though the Princess Naq'd is ugly, mating with her might not have been too high a price to pay for the throne of Babylon."

"Like many a man who made a fool of himself over a comely woman you have wise counsel for others," the captain replied in wrath. "But all women look alike in the dark, and I am man enough to please even the ugliest. I did not refuse the princess because she bears Nebuchadrezzar's features but because she is heir to his mind and will. Through me she would wish to command the army and rule the country, and I am not one to serve a woman. If ever I should wish to sit on the throne of Babylon, I shall not ascend it through a bed. But rather than my lack of good sense we were discussing your son, Nabukasir, whose enlistment I shall in no way hinder!"

"Since I cannot compel your aid I shall remind you of a debt," my master said. "I never spoke to you of having saved your life at Nineveh. But since you will not release my son from the army, I now charge you with guarding his life. Though he cast off my name, my blood flows in his veins and through him my seed shall continue on earth. I ask you before Marduksharusur as a witness that you bring my son back to me, paying me with his life for yours. Should he fall in the land of his ancestors I shall no longer call you, who put this madness in his heart, my friend!"

"This is a grave thing with which you charge me," the captain replied. "But Ziria's youth shall render him safe from the most dangerous missions, which are entrusted only to those who fought in previous wars. I shall ask that he be assigned to my company, where I and Marduksharusur can watch over him."

"Did my lord mention my name?" I stammered, my bowels turning to water. For knowing the captain I knew that his words could mean but one thing.

"Indeed I did," the captain replied. "Are you not a veteran of the first war against Judah? Did you not fearlessly shout the order for surrender to the defenders on the walls of Jerusalem? How could Nebuchadrezzar venture on another campaign against Judah without his favorite and most beloved interpreter?"

"My lord delights in mocking me," I said in despair. "But let my lord remember that I am not as young as I was nine years ago, when my lord first wished this wretched task on me. Now there are many in Babylon who speak Hebrew and who, being younger than I, could be of greater service to the king."

"Why should the king entrust his secret business to a Hebrew interpreter rather than to his loyal subject Marduksharusur?" the captain asked. "Did you not once tell me that strange things might happen in the heart of a man when he set foot in the land of his ancestors? Therefore cease your struggle, neither trouble yourself with inventing more excuses, for the king himself commanded that you come along on the campaign. Also consider young Ziria, who will draw much comfort from your presence. As for your fear of battle, remember that your fate and mine shall not be accomplished until the goddess Ishtar descends from on high!"

And so I proceeded once again to set my house in order. My wealth had now become considerable. There were many contracts to be written over to my master, he being likely to outlive his own son, who had recklessly joined the army. The merchant who invested my silver was more than astonished to learn that I too was going to war. But when he chided me for my folly, as would any sensible man, I replied:

"My lord forgets that I am a slave who must obey orders."

Then the merchant stroked his beard, shook his head and said:

"Knowing well the extent of your wealth, I often wondered why you did not purchase your freedom long ago. You might have moved to another town and lived out your life as a respected freeman."

"Indeed one might marvel at my folly," I replied. "But it is known that wisdom rarely increases with wealth."

Nor would I confess that I had other reasons for not buying my liberty. I had none in the world but my master, with whom I had now lived longer than with my own parents. Indeed I owned him as much as he owned me, he being unable to rid himself of me unless he sold me. And this he had refused to do more than once. Should I not cling to the one person who cared whether I lived or died even if it was in slavery?

Thus I turned my accounts over to my master, who cursed the king for his wars and the Captain Holofernes for his foolish bravery, in which he had ensnared both me and David. Embracing me before I loaded my gear on a donkey to join the troops, my lord begged me to see that his son lacked for nothing on the campaign, and to render harmless by wise counsel whatever folly the Captain Holofernes might put in his mind.

And so, at the age of thirty-four, in the month of Heshvan, in the sixteenth year of Nebuchadrezzar, I bade farewell to my lord Nabukasir and to the great city of Babylon to become once more an unwilling soldier in the king's army.

TEN

Thou shalt make a way, that the sword may come to Rabbah of the children of Ammon, and to Judah in Jerusalem the fortified. For the king of Babylon standeth at the parting of the way, at the head of the two ways, to use divination; he shaketh the arrows to and fro, he inquireth of the teraphim, he looketh in the liver.

EZEKIEL 21:25,26

THOUGH I had thought that I would never again see Damascus, once the troops were encamped there I felt as if I had been to that lovely city but the day before. Now, at the end of the month of Heshvan, when the fierce summer heat was already abated, Damascus lay like a sparkling green jewel in the yellow sands of the Great Desert, the city being watered by the rivers Amanah and Pharpar.

The Babylonian soldiers cast off their armor and garments to frolic in the rivers, among them my master's son, the boy whom I shall continue to call David though he had changed his name to Ziria. His stepfather had furnished him with a costly coat of mail and a fine sword, and thus he strode about like a boy playing at war. The older men would have won his silver in deceitful games of dice or robbed him while he lay drunk of the wine he could not yet hold had not the Captain Holofernes proclaimed that he would hack to pieces any who harmed the boy.

Soon it was known that David was the son of the man who saved the captain's life at Nineveh, and though the soldiers grumbled because of his many privileges, they let him alone. But he, trying to impress the veterans of previous wars, spoke boastfully of the feats he would accomplish—feats to outdo those of his own father—until they turned from him in disgust. For they were men who knew that battle is not what a boy who had never heard the clang of weapons thought it to be.

Perhaps the older men would have given David a sound thrashing in spite of the captain's threats had the Captain Holofernes not been greatly beloved by his soldiers. Many believed that his life was charmed and that no ill fortune could befall them while he fought at their head, for he had never yet been wounded. When he stripped to bathe in the river with his soldiers, I could see that his only scar had remained the one on his wrist, where he had cut off the star-shaped birthmark.

But though the captain's splendid body had not changed and was as firm and lean as nine years ago, he had aged in other ways. His temples and beard were streaked with gray, and the hair on his chest speckled black and white like the fleece of a sheep of mixed color. Nor did he throw back his head in laughter as often as in former times. Though he rarely spoke of his lack of advancement or else made light of it, saying he was happy as a soldier no matter what his rank, in his heart he felt bitter over not having been named commander of the host.

As for Neriglissar, the former captain of hundreds who was now the king's son-in-law, he strutted about giving orders to the Captain Holofernes, who had already been a soldier when Neriglissar was soiling his swaddling clothes. But Nabuzaradan, who shared in the command of the troops, befriended the Captain Holofernes as before, not having forgotten that they stood guard together in Jerusalem and that it was they who had counted the golden vessels taken from the temple.

But when it came to the war council, the Captain Holofernes held equal rank with all the other captains who sat with the king. I too was present at that council, being one of the scribes charged with keeping the records. There I learned that Nebuchadrezzar was weighing in his mind whether to proceed straight to Jerusalem or to go against Rabbath-Ammon first, for there were rumors that the king of Ammon might make a league with Zedekiah. And Nebuchadrezzar consulted his soothsayers and dream diviners, searching for omens while he waited for his spies to return from Ammon. When the spies brought back the report that Baalis, the king of Ammon, did not wish to engage in war, Nebuchadrezzar resolved to proceed straight to Jerusalem that he might bring back the troops to Babylon before the New Year. But the Captain Holofernes asked to be heard and said:

"Let the king and the brave captains listen to my counsel. We all know that even as we have spies in their camp, the Egyptians have spies in our camp. Therefore let us employ a ruse to confound them.

Let us send messengers to the king of Ammon and ask him to permit our armies to pass peaceably through his land, while we pretend that we are marching on Ammon to make war. This will mislead the Egyptians and Hebrews into thinking that they have many days yet in which to prepare for an attack. While the Hebrews still believe themselves safe, we shall proceed from Rabbath-Ammon down to Jericho, from there ascending to Jerusalem to take the city by surprise. Moreover, we must send troops by way of Hebron to Lachish to cut off the advancing Egyptian army. Without Egyptian aid Jerusalem cannot hold out for long—did they not surrender the last time after three months?—and our troops will indeed be back in Babylon for the New Year."

Then the Captain Holofernes sat down to let the other captains have their say. Some praised his plan, while others pronounced it a folly, among them the commander of the host, Neriglissar.

"How long would it take the Egyptian spies to discover our true plans?" he asked. "As for the Ammonites, they are not worthy of trust and might yet betray us to the Egyptians, letting our armies pass through but falling on our backs once we descend toward Jericho. Indeed this mad plan would please the Egyptians so much that one might think this counsel coming from the mouth of the enemy."

Turning pale, the Captain Holofernes jumped up with his hand on his sword. There might have ensued bloodshed had not the king called the captains to restraint. Then Nebuchadrezzar spoke:

"It is true that one cannot hide the destination of an army as large as ours from the enemy. Nor need we use deception, being powerful enough to seal off Jerusalem from all sides. As for the Egyptians, let us see first if they will come forth to engage us in battle, for they are known to arrive late or not at all, as they did at Nineveh."

But still smarting from the derision Neriglissar had heaped on him, the Captain Holofernes rose again and pleaded with the king to let him lead half the army south by way of Ammon, or even ten thousand men, or—when Nebuchadrezzar refused him that number—five thousand. And when Neriglissar said that five thousand soldiers were too small a force to take Lachish and too large a force to waste on a folly, the Captain Holofernes exclaimed:

"Then let the king give me a thousand men and see what I shall accomplish with them!"

At that the captains began to shout loudly, all speaking at the same time. The king angrily dismissed them from his tent, but he bade the two commanders of the host, the Captain Holofernes and two scribes remain behind, for he would keep a record of all that was said. I hardly need confess that I was one of the scribes, for how else would I know what was discussed? When the captains were departed, Nebuchadrezzar turned to the Captain Holofernes and asked why he would do this brave and dangerous thing. And the captain replied:

"Nine years ago the ruling king of Judah was killed and a boy of eighteen put on the throne that he might surrender without losing face. But today matters are different. Pharaoh Hophra wishes to gain back the power that once was Egypt's, and this time the Egyptians will assuredly come to the aid of the Hebrews. Therefore let us stop them with boldness! The captains may scoff at my plan—but has the king forgotten how the captains scoffed at his plan of entering Nineveh below the Water Gate? Did my lord not plead with his father to let him try this ruse with a few brave warriors? And did it not gain my lord Nineveh and an everlasting name? Then why would the king not grant me my request and give me these thousand brave men? Even if we cannot take Lachish, we shall lie in wait along the road in the mountains and fall onto the flank and back of the Egyptians, throwing their ranks into confusion. Indeed they will believe our numbers much greater than they are!"

And the captain proceeded to reveal how this deception was to be accomplished.

"Let us muster out soldiers as if we were dividing the army to take half the troops against Ammon. No doubt Pharaoh Hophra will soon learn of this strategy. But while his spies in our camp wait for the departure of the troops, my own men—whom I shall select during these preparations without much notice—will steal out of the camp at night and start on their way. Seeing the rest of the troops remain encamped, the spies will send messages to Egypt of our changed plans. These conflicting reports will greatly confuse the Egyptians. When we swoop down on them from the mountains and fall onto their flank, they will remember the first message and believe half the Babylonian army descended on them. This might soon turn them to flight, for the Egyptians care little about fighting a powerful foe and are better at making promises than in doing battle. Thus they will be prevented from going up to Jerusalem and breaking the siege of our army."

During the captain's speech Nebuchadrezzar rose from his throne in the tent and paced back and forth, for he could bear sitting still even less than in former times. He was quite stout now and nearly bald, and he panted as he moved about. His face was bloated and red, and it was rumored that he drank much when he could not fall asleep, for he was unable to find relief in the arms of a woman. His eyes were bloodshot from lack of sleep and from reading the many reports of his vast kingdom, and the trembling of his once steady sword hand had increased since the time his own captains had risen up against him.

"You know well that you and all your soldiers might be killed in this venture," Nebuchadrezzar said when the captain had finished. But in spite of these words of caution his eyes betrayed envy. "If only I were younger I would join you in this folly, for I never remained behind the first of my troops. But my youth is gone from me and I no longer consider death lightly. Nor should you despise life, Holofernes."

Looking the king straight in the eyes, the captain said softly:

> " 'Who, my friend, can scale heaven?
> Only the gods live forever under the sun.
> As for mankind, numbered are their days;
> Whatever they achieve is but the wind!
> Even here thou art afraid of death.
> What of thy heroic might?
> Let me then go before thee,
> Let thy mouth call to me, "Advance, fear not!"
> Should I fall, I shall have made me a name—' "

While the captain spoke these famous words which I knew so well, Neriglissar's face turned darker and darker until he burst out in a fury:

"Will the king suffer such insolence proclaimed to his face?"

Nebuchadrezzar sighed and said:

"Neriglissar is a brave warrior and a good husband to my daughter Naq'd, having already begotten a fine, strong son upon her. But it would harm him little if at times he turned his mind to our old poetry. Then he would know that the words the Captain Holofernes recited were the same Gilgamesh spoke to his friend Enkidu when he proposed that they do battle with the monster

Humbawa. And now I would have you all withdraw and leave me alone with the captain that we might discuss matters which are understood only by old comrades-in-arms!"

We all bowed and retired, leaving the king alone with the Captain Holofernes. But when we stepped outside the tent Neriglissar muttered bitterly:

"Nebuchadrezzar will always cherish those who fought with him at Nineveh, even if they should plot to stab him in the back."

Then the Captain Nabuzaradan spoke up and said:

"I served under Holofernes in the last war against Judah and know him to be loyal to the king. Nor do I see why you would want to throw suspicion on him, Neriglissar!"

"Should I not suspect a man who lusts so deeply after glory that he would gamble on it his life and the lives of a thousand soldiers? Would not one who plans to rout the Egyptian army with such a small force think he might seize the throne of Babylon in the same manner? Neither tell me that such a thing was never done, for more than one captain of the army reached for the royal crown! Was not the king's own father, Nabopolassar, a captain before he became king?"

"I doubt that Holofernes has set his sights on the throne," Nabuzaradan replied. "Nor do I believe that the king will grant him a thousand men that they might all be killed, for Nebuchadrezzar greatly values his veterans."

"In this too you are mistaken," Neriglissar said. "The king knows well that an ambitious man at the head of a thousand loyal soldiers might serve him better dead on the soil of Judah than alive in Babylon."

And when a short while later the Captain Holofernes emerged from the tent to disclose with shining eyes that the king had granted his request, Neriglissar said with a sly smile:

"Truly there is no end to Nebuchadrezzar's wisdom!"

The Captain Holofernes had requested my services as a scribe. While I sat preparing the clay tablets on which I would record the names of the thousand recruits, the captain spoke to me of what was said between him and Nebuchadrezzar. For he did not differ from other men in that he wished to boast of the king's confidence.

"Nebuchadrezzar is become a bitter man, having suffered grievous disappointments with the males of his family," the captain said.

"Though the crown prince Amel-Marduk is old enough to draw a sword, he will not go to war but hides behind the queen's skirts as in former times. Even this youth Nabonidus, who would sooner dig up old temples than get drunk or lie with a woman, has put aside his pastimes to serve his country. But Amel-Marduk said to the king: 'Why should I learn to wield a sword if my lord has already conquered all the nations? There is nought left for me to accomplish, and I shall be known forever as the son of the great King Nebuchadrezzar.' Then the king said to me: 'How can I go into battle and risk my life if I have none to sit on the throne after me? My worthless son spends more time in the house of my prisoner Jehoiachin, the former king of Judah, than in the house of his own father. If he but went there because of the princesses I should not be displeased, for the royal house of Judah is of ancient lineage worthy to be grafted on the house of Babylon. However, my son does not covet a Hebrew princess but a Hebrew prince, and no offspring can come of such a union. If I were to die in battle, the queen might rule the land until Naq'd's son was old enough to sit on the throne— my own son not being worthy of kingship. But the queen is more concerned with furnishing her palaces than with the welfare of our country. As for my son-in-law Neriglissar, though he is a brave warrior, one who knows how to lead men in war does not of needs know how to lead a nation in peace. Should I be called to my fate, the only one fit to sit on the throne after me is the Princess Naq'd, who always knew more about matters of state than her brother. However, custom forbids that I name her my successor, for women were not meant to be rulers. Therefore I shall not accompany the troops to Jerusalem but shall remain in Riblah, for if I heard the clang of weapons my blood would boil like that of an old war horse and I would rush into battle, perchance to fall before my task on earth is accomplished. But I have vowed to complete all the great buildings I began in Babylon and to unite my vast kingdom in peace and prosperity. As for you, Holofernes, select those thousand brave warriors and may Marduk bless your weapons and grant you victory!'"

For days the camp was in turmoil while troops were assembled as though they would soon march off to Ammon. The king himself cast the sticks and examined the livers of sacrifices to learn the day propitious for commencing the campaign. In the end not even the most clever spy could suspect a ruse, nor did any observe the Captain Holofernes, who spent the days in his tent mustering his thousand soldiers.

The call had gone out among the men that the Captain Holofernes wished to assemble a troop of valiant veterans, but for what purpose none was told. Yet many more men came than were needed. Not only would they serve under the captain's command, they also believed that no harm could come to them while they followed him. Thus it was for the captain to select those he thought best fit for the dangerous mission.

While I sat writing down their names, their ages, the cities from which they came and whether they were married or single—that their families might make a mourning for them should they fall in battle—the captain questioned them about the wars in which they had fought. But he did this so swiftly, not wishing to lose much time, that I could barely complete one entry before commencing the next, nor could I raise my eyes to gaze at the men. Thus to me they were only names, ages and places where they had fought. Many had been on the previous campaign against Judah. Some had fought in Elam and Lebanon, and a few even at Carchemish. I found that the captain preferred younger men over older, and single men to those who had wives and children.

Though we worked from sunup to sundown, it took several days before all the soldiers were mustered. And still men were lining up outside the captain's tent to be assigned to him. Toward the middle of the fifth day, when my fingers ached so that I could barely hold the stylus any longer and my eyes were red and swollen from gazing at my clay tablets, the captain suddenly paused in his questioning of the men. Too weary to look around, I just sat with my shoulders hunched, waiting for him to continue. But rather than resume his dictation, the captain said:

"You have come to the wrong tent, grandfather. This mission is meant for younger men."

The soldier who stood behind me replied:

"Though I may not be newly weaned from sucking the milk of my mother—as are most of these youths the captain selected—I can still outmarch and outride any of them. Moreover, I fought in many wars, not only in Judah, Syria and Elam, but also at Gaza, Carchemish and Harran."

"Indeed you appear old enough to have fought at Nineveh," the Captain Holofernes said.

"And if I fought at Nineveh—did not the captain also fight at Nineveh? And does the captain think himself too old to do battle?"

Instead of the curse I expected at such insolence, I heard the captain break into roaring laughter. But when the soldier who had spoken so boldly joined in the laughter, the hair rose on the back of my neck. Though it was many years since I had heard the same gruesome laughter at Nineveh, I would not forget it as long as I lived. Dropping the stylus, I turned around to stare at the man who stood before the Captain Holofernes.

His hair and beard had turned the gray of iron. Indeed he might have been a kindly grandfather had not the expression of his eyes and mouth remained as cruel as before. Where the deep gash had been on his forehead there was an ugly red scar, like the one God put on Cain to mark him forever. Looking at the man I trembled so hard I thought I would faint, for I had long given up hope of ever finding my father's slayer. However, I had not forgotten the oath I had sworn by Yahweh, and such an oath must not be broken. But how I would avange my father's death and my sister's shame on this monster who struck terror into my soul even now that he was become old I did not know.

Not until the Captain Holofernes raised his voice in anger did I perceive that he had resumed his dictation. I collected myself and took up my stylus, but my hand continued trembling so that I spoiled one clay tablet and had to find another before I could record the murderer's name. He was called Bania the son of Kimutu, and he came from Cutah, which I thought most fitting, this being the city where dead men are said to go.

After recruiting Bania the captain mustered still more men. But though my fingers recorded their names, the sound of the captain's voice was like the sound of the wind in my ears, for I still thought of the man whom God had made cross my path after all these years. And even I, who had long ceased to believe in such things, thought it an omen.

Nor was there an end to omens. No sooner had the Captain Holofernes mustered his men than some came to accuse a one-eyed soothsayer who went about predicting the same future for all.

Indeed he prophesied that the goddess Ishtar would descend from on high to lead them to their fate!

Hearing this, the captain smote his thigh and exclaimed:

"Then the old scoundrel is still alive!"

And he commanded that the soothsayer be brought before him. I too was curious to see the man who had foretold my fate as though the future held no secrets for him. When he was brought before the Captain Holofernes I drew near that I might hear what excuses he would invent this time for his strange prophecies.

I could see that he had done well in his calling. Whereas he had been dressed in tatters when he predicted my future in Harshinana's kitchen, he now wore costly robes of fine wool, and on his head the tall hat of the dream diviner. The empty socket of his eye was covered with a golden disk in the shape of the eight-pointed star of Ishtar, set with precious stones. Not having been told why he was summoned, he bowed down low before the captain and said:

"My lord has heard of my renown and would learn his future from me!"

"Indeed I heard of your renown, scoundrel," the captain replied. "As for revealing my future to me, you did that long ago, before your eye was scratched out by the priestess whom you observed undressing."

The soothsayer turned pale and stumbled backward as though he had seen an evil spirit. But the captain continued:

"And now you are preying on the troops and amassing much silver from these ignorant soldiers who pay you for your lies. Nor are you abashed to make them all the only prediction you know— the same you made not only me but also the scribe who stands beside me."

The soothsayer fell on his knees, covered his good eye with his hand and exclaimed:

"It is indeed a black day when such portents meet together!"

"For once you have spoken truly," the captain said. "Unless you cease from weakening the hands of my soldiers with your lies, you shall forever remember this day as a black day!"

"Let Ishtar be my witness that I never pronounced a prophecy that was not truly revealed to me," the soothsayer said, placing his hand on his heart. "As for the prediction concerning my lord's soldiers, I made it but twice before this day: once to a youth at

Uruk who was born with the sign of Ishtar on his wrist, and once to
a young slave at Borsippa who had just been made a eunuch. If the
scribe beside my lord is that eunuch, my lord must be the youth
from Uruk who was then an acolyte at the temple of Ishtar!"

"I am indeed that former acolyte," the Captain Holofernes said.
"But as for the sign of Ishtar you speak of, this is another of your
lies, as you can see for yourself."

And the captain slipped off his broad silver bracelet and stretched
forth his arm. Seeing the scar on his wrist, the soothsayer screamed
with horror, threw himself flat on his belly so that his tall hat
toppled to the ground, and clasping both his hands over his head he
moaned:

"By cutting off her sacred sign the captain has earned the everlasting wrath of Ishtar! The goddess never relinquishes what she has
marked as her own! Nor am I any longer puzzled by the odd behavior of my divining rods. Surely the fate of my lord's soldiers will be
accomplished together with his. Therefore let the captain repent
and sacrifice to the goddess that she may remove her curse from
him!"

Turning pale with rage, the captain bent down, lifted the soothsayer from the ground and seized him by the throat.

"If you persist in this prediction I shall have you driven from the
camp!" he shouted. "But you would soon find new victims to stuff
your bag with silver. Indeed I know a better punishment for you. I
shall have you assigned to my troops that you might accompany
them into battle. And if you will not predict victory for us, I will
rip out your lying tongue with my own hands!"

Now that all was prepared for the secret mission, it would be but
a day or two before the men left the camp under cover of darkness.
Nebuchadrezzar had sent a mounted messenger with rich gifts to
Baalis, king of Ammon, asking him to let a thousand Babylonian
soldiers pass peaceably through his land. But should Baalis refuse,
Ammon would be turned into a heap of ruins. None thought of
waiting for a reply, for surely the king of Ammon would not wish
to incur Nebuchadrezzar's wrath by refusing such a modest request.

The Captain Holofernes had told his soldiers that they were to
advance before the army, but he had not revealed their destination
to them. There was some discontent among those he had rejected,

none being more disheartened than David when he learned that he was not to be among the captain's troop. When I spoke sensibly to the boy, reminding him that he had never yet carried his weapons into battle nor was he strong enough to march with these hardened veterans, he stamped his foot, pouted and all but wept like a child. Nor would he be comforted by my promise that I would look after his comforts as before.

"I did not join the army to have you run after me like a nurse-maid!" he cried.

But I never knew him to refuse the special food and drink I procured for him, for he had been greatly spoiled by his mother and his stepfather.

When I discussed the boy's unhappiness with the Captain Holofernes and inquired what provision he wished me to make for his ward, the captain replied:

"I already commended Ziria to the Commander Nabuzaradan and charged him with keeping the boy from danger because of the debt I owe his father. So you need not concern yourself with his welfare, nor will you be able to look after him since you are to come with me as my interpreter."

Hearing this gruesome proposal, I raised my hands in supplication to the captain and exclaimed:

"Was I not appointed the king's own interpreter? And would my lord now drag me along on this mission, knowing that the dangerous task requires great valor and skill at war? How am I to follow these soldiers who ride with the swiftness and fury of demons of the nether world—I, who cannot even ride upon a gentle donkey without having the blood squirt from my buttocks after a day? Was not this mission meant for only the most hardened veterans?"

"And are you not a veteran of the previous war against Judah?" the captain asked. "Did you not brag on many occasions of how you fearlessly shouted the order for surrender to the defenders on the walls of Jerusalem? As for us, we shall reach Judah long before the army and shall be in great need of an interpreter whose boldness is surpassed only by his knowledge of Hebrew! Though I do not plan to engage my troops in battle but shall rather advance by night, we might have to take some Hebrew hostages to guide us through their wretched hills. How shall we speak with them if not through an interpreter? Thus, knowing your fearless heart, I requested your services of the king. Nor have I forgotten your tender buttocks but ordered that a basket such as is used for the transport of women be placed upon a swift camel to spare you the discomforts that strengthen real men, for I would not have you perish before you have been of use to me. And now go and bid your master's son farewell, but beware of revealing to him our true mission. He is only a boy who might rashly boast of his knowledge."

I knew then that it would be vain to reason with the Captain Holofernes, nor could I cease thinking of the dreadful omens—the appearance of my father's slayer and of the soothsayer who had predicted our common fate.

As for this soothsayer, I nearly stumbled over him when I went to my tent to collect such things as I would carry with me. He had rent his garments, sprinkled dirt on his head and sat on the ground swaying back and forth as if in mourning. But when I inquired whose death he was bewailing, he said it was his own.

"Today I read my own fate," he said, "though this is thought bad practice among dream diviners, for a man might be swayed in his predictions by the desires of his heart. But what man would wish for his own death? Yet though I examined a ram's liver, cast the sticks and poured oil on water, I could not prevent the star of Ishtar from appearing in the omens time and again. Thus I know that my fate shall be the same as yours, the captain's and that of the thousand men who are to go with him—may Ishtar grant us life!"

ELEVEN

And it shall be unto them as a false divination in their sight, who have weeks upon weeks! but it bringeth iniquity to remembrance, that they may be taken.

—EZEKIEL 21:28

IN the month of Heshvan we heard that the Babylonian army had reached Damascus (the old woman Tamar said to the young scribe). But even then none knew whether they had come to make war on us. The Egyptians spread rumors that Nebuchadrezzar was to go first against Rabbath-Ammon, and that there were still many weeks left in which to prepare Jerusalem for an attack.

As always in such uncertain times, people were divided against themselves. Some advised submission, some advised war, and some advised patience until one learned Nebuchadrezzar's true plans. If there was disagreement in Bethul, there was all but open strife in Jerusalem. The princes who were in league with the Egyptians counseled King Zedekiah to resist the Babylonians. But Jeremiah, who walked about freely at that time, advised surrender. Nor was he alone in speaking for peace. Ezekiel the son of Buzi, who had been carried into captivity nine years before, had returned to plead the cause of Babylon. Many proclaimed Jeremiah and Ezekiel traitors who had sold their tongues to Nebuchadrezzar for silver, and asked that they be put to death. But others knew that the prophets spoke out of true concern, for they would not see all Judah turned into heaps of ruins.

As for the inhabitants of Bethul—they had no prophets but relied on the words of the elders who sat in the gate. And when the elders confirmed their belief that the Babylonian army would never come against Bethul the people rejoiced, for they were told what they wished to hear. Only Judith was scornful and stepped before the elders to debate with them the wisdom of their verdict.

"Someday the blood of helpless women and children will be on your heads," Judith said. "If the Babylonians come against Jerusalem they will assuredly not spare Bethul. Though we have but few men who draw the sword, we could resist half the Babylonian army if only we strengthened our walls and repaired the breaches that have long been neglected. But above all we must complete the shaft my father began and bring in water from the spring!"

Then the elders replied:

"Though you did well at many tasks requiring the hand and mind of a man, Judith, it is not seemly that a woman advise men on war, nor was such a thing ever done."

"Did not Miriam cheer on the children of Israel?" Judith asked. "Did not Deborah lead the Hebrews into battle? Was it not Yael who drove a tent pin into Sisera's temple, and a woman of Thebez who tossed a millstone down on Abimelech, killing him? Why, then, would *you* despise the counsel of a woman in matters of war?"

Much dismayed by these words, the elders replied:

"All these ladies lived in times of yore, nor do we know if they truly achieved those great deeds."

"Even if you would doubt the deeds of these women, you must grant that it is women who suffer most in war," Judith said. "They lose their husbands and sons, and are made slaves and harlots by the conquerors. Why, then, should they not show concern? I do not ask that you march off and engage the Babylonians in battle! I only would have you repair the walls and ensure that we have water in case of a siege."

"Even if we repaired our walls they would never withstand the Babylonian battering rams," the elders replied. "And as for water, did not the rains commence early this year so that our cisterns in town are nearly filled to the brim?"

"Though some rain fell last month, it has not rained since," Judith said. "My father taught me that if the first rains came too early in the season there would be a drought right into winter. Therefore let us complete his shaft!"

Greatly vexed with Judith, the elders said:

"When your father died you were still half a child, Judith. You may remember many things he never said. Moreover, it is known that the Babylonian army is headed for Rabbath-Ammon. Even if they proceeded from there to Jerusalem, they would go by way of

Jericho. But to attack Bethul they would have to traverse the wilderness, and this thing cannot be done."

"Did not David and his brave warriors traverse the wilderness?" Judith asked.

The elders sighed and gazed at each other.

"It is harmful to let a woman have learning," they said. "David traversed the wilderness with a handful of men! Even the mighty Nebuchadrezzar could not carry his army with all their chariots, siege towers and battering rams across our mountains! But if by some miracle he could, we would assuredly have to surrender to him."

Then Judith turned away in wrath, muttering:

"It is good that my father died before hearing such speech come from the mouths of the last remnant of Simeon, the tribe that was known for its mighty men of war! As for me, I shall do what I think right even without the aid of these cowards."

Afraid that time was growing short, Judith did not delay in carrying out her plans. Since none of the villagers would assist in digging the shaft, she thought to conceal at least the approach to the spring.

"If the enemy come, they will be in as much need of water as we, for these hills are dry unless one knows where to find wells. Let us erase all traces of the path that leads to the spring and disguise the entrance to the cave in such an artful manner that none might suspect a source of water behind it."

Then Judith commanded her own servants to bring pickaxes, shovels and wicker baskets in which to move trees and shrubs. And she herself stood over them, in her plain widow's garb, to direct the spading up of the path and the moving of bushes and small trees. Nor was this an easy task, for after the early rains the ground had dried again and was now hard and caked, refusing to render up the shrubs. After they were transplanted it took much raking over to conceal the holes. And for days many pitchers of water had to be hauled from the spring to moisten the ground that the newly planted bushes might not wither and die.

When the task was completed, the women of Bethul cursed Judith roundly. Now they had to pick their way to the spring through the shrubs, using a different approach every day that they might not tramp down a new path. Nor was it easy for them to find the entrance to the cave so well had Judith seen to its concealment.

But in town one was telling the other that Judith was going mad from having too much wealth and no husband. Her storehouses were filled with grain, her cellars stocked with jars of wine, and her coffers stuffed with silver and the deeds to all the land she had acquired. As for a man—there was none who dared court her save Joab, who still spoke to her of marriage though she had refused him many times.

But when Joab came to call on her this time, Judith descended from her chamber on the roof instead of having me turn him away with some lie about her ill-health. She had tied her thick, red hair at the nape of her neck that it might not fall into her eyes when she bent over to help with the work, and her widow's garb was soiled at the hem from toiling with spade and hoe as the least of her servants. But even though there were dark circles under her eyes from working hard and sleeping little, she was still very beautiful.

Joab gazed at her with the eyes of a sick calf—and he already the father of five daughters—and said:

"Must a woman of your wealth kill herself working like a slave, Judith? Do you truly believe that the spring could save us if the Babylonians came against Bethul?"

"Are you as much of a coward as the other men who speak of surrender?" Judith replied. "You to whom my father gave his own sword nine years ago, when he could no longer go out into battle but would still bend a bow and shoot an arrow to keep the Babylonians from our gates!"

"What could one man alone do with your father's sword even if he were willing to fight?" Joab asked, for he would not be called a coward by Judith.

"Alone you could do little," Judith replied. "But if you went around strengthening the hearts and hands of the other young men, much could be accomplished by even a few. Did not Gideon rout a whole army with three hundred warriors?"

"Gideon did not rout an enemy armed with weapons such as are known to the Babylonians," Joab said. "Nor do we have three hundred men who draw the sword but barely a hundred—if they would fight. Hardly enough to stem the onslaught of Nebuchadrezzar's troops! But then these troops will never come against us."

"If it be the will of God they will not come," Judith replied. "But if they do come, remember that miracles happened in these hills!"

TWELVE

How say ye: 'We are mighty men,
And valiant men for the war?'
                                        —JEREMIAH 48:14

IT was in the month of Kislev, at the time of the new moon, that the Captain Holofernes and his troop stole away in the dead of night (the old man Isaac said to the young scribe). They had tied their horses near the edge of the camp, from where they could be led away subtly. Each of the chosen warriors was a skilled horseman, but when they stole out of the camp they led their horses by the bridle lest the noise of men galloping off into the night should rouse the Egyptian spies.

Nor were the horses their only beasts. There were pack asses with provisions, my camel with the padded basket on its back, and a mule as a mount for the wretched soothsayer. If the latter did not weep aloud in his despair, rousing all the camp, it was because the captain had threatened that the first sound coming from his mouth should also be his last. As for me, I had long learned that a man cannot quarrel with his fate. Thus I sat huddled upon my camel, which a soldier led along with his left hand, while he guided his own horse with his right.

In the dark the silently moving men seemed like ghosts from the nether world. There was no word exchanged between them until they were far from the camp, nor could their faces be seen in the black of night, only here and there the glimmering of a helmet. The pack animals had been placed in the middle, surrounded by the horses, lest they break away and be lost. They carried enough dried meat and pulse, dates and bread to last us until we reached Rabbath-Ammon, where we would replenish our supplies. As for water, it could be bought for silver along the way where there were wells.

The donkeys also carried many tents, more indeed than were needed for the soldiers. Though the Captain Holofernes planned to proceed by night, avoiding all settlements in Judah until he reached Lachish, once he pitched camp he would have the enemy think our numbers greater than they were in truth.

The men marched on foot until dawn, when a spot safely concealed from view was found. There they posted sentries and sank down on the ground to sleep through the day. I too slept until the following night, when the Captain Holofernes roused his soldiers to continue the march. Though he thought it safe now to let them mount their horses, we still progressed slowly. Instead of taking the highway from Damascus to Rabbath-Ammon we traveled through abandoned parts, where the horses slipped and stumbled in the darkness. After riding all night on the unsteady beasts the men again spent all day sleeping. Thus it was not discovered until nightfall, when the troops assembled to refresh themselves around the camp-fires before departing, that the boy David was among them.

He had stolen a horse, tied a false hairpiece to his beard that it might look fully grown, and in the dark had slipped out with the rest of the men. The Captain Holofernes swore horribly when two of his soldiers dragged David before him and he saw how the boy had disguised himself. But though he trembled before the captain's wrath, David spoke with the insolence of youth:

"Did not my lord tell me how *he* pasted the beard of a he-goat to his chin when he took the place of his elder brother?"

Smiting his thigh with anger, the captain replied:

"When I disguised myself to look older it was not to go on a secret mission but to become a recruit in the king's army. Nor did I see combat until I had been hardened for many months that I might not be a burden to my comrades. As for joining the foremost troops, this was denied me until I fought at Nineveh, when I had been a soldier for four years and knew more about war than you will learn if you live to be a hundred. Ah, if only I had listened to your father when he begged me to have you discharged from the army because of your youth! Nor do I know yet how I shall deal with your disobedience."

Then the man Bania, who had slain my father and ravished my sister, drew near the captain and spoke:

"Why should the boy not be punished as other soldiers are punished for disobedience, seeing that he passed himself off as a veteran?"

His cruel eyes shone with pleasure at the thought of seeing David tied to a stake to receive forty lashes upon his bare back, as was the common punishment. At that the boy turned pale, while I, knowing that David could never endure the whipping, threw myself at the captain's feet to plead for his mercy.

"If not for the debt of honor I owe Nabukasir, it would go badly with his son," the captain said. "But since Ziria is now among men he had better act like one, for I shall make no more allowances for his youth. It were better if I sent him back to Damascus, but he cannot return alone, neither can I spare any men to escort him back to the camp. As for you, Marduksharusur, you need not offer yourself for that task—as surely you would the moment I close my mouth—for I cannot spare you either. Nor do I believe that Ziria could be trusted to remain silent now that he knows our destination, for he has the mind of a child. But let him act like a man henceforth, lest he bring disgrace to his father's name."

With these words the captain dismissed David from his presence. I escorted the boy back to the mount he had stolen, chiding him for rashly risking his life, which was as precious to me as to his own father, he being the only son I had ever known. But instead of thanking me for saving him from the whipping he so well deserved, David sulked and said:

"Why did the captain shame me before all the soldiers, revealing that my father wanted me discharged from the army? But though I knew nothing of this I am not astonished by my father's baseness. He would not have me serve Nebuchadrezzar now that his own heart is turned against the king, nor would he have me show bravery where he showed cowardice!"

Then I too became angry with David and said:

"Your father always abhorred war, but where it concerns bravery you may be proud if you ever equal even the least of his feats. As for your foolish speech, I can see from it that your mind has not grown since you ran after me nine years ago, shouting: 'I too shall go to war against Judah, I too shall go to war against Judah!' And you the son of a Hebrew!"

My heart was heavy when I seated myself in the basket upon my camel for the third night's trek. In spite of my harsh words, my concern for David was no smaller than before, and I feared he would not show the required fortitude on this dangerous mission. Neither did I dare contemplate how the captain would deal with the boy if he proved a hindrance to him. For by the way the captain drove his men I could tell that he would accomplish the task he had set himself at all costs.

On the third and fourth nights we continued advancing swiftly into the mountains of Ammon. And when on the fifth morning the walls of Rabbath-Ammon came in sight, even the most hardened soldiers felt faint with weariness. But the thought that soon they would be able to refill their nearly empty waterskins, savor once again the taste of freshly slaughtered sheep, and know the pleasure of a harlot's company, restored their strength.

However, from the moment we sighted Rabbath one strange occurrence followed upon the next. Though it was already the month of Kislev, the many hills about the city looked parched as if no drop of rain had yet fallen. The beds of the springs which rose north of Rabbath to feed into the River Jabbok were empty wadis in the cracked, yellow soil. Nor did the people welcome us with greetings, but all seemed to have fled behind the barred gates of Rabbath. At once I was filled with deep misgivings. If the people of the land had received Nebuchadrezzar's message of peace, why should they show such fear at our approach?

The Captain Holofernes called his troop to a halt while he too gazed thoughtfully at the barred gates of the city. We had left on this mission without waiting for an answer to Nebuchadrezzar's request. And though the captain trusted in the powerful name of the king of Babylon, he could not be certain that we would be treated as friends. Thus he ordered all the tents pitched that the Ammonites might think we had come in great numbers. Then he had our beasts and supplies gathered into the midst of the camp and double sentries posted all around, for he would not risk losing what little we had left. Though there were no Ammonite troops without the walls, we did not know whether armed soldiers were not hiding within to take us by surprise.

Having seen to all these precautions, the Captain Holofernes said:

"And now let us approach the gates of Rabbath and discover whether these wretched Ammonites will deal with us peaceably."

Because I was cursed with this gift of many tongues, it was again my task to draw near the wall and interpret to the men upon it the captain's words. To show that he had come in peace he had taken with him only twenty soldiers, nor did they raise their shields in approaching the wall to display their trust. Though I feared that such bold behavior would get us all killed, not an arrow was shot at us from the wall. But neither were the gates flung open, nor did any of the Ammonites hail us from above.

Then I shouted up the message of the Captain Holofernes, proclaiming that we had come in peace and would pay in good Babylonian silver for food and water. And when still none would answer, I spoke of the request Nebuchadrezzar had sent to their king. In the end one of the men upon the wall took heart and shouted back that they knew of no message from the king of Babylon, but that they would inquire of King Baalis in his palace.

We sat down on the ground some distance from the wall to wait for an answer from the Ammonite king. Morning passed into noon and still there was no reply. Some of the men fell to rolling dice, which one or the other always carried with him, while others dozed beneath their shields. The heat increased as the sun rose into the cloudless sky, and the parched ground on which we sat seemed to dry out even more and crack before our eyes. It was much too hot for the month of Kislev in this part of the land. Soon the gambling soldiers also sought shelter beneath their shields. The only one who remained upon his feet was the Captain Holofernes. He paced back and forth, his boots churning up clouds of dust while he glowered at the barred gates of Rabbath.

"It is folly to promise peace if one can bend a foe to one's will by the use of force," he muttered. "If I had my five thousand soldiers I would break down the gates of this wretched city and slay every last male in it for detaining me on my course!"

And the captain tugged at his beard, striding back and forth even more furiously. But I saw that he was mad with the zeal of one whose youth is fled from him and who has not yet made himself a name.

It was not until the sun was in our eyes, having moved west toward its setting, that a troop of Ammonite soldiers with their weapons at ready took up their posts atop the wall. Our own men jumped to their feet with their shields raised, while I wisely hid behind them where I might be the first to take flight. But again no arrow was shot at us, neither was a spear flung down. Instead there was a sound of trumpets, and then there appeared a sumptuously clad figure among the soldiers that could only be Baalis himself, the king of the Ammonites. Beside him stood a young man whom I would have taken for the king's interpreter had he not worn garb almost as costly as that of the king. This young man shouted down to us in the Babylonian tongue, which he spoke well:

"Let your leader come forward and let him repeat the message he sent to my father, the king, for we have been much puzzled by the report of our men, never having received word from the king of Babylon!"

We knew then that the young man was one of the Ammonite princes, perchance the crown prince himself. But the Captain Holofernes mumbled before stepping forward:

"No doubt these wretches received both Nebuchadrezzar's message and gift but would now deny all knowledge of it."

While he repeated in Babylonian all I had said before, I wondered whether the young prince had not spoken the truth. Neriglissar had been one of the few who knew the captain's plan. Remembering his hatred of the Captain Holofernes, I thought that he might have waylaid and slain the king's envoy. If the Ammonites were not warned of our peaceful coming, they might easily fall upon the thousand men and slaughter all, including the Captain Holofernes.

When the captain had finished, the young prince on the wall exchanged words with his father. Then he replied:

"We never received either message or gift from the king of Babylon. Nor are we at war with Judah or Egypt. How should we answer to their ambassadors if we supplied you with food and water to strengthen your hands against them? But if you will go your way we shall let you pass peaceably and pretend we never saw you, for we would not have war with Babylon either!"

The young prince and the king turned as though to leave the wall. But the captain called after them to tarry a little longer, while he discussed with his officers this strange turn of events. And drawing his men about him, he said softly:

"I do not trust these Ammonites in our backs while we descend toward Jericho. If they fall upon us they will be on the heights above and we shall lose many men fighting them uphill. Even should we make good our escape they might pursue us to the Jordan, where we would have to make a stand, not being able to retreat swiftly across the river. But if we could seize some Ammonite hostages—perchance the young prince himself—they would not dare attack us. However, to accomplish this feat we shall have to use a ruse."

And turning back to the wall, the captain shouted:

"I can well understand that my lord would not arouse Egypt's ire by aiding us. But would my lord deny me and my officers to enter Rabbath and spend the night with some harlots before continuing on the morrow? It is many days since we left Damascus and any of us has lain with a woman. Surely my lord, who has great understanding of such matters, would not have to defend this action before Egypt!"

Then the prince, being young and easily flattered for his knowledge of women, replied:

"In this not even the Egyptians could accuse us of having strengthened your hands in war! As for me, I shall be honored to entertain you as my own guests!"

At that the Captain Holofernes smiled grimly beneath his beard and said:

"Truly Ishtar must be with us to deliver this fool into our hands!"

Seeing that I was a eunuch, the Ammonites showed no suspicion when I did not enter the city with the other soldiers to lie with a harlot. While the gates of Rabbath were flung open to the Captain Holofernes and his officers, I hurried back to our camp. There I approached the highest officer who had remained behind and revealed to him the captain's orders: as soon as it grew dark all tents were to be dismantled and loaded on the pack asses, together with the remaining supplies. As for the men, they were to stand ready for a swift departure as soon as the Captain Holofernes and his soldiers returned with their hostage. If they did not return until dawn, the officer would know that they had been slain. Then he had better prepare for a battle if he wished to die honorably, or turn to flight if he would rather perish from a wound in his back. For there was little doubt that the much larger Ammonite forces would vanquish the thousand Babylonian soldiers.

By good fortune the crescent moon in the sky did not shed much light. Thus the sentries on the walls of Rabbath did not see our soldiers break camp subtly and prepare their horses for a swift departure. But it was not until after the middle watch, when fear and doubt began to arise in the hearts of the soldiers, that the Captain Holofernes returned with his men. They all smelled of wine, and more than one among them was barely able to stand upright. However, they had achieved their aim, for they carried with them the young Ammonite prince. He was even more drunk than the rest and was singing gaily as though he did not know what was to be his fate. Indeed he seemed to have followed the Captain Holofernes of his free will, there being no mark of violence on him. But there was no time to reveal how this had been accomplished.

Now every man swung himself upon his saddled horse, while I was made to share the soothsayer's mule that the prince might be placed into the basket on my camel, for he was too drunk to ride. Thus we stole away like thieves in the night to begin the descent toward Jericho.

We were still upon the mountain heights when the sun rose behind us, shedding light over the hills on the other side of the Jordan. We could see Jericho in the valley below, and the twisting riverbed dividing the eastern and western part of the plain. Not far beyond Jericho the mountains reared up like a sudden wall, lying barren, dusty yellow and forbidding between us and the coastal plain. As the sun rose higher we could perceive in the west a dark-blue streak beyond the white sand dunes in the distance and a glinting here and there that revealed to us the Great Sea. The Egyptians would march north along this coastline before turning inland by way of Lachish, where the captain planned to waylay their troops. But gazing across the vast mountainous wilderness, I thought it a distance none could traverse. Nor were the soldiers elated by the sight, for they were men of the plains who feared and hated the hills.

But the Captain Holofernes paid no heed to the muttering of his soldiers. He summoned me to his side and said:

"Prince Hanun—for that is his name—will soon wake from his drunken stupor and wish to know where he finds himself. I would have you go and soothe him in his own language lest he rashly cause us to slay him, for he is of no value to us dead. Also remind him that he followed us of his own will, even bidding the guards to unlock the gates for us. Nor shall he be harmed while his people desist from

falling on our backs. But after our mission is completed he shall be
safely returned to his home."

The captain had charged me with this errand none too soon. Even
as I approached my former mount, Prince Hanun sat up in the
basket and loudly demanded to know what had happened. When I
gave him the captain's message his face turned dark, and holding his
head in both his hands he said:

"Last night I drank too much and did not know my own actions.
But I was not so drunk as to forget how I was deceived by your
captain, whom I welcomed in my house as an honored guest. As our
spirits grew gayer with the wine, your captain spoke to me of
certain clay tablets he had in his camp—tablets on which were
depicted naked women comporting themselves in a manner I had
never beheld. He offered to show me these tablets if I followed him
and his men to the camp. I roused my companions—those who had
not yet fallen under the table—that they might join me on this
delightful visit. But no sooner had we reached the gates and I had
given orders to unlock them than all my companions were overcome by the wine, falling to the ground, where they were soon
joined by the guards. As I think back on it now I have grave doubts
that they were drunk. Rather I believe that they were brought
down by treachery, even as I was brought down by treachery. But
let your captain know that the gods abhor one who betrays his host,
neither will my father let this sin go unavenged!"

When I returned with this message to the Captain Holofernes, he
only laughed and said:

"Truly it was not wine but folly that did those men in! However,
we killed none but only left them bound and gagged that they
might deliver my message to the king when he discovered his son
missing in the morning. Surely King Baalis will value his son's life
above an act of vengeance, more so since he need not require of us a
blood guilt."

And again the captain laughed as if abducting a crown prince
were a small matter. But when I returned to take my place on the
mule behind the soothsayer, I found him greatly distraught by the
tale he had learned from the other officers.

"Was there a dearth of ill omens that the Captain Holofernes had
to incite the gods to further wrath by betraying his host?" he asked.

And though I did not believe in heathen gods, for once I agreed
with him.

As for the Captain Holofernes, he considered only the good omens. Gazing down into the valley of the Jordan, he said:

"It is fortunate that the rains are late this year, for they clear the air so that looking across from Judah one can discern all movements on the slopes of Ammon. But since there has been no rain, the haze and dust will soon form a yellow curtain which will conceal us even in broad daylight. Still let every man remove his helmet and his shield, place them on his horse and cover them with his cloak that they may not catch the rays of the sun and betray by their glinting our course."

When his soldiers muttered again—having hoped that after their brief rest the previous night they would be allowed to sleep in the daytime—the captain told them that it was better to be weary than to be dead, for they were not yet safe from pursuit. If they continued their descent they would reach the edge of the plain shortly before nightfall. There they would wait for complete darkness, when it would be a simple matter to cross the plain. Once across the Jordan they would be safe from the Ammonites, who would not dare pursue them into Judah.

Then the men did as the captain commanded. They dismounted, hid their helmets and shields, and led their horses by the bridles, for the path downhill was treacherous with loose stones. Even Prince Hanun was made to dismount the camel, but the captain had himself chained to his prisoner that he might not try to escape. Only the soothsayer and I remained seated upon our mule until his forelegs buckled under him and we both rolled off, head first, to the great glee of the soldiers. After that we too were forced to climb downhill like goats.

Proceeding at the head of his troop the captain did not halt until we had reached the last hill from which we would descend into the valley. Though he gave his soldiers a respite he would not sit down but walked about among them, kicking awake those who had dozed off and saying:

"Let us first cross over the Jordan and gain the western hills. Then you may sleep as long as you like."

No sooner had darkness fallen than the captain roused his weary men to continue their descent, he lashed to his prisoner, the soldiers leading their horses, the soothsayer and I leaning upon each other for support, dragging each other down as we stumbled, and cursing the fate that had delivered us into the hands of a madman such as the Captain Holofernes.

When we reached the eastern edge of the valley the crescent moon had risen into the sky, shedding a pale-blue light in which the barren, deserted plain looked like a region of the nether world. Jericho still lay some distance to the north and west of us, beyond the Jordan. But the Captain Holofernes would not allow his men to mount their horses, fearing that if they were weighed down their hoofbeats would carry far in the still of the night. Thus it was near the middle watch when we finally entered the thicket of shrubs and reeds at the eastern bank of the Jordan. Save for a brief rest the soldiers had marched since dawn, nor had they eaten, for the captain had ordered that our dwindling supplies be used sparingly. But worse than the hunger was the thirst that plagued us all. Most waterskins were empty, for all the springs in the mountains had dried up, nor had we dared approach any wells to buy water. Even those soldiers who feared the ghosts that lurk near rivers in the dark waded down into the Jordan, scooping up water with their hands to slake their thirst. The horses plunged in after them and would have rolled over on their backs, losing their loads of helmets and shields, had not the men prevented them in time.

Still chained to his prisoner, the Captain Holofernes refreshed himself and bade Prince Hanun wash his face and chest, for having had too much wine the day before, the prince had vomited on the way. But I, on soles smarting with blisters from the long downhill climb, scurried about in the dark to discover David and see whether he was not lost on the mountain path.

I found him sitting under a bush near the riverbank, his face hidden in his hands as he sobbed softly. When I inquired as to the cause of his grief, he said his weariness was such that he would sooner remain lying in the thicket by the Jordan than cross the plain to climb the mountains at its western edge.

But I implored the boy to consider his mother, who would surely perish of grief if he died, his older sister, whose first-born he would not live to see, and his father—even though he hated him—to whom his son's life was more precious than his own. Surely if I, a feeble eunuch, could prevail, so could he who was the son of a brave warrior. Thus, when the Captain Holofernes gave the order to cross the river, David rose to his feet to follow the other men.

Again the captain proclaimed that the gods were with us. The Jordan, swift and deep at other times, ran low and sluggishly because of the drought, the water reaching barely higher than the soldiers' thighs. The men led their horses with one hand, while with the other they held their swords above their heads to keep them dry. All this was done in deep silence. Only now and then a horse snorted as it lowered its head for one last drink.

We had marched so many hours during the night that our eyes had become accustomed to the darkness. Thus, once across the Jordan and out of the thicket along the riverbank, we could see to the north of us the ragged, black outline of palm trees marking the place where Jericho was fed by a spring of sweet water. But we swiftly moved away from that beckoning oasis, heading south and west toward the mountains.

When we reached the foot of the outermost range behind which lay the wilderness of Judah, the sky began to brighten in the east. And still the captain would not grant his men a rest but drove them into the hills, lest they be observed from Jericho when it grew light. All night long the faces of the men had been concealed by darkness. But as dawn broke I could see that they were gray and furrowed with weariness, and their beards and hair caked by the dust of the mountains that had mingled with the water of the Jordan.

Not until the sun rose over the ridge of the mountains did the Captain Holofernes allow his soldiers to pitch camp. They hastily put up a few tents for shade and fell down in heaps without first unbuckling their armor. Soon their snoring was the only sound heard in the eerie silence that lay over the mountains. All around us were barren hills, some rounded, some shaped like pyramids as if to suit the whim of some pharaoh. The limestone glared white in the sun, but here and there a bright red streak ran like blood across the face of the rock. Again I was taken by the thought that this might be the landscape of the nether world. But I too was so weary that I would have fallen asleep beside the soothsayer, who clung to me for comfort, had not the Captain Holofernes sent the man Bania to fetch me.

While I stumbled over the sleeping soldiers, trying to keep my distance from the one man on earth whom I hated above all others, Bania turned around and with many horrible oaths urged me to hurry.

"The captain tried to question Prince Hanun about a way through these mountains, which the Ammonites must know well, having waged many wars against the Hebrews. But this accursed Hanun pretends of a sudden to have no understanding of the Babylonian tongue. I could think of many ways that would swiftly restore his memory, but the captain forbade me to use them. Rather he would have you speak to this wretched prince, whose life would be worth nothing if our numbers were five times what they are."

When we arrived at the captain's tent, I found him angrily pacing back and forth. Though he was older than most of his men and had marched with them all night, he still had the strength to stand upright, and so had this monster Bania. But Prince Hanun sat on the ground with his face in his hands. Hearing us enter he raised his eyes, and now that I beheld him from nearby I saw that he was barely older than the boy David. But even in his weariness he looked proud and stubborn, for he was born to reign over others, and such a habit is not broken overnight. When I repeated to him the captain's question in his own language, the prince only shook his head and replied:

"There are no paths through the wilderness. Nor must one follow the wadis in the month of Kislev, for they fill with rushing waters when the rains commence and sweep all those who would traverse them to destruction."

When I translated this answer to the Captain Holofernes, he glanced up at the sky and said:

"There is not a cloud in the sky, and the earth here is as dry and barren as a woman past the childbearing age. But in spite of himself this boy revealed to me what I would know by telling me where one must *not* go, though he offered this counsel to deceive me. We shall soon break camp and continue south, for if the people of Jericho discover our tracks across the plain, they might send word to Jerusalem for troops to pursue after us. But they will not follow us into the wilderness, which they say cannot be crossed by an army."

Having made these plans the captain rubbed his red, swollen eyes, sat down on the ground beside his prisoner, leaned his head against the tent post, and with his hand on his sword fell asleep. But the man Bania remained awake to stand guard over them, reminding me of the monster Humbawa who needed no sleep.

We wandered about in the wilderness for three days, now following one wadi and now another without making much progress. Most
wadis ran from east to west, whereas the Captain Holofernes wished
to proceed south. In the end I began to think that we would meet
the same fate as the Israelites in the wilderness of Sinai. But while
Moses had procured for his people water and meat when they
clamored for them, the Captain Holofernes could not equal those
miracles. Thus our water dwindled away in the skins that had last
been filled at the Jordan. As for game, the only beasts that crossed
our path were foxes with pelts the gray color of the rock, who
could vanish from sight simply by standing still. Now and then a
man shot down one of the black crows that mocked us from above.
But they could not drive away the vultures which followed our trail
as if they knew more about our fate than we. Soon the men began
to slaughter the pack animals, for the burdens these beasts had
carried had long been consumed. All that was left were the many
tents we had taken along. Nor would the captain abandon them now
but commanded that they be loaded on the horses, while the men
had to make their way on foot.

Every day the muttering of the soldiers increased. They thought
themselves lost in the wilderness and feared that they would perish
of hunger and thirst. All the mountain springs had dried up, and
though at times we saw dark rain clouds gathering in the sky, they
were always scattered by the wind. Many of the soldiers wanted to
turn back, and in the end some officers approached the Captain
Holofernes with that proposal.

But the captain replied that they could not return to Ammon
after having abducted the crown prince, nor were they strong
enough to assault and take Jericho. Rather they must proceed south
through the wilderness and then head west to discover a small
village that might be captured by a thousand soldiers. Once they
had seized such a village there would be enough meat and grain,
water, wine and even women for the men. Also they might turn this
village into a stronghold if any escaped to summon the Hebrew
forces.

Learning the captain's answer, the soldiers became even more
disgruntled than before. They were weary from climbing through
the desolate mountains and weak from lack of food. It should take
only the smallest spark to set off a rebellion among them. As for me,

I do not know what made me prevail save the desire not to perish in the wilderness. In my heart I hoped that someday I might still return to Babylon, where I held a high position at court, owned much silver, and had a master who shared with me my love for the old writings. But dragging myself over the mountains on bleeding soles, weeping with weariness whenever we were allowed a brief rest, covered with filth and emitting a foul stench, I thought this memory but a blissful dream.

The one who reminded me that my former state was not a dream was the boy David. All his brashness had abandoned him, and he often came to me crying for food and water. But I could not procure for him what the others lacked, nor would I have dared arouse the men, for their mood became blacker from one hour to the next.

On the fourth day after crossing the Jordan we followed a wadi that seemed to lead south but then turned west to dwindle among the mountain ranges. We reached the end of that wadi at noon. Though it was the month of Kislev, the sun beating upon the bare, white rock gave off much heat and made the tongues of the men cleave to the roofs of their mouths. Their water was become so scarce that now they drank but once a day. Walking behind their thirsty, stumbling horses, they sullenly dragged their spears along in the dust.

When they reached the end of the wadi, the captain ordered the men to retrace their steps to the point from which they had started out. They halted, one looking at the other without moving on. But David, who had limped along beside me, sat down on the ground, put his face in his hands and moaned:

"I can no longer go on. You should have abandoned me by the bank of the Jordan, for there I would not have perished of thirst. Even here it is better to die quickly than to continue in this slow death."

When all my pleading with him proved to no avail, I hastened after the Captain Holofernes as swiftly as my much diminished strength allowed. The captain had proceeded toward the end of the column that those who had been last might now be first in going back. When he learned of David's weakness he cursed terribly, but reminded by me of the promise he had made my master, he followed me to the spot where David had fallen on the ground.

Standing over the boy, the Captain Holofernes ordered him harshly to get to his feet. But David replied:

"I cannot. Just leave me here to die and continue on your way, for if I do not die today I shall die tomorrow."

"You may die today or tomorrow," the captain said without mercy, "but while you are still alive you must not remain behind. Some Hebrew shepherd straying with his goats into these hills might discover you and make you reveal to him our strength and destination."

David looked up pleadingly at the captain and replied:

"Even if I were to survive—which I doubt, being faint unto death—I would never betray my comrades and my country!"

At this the captain said with a bitter laugh:

"Would you have me believe that one who whimpers after a few days of marching would withstand much greater pain? I have seen stronger men than you break under torture, neither would the Hebrews show you mercy! Up now, and do not put your father's name to shame before me!"

But David remained sitting on the ground, his head sunk between his shoulders. When the soldiers saw him defying the captain's order, first one sat down, and then another and another, until all those who were close enough to have heard the words exchanged between the captain and David sprawled on the ground, with their spears and shields lying in the dust beside them.

Seeing that the weakness of one boy might turn his whole troop to rebellion, the captain blanched and kicked David with his boot, while he sharply repeated his order. But the boy only shook his head.

"If you will not leave me behind, kill me then, for I cannot go on," David said, knowing the promise the captain had made his father.

The captain gnashed his teeth loudly enough to be heard in the stillness that had fallen over the men. Then he spoke softly and fiercely:

"I made your father, a man unfortunate enough to have sired a coward, a solemn promise. But I also swore before the king to protect the lives of the soldiers he entrusted to my command, and their lives are a thousand against one. Nor would I risk them for a weakling. But I will not have it said after me that I struck down a whimpering boy sitting at my feet in the dust. Therefore if you would have me kill you, stand up and defend yourself like a man!"

The blood fled from my face when the captain drew his sword, for I could see that he had spoken in earnest. I should have thrown myself at his feet to plead for mercy, but I feared that even if he did not strike me dead the other soldiers would tear me asunder. They all observed David and the captain with stony faces, waiting for the outcome of the contest. And still the boy did not move, neither would he raise his eyes to meet the captain's gaze.

"Up and defend yourself!" the Captain Holofernes repeated. And when David failed to respond, the captain shouted, nearly weeping with rage: "Get to your feet and fight, you Hebrew bastard!"

At that David raised his head, his face contorted with shame and rage. Pushing himself off the ground with his left hand, he drew with his right the precious sword that had been a gift from his stepfather. The Captain Holofernes stood motionless, his own sword held pointed before him. Now the boy raised his weapon as though to strike and stumbled forward, but his weariness was such that even before he reached the captain his arm was pulled down by the weight of his sword. Still he staggered on until he came to within striking distance of the captain. And when the Captain Holofernes remained motionless with his sword extended before him, David closed his eyes, pitched forward and impaled himself on the captain's sword.

And thus, by the unfathomable will of God, the first Babylonian soldier to die in this war on the soil of Judah was a Hebrew.

Seeing the blood gush from the boy's chest, I had emitted a piercing shriek and had fallen into a faint. But my merciful state of blackness was brief. When I opened my eyes the Captain Holofernes still stood in the same spot as before. Blood was dripping from his sword onto David's body, which now lay at his feet. None had as yet uttered a sound, while the captain glowered fiercely from soldier to soldier as if challenging them to rise and do battle with him. It would have been easy to slay him, for he was one against a thousand. But knowing that David was the son of the man who had saved the captain's life at Nineveh, the soldiers understood what the captain had done for them. As silently as they had sat down before they now rose to their feet, picked up their weapons and faced back whence they had come. Forming a column they began to march along the wadi, passing to the left and right of the captain, who still stood with his dripping sword over David's body as if he were turned to stone. But when Bania said loudly that the boy would make meager pickings for the vultures, the blood returned to the captain's face. Calling the troop to a halt, he said hoarsely:

"Though I had to slay Ziria he shall not be carrion for the vultures. Let us dig a grave and bury him with his sword under his head, as befits a soldier fallen in battle."

The soldiers gaped with amazement but did the captain's bidding. While he observed them with lifeless eyes, they carved out a grave in the hard, dry soil. But I lay weeping on the ground and did not raise my eyes until after they had placed David in the hole and had covered him with earth. Now he was become part of the hills that engulfed us on all sides like storm-tossed waves of white and yellow rock.

When the hole was filled, the captain had the men pile a mound of stones on it to mark the grave. Then, pushing his sword into the ground to cleanse it of blood, he gave the order to move on. I too rose to my feet and joined the moving column, for a man will cling to life though all those he loves die around him. But before the next bend of the wadi I turned around to throw one last glance at what was left of David: a small, white mound of rocks among the many large mounds of the wilderness of Judah.

By the time we had traced our course back to the entrance of the wadi darkness had fallen over the mountains, and the captain allowed his soldiers to pitch camp. They huddled together for warmth, the night being as cold as the day had been hot, and for shelter against the evil mountain spirits. Nor was their fear lessened when the moon rose in the sky, for the black patches and stripes in the valley looked even darker against the pale purple slopes which were bathed in moonlight.

But I, wishing to make a mourning for David, walked away from the soothsayer, whose wretchedness was but increased by what he had witnessed that day. I rent my clothes, sat on the ground and sprinkled dirt on my head, for the boy who lay buried in the harsh hills of his forefathers was the same I had rocked on my knee while I told him tales about the happy land of Dilmun where the lion did not kill, the wolf did not tear the sheep, and there was neither sickness nor old age nor death.

I do not know how long I sat there rocking back and forth when I heard the approach of unsteady footsteps. Fearing that the soothsayer had come to plague me with his lamentations I opened my mouth in anger when I recognized the Captain Hollofernes. He stood swaying as though tossed back and forth in the night breeze, but then the wind carried to me a whiff of wine. Where he had obtained enough to drink himself drunk I did not know, but he might still have had a jug concealed on one of the pack asses.

"What are you doing alone in the dark, Mardukshasusur?" he asked in a thick voice. "Are you perchance thinking of deserting?"

"And where would I go alone in this wilderness?" I replied. "I only sought solitude to bemourn the son of my heart who found such a cruel and untimely death. Nor do I know how I shall bring back this evil news to my master."

"You shall tell Nabukasir that his son fell in battle," the captain said. "But if you dare reveal what happened today, I shall rip out your lying tongue with my own hands."

"I would surely not increase my lord's sorrow by telling him that the man who slew his son was the same who promised to bring David back alive," I said.

"Only because there are no witnesses to your speech will you go unpunished," the captain said. "It is true that Nabukasir charged me by our friendship to bring his son back alive. But I also swore to guard the lives of my soldiers, and an oath to the king ranks above one to a friend. Nor will I pretend that Ziria stumbled upon my sword, for I could have stepped aside that he might fall on the ground. But I did not kill the boy lightly. It is a small matter to slay one you hate. To kill one you love for the safety of others takes great courage. And if I fulfilled my duty to my king, the Hebrew god should be equally pleased with my deed, for it is known that he requires human sacrifice."

Then I screamed as I had nine years ago, when the Captain Holofernes first proclaimed this terrible lie:

"It is the Canaanites who commit this abomination, not the Hebrews!"

"I do not see that they are lesser savages than the others," the captain said in sullen drunkenness. "Did they not celebrate the New Year when the earth lay dead and fallow, until we taught them to count the months from the time nature returns to life? But then this land is barren in the best of times. Why a nation of madmen should force us to fight them for it not even their bloody god knows!"

Raising my hands in supplication, I exclaimed:

"Let my lord not curse the Hebrew god in his own mountains, or we may never escape alive from this wilderness!"

"Have no fear, Marduksharusur," the captain replied. "Your fate and mine are in the hands of Ishtar. As for this Hebrew god, the taste of the blood I spilled in his hills is still sweet in his mouth and he shall not require our lives of us."

Indeed the following day our wanderings in the wilderness came to an end. At dawn we discovered a track that led south and later turned west, rising toward the ridge of the mountains, from where the slopes dropped down into the western lowlands. Before we gained the summit, the captain called his troop to a halt and selected three men whom he trusted to spy out the land on the other side of the mountains.

The three spies did not return until sunset, when many of their comrades thought they had been induced by their good sense to desert. They were weary from much climbing but their eyes shone, for they brought back good news: looking down from the ridge they had spied a village in the distance, where the wilderness changed into rolling hills surrounded by flat farmland. The village, though small, sat atop a steep hill and was surrounded by a wall. Hearing this, the Captain Holofernes was greatly astonished, for he knew of no fortified towns in this region. He bade me inquire about this village of Prince Hanun, who being a neighbor of the Hebrews would surely know about it.

However, the Ammonite prince refused to answer my questions, saying:

"Though I will not speak Babylonian, I can well understand the speech of the soldiers around me. I know that the boy slain by the Captain Holofernes was the son of his best friend. How much would my own life be worth in the hands of this man? Why should I aid him if surely he will slay me too when he no longer has need of me?"

I reasoned with the prince, telling him that the captain had not killed David for sport, nor was he a man wholly without honor. Rather he ranked an oath to a king above an oath to a friend—and had he not promised the king of Ammon to return his son? Therefore if Prince Hanun wished to see his father again and follow him on the throne, he had better tell the captain what he would know. And so deeply do people believe that their own lives will be spared even if all those about them are slain that in the end Prince Hanun answered my request.

"The name of the village your spies saw is Bethul," he said. "It is inhabited by Hebrews of the tribe of Simeon, whose ancestors lived in the cities of the Negev before they moved north to dwell among the tribe of Judah. Their numbers are small, but they are known to be mighty men of war who will defy even their own kings. Nor do they welcome strangers but prefer to keep to themselves. As for the wall about the village, I believe it to have been erected long ago by the Hebrew king Rehoboam, who sought to fortify the mountains east of the lowlands."

"And does my lord think this wall strongly manned?" I asked, knowing that the captain would wish to learn this above all else.

"I doubt that there are in Bethul more than a hundred men who draw the sword," Prince Hanun replied. "But even if they would not defend Bethul out of pride they will surely defend the village because of their women, whose repute of beauty is such that we have heard of it even in Rabbath-Ammon!"

The Captain Holofernes was well pleased with my report.

"These villagers will never dare defy us with a hundred men," he said. "But should they choose to fight, the thought of their beautiful women will spur my own soldiers to great deeds. As for me, I should sooner see the men of Bethul display good sense and not engage us in battle, for I would save our strength for the Egyptians. And now let us proceed swiftly that we may reach the lowlands at nightfall. There we shall subtly pitch all our tents so that upon awakening the people of Bethul will think themselves surrounded by half the host of Babylon!"

THIRTEEN

Who is she that looketh forth as the dawn,
Fair as the moon,
Clear as the sun,
Terrible as an army with banners?

—THE SONG OF SONGS 6:10

I T is here that Isaac's story and mine become one (the old woman Tamar said to the young scribe). For it was in the month of Kislev, at the time of the increasing moon, that the people of Bethul awoke one morning to loud shouts from the watchtower. And when all hastened into the street in their nightclothes, the watchman called down from the tower that they were surrounded by the Babylonian army.

At first none believed his words, and he was accused of having spent the night drinking with his companions upon the wall. How could the Babylonian army have surrounded Bethul when the night before there had been no sign of them? But the watchman implored the people to climb the tower that they might see the proof of his truthfulness.

The only woman to join the elders was Judith, nor did any question her right, for there were few among them who were not indebted to her in some manner. But since it was unseemly that she be alone with all these men I went with her, lest the other women accuse her of brazenness.

Though the sun was still hidden behind the Mountains of Moab as we approached the tower, the sky was brightening. Soon the chill of early morning would be followed by another day too warm for the season. The sky was cloudless, nor had there been any more rain since the month of Tishri. While before the elders had sneered at Judith's concern about the drought, they now gazed worriedly up at the unblemished sky. But none spoke until they had ascended the tower and peered down from behind the battlements. Then the elders broke into loud lamentations, for the tents pitched in the fields below made it appear as if half the host of Babylon had come against Bethul. After one of the men regained his composure, he said:

"Though this is a sight to strike terror into our hearts, matters may not be hopeless. Indeed I have little doubt that the Babylonians will spare our lives. Had they wished to take Bethul by force they would have done so at night, breaking down the gate and setting fire to our houses before any of our soldiers could be roused to battle. Therefore let us surrender while the Babylonians are still kindly inclined toward us! Surely none will hold it against us if we bow to such superior numbers."

Then Judith said:

"Would you throw open the gates of Bethul even before the enemy demanded our surrender? Think of what will befall the women if these savages enter our town!"

And she rubbed the scar on her neck until it turned a dark red.

"Whatever may happen to the women will not attain in terror to what would befall them if Bethul were seized by force," replied the elders, all men well gone into their years whose concern was for their lives rather than for the honor of their women.

But gazing down into the valley with narrowed eyes, Judith said scornfully:

"Had the Babylonians wished to seize Bethul by force, they would indeed have done so by surprise. But their numbers may be smaller than they seem, for the tents around Bethul are well spaced out. And though there are horses tied to the tents, there are few pack animals and no cattle, neither do I see any battering rams. Might not their absence mean that these troops are ill armed and short on food? Moreover, since most mountain springs have run dry, these soldiers must be in even greater need of water than we, who still have some left in our cisterns. Nor will the enemy discover our spring, for the entrance to the cave is well concealed and what little water seeps out is soon consumed by the dry soil. Therefore let us hold out a few days and see whether these men are not too weak to force a battle. Meanwhile let us send to Lachish for troops to help us drive the Babylonians back into the wilderness that they might all become carrion for the vultures!"

After Judith's speech, the elders looked down once more into the valley and saw all the things they had not seen before. And though they were loath to concede wisdom in a woman, they granted that Judith had spoken sensibly.

After the elders and Judith descended from the tower, each went his way to do what he thought best: pray to God for a miracle, caution the people against a siege, and call up the fighting men. Though the last was no task for a woman, it was the one Judith chose for herself. She bade the men burnish their swords, which had grown rusty from lack of use, string their bows, repair the plaiting of their shields and the scales of their armor, bring out their spears, slings and the heavy stones that could easily kill a man when hurled from the wall, each stone being the size of a pomegranate. And she commanded the women to split kindling for firewood that they might rain down flaming death on the attackers should they attempt to storm the wall.

"Let us hope that the Babylonians will not engage us in battle before we have summoned help from Lachish," Judith said as she went about fanning the courage of the men. "But should they decide to storm our walls, let them come up! We are upon the heights and can make them pay dearly for an assault."

So great was Judith's zeal that her eyes shone as they had not in many years, the color of her cheeks was heightened and her red hair became undone, spilling over her shoulders. If the hearts of the men were not strengthened by her brave words they were inflamed by her beauty, and they would have fought to prevent strangers from possessing what was denied them.

As for the women of Bethul, they did not relish the sight of their husbands rallying around Judith. In the end they dispatched her aunt Sarai that she might call her to restraint. And Sarai came with her hair disheveled and her hand upon her head to speak with Judith in her house.

"Why are you doing this thing, Judith?" she exclaimed among loud lamentations. "It is the task of the elders—all wise and sober men—to decide whether Bethul should fight or surrender peaceably. But then the spilled blood of our men means little to you, who have neither husband nor son. As for my own daughters, they have husbands to consider and also young children, who will be dashed to pieces if the Babylonians take Bethul by force. Therefore cease from inflaming the men before we are all killed because of your folly! Nor do I see why you wish to defend King Zedekiah's cause, having spoken of him with contempt on many occasions."

"I care little about King Zedekiah's cause," Judith replied. "But I care greatly about my country. And the fate of all Judah might be determined by whether we make a stand or surrender without a battle."

"Your speech is bold only because your womb is barren," Sarai said. "If you had children, your first concern would be for their lives."

Then Judith tossed her head in anger, bit her lips and said:

"Small wonder they say a woman's nation is encompassed by the four walls of her house! But you had better return to your home and see that your people deal frugally with food and water, for we might have to hold out a fortnight before relief arrives from Lachish."

Then Sarai smote her thigh in anger, and walking out she muttered that her mad brother's greatest folly had been to raise his daughter as if she were a son. Nor was her wrath diminished when her son-in-law Joab entered the house just as she was about to depart.

"No doubt you rejoice in our misfortune," she said to Joab, "for it has provided you with one more cause to visit Judith!"

She gained the street before Joab could reply, nor had he the mind that would furnish him with a swift answer.

Though on other occasions Judith displayed little joy upon seeing Joab, she said now:

"It is a good thing you are come. We must climb the tower together and see how our few fighting men might best be deployed if the enemy were to attack. Tamar too shall come along lest your wife suspect us of behaving indecently atop the tower. For knowing your wife, I know that her heart is more troubled by such thoughts than by the great danger surrounding us."

It was past noon when we climbed the watchtower for the second time that day. The Babylonians had not yet sent a messenger to demand our surrender, nor did they seem to prepare for an attack in the camp below. We could see the soldiers idling about, some sitting on the ground, some strolling, some polishing their weapons or grooming their horses, whose black and brown coats gleamed in the sun. Most of the men wore no helmets as though they were little concerned about being attacked, nor did they throw more than occasional glances up at Bethul.

"These savages pitched their tents in my fields and are trampling the ground my father cleared with his own hands," Judith said through clenched teeth. "Also I see a horse tied to the doorpost of my summer house and two sentries standing guard beside the entrance. No doubt their commander reposes even now upon my bed, roaring with mirth at the thought of how we shall come crawling to plead for his mercy. Ah, if I were a man I would go down alone to slay the monster with my own hands!"

Judith's cheeks, pale only a moment ago, grew flushed again as she stood rubbing the scar on her neck. But Joab, gazing at her the way men looked at Judith, said:

"It is a good thing you are not a man, Judith. Your brave words would be folly in the mouth of a man, for none can steal alone into the Babylonian camp. He would be slain by one of the many guards, or die a slow death if captured alive. No, if we would fight we must wait for the enemy to attack us! Our position atop the hill is our sole advantage over them, for they easily outnumber our fighting men a hundred to one."

"Do you truly believe there are ten times a thousand soldiers in the camp below?" Judith asked. "How could such a number have traversed the wilderness unseen and unheralded? But if there are indeed so many of them, they will perish even sooner of hunger and thirst. Though they might discover some grain in the pits by the threshing floor, and a few jugs of wine in the caves near the vineyards, it would not suffice them for long. I wish there were more wine in the caves, for it is new wine that makes men ill if they drink too much. If the Babylonians lay drunk in their tents, our men could easily fall upon them and slay all."

"Your father would be proud to hear your words," Joab said. "Indeed you are his equal in spirit, though he was not your equal in beauty."

"My father was handsome as a prince, nor shall I ever see such a man again," Judith replied. "But I must not fail him even in death, for he taught me how one serves one's country. Did he not return from Megiddo a cripple for life? If only I knew the plans of these

Babylonians! But wait, there is a man emerging from my summer house, followed by more men. And now they swing themselves upon their horses—"

"If this be an attack, the tower is no place for a woman!" Joab cried, seizing Judith from behind to pull her back. But she shook off his hands, saying:

"Do not speak folly, Joab. These ten men who are approaching the foot of the hill cannot attack us without their soldiers. Rather I think it is the Babylonian commander and his captains come to ask for our surrender. See, now they are joined by yet another man who does not appear a soldier, for he has neither helmet nor shield, nor does he ride upon a horse but upon a mule."

"Should not the watchman sound the alarm?" Joab asked.

"Not until I give the order," Judith replied. "The elders might lose heart when they see the Babylonians from nearby. But we shall listen to their words in silence."

When he saw the Babylonian warriors wend their way up the hill, the watchman turned pale and set the horn to his mouth. But he did not dare stir Judith's wrath, for he had borrowed grain from her for which he had not yet paid. Thus he remained silent, while Joab, who would not display fear before Judith, pulled an arrow from his quiver. But Judith bade him not waste arrows until they learned the demand of the Babylonians. Indeed the riders had halted out of the range of an arrow, but close enough that we could see them clearly. Though I had promised Merari in his dying moment that I would never take a husband, I had not been struck with blindness concerning men. Thus I exclaimed before I could curb my tongue:

"Ah, what splendid young men!"

But Judith turned on me in wrath, saying:

"Keep your harlot's thoughts to yourself! Are you no better than all the other women who lust for these Babylonians?"

And she angrily rubbed the scar on her neck with one hand, while with the other she shaded her eyes to see the better.

The warrior whose costly armor and helmet revealed him as the leader had turned to the rider of the mule and spoken to him. When that one dismounted we saw that he was short and fat, neither did he have a beard though he was no longer a youth.

"Would they send a eunuch to demand our surrender?" Joab asked, as the fat man drew closer to the wall. But Judith replied:

"It might be one of their scribes who knows our language."

Having approached as closely as he dared, the eunuch formed a funnel with his two hands and shouted up in Hebrew:

"Men of Bethul, hear me! Why have you barred your gates and fled inside your walls though we have come to you in peace? Surely if our troops wished to seize Bethul by force it would be a small matter to them, they being without number like the sand of the sea, while you have but a hundred fighting men! Therefore listen to the message of the Captain Holofernes, the commander of this huge army! If you will open your gates before nightfall and let the troops of the great King Nebuchadrezzar enter Bethul peaceably, not a hair shall be harmed on the heads of the inhabitants. Neither shall our soldiers lay claim to any cattle, wine or women without paying for them in good Babylonian silver. But if you will not open your gates to us, thus says the Captain Holofernes: we shall throw up earthworks around Bethul that none might come in or go out, neither will you be able to obtain water, for we know that the springs that nourish you are in the valley. But you shall soon perish of thirst, and those who survive shall be slain with the sword when we come up to take your town! As for the women, they shall be a spoil and sport to our soldiers! Therefore surrender peaceably while there is yet time!"

The man dropped his hands from his mouth, waiting for an answer, for he did not know that there was none upon the tower but our small group. But Judith said softly:

"Answer him not."

And Joab said just as softly:

"This man speaks Hebrew well, though in a strange manner. Might he be one who was carried away from Jerusalem nine years ago?"

"It is shameful to lend himself to this task if indeed he be a Hebrew," Judith said. "But then he is not a man. However, lest the Babylonians think that all our males resemble this slave, let us send them a message of our own. How far will your arrow fly, Joab?"

"Far though it may carry, I fear it would lose its strength to kill the dog," Joab replied.

"I do not seek his life," Judith said, "for of what value is the life of one like him? Rather I would send a reply to the great Captain Holofernes, who demands our surrender. Is there anything in the tower on which I might write?"

But there was not even a piece of potsherd, neither was there pen and ink. Then Judith bent down, ripped a piece off her undergarment, took Joab's arrow and bade the watchman pour wine from his flask over its tip. With it she wrote some words, the red letters on the white linen cloth looking as though they were traced in blood.

"What is this message you wrote?" Joab asked when Judith swiftly rolled up the strip of cloth.

"If I showed it you, could you read the words?" Judith replied, knowing that Joab had never mastered writing. "You must trust me in this matter as I shall trust you to shoot your arrow at the very feet of this slave!"

And tying the strip to the arrow, she handed it to Joab. He knelt down behind the battlement, bent his bow and sent the arrow flying toward its target. Since his arm was strong and his aim good, the arrow landed barely a pace from the eunuch. But that one, not having perceived what had happened until it was too late, stood swaying back and forth as if about to faint with terror.

While Judith smote her thigh with mirth, the Babylonian commander jumped off his horse, darted forward, seized the arrow and carried it back with him to a safe distance. From the tower we saw him unroll Judith's message, gaze at it and beckon the eunuch that he might read it for him. Having heard the message, the captain threw back his head, shaded his eyes with his hands and stood looking up at the wall a long time. Then he swung himself upon his horse and led the other men back to the camp.

But Judith would not reveal to us what she had written.

When I read the message shot at us from the walls of Bethul I did not trust my own eyes (the old man Isaac said to the young scribe). Moreover, I was still stunned by the terror of having barely escaped death, for the arrow had missed me by no more than a hair's breadth. Thus it required sharp words from the Captain Holofernes before I translated the message, which was written on a white strip of cloth in a red substance that looked like blood. And these were the words:

"Let him who puts on his armor not boast himself as he who takes it off. Your threats do not deceive us, nor are your numbers as great as you would have us believe. But while we still have much water and cattle in Bethul, you lack both. You shall yet eat your own dung and drink your own piss before we surrender!"

Hearing this message, the Captain Holofernes smiled grimly and said:

"There are braver men within Bethul than I thought. Indeed I would sooner fight them than break them by siege, for I never shirked a battle with bold warriors. But my men are weary from the long trek across the wilderness and weak from lack of food. Nor do we have the proper weapons for an assault, though even two battering rams should suffice to bring down these ancient walls. But since we cannot procure by wishing what we lack, we must break the enemy with what we possess. We cannot move on before seizing Bethul, for these people would soon alert all Judah to our presence. But if we take Bethul, slay all the fighting men and disarm the rest, a small garrison might prevent any from slipping out while the rest of us proceed."

The captain mounted his horse to lead his officers back to the camp, while I tarried to gaze once more up at the walls of Bethul. I remembered the shame I had felt nine years ago, when King Jehoiachin and his nobles had come forth from Jerusalem to prostrate themselves before Nebuchadrezzar. But now, looking up at these crumbling walls which a hundred Hebrews would defend against a host of seasoned warriors, I felt as if I were again growing whole in my parts. And though I might be killed if the men of Bethul succeeded, I wished them victory.

Then, with dread and hope mingling strangely in my heart, I mounted my mule and followed my Babylonian masters back to their camp.

The Captain Holofernes had seized as his quarters the hut that was discovered in the morning among the Babylonian tents. The bolted door was easily forced, never having been meant to withstand the powerful thrust of a soldier's shoulder. If the captain had hoped to find food in the hut, he was disappointed. The pots and jars that were stacked beside the open hearth in the kitchen were empty. There was neither grain nor wine nor even a drop of oil in any of them. Again the captain proclaimed that he could not fathom why the Hebrews would shed their blood for this land, where they could ill afford to waste even a morsel of food.

No Babylonian would have taken the hut for the home of a wealthy person. There was a bed covered by a worn throw in one

of the small rooms, a mat on the floor in the other, and in the third
some tools to work the fields and an old harness, as if the people
who lived in the house had once owned a horse.

"Even if this wretched shack lacks other comforts, at least there is
a bed on which to repose after all these weeks in the field," the
captain said.

And he stretched out on the bed with his arms beneath his head as
a pillow. Thus he remained until noon, waiting for an offer of
surrender from Bethul. But when the sun passed through its highest
point and no messenger came, the captain summoned his officers for
a council.

"The people of Bethul may fear that we would slay any who
comes forth," he said. "Therefore let us go up to them and reveal
our peaceful intentions. Little would be gained by waiting yet
another hour when we could be entering the town to fill our
stomachs and have our soldiers enjoy the company of women,
which they have lacked for so long."

I did not relish the thought of approaching still another wall as
interpreter, but remembering the two previous occasions on which I
had returned unharmed from that errand, I took heart. Thus my
fright was even greater when I found myself the target of an arrow
shot from the wall.

If after our return to the camp my own heart was divided, the
captain's mood was all grim. He bade his officers put their men to
digging a deep moat and throwing up earthworks around Bethul,
while he himself went in search of the spring. Though we might
find some game and birds in the woods and even slaughter the horses
if need be, our water was all but gone.

The men looked grim when they learned that this was not to be
an easy conquest but a siege, nor did they rejoice at the thought of
digging a moat in their weakened state. So as not to arouse their ire
by my idleness I retreated into the hut, which the captain had left
unlocked. Soon I was joined there by the soothsayer, whose dignity
and exalted station forbade him to engage in the digging of ditches.
Removing the golden disk that covered his empty eye socket, he
sank down beside me on the rug by the hearth. While he used the
hem of his garments to polish the precious stones that formed the
eight-pointed star of Ishtar, he sighed and spoke mournfully:

"Even you, Marduksharusur, can no longer scoff at my predictions. There is little doubt that we shall all perish here, as the omens foretold."

"Did not the omens predict that the Goddess Ishtar would descend from on high to lead us to our fate?" I asked spitefully, though in my heart I too was certain of our doom.

"The meanings of omens are mysterious and may be read in more ways than one," the soothsayer replied. "If our minds became clouded by thirst, might we not have visions of Ishtar before we perish?"

Since I had heard tales of how a man might go mad when his water gave out, I could not sneer at the soothsayer's words. Indeed it mattered little to me what I should see before I died of thirst. Nor was it unlikely that I would meet this gruesome end.

Though the Captain Holofernes and his men had searched the woods and the brush at the foot of the hill, they had failed to discover a spring or even a well. All they had found were a few bushels of grain in a pit, and some jugs of wine concealed in a cave near the vineyards. Tasting the wine, the captain said surly:

"Why some people value this Judean wine I do not know, for unlike our own sweet date wine it is tart and burns the palate. However, there may be enough for each soldier to make him forget his thirst until we discover the spring. Nor do I doubt that there is such a spring. The people of Bethul cannot have much water left in their cisterns, the land having suffered a drought. Therefore let us watch for any who might sneak out after dark to draw water. But beware of killing him before he has led us to the spring!"

The captain ordered the number of sentries increased fourfold for the night. But no Hebrew approaching the spring was discovered, though two soldiers heard a rustling in the brush. When the creature did not answer their challenge but fled they gave chase, one of them releasing his arrow at the form he saw moving in the dark. But when they approached the fallen prey they found that they had killed a deer. Though this meant fresh game for the officers, the Captain Holofernes was filled with wrath.

"Fools, did I not give orders to refrain from shooting?" he roared. "Even this deer might have led us to the spring if it had come in search of water!"

But for the grim mood of the soldiers, the captain would have had the two offenders flogged. Thus he only sent them back to throwing up earthworks, for the men had not completed the task on the previous day, being used to the aid of slaves in this labor.

When the deer was skinned and dressed, the officers begged the Captain Holofernes to have the soothsayer read the omens from the beast's liver. Though the scoundrel's mien betrayed what misfortune he saw there, he did not dare reveal it to the captain. Rather he predicted that in a few days the people of Bethul would surrender of their own accord. Nor were these words folly, for in a few days the villagers too would have no water left. But by then we would all have perished of thirst. However, when the soothsayer asked that a portion of the deer be offered in sacrifice to Enlil, who gave rain, the captain Holofernes seized him by the throat and said in a fury:

"Would you make us waste good meat to pray for what would bring more comfort to the enemy than to us? Better let us all perish of thirst than be forced to besiege this wretched village for months and become the laughingstock of all Babylon! Our task was to trouble the Egyptian army, nor shall we fail after we have come so far. As for this wretched spring—may Ishtar strike me dead if I rest until I have discovered it!"

Before we descended the tower, Judith commanded the watchman not to open his mouth to anyone (the old woman Tamar said to the young scribe).

"Let the elders not hear of the offer," Judith said. "Their courage is no stronger than the shell of an egg and might easily be crushed. Once we are assured of help they may learn the truth. But first we must find someone to carry the news of the siege to Lachish."

Joab at once offered himself for that perilous task, but Judith replied:

"You have a wife and five daughters to consider, nor are you as young and fleet of foot as in former times. This task calls for a youth of supple body and lithe tread that he may slip unobserved through the Babylonian lines."

"And what would keep such a youth from tarrying in Lachish to save his life rather than bring back their answer to Bethul?" Joab asked with hurt pride.

"I have heard it said that a man would abandon his parents, his wife and his children, but would gladly risk his life for the woman he desires," Judith answered. "Therefore we shall make certain that the one we choose loves a maiden in Bethul. Tamar shall inquire about this of her mother, for though Dinah has forsworn sorcery, those in love still come to her for potions. Surely she can help us find such a youth. As for me, I must go and bid the women set some water aside for their cattle. As long as the cows stay alive we shall at least have milk for the children."

While Judith set out on this errand, I returned to our house in Bethul. There I found that my mother had put the men to building a fence around our cistern, which was to be covered with a wooden plank. When I asked if the cover would not prevent the rain from filling the basin, my mother glanced up at the sky and said:

"Where is this rain you speak of? There has not been a cloud in sight for days, and those which appeared before were scattered by the wind. Though it rained over other towns it did not rain over Bethul. I would sacrifice to the goddess that she may not punish us with thirst for withholding her libations. But since our mistress trusts in Yahweh alone, we must guard against the day when neighbor will slay neighbor for a mouthful of water."

Then I replied that Judith also trusted in help from Lachish, and I asked my mother for the name of a youth who might be sent there with a message.

"Let Ira the son of Othoniel go to Lachish," my mother said. "The maiden he loves was promised to another man, for Ira cannot raise the bridal price. But if he performed this perilous task her father might give him his daughter as reward, though most fathers prefer silver to great deeds."

Dispatching me to fetch Ira, my mother bade me not reveal to him why he was summoned. When the youth returned with me to the house, he exclaimed:

"Have you got the potion to gain me my heart's desire, Dinah?"

But Judith, having come home, overheard his words in the next room and called out scornfully:

"Dinah's sorceries shall serve you for nought, Ira. But if you would perform a great deed for Yahweh, your wish might yet be granted."

And she told Ira what she would have him do. To gain his love the youth was willing to risk his life, but he wondered how he might leave the besieged town. Surely the danger of attack was too great to open the gates for even a moment.

"Any man would know of another way to get beyond the wall,"
Judith replied, looking Ira straight in the eyes.

The youth turned crimson, for he understood that she meant the
window in the harlots' quarters, nor had he thought that Judith
knew of such matters.

"Take care, walk lightly, and make haste to return with good
news from Lachish," Judith said. "Now go and may Yahweh
protect you!"

Just before darkness fell Judith once more ascended the tower.
She returned with the news that the Babylonians were digging
trenches and throwing up earthworks to prevent us from summoning help.

"But they labor slowly, nor will they complete the task before Ira
returns," Judith said. "No doubt they are parched by thirst and so
are their horses, which stand about with their heads drooping. I am
certain that they have not yet discovered our spring. But when the
troops from Lachish come to our aid, the Babylonians will fall
before us as ripe barley falls before the reaper's sickle!"

That night we sat up praying and listening into the dark for the
scream of one deadly wounded or one being tortured. If Ira was
captured the enemy would wish to learn from him the strength of
our defenses and the location of our spring. But we heard nothing
all night.

The following night, long after the middle watch, Ira returned
from Lachish. The youth staggered into Judith's house, his legs and
arms covered with bleeding scratches. He had crept on his belly
uphill through the brambles and had been hoisted by a rope through
the window of the harlots' quarters. But when we exclaimed in
horror at his bloody appearance, he only shook his head and said in a
weak voice:

"If this were the worst that befell me it would matter little. Last
night when I left Bethul some Babylonian sentries heard me creeping through the brush. But when they began to hunt about I lay low
until a deer lured them off my track. Nor did I go unobserved upon
my return. I am certain that I was followed halfway up the hill in
the dark. Why the Babylonians refrained from killing me I cannot
fathom, unless they wished me to bring you the message that we
shall all soon perish together, either of thirst or by the enemy's

sword. There are to be no troops from Lachish! Not only did they refuse me help, but they mocked me when I told them that we were surrounded by half the Babylonian army. 'It is known that the Babylonian army has not yet left Damascus,' they said. 'Only yesterday our commander of the host, Coniah the son of Elnathan, passed through Lachish on his way to request help from Pharaoh Hophra. Meanwhile Jeremiah is sending us pleas to surrender if the Babylonians come against Lachish. But our soldiers are loyal to King Zedekiah, nor can we spare any to help you drive away a band of Moabite raiders who might appear to you like half the host of Babylon! Any sober person knows that the eastern mountains cannot be crossed by troops. Therefore return to Bethul and tell your townsfolk to abstain from wine that they might not have visions of great armies coming forth from the wilderness!' And they drove me from their presence in scorn. Many another in my place would not have returned to Bethul. But rather than save my life I would die in the arms of my love, whom her father will not deny me now that it matters little whether her bridegroom be rich or poor."

Promising that she would speak to the maiden's father, Judith bade the youth spend the night in our house. But when Ira's eyes had closed with weariness, she whispered to me:

"Even in the face of death men think of nothing but whoredom." And she rubbed the scar on her neck. "But we must turn our minds to weightier matters. Now that we know that there will be no troops from Lachish, we must be still more frugal with our water. Soon the Babylonians will be so weakened by thirst that even a hundred men might beat them if they fell upon them by night. But should the rains come, we can prevail until our foe have eaten all their horses. Then they will depart or perish of hunger, sparing us the need to do battle with them. Either way we must remain victorious, for having defied them we would all be slain if they won."

On the third day of the siege Judith's face was ashen when she returned from the watchtower. Shutting the door behind her that none might overhear her words, she said:

"This morning I went to observe the clouds above and the enemy below. There was no change in either, the clouds still gathering in the distant west and the Babylonians still encamped in the valley below. But as I stood scanning the trench and earthworks that now encircle our hill, I saw a thing that made my blood run cold. Not having been watered since the enemy sealed us within our walls, the shrubs and trees which we moved to conceal the path to the spring have begun withering. Soon they will shed their leaves to form a brown line that will point the way to the spring. Therefore let us pray that the clouds I saw in the west will move east and burst over Bethul!"

My mother glanced at Judith, opening her mouth without daring to speak her thoughts. But after Judith had gone up to her room to fast and pray, my mother muttered:

"Judith has fasted many days since her husband died, but all she accomplished was to grow thin. The gods do not reward us for what we deny ourselves but only for what we offer them. But Judith will not see this until she has led us all to destruction."

On the second day of the siege, the Captain Holofernes made another fruitless search for the spring (the old man Isaac said to the young scribe). By then what little wine had been found in the caves was gone, and the water for the horses had long been consumed. Here and there one of the beasts tottered and fell to the ground, but the men quickly dragged it out of sight that it might not be observed from the tower of Bethul.

By nightfall the soldiers were quiet and sullen, sitting on the ground with their heads sunk between their shoulders. They did not discuss women, as they were wont to do, nor did they roll dice. I felt as feeble as the rest but was more fortunate, being allowed to share the captain's hut. He had put Prince Hanun in one of the rooms and would have me at hand when he wished to speak with him, the prince refusing to reply in Babylonian. But that night the captain had no desire to converse with his prisoner. When the full moon of Kislev rose high enough to shed its blue light over the besieged hill, the captain set out once more in search of the spring, still hoping to be led there by some thirsty beast. Thus I was left alone in the hut with Prince Hanun.

When we pitched camp at Bethul the young man was put in fetters but was allowed to roam about freely, for with his clinking chains he could not steal away unobserved. While the Captain Holofernes was out hunting for the spring, Prince Hanun came into the kitchen of the hut, where I sat dejectedly beside the cold hearth, and said:

"The wrath of the gods fell swiftly upon these treacherous Babylonians. They shall all perish of thirst here!"

"My lord should not find this a pleasing prospect," I replied. "If the Babylonians perish of thirst, so will he."

Prince Hanun glanced over his shoulder toward the door, and finding that it had been left unguarded since I was thought guard enough for a shackled man, he crouched down beside me and whispered:

"You and I need not perish with the rest. If you were to strike off my chains, we might slip away while the captain is out hunting for the spring. Without my chains the men will not recognize me in the dark but take me for one of the soldiers. I know a short way through the hills that will lead us back to Ammon. Surely my father would reward you richly for saving the life of his first-born!"

Let me confess that this prospect did not fail to tempt me in the face of a wretched death. I might have given in had not the chance of success appeared dim to me.

"Even if there were such a path as my lord says, how are we to make our way back to Ammon without water?" I asked.

"There are some villages along the way," Prince Hanun replied. "Though they might not open their gates to an army, they would not fear to let two solitary strangers draw a drink from their wells. Indeed they might help us even more if we revealed to them the presence of a thousand weary Babylonians, who might easily be overcome."

"First my lord spoke to me of flight," I said. "But what he proposes now is treason. If I committed such an act I would never dare return to Babylon, where I still own much silver."

"Does your greed exceed your love of freedom?" Prince Hanun asked with contempt. And when I made no answer, he continued: "Though you wear your hair long and there is no slave mark on you, I learned from the soldiers that you are an Assyrian slave whom Nebuchadrezzar raised to the rank of royal interpreter. As for your fortune, it will someday be your master's inheritance. But if you lived in Ammon as a free man, you might leave your silver to the heir of your choice."

Then I remembered that the heir of my choice lay buried in the wilderness of Judah, and I lowered my head and wept for all those I had loved and lost to violence. Remembering my father and my sister Abigail, I thought of what Bania had done to them and of the

oath I had sworn. Perhaps I might find the courage to kill Bania
with my last strength when he had become weak of thirst. Thus I
answered the prince:

"Even if my lord offered me freedom and my own weight in
silver—which was great before I went on this wretched campaign—
I could not accept his offer. I swore a solemn oath before my god
concerning a certain matter, and such an oath must not be broken."

"What matter could be of greater importance than one's freedom?" Prince Hanun asked bitterly, rattling the chains that made
him too a slave.

But I would not reveal to him the nature of my oath, nor could
we exchange further words, for the Captain Holofernes returned
from his errand. He entered the hut without greetings and began to
pace back and forth, halting now and then to peer into one of the
empty jugs, as if he thought it might miraculously have filled with
water. But though his lips were cracked and his eyes feverish, his
strength prevailed. After more pacing he dispatched a sentry to
summon his officers to the hut. When all were assembled, the
captain said:

"Unless we discover the spring before dawn, we shall attack
Bethul at daybreak. If we would take the town by force, it must be
done while our soldiers still have the strength to storm the walls!"

Between the middle and the morning watch a soldier entered the
hut to report that he had heard rustling in the brush and had followed the sound up the hill to Bethul. But since the Captain Holofernes had repeated his order not to shoot at anything moving in the
dark, the soldier had not dared bring down his quarry. Thus it was
not known to him whether it had been a man or a beast.

Except for that soldier none heard any suspicious movements, nor
was the all-night search for water fruitful. When the first sign of
dawn edged into the eastern sky, the Captain Holofernes had all his
soldiers roused. This was done in deep silence so as not to alarm the
watchers on the walls of Bethul, nor would the captain let his men
mount their horses.

"Horses serve only in open combat," he said. "The storming of a
defensed city must be done by brave men. Since we have no battering rams we shall have to use sappers to tunnel under the wall, and
many will not live to see the sunset. But those who fight valiantly

and survive will have their fill of food and drink before the day is over, and also the spoils and the women of Bethul to share. At any rate it is better to fall in battle than to perish of thirst while the enemy mocks us from the wall!"

The captain's message greatly cheered the soldiers. Though they did not desire to die, if this was to be their fate they would rather die fighting. Moreover, many believed that no harm could come to them in a charge led by the Captain Holofernes, whom all knew to be invulnerable.

But the captain returned to the hut as grim as before, saying to me as he strapped on his armor:

"I would still prefer to seize this wretched village without a battle. If half my men are killed or maimed, the rest will be but a gnat in the hide of the Egyptian army. As for Neriglissar, he will delight in spreading the tale of how I bravely conquered a village defended by a hundred Hebrews."

When the captain stepped out of the hut in full armor, the sky had turned a milky white above the hills of Judah. Though there was a slight breeze, the air was as dry as if it had not rained in the land since the beginning of time. The grass and flowers in the fields had long turned brown, but the shrubs and trees on the hillside were still green.

"If only we could suck water from the deep soil like these trees!" the Captain Holofernes exclaimed. "In another week we might take Bethul without spilling one drop of our blood."

He shaded his eyes to gaze up at the hill on which many of his soldiers would die this very day, trying to take in every rise and gully. Suddenly his expression changed and he drew a deep breath as though in surprise. However much I strained my eyes looking in the same direction, I could perceive nothing. But the captain turned to the officers beside him and said:

"Is it not strange that yesterday all the trees on the hillside were green, but overnight some were seized by a blight that leapt from tree to tree, forming an unbroken line down the hill? I, who was raised among peasants, know that trees are not wont to wither in such an orderly fashion. Why would only some turn brown, and why should they trace a curving line down the slope such as might be formed by a path? Ah, but I shall soon discover the cause of this mystery! Until I return let no man make a move!"

The captain flung himself upon his horse and galloped off toward where the brown line dipped from the hill into the valley.

Long before those near the hut could see him, his return was heralded by loud cheers from the soldiers. When he finally came in sight we knew what had caused the joyful noise from the troops. The captain's hair and beard were dripping wet as if he had doused himself, and under his arm he carried his helmet filled with water. Pouring out the water on the ground as a libation, the captain threw back his head, opened his mouth in laughter and shouted:

"Ishtar be praised, I found the spring! Let the men unbuckle their armor and return to their tents, for we shall not lose a single soldier now. If the drought persists but a few days longer, these stubborn Hebrews behind the walls of Bethul will fall into our hands as ripe dates drop into the open mouth of one who lies snoring beneath a palm tree!"

On the fourth day of the siege the people of Bethul thought themselves vanquished (the old woman Tamar said to the young scribe). For on that day the Babylonians discovered our spring.

We first learned the bitter news from the watchman on the tower, who shouted down to us that the Babylonians were hauling buckets full of water into their camp. Soon we could hear their gleeful shouting and singing as they bathed themselves and watered their horses. None could fathom how the enemy had discovered our spring, for in looking down the hill the brown line of withered trees could not be plainly seen. But when the elders proclaimed that the discovery of the spring was a sign from God that He favored the Babylonians over us, Judith replied with scorn:

"Are you prophets to interpret signs from God? Perhaps God does not favor our foe but only wants to lull them into carelessness. Having found the spring, they will post fewer sentries tonight. If our fighting men were to steal down under cover of darkness, slit the throats of the sentries and fall upon the sleeping soldiers in their tents, they might inflict great losses upon them before fleeing back within our walls!"

"And all this you would accomplish with a hundred warriors, while our enemies number in the thousands?" the elders asked in dismay.

"Did King Josiah consider the number of his soldiers when he went up against the Egyptians at Megiddo?" Judith replied.

"And was not Josiah slain for his folly?" the elders said. "And has Judah known anything but misery since his death? No, we must surrender to the Babylonians while there is still time, for nothing can save us now!"

"Surely God can save us," Judith said. "There is still some water in our cisterns, and the month of Kislev is almost past. Any day now the rains must commence. At least let us wait until our water gives out before we surrender!"

Loath to see a woman display greater faith than they, the elders replied:

"Let us wait another week then. If God has sent us no rain by next Sabbath, we shall throw open our gates to the Babylonians and trust in their mercy."

"It is arrogance to challenge God's mercy," Judith muttered. "But it is better than surrendering, for much can happen in one week."

One day passed, and a second, a third and a fourth, and still it did not rain. To save the water for the children and cattle, people took to drinking wine, and even those who remained sober were in a drunken fever from the waiting and worry. Some proclaimed that, unlike the cruel Assyrians of yore, the Babylonians were known to be merciful, while others said that all conquerors were alike. The Babylonians too would kill the men, slay the children and ravish the women, and therefore they must make the most of the brief time left them. Then they would drink themselves drunk, and when darkness fell there was much scurrying back and forth between houses. Husbands lay with their neighbors' wives, and many a maiden resolved not to save for the enemy what she would sooner surrender to the youth of her choice.

Knowing this, Judith ranted as she paced back and forth on the roof of her house.

"Instead of purifying themselves that they might merit the mercy of God, the people commit even more whoredom than before! Small wonder that Yahweh withholds His rain when the inhabitants of Bethul are more rotten yet than those heathens who sing their lewd songs in the valley below!"

And Judith rubbed her scar until it was a deep red.

Every night we could hear the Babylonians singing, and though we did not understand the words, the raucous tone betrayed them as

soldiers' songs. But after the camp had fallen silent and the red glow
of the fires vanished from the sky, there were always a few left who
sang the sad songs of soldiers far away from home, who long for
their mothers and wives.

But Judith would cover her ears to shut out the voices of these
men, while she fervently prayed for a sign or miracle from Yahweh.

After the spring was discovered on the fourth day of the siege
(the old man Isaac said to the young scribe), the Captain Holofernes was certain that Bethul would surrender before sunset. He
ordered his soldiers to fill every empty vessel, flask and jug, and to
haul the water into camp that the besieged might know their secret
uncovered.

I too went with the soldiers—not to haul water but to slake my
thirst, wash my face and see for myself how this spring had been
hidden that none had found it sooner. Whoever had concealed it
had done so artfully. The entrance to the cave where the water
bubbled from the rocks was overgrown with thick brambles that
had not yet shed their leaves, for the bushes were nourished by the
moisture seeping from the cave. But following the brown line of
withered trees, the Captain Holofernes had arrived at the proper
spot, and hacking away the brambles with his sword, had discovered
the cave.

Though the cave was of some depth it was barely higher than a
man, its damp walls overgrown with moss and lichen. The flow of
water was much diminished by the drought. What little trickled
forth collected in a basin in the rock, the overflow vanishing into
the dry soil. Thus it took some time before the soldiers filled all
their vessels.

While they were engaged upon this task the Captain Holofernes
stripped off his armor and garments to wash his body, for he was
filthy and stank like the rest of us. He sang lustily as he poured
water over his head and his hairy chest, scrubbing his back and
armpits with a brush such as was used for grooming the horses.
When he removed his loincloth to wash his buttocks, his belly and
his thighs, I turned pale with envy, for he had much of what any
man would desire. Even his soldiers observed him with awe, one
winking at the other, for by such things are men impressed. Having
completed his ablutions, the captain shook the water from his hair

and beard, raised the amulet he wore on a chain about his neck to his
lips, kissed it and exclaimed:

"For this, lady, I shall make sacrifice to you when I return to
Babylon, even though you are neither less fickle nor less faithless
than other women, on whom all gifts are wasted!"

At these words the soldiers blanched in terror of Ishtar's wrath.
But when no bolt of lightning struck from the blue sky, they
grinned at each other in relief. Only the soothsayer, who knelt
beside me washing himself, moaned with despair:

"This madman will not cease from provoking the gods until death
seals his blasphemous lips."

As for the Captain Holofernes, he gave little thought to death
now that the spring was discovered. When all the water was hauled
back to camp and a great display had been made of washing the
horses, he ordered a few of the beasts slaughtered. He would have
his men eat and drink well that they might enter Bethul in a dignified manner without betraying their former plight.

But the sun moved west toward the Great Sea, and yet none came
forth from Bethul to surrender.

"If these people would goad us into attacking them while they
still have their strength, they will find my patience without limits. If
they will not come forth today, they will come forth tomorrow or
the day after. There is only one thing that could force us to attack
Bethul," the captain said, glancing up at the sky. "But even their
own god is against these people, for there is not a rain cloud in sight.
While the drought endures, we can wait."

But five days passed without rain and still Bethul did not surrender. The soldiers, whose hearts had been eased after the spring
was discovered, turned grim again. Soon the cause of their changed
mood became known to the Captain Holofernes. There was a rumor
among the men that the people of Bethul had a secret source of
water that would nourish them while they kept themselves free of
sin in the eyes of their god. In the meantime the Babylonians would
consume all their horses and perish of hunger in the end.

Hearing this the captain swore horribly, for he did not believe in
miracles, nor did he believe that there was a well atop the hill. He
set out at once to learn the source of this rumor that he might
punish the guilty one and discredit his words before the men. It was

soon discovered that the tale came first from the mouth of Prince Hanun, who was allowed to mingle freely with the soldiers.

"I would have acted more wisely in putting a gag in his mouth rather than fetters on his wrists," the Captain Holofernes raged. "As for miracles, this wretched Ammonite had better reveal to me how he recovered his memory of the Babylonian tongue!"

Thus, when Prince Hanun would reply to his questions only through me, the Captain Holofernes struck him across the face, shouting:

"Do not play games with me as you would play with your underlings, neither forget that your life is in my hands! And now confess what you told my soldiers to weaken their hands!"

The blow sent the young man staggering backward and left a dark red mark on his cheek. But Prince Hanun did not cry out, and though he trembled he gazed defiantly at the captain. Then he replied in Babylonian:

"Why should I fear to tell the truth? While they do not break the commandments of their god, the Hebrews think themselves invincible. They tell tales of their god parting the sea for them to pass through, of his causing water to gush forth from the dry rock to slake their thirst, and of food and fowl raining from heaven to quench their hunger. Moreover, they claim that some of their heroes each killed his hundred, or two hundred or even three hundred singlehanded—not that I believe all the lies told by these Hebrews. As for the men of Bethul, they are the fiercest among the fierce, being the last remnant of the tribe of Simeon. They would have one believe that two of their ancestors with a handful of servants slew all the males of Shechem because the prince of that city had ravished their sister when she went to visit the daughters of the land. This they did even though the prince would marry the maiden and pay for her any price they desired. If men did that much to avenge the honor of one maiden, how much more would the men of Bethul do for all their womenfolk?"

"Such tall tales might find belief in the ears of my simple soldiers but not in mine," the Captain Holofernes replied. "If a few men slew all the males of Shechem they must have used a ruse to take them unawares. Nor do I think that they acted wisely, for instead of gaining a powerful ally they retrieved a defiled virgin. As for that virgin—why did she go about the land unescorted if she had two brothers and all their women to watch over her? No doubt she went to meet the young man, only to be snatched by her brothers from the fate she so much desired! More than one such love was broken up with much bloodshed by the kinsfolk of the young people. Or else the brothers used their comely sister to entice the prince of Shechem and conquer his city. But you, Prince Hanun, shall not go unpunished for spreading such tales among my soldiers! However, since I gave my word to spare your life, I shall not bring your blood on my head. Rather I shall deliver you into the hands of the people of Bethul that you might share their fate. If, by spreading tales of our great strength among them, you can make them surrender before the week is over, your life will be spared. But if we have to take Bethul by force, you will be slain with the rest of the males. However, since you consider them invincible, you have nothing to fear!"

"You only pretend to spare my life, knowing well that these Hebrews will kill me if I ascend their hill. You are dishonorable in word and deed!" Prince Hanun said, spitting at the captain's feet.

"Do not think to provoke me into slaying you," the captain replied. "I do not break my word lightly. Nor will you be killed by the Hebrews when they find you in the state in which I shall deliver you to them."

When night fell the Captain Holofernes had Prince Hanun tightly bound in ropes and carried up the hill to be left near the gates of Bethul. There the prince might either perish of hunger and thirst, or else cry out to the watchers on the wall to fetch him into their town.

"But what if this wretched Ammonite speaks against rather than for us?" one of the officers asked.

"I trust more in his hatred of the Hebrews than in his good sense," the captain replied. "We have been at war with Judah only twice, but the Ammonites have been at war with them continually since the Hebrews conquered this part of the land."

Next morning the Captain Holofernes and his officers stationed themselves where they could observe the gate of Bethul from the valley below. They could not see Prince Hanun lying bound among the brambles, but after a while they could hear his feeble cries. He seemed in great discomfort, being unable to move from where he had been cast. But the gate of Bethul remained barred, though one could see figures scurrying behind the battlements of the wall. Suddenly a rope was flung down, and a man swung himself over the battlements to climb down.

"Ah, these people are crafty," the captain muttered not without admiration. "They would sooner risk the life of one man than open their gates to discover the source of the cries."

The man who had climbed down the rope vanished among the underbrush. Soon he returned carrying Prince Hanun upon his back. He had not loosened the prince's bonds but carried him close to the wall, where he fastened under his arms two ropes that had been tossed down. While Prince Hanun was being hoisted up, the man ascended the rope he had climbed down, and he and the prince vanished over the battlements.

But we went back to waiting.

Shortly after dawn the following morning I was awakened by loud cries in our camp. Thinking that a messenger had brought an offer of surrender from Bethul, I hastened toward the source of the noise to see whether my services as interpreter were needed. But instead of a messenger I found a great many soldiers gathered, loudly shouting to each other as they pointed to a woman on the wall of Bethul. One could not tell from the distance whether the woman was young or old, comely or ugly, but there was no mistaking the figure on the wall. Her long hair gleamed red in the morning light as though tinted by the rays of the rising sun. She stood shading her eyes with both her hands in a manner that would have concealed her face even at close range, but all the soldiers proclaimed her to be of great beauty. More than one would have liked to storm the wall, for it was many weeks since any had lain with a woman. As the uproar increased, more men collected in the spot until it appeared as if the entire troop was assembled to gape at the figure on the wall. Even the horses neighed loudly, stirred by the noise, while the camel that had once been my mount rose to its feet and danced around the stake to which it was tied.

The Captain Holofernes had to push his way through the milling soldiers to learn the cause of the tumult. When he was told that there was a woman of great beauty on the wall of Bethul, he jumped up on a rock where he stood above his soldiers and shouted:

"Fools! You have gone without women for so long that anything with long hair would appear beautiful to you! Do you not see that these people would goad us into an attack that they might slay many of us while they still have their strength? Have you forgotten the tales Prince Hanun told you of how the Hebrews use their women to beguile their foes? But if you will be patient another day or two, you need not spill your blood for the pleasure of having a woman! Now return to your tents and keep your peace until I call for an attack! Nor let any man approach near the wall lest I have him slain as a deserter!"

The soldiers grumblingly obeyed the captain's order. But he remained gazing up at the wall, calling the woman upon it all manner of names. She remained at her post until all the soldiers had scattered. Then she vanished behind the battlements.

"We have water and food to last us for some time," the captain said. "But for my soldiers nothing can take the place of women. Now I wish that I had some harlots following my troops, for it is harder to bait a sated lion than one who is hungry!"

After the soldiers had seen the woman there was little else they discussed, each picturing what he would do with her when he entered Bethul. There is no need for me to repeat their words, such things being known to all men. The worst braggart among them was Bania, the man who had slain my father and ravished my sister. As he boasted of what he would do with the first woman he seized, saliva trickled into his beard so that he resembled a dog lusting for a bone. But when I fled from his presence with my hands clapped over my ears, he laughed and shouted after me:

"Are my words too coarse for the delicate ears of the royal interpreter? Ah, but he shall yet witness things he could not picture even if he had what is needed between his legs!"

Then I fell down on my knees, praying to God for a miracle that would rid the world of this monster, even if his death would also require mine.

Five days of the week Judith had begged of the elders passed, and still there was no rain cloud in the sky (the old woman Tamar said to the young scribe). All the water had been consumed, and wine too was become scarce. People gathered to stare with dull eyes into the shallow shaft Merari had left behind, some even climbing down with spades, as if by scraping in the dust they could draw water. As for the cattle in town, they would soon have to be slaughtered to keep them from dying of thirst. Some people whispered of drinking the blood of the slaughtered beasts, though such a thing is an abomination.

But Judith continued fasting and praying to induce God's mercy. She no longer left the house, for it was she who had called the people to resistance, and she could not bear to look upon their suffering. Nor would it have been wise if she showed herself in the street, for the women were greatly incensed against her for having stirred up their men.

But on the sixth day of the siege a man came at sunrise to summon Judith to the tower. When he would not reveal why she was called, my mother would detain her, but Judith consented to go with the messenger. Then my mother pulled me aside, saying:

"Follow after them, Tamar, and if any threatens Judith, return and fetch me. Though Judith trusts in Yahweh to protect her, the people of Bethul have greater fear of my curse."

I sneaked out of the house, trailing Judith and the man until we reached the wall. There I concealed myself behind a stable, where I could peer around the corner and hear what was said.

Since the siege began the guards upon the wall had been doubled for fear of an unexpected attack. But now many of them had come down and stood surrounding their captain, Joab. When Judith approached, he said to her:

"It is good you are come, for we have need of your counsel, Judith. There is a man outside the wall calling for us to fetch him out of the brambles, where—he says—he lies bound tightly in ropes. Though he speaks Hebrew he proclaims himself an Ammonite, who was cast out by the Babylonians for praising our boldness to their faces. But we cannot see him, neither do we know whether this is not a ruse by the enemy to make us open our gates. Half their troops might have crawled up the hill under cover of darkness and now lie concealed in the shrubs, ready to rush the gates the moment they are swung open. But then again the man crying out to us might be speaking the truth. Moreover, he promised to reveal to us many things about our foe if only we rescued him from a wretched death. What, then, shall we do, Judith?"

"Why ask my counsel? Why not inquire of the elders?"

But Judith knew well that the young men who would fight no longer wished to be counseled by the old men, who would surrender. Therefore she gave them the desired answer:

"Let us rescue this Ammonite, for what he might tell us could save our lives. Nor need we open the gates to fetch him. All we need is a rope lowered from the wall, and a brave man who would risk his life. If this is a ruse, the Babylonians will slay him as he approaches the bait. But if the man in the brambles speaks the truth, it should be a small matter to carry him near the wall and hoist him up with ropes."

While the men acclaimed Judith's wisdom, Joab offered to climb down and fetch the Ammonite.

"But there is one thing I would have you do," he said. "If this be an ambush, do not let the enemy take me alive. Rather let one whose aim is good kill me with an arrow that I might not be tortured and degraded by our foe."

Regarding Joab warmly, Judith replied:

"When my father rode off to fight at Megiddo, his uncle Shallum said: 'God in His infinite wisdom created brave men fools lest they have the good sense to be cowards.' If ever I called you a fool, Joab, let me beg your forgiveness now. In this time of travail we have great need of fools!"

Then all entered the tower to ascend the wall, while I remained hidden behind the stable to wait for their return. I heard no cries from the wall that would have betrayed an ambush, nor did I hear the whirring of arrows being discharged. After a while the murmur of voices came from the tower, and then Judith and the men emerged into the open square inside the gate, carrying in their midst a young man bound in ropes. When he was put down and the ropes cut off him, he stood rubbing his arms and legs where the thick twine had cut into his flesh. But his eyes were on Judith as he spoke:

"What I heard in Rabbath-Ammon about your women is true. If the Babylonians knew that there is such beauty within your walls, they would long ago have stormed Bethul!"

"Is there no graver matter troubling my lord's mind, seeing he is but newly escaped from death?" Judith asked, rubbing the scar on her neck. "Nor is it seemly that he should speak thus to a widow many years older than he!"

The young man's answer betrayed his courtly breeding:

"As age improves good wine, so does it improve the beauty of a truly beautiful woman. As for your being a widow, this news pleases me greatly, for I would take you with me as my wife when I return to my land."

"This is neither the time nor the place to discuss such matters," Judith replied. "However, let my lord know that after my husband's death I vowed never to take another in marriage."

"Not even the crown prince of Ammon?" the young man asked. While the men gasped with astonishment, Judith said:

"Not even the crown prince of Ammon. Moreover, if I were to take another husband, this right belongs to my kinsman Joab, who rescued my lord from the brambles."

"I would pay any price to buy this right from him," the prince said.

"There is no sum which could pay for that right," Joab replied. "But let us not bargain over a woman who would have neither of us. Rather let us go and rouse the elders, for this new event cannot be kept from them forever."

While the others went to wake the elders, I returned home to tell my mother all I had heard.

"Is it not like Judith to refuse a royal prince?" my mother said. "Though others may think her to act from grief, I know she will not wed for fear of another husband like Manasseh."

But when Judith returned home there was no more talk of husbands. She would speak of nothing but the siege.

"Prince Hanun revealed to us many things about the Babylonians," she said. "But the elders distrust his words and would have him repeat what he said before the people that they might decide by acclaim whether they would fight or surrender. Even now a messenger is summoning all the men to the square by the gate. Nor should the women tarry behind, for is not their fate at stake too?"

When we left the house we found the streets thronged with people, all running in the same direction. Anyone not too feeble to walk, young and old, men, women and children, maidservants and menservants would see this prince who had come within our walls. But when the young man approached with the elders, a murmur of disappointment rose from the crowd, for the Babylonians had stripped him of his princely robes before casting him out. Also he seemed young to offer advice on matters of war and peace, such counsel sounding better in the mouths of graybeards. But leaping up on one of the stone benches by the gate, he addressed the assembled crowd with great passion:

"Men of Bethul, hear me! Though our countries have often warred, we must now join to resist a common foe! Therefore give credence to my words even if you think me your enemy! Do not surrender to the Babylonians but defy them! Neither trust in their promises of mercy, for they are led by a man wholly without honor whose word has no more weight than chaff in the wind! I know whereof I speak, having been a prisoner of the Captain Holofernes. Not only did he abduct me from my palace, where I entertained him as my guest, but he also cast me out to die of hunger and thirst when he had vowed to return me home alive. But can one expect better of a man who would slay the son of his best friend? Surely no man shall escape alive if the Babylonians enter Bethul, and as for the women, their fate too is sealed. Indeed we would not let the Babylonians enter peaceably into Rabbath-Ammon, for they are wont to buy the women's favors with trinkets and food, thus turning even the chaste to harlotry. As for the women, they dote on these Babylonians, who never having known hunger are fat and handsome—though I do not believe the lies they tell about their rich crops. Moreover, they spread tales which fill our women with discontent and the desire to snare for themselves Babylonian husbands. While we may take many wives and may send off any with a bill of divorcement if she no longer pleases us, the Babylonians may take only one wife at a time. But if they would divorce her they must give her much silver—it is their law!—even if the wife seeks the divorce. Indeed it is rumored that there are in their country women who have become wealthy from marrying often. For that alone we ought to keep the Babylonians away from our homes!"

With these words the young prince proved once again that men are fools who often speak as if women had no ears to hear. But while the women gazed at each other in amazement, the men of Bethul acclaimed Prince Hanun's words. Then he continued:

"There are in the camp below no more than a thousand soldiers, who have neither battering rams, nor ladders with which to scale your walls. Therefore you would do well to goad them into an attack, for your archers might kill a great number with arrows, thus rendering them unable to take your town!"

And when the men would know how this could be achieved, the prince said:

"Though the Babylonians have water and horsemeat, there is one thing they lack: women. Nor can the rolling of dice assuage their boredom, for they must continually have new diversions, as is the custom in their own land. If some of your women showed themselves on the wall, these soldiers would become so maddened by lust that they might rush blindly into an attack. But if they proceeded without the Captain Holofernes they would soon be vanquished, for they are invincible only while he fights at their head. Thus, by using the beauty of your women, you might achieve an easy victory!"

At that the men fell silent, one looking at the other to see which would offer his wife or daughter or sister to show herself on the wall. And when none came forward, the men of Simeon being very jealous of their women, Judith, who had neither father nor husband, said:

"I shall go."

But Joab exclaimed:

"I forbid you!"

"By what right?" Judith asked.

"By being your dead husband's kinsman," Joab replied.

"Being my dead husband's kinsman does not make you my husband. Go be master in your own house! As for me, though I am a widow I never took bread from the hand of anyone and am free to do as I please!"

And Judith turned to leave the square. But Joab pushed his way through the men to pursue after her, while his wife, who stood among the women, stamped her foot and smote her thigh in anger. When Joab seized Judith from behind, she halted and said:

"You have soon made me forget my promise not to call you a fool again, Joab. Indeed I do not know who is the greater fool, you or this Ammonite prince who thinks of nothing but women. Surely he must be an utter simpleton to have let the Babylonians abduct him from his own palace! Still I shall follow his counsel and show myself on the wall tomorrow, though not to goad the Babylonians into an attack, for I doubt that they would be enticed by such a simple ruse. Rather I shall attempt to count them as they come forth from their tents one by one to relieve themselves in the morning."

"It is unseemly that a chaste woman should observe such a thing," Joab said.

"One cannot break a grown ass of his habits, nor a fool of his folly," Judith replied with a sigh. "Know, then, that I do not wish to spy on these men as they uncover their parts. Rather I would make certain that Prince Hanun spoke the truth. If there are of them no more than a thousand, we might dare attack them by night, when each of our men might kill his ten in the dark. Did not Prince Hanun say that these soldiers might easily be routed if they found themselves bereft of their leader?"

"But then one would have to slay him first!" Joab exclaimed. "And how could this be accomplished, he living in your house in the midst of the camp?"

"How this might be accomplished I do not yet know," Judith replied. "But I shall closely scan the camp tomorrow to see if it can be done. At any rate, I know my own house well, and every path by which it might be approached."

Halting in his tracks, Joab caught Judith by the arm and said softly:

"This plan which is in your mind—think of it no more, for I will not permit it."

"There is nothing in my mind but what I shall do in the morning," Judith replied calmly. "As for the rest, it is in God's hand. Who knows but that tomorrow the heavens will open to pour down rain on us? Then we shall be able to hold out forever!"

But when Judith left the house early next morning, the sky was as cloudless as before. Though night had not yet ceded to dawn, the streets were thronged with people streaming toward the wall. The men of war had armed themselves against an attack. All carried bows and swords, but not half of them owned coats of mail. As for their helmets, those were old and battered, having been passed down to them by their fathers and grandfathers. Yet their spirits were good, for they had fortified themselves with wine, of which the largest portion had been set aside for the fighting men. Behind them followed the males too old or too young to do battle, and behind them the women and children. But Judith walked before the men that she might be the first to ascend the wall. She had wrapped herself in a cloak that shrouded her from head to toe save for her pale face, from which her green eyes peered somberly. Whether the

Babylonians moved to attack or not, she knew this to be a day of decision—the last of the week which the elders had granted her.

Judith and the warriors entered the tower to take their places on the wall, but the throng remained in the square below, waiting for news. Many stood praying while much time passed and nothing happened. Then a man shouted down from the wall that the Babylonians were slow in coming forth from their tents, staggering about as if still caught in sleep. Not until the sun rose above the mountains of Moab did our lookout report that the soldiers below had sighted Judith exposed in the bright light. But then he returned to his battle station, leaving those in the square greatly perturbed. We could hear the men on the wall shouting back and forth, but we could not make out their words. Some thought the shouting meant an attack and would have us act as if the enemy were already upon us, while others advised calm until the truth was known.

After a while the shouting subsided, and then our young men descended one by one, looking weary from having braced against an attack that never came. The last to emerge into the square was Judith. She had tossed her cloak over her shoulder, and her red hair gleamed in the sun. When she saw the curious faces of the people, she stood in their midst and said:

"Some of the things Prince Hanun said are true, while others are not. It is true that our foe is not as numerous as we feared. It is also true that they lust for women, for all came running to gape at me until the whole troop was assembled. But it is not true that the Babylonians are fools who would blindly rush the wall. Indeed when their captain jumped upon a rock to exhort them, they all returned to their tents. Surely this man has great power over his soldiers and must be weighed in our plans."

But one of the elders in the square spoke up, saying:

"There is nothing more to plan. The ruse Prince Hanun proposed has failed. We might as well divide the wine among ourselves, for there is to be no battle. As for our cattle and sheep, they are dying of thirst, neither is there anything left for the children to drink. Nor has any of us washed his body or garments in days so that we shall soon rot in our own filth. Truly none can blame us now for coming to honorable terms with the enemy!"

"There are no honorable terms with an enemy," Judith replied. "It is better to die as free men than to live as slaves. Nor have I yet tried everything in the week you granted me. There is still one day left."

"And what would you accomplish in one day that was not accomplished in six?" the elders asked.

"I would attempt one more thing," Judith said. "But this is not the place to discuss it. Let my lords and Joab come to my house that we may speak in secrecy. I would also ask some questions of Prince Hanun before I make you my last proposal. Should this one fail, you will still have time to surrender. But I shall not live to witness this shame."

When the men were assembled in Judith's house, she turned to Joab and asked:

"If a way were found to slay the Babylonian commander, would your soldiers be willing to attack the camp?"

At this question the elders placed their hands upon their heads, but Joab replied:

"They would be willing. However, the deed you propose cannot be accomplished."

"This we shall see in time," Judith said. "But first let Prince Hanun tell us why the Babylonian soldiers have such great faith in their captain."

"Because the Captain Holofernes was never yet wounded in battle," the prince replied. "I know this to be true, for I have seen him strip to bathe and found not a blemish on his body. Also there is an oracle that he shall not meet his fate until the goddess Ishtar descends from on high. As for the captain, he believes in neither gods nor demons but only in the strength of his sword arm. If ever a man thought himself immortal it is he, nor does he believe that he can be slain by a man."

"Might not a woman accomplish what a man cannot do?" Judith asked calmly.

At that the elders wailed even more loudly than before, while Joab jumped swearing to his feet. But gazing at Judith the way men looked at her, Prince Hanun replied:

"Though Judith's beauty is great, the Captain Holofernes should not be easily beguiled. His soldiers tell many tales of women pursuing him wherever he goes. Indeed they claim that in Babylon an armed guard protects the door of his house—not to shield him against assassins but to drive away the ladies. Nor has he taken a wife, having the wives of many other men. And though the Captain Holofernes is no longer young, Judith should not esteem him lightly, for his appearance is gorgeous and he might entice even a virtuous woman."

Before Judith could reply, Joab exclaimed:

"This monster shall not entice Judith, for she shall not go down to him! Moreover, if the other soldiers saw her beauty they would seize her for themselves long before she reached the captain's quarters!"

"This too I considered," Judith said when Joab ceased shouting. "Indeed I cannot go down alone but must have a number of women accompany me that they may distract the soldiers while I seek out their captain. Let my lords not fear that I shall invite their virtuous wives and daughters, though there might be among them more than one who would gladly consent. Rather I shall ask the help of those to whom it matters little whether their hire comes from the hands of Hebrews or Babylonians. Moreover, these women know how to please men and will not soon be wearied by the multitude. But while they keep the soldiers amused I will deal with their captain!"

"You shall do no such thing!" Joab cried. "But if it must be done, I shall disguise myself as a woman—though I loathe the thought— and descend with the harlots to do the deed myself!"

Then Judith smote her thigh in mirth, exclaiming:

"Disguise yourself as a woman—you whose arms bulge with muscles and who walks with the tread of an ox pulling a plow! There are in Bethul some youths who might pass for women, being delicate and of a mincing walk, but they lack the stout heart required for this deed. No, I am resolved to do this thing myself!"

"I would slay you first before I allowed you to be defiled by this heathen!" Joab shouted.

"He shall not defile me," Judith said calmly. "He shall not touch me. I fasted and prayed for many days, and I had signs."

"What signs?" Joab asked with distrust.

"It is not for you to know what God revealed to me," Judith replied. "Neither can you keep me from my purpose. If I be killed, there is none to whom you need answer for my life. And if I live, my life will have been for some end. But we must not waste time, for our store of wine is nearly gone. Therefore let me go and inquire of the harlots if they would come with me. And now let my lords return to their homes, but let them keep my plan from the women lest they spoil it with their unrequested help. As for you, Joab, stand ready with your warriors until I send word appointing the time for you to fall upon the enemy camp!"

After the men had departed from our house—the elders muttering among themselves, Prince Hanun praising Judith's boldness, and Joab weeping with rage—I asked Judith whether she had in truth received signs.

"Has not my whole life been a sign?" Judith replied. "Did God not shield me from harm more than once, showing me that my beauty was meant not to please men but to kill them?"

I staggered backward in horror, whispering:

"You have gone mad from fasting too much. God never gave you such signs!"

"Even you who were with me on those occasions would deny God's hand!" Judith exclaimed. "Have you forgotten the night of the wine festival, when your mother first bade you sleep beside my bed? While you lay snoring from too much wine and dancing, I was awake. I knew well who was the man entering my room in the dark, for I heard him dragging his lame leg. And though I knew why he had come I did not cry out. Suddenly you, who lay snoring only an instant ago, woke with a start and drew your mother with your screams. Thus I was saved that night. But my father died refusing to give me up to a husband. And was it not a sign that I was cursed with a husband like Manasseh? As for my lewd father-in-law, I knew his thoughts when he sent you from the stable the day the mule was born. Had I believed his lies, I would have gone with you to see your mother. Instead I thought: let it be the father if not the son. But when he came near me, whispering in my ear with his moist red lips: 'Come, Judith, let us lie together that I may be the father of my grandson!' I pushed him away, maddening Hadad with my screams. Was it less than God's hand that led a blind horse to save my virtue? And do you remember the night we came down from the hill after the rites, when I would not return to my house but went to seek out Manasseh in town? If I said then that I wanted a son, I lied. For in my heart I asked: shall my youth go from me before I have known a man's embrace? And though Manasseh fled from my nakedness, he was dead next day. Thus I am still a virgin at thirty, while all the men who touched my life lie buried in the ground. What could be the meaning of my barren life but that God spared me for this day? He need not speak to me from a flaming bush to reveal His will more plainly! And now detain me no longer, Tamar, for I must go and speak with the harlots. Also I would borrow from them ointments and kohl that I may paint my face to appear as one of them. But you and your mother shall fetch my bridal garments and jewels from Manasseh's house. Let me adorn myself for the Captain Holofernes that my beauty may blind him even if he has lain with all the comely women in the world!"

While Judith sought out the harlots, I went with my mother to Manasseh's house. When we unlocked the door that had been bolted for two years, the smell beyond it was that of a grave. I thought of Judith's signs, but I did not speak of them to my mother. Rather I helped her place the garments and jewels in two baskets, which we carried back to our own house. There we unfolded the robes Judith had last worn at the rites of the goddess, shook out the dust and hung them in the yard to be aired of their musty odor. Then we each fetched a soft rag to rub luster into the tarnished jewels. While we were thus engaged, I asked my mother:

"Do you believe that Judith will succeed in her plan? Was ever such a deed accomplished by a woman?"

"Did not the goddess Anath avenge the death of her brother Baal with the sword?" my mother replied. "Did she not slay the villainous Mot, did she not hack his body to pieces and scatter it over the fields so that the earth, which had lain dead and fallow, returned to life? Even so shall Judith free our fields from those who are trampling them to death!"

I quickly glanced at the door and whispered:

"Let Judith not hear your words, for she would do this deed for Yahweh!"

"Judith may serve her god, but I shall pray to mine," my mother replied, mumbling spells and incantations as she polished the jewels. But she fell silent when Judith entered the house, bearing the ointments and paints she had borrowed.

"The harlots will gladly come with me, for they too heard Prince Hanun's tales," Judith said. "Also their patrons are few since the siege began, the favors of virtuous women being cheaper than theirs. But rather than gossip let me prepare for my task. How I wish for a bath that my stench may not repel my victim!"

Then my mother said:

"I still have a jug full of water which I hid against a day of great need."

"You sinned in hoarding what others lack!" Judith exclaimed. "But I would sin even more in bathing myself while children go thirsty!"

"Must not the holy tools be purified?" my mother asked.

And she went to fetch the jug from its hiding place, while Judith disrobed to be purified. I had not seen her naked since the night she stood with her hands on the pillar of Ashtoreth. Though her body was thin from fasting, her breasts were fuller than they had been then. Her skin was still smooth and unblemished, white against her lustrous red hair, that fell down to her hips. My mother's lips moved silently as she poured water over Judith's back, but Judith did not see her. She dried and anointed her body, slipped into her clean linen garments, and sat by the table to paint her face. But though she reddened her mouth and cheeks, and rubbed kohl around her eyes, she did not look like a harlot. Her eyes betrayed that she knew nothing of men, nor did her mouth look like the mouth of one who had known many loveless kisses.

I fetched her bridal gown and the gold-bordered gossamer veil that fell down to her ankles, while my mother handed her the jewels that lay glistening on the table—the bracelets and earrings and rings set with beryl and lapis lazuli, the silver chains and golden beads for her neck, and the sparkling bridal crown to place atop her sheer veil. On her feet Judith put her fine embroidered slippers, but she would not wear bells around her ankles lest she be heard approaching the enemy camp.

When Judith was thus attired, her beauty would have dazzled a king even if he had a harem of thousands. Just then our door was flung open and Joab stormed into the house. Seeing Judith, he gasped and posted himself with outstretched arms before the door.

"You shall not leave this house to be made a whore by that heathen!" he cried.

"I shall not be made a whore, Joab," Judith said gently. "I had signs. Ask Tamar if I speak truly!"

When Joab gazed at me I nodded, for had I not witnessed these signs? But Judith continued:

"Still it is good you are come, Joab, for you must do certain things. Have the gate opened after the sun is down and the moon not yet risen, while it is still dark. It would be wise if you doubled the guard, for one never knows the enemy's moves and tricks. While the harlots slip out and descend together, I shall let myself down by a rope from their quarters and approach the camp from the opposite side. There I shall wait concealed in the bushes until I know by their shouts that the Babylonian soldiers have sighted the women. No doubt even the posted sentries will run to meet them. Then I shall slip into the camp and swiftly make my way to my house, there to wait for the captain, who will have gone to discover the cause of the tumult. How he will deal with me I do not know, but if he looks at me as do you, Joab, I have little fear that he will slay me."

"Nor do *I* fear that he will slay you," Joab said grimly. "Rather I fear for you a worse fate!"

"Fear not," Judith said. "I have made provision. I shall take with me a large jug of wine, for there is none left in the Babylonian camp. Surely the great Captain Holofernes will not refuse to share with me a cup or two, or even three. But while I fill his cup, I shall only pretend to fill mine. Thus he will be too drunk to harm me on the first night. While he lies snoring, I shall observe when the sentries begin to nod at their posts and learn the best time for killing the captain, which must be done shortly before the camp is attacked."

"But how shall *I* know that the deed was accomplished?" Joab asked.

"I shall send word to you beforehand," Judith replied. "Though I am taking wine with me, I am not taking food. If I find favor in the eyes of the Captain Holofernes, he will surely not wish me to starve to death. But I shall refuse to eat his unclean food and ask that he send one of the harlots for victuals into town. Then let Tamar bring me food in a basket, and also my own clean dishes. While she serves me I shall whisper to her the appointed time for the attack, for I would not trust a harlot with this message. I shall kill the Captain Holofernes no later than on the third night, for I know that the wine in Bethul will last no longer."

Joab gazed at Judith a long time before he said:

"You thought well of everything, Judith. But one thing you

failed to consider. What if your heart should be softened by this comely captain?"

Turning pale with wrath, Judith replied:

"What cause have you to doubt my virtue, Joab? But to ease your mind, I shall swear a holy oath before you. If I fail to kill the Captain Holofernes within three days—if I fail to redeem my oath before Yahweh—may my fields be sown with salt and my vineyards be heaped with hailstones, may my houses be struck by lightning and burn to the ground with all my possessions in them, and may all the enemy make me their harlot and cast me out to die when they had their fill of me! Now stand back from my door, Joab, for you made me swear a terrible oath, and such an oath must be swiftly redeemed!"

Came the sixth day of the siege and still Bethul did not surrender (the old man Isaac said to the young scribe). But why the villagers would continue their defiance none could fathom, for there had been not a drop of rain.

The Babylonian soldiers were beginning to grow restless from the long idleness. There were no more trenches to be dug, no more wine to be drunk, and many had lost what little silver they had in the endless dice games. As for food, it was horsemeat day after day, except when one of the soldiers shot a deer or a hare. The men spoke longingly of honey cakes, of thin sesame loaves and good leavened bread, for it was many weeks since they had tasted anything baked. But after discussing the delicacies they craved they returned to discussing women.

"The captain bade us be patient another day or two," one reminded the other. "May the gods grant that his words become true lest we turn back into boys whose hands know their own parts better than those of women."

All through the sixth day the strong wind and swirling dust confined the Captain Holofernes inside his hut. He had granted me leave to sleep on the mat in the kitchen, for he liked to converse with me, having known me longer than any of his fellow officers. Toward evening he bade me recite for him some of the old poems I knew by heart, claiming that they would soon lull him into blissful sleep. But no sooner had I settled down by the hearth than a loud uproar was heard at the outermost edge of the camp.

The Captain Holofernes seized his sword and helmet and dashed outside, shouting for me to bring him a lighted torch while he mounted his horse. Snatching the torch from my hand, he galloped off toward the source of the clamor. As I stood watching the red streak of the flame vanish into the dusk, more and more men ran past me in the same direction, some clad only in their loincloths as they had lain in their tents. When I detained one to ask him questions, he shook me off fiercely and shouted back over his shoulder:

"Have you not heard that there are some Hebrew harlots come down into our camp? Hurry, for the men will soon draw lots to see who shall lie with them first, and who later!"

And he ran on like one bereft of his senses. But I thought it all a prank by one of the soldiers. And even if it were true—how was I to profit by the presence of women except they knew how to prepare horsemeat in a novel manner? Thus I remained near the house to wait for one sane enough to tell me the truth.

The moon rose in the sky and none of the soldiers returned, neither did the Captain Holofernes. My feet grew tired from standing so long in one spot, and I resolved to wait in comfort inside the house. But turning toward the door I beheld a sight that made my knees knock together. Near the house stood what looked like the figure of a woman. But I had never seen a woman that tall, nor had I heard her approach. When I saw the glitter of many jewels in the pale moonlight, and the sparkling crown on the head of the tall figure, I remembered the oracle concerning me and the Captain Holofernes. Seeing the apparition draw near the hut where we dwelled together, I fell on my face in terror, for I thought my time had come. But as I lay with my hands clasped over my head, a woman's voice addressed me in Hebrew:

"Why do you grovel before me on the ground? If you understand my speech, rise and tell your captain that I have come to see him. I am accustomed to traffic with men of standing and would not waste my art on the common soldiers."

"Who are you?" I asked in a quavering voice, having heard that gods sometimes play tricks on mortals.

"I am one of the harlots fled from Bethul. Why should I perish with those who despise me for my calling if I can live serving one who would reward me well?"

"Are you truly a mortal woman?" I asked through chattering teeth.

"What else would I be? And you, are you not the Hebrew eunuch who shouted up the order for surrender?"

I knew then that she spoke the truth. But I would not have any hear her call me a Hebrew, therefore I answered:

"I am an Assyrian by birth, and by profession a scribe and interpreter who speaks many tongues with equal ease, Hebrew being but one of them."

"Whoever you may be, go announce me to your captain!" the woman said in a tone of one accustomed to give orders.

When I told her that the captain had ridden off to discover the cause of the uproar in his camp, she approached the door as if to enter by herself. Jumping to my feet—for I was still lying in the dust—I exclaimed:

"You must not enter the captain's house without his leave!"

"The *captain's* house," the woman said in a strange voice. "Has he acquired a deed to it that I need his leave to enter?"

Not knowing what to make of this question, I was relieved to see a flame streaking through the dark which heralded the captain's return. He reined his prancing horse some distance from me, shouting:

"It cannot be much longer now before Bethul surrenders, for the whores are already fleeing the town! Some painted and perfumed harlots came into our camp, and though they cannot speak our language they have made their purpose known by signs, nor does their business require many words. At first I thought the men would tear them asunder in their zeal, but in the end their good sense prevailed. By treating the whores gently they will have their use more than once, though it may take days before each harlot has pleased the men assigned to her. As for me, I had a woman in Rabbath-Ammon, nor am so young that I cannot wait my allotted turn."

Then I said:

"The captain will not have to wait his turn. There is a woman here who would not deal with the common soldiers."

And I pointed to the tall figure concealed in the shadow of the house. When she saw me beckoning, the woman came forward and stood where the moon lent glitter to her jewels. But her face was still in the shade.

Raising the torch above his head to spread its circle of light, the captain roared:

"I shall have all the sentries flayed for their slack vigilance! Who is this harlot and how did she slip into camp unobserved?"

Though I repeated the question in Hebrew, the woman remained mute. She still stood outside the circle of light, her face turned toward the captain, who was fully revealed in the glow of the torch. His helmet gleamed, his eyes flashed with fury, and the muscles of his right arm bulged as he reined in the prancing horse.

"Why does she not answer?" the captain shouted. "Has she no tongue, or has she never seen a man on horseback?"

And when in my terror I translated this question word for word, the woman replied softly:

"I have seen a man on horseback before. As for who I am and how I came here—my name is Judith, and I entered the camp from the east, knowing that the captain would not wish me seized by his soldiers before he knew my company."

Hearing this answer, the Captain Holofernes said:

"I rarely met a woman who did not know her worth. Let me see why this one considers herself of such value."

And holding the torch before him, he rode near the tall figure. As the glow of the flame fell over her, I saw her face for the first time. Though I had seen women of all nations in Nineveh and Babylon, and had glimpsed some in the king's own harem, I gasped in wonder. Even the Captain Holofernes sat motionless astride his horse, gazing at the woman for a long time. Then he said softly:

"Not all of Prince Hanun's tales were lies. There are indeed women of great beauty in Bethul. But I did not seize this one as my booty. She came to me of her free will, and I have nothing to offer her for her favors, whose price must be very high."

Having heard these words from my mouth, the woman replied:

"Let the captain not concern himself with my hire, for I can see that he is a man of honor who will not refuse me my due. Rather let us enter the house and repose, for I have brought with me a jug of wine that we might drink together before we taste of greater delights!"

Being needed as interpreter, I followed the captain and Judith into the house. The captain stuck the torch into a metal ring beside the hearth so that the flickering flame filled the kitchen with a red glow. Judith put down the wine jug she carried on her shoulder and went to fetch two cups from the shelf. Though she was very tall she walked lithely, her giant shadow on the wall mimicking her every move. Her chains and bracelets jingled as she bent over to pour the wine, but she would not meet the captain's gaze as she handed him his cup.

The Captain Holofernes had taken off his helmet but had kept his sword strapped to his waist. Holding the cup in his hand, he said to me:

"This woman moves about the house as though she knew it well. When she went to fetch the cups, she did not first turn around to search for the cupboard. Neither does she walk like a harlot, flaunting her hips and breasts, nor does she flutter her lids and throw me languid glances. And now that she is fully revealed in the light, I see that she knows little about painting her face, having marred its beauty rather than enhanced it. I do not believe that she is what she pretends to be, for I have been a man long enough to know a virtuous woman from a harlot. But I shall soon discover the meaning of this strange visit!"

Raising his cup, the captain bade me tell Judith to join him in drinking. As he stood waiting for her to taste the wine before him, she said with a smile:

"Your captain need not fear that I brought him poisoned wine. See, I am not afraid to drink of it!"

She put the cup to her lips and bent her head back, drinking deeply. The captain's face changed strangely as he looked at the curve of her fine, white throat. With two swift steps he approached her, and even before she could take the cup form her lips, he put his left hand on her breast and pressed his mouth to her smooth neck. Being taken unawares, Judith dropped the cup and pulled back, raising her palms to cover her burning cheeks.

"Did I not tell you that this woman is not a harlot?" the captain exclaimed, his right hand reaching for his sword as though it could sense danger even before his mind. "And did the men of Bethul think to snare me with this woman's beauty, which in truth is great? Would they use her as their ancestors used the maiden who bewitched the prince of Shechem? If they are foolish enough to believe their own fairy tales, they had no right to take me for a like fool! As for this woman, she had better reveal to me the true purpose of her visit, or in spite of her beauty it will go badly with her!"

When I repeated his words to Judith, she replied:

"What should be the purpose of my visit but to please the noble captain?"

"Then let her please me!" the Captain Holofernes cried, putting down his cup to seize Judith with both hands. But again she moved out of his grasp.

They stood no more than a pace apart, their eyes at the same level as they glared at each other. Though the Captain Holofernes was thought tall among Babylonians, with her crown on her head Judith was taller than he. She shuddered, though seemingly not from fear, and her breath came hard as if she had been running. But the captain bit his lips, furrowed his brow and turned from her, muttering:

"I must not permit this woman to stay with me in the house. She might make me forget that I never yet forced a woman, not even when I was still a beardless recruit. But I cannot deliver her to my soldiers, who might fall to killing each other over her, nor can I bear the thought of destroying such beauty. Therefore I shall show her mercy even though she tried to deceive me and let her return unsullied to Bethul."

Hearing this generous offer, Judith only shook her head.

"Your captain cannot make me return," she said. "I would sooner have him kill me, for I swore a holy oath before my God, and such an oath must not be broken."

Though I did not know the nature of her oath, my blood ran cold at this answer, nor would I translate her words until the captain had prodded me with many curses.

"Whatever she swore before her god, let her return home and forget her folly," the captain said.

When I translated his words to Judith she turned pale and said softly:

"Tell the Captain Holofernes that I swore before my God to kill him, and see whether he would still send me back to Bethul!"

But my teeth chattered so loudly that I could not emit a word, though the captain shook me and even slapped my face.

"Imbecile!" he roared. "What did the woman say to fill you with such terror? Ah, how I wish I understood her without having to suffer your babbling!"

Seeing that he would strike me again if I did not translate Judith's words, I stammered:

"Let the captain know that the people of Bethul rid themselves of a madwoman who claims that she has come to kill the captain!"

The Captain Holofernes released me and gaped at Judith, who calmly returned his gaze as one resigned to her fate. But instead of drawing his sword, the captain threw back his head, opened his mouth in laughter and exclaimed:

"The men of Bethul could hardly have sent me a better diversion! Ask her how she would kill me, since she did not poison the wine in the manner of women. Would she choke me with one of her chains, or did she bring a dagger concealed in her garments?"

I did not know then who was the madder of the two. But not daring to disobey the captain, I repeated his question to Judith.

"It is told of our second king that he stunned a giant with a sling stone and then slew him with his own sword," Judith replied. "Is there a dearth of weapons in the Babylonian camp that I should have brought my own?"

At this answer the captain laughed even harder than before.

"Would she stun me with her beauty before wresting my sword from me? And does she know how to wield a sword? I had better teach her that she may not falter at her appointed task!"

When he unstrapped his sword and handed it to Judith I was certain that his reason had left him. Neither did Judith know what to make of his action. She took the sword from him, only to find that she could barely lift it, the captain's sword being fashioned to suit his great strength.

"This is not the way to hold a sword, Judith!" he exclaimed with mirth. "Come, let me teach you!"

And moving behind her, the captain seized her around the waist with his left arm, while with his right he raised her right, in which she held his sword.

"You slash like this and then you stab like that!" he shouted, moving her arm as he held her tightly against him.

I had not seen his eyes flash in this manner since I observed him doing battle in Nebuchadrezzar's palace court, when he helped quell the captains' rebellion. But now he seemed doubly roused by holding a sword *and* a woman. As for Judith, the lustful look in her eyes did not seem caused by lust for murder, nor her panting by the effort of swinging the sword.

When they halted, the captain gently wrested the sword from Judith, pushed it back in its scabbard, and said:

"If she would slay me with my own weapon she must approach near my bed. I unstrap my sword only at night and place it on the floor beside my right hand. But she will have to come to me of her free will. I shall not force her."

And Judith replied through my mouth:

"If it be my God's will that His spirit enter into me, I shall find the strength to do this great deed."

The Captain Holofernes smiled at her answer and said:

"I have taken many women from men, but I have never yet taken a woman from a god. If her god's spirit can enter into her, so do I have means of entering into her. And if her body must be our battleground, so be it. But let her god know that I am wont to remain the victor. And now let us sit down and drink to rouse our spirits to combat!"

But I translated only the last part of the captain's speech, for I would not have his words pass through my mouth to blaspheme Yahweh in His own hills.

The Captain Holofernes soon discovered that whenever Judith filled his cup she poured but a few drops into her own. But he pretended not to see through her plan, while he observed her with a strange smile. As for Judith, she rarely raised her eyes to meet his glance. When she did, her cheeks would flush and she would put her hand to her neck, rubbing her skin beneath her many chains. But though she drank sparingly, the wine soon sparkled through her eyes. Then the captain's smile deepened, and he said to me:

"This woman does not know that I outdrank my comrades on many occasions. Even if she takes only a mouthful to my every cup, she will be drunk long before me. But let us pass the time with discourse, for though I cannot understand her speech, the sound of her voice is pleasant in my ears. Now that the wine begins to cloud her mind, she may tell us how she knew where to find the cups without searching for them."

To this question Judith replied:

"Why should I not find the cups in my own home? This house, the land on which it stands, the fields around it and all the vineyards stretching up the slopes are mine. I am the richest woman in Bethul!"

Her words were proud, but it was the wine speaking through her mouth, for her tongue was thick and would not do her bidding. The captain gently shook his head and said:

"Is it not strange—my father owned as much land outside Uruk, and I always thought us poor? But then the people of Judah have never known true wealth. I would like to see this woman's face if she beheld our rich, black soil and the crops it bears us! Had I taken her captive I would carry her with me to Babylon, for her beauty makes her worthy of a better place than this wretched village. But not being my prisoner, she will have to follow me of her own will."

"What makes the captain think that Judith would follow him?" I asked. "Did she not confess that she came to kill the captain?"

"And does she look to you like a woman about to kill a man?" the captain replied.

Glancing at Judith, I saw that she was very drunk. She had propped her elbows on the table, cradling her cheeks in the palms of her hands. Whereas before she had avoided the captain's eyes, she now searched his face as if trying to remember some forgotten matter. Then she spoke without first having been asked a question:

"It is a long time since a man sat drinking wine in this house."

"Does she have a husband then?" the captain asked. "And what man would let such a woman seek out another, even to kill him?"

But Judith replied to my question:

"I have no husband. I am a widow these two years."

"Surely the stars favor me tonight," the captain said when he heard her answer. "Though most men would prefer a virgin, I would sooner have a widow. Nor must we waste more time, for Judith had a long fast, and her eyes tell me that her hunger is as great as mine. But lest we forget that she came to kill me, let me remind her of the promise she made her god!"

And rising, the captain ungirded his sword and held it out to Judith as he backed toward the door of the bedchamber. Judith too rose and followed him slowly across the room. The torch had nearly burned down. The two figures facing each other through the open door of the bedchamber looked like two tall shadows, save for Judith's glittering jewels and the gleaming blade of the sword.

Then the captain said to me:

"Go find yourself another place to sleep tonight, Marduksharu-sur. I have no more need of your services, for the cries of pain and the moans of lust are the same in every language."

I do not know how long I wandered about the camp. Though I was tired I could not find sleep. There were many fires burning through the night, while the men waited their turns outside the harlots' tents. As the soldiers stood laughing and trading coarse talk, it seemed as if they had forgotten what had brought them to this place. But I, not having what could be eased by the company of women, did not forget.

Outside one tent the man Bania had fallen into a quarrel with another soldier. When the man ahead of him would prevent him from entering the tent, Bania struck him down and passed on before him. I hoped that the other soldiers would fall upon him and slay him, thus releasing me of my oath. But their fear of Bania was almost as great as mine. Nor did any of them wish to converse with me, for I could not join in their banter. Even the soothsayer, who often had clung to me like my own shadow, barely glanced up when I addressed him, his good eye never leaving the flap of the tent before which he had taken up his post. I would have liked to tell him how Judith appeared before me, but since he paid me no heed I went my way.

Fearful that the soldiers would drive me out if I sought shelter in one of their tents, I crouched down near a fire. But I did not feel warmed by the flames, nor would sleep come to me though I closed my eyes. Thinking of Judith and the Captain Holofernes together in the house, I tried to recall how it had been when I lay with the lady Harshinana. But the memory had long faded, nor had it been worth the punishment it brought me.

As for risking one's life for one night—need not a man be utterly mad to lead a woman bent on murder to his bed? But then my master had told me long ago that if the Captain Holofernes could not challenge death on the battlefield he would seek it in the bed-chamber. And what if indeed he were found slain in the morning? What would happen to me, who alone knew of Judith's presence? Should not the other officers accuse me of having aided her and slay me in their wrath?

This thought so frightened me that I roused myself from my half-sleep. Gazing up at the sky, I saw that it was growing brighter in the east. I quickly leapt to my feet and hastened back to the house. If I found the captain dead, I might still escape from the camp before the guards of the morning watch had rubbed the slumber from their eyes.

When I reached the house, I softly opened the door to listen whether one or two were breathing in the bedchamber. But I discovered the Captain Holofernes standing in the kitchen, an oil lamp in one hand and a cup of wine in the other. He was naked save for the amulet around his neck, which he did not take off even in bed. Seeing him thus revealed in the glow of the lamp, his strong, manly body as hale as before, I exclaimed:

"Then my lord is not dead!"

"Is it you, Marduksharusur?" the captain asked, squinting at the door, where I stood half hidden by the darkness. "And why should I be dead? Though I am not as young as in former days, neither am I so old that one night in a woman's arms would kill me! But why are you returned when I sent you away, unless you wanted to be the first to see me lying in my blood?"

And when I vowed that it was concern for the captain that had brought me back, he laughed and said:

"It was not my blood that was spilled last night but that of the woman who came to seek my life. Do not shrink in horror, Marduksharusur, for I drew her blood using only the weapon that nature bestowed upon me. As for Judith's husband, he was not much of a man unless he left her a widow before setting foot in his bridal chamber. But since you are returned, go fetch us some food, for Judith will be hungry when she wakes!"

When I returned from my errand, the Captain Holofernes was still in the kitchen. He had put on his boots and the short kilt he wore beneath his coat of mail, but his hairy chest was bare. He stood scratching it and yawning when I entered bearing cooked horsemeat and a jug of water. Smelling the meat, the captain held his nose in disgust and said:

"Those who prepare our food deserve to be strung up by their thumbs! I hope Judith can cook, for if she cooks as well as she loves, she should be the prize any man desires. I might even take her with me as my wife to bear me the seven sons my mother wished me to have! Would not your master smite his thigh with mirth if I brought back a Hebrew wife?"

I only gaped at the captain, for he had never yet spoken of taking a wife. Nor could I imagine what spell Judith had cast over him to alter his mind in one single night. But when she emerged from the bedchamber, I saw what had captured the captain's heart. She wore neither jewels nor precious raiments but only her simple linen garment. And now that all the paint was kissed off her face, she was even more beautiful than before. Her long red hair had become undone and was spilling over her shoulders, and the skin of her face and arms was an unblemished white. When she saw me she blushed deeply, for had she not uttered great threats through my mouth last night? Nor did she speak until the Captain Holofernes bade me offer her food. Then she shook her head, averting her face so that she need not look at me as she mumbled:

"I must not defile myself with what is unclean."

When he heard her refusal, the captain exclaimed:

"Would she share my bed but not my food? See if you cannot dissuade her of her Hebrew stubbornness, for surely she must be hungry after such a night!"

And he fell to the food, while I tried to coax Judith to eat with him. But she went on shaking her head though she swallowed hard as she stood watching the captain. When his gaze met hers she flushed more deeply than before and rubbed her neck, on which could be seen a thin, red mark now that she had taken off her chains. Frowning at the mark, the captain put down the piece of meat he held in his hand, approached Judith and gently touched her neck with his finger. When she gasped and pulled away, he said:

"If I caused this bruise on her lovely neck, let me make amends. I have with me nothing I value more than the amulet my mother gave me to hang about the neck of my bride. I never took it off in all the years, but now I shall give it to Judith, for if ever I wanted a woman to bear me sons it is she. Can you not imagine what splendid warriors should come forth from the womb of one who has the courage of a man and the beauty of a goddess? I would not be amazed if someday one of them sat on the throne of Babylon!"

Then I saw that a single night had turned the Captain Holofernes as mad as a youth who had lain with his first woman and who thought that he had discovered between her thighs the gateway to

Eden. And I also saw that love could make a man dream dangerous dreams. But the captain took off his chain, slipped it over Judith's head and hung it around her neck.

Judith, whose cheeks had been flushed only a moment ago, turned ashen. Her hand went up to the image of Ishtar on her breast, her fingers closing over it as if she would tear it off. But then her hand went slack, and she fell to the ground in a faint.

The Captain Holofernes knelt down beside her, cradled her head in his arms, and looking up at me he asked in amazement:

"Could she be with child after just one night?"

Seeing that he was no less a fool than many another man who was smitten by a woman, I replied:

"She cannot be with child so soon. Rather she drank too much last night without eating a morsel, nor do I think that my lord gave her much rest. Therefore we had best ask her when she recovers where we may find such food as she would be willing to eat!"

Joab sat up with us all night to pray and wait for word from Judith (the old woman Tamar said to the young scribe). Toward morning his wife came weeping, for she did not know where Judith had gone, and she thought Joab had spent the night with her. They quarreled in my presence, but in the end Joab went home with her, for he was sworn not to reveal Judith's plan. Thus he was not in the house when the harlot came with the message.

My mother and I were sweeping the lower chambers when the woman walked in. She had not knocked on the door but had entered the house as if she were a familiar friend. My mother stopped sweeping and glared at her, for no woman of her calling had ever set foot in our house before, and this one comported herself in an insolent manner. Only after she had stared her fill did she deliver Judith's message.

"Your mistress bids you slaughter a fowl and stew it for her. But make haste, for she is starved after her night with the captain!"

"Curb your insolent tongue," my mother replied. "These walls are not accustomed to shelter the likes of you."

"Am I worse than Judith because I lay with the common soldiers and she with the captain?" the harlot asked.

"Neither slander Judith, lest I put on you a curse to prevent you from ever lying with another man!" my mother said.

Backing away in terror, the harlot exclaimed:

"Let Yahweh be my witness that I speak the truth! When I saw Judith this morning she looked more spent than I, though I had to please many and she merely one. But let me return to the camp, for the Babylonian soldiers yearn for my company and have given me many presents. Indeed I earned more in one night than I earn in Bethul in many months!"

And the harlot hastened away, while my mother and I remained looking at each other.

"Surely she lies," I said in the end.

But my mother did not answer. She went out in the yard where the fowl were scratching, and when I heard the wild cackling of one come to a sudden end, I knew she had wrung its neck. Then she brought it inside, and together we plucked it, bled it, disemboweled it, and put it to stew in a kettle on the hearth. My mother fetched some water from yet another jug she had hidden, and tossed greens and herbs into the pot with the fowl until the kitchen was filled with a savory odor.

While the stew simmered on the hearth I went and dressed myself in my best garments to go down into the Babylonian camp. Seeing that my mother was engaged in the kitchen, I stealthily took Judith's paints to redden my lips and cheeks, and to daub kohl around my eyes. My heart pounded as I gazed at myself in the mirror, for I too was comely then. And if I had promised Merari to keep myself from men, could any blame me if one of the Babylonians seized and forced me, he being the stronger and I being alone in the enemy camp?

When I went to fetch the basket with the pot of stewed fowl from the kitchen, I kept my face averted lest my mother notice what I had done. But she, knowing the hearts of women, raised my chin with her hand, and seeing my painted face slapped me hard across the cheek.

"Go wipe your face clean and do not think to play the harlot among the Babylonians!" she cried.

When she was pleased with me she put the basket in my arm and took me to the gate. On the way we chatted with some of the women, pretending that the basket was meant for one in childbirth. Each woman told another tale of woe, of children crying with thirst, of men quarreling over the last of the wine, and of cattle perishing in the stables. Many were gathered around the shaft Merari had dug long ago. They would stare down into its dry depth and then gaze up at the sky, where the sun was lapping up the few white clouds. Regarding their ravished faces, my mother whispered to me:

"Let Judith redeem her oath speedily, lest we all die of thirst."

She said no more until we reached the wall. Joab had told the watchman of my errand, and he unlocked the gate to let me pass. My mother muttered a blessing as I slipped out through the narrow crack, and then the heavy doors creaked shut behind me. As I gazed down on the tents in the valley below my knees trembled. I would have liked to flee back within the walls, for what had seemed enticing before now loomed like a threat. What if the soldiers fell upon me and ravished me until there was no life left in my body? Had we not heard of such deeds? But trusting that Judith had made provision for my safety, I began my descent.

As I approached the camp it seemed to shrink in size, for now I could see only the tents nearest me. Halting, I gazed fearfully at the sentries, the first Babylonians I had ever seen from close by. They seemed neither the wild beasts our men had pictured nor as handsome as the women had thought them. But for their longer beards and sturdier build they might have been Hebrews. Still I trembled as I approached the sentries, not knowing how to address them if they challenged me. But having been warned of my coming, they waved me past them with their spears. Nor did any of the other soldiers raise a hand against me, though they made lewd signs and shouted words whose meaning I could well imagine.

Barely finding my way through the maze of tents, I walked faster and faster until I ran the last part of the stretch to our summer house. When I burst into the kitchen I had no breath left to exclaim at the sight of Judith. She had put off her jewels and fine garments, tied back her hair with a ribbon, and stood sweeping the floor like a housewife whose husband was gone for his day in the field. When she caught me staring at her she blushed deeply. Then I knew that the harlot had spoken the truth. Judith and I had sucked the same milk, and there was no change in her that would escape me. She looked wearier this morning than after a hard day in the fields, but also more beautiful than I had ever seen her. I would have gaped at her forever had not the eunuch who shouted the order for surrender entered the kitchen and said to me:

"Make haste, woman, and lay out the food for your mistress. She fainted from hunger this morning, not wishing to eat our Babylonian food. But the Captain Holofernes would have her well fed that she might regain her strength before he returns to enjoy her company."

Judith's cheeks turned more crimson yet, and when her hand went up to her scar I noticed the golden chain around her neck. It hung down heavy as though weighted by a pendant, whose shape I could not discern, for it was concealed beneath her garment. And still she said no word but stood observing me with the broom in her hands as I laid out her plate on the table and took the covered pot from my basket. When I raised the lid, the fine strong odor of the fowl rose from the pot. The eunuch's eyes nearly popped from his face, and though he swallowed hard, saliva foamed in the corners of his mouth as he exclaimed:

"Who would have dreamed that I, who have lived off horsemeat these many days, would ever again smell a stewed fowl such as my mother used to prepare on a Sabbath eve!"

No sooner had the words escaped his lips than he clapped his hand over his mouth and glanced at Judith in terror.

"Then you lied to me last night," she said with contempt. "You are not an Assyrian but a Hebrew turned against his own people!"

"Am I worse than you who spoke great words and swore a holy oath?" the eunuch replied, having regained his insolence.

I gaped at Judith appalled.

"What does he know of your oath?" I asked.

"He knows nothing," Judith replied coldly. "What would one such as he know of holy oaths? And now let him leave us alone that I may eat my meal in peace."

But the eunuch lingered in the kitchen, licking his lips as he looked at Judith's stew.

"The Captain Holofernes bade me stay with you," he said. "But if you would give me of your stew, I might step outside for a while to relieve myself."

Judith pulled a leg of fowl from the pot and tossed it at him as one would throw a dog a bone. He caught it in his hands and greedily began to tear at it even before he was through the door.

"That scum is no better than Esau, who sold his birthright for a mess of beans," Judith muttered.

But no sooner had the eunuch shut the door behind him than Judith sat down by the table and fell to the food. She snatched up pieces of meat, gnawed each bone until it was shining clean, drank the broth from the pot and finished by licking her fingers. Observing her, I wondered whether the Judith who sat devouring her meal ravenous as a bride was the same who had always eaten so sparingly. She glanced up, but she could not meet my eyes and quickly looked away again.

"And what of your signs?" I asked in the end. "What of your sacred chastity?"

"He was stronger than I," Judith mumbled. "And we were alone in the house. What could I do?"

But she did not look like a woman who had been forced, and I remembered my own thoughts of the morning. However, I did not speak of them but said:

"You had better make haste to redeem your oath now that you have beguiled the Captain Holofernes. The people of Bethul suffer greatly from thirst, and Joab wishes to know when he and his men are to storm the camp."

Turning pale, Judith replied:

"I have not yet discovered how often they change the watch, nor the posts of all the guards around the camp. When the captain returns I shall beg his leave to go and wash at the spring. In walking about I shall discover more than is known to me now. There is still enough wine left for our soldiers to last them another day. As for you, return to Bethul but bring me more food tomorrow. Until then there is nought I can say or do."

As I turned to leave, the door flew open admitting the Captain Holofernes. Then I knew what had changed Judith's heart, for I had not seen such a man since Merari died. The captain was clad in his coat of mail, but his arms and legs were bare as those of a common soldier. His flesh was the hard flesh of one who had marched and ridden all his life, and though there was silver in his long, black hair and beard, he did not look like one whose youth is fled from him. His eyes flashed, and there were around them lines as if he had known much laughter in his life. He approached Judith, gazed down on her plate piled with clean bones, lifted the lid of the empty pot and sniffed at it. Then he smiled at me and spoke some words I could not understand. I blushed deeply under his gaze, for his eyes were the eyes of a man who had known the embraces of many women. And I understood why Judith's signs had fled before him as dew before the sun.

Judith did not dare look at him for fear of betraying what was in her heart. But when he took a strand of her long hair between his fingers, she trembled as if she could feel his touch. I remembered how often Manasseh had played with her hair, putting it up in artful curls. But he had never stirred her, while the captain's finger brushing the tip of her hair made her shudder as though he had clasped her in his arms.

Smiling at Judith, the Captain Holofernes tugged at the chain about her neck, pulling the pendant out from beneath her garment. At the sight of it I turned pale, for it was the image of the goddess. Seeing my horror, Judith also blanched, but the voice in which she addressed me was cold and firm:

"Do as I bade you. And if you would keep my love, tell none what you saw here—not even your mother."

Then I turned and left the house, for I knew that there was no room in it now but for the two of them.

After Judith had thrown me the leg of fowl, I left the house and sat on the ground beside the door to consider what I had done (the old man Isaac said to the young scribe). I had not thought to betray myself as a Hebrew, but God had twisted my tongue to make it form the words I would not say. Perhaps He would provide Judith with an ally, though I doubted then that she would carry out her threat. I had seen her face in the morning, and I knew that she loved the Captain Holofernes as a woman loves a man who has brought her boundless pleasure.

At the captain's approach I tossed away the bone from which I had sucked even the marrow, and rose to my feet arranging my clothes as if I had just completed an errand of nature. But when I would follow the captain into the house he waved me away. I remained outside the door until Tamar emerged with the basket on her arm.

"What are they doing inside?" I asked her in Hebrew.

Scowling at me, she replied:

"They are doing the thing you cannot do, as you well know, having acted the pander for them."

"The Captain Holofernes requires no pander to gain the favors of women," I exclaimed in anger, "neither would your mistress do what was not in her heart!"

Then Tamar cast down her eyes and went her way, covering her ears as she passed the soldiers who called out to her such offers as all women understand though they be in a foreign tongue. I would have run after her and begged her to bring me another piece of fowl tomorrow—for which I would gladly pay with what silver I still had left—had not the captain summoned me inside.

"There is something Judith wants of me, but I cannot understand her words," the captain said.

While he spoke Judith emerged from the bedchamber, shaking out her skirts. But now she showed little shame and spoke to me like a concubine to a eunuch in a harem:

"Tell the captain that I would wash at the spring that my body may be clean for the night."

Hearing her plea, the captain replied:

"I wish I could offer her precious ointments to salve her body, but lacking these the water of the spring must suffice. However, I would not have her walk about the camp alone. Her beauty might make my soldiers forget themselves and they might risk my wrath to possess her. But it is not seemly that I guard her myself. Therefore I would have you go with her, Marduksharusur, and stand before the cave while she bathes. Do not let her out of your sight, but do not look upon her nakedness if you would not have me gouge out your eyes!"

I knew then that the captain's madness was still increased since the previous night. How could I observe Judith without looking upon her nakedness, and what did it matter if such a one as I saw her disrobe? But rather than question this order, I asked:

"And what shall I do if a soldier attacks her—I who never held a weapon in his hands?"

"Though they cut off your parts they did not rip out your tongue," the captain replied. "You can scream for help! As for me, I shall follow you and find some employment not far from the spring that my soldiers may not laugh at my folly."

Having received the captain's leave, Judith fetched a large basin in which to bathe at the spring. I followed her outside, not at all convinced that the soldiers would respect my person. Indeed the first to cross our path was the feared Bania. When he saw Judith he halted and gaped at her as though he had been turned to stone. But before one coarse word escaped his lips, I said:

"You had better guard your tongue, for this woman belongs to the Captain Holofernes."

Then Bania muttered:

"If there are more like her in Bethul, we should long have stormed the walls rather than content ourselves with the old whores who fled into our camp!"

And he stood scratching between his legs while I quickly led Judith away. But she strode on with her head held high, looking neither left nor right at the soldiers who came forth from their tents to gape at her. They watched her in silence, too awed by her beauty to make lewd remarks. But I thought of what Bania had said, and my hatred for him was greater than before.

When we arrived at the cave of the spring, Judith bade me remain at the entrance. I stood with my back turned while she disrobed, reaching behind me to accept her garments. In the distance I saw the Captain Holofernes mingling with his soldiers, speaking now to one and now to another as if he had come among them by chance. Behind me I heard the splashing of water as Judith made her ablutions, followed by a long silence. Suddenly the quiet was rent by a deep moan. Fearing that a soldier had been concealed in the cave before Judith entered, I whirled around and peered inside, ready to scream for help. But Judith was alone in the cave.

She had fallen to the ground and lay naked on her belly, her nails clawing the earth. I could see the curve of her back and her buttocks in the dim light, and though the sight could not stir me, I knew her to be beautiful beyond words. As I gazed at her she moaned again and her back arched as if she were racked by pain. Then she beat the ground with her fists, and throwing back her head she screamed:

"No, he is mine!"

Terror filled my heart and I whispered:

"Are you ill, Judith?"

She was silent at once and breathed deeply as though she were asleep, but I knew her to be awake. After a while she said in a calm voice:

"You may throw me my garments now. I fell asleep from weariness and had an evil dream."

I turned my back again and listened to the rustling of her robe as she dressed. When she emerged from the cave into the daylight, her face betrayed nothing of her former anguish. But in going back she would not return the way we had come but would take the long way around the camp. Though I knew her will to be stronger than mine, I said:

"You must not wander all over the camp, Judith. The Captain Holofernes charged me with your safety and would have my life if any harmed you."

"None shall harm me," Judith replied, "nor are you the one to guard me. I feel the need to walk, having been shut in the house all day."

And she continued looking left and right, though she would conceal her curious glances from me. Then I said:

"I know what you would discover, Judith. If you persist, you will bring us both to a bad end. But if you return to the house with me, I shall find a piece of potsherd and draw on it what you wish to know."

Gazing at me with deep distrust, Judith said:

"Why should I believe one who would betray his people and his masters? And why would you do this thing for me?"

Then I replied:

"Not all my words are lies. I was in truth born in Assyria. There is in this camp a Babylonian soldier who killed my father and ravished my sister when Nineveh was taken. I swore then that I would kill that man if ever I met him again. And though I had long ceased to believe that this would come to pass, it did through God's will. But I am only half a man and lack the boldness to kill another. Therefore if all the Babylonian soldiers must die that he too may die, so be it. At least let me know that I was the tool to bring about his death."

"And what if I betrayed you to the Captain Holofernes?" Judith asked to test my fortitude.

"I have no fear that you will betray me, Judith," I replied. "You too swore a holy oath, and such an oath must not be broken."

At that Judith turned ashen and muttered:

"You speak truly. Go then and draw me that plan, and may God have mercy on both of us."

I could not accomplish my task until after the evening meal, for the Captain Holofernes would have me about while he and Judith were awake. Judith joined him at the table but refused to touch his food, nor did a drop of water pass over her lips, though she had used it for washing her body. But when it was time for bed, she followed the captain of her own will.

No sooner had the door of the bedchamber closed behind them than I slipped out of the house. Being the captain's scribe, I aroused little suspicion by carrying a damp clay tablet and a stylus with me. I halted here and there to chat with one of the guards, who did not know that what I marked on my tablet might well be his death sentence.

Again the campfires burned late while the soldiers stood waiting their turns before the tents of the harlots. The night was the darkest yet since we had entered Judah, the moon being hidden by clouds for the first time. I hoped that those who lay snoring in their tents would sleep as deeply tomorrow, for I had little doubt that it was then the men of Bethul would fall upon the camp. Why else would Judith have wished to learn the position of all the guards? And I also knew in what manner she thought to deliver the plan to Bethul, for though I was bereft of my manhood I was not bereft of my good sense.

It was past the middle watch when I slipped back into the house, not wishing to spend another night in the open. I had concealed the dangerous plan I had drawn beneath my garments near my body that none might discover it while I lay sleeping. I paused to listen whether there were still sounds of love coming from the bedchamber. But all was quiet, and I bedded down beside the warm hearth, where I slept until Judith entered the kitchen in the morning.

As on the previous day she looked both weary and beautiful. She would not return my meaningful glances until the Captain Holofernes left the house for his morning ablutions, and even then she did not address me until I whispered to her:

"The thing you wanted—it is ready for you."

But when I reached inside my garments to hand her the plan, she backed away in dread.

"Let me first reason with the captain," she said. "He might yet raise the siege and move on, sparing us much bloodshed. Surely some of our own soldiers would fall in this battle, and there is among them none who is not a husband and father."

But she would not meet my gaze while she spoke, and I saw that another night in the captain's arms had weakened her resolve. And yet she had sworn a holy oath. But when I reminded her of it, she said:

"If my people be saved from destruction, have I not redeemed my oath?"

"And do you truly believe that the captain might be persuaded?" I asked in reply.

"At least let me try," Judith said.

It took some time before the Captain Holofernes returned. Every morning he walked about the camp and spoke with his soldiers to keep their spirits from flagging during the siege. But Judith paced the room like a lioness, for the longer she waited the shorter grew the time until Tamar would bring her midday meal. When the captain finally entered the house, Judith barely allowed him to take off his helmet before she bade me speak to him.

"I would make a bargain with the captain," she said. "If he raised the siege and moved on, I would follow him as his slave and concubine. But let him spare my town and my people!"

I would not trust my ears. Was this the woman who only two nights before had proudly proclaimed that she had come to kill the Captain Holofernes? But seeing the captain's eyes on my lips, I told him Judith's words. He smiled and shook his head, saying:

"I do not want her for my concubine. I shall carry her with me as my lawful wife that she may bear me seven sons. I shall take her away from this grim country where people fear to laugh lest they offend their god, and bring her to Uruk, the city of music and laughter, where men and women dress gorgeously and love life! Now that I have found the woman with whom I would live out my years I would return to the city of my birth. There I own many fields, which the king bestowed upon me for my services and which are being tended by my brother. Let Judith oversee this work if such labor pleases her, though a woman of her beauty might better spend her days reclining upon a perfumed couch! As for me, I have faithfully served in the king's army for more than thirty years. Surely Nebuchadrezzar will not refuse to release me now that I wish to raise sons to brighten my latter years!"

At this long answer Judith's eyes filled with dread. When I translated the words for her she turned paler yet and said:

"The captain said nothing of raising the siege. As for buying me

with promises of marriage and many rich fields—does he not know
that all the fertile fields of Babylonia could not replace in my heart
the land that my father cleared with his own hands? But do not tell
him this. Rather ask him again about raising the siege."

"Ah, what stubbornness," the captain said with a sigh. "I cannot
raise the siege without befouling my honor. But if these wretched
men of Bethul surrendered of their free will, I would grant them
peace and spare the lives of all save those who counseled them to
resistance."

Hearing this answer, Judith turned to stone.

"Let the captain know that if he would slay those who roused the
people of Bethul to resistance he must slay me first. It was I who put
them on this course! Indeed it was I who wrote the message that
was shot down from the tower of Bethul!"

In all the years I had known the Captain Holofernes I had never
heard such curses come from his mouth as now.

"Why can women not tend to the task for which the gods fashioned them?" he roared. "Why must they mix in the affairs of men
rather than let them wage their wars in peace? Should I, who killed
his best friend's son for fear of being delayed one single day, pardon
a townful of Hebrews who delayed me for many days? Should I let
them escape unpunished only because one of their women possesses
the looks of a goddess?"

But I knew that a man will sometimes do for a woman what he
would not do for his best friend. In the end the captain shouted that
he must think on the matter another night and stormed out of the
house, where he would not have to look upon Judith's face. While
he leapt on his horse and galloped off in a fury, Tamar entered
through the door which he had left ajar.

Seeing the covered basket on her arm, I was reminded of her
purpose. I slipped my hand inside my garment, pulled forth the
tablet with the plan and swiftly pressed it into Judith's hand. Then I
fled from the house, knowing that I had done my part. As for the
rest, it was between Judith and her God.

Having learned how Judith passed her first night in the Babylonian camp, I returned home (the old woman Tamar said to the
young scribe). Once the tents of the enemy were behind me I made
my ascent slowly, for I had to consider what I would say. If Joab

discovered the truth he would want to attack the camp in broad daylight, causing the death of many men for the lost virtue of one woman. And though I had no husband, there was among the soldiers my own younger brother. Did it not suffice that my mother had lost her husband at Megiddo? Must she now lose her only son at Bethul? But if time were gained Judith might still redeem her oath, for she swore by Yahweh, and such an oath must not be broken.

When I reached Bethul I had resolved in my mind what I would tell the men. No sooner was the gate bolted behind me than the guards and soldiers crowded around, each wishing to learn the hour of attack. But I would speak only to Joab, who sat in the chamber beside the gate, drinking wine with Prince Hanun. When I entered, Prince Hanun addressed me before Joab:

"Has your mistress wrought her wiles on the great Captain Holofernes or has he dealt with her as he deals with all women?"

Seeing Joab's face darken, I replied quickly:

"Is Judith a woman like others that any man should treat her basely? Indeed the Captain Holofernes honored her as one whose virtue outshines even her beauty! Not only did he have her own food fetched for her, he set aside a tent where she slept guarded by a eunuch that none of the soldiers might trouble her. Moreover, when Judith told the captain that the people of Bethul could not hold out much longer, he believed her words. As for the time of the attack, Judith had not yet learned all she would know. Tonight, after the captain falls down drunk, she will slip outside and observe what she could not discover before. But tomorrow, when I take her again her food, she will whisper to me her orders, for she vowed to accomplish her task no later than on the third night."

Thus I spoke boldly to the men, hoping in my heart that my lie would turn to truth. I even looked my mother straight in the eyes when I told her the same tale, though I had never before dared lie to her. She gave no sign that she did not believe my words. But when she placed the pot with the stewed fowl in my basket next morning, she said to me:

"Tell Judith that the people are parched and the children cry with thirst. Neither let her be deceived by the clouds that covered the sky last night, for when men break their oaths the gods withhold their rain."

And at the gate Joab said to me:

"The soldiers have drunk the last of the wine. Tell Judith it must be tonight."

As I approached our summer house I saw the Captain Holofernes storm out the door, jump upon his horse and ride off in a fury. My heart froze within me, for I feared that he and Judith had quarreled and might not spend the night together. Nor did the captain's eunuch act in a manner that filled me with faith. I had barely entered the kitchen when he pulled something from his garment, pressed it into Judith's hand and fled from the house. But she stood clutching that thing in her fingers and staring at me with dread as if I were the bearer of ill tidings. While I laid out her plates she did not say a single word, nor did she fall to her food as on the previous day. In the end I spoke to her first, saying:

"The people thirst and the children weep."

And she replied:

"I offered to follow him as his slave if he raised the siege. He may still show mercy."

And I said:

"The soldiers drank the last of the wine."

And Judith replied:

"He would think on it one more night."

And I said:

"It cannot be."

And Judith replied:

"Though I offered to be his concubine he would take me for his wife that I might bear him seven sons."

And I said:

"The women of your house do not bear sons. And those who do die in childbirth."

And she replied:

"He is strong. He might break the curse. Give me one more night."

And I said:

"It must be tonight."

And Judith replied:

"He would take me with him to Uruk, where there is laughter and music and love of life."

And I said:

"Would you abandon the land your father cleared with his own hands to become the whore of a heathen?"

And Judith replied:

"Having seen him, what would you have me do?"

And I said:

"You swore by Yahweh."

Then Judith shut her eyes, opened her hand and held it out to me.

"Take this tablet," she said in a dead voice. "On it are drawn the posts of all the sentries. Tell Joab to fall on the camp before dark cedes to dawn, when the guards of the middle watch have dozed off and those of the morning watch have not yet rubbed the sleep from their eyes. Let our soldiers subtly cut the throats of all the sentries. Then let them attack the camp with a great clamor in the manner of Gideon to deceive the Babylonians into thinking their numbers swelled by troops from Lachish."

"And will the Captain Holofernes live to rally his soldiers to defense?" I asked.

Judith opened her eyes, but her gaze was like that of one who has entered the nether world.

"I swore by Yahweh," she said. "Who would dare break such an oath?"

When the woman Tamar hastened past me without giving me a glance, I knew that Judith had delivered to her my tablet (the old man Isaac said to the young scribe). I observed her as she ascended the hill to Bethul until she was lost from my sight. Only then did I dare consider my treason safe from discovery. But I froze with fright when the man Bania, who had seen me look after Tamar, asked:

"What is there about this woman that one such as you should stand gaping after her?"

I swiftly recovered my wits and replied:"I see in her not the woman but the cook, for the food she prepares is truly fit for the gods. But let me return to the house lest her mistress consume all without offering me a morsel!"

And I retreated behind the door, hoping that Bania would soon forget what he had seen. The sight inside the house was not one to gladden my heart. Though a savory odor rose from the stewed fowl,

Judith stood by the table staring at it with empty eyes. When I asked if she would not eat, she replied that her hunger was gone.

"After my husband died, people thought I fasted from grief," she said. "But in truth I gagged at the sight of food, for there was much to trouble my memory. Yesterday I thought myself cured, but today my sickness returned worse than before. However, I would not have the captain discover my untouched meal lest he question what took away my hunger. Therefore sit you down and eat your fill, for I see you devouring with your eyes what I cannot put in my mouth."

"Will you not be too faint for the night?" I asked, though I trembled with greed.

"Is the bride too faint though she fast all day?" Judith replied. "Let me prepare myself as for my wedding. Tonight I shall seal my contract with the Captain Holofernes."

At her words the hair rose on the back of my neck. But I sat down and devoured her food, for while a man lives his stomach knows nothing of death.

When the Captain Holofernes returned, having ridden off his fury, he found Judith's plate piled with clean bones. Gazing fondly at her, he said:

"There is nothing I would refuse this woman save the thing she asked of me. However, I shall soften my conditions. Let her return to Bethul tomorrow and plead with the men for a peaceful surrender. If for each day I lost one came forth to accept the guilt of the rest and die for them, I would raise the siege and spare the others. It is asking little enough for the delay they caused me!"

Hearing this offer, Judith replied somberly:

"I shall spare no effort to bring an end to the siege of Bethul."

Only after I had translated her words did I grasp their true meaning. But the captain took Judith's face between his palms and spoke to her slowly as one speaks to a deaf person, hoping she would understand without the words having to pass through my mouth:

"They say a man's fate is written in the stars. And though I do not believe in such things, it must have been in the stars that I should discover the mother of my sons in a village in Judah. Surely it was more than hunger for glory that drove me on this mad mission! Nor did I ever before long for the end of war. Let your wretched King Zedekiah surrender speedily when our army comes against Jerusalem that you and I may return to Babylon for the

New Year Festival. I shall deck you in jewels and precious raiments, and together we shall descend to the wharves of the Euphrates and watch the barge that carries Nebo upstream from Borsippa, while the crowd cheers and the doves of Ishtar rise white into the blue sky. And before the year is passed you shall bear me a son fit to sit on the royal throne! We shall live in Uruk then—a city from which mighty kings have gone forth—and you will have forgotten this wretched village that spawned you, even as a precious jewel forgets the barren rock from which it was carved!"

Looking into Judith's eyes as he spoke, the captain did not bid me translate his words. Nor did I offer my services, for it was better that Judith did not know what he had said. But I could see in her eyes that even though her ears could not understand his speech her heart did.

That night the Captain Holofernes did not send me away. He and Judith were become as man and wife, who would lie in each other's arms untroubled by a stranger's presence in their house. But I found no sleep on my mat by the hearth, barely daring to breathe as I listened for sounds from the bedchamber. I heard neither sigh nor moan nor the clang of metal, and in the end I slid into slumber. I was startled awake by a white-clad figure standing above me. Before I could scream with fright, a hand sealed my lips.

"What time is it?" Judith whispered in my ear.

Instead of answering her question, I asked:

"Is it done?"

"Not yet," she said softly. "How long until the morning watch?"

"I think the night watch is three parts over," I replied in a whisper.

"Then there is still time," Judith said.

I could see her crouch down by the hearth and clasp her arms around her knees.

"Should you be here?" I asked. "What if the captain wakes and finds you gone from his side?"

"He will not wake," Judith replied. "He slept with a smile on his lips as a child sleeps in his mother's arms. As for me, I cannot sleep, nor can I look upon his face now."

She was silent, stretching forth her hands as if to warm them over the still-glowing embers. After a while she whispered:

"All my married years I lived as a widow. But now that I have no husband I am become a wife. However, tomorrow my widowhood will be renewed. I have but a brief span to learn what a wife might learn in a lifetime. Tell me about him!"

"What can I tell you at this late hour?" I asked in despair.

"Tell me of the child and youth he was before he became the man I know," Judith said.

I did not know why she would hear these things—whether she hoped to learn from my mouth tales that would make her loathe her lover, or whether she would tear out her own heart before she stilled his. But I did as she bade me. I told her tales true and false about the Captain Holofernes, those I had witnessed and those I had only heard. I told her that he was a man of the south, even as her own forefathers were men of the south. I told her how he had become a soldier at sixteen, and how war had remained his life. I told her how he was saved at Nineveh by my master, who in turn was saved from the flames by the crown prince Nebuchadrezzar. I told her of how these three men loved and hated each other, and how their lives remained enmeshed though they went their different ways. I told her how the captain had followed Nebuchadrezzar into Yahweh's temple, and of the blasphemies he had uttered there. And yet he was not struck dead that day.

I saw Judith shudder in the dark.

"Yahweh's wrath is terrible and His memory without end," she said. "Nor can His will be defied. But tell me more about the captain!"

I told her then how the Captain Holofernes had fought with Nebuchadrezzar's treacherous brother. How he had saved my master from the jealous Chaldeans. How he had helped snatch Shadrach, Meshach and Abed-nego from the fire. And how he had battled a lion face to face, rescuing me from certain death.

Moaning deeply, Judith said:

"Can you not tell me tales to make me hate him?"

"I knew the captain only in peacetime," I replied. "What he did in the many wars in which he fought I do not know. But no doubt he did what all soldiers do in war."

"Must you add to my torment?" Judith asked. "Is there truly no tale that would ease my task?"

Then I knew that I must reveal what I had buried in my heart to escape the memory. And I told her about the boy David, whom I had loved like a son and whom the captain had slain in the wilderness of Judah.

"If he felt no mercy, why should you?" I asked when I had finished.

"Perhaps he did not love the boy," Judith muttered.

"In this you are mistaken," I replied. "The Captain Holofernes loved David dearly, having known him since he was a babe at the breast. But let me repeat to you what the captain said after slaying the boy. 'It is a small matter to kill one you hate. To kill one you love for the safety of others takes great courage.' "

Judith sat silent for a long while. Then she rose heavily to her feet and said softly:

"It is good that he taught me how to wield a sword. Thus I shall not cause him needless pain."

She said no more. But I sat shuddering as I watched the white figure glide across the room like a spirit of the nether world and vanish through the door of the bedchamber.

FOURTEEN

And fields shall be bought in this land,
whereof ye say: It is desolate, without man
or beast; it is given into the hand of the
Chaldeans.

—JEREMIAH 32:43

THE old man Isaac fell silent. Then he rose, walked over to where the old woman stood stirring the stew on the hearth, dipped his finger in the broth and licked it.

"Ah, Tamar's cooking surely was worth betraying myself as a Hebrew," he muttered, closing his eyes in ecstasy. When he opened them again, he saw that the young scribe had not taken down a single word of what he and the old woman had told him.

The youth sat gazing at them in disbelief. In the end he asked:

"And what happened after the door of the bedchamber closed behind Judith?"

"Does not every babe know what happened then—how Judith struck off the captain's head, and how the men of Bethul fell upon the Babylonian camp like eagles—"

"Why do you lie when you promised to tell the truth?" the old woman Tamar broke into Isaac's speech. "Judith never struck off the captain's head!"

"And how would you know this, having remained in Bethul while I was in the camp below?" the old man asked crankily.

"Because when I came down at night I saw the captain lying whole upon the bed!" Tamar replied.

"Then Judith did not kill him?" the young scribe asked in amazement.

"Of course she did," Isaac replied. "Had she not sworn a holy oath? But it is true that Judith did not strike off the captain's head, for such a deed requires great strength and great hatred. If Judith possessed the first, she lacked the latter."

As for me (the old man Isaac said as he settled back to finish his tale), I did not enter the bedchamber to witness the slaying but remained in the kitchen to listen for the clamor of the attack. When I heard the fighting men of Bethul raise their battle cry, I disheveled my hair and ran outside shouting that I had discovered the Captain Holofernes dead upon his bed, and his head was not on his body. As for the Hebrew woman who had been with him, she had vanished into the air, for though I had spent all night inside the house, I never saw her leave.

As fate would have it, the first to hear me proclaim this lie was the soothsayer, who joined in my lament, wailing:

"Ishtar's wrath has fallen on us! The oracle has come true!"

And tearing his hair he ran out among the tents to spread this grim news. In the darkness and confusion none thought of searching the house to see if he spoke the truth. The Babylonian soldiers came tumbling from their tents half clad. Few had found time to don their coats of mail, and many came forth unarmed to find the camp overrun by the foe. Nor did they know that the attackers, who slashed left and right with a great noise, were but a hundred men. And while the Hebrews had a password to make themselves known to each other in the dark, the Babylonians had none. Thus the soldiers who had seized their weapons slew many of their unarmed comrades, unwittingly swelling the enemy's ranks. As for me, I escaped with my life because I hid in a tent while the battle raged and did not creep forth until the clang of weapons had ceased.

By the time the sky grew lighter in the east the ground between the tents was littered with dead and dying Babylonian soldiers. Many had tossed away their swords and had fled when they learned that their captain was killed, but the Hebrews pursued after them to slay every last one of their foes. Save for the moaning of those not yet dead, the camp was deserted and silent when on my way back to the house I stumbled over Bania. Though he lay on the ground he was not gravely wounded, nor was the fight yet gone out of him. Seeing me in the pale light of dawn, he whispered:

"Help me to my feet, Marduksharusur, and let us hide in the brush until nightfall, when we can make our escape from these Hebrew dogs. Though matters may look grim now, I have survived more than one hopeless battle!"

My heart froze and my bowels turned to water as I watched the monster whom I had hoped dead creep toward me. He pushed himself forward with one hand and one leg—having been wounded in the other—while he dragged his sword behind him in his right hand.

"Are you become stone to stand gaping at me? Here, help me up!" he whispered in a hoarse fury.

But backing away from him, I replied:

"You may have lived through many hopeless battles, Bania. But you shall not live through this one!"

And though I had never held a weapon in my hands, I bent down to seize the sword from one of the fallen soldiers. For I too had sworn a holy oath, and such an oath must not be broken.

Bania halted in his advance, regarding me as if I were a madman.

"Has the sight of blood crazed you so that you would slay your own countryman, who might help you save your wretched life?" he exclaimed.

"It is not the saving of my life but the taking of yours that concerns me now," I replied in a voice that sounded strange even to me. "I swore long ago that you should pay for the old man and the young maiden in Nineveh!"

"Why must the gods curse me with a madman in this hour of travail?" Bania howled, writhing angrily on the ground. "Who are this old man and this maiden you speak of?"

"Do not pretend having forgotten the old man you slew and the maiden you ravished at Nineveh!" I cried in my fury.

"And would you have me remember at this time every old man I slew and every maiden I ravished?" Bania asked.

Then I saw that the dreadful deed that had seared my mind forever was but one of many in this monster's life. And firmly grasping the handle of the sword in both my hands, I spoke:

"The man you killed and whose member you struck off at Nineveh was my father. And the maiden you ravished was my sister. As for me, I am not a Babylonian but a Hebrew who swore long ago by his God to avenge this deed. And now the time has come, Bania!"

But rather than cringe in fear, Bania raised his sword from the ground and roared:

"Then it was you who betrayed us and delivered the captain into the hands of the Hebrew whore who slew him! And though I may be wounded, I still have the strength to kill a cur such as you!"

On any other day I should have taken flight. But on that day I remembered what Judith had done for her God and her people. I raised the sword to my chest with both my hands, and putting all my weight behind it I staggered forward, thrust down and ran Bania through. As the blood gushed forth from his chest and his ugly face contorted in the grin of death, the sword slipped from my grasp and I fell to the ground in a faint.

It was this deed and my fainting that saved my life (the old man Isaac said). When the shouts of the returning Hebrews roused me from my stupor, my face and my garments were smeared with Bania's blood, for I had fallen over him. And since I wore no armor and replied in Hebrew when the men of Bethul called out to me, they took me for one of them. But I rose and hastened back to the house to plead for Judith's protection before I was found out.

When I saw the door of the house standing ajar I halted, afraid that Judith might have been slain. For I did not yet know that all the Babylonians were dead. But when I heard one shouting inside in Hebrew, "Judith, are you well, Judith?" I too entered the house.

The open door of the bedchamber revealed to me a gruesome sight. The Captain Holofernes lay dead upon the bed, his garments soaked with blood, his right hand hanging down and resting on the floor where he was wont to keep his sword. But the sword was gone from its place. Following a trail of blood across the room, my eyes were drawn to where Judith leaned against the wall. The hem of her skirt was stained with blood, and she kept her right arm extended from her body, her fist clutched around the handle of the sword as if her fingers were grown to it. Her face was ashen, and though her eyes were wide open they seemed sightless, nor did she blink when the Hebrew who had entered the room called her name over and over again. She must have stood thus for a long time, for there was a dark pool on the ground where the blood had dripped from the sword.

"We won the battle, Judith!" the Hebrew shouted again to rouse her from her stupor. "We beat those wretched heathens to nonexistence! And now let me strike off their leader's head that we may mount it on the wall for all the people to see!"

But when the man raised his sword as though to perform this

deed, Judith opened her mouth and spoke in a voice that sent
shudders down my back:

"Do not touch him, Joab. He is mine. I gave to God what I
promised God. What is left belongs to me."

And she slowly moved away from the wall and stood before the
bed with the sword in her hand like a sentry. As understanding
dawned in Joab's eyes, so did horror.

"Then the monster defiled you!" he exclaimed.

"Weigh well the words you speak to my face," Judith said in her
terrible voice. "It was my beauty that deceived him. But he did not
defile me."

"Then let me strike off his head and mount it on the wall," Joab
repeated.

I saw that his thirst for revenge was so deep that nothing but this
deed could quench it. But Judith stood guard before the captain's
body, saying:

"If you must show the people a head, the head of any Babylonian
soldier will serve. There is in Bethul none save Prince Hanun who
knew the Captain Holofernes, nor would he recognize a severed
head smeared with blood. And now leave me alone and lead your
men back to Bethul for the victory feast!"

"Will you not come with us? What if the people clamor for
you?" Joab asked.

"If the people clamor for me, tell them that I shall remain in my
house for three days until I have become purified from touching the
dead. None is to visit me but Tamar and her mother. Through them
I shall send word of what I would have you do next. Let none break
my command, for having killed one man I would find it a small
matter to kill another!"

The old woman Tamar lifted the pot with the stew from the fire
and moved it to the rim of the hearth, where it would remain warm
without being scorched. Then she drew near the table to continue
the tale:

While our soldiers crept down the hill in the dark, the women
mounted the wall to observe the battle below. But though we
could hear the shouting, the neighing of horses and the clang of
weapons, we saw nothing until the sun rose over the mountains of
Moab. Then we discovered that the ground between the tents below
was strewn with the bodies of dead Babylonians. As for our men,

they were still pursuing after those who had escaped, nor was it difficult to overtake the foe in our own hills. When our soldiers drifted back into the camp, we found that their numbers were not diminished. But none of us was astonished—for was this not the day of a great miracle? Now that we had gained victory, the elders prided themselves on their wise judgment and praised Judith for her valor. The people would have descended to fetch her with timbrels and dances had not Joab returned with her message, carrying mounted on a pole a bloody head.

At the sight of it I shuddered, remembering how handsome the Captain Holofernes had been and how Judith had adored him. However, the other women shrieked with glee as they danced around the head and befouled it in the most loathsome manner. But the face, the hair and the beard were caked with so much blood that the added filth was barely noticed.

When the head had been mounted on the wall, the women descended the hill in triumph to fill their jugs with the water for which this battle had been fought. For though the sky was covered with clouds, not a drop of rain had yet fallen. While the women quenched their thirst and splashed each other with the precious water, our men stripped the dead foes of their weapons and their silver bracelets, dismantled the tents, rounded up the remaining horses and carried the booty up to Bethul. Before the day was over nothing was left in the fields below but the naked bodies of the slain, and Judith's summer house standing solitary as it had stood before the enemy tents surrounded our hill.

Then my mother and I went down, carrying food and wine to Judith. She had locked herself into the house and would not open up until all the people were returned to Bethul. Nor would she let us in until we had vowed that we had come alone. Only then did she release the bolt on the door.

When I saw her I cried out in horror. She still carried the captain's sword in her right hand and her eyes were like those of one bereft of reason. As we entered she backed toward the door of the bedchamber, to guard it like a sentry.

My mother put down her basket, pulled from it a jug, and pouring wine into a cup she held it out to Judith.

"Drink this to cast out the memory," she said. "Then let me help you off with your bloody clothes!"

"Do not touch my robes while his blood on my skirts is still warmed by mine," Judith replied, striking the cup out of my mother's hand and keeping her at bay with the sword.

"You are madder than I feared," my mother said. "I never believed that the captain did not touch you. But neither did I believe that you would shut yourself in the house with his headless body."

Judith laughed terribly and moved away from the door to display the Captain Holofernes lying whole upon the bed. Though his chest was pierced through, there was a smile on his lips, witnessing his swift death. But when my mother would enter the room, Judith again barred her way. Then my mother said:

"Will you keep him here until his body rots and a worm falls out of his nose? Better cast him into the fields that the vultures may make an end of him!"

"Did I refuse the people of Bethul his head to cast his body out to the vultures?" Judith asked. "No, he is mine. I shall bury him as a wife buries her husband."

When she told us where she would bury the captain, my mother turned ashen.

"How would you carry him there?" she asked. "And how would you roll away the stone from the mouth of the cave, when this task requires the strength of three men?"

"His horse—which I shall claim as my booty—shall carry him there. As for rolling away the stone, have I not shown today the strength of a man? You and Tamar together might have the strength of another. As for a third, there is one here in the house with me, though he is only half a man."

And Judith called forth the eunuch who had concealed himself beneath a bundle of rags in one of the chambers.

"Have you, madwoman, kept one dead and one living Babylonian with you?" my mother exclaimed in horror.

"Though he calls himself Marduksharusur, the one alive is a Hebrew," Judith replied. "Having been the captain's slave, he too is my booty. And now let Tamar return to Bethul and claim my horse, for we must bury the captain tonight."

I did as Judith bade me. Our men had shut all the horses in a corral within Bethul. It took Joab's order to make them release one, for though they had no wine they seemed drunk from water. There was much revelry in the streets, and Joab whispered to me before unlocking the gate:

"Let Judith rid herself of what she has in the house before the night is over. I do not know how much longer I can detain the people from going to fetch her."

He did not say what Judith ought to do with the captain's body, nor did I reveal to him her plan. My strength was greatly taxed by leading the prancing horse down the steep path. I had not been near a horse since Hadad died, and then not very near. After tying the horse to the doorpost I entered the house to find that Judith had dressed the captain in his armor. But though she would bury him as one fallen in battle she would not place his sword under his head but kept it for herself.

When the captain was laid out, my mother mumbled that she had not seen such a man since Merari lay dead upon his bier. However, Judith seemed deaf and blind to everything about her, though she calmly did whatever task was required. She wrapped the captain's body in the bed cover and bade my mother and me grasp the foot end, while she took hold of the other. As for the eunuch, he ran this way and that, making a great display of doing nothing. Thus we three women carried the body outside and placed it across the saddle on the horse.

Night had fallen on the fields, with not a star shimmering through the heavy clouds. The air was cold with a hint of dampness on the wind, but yet there was no rain. Judith led the horse across the fields, while the eunuch followed close behind her, seeking shelter in her shadow. I was no less afraid than he, for I saw black shapes moving in the fields. Though they were perching vultures, I feared in my heart that they might be the ghosts of the fallen dead.

Nor did my terror diminish when we ascended the hill to the burial caves. It was a place I dreaded in the daytime and more so tonight, when the spirits might rise in wrath against the one we would lay to rest among them. But Judith climbed upward as though she could see in the dark, pulling the horse behind her. When we arrived at the caves she slowed her pace to count the sealing rocks until she came to the one she was searching for. There she bade us put our shoulders to the rock and help her roll it away from the mouth of the cave. Again the eunuch panted much but helped little, and I could hear his teeth chatter with terror.

When the stone was moved we lifted the captain's body from the horse and carried it to the entrance of the cave. Letting the blanket drop to the ground, Judith slipped her arms under the arms of the dead man and pulled him inside. I was glad that she did not ask my help, for I would have died of terror if I stumbled in the dark over the bones of the other one who lay buried in the cave.

We waited a long time shivering in the dark. When I began to fear that Judith might have done herself some harm, she came forth from the cave, bade us help her roll the stone back before the entrance, gathered up the blanket from the ground, grasped the horse's bridle and led it back to the house. Then, without changing her bloody garments, she carried the jug of wine which my mother had brought into the bedchamber and sat on the floor before the empty bed. There she remained all night, staring at the bloody sword she had leaned against the wall and drinking herself drunk.

Observing her through the open door of the bedchamber, my mother said:

"She is truly her father's daughter. Just so did Merari sit drunk on the ground after Shoshanna died, moaning 'I killed her, I killed her.' "

When Judith fell asleep on the floor toward dawn, I opened the door to let in the fresh morning air. But I did not dare cross the threshold, for there was a multitude of vultures in the fields, flapping their black wings and screeching at each other as they fought over the carrion. Now that the tents were gone, I saw how the ground was tramped by the hoofs of horses and the boots of a thousand men. Though it was already the month of late planting, there had been no rain to soften the soil, and the dark clouds above only seemed to mock the dry earth below. I wondered whether our fields would yield this year a crop other than the dead bodies of our foes.

Judith lay in deep slumber until at even a loud pounding on our door stirred her awake. She sat up gazing about her, and when her mind cleared she bade me send the caller away. But it was Joab come with the news that they had seen fire signals from Lachish and Azekah, warning them that the Babylonian army had reached Jerusalem.

"You had better come up to Bethul, for this house is no place for three women alone!"

However, Judith would not listen to Joab's pleas, and in the end he went away, while she remained with her face hidden in her hands, moaning:

"Surely the Babylonians will search for the troops that went before them! Though my head aches I must think, for I did not commit this deed that my people might be slain in reprisal and Bethul razed to the ground. Tomorrow at daybreak let all those who can wield a spade come down from Bethul. Let them gather up the slain, cast them in the trenches the enemy dug in our fields, scatter earth over them and level the ground. As for the booty they seized, let them burn the tent posts, cut up the hides of the tents, melt down the Babylonian silver bracelets, slaughter the horses that bear Nebuchadrezzar's brand, and bury the captured weapons beneath the floors of their houses. Should the Babylonians send spies to discover the fate of their lost troop, we shall pretend that we never saw any of them. Let Nebuchadrezzar search the wilderness for his soldiers! While he finds no trace of them here he will not trouble us, for of what value is our small village to the ruler of all nations?"

When I delivered this message to Bethul I barely escaped with my life, so incensed were the people over what Judith would have them do. But in the end Joab and the elders prevailed upon them to obey her command.

Next morning the people came down with spades to battle the vultures for their prey, cursing the day they must bury their slain foes. Nor was this an easy task, for the earthworks the enemy had thrown up had hardened, requiring much labor before they were leveled. It took three days to accomplish the work. Every night there were fire signals from Lachish, and every day fewer people came down from Bethul, for they feared being caught in the open field by the Babylonian soldiers. Judith might have roused the people to courage, but having thought of what must be done she went back to drinking, while my mother and I remained near her to tend to her needs.

When all the slain had been buried, a great silence settled over the fields. Our people had fled back within the walls of Bethul, and the vultures had flown away. Toward evening the silence became weighted with a blackness that filled me with dread. My mother and I huddled near the hearth, together with the eunuch. He had remained with us, fearing that the men of Bethul would slay him if he showed himself. Only Judith sat apart, drinking.

Suddenly there was the sound of a strong wind rushing over the fields, and a pounding on the roof such as we had not heard in many months. Judith stirred from her stupor, pushed away the wine jug, and rising from the ground she staggered to open the door. A gust of wind drove the rain into the kitchen, but Judith spread her arms as though to embrace the downpour and ran out into the night.

Leaning against the wind and the driving rain, I stepped before the door and shouted her name into the darkness. She did not answer, and all I heard was a roaring in the night as if God had unleased another deluge.

When Judith returned, her cheeks—which had not been stained by a single tear—were wet from rain and her tangled hair hung down in dripping strands. Her garments were soaked, the dark bloodstains on them merging with the darkness of the wet cloth. The cold water washing over Judith's face had cleared her head and she said soberly: "The drought is broken. The rains have come. Tomorrow we shall plow!"

It is true that I feared to show myself before the men of Bethul (the old man Isaac said to the young scribe). I did not know what lies Prince Hanun had told them about me, nor would I face them before they were sobered from their thirst for blood. Thus, while Tamar and her mother went to summon the men for the plowing, I approached Judith to tell her of my plight.

She was sitting on the bed in her chamber, cradling the captain's sword in her arms as one would cradle a child. I feared that she had fallen back into madness, but her eyes were clear in her pale face. Then I begged her to shield me from the wrath of the people, nor would saving me be her loss, for was I not her rightful booty?

Regarding me thoughtfully, Judith replied:

"Even in my grief and drunkenness I pondered your fate. No Hebrew should be a slave for more than seven years. And though it was not I who owned you, you have been a slave long enough. Therefore I shall set you free that you may learn the meaning of liberty. But first I must change your name, for it is not seemly that a Hebrew be called Marduksharusur."

"Lest you do what was done to me twice before, let me reveal to you that I have a Hebrew name. My mother called me Isaac, hoping that I should bring joy and laughter to her latter years. And though my name was turned to mockery I would keep it, since it was given me by the one who gave me life. But now let me throw myself at your feet to thank you for giving me the greatest gift next to life!"

How long I would remain free in a Judah beleagured by the Babylonian army I did not know. Nor did I dare consider my fate if upon my capture it was discovered that I alone of the lost troop had escaped alive. But soon my mind was turned to other troubles.

The two women returned from Bethul, bringing with them a team of oxen laden with sacks of seed, and a freshly honed plowshare. But they also brought the news that the men of Bethul would not come down to till the land.

"They fear being caught by soldiers in the open field, nor would they waste good seed," Tamar said. "For even if the enemy does not come now, he will surely come to burn the crops."

Then Judith roared with rage:

"They are like children who forget the lesson when the rod is put away! Did I save them from death by thirst only to see them die of hunger? Nine years ago Jerusalem fell after three months. But what if this time they hold out for years? Whence shall come our food if we do not sow? And shall my sacrifice have been for nought? No, the people shall live even if I myself must plow the fields!"

"Would you do man's work?" Tamar asked.

"Have I not done man's work before?" Judith replied, striding out of the house in anger.

We followed her outside and watched in awe as she hitched the plow to the team of oxen. Then she poured grain from one of the sacks into the seeder and bade Tamar hand her the whip. Cracking it over the fat rumps of the beasts, she prodded them into a slow walk. Once the oxen were set on their course, Judith grasped both handles of the plow and bore down with all her might to open a furrow in the damp soil. But we stood gaping after her as she stolidly followed the oxen, her arms taut with the effort of guiding the plow, her face set against the cold wind, and her skirt turning dark at the hem where it brushed the sodden clods of earth.

Nor were we alone in observing her. The people of Bethul had gathered on the wall, now one and now the other forming a funnel with his hands to shout down words she could not hear. But none came forth to aid her, not even Joab—though later we learned that his wife had detained him with threats of hurling herself off the wall if he went.

As for Judith's strength, it did not fail but increased miraculously. She plowed furrow after furrow, walking steadily behind the swaying oxen, while the wind billowed her garments like a sail and her red hair blew across her face. I thought myself caught in a dream, for I had never seen a woman do such work. But neither had I seen a woman who had killed a man with his own sword.

When Judith steered the oxen across the field toward the house, I thought she had done for the day. But she halted beside me and said:

"It is your turn now."

Turning pale, I exclaimed:

"Would you have me plow with these hands that in twenty years held nothing heavier than a stylus?"

And I stretched forth my hands, which were white and soft except where the stylus had calloused one of my fingers. Regarding me with contempt, Judith said:

"At the time of plowing one farmer is worth ten scribes. And if a weak woman can plow, so can you who are a man!"

But fearing hard labor almost as much as death, I replied:

"Your word cannot restore my manhood, nor your command teach me skills I never knew. Even when I was a slave on a farm outside Borsippa I was given no heavier task than feeding the fowl! Did you set me free only to work me harder than the least slave?"

Then Judith bit her lips, pulled the whip from its holder, and stepping near me she said softly:

"Though I set you free, you speak as a slave in that you believe freedom means idleness. But I shall teach you the burden of freedom!" And striking me across the face with the whip, she shouted: "And now you shall plow!"

And so I plowed. I shall not describe to you my aching arms and legs, nor my blistering palms. Neither shall I make long mention of the laughter on the wall when I stumbled after the oxen, trying to hold down the plow while Judith walked beside me with the whip in her hand. But lest you think that I had no profit from my work, let me tell you that my plowing in the sight of all the people inclined their hearts toward me. For even if they did not believe that I had drawn up the map of the Babylonian camp for them, they could not deny what they witnessed with their own eyes. And thus I came to be accepted by the people of Bethul.

That night I slept so deeply I would not have waked if all the host of Babylon had descended on the house and burned it over my head. But the one who woke me next morning was no less terrible, nor did she show me mercy though I wept at her feet and begged her to let me rest.

"The price of freedom is high, as I can attest," Judith said. "But without it one might better be dead."

After the second day of plowing I thought I would soon be both free and dead. Judith made me take turns with her at the plow, and when I fainted by the way, she put Tamar and her mother to the task. But Tamar was too weak and her mother too old, and in the end Judith did most of the work. Whence came her strength I do not know, but then one must not question miracles.

On the third day Tamar again ascended to Bethul to fetch more seed, and also food for our household. When she was ready to drive the oxen up the path, Judith emerged from the house with a basket on her arm. Handing it to Tamar, she said:

"Bring me my widow's garb from town." For she was still dressed in the fine robes in which she had come into the Babylonian camp, though now they were soiled with dried blood and caked with earth. "And return these things to the place where you found them. I would never set eyes on them again."

As the sun broke through the clouds, I saw a glittering in the basket before Tamar wrapped her scarf around it.

When she returned from Bethul she had new tales to tell. In their shame over seeing Judith toil in the fields, the men had resumed work on Merari's shaft. Taking turns at the digging, they had nearly doubled its former depth. But Judith only mumbled:

"Some fools will provide for a need after they suffered it. If they were wise they would plow, but then they have not yet known hunger."

Nor would they this year, for Judith and I tilled not only her own fields but also those of the others. If her strength sprang from faith, mine sprang from fear of her. But together we prevailed and God was with us. Dry days followed upon rainy days. And though the Babylonian army had spread over all the open land around Jerusalem, they did not come against Bethul.

Where only a short time ago there had been a battlefield seeds began to sprout. Not since I had lived on Iddina's farm had I seen a green carpet of tender shoots cover the black soil. Now that the raw flesh on my palms was healed I took pride in the work I had so unwillingly done, nor was weeding the fields hard labor after the plowing. Though I had always slept late in winter I soon fell into the habits of a farmer, rising early with the women.

It was on such a morning four months after the plowing that Judith stood in the open door to scan the fields. She stood leaning with her back against the doorpost, her red hair gleaming in the sun, the breeze that rippled the young green stalks of grain billowing her garments. I sat by the table, waiting for Tamar's mother to give me a piece of the bread she had baked before dawn. My mouth watered at the savory smell, and so intent was I upon my greed that I paid scant heed to the old woman's mutterings.

"She descended like Anath to slay Mot. Instead she slew Baal. But Baal always returns to life in spring. Behold, he rises again in her own body!"

I had always thought the old woman a witch, but now I thought her mad. However, gazing more closely at Judith, I saw that it was not the breeze swelling her garments.

She was with child.

Until that morning I knew as little as Isaac (the old woman Tamar said to the young scribe). Judith herself must have known from the day she missed her time of the moon. But if she felt faint she pretended it was from hard work, and if the sight of food made her sick, it had done so before. As for the puffed skin under her eyes, I thought it caused by her sleepless nights. Thus I did not know that she was with child until my mother spoke of it.

"When I first feared this," my mother said, "I mixed her a potion to make her cast off the fruit of her womb. But she struck the cup out of my hand, saying: 'He would have me bear him seven sons. Let me at least bear him one to continue his seed on earth!' Seeing that she wanted the child, I told her to pray for a daughter if she would live. But she replied: 'Let me die then! I made provision for my people. At any rate I shall die after the harvest.'"

I was glad then that the villagers had shut themselves within the walls of Bethul. Though they had sung Judith's praises, I feared they would deal harshly with her if she bore a Babylonian bastard. Thus when they inquired about Judith, I said she was well.

But the people of Bethul continued their lives as before. They ate, drank, slept and begot. Some married, some gave birth, but none died during these months, and so there was no need to open the gates. Though every night there were fire signals from Lachish and Azekah, the war seemed far away. Many believed that God had made a covenant with Judith, promising her that Bethul should be spared. That she kept herself concealed made her even more holy in their sight.

Now that Judith was past her months of sickness, her beauty still increased. The skin of her face was smooth again, and her full white breasts would have been a husband's delight. But the one who had made her blossom lay buried in the hills.

As the child began to stir within her, she grew restless. She would leave the house to roam through the fields in which the barley now stood golden, the high stalks concealing her ripe belly from any who might look down from the wall. At times I would follow Judith to aid her if she grew faint from the heat. But she walked about undaunted, nor was the sun as fierce as three years before, when Manasseh had died at the time of the barley harvest. The coolness of night lingered into the morning until the milky sky turned blue and the singing of birds grew fainter. The wildflowers on the slopes had not yet withered and the poppies in the fields were a deep red as though tinted by the soil from which they grew. Never before had the barley stood so high after a late planting, never had the blades grown as broad as a man's hand. Marveling at that miracle of plenty from the wall, the villagers told each other that God had truly blessed Judith's work. But my mother proclaimed that the soil had been rendered fruitful by the thousand men whose blood and bones had been scattered over the fields like dung.

Sometimes Isaac walked with us in the fields. His white scribe's hands had hardened, and the color of his face had turned ruddy. He who had never before seen the hills of Judah in springtime said he knew now why the Hebrew captives mourned for their homeland. And yet at times he confessed that his own heart longed for Babylon, though there would be no festivals this spring.

Nebuchadrezzar's hopes of bringing the troops home for the New Year had come to nought, and the king of Babylon remained in Riblah. The siege of Jerusalem continued until the Egyptian army came forth from their land. Then the Babylonians broke up from Jerusalem to drive back their more dangerous foe.

This happened shortly after we began harvesting. Again it appeared a miracle meant to save us. Now the heat increased from day to day, and if the grain was not cut in its fullness it would wither on the stalk. Judith was too big with child to labor as at the time of plowing, nor would she show herself in the fields once the grain was cut. But when Nebuchadrezzar's troops broke up from Jerusalem, the men of Bethul regained their courage to come forth from the walls to harvest. Then Judith said to me:

"Go tell the men that though I planted their fields, the grain I sowed was mine and so are the crops. Let them pay me if they would eat the fruit of my labor! The day to reward idleness and cowardice is not yet come!"

The men could easily have defied Judith, but they feared that God would turn the grain to dust in their hands if they refused her demands. Thus each paid in his manner—some with the silver they had stripped off the Babylonian soldiers and others, whose loot had been poor, with deeds to their land. When the harvest had been gathered and the grain taken to the threshing floors, Judith was richer than before. But she continued concealed in her house and would speak to none.

After the Babylonian army broke up from Jerusalem, Prince Hanun returned to his own land. For it was safe now to travel through the hills. But before setting out on his journey home, the prince came to Judith's house, knocked on the door and entreated her to come with him as his wife. When she would not answer, he shouted:

"If ever you change your heart, Judith, the borders of my land will be open to you! Indeed they will be open to all Hebrews who wish to escape from Nebuchadrezzar. For they treated me kindly and did not slay me when I was delivered bound into their hands."

Later many were to flee across the Jordan, where King Baalis gave them safe refuge because of his son. Thus the two enemies of yore were joined in their hatred for the Babylonians. But not all who fled went to Ammon.

One day we heard in Bethul that Jeremiah had been detained as he tried to leave Jerusalem to go to the land of Benjamin. And when they accused him of falling away to the Babylonians, he said he had left town only to claim a field in Anathoth that had become his inheritance. But none believed him, and the only one who would have dared swear to the truth of his words was big with child and concealed in her house.

In the end King Zedekiah let the prophet go. However, in these times a man was detained one day, set free the next, and detained again on the third day. No sooner was Jeremiah released than he predicted that the Babylonian army would return victorious to destroy Jerusalem. When he called again for surrender, he was cast into a pit filled with mire, where he would surely have perished had not an Ethiopian officer at court pleaded with the king for his life. This same officer, Ebed-Melech by name, lowered ropes into the pit and gently hoisted the prophet from the slimy depth. But when we professed amazement that of all the officers at court an Ethiopian should have shown such mercy for a Hebrew prophet, Isaac said:

"You, who know nothing of the world, may be amazed. As for me, I would have perished long ago had not an Ethiopian carried me on his back from Nineveh to Babylon!"

But you must remember that Isaac told many lies in his life, nor was there ever a tale that he would not wish to surpass with one more astounding.

Neither the jailing of Jeremiah nor the threat of death could prevent his words from coming true. When the Babylonians returned to surround Jerusalem, there was no hope left that the siege might again be broken. For after defeating the Egyptian army, Nebuchadrezzar's troops had stormed the two mighty fortresses that guarded the road to Jerusalem. We could still see fire signals from Lachish, but we could no longer see Azekah. When it became known that Lachish too had fallen, the people of Bethul fled back within their walls. Now all the land south of Jerusalem was in the hands of the enemy. Jerusalem was sealed off from every side so that none could go in or come out. But though we no longer received news from the capital, we knew that they would soon suffer famine. For unlike us they had not been able to sow and reap this year. Our harvest of barley was safe within the walls of Bethul, and it was not yet time to pick the olives and gather the grapes.

While the summer heat lay heavily on the cropped fields, we left the house only after dark or before dawn. Then Judith and I went to the spring to draw water. Now that all the people were fled into town we stood in no danger of being observed. Judith was become heavy and her ankles swollen. She often bade me fill a basin with cold water, and she would sit on a rock soaking her swollen feet. In the dark the splashing of the spring sounded louder than in olden times. While they had still dared come down into the fields, the men had deepened the pool in which the water collected. Moreover, they had begun digging a tunnel beneath the hill of Bethul. When the Babylonians returned, they had halted the work. But they vowed to complete the tunnel from within the hill until it joined with the part they had dug from without. Sometimes, in the silence before dawn, we could hear the scraping and knocking through the rock. Then Judith would sigh and say:

"Had they shown such zeal a year ago, my life would have taken a different course."

I was not certain that in her heart she really wished it so. If she had remained a chaste widow, how could she be with child now? And her mind was wholly upon the child in her womb. She bade me fetch her fine linen robes from town and tore them up for swaddling clothes. And she had me bring down a cow, fearing that she would lack milk to suckle her child. For she was too old to bring forth her first-born.

My mother observed Judith with sorrow, but she spoke her fears only to me:

"To prepare as Judith does means tempting the gods. And if the child lives, she cannot conceal it forever from the people. But men's gratitude is even shorter than their memory. They will surely stone her if they discover that she did not save them by a miracle but in the manner of mortal women."

When I warned Judith about this, she said she would pretend that a maiden from another village had left her bastard on our threshold one night. Surely none would prevent her from raising the infant, since she had no child of her own.

As the time of the grape harvest drew near, so did the time of Judith's confinement. But the grapes turned dark and heavy on the vines and still she did not give birth. Her belly grew bigger every day, and she could barely walk. My mother wailed that even one on whom there was no curse could not hope to live bearing a giant.

When the grapes were ripe for the picking, Judith bade us go up into vineyards with baskets. But my mother refused to leave her alone in the house.

"What if your pangs seize you while we are away in the hills?" she asked.

"The first child does not come quickly," Judith replied. "Nor is there much you can do when the pains commence. But to let the grapes rot on the vine is a sin. None will come down from Bethul to do the picking, and we must not lose the harvest!"

And she drove us from the house, placing the needs of the land above her own. Every day my mother, Isaac and I ascended the slopes to gather the grapes. It was the fifth month of the year, and though we began work at daybreak it soon became hot. But we did not dare cease before we had filled many baskets. I carried most of the burden, my mother having become too old for such work, and Isaac lamenting as in the days of the plowing. But while the earth had been black and wet then, it now turned yellow and cracked in the heat. We could plainly see in the valley below where the soil had sunk down into the trenches that were the graves of a thousand Babylonians. Then we would gaze fearfully toward the north and west, for if a troop of soldiers suddenly came upon us our lives would be worth less than a basket of grapes.

But when we spoke to Judith of our fears, she replied that those who observed the wind did not sow and those who watched the clouds did not reap.

Indeed the Babylonians seemed to have forgotten about Bethul, or if one were to believe Isaac, they had never even heard of our town. Thus we filled many more baskets with grapes and carried them up to Bethul. Nor did we neglect to take receipts for every basket we delivered into town. These Judith stored in an earthenware jar against the day when she would demand payment from the people.

As for her giving birth, it seemed that she would carry the child in her womb forever. But one evening when we returned home weary from the day's work, we found Judith lying upon her bed, her face ashen and her forehead covered with sweat.

"You had better prepare what needs preparing," she said to my mother. "The pangs commenced at noon."

Bending over Judith to feel her belly, my mother said it would be some time yet before she gave birth. But she bade me lay out the swaddling clothes, set a kettle with water on the hearth, and shut the door tightly that none might hear Judith's screams in the still of the night.

Then we settled down for the waiting. The hours passed, and though the pains were strong they were far apart. Judith reclined on her bed, her head against the wall on which she had hung the captain's sword. She had not pushed it back into its scabbard, and the tip on which the blood had dried to a dark brown was no more than a hand's breadth above her head. Whenever she reared up in one of her pangs, I thought the sword would pierce into her brain. But then she would sink down again, panting yet unharmed. And still the child would not come. When toward morning Judith asked how much longer, my mother replied that it might not be until the sun set again.

"How will I bear it?" Judith moaned.

But she did not scream once, though her torment was great. When her pains still increased she pulled from beneath her garments the amulet which the captain had given her—for she had never taken it off—and bit on it to keep from crying out. I feared she would break her teeth, but her teeth proved stronger than the metal and left their sharp marks on the goddess.

In the end I could no longer bear to witness her agony and went outside to seek comfort with Isaac. I discovered him sitting on the ground beside the door, his hands clapped over his ears. When I asked him what he was doing, he replied:

"Though I was near a woman in travail but once, the sound of her screams is still in my ears."

"There is no need to cover your ears now," I said. "Judith will not scream. But we had better go inside and shut the door, for the heat is turning fierce and we must not let it fill the house."

After the glare of the sun, the dimness of the kitchen was soothing. I moved the kettle from the flame, for the water was boiling and the child not yet born. Isaac huddled in a corner with his face to the wall, swaying back and forth. Had I not known him to be a eunuch, I would have thought that he was praying for the birth of a son.

And still there was no cry of an infant from Judith's bedchamber, only her soft moaning. I took heart and again approached the door. My mother had made Judith rise from the bed and sit upon her knees with her legs spread wide, urging her to press down with all her might. But Judith only shook her head and shut her eyes, gripping my mother's shoulders so hard that I feared she would crush her bones. The heat in the room was stifling, and the garments of both women were soaked with sweat. Their faces gleamed wet, and Judith's hair stuck to her head as if she had walked in the rain. When she recovered her breath, she opened her eyes and said:

"I know it is a son. He is trying to kill me for what I did to his father."

"You did what you did for your people and your god, may he grant you life," my mother replied. "And now press down!"

I remained in the room then, now wiping the forehead of the one, now of the other with a rag dipped in cool water. It was past noon and Judith had been in travail for more than a day. And still the pains were far apart. Toward evening she said:

"If I die and the child lives, you shall name him Merari. Now let Isaac find a piece of potsherd and put it in writing that the child is to be heir to all I own. I shall sign my name to it while I am still in my senses, and you and Tamar shall bear witness."

Then she returned to her bed, saying it was not seemly that Isaac should see her sitting on my mother's knees with her legs spread wide. But even so he was in terror. Whenever Judith was seized by a pang his face turned ashen, and his fingers trembled so that he could barely record her words. No sooner had Judith signed her name and we made our marks than he fled back to the kitchen, where I heard him retch and moan as if he were giving birth.

After midnight the span between Judith's pangs grew shorter. But she would not resume her place on my mother's knees.

"Let me give birth on the bed where he drew my blood and I his," she said. "And if I am to die, let me die on the same bed."

How she kept from screaming then I do not know. Every time her body arched in pain I shrieked until my mother slapped my face. When Judith's water broke toward morning, my mother drove me out to ready the bath for the babe. In the kitchen I found Isaac prostrate on his belly, his hands shielding his ears. He had mistaken my shrieks for Judith's. But rather than speak to him I hastily filled a pan with water and ran back into the bedchamber. As I entered, Judith let out her only scream and brought forth her child amidst blood and excrement. Then she fainted.

I stood with my hand clapped over my mouth as I watched my

mother lift the child from between Judith's legs. Though the babe
was still covered with slime and blood, I could see it was a boy. My
mother raised him up by his feet, shook him, slapped him and
splashed him with water. But she could not restore his breath.

As for Judith, she lived.

When she recovered her senses, she raised her head to look across
the room.

"Where is my son?" she asked.

My mother had taken the small body to the kitchen, and I did not
dare answer Judith.

"It *is* a son?" she asked then.

While I still stood with my hand over my mouth, my mother
returned from the kitchen.

"Where did you take my child?" Judith shouted, though she was
weak. "Bring him to me that I may feast my eyes on him!"

I thought my mother would tell her then, but she went to the
kitchen and fetched the child. Now that she had cut the cord of the
afterbirth and washed the babe, I could see how handsome a child
he was. His head was covered with hair. His limbs were perfectly
formed, and there was no blemish on his body. My mother held him
up for Judith to see.

"Is he asleep so soon?" Judith asked.

"He is dead," my mother said.

Her eyes filled with disbelief, Judith pushed herself up on her
elbows to see the better. When she saw that my mother had spoken
the truth, she threw back her head and howled like a beast.

"God," she cried, "was it not enough? Must I plow and sow and
reap and bear men and slay them and bury them? Did it not suffice
that I gave you what I treasured most? Must you also take my first-
born, the fruit of my body, for the sin of my soul?"

And she struck the bed with her fists and cursed God in a manner
that made my blood run cold.

My mother handed me the child's cold body, and filling a cup, she
put it to Judith's lips. Judith struggled and coughed, but in the end
she swallowed the potion. She was calm almost at once, and when
her eyes closed I thought her asleep.

"What shall we do with the babe?" I whispered to my mother,
loath of holding the dead child much longer.

But Judith was not yet asleep. She opened her eyes, and looking at me she spoke with great effort:

"Bury him with his father. And put this in the grave with him."

She held out to me something that glittered dully in the palm of her hand. It was the image of the goddess.

Without the ox we took along, we could never have moved the heavy rock from the mouth of the cave (the old man Isaac said to the young scribe). With the child we buried my hope for one who would take in my heart the place of the boy David. I had indeed prayed for a son. I should have rocked him on my knees, taught him to read and write as he grew older, and told him tales of the happy land of Dilmun where the lion did not kill, the wolf did not tear the sheep, and there was neither sickness nor old age nor death. Instead I carried him in a basket to the burial cave in the hills. The old woman had wrapped him in his swaddling clothes and hung the amulet around his neck. And he slept with his fathers.

As for Judith, she rose from her couch after three days, saying that she was not a city woman to lie abed for weeks. She bade Tamar wash the bedcover, but the bloody stains of love and death and birth had left their marks forever. You can see them to this day.

Soon Judith followed us into the hills to gather the grapes, for the harvest was not yet completed. If she still lacked the strength to fill many baskets, she was strong enough to drive us on. But when it came to delivering the baskets into town, she would not go with us.

Now that I was known and trusted in Bethul, none prevented me from walking about freely. I went to look at Merari's shaft, which seemed bottomless, with steps cut into the rock running round the sides like a spiral. The men had completed the tunnel from within the hill and had hollowed out a large chamber below, where the water from the spring ran into a pool. Bending over the shaft, one could feel the cool vapor rising from the damp earth. Had it been completed a year before, both Judith's life and mine would have taken a different course.

As for the people of Bethul, they were glad of the lies we told them about Judith when they inquired after her. Indeed they added many more tales to ours until in their minds she ceased to be mortal.

Thus they were less ashamed to write over to her their fields and houses for the grain and wine she sold them. Moreover, they said:

"What good are our fields to her, who has no son? After the war she will surely restore them to us! But if the Babylonians come, they will slay Judith, burn Bethul and lead us away captive. Then the land will be lost to her and to us."

Like fools they did not consider that Judith had kin, even one male kinsman by her husband. Someday Joab might take it into his mind to claim the land, for even honest men have been known to be altered by the scent of wealth.

But it was my task to take pledges, not to offer counsel. As we delivered the rest of the harvest—the olives and the summer fruit—the receipts grew in number until Judith had filled many jars with pieces of potsherd. And before the war was over she owned every field, every house and every person in Bethul.

Later people would say that they had given her all the lands as a reward for her great deed, for they would not admit their cowardice before their children.

By the time the early rains came and the air turned cold, Judith had recovered her strength. But the past year had left its mark on her. Though her beauty was still great, there were hard lines in her face and she began to look like a peasant woman. When the sun struck her hair as we worked side by side in the fields, I could see a glint of silver among the red. But otherwise Judith was as unaltered as the land that swallowed up the dead and went on living.

When the next harvest time came around, the Babylonians were still besieging Jerusalem. But they did not come against Bethul, for the fates of war did not turn on a small village in the hills. That year the men and women came down for the reaping. The early rains and the late rains had come in their season, and the harvest was even richer than the previous year. Now that she was no longer with child, Judith mingled freely with the people, appointing them tasks as if all were her servants. But even the men obeyed her orders, as if by slaying one she too had become a man.

Only Joab still thought of her as a woman. When the harvest was hauled into town, he pleaded with her to return to Bethul lest she be slain in the fields. But Judith replied:

"What more can the Babylonians take from me than my life? Have I not lost all I held dear?"

When Joab understood whereof she spoke, he said bitterly:

"The one thing you love better than any man you kept."

And he went his way, seeing he could not wrest her from the land.

As for me, I was become a farmer. In one year I had learned to observe the clouds, to pray for rain, and to dread the cankerworm and the drought. If not for the receipts I wrote out, I would have forgotten how to hold a stylus. I often wondered whether all my learning had been for nought. Had I wasted the tears I shed while studying Sumerian? Had it been folly to practice my Greek letters? Had I mingled with sages and courtiers only to end up plowing the fields around Bethul, the freed slave of a mad Hebrew woman?

But while the enemy was still troubling Judah I did not dare confess that I longed for Babylon.

Nebuchadrezzar's troops had besieged Jerusalem in the tenth month of the ninth year of Zedekiah's reign. Now we were in the fourth month of the eleventh year. Twice the fields around Jerusalem had not been planted, and by now there was famine in the city.

One dark night in the fourth month there was a knock on our door. Sleeping in the kitchen, I was the first to hear it. My bowels turned to water and I crept deeper into a corner, fearing that the Babylonians had sent patrols into all the villages to seize them by surprise. In the end Judith awoke and opened the door, while the other two women huddled in terror against the wall. But the man who entered was a Hebrew.

He staggered in, covered with dust and blood, nor was he able to speak until he had refreshed himself with wine. Only then did he reveal to us the dreadful news.

In the fourth month the famine had become so sore in Jerusalem that there was no more bread left for the people. Even the king and his court were starving. Then, on the ninth day of the month, a breach was made in the city, but the king with all the men of war fled by night through the gate between the walls, which was by the king's garden. Now the Babylonians were all about the city, but Zedekiah and his troops went by the way of the Arabah. However, the Babylonian troops pursued after them and overtook Zedekiah in the plains of Jericho, scattering all his army from him. The king was taken prisoner while some of his soldiers escaped, the bearer of this news being one of them. He had fled south along the Jordan and then crossed the hills, following the paths of mountain goats and nourishing himself from whatever wild fruit and grain he could find. That he had arrived at our house alive was no less than a miracle.

When I led the man up to Bethul next morning, he asked:

"How is it that a woman of such beauty dwells alone in the fields in these times?"

I replied that there was no need for me to tell him the tale, for he would hear no end of it in Bethul. And leaving him at the gate, I returned to Judith's house.

That man was not the last to knock on our door. A few of the Hebrew soldiers had escaped across the Jordan into Ammon, but others wandered for days through the wilderness, some to perish in the barren hills, some to find their way to our house. Still others escaped from Jerusalem after the Babylonians seized the city. These brought us further grim news.

The king, his sons and his nobles had been taken to Nebuchadrezzar in Riblah. And the king of Babylon passed judgment on Zedekiah for having broken the holy oath he swore before him, when he made him king of Judah in the throne room of his father. And he slew the sons of Zedekiah before his eyes. He also slew all the princes of Judah in Riblah. And he put out Zedekiah's eyes, bound him in fetters and carried him to Babylon, to be kept in prison until his death.

Then I remembered how eleven years ago Nebuchadrezzar had refused to slay King Jehoiachin and his sons, saying that he would not show fear before a mere boy and unborn children. But much had happened since to teach the king of Babylon fear. And I also remembered my master's prediction that great power did not make a man stronger and nobler but weaker and baser, and that in the end he would do what he had forsworn.

In the fifth month, on the ninth day of the month, the sky in the north turned a deep red though the sun had already set. The darker it turned the brighter became the sky, as if God in His wrath had filled the heavens with fire. And we knew Jerusalem was burning.

I had seen another great city burned by the Babylonians, and I knew that they made of it a thorough task. Of Sennacherib and Ashurbanipal's palaces no stone was left standing upon the other, nor of the temple of Nebo and the great library where I had learned to read and write. But all was turned into heaps of ruins.

Looking up at the flaming sky, the women wrung their hands and wailed:

"Ah, the monsters, ah, the beasts!"

But having lived among the Babylonians, I knew that they were neither monsters nor beasts. They worshiped their gods, obeyed their laws, loved their wives and spoiled their children, nor did they buy or sell without signing contracts before many witnesses. And they all honored their great king who put up inscriptions on every wall professing his love of peace. Truly the Babylonians were no monsters. And that made what they did in Jerusalem on this ninth day of Ab all the more dreadful.

Later we learned that the Captain Nabuzaradan was charged with sacking Jerusalem. This was the same Nabuzaradan who together with the Captain Holofernes had measured the thickness of the brazen pillars before the temple. And Nabuzaradan broke down the pillars cast by Hiram of Tyre, whom Nebuchadrezzar had proclaimed the greatest craftsman born in a thousand years. He also seized all the brass pots and shovels and pans, and the vessels of silver and of gold that had not been carried away eleven years ago. When he had plundered Jerusalem he burned the temple of Yahweh, and the king's palace and the houses of all the people. And he broke down the walls that Jerusalem might never again be turned into a fortress.

But Nebuchadrezzar remained in Riblah, for he had sworn not to look upon the destruction of another city, and a king of Babylon does not break his vow.

Then Nabuzaradan seized all the high officials that were still found in the city and brought them to Nebuchadrezzar that he might judge them for having caused the war. And the king of Babylon put them to death in Riblah, in the land of Hamath. And Nabuzaradan also carried away the common people from Jerusalem, but their number is disputed to this day. He left only of the poorest of the land to be vinedressers and husbandmen, and he gave them fields and vineyards in those days. Then the poor blessed the conquerors, for land was more precious to them than the temple into which few had ever set foot.

Only two men of standing were set free to go whither they pleased—Jeremiah and Ezekiel, whom many called traitors. Jeremiah chose Judah over all the honors Nebuchadrezzar offered him in Babylon, but Ezekiel followed the captives. Some said he was maddened by grief over the death of his young wife and thought he would find her alive in Tel-Abib. But others proclaimed that he would not remain behind with the poor, while all the men of learning were carried to Babylon.

As for me, I envied Ezekiel his fate. However, I had no choice but to remain in Bethul and work for Judith. A year had passed almost to the day since Judith had lost her son to the day the temple was burned. Though it was a year of grief, the earth continued to bring forth. There was a great abundance of wine and summer fruit all over Judah. The Babylonians had sacked and burned the great cities, but they had not cut down the groves or pulled up the vines. For they were men who came from a land of plenty, and though they would kill people they would not see them suffer hunger.

Even now Nebuchadrezzar did not set a Babylonian governor over Judah but appointed Gedaliah the son of Ahikam to rule over those who were left behind. And Gedaliah called upon the people to harvest and to dwell in the cities that were left standing.

Now, when all the captains of the forces that were in the fields heard that Gedaliah was made governor over Judah, they went to dwell with him in Mizpah, the city he had made his seat. And all the people who had fled to Ammon and Moab and Edom returned to Judah. But there were among those who returned some who would not serve a governor set over them by the Babylonians.

It was in the seventh month, after the harvest was completed and the people were working the wine and olive presses in town, that eleven men came riding to our house. We could see them approaching from the distance, for the day was clear and the fields were covered with only a short, brown stubble. The men were in full armor, the sun striking glittering sparks from their helmets and shields. We had not seen armed men since all the Babylonians were slain, nor did we know whether those approaching were friend or foe. I would have fled inside the house and bolted the door behind me, but Judith remained outside, shielding her eyes with her hands as she observed the warriors draw near. When they came close I recognized them as Hebrews. Though I was poised for flight I lingered by the door, curious to learn why they had come armed as for war.

The one who rode at their head reined his horse and regarded Judith, who stood facing him boldly. Then he addressed her:

"What Prince Hanun said about your beauty, Judith, was true. He also spoke the truth concerning your boldness, for few women would dare meet a band of armed men in the field these days. I have little doubt that you will aid us in our task!"

"And who may my lord be, and what task does he mean?" Judith asked, gazing steadily at the stranger.

"I am Ishmael the son of Nethaniah, of the blood royal," the man replied. "I have come to restore the rule of Judah to those who were appointed to it by God."

Hearing this, I wondered whether there was in Ishmael's veins more royal blood than in mine. Had not my grandmother's father sat on the throne of Judah? Nor did I like the manner in which he would burden God with his heart's ambition. But seeing that Judith would ask no questions, Ishmael continued:

"Prince Hanun told us how you dealt with the Babylonians. Surely you would not suffer a puppet of these same Babylonians to rule Judah! Therefore raise your battle cry, Judith, and summon your hundred brave warriors that they may ride with us to Mizpah and slay this accursed Gedaliah! If your men would fight, King Baalis would furnish them arms and horses, for he has not forgotten how a base Babylonian dealt with his son."

Then Judith sighed and said:

"Does it not suffice that our land was laid waste by our foe? Must now Hebrew slay Hebrew? Are men like lions that they cannot have their fill of blood once they have tasted of it? As for me, I would not goad brother to kill brother. What tales Prince Hanun told you of me I do not know. But one thing I do know: war is not the invention of women. All I ever wanted in my heart was to work my land in peace, raise my cattle, bear my sons and have a husband to share my bed at night!"

As Judith spoke, the color rose in her cheeks, her eyes flashed, and she was as beautiful as in former times. Gazing at her with lust, Ishmael said:

"Soon you shall have all your heart desires. If you will help us, I myself shall take you for my wife, and you shall bear me a son to sit on the throne of David!"

Then Judith bit her lips, rubbed the scar on her neck and replied softly:

"There was another man who offered to make me the mother of a king. I slew him in his sleep. Knowing this, would my lord dare close his eyes beside me? No, I shall never bear a son to sit on any throne, nor shall I ever take another husband. But I beg my lord to ride on and leave my people in peace. They have done their share of fighting and will not stain their hands with the blood of Hebrews!"

Had Ishamel not feared that he and his band were being observed from the wall of Bethul, he would have slain us in the field that day. For—as is known to all now—he was a man to whom the shedding of blood was a small matter. Thus he only scowled and warned us not to speak to any of what we had heard. And swinging his horse around, he galloped off with his troop behind him.

No sooner had they vanished over the hills than Judith sent Tamar up to Bethul with word for Joab, bidding him to dispatch a warning to Gedaliah in Mizpah. But it was the fate of messengers from Bethul not to find credence. Indeed Gedaliah accused those who would warn him of slandering Ishmael, proving himself an honest man who cannot conceive of another's baseness. Thus Gedaliah the son of Ahikam suffered the fate of an honest man, being slain by Ishmael in his own house, where they ate bread together. Ishmael also slew the Hebrews that were with Gedaliah, all the Babylonian garrison, and fourscore men from Shechem, Shiloh and Samaria who were come to sacrifice at Mizpah. Then he cast the bodies into a pit, and carried away captive the rest of the people that were left in Mizpah to go over to Ammon. These captives in turn fled from him when Johanan the son of Kareah and all the captains of the forces that were with him came to fight with Ishmael by the great waters in Gibeon. But Ishmael escaped from Johanan with eight men and returned to Ammon.

Then Johanan took the remnant of the people he had recovered from Ishmael and assembled them in Gerut Chinham, which is near

Bethlehem, to go down into Egypt. For they feared Nebucha-drezzar's wrath because his governor had been slain. Many from all over Judah came to join them. Even a few from Bethul said it was better to dwell in Egypt, where they would see no war, nor hear the sound of the horn or know hunger. These left Bethul though Judith cursed them. But she could not detain them, even as Jeremiah could not prevent Johanan and all his people from going down into Egypt. Indeed they carried the prophet with them against his will, together with his scribe, Baruch the son of Neriah. And Jeremiah continued to prophesy in Egypt until he died.

When all who would stir up trouble were departed, there was peace in the land. The soldiers and nobles and men of wealth were gone, but those who lived off the soil remained.

We plowed and sowed and reaped at the appointed seasons, we gathered the grapes and beat the olive trees and picked the summer fruit. All the land around Bethul belonged to Judith, and she was mother to all. As pay for their labor she doled out enough to the people that none suffered hunger, nor was there ever a famine, for she laid up stores for the lean years. The surplus yield of her fields she filled in sacks and sold in villages whose harvests had been poor, as she had done in former times. But though her wealth increased she continued dwelling in her hut in the fields, where she had known the husband of her heart and born her son.

In town they revered Judith for her modest manner of life and her piousness. Nor did any dare protest when after old Dinah's death she went up into the sacred grove to cut down the pole of Ashtoreth and smash her altar. From then on only Yahweh was worshiped in Bethul. But the women wear amulets of the goddess beneath their garments to this day.

As the years passed, I forgot my Sumerian and Greek. Indeed I would have forgotten how to speak Babylonian had Judith not taken me with her when she went to sell her grain in the villages near the Sea Road. It was there that the caravans from Babylonia passed in the spring on their way down to Egypt, to trade between wars.

I would wait by the road for the camel trains bearing silks and spices from India, fine woolen cloaks from Babylon, carved ivory

and wrought jewelry from Hamath, purple cloth from Sidon, and
sacks of barley and wheat from the rich Euphrates Valley in the
years when the harvest was poor in Egypt. For there is no dishonor
in feeding one's foe at a good profit. From these merchants I begged
news of Babylon, pretending that I had often traveled there on
business before the war. For I would still keep it a secret that I was
the only one left alive from that ill-fated campaign.

The merchants were pleased to discover one who spoke their
tongue in this distant land. They told me how Nebuchadrezzar had
warred against Ammon to prevent King Baalis from stirring up the
smaller nations against him, for he would have peace in his vast
realm even if he had to gain it by waging war. The king of Babylon
also had laid siege to Tyre, hoping to seize that city's fleet and sail
for Greece before the Greeks took it into their minds to sail for
Babylonia. But Tyre would not surrender to the great king. One
year passed, and a second, a third, a fourth and a fifth, and
Nebuchadrezzar's troops were still encamped before Tyre, the city
that stood an invincible fortress in the sea.

When Tyre finally fell after fourteen years, Nebuchadrezzar was
too old to accomplish his great design. Also it was rumored that his
reason had left him. His fear of assassins had become so great that
none bearing arms was allowed in his presence. He would not even
let his barber near him, nor would he eat food prepared in his
kitchen but only what he picked with his own hands. His hair and
nails grew wild as the feathers of an eagle, and he fed on raw fruit
and greens, like the beasts of the field.

There were some at court who wished to make the crown prince
Amel-Marduk regent. But the Princess Naq'd would not suffer a
weakling like her brother to sit on the throne while her father lived.
And since her husband Neriglissar commanded the army, she could
force her will on the courtiers. Thus the words of the Captain
Holofernes had come true, and the Princess Naq'd ruled the land
through her husband.

But in the end Nebuchadrezzar's madness passed from him, and
he still lived to complete many of his dreams. The merchants who
went down to Egypt spoke to me of their joy when upon returning
to Babylon they could see from afar the top of Etemenanki gleaming blue in the sun. The trees in the queen's garden had grown so
tall that a dense forest seemed to be rising above the white roofs of

Babylon. On the blue-tiled walls of the Processional Road golden lions marched in relief, sixty lions on each side, one hundred and twenty in all. As for the mighty arches of the Ishtar Gate, these too were sheathed in glazed blue tile and adorned with golden bulls and dragons in relief, one row above the other, nine rows in all. And so were the walls of the king's throne room covered with glazed blue tile and adorned with scrollwork, trees of life, borders of white and golden daisies, and marching lions. But nowhere was there depicted a battle scene, for the great king of Babylon was a lover of peace.

Hearing these wondrous tales, I longed to spend one more spring at the banks of the Euphrates, to wait for the great barge bringing Nebo from Borsippa, to hear the whirring wings of doves as they rose white into the blue sky, and to feel in my nostrils the glorious stench of a big city. I would stroll once more with my master through the artisans' quarters, turn in to a wineshop and listen to the tall tales of the sculptors, painters and vendors of songs who thought their wares superior to anything done in the king's own palace.

But, since this was denied me, I would at least discover the fate of my former master. After some years had passed and I was become friends with one of the merchants, I begged him to inquire after one Nabukasir, who had last dwelt in the artisans' quarters of Babylon.

The following spring I waited eagerly for the caravans from Babylonia. But the merchant whom I had begged to bring me news of my master glared darkly at me and said:

"May you entrust my enemies with such errands! I was nearly detained when I inquired after this man!"

"Then he resumed his writing and was discovered!" I cried in dismay.

Regarding me strangely, the merchant replied:

"Of his writing I know nothing. But it was discovered when two landowners sued each other in court that this Nabukasir had sold to one royal crown lands. Only because he had fought at Nineveh did Nebuchadrezzar spare his life. But the king seized all the silver this Nabukasir had inherited from a slave who bravely fought and fell in the war against Judah, and banished him from Babylon forever. It is said of Nabukasir that he went mad, proclaimed himself a Hebrew and went to live with the captives at Tel-Abib. As for me, I would rather not be sent to inquire about thieves and madmen in the future!"

Thus I learned that I had bravely fallen in battle and that my wealth had ended up in the hand of the one who needed it least. I also saw that it was safer to speak treason than to sell crown lands. For it could always be reasoned that a man speaking treason was bereft of his senses, but to tamper with the king's lands was unforgivable.

More years passed. Though I still went down to the Sea Road in spring to hear news from Babylon, I had long given up hope to return there. But one spring the merchant who had remained my friend in spite of the bad turn I had done him brought a letter for someone in Bethul. When he handed it to me I turned pale, for one who committed treason is never again free of fear. However, it did not bear the king's seal, as I had feared, but was addressed to Judith. I hastened back to the inn where we had stopped for the night, eager to learn what news it might contain. But Judith was not as curious as I. She turned the envelope back and forth in her hand, muttering that she knew none in Babylon.

"At least let us break the seal and read the letter!" I cried in despair.

In the end she consented. I broke the clay container and handed Judith the tablet that fell out. But she returned it to me, bidding me translate the words for her, for she could not understand them. This is what the letter said:

"To Judith the daughter of Merari, Peace.

"Our father Aaron, being full of years, went to his fate in the month of Adar. But before he closed his eyes he said to his sons: when we were carried into captivity in the first year of Jehoiachin, my brother Merari, a farmer, remained behind in the village of our birth. He may have died since, but his daughter Judith might still be alive. I cannot go to my grave with the thought of our kinswoman living in wretched poverty, while our wealth increases from day to day. Therefore swear to me that you will make inquiry and bring her to live with you in Babylon.

"Now if you, Judith, still be alive and receive this letter, know that things have gone well with us. Because of our skills we were allowed to leave Tel-Abib that we might work on Nebuchadrezzar's great buildings. Through shrewdness and foresight we also acquired land in the New Town, where we erected many houses for those who no longer wished to live in the cramped quarters of the Old Town. As our wealth increased we opened banks, one of us remaining in Babylon, one moving to Nippur and the third to Borsippa, so that now we finance commerce in half of Babylonia. Indeed it is not seemly that a kinswoman of ours should live in poverty in Judah.

"Therefore, if it seems good to you, take those of your household you would bring along and join the caravan when it returns from Egypt. Neither concern yourself with the cost of the journey, for any Babylonian merchant will honor the seal on this letter. If you come to Babylon you shall have a roof to shelter you until your dying day, nor shall any member of your household ever suffer need."

The letter was signed with a Babylonian name that might once have been Hebrew. When I had finished reading the message, my heart pounded with joy and I exclaimed:

"When shall we leave, Judith?"

But scowling at me, Judith replied:

"After all these years they dare send me such a letter—me, the richest woman in Judah! They would give me a dank room in their house, a bowl of curd to still my hunger, and the right to tend their spoiled children! Do they think I am like them—who have become merchants and moneylenders, who have forgotten the land of their birth and no longer know how to write Hebrew?"

And she flung the tablet on the floor. But it was made of good Babylonian clay and would not break. Then Judith picked it up, carried it into the yard outside, borrowed an ax and smashed it to pieces, as she had smashed the altar of Ashtoreth.

And we remained in Bethul.

However I did make a journey that year.

It was after the grape harvest, in the seventh month, in the twenty-fifth year of the captivity of Jehoiachin—for those who believed that Judah would be restored continued reckoning time by his reign—that a traveler from the north brought us strange news. Passing by Jerusalem, he had heard from some who still lived there that they had seen a man with a measuring line climbing about the ruins of the temple. This man, they said, was of a striking appearance, with flaming red hair and a red beard. He had seemed utterly mad, pacing the ground on which nothing would ever again be built, and the children had mocked him and thrown stones at him.

Hearing this tale, I said to Judith:

"There is only one who would fit this description: Ezekiel the son of Buzi! Perhaps now that he is become old Nebuchadrezzar repented of destroying the temple and would rebuild it. And was it not Ezekiel who recited all the measurements to the king of Babylon? Let me go and discover if he returned to draw up the new plans!"

Though Judith scoffed at the thought, she let me saddle an ass to ride up to Jerusalem. I thought to stop overnight in Bethlehem, where with luck I might find room at the inn. If I continued at dawn next morning, I would reach Jerusalem by noon.

The weather was fine and dry, as it is before the onset of the early rains. Though the earth was parched after the summer, and the grass and herbs withered, the woods through which I rode were a shady green. Now and then I startled a deer from the underbrush. Since the war not many people traveled through these parts, Jerusalem having ceased to be a place of pilgrimage.

It had been dark when I left Bethlehem, but as I approached Jerusalem the sun stood high. Though the woods were behind me now and the heat was great, I felt cold with fear. From the next crest the land dipped down into the Valley of Hinnom. Soon I would see Jerusalem.

When I gained the heights I reined my ass to gaze across the infamous valley, recalling how twenty-five years ago I had halted on a hill not far from the one on which I found myself now. Then the walls of Jerusalem had still stood high and strong. Behind them the houses had climbed up the slope of Moriah, where Solomon had built his own house and the house of Yahweh. No mighty destroyer had brought down palace or temple in more than three hundred years.

What offered itself to the eye now was a sight of horror. Where once the walls had stood, a ring of broken, scattered stones surrounded the city. Behind these rose charred ruins, houses standing blackened as they were left thirteen years ago, here a leaning wall, there doorposts supporting nothing. Atop the hill, where the palace and temple had stood, there was a vast emptiness, like a terrible monument to the wrath of God. Remembering how I had prayed that I might never see Jerusalem destroyed, I wished in my heart that I had not returned to this site.

But I had come too far to turn back. Riding down the hill to cross the valley and ascend the opposite slope, I wept all the way. Whenever a breeze rose it stirred up ashes and the smell of smoke, even after all these years. There were no gates left through which to pass, only rubble around which I guided my ass into what had once been teeming streets. I rode up all the way to the forecourt of the palace, where one had entered through the porch of pillars into the inner court. The big foundation stones lay broken upon the ground, and of the mighty cedar pillars only charred stumps were left, as though a fire had raged through a forest. Where I had walked in wonder my ass now picked his way through sand and ashes, across the heap of ruins that had been the house of the forest of Lebanon, into the temple court.

There the devastation was even greater. What had been made of wood was burned, what had been made of stone smashed, what had been made of brass and precious metals carried away. All that was left were the foundations of the temple, and down below toward the south the ruined city. Even Ezekiel could not be so mad as to believe that what had been destroyed could ever again be rebuilt. I dismounted from my ass, rent my garments, scattered on my head ashes of which there was no dearth, and sat on the ground in mourning for the city that I had once seen in its glory.

But when I rode back down by a different way I saw that the city was not wholly dead. Here and there people had cleared away the rubble, had rebuilt a house, whitewashed the walls and planted a garden. I saw smoke from a hearth rising through an open door, and heard the sound of a hammer, the laughter of a woman, the shout of a child. And I knew that even in this desolation men had embraced women and begotten children, who laughed and played among the ruins. And there were roses growing from the rubble.

I stopped by one of the houses to ask if any had seen a red-haired man with a measuring line. One of the children said he had, but his mother chided him from spreading a tale the boys had made up among themselves. And when I asked in another house, some confirmed the rumor and some denied it, until in the end I did not know what to believe.

By the time I was done asking around it was too late to embark on my homeward journey. I spent the night in one of the houses where

I was offered shelter. But I could not sleep for the acrid smell of smoke, and I lay awake all night listening to the barking of dogs, howling of cats, and crowing of roosters that rushed dawn. And next day I returned to Bethul.

The temple was not rebuilt. If Ezekiel had indeed been there, he was never seen again. A year went by, and another and another, until eleven years had passed since I rode up to Jerusalem. That year the foundations of the earth shook, for in that year Nebuchadrezzar died. He had sat on the throne of Babylon forty-three years. During his reign his kingdom had grown until it stretched from the Great Sea to the Lower Sea, from the upper Tigris to the Cataract of Egypt, encompassing what had been Assyria, Elam, Hamath, Ammon, Moab, Judah, Syria, Tyre and nearly all of Egypt. He was become the greatest king that ever lived. None of those who followed after him attained to his glory.

His son Amel-Marduk sat on the throne but three years. Though some Hebrews praised him for raising Jehoiachin to a high position, the Babylonian courtiers held him in low esteem. While his father lived, Amel-Marduk had never led the army in battle. Moreover, it was whispered that the clemency shown the Hebrew king was caused by Amel-Marduk's sinful love for one of the Hebrew princes. Indeed there was little in his conduct to gain him the esteem of those who still recalled Nebuchadrezzar's restraint. When Neriglissar wrested the reign from him, all Babylon rejoiced.

Though Neriglissar reigned barely four years before he died, he led a successful campaign against Silicia, restored the temples in Babylon and Borsippa, strengthened the eastern bank of the Euphrates and added many new canals around Babylon. In all this his hand was guided by Queen Naq'd, in whom her father's spirit was strong. She made Neriglissar restore an old palace on the riverbank for his own use, thinking it unwise for him to dwell in the shadow of his great predecessor. And so the man who had accused the Captain Holofernes of coveting the crown sat on the throne of Babylon.

When he died, his young son Labashi-Marduk ruled but briefly. Even his mother could not save his throne. For now the queen had to contend not only with the powerful men at court but with another strong-willed woman who would see her son king. This was the same woman whom I had observed walking with her arm about her son's shoulder many years ago. Married to a priest and herself a former priestess, Nabonidus' mother was greatly esteemed by those whose power rivaled that of the captains. It was with the aid of the priests that Nabonidus deposed Labashi-Marduk. His mother had also gained him support among the older captains. Though she had always denied the rumor while Nebuchadrezzar lived, she now made it known that Nabonidus was the true son of Nabopolassar, conceived when the old soldier king first brought her from Harran to Babylon. Thus my kinsman on my grandmother's side sat on the throne of Babylon, while I lived as a peasant in Bethul.

But Nabonidus did not fulfill the hopes of those who had put him in power. Every spring the caravans brought new tales of outrage from Babylon. Instead of concerning himself with matters of state, Nabonidus wasted his time and his country's wealth on digging up old temples. Soon he fell out with the priests over rebuilding the temple of the moon-god Sin at Harran, where once his mother had been high priestess. Nor would Nabonidus celebrate the festivals of the other gods until this task was completed. So incensed were the priests that they accused him of an unnatural love for his mother. In this, however, they spoke utter folly, for the lady was then nearly a hundred years old. While she lived, Nabonidus worshiped her like a goddess, and when she died at the age of a hundred and four he gave her a royal funeral. It was told of her that her sight and hearing remained keen, her vigor undiminished, and that until the end she retained the stomach of a vulture and the bowels of a camel.

As for Nabonidus, he left Babylon and went to live in Teima, in the Arabian desert. There he built a temple to Sin, to worship the god of his choice. Thus, by his absence, he imposed his will on the priests, for while the king was away the temples in Babylon remained closed and the New Year Festival could not be celebrated. For though he left his son Belshazzar behind as regent, the festivals required the presence of the king.

Of Belshazzar it was told that his conduct was even viler than that of Amel-Marduk. There was no end to banquets in the palace, with much drinking from golden vessels and debauchery such as could never have taken place in Nebuchadrezzar's time. But Nabonidus remained in Teima for seven years, while matters in Babylon grew worse. The pilgrims no longer came into town for the New Year

Festival and commerce declined. The value of gold decreased, while the price of land went up until the sum that had formerly bought a hundred gar now bought only ten. A slave that had cost forty shekels in Nebuchadrezzar's time now cost fifty, and the price of grain increased in like manner.

One year the caravans brought the news that the rivers had flooded late, causing the crops to fail. Grain was become so dear that there was a famine in the land that had never known hunger.

All the predictions made by my merchant friend of yore had come true, and Babylonia had been ruined by her own wealth. But while the greatest nation on earth went into decline, a new star rose in the east.

Cyrus had made himself king of the Medes.

When Nabonidus returned to Babylon in the sixteenth year of his reign, it was too late to save his kingdom. By then Cyrus had conquered Lydia and captured Croesus. The following year Cyrus marched into Babylonia, fighting one single battle, at Opis. When the people of Sippar learned that Cyrus was near, they rose in revolt against Nabonidus and surrendered to the Medes. But Nabonidus escaped and fled to Babylon.

Two days later Babylon—around which Nebuchadrezzar had built high walls that no conqueror might approach near the city—threw open its gates to welcome Cyrus. Before him had flown rumors that he would restore the old worship, return the plundered gods to their rightful dwelling places, and let the captives go. People danced in the streets when Cyrus' troops entered Babylon and spread palm leaves in his path. No weapons defiled the holy temple precincts. The city of Babylon was not sacked. No women were raped—at least not without their consent. Nothing was taken without payment. Indeed Cyrus ordered that all the decayed houses in Babylon be restored at his cost. But this last I refuse to believe, for was there ever a conqueror who would rebuild the homes of his vanquished foe?

As for Nabonidus, he was captured on his flight to Borsippa. When Cyrus saw that Nabonidus was old and harmless, nor would he stir up trouble if he were left alone to unearth ancient temples, he set him free. But he had Belshazzar slain in the dark of night. For he heard that the prince had used the sacred vessels of the captives for his banquets, and one who did not fear the gods would not honor a holy oath of allegiance.

The only one who continued at court from Nebuchadrezzar's time was Daniel, proving that kings come and go, but wise counselors remain in office and write books. It was he who revealed to Cyrus that there was a list made when the holy vessels were taken from the temple in Jerusalem, and the king promised to restore them accordingly. In all other matters Cyrus also kept his word. He set the captives free—those who would return to Judah to return and those who would remain in Babylon to remain. He allowed them to take along their possessions, their women, their slaves, their cattle, their silver, their gold and all the freewill offerings given them by those who chose to remain behind. And he put it all in writing, for though a king's word is sacred, a signed and sealed edict is better.

EPILOGUE

Thus saith Cyrus king of Persia: 'All the kingdoms of the earth hath the Lord, the God of heaven, given me; and He hath charged me to build Him a house in Jerusalem, which is in Judah. Whosoever there is among you of all His people—the Lord his God be with him—let him go up.'

—SECOND CHRONICLES 36:23

AS for the captives, I heard that they have already set out on their journey to Judah," the old man Isaac said to the young scribe. "Therefore if you would write for them the tale Tamar and I told you, you had better commence!"

"But what about Judith?" the young scribe asked.

The old man blinked, surprised like all those who set out to sing the praise of others only to end up singing their own.

"What more would you know about Judith? She dwells alone, she tends her lands, she feeds her people and judges their quarrels. For they still bring their suits before her."

"And is she as beautiful as in former times? And what will become of her great wealth?" the young scribe asked.

"Judith and Tamar were born within a fortnight," Isaac replied. "And does Tamar look beautiful to you? As for Judith's wealth, she made provision that there should be nothing left to claim by those who might think themselves her heirs. This year—which is the fiftieth since the Babylonians besieged Bethul, the year of the jubilee—Judith broke all the deeds she held to the fields and houses and people, as the law prescribes. But her silver will go as a sin offering toward rebuilding the temple, for the blood she shed. For Judith was a killer of men. Two of them she has long forgotten. But every year at this time she spends a night outside the cave that holds the three she loved: her father, who died not wishing to give her up to another man; her lover, whom she slew with his own sword; and her son, whom she choked to death in her womb."

The old man paused to gaze at the young scribe, who still sat with his hands folded in his lap, while his scroll of parchment lay untouched before him on the table. But when Isaac inquired why he had not written down a word, the youth replied that he would be ashamed to record the words of one who made mirth even of suffering and death.

"God forbid that I make mirth of such grave matters!" the old man exclaimed. "And if I laugh, I only laugh lest I cry. Some say that life will be better now, for there was never before a ruler like Cyrus. But was not the same said of the young Nebuchadrezzar? And even if Cyrus showed his foes mercy, will he not fail like all the others before him? For nations are like women—they respect the one who forces them more than the one who buys them, and they do not love either. My wise friend Tarqu often said: 'Those who come after us repeat our follies. The day before yesterday is the day of tomorrow.'"

"Is this what you would have me record for the returning exiles?" the young scribe asked. "And if they ask me what is the meaning of this parable—and surely they will, as is the custom among our people—what shall be my answer? That the Captain Holofernes was a fool, that Judith was a woman driven by lust and greed, and that all rulers are vain and weak and grow mad with age?"

"Is this what you gathered from my tale?" Isaac asked with amazement. "But then each man hears in the words of others only the echoes of his own thoughts. As for me, I have lived too long to pretend that the weak who have faith are stronger than the mighty who scoff at God. But if you must answer those who ask questions, you might say: Is Judith not like the land that killed the fathers, the sons and the strangers who came to possess it in love and war, and yet it lives? And if they would know the meaning of the strange prediction concerning the fate of the Captain Holofernes, tell them that Ishtar is the goddess of love and war. And was it not love and war that killed the captain? However, you need not concern yourself with impressing the exiles, for those who once lived in Babylon are not easily amazed. They will scorn the way we plow our fields, cook our food, wear our clothes and speak the Hebrew tongue, proclaiming that all was done better in Babylonia. Nor will it matter to them whether Judith did her great deed for lust or greed or love of her God and her people!"

"You see all others reflected in the mirror of your own weakness," the earnest young scribe said with contempt. "As for me, I prefer to believe the glorious tales I heard about Judith all my life!"

"Nor can I blame you for your belief," the old man said. "Indeed such is the spell cast by an often-told tale that even I, who was in the house when Judith lay with the captain, at times believe that she remained pure. Go then and write the story people would hear—of the chaste widow who slew the Captain Holofernes for the glory of her God and the honor of her people. And perhaps it *is* the truth—for what is the truth but what one comes to believe in the end?"

AUTHOR'S APOLOGIA

THE LEGEND OF Judith who slew Holofernes has been in the public domain for almost two thousand years. The material is so dramatic that it has proved irresistible to many writers, painters and dancers—and I am as open to temptation as the next person.

The Book of Judith, as it appears in the Apocrypha, is riddled with historical inconsistencies and contradictions. Fiction writers of that time were not yet afflicted with scholarly critics. Alas, we are no longer so fortunate. I have therefore diligently done my homework. For my sources I relied on the *Holy Scriptures According to the Masoretic Text*, the Book of the Apocrypha, and numerous volumes on Jewish, Assyrian and Babylonian history, customs, literature and religion, all available to any fanatic willing to bury himself for months in the Public Library. I also visited all the historic sites accessible to one of my sex and religious persuasion.

Let me state that I am well aware that the Book of Judith was probably written in the first century A.D. and that its locale is thought not to be where I placed it. I am also aware that Daniel is not a historical personage, and that the legends contained in the Book of Daniel were recorded some four hundred years after Nebuchadrezzar's times. Some of the historical material originally contained in my book had to be deleted. Any scholar who might be seduced into reading a novel would be familiar with it, while it would only tend to confuse the layman.

On two occasions I deviate knowingly from my sources: the

date for the destruction of Jerusalem is given in II Kings as the seventh day of the fifth month; in Jeremiah as the tenth day of the fifth month. I have compromised on the ninth day of the fifth month, the official day of mourning for the destruction of the temple. The ruse to which I ascribe the conquest of Nineveh is mentioned in Herodotus in connection with the fall of Babylon. However, neither the Nabonidus Chronicle nor the report by Cyrus, both of which thoroughly cover the fall of Babylon and largely coincide, bear out Herodotus. On the other hand, we have in verse 2:7 of Nahum's description of the fall of Nineveh a reference to "the gates of the river" being opened. There is a tradition that the river gates were swept away by a flood, but it does not seem plausible to me that an army could have crossed a rampant river. I have therefore played a novelist's hunch in assuming that Herodotus might have been —not wrong but misinformed. If I am mistaken—*mea culpa.*

If, out of the many choices open to me, I selected the time of Nebuchadrezzar's second campaign against Jerusalem for my story, I did so because this period seemed to offer the most dramatic possibilities. Many a writer before me has interpreted the legend of Judith in the light of his times, and so must I interpret it in the light of our times. I have, therefore, tried to make my story historically plausible rather than accurate—though I refrained from tampering with any *truly* established historical facts. As an apologia for my interpretation I should like to borrow from *The Republic* the words Plato put into Socrates's mouth:

"Because we do not know the truth about ancient times we make falsehood as much like truth as we can, and so turn it to account."

S.W.

ABOUT THE AUTHOR

STELLA WILCHEK was born in Vienna and attended the Real Gymnasium in Vienna until the outbreak of World War II. As a refugee from Hitler, she fled to South America, where she remained for eight years before coming to the United States.

Her first novel, *Ararat*, published in 1962, was a Harper "find." She is also the author of *Tale of a Hero*, a novel published in 1965. She presently lives in New York City with her husband.

Set in 10 on 12 Janson
Composed, printed and bound by AMERICAN BOOK–STRATFORD PRESS, INC.
HARPER & ROW, PUBLISHERS, INCORPORATED